The Storyteller

or

The Hakawati

Rabih Alameddine was born in Jordan to Lebanese parents and has lived in Kuwait, Lebanon, England and the United States. He is the author of two previous novels and a collection of short stories, and is the recipient of a Guggenheim Fellowship. He lives in San Francisco and Beirut.

ALSO BY RABIH ALAMEDDINE

I, The Divine

The Perv: Stories

Koolaids

The Storyteller

or

The Hakawati

Rabih Alameddine

PICADOR

First published 2008 as a Borzoi Book as *The Hakawati* by
Alfred A. Knopf, a division of Random House, Inc., New York.

First published in Great Britain 2008 as *The Hakawati* by Picador

First published in paperback 2009 by Picador
an imprint of Pan Macmillan Ltd
Pan Macmillan, 20 New Wharf Road, London N1 9RR
Basingstoke and Oxford
Associated companies throughout the world
www.panmacmillan.com

ISBN 978-0-330-45447-6

Grateful acknowledgment is made to the following for
permission to reprint previously published material:

Lili Fabilli Osborne: Excerpt from *The Passionate State of Mind
and Other Aphorisms* by Eric Hoffer (New York: HarperCollins, 1955).
Reprinted by permission of Lili Fabilli Osborne, literary executor
of the estate of Eric Hoffer.

Penguin Group (UK) and Assírio & Alvim: Excerpt from *The
Book of Disquiet* by Fernando Pessoa, translated by Richard Zenith
copyright © 2001 by Richard Zenith (London: Allen La
The Penguin Press, 2001). Reprinted by permission o
Penguin Group (UK) and Assírio & Alvim.

The Arabic word for *al-hakawati*, which appears on the title
was designed and drawn by Dr. Sami Makarem.

FT PbK

Chapter 10 was previously published in *Zoetrope*,
in slightly different form, as "In-country."

A CIP catalogue record for this book is available
from the British Library.

Printed and bound in the UK by
CPI Mackays, Chatham ME5 8TD

For Nicole Aragi

Demon Destroyer

Luscious Dove

BOOK ONE

BOOK ONE

Praise be to God, Who has so disposed matters that pleasant literary anecdotes may serve as an instrument for the polishing of wits and the cleansing of rust from our hearts.

Ahmad al-Tifashi, *The Delights of Hearts*

Everything can be told. It's just a matter of starting, one word follows another.

Javier Marías, *A Heart So White*

What Hells and Purgatories and Heavens I have inside of me! But who sees me do anything that disagrees with life— me, so calm and peaceful?

Fernando Pessoa, *The Book of Disquiet*

— One —

L isten. Allow me to be your god. Let me take you on a journey beyond imagining. Let me tell you a story.

A long, long time ago, an emir lived in a distant land, in a beautiful city, a green city with many trees and exquisite gurgling fountains whose sound lulled the citizens to sleep at night. Now, the emir had everything, except for the one thing his heart desired, a son. He had wealth, earned and inherited. He had health and good teeth. He had status, charm, respect. His beautiful wife loved him. His clan looked up to him. He had a good pedicurist. Twenty years he had been married, twelve lovely girls, but no son. What to do?

He called his vizier. "Wise vizier," he said, "I need your help. My lovely wife has been unable to deliver me a son, as you know. Each of my twelve girls is more beautiful than the other. They have milk-white skin as smooth as the finest silk from China. The glistening pearls from the Arabian Gulf pale next to their eyes. The luster of their hair outshines the black dyes from the land of Sind. The oldest has seventeen poets singing her praises. My daughters have given me much pleasure, much to be proud of. Yet I yearn to see an offspring with a little penis run around my courtyard, a boy to carry my name and my honor, a future leader of our clan. I am at a loss. My wife says we should try once more, but I cannot put her through all this again for another girl. Tell me, what can I do to ensure a boy?"

The vizier, for the thousandth upon thousandth time, suggested his master take a second wife. "Before it is too late, my lord. It is obvious that your wife will not produce a boy. We must find someone who will. My liege is the only man within these borders who has only one wife."

The emir had rejected the suggestion countless times, and that day would be no different. He looked wistfully out onto his garden. "I cannot marry another, my dear vizier. I am terribly in love with my wife. She can be ornery now and then, vain for sure, petulant and impetuous, silly at times, ill disposed toward the help, even malicious and malevolent when angry, but, still, she has always been the one for me."

"Then produce a son with one of your slaves. Fatima the Egyptian would be an excellent candidate. Her hips are more than adequate; her breasts have been measured. A tremendous nominee, if I may say so myself."

"But I have no wish to be with another."

"Sarah offered her Egyptian slave to her husband to produce a boy. If it was good enough for our prophet, it can be good enough for us."

That night, in their bedroom, the emir and his wife discussed their problem. His wife agreed with the vizier. "I know you want a son," she said, "but I believe it has gone beyond your desires. The situation is dire. Our people talk. All wonder what will happen when you ascend to heaven. Who will lead our tribes? I believe some may wish to ask the question sooner."

"I will kill them," the emir yelled. "I will destroy them. Who dares question how I choose to live my life?"

"Settle down and be reasonable. You can have intercourse with Fatima until she conceives. She is pretty, available, and amenable. We can have our boy through her."

"But I do not think I can."

His wife smiled as she stood. "Worry not, husband. I will attend, and I will do that thing you enjoy. I will call Fatima and we can inform her of what we want. We will set an appointment for Wednesday night, a full moon."

When Fatima was told of their intentions, she did not hesitate. "I am always at your service," she said. "However, if the emir wishes to have a son with his own wife, there is another way. In my hometown of Alexandria, I know of a woman, Bast, whose powers are unmatched. She is directly descended, female line, from Ankhara herself, Cleopatra's healer and keeper of the asps. If she is given a lock of my mistress's hair, she will be able to see why my mistress has not produced a boy and will give out the appropriate remedy. She never fails."

"But that is astounding," the emir exclaimed. "You are heaven-sent, my dear Fatima. We must fetch this healer right away."

Fatima shook her head. "Oh, no, my lord. A healer can never leave her home. It is where her magic comes from. She would be helpless and useless if she were uprooted. A healer might travel, begin quests, but in the end, to come into her full powers, she can never stray too far from home. I can travel with a lock of my mistress's hair and return with the remedy."

"Then go you must," the emir's wife said.

The emir added, "And may God guide you and light your way."

✤

I felt foreign to myself. Doubt, that blind mole, burrowed down my spine. I leaned back on the car, surveyed the neighborhood, felt the blood throb in the veins of my arms. I could hear a soft gurgling, but was unsure whether it came from a fountain or a broken water pipe. There was once, a long time ago, a filigreed marble fountain in the building's lobby, but it had ceased to exist. Poof.

I was a tourist in a bizarre land. I was home.

There were not many people around. An old man sat dejectedly on a stool with a seat of interlocking softened twine. His white hair was naturally spiked, almost as if he had rested his hands on a static ball. He fit the place, one of the few neighborhoods in Beirut still war-torn.

"This was our building," I told him, because I needed to say something. I nodded toward the lobby, cavernous, fountain-free, now perfectly open-air. I realized he wasn't looking at me but at my car, my father's black BMW sedan.

The street had turned into a muddy pathway. The neighborhood was off the main roads. Few cars drove this street then; fewer now, it seemed. A cement mixer hobbled by. There were two buildings going up. The old ones were falling apart, with little hope of resuscitation.

My building looked abandoned. I knew it wasn't—squatters and refugees had made it their home since we left during the early years of the civil war—but I didn't see how anyone could live there now.

Listen. I lived here twenty-six years ago.

Across the street from our building, our old home, there used to be a large enclosed garden with a gate of intricate spears. It was no longer a garden, and it certainly wasn't gated anymore. Shards of metal, twisted rubble, strips of tile, and broken glass were scattered across piles of dirt. A giant white rhododendron bloomed in the middle of the debris. Two begonias, one white and the other red, flourished in front of a recently erected three-story. That building looked odd: no crater, no bullet holes, no tree growing out of it. The begonias, glorious begonias, seemed to burst from every branch, no unopened buds. Burgeoning life, but subdued color. The red—the red was off. Paler than I would want. The reds of my Beirut, the home city I remember, were wilder, primary. The colors were better then, more vivid, more alive.

A Syrian laborer walked by, trying to steer clear of the puddles under his feet, and his eyes avoided mine. February 2003, more than twelve years since the civil war ended, yet construction still lagged in the neighborhood. Most of Beirut had been rebuilt, but this plot remained damaged and decrepit.

There was Mary in a lockbox.

A windowed box stood at the front of our building, locked in its own separate altar of cement and brick, topped with A-shaped slabs of Italian marble, a Catholic Joseph Cornell. Inside stood a benevolent Mary, a questioning St. Anthony, a coral rosary, three finger candles, stray dahlia and rose petals, and a picture of Santa Claus pushpinned to a white foam backboard.

When did this peculiarity spring to life? Was the Virgin there when I was a boy?

I shouldn't have come here. I was supposed to pick Fatima up before going to the hospital to see my father but found myself driving to the old neighborhood as if I were in a toy truck being pulled by a willful child. I had planned this trip to Beirut to spend Eid al-Adha with my family and was shocked to find out that my father was hospitalized. Yet I wasn't with family, but standing distracted and bewildered before my old home, dwelling in the past.

A young woman in tight jeans and a skimpy white sweater walked out of our building. She carried notebooks and a textbook. I wanted to ask her which floor she and her family lived on. Obviously not the second; a fig tree had taken root on that one. That must have been Uncle Halim's apartment.

The family, my father and his siblings, owned the building and had lived in five of its twelve apartments. My aunt Samia and her family lived in the sixth-floor penthouse. My father had one of the fourth-floor flats, and Uncle Jihad had the other. An apartment on the fifth belonged to Uncle Wajih, and Uncle Halim had one on the second floor—fig tree, I presumed. The apartment on the ground floor belonged to the concierge, whose son Elie became a militia leader as a teenager and killed quite a few people during the civil war.

Our car dealership, al-Kharrat Corporation, the family fountain of fortune, was walking distance from the building, on the main street. The Lebanese lacked a sense of irony. No one paid attention to the little things. No one thought it strange that a car dealership, and the family that ran it, had a name that meant "exaggerator," "teller of tall tales," "liar."

The girl strolled past, indifferently, seductively, her eyes hidden by cheap sunglasses. The old man sat up when the girl passed him. "Don't you think your pants are too tight?" he asked.

"Kiss my ass, Uncle," she replied.

He leaned forward. She kept going. "No one listens anymore," he said quietly.

I couldn't tell you when last I had seen the neighborhood, but I could pinpoint the last day we lived there, because we left in a flurry of bedlam, all atop each other, and that day my father proved to be a hero of sorts. February 1977, and the war that had been going on for almost two years had finally reached our neighborhood. Earlier, during those violent twenty-one months, the building's underground garage, like its counterparts across the city, proved to be a more than adequate shelter. But then militias had begun to set up camp much too close. The family, those of us who hadn't left already, had to find safety in the mountains.

My mother, who always took charge in emergencies, divided us into four cars: I was in her car, my sister in my father's, Uncle Halim and two of his daughters with Uncle Jihad, and Uncle Halim's wife, Aunt Nazek, drove her car with her third daughter, May. The belongings of three households were shoved into the cars. We drove separately, five minutes apart, so that we wouldn't be in a convoy and get annihilated by a stray missile or an intentional bomb. The regathering point was a church just ten minutes up the mountain from Beirut.

My mother and I reached it first. Even though I'd gotten somewhat inured to the sounds of shelling, by the time we stopped my seat was sopping. Within a few minutes, as if announcing Uncle Jihad's arrival, Beirut exploded into a raging cacophony once more. We watched the insanity below us and waited warily for the other two cars. My mother was strangling the steering wheel. My father arrived next, and since he was supposed to be the last to leave, it meant that Aunt Nazek didn't make it somehow.

My father didn't get out of his car, didn't talk to us. He kicked my sister out, turned the car around, and drove downhill into the lunacy. Aghast and eyes ablaze, my sister stood on the curb, watched him disappear into the fires of Beirut. My mother wanted to follow him, but I was in her car. She yelled at me: "Get out. I need to go after him. I'm the better driver." I was too paralyzed to move. Then my sister got into the car next to me, and it was too late to follow.

We were lucky. Aunt Nazek's car had died as soon as it hit the first hill. Always a good citizen, she parked the car on the side, even though there were no other cars on the road. My father had driven past on the way up and hadn't noticed. He found them, and my cousin May jumped into his car, but he had to wait for Aunt Nazek as she tried to remember where she had put all her valuables. He returned them to us safely, but while he was driving back, a bomb fell about fifty meters away from them, and a piece of shrapnel hit the car's windshield and got stuck there. No one was hurt, though both Aunt Nazek and May lost their voices for a while, having shrieked their throats dry.

My cousin May said that my father shrieked as well when the shrapnel hit, an operatic high note. However, both my father and Aunt Nazek deny that. "He was a hero," my aunt would say. "A real-life hero."

"It wasn't heroic," my father would say, "but cowardly. I'd have been too afraid to show my face to my brother if I hadn't gone back after his wife."

That day was twenty-six years ago.

Fatima was waiting outside her building, which was covered head to toe in black marble, one of the newer effronteries that have risen in modern Beirut. As if to compensate for the few neighborhoods that had not been upgraded since the war, Beirut dressed itself in new concrete. All over the city, upscale high-rises were being built in every corner, nouveau-riche and bétonné.

"Sorry I'm late," I said, grinning. I could usually predict her reaction, since she was an old friend and confidante. I was about to get a pretend tongue-lashing no matter what I said.

"Get out of the goddamn car." She didn't move to the passenger side, stood with arms akimbo, her blue-green purse dangling from her wrist almost to her knees. She was dressed to dazzle; everything about her flashed, and the ring on her left hand screamed—a hexagonal mother of an emerald surrounded by her six offspring. "You haven't seen me in four months, and this is how you greet me?" I got out of the car, and she smothered me, covered me in her perfume and kisses. "Much better," she added. "Now let's get going."

At the first sign of traffic, she slid open the visor mirror and interviewed her face. "You have to help me with Lina." Her words sounded odd, her mouth distorted as she redecorated her lips' outline. "She's spending the nights sleeping on the chair in his room. As ever, your sister won't listen to reason. I want to relieve her, but she won't let me."

I didn't reply, and I doubted that she expected me to. Both of us understood that my father wouldn't allow anyone other than my sister to take care of him and was terrified of spending a night by himself. He had nightmares about dying alone and uncared for in a hospital room.

"When we arrive," she said, "kiss everybody and go directly to his room. I don't think there will be a lot of people, but don't allow the rest of the family to delay you. I'll stay with the visitors, not you. He'll be offended if you don't rush in to see him."

"You don't have to tell me, my dear," I said. "He's my father, not yours."

❧

Fatima left the green city in a small caravan with a retinue of five of the emir's bravest soldiers and Jawad, one of the stable boys. She understood the need for Jawad—the horses and camels had to be looked after—but she wondered whether the soldiers would be of any use.

"Do you not think we need protection?" Jawad asked as they started their journey.

"I do not," she said. "I can deal with a few brigands, and if we are attacked by a large band, five men will be of no use anyway. On the contrary, their presence may be a magnet for that large group of bandits." She felt the emir's fifty gold dinars that she had hidden in her bosom. "If it were just you and me, we would invite much less attention. Well, nothing we can do now. We are in the hand of God."

On the fourth evening, in the middle of the Sinai Desert, before the sun had completely set, the party was attacked just as Fatima had predicted. Twenty Bedouins dispatched the city soldiers. Finding little of value among the belongings, the captors decided to divide the spoils evenly: ten would have Fatima, and ten would get to use Jawad.

Fatima laughed. "Are you men or boys?" She stepped forward, leaving a visibly nervous Jawad behind. "You have a chance to receive pleasure from me and you choose this stripling?"

"Be quiet, woman," said the leader. "We must divide you evenly. We cannot risk a fight over the booty. Be thankful. You would not be able to deal with more than ten of us."

Fatima laughed and turned back to Jawad. "These desert rats have not heard of me." She took off her headdress; her abundant black hair tumbled around her face. "These children of the barren lands have not sung my tales." She unhooked the chain of gold coins encircling her forehead. "They believe that twenty infants would be too much for me." She took off her abayeh, showing her seductress's figure, stood before the Bedouins in her dress of blue silk and gold. "Behold," she said. "I am Fatima, charmer of men, bewitcher of the heavens. Look how the moon calls his clouds; see how he crawls behind his curtains; watch him hide in shame, for he refuses to reveal himself when I show my face. You think you peons will be too much for me, Fatima?" She raised her hands to the vanishing moon. "Think whether twenty of you would satisfy me, Fatima, tamer of Afreet-Jehanam." She glared at the men. "Tremble."

"Afreet-Jehanam?" the leader cried. "You conquered the mighty jinni?"

"Afreet-Jehanam is my lover. He is no more than my plaything. He does my bidding."

"I want her. I refuse to have the boy. We have to redivide the spoils. This will not do."

"No," the leader said. "We cannot have everyone get what they want. That is not the Arab way. It has already been decided."

"I want the woman as well," cried another man. "You cannot keep her to yourself and give us this waif of a boy." An argument ensued. Everyone wanted Fatima, except for one man, Khayal, who kept insisting, "I really want the boy," to anyone who would listen. But no one listened. The nine men who were given Jawad but wanted Fatima grew livid. Rules or no rules, they had been cheated. They had no idea Fatima was so talented. They had been deceived and wanted their appropriate share. The goods, as any idiot could see, had not been divided equally. Battle lines were drawn, swords unsheathed. Quickly, the ten killed the nine.

"I think the boy is winsome," said Khayal.

Twenty lustful eyes stared at Fatima.

"Now, now, boys," she said coyly. "Was that really necessary?"

"It is time, Sitt Fatima," the leader said. "We are ready."

"Well, I am not. I must choose who goes first. The first lover is very important. He will help me set the stage for what is to come. Should I go with the one who has the biggest penis? I like that, but sometimes he who has the biggest is the worst lover, and that will force me to work harder. This should be amusement, not labor. Which of you has the smallest penis? A man with a small member would be more eager to please me, but then, as hard as it is, it is not as satisfying. Choosing the first lover should not be taken lightly. I have much to consider."

The leader huffed and puffed. "There is nothing to consider. I go first. I am the best lover, and the rest can take turns after I am sated."

"You are not the best lover," another brigand said. "If you were, your wife would not be leaving her house in the middle of the night." Those were the last words that man uttered. The leader unsheathed his sword once more and cut off that man's head.

"You should not have killed him," another cried. "It is not right that you go first. We should let Sitt Fatima decide. She is the expert, not you. She should decide on the order. Since I have the biggest penis, I believe I should go first."

"You do not have the biggest," argued another. "I do." He lifted his desert robe. "Look here, Sitt Fatima. I have the biggest, and I promise you I am not a bad lover. You must pick me."

"Put that tiny thing away," the leader said. "I am the leader, and I go first."

"It is thickness that matters, not length."

"I still want the boy. I just want the boy."

"Your member is no bigger than a thimble."

"You take that back. Admit that mine is bigger than yours or prepare to die."

And the men fought till death. The leader was left standing—the leader and the boy-lover, who had remained out of the fray. "The best of all men awaits you, your ladyship." The leader puffed up like a pigeon. "Let us begin."

"Let us," she said. "Undress and show me my prize."

"Come to me," he said once he was nude. "Look. I really have the biggest one."

"No," Fatima said. "Mine is bigger." From under her dress, she took out her knife and cut his penis off and slit his throat.

"Pack everything back into the caravan," Fatima told Jawad. "We have some way to go before we settle for the night. Gather these dead men's horses. I will go through their things. We will leave this arid wilderness richer than we arrived."

"But what shall we do with this man?" Jawad gestured toward his admirer.

"By your leave, I would like to invite the boy into my tent," Khayal said.

"The boy is neither captured nor a slave," Fatima said. "Since he has free will, you must convince him, charm him into your tent. We have seven nights before we reach my home city, Alexandria. You have seven nights to seduce him. You may begin tomorrow."

And Fatima looked up at the sky and its stars and thanked the moon for his help.

And Fatima, Jawad, and Khayal led their numerous horses, camels, and mules into the night.

"Ah, the smell of salt and sand," Fatima told her companions. "There is no elixir on this blessed earth like it."

During the day's march, our three travelers reached the blue-tongued shores of the Mediterranean. That night, they camped on the beach. Much to Khayal's disappointment, Jawad unfurled his own tent after watering, feeding, and brushing the pack animals. After a dinner of bread, dried meat, and dates, Fatima poured herself a cup of wine. "Shall we begin?"

"Begin?" Khayal wondered. "You mean my seduction? Am I supposed to perform publicly? I would prefer to talk to Jawad in private." He bent his head. "I am, in large measure, a discreet man." He lifted his head and looked at Jawad, sitting next to Fatima. "You would appreciate a discreet man, I am sure."

Jawad shrugged. Fatima said, "Discretion is boring."

"My lady," Khayal said, "our agreement was that I seduce the boy in seven nights, not that I perform the seduction publicly. That would be unfairly humiliating."

"Love is unfairly humiliating."

Jawad nodded. "I do not know much of love, but I do know that it is humiliating."

"I must protest," Khayal said. "The Prophet—may the blessing of God be upon him—said, 'He who falls in love and conceals his passion is a worthy man.' "

"Being a bore is in itself unappealing," our heroine said. "Being a bore and a liar to boot makes a man rebarbative, as well as dishonored. Lying with the Prophet's words? You might as well remove your head-dress and shave your beard. The Prophet, peace be upon him, said, 'He who falls in love, conceals his passion, and is chaste, dies a martyr.' If you wish to become a martyr, that can be arranged easily, but it is already too late to conceal your passion."

"And chastity is not what he is after anyway," Jawad added.

"The desert nights are long and bare," Fatima said. "Entertain us, or begone. If you desire to possess this boy, you must convince him."

"Convince me."

"Move him."

"Move me."

"Wait." Khayal stood up. The light of the fire cast flickering shadows on his long white robe. He was a thick-shouldered man, with a hawkish beak and full, heavy eyebrows. "I will do what you ask if I have to, but allow me one final attempt at convincing you that discretion works best in matters of love. I can tell you the story of Bader, son of Fateh."

"I am not sure I am willing to be convinced. Are you, my dear Jawad?"

"Well, I do like stories."

"There you go. The boy likes stories. Tell us the tale of this Bader."

Khayal said, "There was a Córdoban, from a great family, by the name of Bader ben Fateh. He was a man of faith, circumspect, a gracious host, well mannered, a beacon of good breeding. I was traveling in Játiva when I began to hear of his exploits. It seems he had lost all modesty by falling in love with a musician by the name of Moktadda. I knew this boy, and I can tell you he did not deserve Bader's love; he did not deserve the love of one of Bader's slaves. Bader spent a fortune on this honorless dullard, welcomed him into his house, and closed it to his other guests. He plied the peasant with the most expensive wines. I heard that our man had removed his kaffiyeh, unwound his head-rope, showed his full face, rolled up his sleeves.

"He cast off the leash of propriety. He fell prey to that ravenous beast, desire. He became the subject of gossip, a notorious story in the harems, a news item in the diwans. His reputation became the object of derision. He lost his standing, his honor, his respect.

"The young musician had not wanted his indiscretion revealed, and Bader's loss of social standing made him a less desirable partner. The object of his passion ran away from him altogether, and refused ever to see him again.

"Had Bader valued discretion, had he folded his secret in his heart, couched his desires, he would not have lost everything. He would have worn the robe of well-being, and the garment of respectability would not have become threadbare. He would have been able to keep both his honor and his lover had he chosen a more circumspect style. Allow me a modest approach."

"Modesty is dull," Fatima said.

"So was the story," Jawad said.

"So true. Didactic stories should only be told to children and to the faithful."

"I weep for the poor children who have to listen to such stories."

"Are you seduced, my dear Jawad?"

"I am sleepy."

"Ah, at least the night passes. I pray that we will be gifted with a better seduction tomorrow. And a good night to all."

My father's face told a different story. He looked wan, haggard, and old—very old. And thin. His wedding band danced upon its finger like a shower-curtain ring. He had spent an hour telling Lina and me that he felt grand. He was happy that I had flown in to spend Eid al-Adha with him, but we should spend it at our home. He wasn't ill anymore. He sounded better. He moved around better. He laughed better. He wanted to go home.

The cast of light in the room was disturbing, slightly nauseating. The antiseptic white walls. The fluorescent lights. It was midmorning, but the sallow curtain diffused a pale gray-green glow. Lina had been going out to the balcony to smoke, always making sure the curtain was drawn so my father wouldn't see her and crave a cigarette.

"I'm doing so much better," my father announced. "I feel formidable."

I pulled back the curtain to let some genuine light in, opened the sliding door for air. It was pitch-perfect weather, two clouds maculating a clear sheet of blue, an early spring in February. I stood for a moment with my back to the room, enjoying the play of the flimsy breeze upon my face. I considered for a moment returning to the waiting lounge to relieve Fatima and Salwa, my sister's daughter, who were entertaining the visitors.

"I know you think I don't know what I'm talking about," my father went on, "but I feel better, and I don't want to spend another night in this godforsaken place."

The Chinese say prolonged illness can make one a doctor. My mother used to say prolonged illness made one a curmudgeon. My mother was wiser. I turned around and looked at the high nightstand, made sure that her framed passport-sized photo was still there, next to her silver locket, which my father insisted brought him luck.

"We have to wait and find out what Tin Can has to say." Lina regarded my father with soft eyes. When she was younger, my sister took after my mother, but as she matured, my father's softer features overcame her face. Lina curled up on the recliner, laid her head back, imitating a Henry Moore sculpture. Her heels poked into the chair's plastic upholstery.

"Talk to him, darling," my father whimpered. He grasped the bed rail, pulled himself onto his side in order to face her. He scratched the small protrusion in his chest where the pacemaker and defibrillator were. I turned around again and watched the sky.

My father could afford the best medical care in the world. Lina had dragged him to Johns Hopkins, to the Cleveland Clinic, to Paris, to London. Yet he always returned to the just-competent Tin Can. He didn't have any illusions in that regard. My father was the one who had dubbed him Tin Can, because he was about as effective a doctor as a tin can. But he was family, Aunt Nazek's brother, my father's brother Halim's wife's brother, and that to my father was more valuable than credentials or prestigious alma maters. In the last few years, he had refused to travel for medical attention and sought only the family doctor.

I heard my voice speak. "And the doctor told the poor father, 'The only way to heal your son is to take his heart.' "

Their voices joined mine. " 'For the evil jinni has made himself a home there.' "

My father laughed. "Don't do this to me." He clutched his heart, pretending pain. "My evil jinni doesn't like to be amused."

"You're still ever so strange," my sister said. "What possessed you to think of that? How long has it been since you've heard that line? Thirty years?"

"More than that," my father said. "My father died thirty years ago, and he wasn't telling those stories of his by then. It must have been thirty-five, maybe thirty-seven years." He took a raspy breath. "God, Osama, you were such a young boy then."

My grandfather actually told me those stories of his until the day he died. He was a storyteller after all, in spirit and in profession. My father tried at different times to get him to stop filling my head with fanciful narratives, but he never succeeded.

"What are you staring at?" Lina asked me. "Turn around and look at us."

"Look," I said. "Look here. March has come in."

The sky was a perfectly cut aquamarine. As in most Mediterranean cities, Beirut's late winter can be either stormy and brumal or magnificently clear, smelling of sun-dried laundry.

"It's still February, stupid boy," Lina said. "It's just a break. The storms will come back."

"A glorious break."

She came up behind me. "You're right. It is glorious." Her arms encircled me, and I felt her weight upon my shoulders.

"I want to see," my father whined from his bed. "Help me up. I want to see." We moved to the bed, helped him sit up, turn around, and stand. He leaned on my sister, the tallest of us three. I dragged the intravenous stand with its deflated balloons behind him as he shuffled the eight steps to the balcony. The cheeks of his rear end jiggled and seemed to droop a little lower with each step. On the balcony, the three of us lined up to admire the false spring and the sun that bathed the sprawling mass of rooftops.

My father catnapped on the hospital bed. Outside, Lina inhaled each puff of her cigarette as if it were her last. She smoked so rapidly that the tip of the cigarette burned into a miniature red coal. She leaned back against the balcony railing, stared up at the sky. I stared down. On the third floor of the hospital, where illnesses were less grave, two women whispered to each other on their balcony like two pigeons cooing. Across the street, in the distance, stood a house that showed severe signs of aging. From where I stood, its shutters looked rotted.

"He's dying," she said, her voice noncommittal.

A thick growth of weeds covered the house's garden. Tall fronds of wild thistle, a few of the tips flowering yellow. "We're all dying," I said. "It's just a matter of when."

"Don't start with your American clichés, please. I can't deal with that now." She shook her head, her black hair covering her face for an instant. "He's dying. Do you hear me?"

"I hear you." Just then, a car trumpeted its horn, one long uninterrupted burst. My sister jumped to check that the sliding door was completely shut. "What makes you think this time is different?" I asked. "He's been dying for so long. He always pulls through."

"He won't always pull through. It gets more difficult each time."

"I know that. But why this time?"

She took a deep breath as she faced me. I could see her chest expand and deflate. My sister was much taller than I. It was with her height that she took after our mother, but Lina was even taller, bigger. Boucher instructed his pupil Fragonard to paint women as if they had no bones. Fragonard could have painted Lina. She was the antithesis of straight lines or angles. Graceful, like my mother.

I, on the other hand, inherited my teeth from my mother, not her height. We both had two crooked upper front teeth. She never fixed hers, because they accentuated her beauty, the flaw making her appear more human, accessible, more Helen than Aphrodite. She didn't fix mine, thinking it would also work for me. It didn't. Alas, unlike her, I had quite a few other flaws.

"Tin Can gives him three months at most," Lina said.

"Tin Can said the same thing four years ago."

"You have to be with him to notice the difference. He's not going to make it, and he knows it." She sighed and flicked her cigarette onto the street below. "I don't know what to do."

The old house across the street must not have been abandoned. A pile of plastic chairs stood outside the door. A stray electric wire, long and lax, stole power from the main city lines. A pigeon settled on the wire, which drooped and seemed about to snap. The pigeon did not last more than a second or two before flying off.

"Shall we begin?" Fatima asked on the second night. She sipped her cup. Sated, with full stomachs, the three travelers sat around the small fire.

"We shall," Khayal replied. "Would my beloved care for a cup of wine to help smooth the rough edges of this evening?"

Fatima raised her eyebrows; her eyes asked if Jawad was interested. He nodded. "One cup only for tonight," she said. "Until you get used to it."

And Khayal lifted his cup. "May my beloved get used to much." He gulped, smacked his lips, paused for dramatic effect. In a sonorous voice, he began to recite:

> *A woman once berated me*
> *Because of the love I feel*
> *For a boy who huffs and struts*
> *Like an untamed young bull*
> *But why should I sail the sea*
> *When I can love grandly on land?*
> *Why hunt for fish, when I can find*
> *Gazelles, free, for every hand.*
> *Let me be; do not blame me*
> *For choosing a road*
> *In life that you have rejected,*
> *Which I will follow till the day I die.*
> *Know you not that the Holy Book*
> *Speaks the definitive truth:*
> *Before your daughters*
> *Your sons shall be preferred?*

"Magnificent," Fatima cried, applauding enthusiastically. "One can always rely on the brilliance of Abu Nawas for entertainment. Who would have thought that a desert dweller would be able to quote the city poet? I am impressed. Are you not, my dear Jawad?"

"Does the Holy Book really say that a man should choose his sons before his daughters?"

"In matters of inheritance, my boy, but the poet took some liberties. More, more, our master reciter. Tell us more."

I no longer wish to sail the sea
I prefer to roam the plains
And seek the food that God
Sends to all living creatures.

"A delight," Fatima said. "How lovely and bawdy that Baghdad poet was. I would have loved an opportunity to drink wine and match wits with Abu Nawas. Was that not marvelous, Jawad?"

"It surely was," Jawad replied. "I, too, am duly impressed. My suitor is learned and sensitive, but his poetry speaks nothing other than his preference for a certain kind of love. That he likes boys does not make him more desirable to me. It simply means he has good taste. His poetry is entertaining but does not move this listener. I do not feel seduced this night either, but I do feel sleepy."

"So true. So wise. We have been dutifully entertained this night, but not seduced. Let us hope for a better temptation tomorrow. And a good night to all."

On the third night, Khayal poured wine into Jawad's cup. He stood before his audience. "I am a vessel filled with contrition. Forgive me, I beg you. Allow me to begin anew."

"There is no need for forgiveness," Jawad said.

"Please," Fatima said, "favor us with your seduction. We sit here, parched earth awaiting its promised thunderstorm. Quench our thirst, we beg you. Begin."

"I stand humble before you," Khayal began, "a once-proud man debased by love." His shoulders slumped. "I may look like nothing much at this moment, but looks can be deceiving." His voice grew. "The cover does not fit the content of the book.

"I am first a warrior. I have fought in God's army. From the coasts off Mount Lebanon to the hills of the Holy Land, heads of infidels have rolled off my sword by the hundreds. I have slain Papists in the west, Byzantines in the north, Mongols in the east. My spear knew no mercy in defending our lands. I am feared in every corner of the world. Europeans use my name to frighten their children. Courage is my companion; honor rides before me, loyalty at my side. My sword is swift, my spear accurate. I am the answer to every caliph's prayers."

"Well said," Fatima called out. "One can see the influence of al-Mutanabbi."

"Who is that?" Jawad asked.

"I will tell you in a little while, my dear. Let us allow our seducer to continue. I am sure he is not done yet."

"I stood upon a hill watching the enemy ships drop anchor along our shores. They were soaked twice, first by milk-streaked clouds that rained upon them announcing my arrival, and then it rained skulls. I rode my steed swiftly, saw our enemy approaching as if on legless steeds. I could not distinguish their swords, for their clothes and turbans were also made of steel. I attacked even though it meant certain death, as if hell's heart pumped all about me. Heroes and warriors fell before me, whereas I remained standing, sword wet and unsheathed. Victorious, I stood with my brethren, faces shining with ecstasy, exchanging smiles of joy. The foreigners had no real experience of the color red. I painted it for them. Blessed are war, glory, and eminence. Blessed is my audience, for allowing me the honor of introducing myself."

"And blessed are you for sharing," Fatima said.

"I feel honored," said Jawad, "and grateful to be in your presence. But tell me, who is this al-Mutanabbi?"

Fatima guzzled her cup of wine. She kept her head back for a moment. She held out the cup, and Jawad poured. And Fatima declaimed:

> *I am he whose letters were seen by the blind,*
> *And whose words were heard by the deaf.*

She paused, smiled at Jawad, and had another sip. "Al-Mutanabbi was the greatest poet of the Arabic language, but more important, he is my favorite. He was blessed with the reckless audacity of imagination, full of astonishing metaphors. He suffered much in his life, because he was born with the two grand infirmities: he was poor and he was Arab. He came into the world early in the tenth century, in Kufa, south of Baghdad. He began to recite poetry of an exquisite beauty that had never been heard before nor has since. He claimed that God Himself inspired his poetry. Hence, the name: al-Mutanabbi, the one who claims to be a prophet."

"Conceit," said Jawad.

"Quite," added Fatima. "As an eighteen-year-old, he was imprisoned and tortured for his heresy. When he was released a few years later, he was once again penniless, powerless, and homeless—the poet in eternal exile. He had nothing to sell but his words, and he was willing. But who would be willing to buy? Most of the city-states were ruled no longer by Arabs, but by Muslims from all over whose native tongue was not Arabic. These princes, whom he wanted to praise, did not fully understand his words. So al-Mutanabbi, full of pride and arrogance, attached himself to the only Arab ruler in the area, Sayf al-Dawlah, the young prince of Aleppo, who was making a name for himself by protecting the northern borders from the evil Byzantine Empire.

"And al-Mutanabbi fought at the young prince's side and praised him, immortalized him in verse so eloquent it has been known to make roses wilt in shame for not matching its beauty.

"But then al-Mutanabbi discovered he had a problem. The young prince, like most Arab rulers throughout the ages, fancied himself a poet as well. He began to compose puerile poems praising himself and belittling the great poet. And al-Mutanabbi could not answer back."

"That is what being a servant is all about," said Jawad.

"The situation did not improve," Fatima went on. "Al-Mutanabbi left Aleppo for Cairo, attached himself to a different ruler, a king by the name of Kafur. The king promised the poet a province if he would sing the king's praises. But Kafur never kept his promise. He was warned by his vizier, a smart man who recognized the poet's genius, that if the king went back on his word he would live eternally as a mocked man, a historical joke. And the king was known to have said, 'You want me to assign a province to this power-hungry poet? This man who claims prophecy after Muhammad, will he not claim the kingdom after Kafur?'

"And al-Mutanabbi left Kafur's court and mocked him, immortalized him in verse so expressive it has been known to make snakes recoil in horror for not matching its venom.

"He wandered to Shiraz, in Persia. He then attached himself to Adud al-Dawlah, but this ruler, too, was unable to satisfy the poet's needs. So the poet tried to return to his Iraq, but was waylaid and killed by brigands along the way. He was the man who in his prime said:

The stallions, and the night, and the desert know me,
And the sword, and the spear, and the paper, and the pen.

But had to say before his death:

> *I am nothing but an arrow, shot in the air,*
> *Coming down again, unheld by its target.*

And he was killed just north of Baghdad, where all poets go to die."

❦

My aunt looked as if she were awaiting a barium enema. Her frail frame didn't settle completely in the chair, and her eyes wouldn't settle on anything. Because of her age and ill health, her fretfulness exhibited itself in erratic slow motion. She opened her handbag, and her bony fingers took out a cigarette.

"What's the matter with you, Samia?" my father asked. "You know you can't smoke in here. One would think you've never been to a hospital before."

"I'm just worried about you." She spoke slowly, gulping for breath. Her speech pattern had changed drastically since her last petite stroke. "I'm afraid that you're hiding things from me. Just tell me, tell me the worst." She forced the cigarette back, crushing it into its box. "My heart is weak, but it can deal with any bad news if it's about my only remaining brother." Lina kept trying to catch my eye. "Don't hide things from me." Lina lifted her eyebrows, grinned conspiratorially. "It's as if I'm not part of this family anymore just because I'm old." Lina mouthed the exact words as my aunt said them: "No one tells me anything."

"There's nothing to tell," my father said. "I'm doing just fine."

I stood up so my aunt wouldn't see me giggle. "I should go to the waiting room. I think the hospital has a two-visitor rule in this ward. I'm surprised the guard hasn't said anything yet."

"Stay here." My sister put her hand up, a border guard stopping an immigrant attempting to cross. "Your aunt's here to visit you as much as your father. Sit back down and tell your aunt all about what you've been doing since she last saw you." My aunt looked bewildered, if not bewitched. "Your aunt would love to hear about your life, I'm sure. Tell her what it's like to work as a computer programmer in the great city of Los Angeles."

When I was a young boy, my aunt used to say that she would be the first of the five siblings to die. She had made that pronouncement to her children, other family members, and random strangers. "Just do as I say," she would tell me when I was seven. "I'll be the first to die, and you'll regret having aggravated me." She was the oldest of the five, born in 1920, and even as a young woman, she wore infirmity like an itchy, gaudy shawl around her shoulders. She stopped saying she would be the first thirty years ago, when Uncle Wajih died.

"How many tranquilizers have you taken?" Lina asked my aunt.

"Have you gained weight?" Aunt Samia replied.

My aunt's eyes almost shot out of their sockets. Her lips and the skin around them seemed to have suddenly been invaded by a thousand lines. The noise in the hallway was that of an approaching army, a police team rushing in for a bust. The bey entered the room, followed by a flock of suits. You would think that in 2003, in post-feudal Beirut, one would have little use for clan chiefs and titled nobles, but traditions are not easily erased in our world. The bey no longer collected taxes, tributes, or royalties, but favors and loyalties were still his to claim. Though this latest incarnation of the bey was thirty, he looked like a boy of seventeen trying on his father's favorite suit. All smiles, he attempted to appear official and officious. He greeted us all perfunctorily, though his eyes never left my father, whereas it was my cousin Hafez, one of the bey's entourage, who held my father's attention.

Fatima, looking furious and threatening, viperlike, followed them into the room. The entourage must have sped past the visitors' lounge or she would have stopped them.

"How are you doing, dear uncle?" the bey said.

My father didn't reply. My sister did, loudly. "How did you all get in here? We can't have this many visitors. There are rules."

Everyone stopped moving. The very air seemed to perspire. A couple of men ahemmed. "It's quite all right, Lina," Hafez said. A nervous laugh escaped his lips. "The guard won't report us. We're here because we care about my uncle." He was a few weeks older than I, but he had the face of a boy.

"Then care outside, in the visitors' room. The guard shouldn't have let you in. I won't allow it. No more than two visitors at a time."

All the men stared at her. Hafez's hands moved from his sides, trembling, up and down. His eyes were those of prey about to be swallowed. "You're overreacting, my cousin. We won't overstay. I'm sure my uncle is happy to have the bey here." He looked to my father for support.

"Only two visitors. Everybody follow me to the waiting room." Lina, with Fatima's help, directed the confused crowd to the door. Fatima actually pushed one of the men out. "Come out with me," my sister said to my aunt. "Help me be a good hostess. You, too, Hafez. Unless you want to be one of the two. Just two people. Everybody else has to leave."

"But I'm not a visitor," Hafez mewled. "I'm family."

Lina turned to me. "Stay." She got closer, bent down to pick up her handbag, spoke softly so no one else would hear. "Make sure he doesn't get excited or emotional. And if the bey asks for money again, come out and get me."

My aunt was still sitting, not comprehending what was happening. Lina helped her up. "Why am I leaving?" my aunt asked.

"I need your wit," Lina replied.

♣

After setting up camp on the fourth night, Khayal began: "I am a poet. By the age of three, I was able to astonish all who heard my eloquent use of our illustrious language. I learned to read and write. I memorized the greats, the not-so-great, and the horrid. I have won more poetry wars in the Syrian countries than anyone has before me. I know panegyric poems, I know love poems. I can recite the entire *Muallaqat*, the qasidas. I am familiar with ghazal poems and khamriyas, the Bacchic songs."

"Tonight the poet offers bravado," Fatima said. "How delightful!"

"I am in awe, but I am not seduced yet," Jawad said.

"I am a lover. Boys from Baghdad to Tunis remember me in their dreams. I am the one whose exploits are recalled fondly by every lad, no matter how many he has had after me. I am the one who has left behind a trail of conquests as long as the Nile itself."

"Boasting and fireworks." Fatima applauded. "Every poet needs to show off."

"I do not find what he said particularly enticing," Jawad said. "I appreciate the technique, but my soul is unmoved."

And on the fifth night, Khayal said, "I must beg your forgiveness. I have been doing this all wrong. I implore you to forget what has come before and allow me a new beginning."

"Go on, please," said Jawad.

"No need for apologies," added Fatima. "You may not have seduced us, but you have certainly entertained us on this long journey, and for that we are grateful. Proceed."

And Khayal began:

> *"My love for you, Jawad,*
> *Leaves me no health or joy,*
> *You are the moon that has taken on*
> *The shape of a boy."*

"Oh, how scrumptious," Fatima cooed. "Back to Abu Nawas. We are going to have an evening of love poems. You will enjoy this, Jawad."

> *"Your face reveals a down so light*
> *A breeze might steal it, or a breath;*
> *Soft as a quince's bloom that might*
> *Find in a finger's touch its death.*
> *Five kisses and your face is cleared*
> *While mine has grown a longer beard."*

"Ah," sighed Fatima, "that must be Latin."

"I am pleased," Jawad said, "but if my suitor finds me beautiful, does that necessarily mean that I should find him so in return? This form of poetry is fun, delicious, but my soul remains untouched. It only increases my longing for the ineffable."

"Your name means 'horse.' My name means 'horseman.' We were meant to ride together. Can you not see?"

"I can see that I still do not feel seduced. My heart flutters not."

❧

"Your daughter is a strong woman," the bey said. His mustache twitched when he spoke, and paralleled his thick brows. He dragged the chair closer to my father's bed. My father refused to look at him, kept his eyes fastened on Hafez, who hovered, unable to control his nervous energy, and seemed torn between opposing overseers. My father followed his every movement disapprovingly. My father's father had been employed by successive beys, treated as one of their many servants. I didn't think my father ever forgave his for that, and it was going to take quite a bit of time for him to forgive Hafez for becoming a toady by choice. "What are you doing here?" my father asked him. "Why didn't you come when you heard I was hospitalized?"

"It's not his fault, Uncle," the bey said, his voice unctuous. "I wanted to come see you, and I wanted him to accompany me. I was a little busy, as you can imagine. Don't blame your nephew. Now, please, tell me about your health. Are you feeling better?"

"So you couldn't come without your master," my father told Hafez.

"I called Lina every day," Hafez said quietly, head bent as if he were speaking to the floor. His tie folded upon itself, bashful.

"But how is your health?" the bey asked.

Lina stuck her head into the room. "Your mother needs you, Hafez," she said curtly, with a disapproving glance at the bey. My father shot her a pleading look. "We'll be right back," she said to him, and to Hafez, "Now."

I knew I should stay with my father, but I could not bear it. I followed them out.

Aunt Samia was agitated and gasping for air. Her respiratory problems belied her true concern. "Is my brother offending the bey?"

"Ah, the illustrious bey, father of all," I said.

Hafez took his mother's hand and glared at me. "You're so American," he said. "Why is it that you're quiet all the time but when you do speak all you do is irritate people?"

"Kiss my ass, Hafez," Lina hissed. "If anyone shouldn't mention the word 'irritating,' it's you, you dumb shit."

"Why do we always resort to strong language?" Aunt Samia asked no one in particular. "It's all my father's fault. He had such a tongue, that one. Shit, shit—that's all he talked about."

Hafez ignored her. "I didn't mean anything, just that he's always so critical. Look, Osama, you know I love you. You know that. But you're forever disapproving. You make it seem that you feel superior to all of us."

I took a deep breath, tried to sound measured and contrite. "From now on, I will watch what comes out of my mouth."

Lina grabbed me by the arm and pulled me aside. "Walk." We walked past the guard and down the hall. "Speak," she said.

"I'm fine. What gets me is the 'You've become American' part. That's what everyone says instead of 'You're fucked up.' They might as well say they hate me."

My sister burst out laughing. "Sweetheart, you're such a treasure. They don't hate you." She began to walk me back to the room, a mother hen who instinctively knew she'd been away from her chicks for too long. "They hate *me*. You're not that important." She chuckled. "You've lived in America for twenty-five years, what are you supposed to become? An orangutan? They're just saying you're different."

"I was different before I left here. And so are you."

"Of course. Me they call the crazy one. They called my mother the bitch. You're just the American."

And on the sixth night, Khayal said, "My lovely. We are but a day away from your destination. I fear I have little time, and I regret how much I wasted of it. It seems that I do not have the ability to charm you, nor have I any skills in seduction. Let me try to convince you by telling you the story of the poet and Aslam."

"I love stories."

"This is a well-known story, which I have read in Ibn Hazm's treatise on love, *The Ring of the Dove*. In the Arab lands of Andalusia, there was a literary man, Ahmad ben Kulaib al-Nahawi, a poet of great stature, well known for his verse, especially his poems about Aslam, the boy whose name means 'to surrender.' Students from all over Córdoba went to al-Nahawi's house to study with him. The boy was one of the students. He was beautiful, refined, well read, earnest, and talented. The teacher fell in love with the student, and soon patience deserted the once-stoic man. He began to recite love poems to him. Tongues wagged. His witty verses of surrender to Aslam were repeated at gatherings in the red city.

"When Aslam heard of the gossip, he stopped visiting his mentor, cut off all classes of any kind. He restricted himself to his house and his stoop. The teacher stopped teaching, did nothing other than walk the street in front of Aslam's house, hoping for a furtive glimpse of his beloved. The dust of his footsteps rose every day and settled only in the evening. Aslam no longer sat on his stoop in daylight. After sunset prayers, when darkness melded into the evening light, overpowering it, Aslam would venture just under the doorjamb for his fresh air.

"When he could no longer lay eyes upon beauty, the poet resorted to guile. One evening, he donned the robes of peasants, covered his head the way they did, took chickens in one hand and a basket of eggs in the other. He approached Aslam, kissed his hand, and said, 'I have come to you, my lord, to deliver this food.'

" 'And who might you be?' Aslam asked.

" 'I am your servant, my lord. I work for you at the farm.'

"Aslam invited the man into his home, asked him to sit for tea, had his slaves take the eggs and chickens into the kitchen. He asked the poet whether the farm was in good shape. The poet replied that all went well. But when Aslam began to ask about the farmers and their families, the poet could not answer.

"And Aslam looked beneath the disguise and saw his nemesis. 'O brother,' he said. 'Have you no shame? Have you no compassion? I am no longer able to attend classes. I have not left my house for the longest time. Is it not enough that I am unable to sit on my own doorstep during the day? You have deprived me of everything that gives me comfort. You have turned me into a prisoner in the jail of your obsession. By God, I will never leave the sanctuary of my home; neither day nor night will I sit on my own stoop.'

"The poet called on his friends, confessed to everything that had happened.

"His friends asked, 'Have you lost your chickens and eggs?'

"Despair descended upon the poet, leaving him ill and bedridden. A friend, Muhammad ben al-Hassan, paid a visit to the poet, saw him looking ashen and feeble. 'Why are you not being seen by a doctor?'

" 'My cure is not a mystery, and doctors cannot heal me.'

" 'And what will cure you?'

" 'A glimpse of Aslam.'

"Pity took root in Muhammad's heart. He paid a visit to Aslam, who greeted him as a gracious host would. After the tea was served, the poet's friend said, 'I beg a favor of you. It is about Ahmad ben Kulaib al-Nahawi.'

" 'That man has made me infamous, the object of salacious jokes. He has besmirched my name, my reputation, and my respect.'

" 'I do understand, but allow the Almighty to be the final judge. All that he has done can be forgiven if you see the state he is in. The man is dying. Your visit would be merciful.'

" 'By God, I cannot do that. Do not ask it of me.'

" 'I must. Do not fear for your reputation. You are but visiting the sick.'

"Aslam begged off again and again, but the friend kept insisting, reminding him of honor, until Aslam agreed. 'Let us go, then,' the friend said.

" 'No. I am unable to do it today. Tomorrow.'

"Muhammad made him swear and left him to return to the poet, told him of the next day's visit. Light returned to the poet's eyes.

"The next day, Muhammad arrived at Aslam's house. 'The promise,' he said as he greeted his host. And they left for the poet's house. But when they reached the door, Aslam stopped, blushed, and stuttered, 'I cannot. I am unable to move my foot forward. I have reached the house, but I cannot enter.' And, swift as a racehorse, he ran away.

"The friend ran after him, grabbed Aslam by his cloak. Aslam kept running, and a piece of cloth remained in Muhammad's hand.

"One of the poet's servants had seen the guests approaching the house and had informed his master, so when Muhammad entered the house alone the poet was gravely disappointed. He snatched the piece of cloth. He insulted Muhammad, cursed at the world, swore at fate, yelled in anger, wept in sorrow. His friend withdrew to leave, but the poet grasped his wrist.

" 'Go to him,' the poet said. 'Tell him this:

> *Surrender, O lovely one,*
> *On the sick, have pity.*
> *My heart desires your visit*
> *More than God's own mercy.'*

" 'Do not stray from the Faith,' Muhammad admonished. 'What is this blasphemy?' He left the poet in anger, but had barely reached the street when he heard the wails of mourning. The poet, Ahmad ben Kulaib al-Nahawi, had died, clutching torn wool in his bony fingers.

"And this is true: years later, on a horribly rainy day, when only ghosts and jinn could walk unprotected, the cemetery warden recognized Aslam, who by then had become a grand poet himself, sitting on the grave of Ahmad ben Kulaib al-Nahawi, paying his respects, visiting the dead, utterly drenched. Rain streaked his face like tears."

And Fatima's face was wet as well. "That is a cheerless tale," she said.

"I feel sad for the poets," Jawad said. "My heart is in pain. I am touched." Jawad looked mournfully at his companions. "But I am not seduced."

❧

The bey made small talk, tiny talk, and my father replied with monosyllables or grunts. He was saved by my niece and a nurse entering the room. I knew for a fact that Salwa disdained the bey and all the traditions he represented, but from the look she gave him, the bey would have thought her an acolyte. Far along into her pregnancy, her wavy black hair forming a halo about her beatific, motherly-to-be face, she announced that my father needed some blood drawn. The nurse nodded. I noted that he didn't have any syringes or needles or tubes. My father closed his eyes, unable to disguise his relief, or not caring to.

I walked the bey to the elevator, and as we passed the waiting room, all his sycophants hurried out. When the elevator doors opened, he didn't enter. He finally decided to talk to me. "Your father is a fine man." He wanted to sound mature, but it was difficult since he looked like a marionette. "You should be proud of him."

I looked at him. One of his men was holding the elevator doors open. There were at least six other passengers, but not one complained.

"You should also be proud of your grandfather," he said. I noticed all eyes on me. The elevator doors kept trying to close. "I always liked you. You should come and visit." He stepped into the elevator and disappeared behind the closing doors. I stared at the spot where he'd been.

"Why does your father have to be rude?" Hafez said. He was holding his mother, acting as her cane. "Would it hurt him to be nice to the bey? The bey loves him, always says great things about him. We owe the bey so much. He shouldn't treat him that way."

Hafez was the closest cousin to me in age, and the family had assumed that we'd have so much in common, we'd grow up to be twins. We actually turned out to be total opposites. We were supposed to be best friends, but we barely got along. He was an insider, and I an outsider.

His mother chided him: "Don't talk about your uncle like that."

"He's just like Grandfather," he said. "Obstinate."

Hafez didn't know what he was talking about. My grandfather had an altogether different kind of obstinacy from my father's, which is why they could hardly speak to each other. Each wanted the other to see the world his way, but neither was willing to share spectacles. As I turned around, I heard Hafez say, "Why does Uncle disrespect me so? It's not as if his children made anything out of themselves."

Back in the room, I heard the same comparison. My father was apoplectic. My sister was trying to calm him down. "He's just like his grandfather," my father mumbled. "Obsequious, ass-kissing dimwit. Just like his grandfather. Son of a whore."

Ah, my grandfather, the progenitor of this mess we called family.

❦

And on the seventh night, outside the gates of Alexandria, Khayal knelt before his adored, defeated. "I have nothing more to offer, nothing but myself. If you want me to leave you, I will depart before the dawn, but if you take my hand, I will make you the same covenant that Ruth made with Naomi: Where you go I will go, and where you stay I will stay. Your people will be my people and your God my God. Where you die, I will die and there I will be buried."

Jawad took Khayal's hand.

— *Two* —

L ook here," my grandfather said, pointing at the only colorless spot on the map spread across the wooden table. I sat beside him, but my head couldn't get close enough for me to see. I stood on the chair, put a knee on the rickety table, felt as if I were floating atop a world of color. I saw Lebanon. I was able to recognize my country in faded purple, but his finger was farther north, above Tripoli. Turkey in yellow ocher. The exact spot discolored, bleached. "This is where I was born." He didn't look at the map, as if his fingers could find his birthplace by touch. "Urfa, it's called. Now they call it Şanliurfa. Means 'glorious Urfa.' Damnable Urfa is more like it."

He cursed easily, smoothly, one reason my mother didn't want me spending too much time with him. But Aunt Samia always insisted on it. He was family. I was a descendant. She was headstrong. That day, she had driven her three sons and me up from Beirut, dropped us at his house in the morning, and left to make her monthly visits in the village. My cousins preferred to play with the bey's nephews. As was their habit, Hafez, Anwar, and Munir walked up to the bey's mansion the instant their mother drove off. My grandfather did not allow me to leave him.

"I am of a time when maps had fewer colors," he was saying. Shaggy white hair sprouted as profusely from his ears and brows as it did from his head. He wasn't in a good mood.

I didn't always understand what he said, but that never stopped him. He stood up. I remained above the map, hovering in its sky. He gesticulated wildly; the floorboards creaked beneath his pacing, an off-key Morse code. "They say Şanliurfa has a mixture of Turkish and Arabic cultures. Sometimes they might even mention the Kurds. But never, if you see all the brochures and travel agents, never do they mention the Armenians. As if we were never there."

"Who are they, and who are we?" I asked

He stopped and stared out the grimy window into the distance as pinecones crackled in the iron stove.

Ah, Urfa, city of prophets. Jethro, Job, Elijah, and Moses spent part of their lives there, but it will always remain the city of Abraham, his birthplace. Yet Urfa's history is far more complex than mere myths, mere tales. It is Osrhoe, it is Edessa. It is in the Bible, the Koran, the Torah.

In the days of the mighty King Nimrod, there lived a young man named Abraham, son of Azar, an idol-maker. Out of wood, Azar sculpted beautiful gods that the people loved and worshipped. Azar would send his son to market with the idols, but Abraham never sold any. He called out, "Who'll buy my idols? They're cheap and worthless. Will you buy one? It won't hurt you." When a passerby stopped to look at the beauty of the craftsmanship, Abraham slapped the idol. "Talk," he said. "Tell this honest man to buy you. Do something." There would be no sale.

Of course, his father was upset. He was losing money and had a nonbeliever for a son. He told Abraham to believe in the gods or leave the house. Abraham left.

Abraham walked into a temple while all the townsfolk were in their own homes preparing for an evening of worshipping their beloved gods. Abraham held out food for the gods. "Eat. Aren't you hungry? Why don't you talk to me?" Again he slapped their faces, one by one. Slap, move over, slap. But then he took an ax and chopped the gods to pieces, some as small as toothpicks. He chopped all but the largest, and put the ax in this idol's hand.

When the people came to worship their gods, they found them in a large pile around the chief idol. They bemoaned their fate and that of their gods. "Who would do this?" they cried in unison, a chorus of wails.

"Surely it was someone," Abraham exclaimed. "The big one stands there with a guilty ax in his hand. Perhaps he was envious of the rest and chopped them up. Should we ask him?"

"You know they don't speak," the priest said.

"Then why do you worship them?"

"Heresy," the people called, and took him to see his king.

My grandfather was the product of an indiscreet affair. His father was Simon Twining—like the tea—an alcoholic English doctor, a missionary helping Christian Armenians in southern Turkey. His mother, Lucine, was one of the doctor's Armenian servants.

My grandfather's first name, Ismail, was predetermined. What would you call a son of your maid if you lived in Urfa? His last name was not Twining. The doctor's wife wouldn't allow that. It was Guiragossian, his mother's name. He received his full name, our family's bane, in Lebanon, as a full-fledged hakawati.

What is a hakawati, you ask? Ah, listen.

A hakawati is a teller of tales, myths, and fables (hekayât). A storyteller, an entertainer. A troubadour of sorts, someone who earns his keep by beguiling an audience with yarns. Like the word "hekayeh" (story, fable, news), "hakawati" is derived from the Lebanese word "haki," which means "talk" or "conversation." This suggests that in Lebanese the mere act of talking is storytelling.

A great hakawati grows rich, and a bad one sleeps hungry or headless. In the old days, villages had their own hakawatis, but great ones left their homes to earn fortunes. In the cities, cafés were the hakawatis' domain. A hakawati can tell a tale in one sitting or spin the same tale over a period of months, impregnating it with nightly cliffhangers.

It is said that in the eighteenth century, in a café in Aleppo, the great one, Ahmad al-Saidawi, once told the story of King Baybars for three hundred and seventy-two evenings, which may or may not have been a record. It is also said that al-Saidawi cut the story short because the Ottoman governor begged him to finish it. The city's despot had spent every night enthralled and had been recalled to Istanbul for growing lax with the affairs of state, even neglecting the collection of taxes. The governor needed to know how the tale ended.

The bey first met my grandfather, a waiflike, hungry thirteen-year-old hakawati, in a sleazy bar in the Zeitouneh district of Beirut before the Great War. My grandfather had been eking out a meager living by entertaining customers in between various salacious or pseudo-musical acts. The bey was inordinately charmed by the witty stories. When he inquired after my grandfather's background, the young Ismail provided three different improbable tales in a row. On the spot, the bey hired my grandfather to be his fool, and from that point on referred to him as "al-kharrat," the fibster, or "hal-kharrat," that fibster. One day, feeling generous, the bey decided to give the rootless boy some dignity. Since my grandfather had no papers, no documented father, the bey called in favors, paid bribes, and offered his boy a new birth certificate, baptizing him with a fresh name, Ismail al-Kharrat.

The little hakawati arrived in our world in the early evening of January 16, 1900. Simon Twining was telling the tale of Abraham and Nimrod to a rapt audience of his wife, his two daughters, his two Armenian maids, and four Armenian orphans in his care.

"Abraham stood defiantly before his king." The language English, the tone rising, the voice smooth. "King Nimrod grew nervous, since it was his first encounter with a free soul. 'You are not my god,' Abraham told Nimrod."

Lucine felt the first pang of pain; a wave of nausea swept through her. She breathed deeply, dismissing the pain as transitory, because the baby had one more month to go. She steadied herself, felt grateful that the stool was four-legged. The doctor believed three-legged furniture to be the work of Satan. It was unstable and mocked the Trinity.

"The young man grew in stature when he defied the hunter-king Nimrod. 'Who is this mighty God you speak of?' asked the frightened king." The doctor picked up the long-handled broom leaning on the corner behind him, lifted it above his head. The handle almost knocked off a small box that he had placed below the angle of a ceiling beam to catch the droppings of a pair of swallows nesting there.

Lucine's second shot of pain arrived three fingers below her belly button, four to the right. She struggled for breath but made no sound.

"Abraham was resolute. 'He it is who gives life and death,' he answered, his gaze unwavering. The king said, 'But I too give life and death. I can pardon a man sentenced to die and execute an innocent child.'" All the children gasped. Lucine felt flushed and dizzy. "Abraham said, 'That is not the way of God. But can you do this? Each morning God makes the sun rise in the east. Can you make it rise in the west?' Nimrod grew angry, had his minions build a great big fire, and ordered Abraham thrown into it. The men came to carry Abraham, but he told them he could walk."

Just at that instant, as Abraham walked into the blazing fire, Lucine's scream was heard throughout the valley. Water spread beneath her four-legged stool, on the scrubbed stones, collecting in the grooves that acted as miniature Roman aqueducts.

A hakawati's timing must always be perfect.

Ah, births, births. Tell me how a man is born and I will tell you his future.

A seer had told King Nimrod that one shortly to be born would dethrone him. The king beheaded the seer as the bearer of bad tidings. He called his viziers into the throne room and commanded the death of all newborns.

What to do? Adna, pregnant with baby Abraham, left her home in Urfa without having time to pack, walked carefully across town, and headed toward a cave in one of the surrounding hills. There she gave birth. Abraham arrived with eyes open, inquisitive and watchful. The baby did not cry. Adna had no milk. The baby reached for her hand, placed two of her fingers in his mouth, and suckled. One finger supplied milk and the other honey.

And now you want to know how the hakawati was conceived, so listen.

The spring before his birth in Urfa. The sun was setting, the temperature had cooled, and the last birds were settling in the highest branches. Dr. Twining was walking home when he saw his maid, Lucine, standing on an unstable log, trying to cover the outhouse with dry palm branches, a seasonal chore: a true ceiling would trap odors, so sun-dried branches mixed with lavender and jasmine covered the top. The faux plafond protected from the elements, provided a botanical sweetness, and allowed God the choice of not looking directly at a family excreting.

The colors deepened at that time of day, allowing Dr. Twining to see his maid, with her back to him, as a mirage—ephemeral, shimmering, divine. Turkeys, chickens, rabbits, geese, three dogs, and two tortoises could all be seen moving around the perched Lucine. She was their daily feeder, and they were waiting for her. The doctor was grateful that he could provide selfless service to all the unfortunates, to the needy and the meek. A solitary swallow flew low in front of him. He saw the forked tail clearly. He fixed his gaze on Lucine, saw that she wasn't a mirage; she moved back and forth on the unsteady log. "Lucine," he called out. The chickens dispersed at his shout. Lucine looked back, her eyes surprised, as if they were questioning the reason for all this. She lost her balance. She opened her mouth to ask for help, swayed forward once, then stiffened, rigid as a column, and fell. Turkeys and geese scattered in all directions.

By the time he reached her, she had still not uttered a sound. She leaned against the gray wall of the outhouse, holding her bare ankle, having pulled up her skirt slightly to look at it. He bent down to examine it. "Are you all right?" he asked. "Let me see." She removed her hand, and his took over, pressing gently. She shuddered. "That hurts?" he whispered. She nodded. His fingers pressed below the joint, gently stroked her sole. She remained quiet. "I think it's a sprain." His thumb and forefinger formed a gentle vise, massaging her calf. "Does this hurt?" She shook her head. Her eyes were new to him. He held her ankle with his right hand. His left massaged up farther, almost to the knee. "Does this hurt? And this? This?"

Fate, I tell you.

He consumed her right then, uncomfortably, outside the outhouse, the faint malodor acting as an aphrodisiac.

"Why would Abraham want to kill Ishmael?" I asked my mother as she undressed for the night. I, already in my pajamas, lay in bed waiting for her, trying to make my small body fit the large indentation my father had worn into the mattress.

"God asked him to sacrifice his son, but then God allowed him to substitute a sheep." She put on her blue cotton nightgown and, in a maneuver that I always considered the height of acrobatic achievement, removed her brassiere from under the nightgown.

"Was it a boy sheep?"

"I assume so." She finally smiled at me, chuckled, and shook her head. "Only my little Osama would wonder about that."

She sat at her vanity to remove her makeup, which still looked wonderful. The entire family had been at Aunt Samia's apartment to celebrate Eid al-Adha, Abraham's sacrifice, the only holiday the Druze celebrate. I loved Eid al-Adha. Kids got money from adults during the holiday. All I had to do was walk up to any relative and smile, and I would get coins that jingled in my pockets.

"Why would God ask him to do that?"

She poured démaquillant onto a cotton ball and delicately wiped her face, sliding her hand from top to bottom. "It was a test," she said, looking in the mirror. "He wouldn't have let him kill his son."

"Did he pass the test?"

"Yes, of course, dear. That's why it's a holiday and we get to eat so much and get fat. Two whole lambs, and nothing left. I think that's a record."

I propped myself on my elbow to watch her more easily. Usually when I moved around in bed, she would tell me to keep still so I could fall asleep faster, but not tonight, probably because of the holiday.

"But what if God didn't stop him? Would he have killed his son?"

"Is that what's worrying you?" Finally done, she walked to her side of the bed. She looked quite different without makeup, more girlish. "It's just a story, Osama. It's not real." She slowly got into bed. "Stories are for entertainment only. They never mean anything."

"Grandfather said it happened on a mountain and God stopped Abraham's hand just as he was about to cut Ishmael's throat. He was on a mountain that was close to the sky, and it was a clear day, too, so God was able to see everything."

"Your grandfather says many things that aren't true. You know how wild his stories are. You know he never went to school or anything like that. It's not his fault. But you don't have to believe the same things he does. If you think something he's saying is too foolish to be true, then it is." She stretched, clicked off the light switch on the wall. "Don't let his stories trouble you. Don't let any story trouble you." She turned me around and hugged me. We were together like quotation marks. "Now go to sleep."

"I don't like Abraham's story," I said to the dark. "It's not a good one."

After a slight pause, "I don't like it, either."

I thought about the story. "If God asked you, would you kill me?" I felt her shudder.

"Now you're being silly," she said. "Of course I wouldn't do such a thing. Go to sleep and stop thinking."

"But what if God asked you to?"

"He won't ask *me*."

"What if he asked Dad to kill me? Would he do it?"

"No. Now, don't be annoying."

I could not stop thinking. "What if God told someone to kill another person—would that be okay? You couldn't put the killer in jail if God told him to do it. What if God told someone to kill a lot of people? Like how about the Turks or the French? God tells a man to kill all the French, and he goes out and shoots every Frenchman he sees. Bang, bang, bang. Is that okay? Does he get blamed? What if—"

She shushed me. She covered my mouth with her left hand. I could smell verbena, her moisturizing lotion. "God doesn't talk to people," she whispered in my ear. "God doesn't tell anybody to do anything. God doesn't do anything."

"But people believe God talks to them."

"Stupid people, only stupid people."

I heard a mosquito's buzz. I sat up, announced its presence to the room.

"Damn," she said. "I thought the room was sprayed." She stood up, considered ringing the buzzer for the maid, then opened the nightstand drawer and removed one Katol. Without turning on the light, she pushed the green spiral insecticide into its stand, struck a match to it. In the sudden flare, she looked like a movie star, her dark hair falling around her face.

"You don't believe in God, do you, Mother?" I asked.

She looked at me as if I were a stranger, then blew out the match, throwing her face into darkness. "No," she said, "I don't believe there is a God." I heard the hollow sound of the match falling in the wastebasket. "But I don't want you talking about this with other people. It's not something we talk about. Do you understand?"

"But how do you know there's no God?"

"Because, if there's a God, your father would have been smitten already. Now, for the last time, go to sleep or go to your room."

The odor of the mosquito killer, mixed with verbena, permeated the room.

That night, in the comfortably furnished parlor while everyone else slept, the doctor confessed everything to his wife. His back to the mild fire, he knelt before her, wept. She put down her knitting and listened to his elaborate explanations. He was weak, only human. He didn't know what had possessed him. It wasn't Lucine's fault. It was his. If only he could castrate himself, his life would be so much simpler, he would be a better human being, the husband she deserved. She remained quiet. It would never happen again, he promised her. It was an accident. Inconsequential. He would once again prove worthy of her trust. She was his anchor. She was his faith. Would she forgive him?

"What about her ankle?" his wife asked.

Puzzled, the doctor could think of nothing to say.

"Is her ankle all right?" she asked.

"It's a severe sprain," he responded. "It'll be back to normal in a month or so, but she needs to be off it for three or four days."

His wife went back to her knitting. Looking down at her work, she said, "That's going to be difficult. It's hard to keep that girl off her feet. She's so industrious and loyal. I don't know if she'll be able to stay still for three days."

Her husband walked back to his chair. He took out his pipe and his tobacco pouch. He began his nightly ritual. "We'll just have to force her." He lit the pipe, took a few puffs, waited for the shreds of tobacco to turn amber before blowing out the match. "For her own good."

"You're right. I'll have to find her some chores that don't require her to move about."

He opened his book, and the bookmark fell on his lap. "Just make sure her leg is elevated."

"Yes. The sprained ankle always above her heart, to make sure it doesn't swell too much." She paused, smiled at him; then her fingers resumed their spidery work.

A cast-iron woodstove dominated my grandfather's sitting room. The exhaust pipe, big enough for a soccer ball to roll through, extended all the way across the room to the ceiling on the other side. He removed the stove every spring, yet when he brought it back in late autumn he placed it in the exact same spot, across the room from the hole in the ceiling. He stuffed the stove with split oak, pine, and pinecones throughout the cold season. The sitting room always felt like a slow-burning oven. And whenever the capricious wind changed direction, aggressive smoke puffed back into the room, searing my lungs. If I complained, my grandfather chided me for not liking the scent of burnt pine, for being a spoiled city boy used to gardenias and lavender handpicked from the gardens.

In winter, the stove became the center of his universe. He cooked on it, brewed his maté, his tea, his coffee. He moved his bed next to it. He left his sitting room only to go to the bathroom at the back of the house.

The next day, Lucine's ankle was swollen and her leg blue to the knee. The doctor's wife brought her a pink oleander and placed it in a chipped glass beside her bed. She raised the bottom end of the bed on bricks. She cleaned Lucine's bedpan. Lucine mumbled incoherent apologies, too shy to speak directly to her madame.

Two weeks later, the doctor stood next to his wife in the doorway of the maids' room, watching Zovik, the second maid, help Lucine vomit into a rusty metal pail.

"Make sure the ankle doesn't move," the doctor instructed Zovik.

"This is the will of God," his wife whispered to him.

Lucine's ankle remained swollen for the rest of her life, all thirteen months of it.

"Play me something," my grandfather said. He slumped on his small couch, the cigarette between his fingers a nub, totally forgotten.

"But you don't like what I play," I said.

My grandfather heaved a sigh of impatience. The cigarette burned his finger. He dropped it on the couch. He stared at his hand, astonished. He stamped the cigarette with the palm of his hand. The butt bounced off the cushion, hit the floor already extinguished. "Pfflt. I never said I don't like what you play." He raked his curly white hair with both hands, but it remained as unruly as it always was, as unruly as he was. "You're my flesh and blood." His beard was scraggly but clean. His clothes were unruly as well.

"You said I play like a donkey."

"Well, then, come here and play something different and don't play like a donkey." He patted the cushion next to him, took out his tobacco pouch, and began to roll. I didn't move. Keeping his eyes fixed on his cigarette, he said, "There's nothing worse than a reluctant performer. All this 'I don't know if I can' and 'I'm really not ready' is shit on shit. Someone asks you to play, just play. Enjoy your time in the sun and don't whine about it."

I brought his oud and sat next to him. "I don't like your oud. It has the wrong strings."

His eyes rolled. "Pfflt. Who cares about stupid things? Just play."

I started with a simple scale to limber up my fingers, just as Istez Camil taught me. My grandfather sank deeper into the couch, the collar and shoulders of his black jacket rising above his ears, almost to the top of his head. I moved slowly into a maqâm, but it didn't sound right. The oud was no good. I tried to compensate, but my grandfather stood up suddenly.

He walked to the stove, opened the top, and threw his cigarette in. "You play like a donkey. What has that idiot of a musician been teaching you? Who listens to all that Iraqi crap?"

"People love what I play. Everybody says I play like an angel, like a sweet angel."

"You play like a donkey angel." He scrunched up his face. He lifted his hands to his cheeks, pretended to make them talk. "Plunk, plunk, plunk. I can make music. Look. Tum, tum, tum." He took out his dentures, held them in front of his mouth. "I can play music, that nobody wants to listen to. Can you? Can you?"

I turned my back to him. "I'm not listening to you. You don't know good music and your oud is horrible."

"Why don't you play something interesting?" I didn't have to look at him to know that he had put his dentures back where they belonged. "Play a song instead of that donkey shit. Songs are better. Tell me a story. Sing a story for me."

"I don't want to. You do it."

He picked up his oud and sighed. He shook his head and said, "In Turkmenistan, Uzbekistan, and northeastern Iran, the word 'bakhshi' means a player of the oud, singer, and storyteller. I am a bakhshi, you are a bakhshi. The word comes from Chinese and arrived with the advent of the smelly Mongols." He plucked two notes before going on: "On the other hand, the storytelling musicians of Khorasan in Iran think 'bakhshi' comes from 'bakhshande,' which means a bestower of gifts, because of the musical gift God has bestowed on them. I have always appreciated thinking of the oud player as a storyteller, as a bestower of gifts."

He played horribly, had a lousy voice that was always off-key. He sang a song about a boy who had more luck than brains.

·　　·　　·

In the summer, by Lucine's fifth month, everyone knew she was carrying a boy. The signs were obvious: she had already gained twelve kilos (boys are bigger); her belly was completely round (girls are awkward, the uterus never fills out perfectly); she was constantly in pain, having spent her entire first trimester on her back (boys are always too much trouble); she did not recover easily, her ankle remained swollen (boys are self-centered, draining all the mother's healing energies); she was radiant (boys make their mothers happy).

On a hot day, a hobbling Lucine sprinkled well water on the ground to keep the dust from rising. One of the tortoises retracted into its shell when it felt the water drops. Lucine wanted to make sure that the spot beneath it did not remain utterly dry. She waddled indelicately. She pushed the tortoise with her bare foot and her ankle gave out. She almost stumbled.

She touched her ankle, which had refused to heal, and prayed to the Virgin. She dragged herself over to the mulberry tree and sat in its shade. She stretched her legs, pointed her toes. To test the ankle's strength, she pushed against a rock the size of a melon and moved it slightly. She placed her toes under it and pushed again. The pain this time was piercing, causing her to faint.

"It's the ankle," the wife said.

"I'm not so sure," the doctor said. He massaged Lucine's ankle, noted a red mark on the top of her right foot. He showed it to his wife. "Are the girls inside?" he asked. It did not take him long to find the white scorpion. Under the rock, crushed as thin as a sheet of paper, its sting its last defiant act. "This is not a good sign."

When I told my grandfather I was hungry, he gave me a piece of dry bread sprinkled with sea salt. "Your midmorning refreshment, my little lord. That's what I used to have every morning for a snack when I was your age. All the orphans waited impatiently for this, between breakfast and lunch. Just taste it. You'll like it." I refused to look at him. He moved around incessantly, like a windup toy that never completely unwound. "Here I am trying to infuse you with culture, my flesh and blood, my own kin. You don't want this, you want that. When I was your age, I had to eat what I was given."

I turned. I made sure that my back was toward him wherever he moved.

"You won't eat my bread. There are children who'd kill to have a piece of bread. You have so many things and you're still not happy. I didn't have any toys when I was your age. But I entertained myself. I didn't need toys like you do. I used to make myself slingshots. I'd climb the only high tree in our backyard, a black mulberry, and use the fruit as ammunition against the Muslim boys. I didn't use stones, because I'd have gotten in trouble, but hitting a boy with a mulberry was a lot more fun anyway. The fruit stained a rich purple. Every time I hit a boy, I'd raise my arms like a champion and almost lose my balance, but I never fell. Those boys used to call us names. They called us *unbelievers* and *without history*. I didn't care, mind you, but the doctor's daughters always cried. Barbara and Jane. Those were their names. See, I still remember, even after all these years. I can still remember their names. I haven't lost anything. Or was it Barbara and Joan? It was one or the other. Ah, who cares?"

"I don't."

"Listen," he said. "Listen. Our house was right outside the city walls. I mean right outside—the remnant of the ancient Roman wall was the back wall of our house. The wall extended beyond the house and marked half our garden. I'd climb the wall at night and yell without any sound, yell at the world: I am here. I'm here, like Abraham. I could see Abraham's pool when I stood on the wall. It shimmered in starlight. It bubbled eternally. Full of sacred fish, guarded and fed regularly."

"Who fed them?"

"The Muslims, of course. When Nimrod ordered Abraham into the fire, God intervened and manifested his glory to the hunter-king. The sycophants opened the oven door expecting to see nothing but charred remains, except there the prophet was, as glorious as ever; the young Abraham was singing, sitting indolently on a bed of red roses, red like the color of fresh blood. Thousands upon thousands of crimson rose petals. The courtiers ran away in terror as if they had seen a jinni or an angel. Abraham, unblemished and untouched, walked out of the furnace, smirked as he passed Nimrod, and went home. The king, the mighty warrior, frightened and furious, called his army. He built the greatest catapult the world had ever seen. But no, he said, one is never enough. He built another, an exact replica. In the catapults' cradles, his men put pile upon pile of burning wood. He doused the fire with more oil, added pinecones for sound effects. He gave the order to unleash his fury at his nemesis. But God changed the catapults to minarets. He transformed the fire to water, and the pool of Abraham came to exist. He changed the fagots to carp, and the fish gave life to the pool. For thousands of years, the freshwater pool has given sustenance and nourishment to Urfa's people. The dervish Muslims guard the pool and give back to God by taking care of his sacred fish. I played there when I was your age. I swam with the fish of God."

Sunlight finally broke through the windows. The air smelled sweet and fragrant. "Were they like other fish?" I asked.

"No, of course not." He waved his hand in a dismissive gesture, his pale, bony wrists protruding from frayed white cuffs. "They were special fish. Sparkled like gems at night, colors you'd never see. If only I could show them to you. And the dervishes looked so holy in their traditional outfits, the white robes and red hats."

"Aren't they the ones that dance? I've seen them. They're beautiful and grand."

"They twirl. That's how they pray. And they are beautiful."

"I want a God that makes me twirl." I jumped off the couch. I untucked and unbuttoned my shirt so it would flow like a robe. "Like this. I can do this for God." I held my hands out. I twirled and twirled and twirled. "Look," I said. "Look."

The Dutch painter Adriaen van der Werff, an accomplished, rather sentimental and repetitive minor master, painted a Biblical scene of Sarah offering her Egyptian slave girl, Hagar, to Abraham. Of course, Hagar looks nothing like an Egyptian. Chestnut hair—close to blond, even—and she has the lightest skin of all three figures, Nordic features, too young and beautiful. She is at the bottom of the painting; only her torso is shown, naked from the waist up. A piece of clothing (a petticoat?) and her right forearm cover her right breast. The right hand on her left breast serves to accentuate the sumptuous nipple. She kneels beside the bed, looks down at her naked belly, demure, submissive, excluded from the discussion between Sarah and Abraham.

Sarah, a crone, stands behind Hagar, talking to her husband. She is fully clothed in drab material, her white hair partially veiled. Abraham is naked on the bed, a navy-blue sheet covering everything below his navel. He has a thick brown beard, but his muscular chest is completely hairless, his abdominals defined. His hand rests on Hagar's sensuous bare shoulder beneath him. He looks happy with the offer, smug almost.

"You see," Sarah says, "that the Lord has prevented me from having children. Go into my Egyptian slave girl. It may be that I build my family through her."

Abraham listened to the voice of Sarah and went into her Egyptian slave girl.

Months later, the sky swelled with glory, and the valley began to color and bloom. Abraham's face had lost its winter pallor; his hair remained black, never-changing, with its widow's peak. Sarah's eyes were swollen, full of tears, her face blotchy. She stared at Abraham, hoped he would not notice her. She had urged him to sleep with her Egyptian. God spoke through her. Hagar would provide him with a male heir, and Sarah would be elevated, if not in his eyes, then surely in her own. Sarah never imagined that Abraham would fall in love with the slave, treat her as a wife. He had such affection for Hagar. And she grew. She still behaved herself, but the look on her face was no longer that of a slave. It was more graceful, more self-assured, the look of someone who belonged. The slave had quickly gotten used to salvation.

"You are responsible for the wrong I am suffering," Sarah informed her husband. "I put my servant in your arms, and now that she is pregnant, she despises me. May the Lord judge between you and me."

"She is your slave," Abraham replied. "Do with her what you think best."

"We should call the midwife," the doctor's wife said. "We don't want people to talk."

"Fine. Fine. Call the witch. I will make sure she doesn't make things worse. Tell her to keep her mouth shut. I don't want to listen to her tiresome life story once more."

Zovik interrupted the midwife's supper—boiled rice and lentils with a touch of cumin. She told Zovik she would come soon after she finished her meal, but then she actually heard Lucine's wail. She jumped up off the ground, almost knocking over the brass tray and the dish of lentils. Nimble for a woman her age and weight, she ran out the door, with a concerned Zovik trailing behind. "Why did you wait so long?" the midwife asked. "Why does everybody wait so long?"

A crowd milled outside the doctor's house. Some had come from as far as two or three neighborhoods away to discover the source of the wails and to discuss their significance. The midwife squeezed through the crowd, ran into the house, and found the children clustered outside the maids' room. As she approached, the wail started as a low rumble, rolled forward like a tumbleweed in harsh winds, and reached a crescendo that almost brought her to her knees. The children's faces registered shock, followed by dismay, and then they slowly began to cry. The doctor's wife came out of the room. "I can't take this any-more," she said to no one in particular. "To your rooms, children. You have no business here. Don't forget your prayers, your teeth, and your eye drops. Now go to sleep." She disappeared into the hallway.

Lucine lay in bed, her eyes staring at the ceiling, her lips praying, her brows and forehead anticipating the next contraction. The doctor seemed agitated and slightly bewildered. The midwife asked if the water had broken and whether the baby had begun to reveal itself.

"I don't know what's going on," he said. "I've never seen anything like this."

"It's definitely a boy. Boys don't like to come out if there's another male in the room. Boys like to be enticed into coming out. Boys want to be made to feel special."

"That's nonsense. I wish you'd stop it."

"O Holy Virgin. This boy seems to be having problems finding his way out." She stroked Lucine's belly. Once, twice, three times. "Listen to me, my boy. We want you out here. You're our special boy. If you come, I'll tell you a story. Come."

Once, there was a little boy who lived with his grandfather in a small hut in a small village. This boy was so tiny that everyone called him Jardown, the rat. Jardown loved his grandfather, who in turn loved Jardown more than anything in the world. His grandfather took care of him, cooked for him, and told him stories.

One day in fall, his grandfather told the other village men that he was getting old and could not bring home as much firewood as he used to, and that the boy, Jardown, was too small to carry all they needed for the approaching winter. The other men told him not to fret. They would all send him their sons the following day, and they should be able to collect enough firewood to last for two or three winters.

The next day, all the village boys arrived at the cottage. Jardown's grandfather gave each boy a piece of bread, a piece of chocolate, and two drops of condensed milk. "This is to thank you for helping us. Go into the forest and bring back as much firewood as you can. Take care of Jardown while you're out there. He is younger and much smaller than any of you."

The boys went into the forest, each carrying his bread and chocolate and condensed milk. Some began to collect firewood while others chopped down dying trees. Every boy was doing his share, except for Jardown, who sat on a big rock with his feet dangling above the forest floor.

"Jardown," one of the boys said, "why aren't you cutting wood?"

"My grandfather gave you a piece of bread so you would cut wood for me, too."

So the boys cut more wood. When they thought they had enough, they gathered all the wood in bundles to carry back to the village. Each boy carried his own bundle—each boy except for Jardown, who still sat in the same place.

"Jardown," another boy said, "why aren't you carrying a bundle?"

"My grandfather gave you all a piece of chocolate so you would carry my bundle."

The boys picked up Jardown's bundle and began to leave, but then they noticed that Jardown was not moving. "Why aren't you coming with us, Jardown? We are going home."

"My grandfather gave you all two drops of condensed milk so you would carry me when I got tired."

A boy much bigger than Jardown lifted him onto his shoulders. They began the long trek home. Soon, however, the sun shrank and everything grew dark. The boys walked and walked and walked and walked, but they couldn't find their way out of the forest.

"Which way is the right way?" one of the boys asked.

"This way." "That way." "No, that way." "No, this way."

In the distance the boys heard the vicious barking of a dog. In the opposite direction from the barking, they saw a light. They wondered which they should walk toward, the barking or the light. After much deliberation, they asked Jardown: "Which way should we go, Jardown? In one direction we have a dog barking. Should we go there, or should we go where there is light?"

Jardown, the smart one, pondered the question. He said, "If we go toward the dog, it might bite us. I think we should go toward the light."

The boys walked toward the light, which was coming from a cottage in the middle of the forest. They knocked on the door, but no one answered. They entered and decided to wait there till morning, when they would be able to see their way back.

After they settled in the cottage, the boys heard a loud noise that sounded like a huge wild animal outside the door. The boys scuttled about and hid behind every piece of furniture. Some went behind the curtains, two crouched under the sofa, one even went up the unlit chimney flue. The door opened, and a big, hairy monster walked in—big as in bigger than a camel standing on its hind legs, but not quite as big as an elephant; hairy as in even hairier than a bear and with a big beard and long hair. He walked in, the sound of each step echoing through the house. The monster took a deep breath. "What's this I smell?" he asked. "It smells like I have humans in here. Young, tasty flesh. I love the smell of boys. Where are they? Where are the yummy boys?"

He searched behind the chairs, under the sofa. He found each boy, one by one. He even located the boy in the chimney. The boys huddled in the middle of the room.

"What are you boys doing in my house?" the monster asked. One of them said in a low, quivering voice, "We can't find our way home."

The monster looked at the feast of boys in front of him, the aroma of tender flesh making him drool. He realized that he wouldn't be able to eat all the boys in one sitting, there were so many of them. The best thing to do would be to get the boys to bed and then eat them one by one while they slept. The monster told the boys: "Allow me to be your host. Spend the night here. I know the way back to your village, but I can only find it when there is light. In the morning, I will show you the way back home. No one finds his way in the dark. Sleep here, where it is safe."

The boys relaxed, breathed a sigh of relief, and went off to bed. Not Jardown. Being the smart one, he realized what the monster was up to. He'd stay awake so the monster wouldn't eat them. The monster waited diligently and uncomplainingly outside the boys' room, counting out time. He peeked from behind the door and asked quietly, "Who is asleep and who is awake?"

"Everybody is asleep," Jardown replied, "but Jardown is awake."

"Why is Jardown awake? What does Jardown want?"

"Jardown can't sleep because every night before bed his grandfather bakes him a loaf of bread."

So the monster went into the kitchen, lit the fire, and began to bake a loaf of bread. When he finished, he brought the bread to Jardown and went back out of the room to wait for the boy to sleep. Dawn was breaking when the monster asked quietly from behind the door, "Who is asleep and who is awake?"

"Everybody is asleep," Jardown replied, "but Jardown is awake."

"Why is Jardown awake? What does Jardown want?"

"Jardown can't sleep because every night before bed his grandfather brings him water from the river in a sieve."

The monster thought that Jardown would go to sleep as soon as he brought him water from the river in a sieve. He hurried out of the house to the river. As soon as he was out, Jardown woke all the boys. "Hurry," he told them. "We must run. The monster wants to eat us. We have to get out of here. It is almost light out, and we can see our way back home. Hurry."

The boys ran out of the house. They got to the river and noticed the monster in the distance trying to fill the sieve with water. The boys quickly and quietly swam to the opposite side, the older ones helping the younger ones across. When they had finished, the monster looked up and saw his banquet of boys across the river. He ran after them. "Let me come with you. I know the way back home. I can help you. How did you get across the river?"

Jardown pointed to the millstones near the monster. "The best way to cross the river is to put one of those stones around your neck and walk across. That's how we did it."

The monster put one of the millstones around his neck. He walked into the river, and the heavy stone pulled him down to the bottom. The boys ran home, and Jardown went to his grandfather, who was very happy to see him, having worried all night.

This is the story of Jardown, the little boy who outwitted the big monster, and that is why, in winter, when the river gets rough, if you get close to the white, raging water, you will be able to hear it saying, "Everybody is asleep, but Jardown is awake," followed by a deep, long sigh.

.   .   .

The hakawati, all one and a half kilograms of him, arrived in a lake of blood. His mother had been noisy, but the baby was quiet. After being assured that it was a boy, with ten toes, ten fingers, and an abundance of unruly, matted hair, Lucine took a deep breath and swallowed hard. She asked the midwife if her baby was alive.

"He breathes," she said. "But barely. He's the smallest baby I've ever seen. He's no bigger than a rat." She lifted him by the right leg, shook him, and spanked his behind.

"He's not crying," his mother said. "Why isn't he crying?"

The midwife held the hakawati as if he were a dead ferret. She was about to shake him harder when the doctor admonished her. "Give him to me," he said. Ismail began to cry the instant he landed in his father's arms. The doctor passed him right back to the midwife.

Someone had placed the evil eye on the baby. It wasn't only that he was a bastard, tiny, and not very healthy. He was an ugly baby and would grow up to be an ugly child, an ugly adolescent, and an ugly man. There was no escaping that. But, of course, his mother loved him.

"Let me see him," Lucine said. She reached out her arms for the crying baby. She did not recognize anyone in his face. "What an angry boy."

Oh, and he also had colic.

"Should I try to feed him?"

The doctor thought there was no point yet, but the midwife disagreed. "Feed him. Feed him. Train him to eat. It's never too early. You have no milk yet, but all the activity will get you milky. He will probably get nothing but glue first, but it's all good. He's so small that he needs every drop of food. If you don't produce milk, there's Anahid, but I think you'll cow fine."

Lucine unbuttoned her blouse and took her left breast out. The doctor gasped involuntarily, stared indelicately. The hakawati took to the breast as a hummingbird takes to the air. The breast provided no milk, so he began to cry again. He cried for an hour, for two, for three. The house didn't sleep. The doctor's wife went in to look at mother and child but could offer no solace. She sent her husband.

"I don't think I have any milk yet," Lucine said. In the flickering light of the one candle, she showed him her breast, pushed her chest out toward him, squeezed her nipple. "Look," she said. "Look." He looked. "No milk yet."

He cupped her breast, held its weight in his palm. "Lucine," he whispered, "I can see now why your name chose you." He brushed a callused finger across her nipple. "Lucine, my moon." He bent down and licked it. Milk flowed. She moved his head gently, brought her son's mouth to it. The hakawati suckled.

Do you know the story of the mother of us all?

"Hagar" comes from the Arabic word for "emigrate," and Hagar did so a number of times. She was a princess in the pharaoh's court. A beauty promised to the pharaoh at a young age, she had her own rooms and a coterie of slaves at her command. The pharaoh had decided to save her for a rainy night, and drought still reigned over Egypt. Her master-to-be, Abraham, was in Egypt with his wife, Sarah, whom he was trying to pass off as his sister. She was sixty-five and beautiful. Abraham was afraid that if the pharaoh knew she was his wife he would kill Abraham and take her. The pharaoh, besotted with Sarah, took her anyway. The pharaoh prepared himself for an evening of pleasure. He had Sarah wait for him in the palace's red room, which he reserved for his most special assignations. He walked into the luscious room and found Sarah already naked on red satin. But God made His presence felt again. Suddenly all the pharaoh could see was an old hag, with wilted eyes, withered skin, frizzled gray hair, bosoms like drained yogurt bags. He covered his kohled eyes in horror and disgust and anguish. "Your face has more wrinkles than my scrotum," he said. "Acch. Get out of this room and leave my sacred realm."

However, Hagar, enamored of Abraham's faith, begged the pharaoh to give her to the God-fearing couple before they were forced to flee. The pharaoh asked her why she'd want to leave such luxury. She stood before him, demure, eyes downcast. "Because I believe," she said.

The pharaoh was horrified, confused by this encounter with a faith he didn't comprehend. He wondered whether Hagar would turn into the repulsion that was the other one. "Go," he commanded in an angry voice for all to hear, all including their strange god. "Leave this world and follow your new masters out of my Egypt."

Abraham took her as a slave, a handmaid for Sarah. Hagar left Egypt, becoming rootless, torn, living wherever her master staked his tent. An emigrant.

· · ·

The hakawati cried and cried. "That makes for strong lungs," Zovik said.

He cried, he suckled, he shat, he slept, he cried. By the third day, after the excitement of the new birth had evaporated, Lucine felt the family's tension. The doctor's girls no longer wanted to see the baby. The wife walked more heavily in the house. The baby's lungs grew stronger. His mouth grew stronger as well, hurting her nipples. The baby sucked until her breasts emptied, then screeched for more.

"I think I should bring Poor Anahid," Zovik said. "She can feed him as well."

Anahid's son, ten days old, had died the morning of the hakawati's birth. Anahid's husband, who couldn't afford mosquito nets, had gone to the Harrar Plain to find work. Anahid had gotten up that morning later than she would have expected. It took a moment to register that her baby had not woken her up. When she rose up from the floor where she slept and looked at her baby in his basket, her first reaction was to weep. Crimson welts, rashlike bumps, and minute pink protrusions covered his entire body. She carried her only son, his breathing labored, and left her house, calling for help. But by the time others arrived, her son had taken his last breath.

The gathering crowd discussed who would have been able to place such a powerful curse. Nothing else could explain the number of mosquitoes required to drain all of an infant's blood. There must be more to it. Look, some said, look at this. Some bites were different from others. Someone lifted the blanket from inside the baby basket. At least three heads stared at the straw within. White lice. Anahid remembered that she had brought the straw the day before. She fainted. No one had heard of lice killing a baby, or of mosquitoes killing a baby. Was the combination fatal? Was such a loss of blood possible? What would Anahid's husband say when he came back? Did he have a powerful enemy?

Her husband arrived in the afternoon, heard the news, went into his house, and beat Anahid unconscious. He didn't unpack. He left and wasn't heard from again.

Afterward, Anahid walked out of her house in a daze. When the residents of the Armenian quarter of Urfa saw Anahid—childless, with her two black eyes, swollen lips, the hair on the right side of her head more sparse than on the left—they were no longer able to call her by her first name only. She became Poor Anahid.

And Poor Anahid became the hakawati's wet nurse. Yet four milky breasts weren't enough. Ismail ate and ate, and when there was no more milk, he cried.

"That boy is not human," the wife told the doctor.

The days grew warmer in Urfa. The skies became less dark and menacing. Spring approached. Yet the hakawati still couldn't get enough. His wails kept everyone in the neighborhood awake. He cried, he suckled, he slept, he cried.

Pregnant, tired, and frightened, Hagar lumbered across the bleak desert. She had fled. Earlier that morning, Abraham had kissed her sweetly, left a tingle in her soul. She blushed, returned the kiss, and watched him leave. Content and hopeful, she resumed her chores.

Sarah decided to sharpen the cutlery. She fetched the knives and flint stones. With each stroke, she looked up at Hagar; sparks flew. Hagar was not stupid.

In the desert, she came across no one. The ripening sun dried her throat. She stopped, wiped the sweat out of her eyes. When she reopened them, lo and behold, God stood before her.

"Hagar, servant of Sarah," God called out to her, "where have you come from and where are you going?"

"I am running away from my mistress, Sarah."

"Return to your home, Hagar," God said. "Go back to your mistress and submit to her. I will watch over you. I will protect you. Be not afraid, for you are my daughter. Return and announce to the world that your son will beget many nations. I will so increase your descendants that they will be too numerous to count. You will be mother to the world."

"You are El Roi," Hagar said to God.

"Look," my grandfather said, pointing at his ankle with his forefinger and his hawkish beak of a nose. "Can't you see the scorpion sting? See this mark. It has been there since before I was born." I knelt to look at the mark. The ankle was skinny, bony, and hairless, the skin pale and blue and thin pellucid. "Isn't this proof? Your eyes can tell you the truth. Whose reality is more real?"

"But the scorpion bit Lucine and not you," I said, looking up at him.

"Don't you ever listen to what I'm saying?" He rose off the chair, moved toward the stove. He removed the top lid, stoked the fire with an aluminum spatula. "It was a curse, I tell you. Someone placed a curse on me before I was born. Lucine was stung by a white scorpion, and everyone knows white scorpions are magical. The sting was meant for me. I was born poisoned, which is why I cried and cried, but no one understood me. I was unable to get enough food. I needed all the nourishment to fight the evil poison inside me. It was a costly battle, but I won."

He lifted his right fist in the air like a champion. "Come," he said. "Join me." We walked a victory lap around the stove, cheered by the roar of an invisible crowd, our arms raised in celebration and pride. My grandfather had to crouch to pass under the exhaust pipe.

Long, long ago, a child was born to the prophet Abraham and his slave, Hagar. He was called Ishmael, Abraham's first progeny, and would grow up to be a prophet and the father of the Arab tribes. Abraham loved his beautiful baby, who looked like a miniature version of him. Being eighty-six, he had given up hope of ever holding a child of his own. He carried the infant everywhere. And Sarah boiled with bilious jealousy. One evening, after dinner, Sarah confronted Abraham. "I had a dream. God spoke to me, telling me you should send Hagar and her son into the desert and leave them there for a month."

By the light of the fire, the prophet saw his wife, a woman grown old. "I do not understand why He would ask that. They cannot survive alone out there."

"Who are we to question His commands? Oh, and they should be left there with little food or water. He said that, too."

Lucine realized the chicken soup didn't taste right, but she ate it anyway. What surprised her was that she was the only one who developed diarrhea. She assumed it was because of her weakened condition. Within a few hours, her baby followed suit, and she was no longer allowed to feed him. Poor Anahid was promoted to sole feeder that day. The hakawati wasn't getting enough from four breasts, reduced to two, his wails grew louder, reaching registers few eardrums could tolerate.

Lucine's interminable diarrhea made her weak. She could no longer move or be moved to the outhouse. Bedpans had to be scoured on the hour. By the third day, her skin seemed to collapse about her bones, except for her ankle, which swelled larger. By the fourth day, it became apparent she was not recovering. Her last words were directed to her son: "Just shut up. Just shut up for once."

Lucine Guiragossian, almost seventeen, died of acute amoebic dysentery.

Abraham led his slave and his son across the desert, journeyed for many long and dangerous days and nights, following Sarah's direction. They stopped at a desolate place. Abraham did not know it then, but the place was already sacred. The first prophet, Adam, had built a temple of worship to the one God on that spot. Nothing of the edifice was left standing. All Hagar saw was the hot sand, the bare hills, the yellow sun, the deathly-blue sky. Abraham gave her a little food and water, prepared to leave her there.

"How can you abandon us?" Hagar begged her master. "How can we survive with so little water in this forsaken place? Is this your decision or the will of God?"

"It is His command." Abraham closed his satchel, avoiding her eyes.

"Oh, that's not so bad, then."

Abraham left them to the silent and lonely desert. There was not a sprig of grass anywhere in the valley, not one tree, not a bird in the sky, not one insect. Hagar looked at the two hills that enclosed the valley, but they offered scant protection or provision. When she ran out of water, the baby began to cry, which seared her heart like a branding iron. She ran up one hill, reached the top, scanned the desert for an oasis; nothing but scalding sand. She ran up the other hill. Disheartening, bleak, sandy emptiness. She kept hearing her baby cry, no matter how high she climbed. She descended to comfort him. His throat seemed parched. She laid him down once more, ran up one hill, down again, up the other, hoping she had missed something. Finally surrendering, she returned to her child. They would die together. He lay on the ground kicking the sand with his feet. As he kicked and kicked, lo and behold, water gushed from the ground, tumbled over sand and rock—a cold stream was born. Ishmael quieted down once he drank some water, and he slept peacefully in his mother's arms. Hagar looked up at the sky to thank her Lord and saw flocks of birds. They circled before alighting to drink from the sacred stream. Bedouins and travelers saw the hovering birds, knew that they had found water. The tribes adjusted their routes to find its source. They arrived in the valley, saw how peaceful it was, and were awed by its bewitching beauty. They looked up to where the water source was and saw a comely Egyptian in a blue robe, resting, her infant asleep on her breast, the light of the sun bathing them in a golden sheen. Even though the tribes were still infidels then, they bowed in silence to the mother and child, so as to not disturb them. They decided to settle in the valley. This was the beginning of the holy city of Mecca. When Abraham returned for his Hagar and Ishmael, he found the valley a blooming oasis with hundreds of palms pregnant with juicy dates, and he thanked God for saving his family.

Every year, pilgrims at the hajj remember the story of Hagar and her baby. They arrive from all over the world to worship, to run between the two hills, Safa and Marwa, praying that God will provide for them the same way He provided for Hagar and Ishmael.

The baby didn't stop crying. Poor Anahid fed him, carried him. Zovik carried him. Even the doctor's wife. No change. Finally, the doctor had had it. He walked in on Zovik, who was trying to coo the baby quiet. "Give him to me," he scowled.

Hesitating, but not daring to show reluctance, Zovik handed the hakawati to his furious father. The hakawati stopped crying the instant his father's hands touched him.

The silence was shocking. The hakawati fell asleep in his father's arms. The doctor, unable to look at anything but his baby, stood rooted to the spot, mouth open, eyebrows raised like arches under Roman bridges. He remained there until his wife called him. For the first time, the doctor told his evening story with a baby in his arms.

"From touch to touch," Zovik whispered to Poor Anahid. "From touch to touch."

Three angels came to visit Abraham on his ninety-ninth birthday. Sarah invited them into the tent and crouched outside, listening to their every word. One of the angels informed Abraham that God was happy with him. "God will increase the size of your family," the angels said. "By your next birthday, your wife, Sarah, will deliver a son."

Everyone in the tent heard Sarah's cackling laugh. She tried to control herself, but the idea of being pregnant in her nineties was hilarious. All of a sudden, she was laughing, her body shaking, though no sound escaped her lips. She clutched her throat. She stood up, ran into the tent.

"You will not have a voice until your child is born," the angels said.

Outside, on the other side of the tent, Hagar snickered silently.

"The doctor built a bed for me," my grandfather told me. "You see, he was a carpenter first, then a deacon, then a doctor. He spent hours making the bed, carved each leg by hand, with high sides so I wouldn't fall. On each of the four corners, he carved a horse's head. He ordered the bolts and screws all the way from England. The wood was local oak, and he stained it a dark brown. I had the most beautiful bed in the house. I slept in it even when I was much too big. I would lie with my legs tilted up on the side."

Poor Anahid watched the doctor work on the bed. She couldn't keep still. The baby nestled in the doctor's shoulder satchel. As long as he was in the doctor's vicinity, the baby was as calm as the Mediterranean in early summer.

"Why are you hovering, Anahid?" the doctor asked. "Is there something you need?"

"I suggest that we not use straw," Poor Anahid said.

My mother's long eyelashes fluttered when she slept. It would be wrong to assume you could get away with anything when she first fell asleep: the slightest movement was enough to wake her. When I put my finger close to her eyelashes so I could know what they felt like, she opened her eyes. I closed mine, pretended to be dozing. "Are you asleep?" she asked.

"Everybody is asleep," I said with eyes closed, "but Jardown is awake."

"Jardown will get a spanking and will have to sleep in his own bed if he's not asleep very soon."

.   .   .

"The doctor wasn't a good storyteller," my grandfather said. "Well, he wasn't bad, but he certainly didn't have the gift. And he was English after all."

"What was wrong with his stories?"

"They were just common. He always told his favorite stories from the Bible. Stories with obvious moral lessons are like eels in a wooden crate. They slither over and under each other, but never leave the tub. In my day, I told some of the same stories, but mine soared. His problem was that he believed. Belief is the enemy of a storyteller."

"But he told a story every evening after dinner, and all came to listen to him."

"Pfflt." He waved his hand and lit another cigarette. "I didn't say all came to listen. All the foreigners did. At the time, there were no hotels or inns or anything like that in Urfa, so the foreign travelers stayed with the doctor. Those foreigners were always impressed with the doctor's storytelling. They didn't know any better. If they spoke Turkish, they could have gone to the café in the Eyyubiye neighborhood and listened to a good hakawati. If they spoke Kurdish, they might have had to ride for an hour south, because the best hakawati in the region was in a village up Damlacik Mountain. And the Armenian storytellers, my God, they were all over. But the doctor never listened to any of them, and neither did anyone who stayed at the house. Before I knew any better, I enjoyed the doctor's stories. But then he kept repeating the same ones over and over. No imagination. And heaven forbid, if he should forget something, his wife was right there to correct him. Who needs that? I wish someone had told me about what went on outside the doctor's puny realm. I had to find out on my own—the hakawatis, the pigeon wars, the traditions—I discovered it all by chance. Had the doctor's wife not been wicked, I might never have seen the world, and you certainly wouldn't have been born—now, would you?"

When he left to pee, I ran back to the table, climbed up the chair to the tabletop, and tried to find Urfa again, tried to find the mountain where the best storyteller was.

"You're so ugly," Ishmael told Isaac, "and you sure have the biggest nose I've ever seen." The fourteen-year-old laughed, and in his arms, baby Isaac smiled with him. It was the baby's weaning ceremony.

Sarah took her husband aside. "Look. He mocks my son. I will not have it. The slave's son deems himself superior. Cast him out, I tell you. Cast them both out."

Abraham tried to reason with his wife. They had sent Hagar and Ishmael away once before. It was not right. It was not fair.

"Cast them out again, and this time don't go back for them."

And Abraham sent his son away, never to see him again, father and son separate for eternity. To quell the pain in his heart, Abraham tried to forget his elder boy, distracted himself with extra chores and trivial whatnots, but the boy never forgot his father. When Abraham died, Ishmael returned to bury him. Ishmael and Isaac buried their father in the Cave of Machpelah, in the field that Abraham had purchased from the Hittites.

"This is now the Tomb of the Patriarchs in Hebron," my grandfather said, as his finger settled on the fading map upon the rickety table, "where the sons of Sarah are still trying to cast out the sons of Hagar."

"Tell me the story of Abraham sacrificing Ishmael on the mountain."

"No, I already told you that one. It's common, too common. Boring, even. It was the doctor's favorite story, and he told it so badly. It's so hackneyed and clichéd. A story needs to be bewitching."

Once, not too long ago, there was a little boy, about the same age as you, who lived with his family in a small village, not unlike this one, not too far from here. The family did not have much money. The father was a stonemason, the mother looked after the house, cooked delicious meals. All the children had their own chores to do. Our boy was the family's shepherd.

Every morning, he would take the sheep out to pasture. He watched them graze, made sure they did not wander, and protected them from foxes, wolves, and marauding hyenas. The sheep liked him and trusted him, so they didn't stray far from our boy. His job became easy, and every day he had time to play. At first, he played with sticks and stones: he made a sheep pen by staking twigs in four corners; small stones were his sheep. But then the little lambs came into his make-believe pen, clamoring for his attention. So he stopped playing with sticks and stones and became one of the lambs, jumped with them, bent down and pretended to chew on the wild-lavender bushes, bleated with them.

When he returned home that evening, he wished he were a lamb because he had had fun playing. Before he went to sleep, he heard his parents arguing about money. "We have so many mouths to feed," the mother said. "How can we find enough for all of them?"

"We have the sheep," the father said. "We have some money. I am working. We'll survive. We have for generations."

But they kept on arguing, and the boy slept fitfully.

The following day, he and the lambs played again, watched over by the ewes. The boy and the lambs ran and jumped and jostled each other. He returned home very happy, but when he opened the door to tell his parents all about his day, he found them arguing.

"How could you have promised that?" the mother asked. "We don't have enough to feed our children, and now you want to have a feast? Have you no conscience? Don't you understand how bad our situation is?"

"How dare you?" the father yelled at the mother. "This is the bey we're talking about. It's an honor. When he comes here, the house will be blessed. I don't understand how you can think of not wanting him in your home. Most people would die for the opportunity."

The mother whispered, "What has the bey done for my family?"

The father slapped the mother. The boy ran into his room.

Before he fell asleep, our boy prayed. He wished he were a lamb and could play all day without any worries. He wished his family could be happy. He wished that he could be the one to provide them with happiness. He loved his family so much. He woke up the next day in the sheep pen. He looked around and saw all his friends, the other lambs, happy that he was in their midst, finally one of them. They bleated in joy. All of them pranced up and down.

The father and mother came out of the house together and walked toward the pen.

"Danger, danger," said the eldest ewe. "The evil ones are here."

"No, no," said our boy. "They are not evil. They are my family."

"When those two show up together," another sheep said, "one of us disappears."

The father and mother came into the pen. They tried to figure which lamb to pick.

"Look at me," the boy yelled. "Look at me. Look at me."

"This one," the mother said. "He is noisy."

"He looks plump and juicy," the father added. He placed the noose around his boy's head and walked him out of the pen.

"The poor lamb," the eldest ewe said as the sheep watched him being taken away.

"Daddy, Daddy," the little lamb said. "I'm a lamb now. Isn't this a miracle?"

And his father took out the knife and slit his throat.

And the little lamb watched his own blood leave him.

And his father cut off his head.

And his father hung him from his ankles to drain him.

And his mother began to skin him with her own hands. She would lift a small part of his skin and punch between the skin and body, lift, punch, lift, punch, until she finally cut the last attached skin at his ankles. And she chopped off his feet and hands. And she took out all his insides. And his mother cooked him over a slow-burning fire.

His father waited. His mother cooked. His brothers helped set up the large table under the giant oak. His sisters cleaned the house and cleaned and cleaned. They got dressed in all the fineries. By lunchtime, they were lined up waiting. The mother wondered where our boy was. His brothers suggested he must be daydreaming somewhere as usual. He had gotten out of doing the chores, that sneaky brat. The family waited and waited and waited. Finally, the mayor arrived and said that the bey had decided not to come to the village.

The lamb was placed in the middle of the table. The whole family salivated.

"You outdid yourself," the father told the mother.

"This lamb was particularly succulent," the mother said.

And the boy felt his father tear into him.

"Pass your plates, children," the mother said. "We'll get to have a great meal for a change."

And the boy felt his brothers bite into his flesh. He felt his sisters chew sumptuous pieces of him.

"This tastes so good," his brothers said.

"The best meal we've ever had," his sisters said.

And the mother brought out his stomach. His siblings fought over his intestines.

"You take this, my dear," his father told his mother. "I know you love it."

"And you take this, my dear," his mother told his father, "for I know you love it."

"And I am happy," said the father.

"And I am happy," said the mother.

And the boy felt his mother bite into his testicles.

And the boy felt his father swallow a piece of his heart.

And the boy was happy.

Three

Fatima dressed for her entrance to the city. She covered her hair with a scarf of sheer red silk, around her forehead a chain of gold. Her neck held beads of lapis lazuli, her right breast supported a small brooch of gems, seven rings of silver encircled her left arm. She tightened the twined belt around her waist and made sure it held the sword firm. She wore her heavy robe, which concealed everything underneath.

It was only after she finished dressing that Jawad came out of Khayal's tent. Embarrassed to have been discovered, he blushed, tried to speak, but ended up stuttering.

"I see you have made your choice," she said. "I am pleased. I grew to like our suitor and would have been troubled had we been forced to send him away."

And our three travelers entered the gates of Alexandria. Bast's house was at the northern edge of the city, along an estuary. The healer stood outside, throwing morsels into the water. Fish surfaced, mouths open, snatching the bread before it hit.

"I had expected you earlier," Bast said without turning, still feeding her pets.

"We were delayed," Fatima said.

"And so expertly disposed of. Well handled, if risky, I must say. Not all obstacles will be as easily surmountable. More will be asked of you." When she ran out of bread, she brushed off her hands and turned around. "You are more beautiful than I expected, and it is to be hoped you will become more beautiful still. Follow me, and leave the lovers outside. You will be separated soon, and they should not hear my counsel."

"Why not?" Khayal asked, but the heedless healer had already begun walking toward her house.

"Can we trust her?" Jawad asked.

Fatima raised her left hand to quiet them and followed the healer into her domain.

"Afreet-Jehanam your plaything?" Bast asked. "That is quite a boast. Sit. Sit." She pointed in the general direction of an area where various possibilities for seating existed. A pale fire burned in the chimney but added no heat, since it was cold neither outside nor in.

"Men are gullible."

"True. It is also true that a boast is dangerous. One always ends up paying its price. Now, my dear, what have you brought me?"

"A lock of my mistress's hair. She would like to give birth to a healthy and wise son."

Puzzled, the healer shook her head. "But why did you bring a lock of the woman's hair? That is not of much use. It is the father who determines the gender of his offspring, the mother its traits. I would need a lock of *his* hair to understand the issue, and hers would have provided the solution. You should have known that. Do not look so troubled, my dear. I would not return a resourceful woman empty-handed, for I, too, am resourceful." She stretched on her toes, rummaged through the small cabinets hanging from the ceiling. "I have something that I have not used in a long time." She bent down behind a table, and Fatima could no longer see her, but she heard the sound of heavy objects being dragged along the floor, and then the sharp meow of a cat as it scurried out. "Oh, Cleopatra, how could I know you were lying there? You have to tell me these things." The healer resurfaced, fully erect now. Her chin settled on her hand, and her eyes focused on the ceiling. "I have to remember where I put it. Ah, of course, how stupid of me." She picked up a long wooden spoon and one of the glass vials on the table and walked over to Fatima. "Please stand up, my dear."

Bast knocked the worn cushion off the barrel Fatima had been sitting on and removed the lid. She stirred the contents with the spoon and dropped the vial into the barrel. "Your salvation," the healer said, raising the vial, which was now filled with an amber liquid. "Any woman who drinks this within seven hours after intercourse will conceive a healthy male child. No guarantee on other qualities, though— the parents have to take care of those." She pushed a cork stopper into the vial and put her hand out. From under her breast, Fatima took out a gold dinar and gave it to her.

"No haggling?" Bast asked.

Fatima raised her eyebrows for the Arabic "no."

"Pity. And would you seek any further advice?"

"I cannot seek a husband, my lady," Fatima replied, "for I am but a slave, and I do not wish for one at this time."

"Ah, husbands are what most seek in coming to me. Pardon me, but I must mollify my poor Cleopatra or she will allow me no sleep tonight." Bast walked away and stopped. "Your humility belies an arrogance, Sitt Fatima, but no matter, you will soon grow wiser. You should have asked for my counsel, but I will give it anyway. Rise, Fatima, and leave quickly. Time is of the essence. What you have to face, you must face alone, or others will be hurt. Leave your home city. It is not time for you to be back here. You will not be a slave for long if you make the correct choices, and the correct choices are always the most difficult ones." She took a deep breath, lowered her head, stared at the floor, then looked back at Fatima, who no longer recognized the woman in front of her. The healer's hair began to unfurl, and the air surrounding her head began to shimmer and sparkle. "Show me your hand," Bast commanded. Fatima stepped toward her, but the healer held her palm out. "Stop. Show me your palm." Fatima raised the palm of her left hand, and Bast recoiled. "Fatima's hand. Leave now, quickly, and have courage."

Bast turned away. "Here, kitty. Come here, Cleopatra."

And the three travelers left Alexandria in a hurry. "Could we not have spent the day and seen the sights?" Jawad asked. "Seems a shame. I have never been to any city but my own. Khayal says the lads in Alexandria wear no underpants."

"It is true," Fatima said. "But I could not linger. We must make haste."

For seven days, they rode with little rest, until they had crossed most of the Sinai. For seven days, Fatima felt her doom follow her, but spoke nothing of it. She heard the earth thump a rhythm that matched her heart's. They rode into the deserts of Palestine.

"We cannot keep up this pace, Sitt Fatima," Jawad said. "The horses cannot make it without a rest. We must ease up, or none will survive and neither will we."

Fatima reluctantly agreed. They set up camp before the sun set. And she waited.

Fatima heard her name being called from below. She heard the low rumble before the lovers did, before the pack animals. She felt the tremor beneath her feet, and, as if her soles had ears, she heard the sand speak: "Fatima, I come for you, Fatima."

The horses whinnied. The noise grew louder; the earth shook. The camels fled. Two untied mares joined them. Jawad seemed to struggle. His instinct was to try and corral them, but he was petrified. The mules stood still. That stillness—there was a moment of it, of unequivocal tranquillity, only an instant—and then the earth exploded. Between Fatima and the two lovers a hole yawned, spewing a hot yellow fire. The flames flickered here and there, but did not change color. Unnatural, they were like giant fronds of an anemone. A giant blue head appeared, the fire its hair. The jinni glared with three red eyes and growled, showing two rows of daggerlike teeth.

"Save yourselves," cried Fatima to Jawad and Khayal. Yet she herself remained rooted.

His putrid stench would have suffocated an infant—the smell of months-old eggs, rotting garbage, and decaying flesh. Hundreds of black crows picked at his teeth for bits of food. They flew in and out of his nose, looked like flies because of his size. The hides of seven rhinos made up his loincloth. He wore a necklace of human skulls that hung to his navel, with two loops around his neck like a pearl collar. Through the space between his legs, she could see Jawad and Khayal fleeing.

"So—I am supposed to be a plaything of yours?" His voice poured forth, slow and sibilant, dripping like unsweetened molasses.

She waited until Jawad disappeared behind the jinni's thigh before replying, "I offer you my sincere apologies, sire. I meant you no disrespect. It was said to escape certain death. We were waylaid. I had no other choice."

"It was a boast," he shouted, with a force that shook everything within leagues.

"It was silly. Anyone can tell you are no one's plaything. Why, look at you. You are so grand and powerful, and I am nothing but a helpless maiden. Who would believe what I said?"

"Quiet." His voice almost knocked Fatima over. "You think your wit will save you this time?" He opened his hands, and ten red fingernails sprang out, ten swords, each as tall as she was. "I want to smell your fear, woman. I am Afreet-Jehanam." His blue chest puffed out. "Tremble."

"I have forgotten how." She took out her sword, held it steadily in front of her.

He laughed. The jinni struck with the nails of his thumb and forefinger, and she scampered away, moved the sword from her right hand to her left, ran toward her attacker. But he was Afreet-Jehanam. He nonchalantly flicked his pinkie and chopped off her hand. She fell to her knees. Looked at her sword-clutching left hand on the ground in front of her. Her wrist sprayed blood. She clutched it with her right arm. Raise it above heart level, she remembered, raise it above heart level. Would it matter?

"Tremble," he said.

"Kill me."

He shrugged. He raised a finger. She closed her eyes. She heard the sound of metal hitting metal. Opened her eyes. Jawad was on his back, his sword next to him. "Is today some kind of day of fools?" the jinni asked. "Am I to be attacked by pests?" Khayal arrived running and stopped between Jawad and the jinni, who said, "Yes, definitely the day of dying fools." He raised his arm with its five finger-swords to strike.

"Stop," Fatima yelled. "You have no quarrel with them. I am the one you want."

"This one tried to attack me from behind. He must die. They both must."

"Spare them. Look at the boy. He has just discovered love. Look into his eyes. Do not end his happiness. Be merciful, sire. He has just begun to live. Kill me, not them."

The jinni considered the situation. He raised an arm to the heavens. The crows flew up, circled his lethal fingernails. He moved his arm, and they shot out like javelins into the empty sky. When he brought his arm back down, he announced, "I will not kill the lovers." The crows began a descent, flew as if they were a flock of black pigeons. "I will not end your life, either, for you are not worthy of being killed by me." He picked up Fatima's hand from the dusty ground where it lay and used her sword as a toothpick, sucking the gaps between his teeth, producing a thunderous noise, savoring the taste of his mouth, smacking his lips. "You have begun to bore me. I had expected a better fight. It will be much more entertaining to hear you try to explain how your plaything left you without a hand." He walked toward the crater in the ground. "Much more fun to watch you muddle handless through your ignoble life." He stepped into the hole. "If you think you are worthy of being killed by my hand, come to my world and claim yours." He chortled as his head disappeared. "I am sure you will be able to find your way to the plaything."

Jawad, sweating from exertion and the sun's harsh rays, rushed to check on Fatima's arm. He tore off his sleeve and tied it around the bleeding wrist. He began to tear off his other sleeve, but Fatima stopped him. She pushed the silver bracelets around her arm farther up. When she could not push anymore, Khayal took over. The rings acted as a tourniquet.

"We must leave," Khayal said. "You may not be fit to be moved, but we have no choice."

"The jinni might return," Jawad said.

"Go," she said, her voice labored, her breathing shallow. "I must travel a different path. Leave now. Linger not."

"You cannot make it on your own," Jawad said. "You are weak. Where do you wish to go, in any case? We must run away from here."

She attempted to stand up, faltered, swayed, and sat back down. "I must retrieve my hand. Leave me." She placed her only hand on Khayal's shoulder and used him as leverage to lift herself. "Tell the emir I met my doom." She did not sway. "Or tell him I will be back soon. Or choose not to return. Find your own place in this world. Take care of each other. Either way. I must descend." She looked into the crater. "Now, be a good boy," she said to Jawad, "and find me a staff. The yucca there would do."

"How do you propose to retrieve your hand?" Khayal asked. "Do you think Afreet-Jehanam is going to give it back to you? And what good will it do? You cannot reattach it. Be not a fool, Sitt Fatima. Come with us."

"I must have my hand."

"But it is the devil's hand, and the devil has it now. An unnecessary appendage."

"It is the devil's hand, and it is also mine. And I must take it back."

"Do you know what the Prophet said about left hands?"

"Stop pestering me. I know my religion. I want my left hand so I can wipe my butt."

And Jawad handed her the yucca staff. "May God, the merciful and compassionate, be your guiding light." And Fatima descended into the hole.

❧

A starchy nurse jiggled into the hospital room in white pants and white sneakers. "Who's going to be getting a bath now?" she announced jovially.

My father was glum, his face furrowed. Seeing his nephew as one of the bey's lackeys had enraged and disoriented him. I glanced at the board on the wall to read the nurse's name. With a red felt pen, she had written "Nancy" in a hippie script and had drawn a smiley face, but one eye had gone missing. She was full of inept cheer. She kept up a steady stream of chatter, more river than stream. She began to undress my father, and remove the electrodes, the white and the blue pads that transmitted his vitals to the nurses' station. With a postcard smile that showed a large overbite, she said, "This is private. Don't you think?"

I had only to look at my sister's face to realize something was amiss. My father sat on the bed, back slumped, legs dangling above the bright, sterile floors. When he turned toward me, I saw defeat. He tried to smile. "Don't you have better things to do than hang around here?" he asked, his voice frail.

"Here, Salwa," Lina handed the stethoscope to her daughter. "You're better at this."

"You don't have better things to do, either?" my father asked my niece.

Salwa, almost nine months pregnant, looking about to explode at any moment, sat behind him on the bed. She moved the stethoscope along his back, as if playing an imaginary game of solitaire checkers. She closed her eyes, and her face sagged, strangely serene. "I hear water," she said.

My sister sighed. She hesitated for an instant before regaining her stage persona. "All right," she announced to the room. "We'll have to get more Lasix." Tin Can was on her mobile's speed dial. She spoke machine-gun style, her voiced pitched high. "Done," she said. "He'll call the nurses. We'll get rid of the water." She walked around, then abruptly left the room. She returned with a nurse, who proceeded to inject the diuretic into one of the intravenous tubes.

And my father began to pant. He still had not urinated an hour later. His laborious inhalations gurgled. Shallow breaths. He cracked feeble jokes. He tried to move, but just getting his arm to behave was arduous. Breathe in. Breathe out. Wheeze. Gurgle. He wilted in his bedding, drooped before our eyes. Lina tried to appear composed, but she did not fool anyone.

Salwa held my elbow and walked me out of the room. "He doesn't want you to see him in this condition." I started to go back in, but she held my arm. "Just relax," she said. "He's having a fit of pique. He doesn't want anyone but my mother to see him suffer. He doesn't want me in there, either. He thinks my seeing him will distress the baby."

From the doorway, I could see the lower half of his body, the tension in his legs below the hospital gown, the curling of his toes with each breath.

❧

Fatima felt weak and moved gingerly. It did not take long for the light to dissipate. She realized she had no plan, no weapon, and no energy to speak of, but the one thing she lacked and needed most was a torch. The ground was uneven, but not dangerous, descending at a reasonable angle. She proceeded into the dark until she could see no more. Blind, she became more careful. One tiny step followed by another. The staff tested where her foot was to land. Quiet was the rule of the place. Quiet until, "I believe you might need this, madame," and then there was light.

"It gets more treacherous from here on down," the red imp said. He sat on a protruding burnt-orange rock, four or five times his size—he was no larger than a boy of three, a miniature jinni, with hooves dangling above the ground. He held out a tiny kettle-shaped oil lamp. "Come. Take it." He grinned. "I will not hurt you."

"I would not know how to carry it. I cannot walk without this staff, and I have only one hand. Look," she said.

He jumped off the rock, pranced up to her with no little animation. She jerked her handless arm away. "I just want to see," he said.

She extended her arm. "You can look, but do not touch."

The little demon stared at her wound. "You need a healer. May I remove the bandage?"

She shook her head. "I need my hand."

"Reattaching it might prove to be a problem," he said, laughing. "But let us see if we can figure out a way for you to carry the lamp."

"You can be my light," she said.

"Oh, no. Not where you are going. You received the call." He circled around her. The top of his bald head seemed to move up and down with each step. "We cannot tie it anywhere on your clothes. Oh, but I can slip the handle onto your finger, and you can hold both the lamp and the staff. Here, try this."

"Why are you helping me?"

"Because you need help. Bring down your hand. I cannot reach that high." And he slipped the lamp onto her forefinger. "With this ring, I thee wed."

"It is the wrong finger, and you are the wrong species."

"And you are dying."

"I have not given up yet." She looked ahead.

"I hope you will," said the imp. "Now go. You do not have much time. I must wait here. And when you die, remember me in your prayers. Call me Ishmael."

She marched, the lamp illuminating her descent, until the walls, ground, and ceiling converged on a circular gate. She approached, held up her staff to see the gate better, swept the back of her hand against it. It was black agate. She pushed against it, but it would not budge. "Open, Sesame," she said. The gate did not respond, but there was movement in the shadows.

"My name is not Sesame." The imp was the same size as Ishmael, and just as red. She noted that both had horns but no tail, which she took as a good sign. "It is Isaac," the imp said. "Ishmael is my brother."

"I seek entry," she said.

"And I seek payment," Isaac replied.

"I can pay."

"I know that." He flicked his hand, and the gate creaked open. "I am nobody's fool. You are top-heavy with money. I will lighten your load. I will take fifty gold dinars." He had the same silly gait as Ishmael.

"I will give you ten." She walked through the gate. "You should have asked when you had a better bargaining position, before I came through. I will not overpay now."

"Fifty." He clenched his fists, tensed his stomach, and jumped twice. "Not one dinar less. I do not compromise. Everyone will make fun of me if I do. I was told you are carrying fifty. That is my price."

"Whoever told you I had fifty gold dinars was lying."

"Why do I get the troublemakers? You are dying, and with your last breath you haggle. You must be Egyptian."

"From Alexandria."

"Oy. I am being punished. Give me your money, madame. It is the law. You will not need it where you are going. Save us both the trouble."

"I have forty-nine, one dinar less. I will give it for an answer to a question."

"Ask."

"How many have gotten out of here alive and human?"

"Wrong question. They always ask the wrong question. None. None have gotten out of here alive and human. Now give me the gold." He climbed up her robe, stuck his hand in her bosom, and took the coins. Fatima wanted to admonish the imp, but held her tongue. "I shall help you," Isaac said, counting the gold, "for I am fond of obstinate troublemakers. When you are asked to surrender a belonging, it behooves you to do so without bargaining. Surrender is the key."

Fatima descended farther into the tunnel. The air turned moist, made her feel heavier with each step. She held up her staff and lamp, saw moss the color of emerald filling every crevice, yet her path remained barren. Various night insects roamed the moss, feeding, scurrying, creating a living, ever-changing Persian carpet. She wished she could touch; wished her lost hand could graze upon the surface. And she reached the second circular gate, carved of emerald. She pushed, shoved. "Open, Isaac."

"My name is Ezra." A little orange imp jumped out of a cloud of orange dust.

"I seek entry."

"And I seek payment. I will have your robe."

"But it is much too big for you. You could fit ten of your kind in this robe."

"I have a large family. Give it." He climbed up the robe, unfastened the clasp, shinnied up above her head, held on to the back of her collar, and jumped. Fatima teetered. Ezra dangled in midair, hanging on to the collar. "Let go," he said. "It is my robe."

"Wait, I am wounded. I lost a hand."

Ezra jumped down, ran around. "May I see?" he asked. "Please?"

"You will have to help me with the robe first." She patted the pocket of her dress to make sure the vial of potion was there, and not in her robe.

And the imp Ezra said, "Uncover your wound so I can see."

"I cannot, for I do not have a free hand."

"You need a healer." Ezra bunched up the robe and lifted it above his head, almost disappearing under it. "Proceed with your journey," her bundled robe seemed to say. "Your time is limited. And, for being kind to me, I will offer you help. In this realm, if someone asks you to uncover your wound, do so."

Beyond the emerald gate, the air grew heavier still, reeking of an earthy stew. She came upon the mushrooms. Small at first, multihued, reds, sienna, ocher, browns, and greens. As she marched deeper, the numbers increased. Cuddled and coddled by the moist air, a metallic-blue mushroom grew as big as a shed. Next to it was one with velvet skin the color of avocado. Fatima felt hunger pains. The third gate was of lapis lazuli. "Let me guess," she said to the dark beyond. "Your name is Abraham."

"No," the approaching yellow imp said. "I am called Jacob."

The price of entry was her necklace of lapis beads, and she paid it.

And Jacob said, "I will offer you help, dear mistress. The paths of folly are not always distinguishable from the ways of wisdom. Please, hurry."

Below Jacob's gate, unrecognizable dark fruit seemed to sprout from jutting rocks. The fruit was veined, streaked, with the texture of polished marble. She stopped and reached out with her wounded arm; a bat flew down from above and covered the fruit with its satiny black wings. Its eyeless face snarled at Fatima. Bats everywhere, thousands upon thousands, hanging from fruits, from rocks. Bats flew singly in every direction, creating a barely audible, disconcerting symphony. Yet her path remained clear.

The gate was gold; its keeper was Job, the green imp; and his price for passage was the brooch of gems. The imp Job said, "I will offer assistance, madame, for you need help. Remember, sometimes it is wiser to choose death."

Fatigue possessed Fatima entirely, took root within her soul, flourished, sprang leaves within her veins. She wished to lie down, but the earth beneath her was not inviting. She should have stopped back at the moss, left her body to the insects of the night. She should have lain down in the giant-mushroom beds. She should keep moving.

She came across a small ruby lying alongside her path, and then a sapphire, a diamond, another ruby, and then a pile, and then piles. Gems of all sizes, gold of all shapes, treasure chests that would make kings and queens salivate. And she did not have the energy to reach. She passed a gilded mirror lying against the wall. She watched her reflection, but she did not look like anyone she knew. She moved on.

The gate was mahogany, and its keeper was a blue imp. She wept as she paid with her red headscarf of silk and the gold chain around her forehead. "Your light seems to be dimming," Noah said. "I will offer help. Delete the need to understand. In this world and that of tales, the need is naught more than a hindrance."

Grief approached like an infection, overpowering her gradually and irrevocably. She marched, cried. A tear fell to the ground before every step, her dragging feet deleting any trace of the watermarks. The crows were in Noah's domain, and their food was carcasses. Most of the bodies were human, flayed, hanging from rusty hooks, dripping an endless supply of red. Black birds on the ground drank from brooks of blood flowing on either side of her path. The ravenous crows fought over rotting morsels. She could not lie down here.

Elijah's gate was turquoise. "I seek entry," she said, "but I have nothing more to give."

"I will take your clothes," the indigo imp said. "Your ragged dress, your undergarments, even your shoes. I will be of service to you. I offer you this. Down here, you are always naked."

Past Elijah's gate, the earth upon which the dead walked was muddy ash and smoke, like the remnants of soup stock left to simmer but long forgotten. The walking dead mimicked her, thousands upon thousands—a colony of purposeless ants, they muddled about, bumping into each other, eyeless or eyes not seeing. Men, women, and children; horses, cats, and dogs; lions, tigers, and apes; dwarfs, demons, and giants. Dead. Whatever outfits any wore were frayed, their flesh decayed. She shivered. None crossed her clear path. And she came upon the seventh gate.

"I know who you are," Fatima said to the keeper of the marble gate.

The violet imp looked surprised. "And I know who you are," he said.

"This must be the final gate. I have arrived at the last domain. You are Adam."

"It must be so. Welcome, my lady. Yet I still require payment. I will take the seven rings of silver around your arm. You will no longer need them." He climbed to her shoulder, pushed down on the rings. She felt the flooding pain as they fell, dragging Jawad's bloodied shirt-sleeve. The blood thumped in her arm. It dripped from the stump where her hand used to be, drained slowly. She stared at her wound, felt her fight seep out of it.

"Walk," Adam said. "You do not have far to go." He blew out her lamp. "You do not need this down here. Move. I will help you. I offer this. In the underworld, death awakens."

"And you call this help?"

She marched. As she had expected, snakes slithered everywhere except along her path. Boas, asps, and rattlers. Desert snakes, swamp snakes. She barely noticed them. Naked, helpless, exhausted, and bereft, she staggered forward. Dullness, her sole possession, clung to her.

And the ground fell below her.

And the ceiling lifted higher.

And the walls opened before her.

And Afreet-Jehanam sat on his throne.

"Approach me, seeker," he said.

My father had his eyes closed; his breathing was shallow and slow. An oxygen mask nestled in the skin of his face. He opened his eyes, an effort that obviously exhausted him, and closed them again. My niece and I stood on either side of his bed.

Tin Can arrived with two other doctors. As if they were part of a club, all three had trimmed black beards and short curly hair—Tin Can had the bushiest eyebrows. I didn't recognize the other two, though they obviously knew the family. "You're not looking too well, Mr. al-Kharrat," one of the doctors said. He wore a Titian-red shirt under his white coat. "We can't have that. The Adha holiday is tomorrow, and your family's all here."

My father smiled wanly behind the mask. He tried to remove it but couldn't. Lina leaned over and pulled it down a little. He mumbled something.

"He says maybe Ali and the Virgin can intervene," Lina said. Everyone laughed. I didn't understand the joke, probably the punch line of a ditty making the Lebanese rounds, to which I was yet to be privy.

The doctor in the red shirt said he wanted to look at the vitals and left for the nurses' desk. The third doctor, a pulmonologist with seabass eyes, listened to my father's lungs. Tin Can suggested to my niece that she shouldn't remain standing for so long. The pulmonologist asked why the electrodes were not attached. My sister gasped. Dr. Titian returned and sheepishly announced that there were no vitals, because the monitors had not been recording. Two nurses rushed in. One dragged a portable machine, and the other hurriedly attached electrodes to my father's chest. The overbite nurse who had given him a bath at noon had forgotten to reattach the tabs, and the other nurses and doctors had not noticed in more than five hours. Doctor Titian pressed buttons on the machine. "Something's wrong," he said. He walked over to my father. "The pacemaker has stopped." Dr. Titian looked at the lump in my father's chest. He tapped it twice, went back to his machine, then back to my father's chest, then the machine.

And the jinn returned to my father's eyes. Instantaneous. His face muscles relaxed. His bony fingers ungripped the bed rail. He took a deep breath.

"Don't scare us like that," Tin Can joked.

"Now you can celebrate the holiday," the pulmonary specialist said.

"With your whole family," Dr. Titian, my father's cardiac surgeon, added.

With the palm of my hand, I covered my sister's eyes. I gently forced her to close them. She had a murderous glare. "Breathe," I whispered. "Breathe." She rested her arms on my shoulders. My hand remained on her face until I felt it dampen.

Fatima wanted to tell the jinni to return her hand. She wanted to challenge him. She craved revenge. She genuflected before Afreet-Jehanam. "I have come down to die."

"Yes." His deep, sibilant voice made her soul shudder. "My world is a wonderful place to die." He opened his hand, and sixteen black scorpions slithered across his blue fingers toward her. "Yet do I detect a bit of resistance?"

"No, sire," she replied. "I have seen the light. I surrender."

A forked tongue unfurled out of the jinni's mouth. "Ah, the sweet smell of surrender excites me so." She did not cringe when the scorpions crawled up her body. She wished one of them would sting her. When he stood up, his throne dissolved into hundreds of asps. "You will be *my* plaything." She did not flinch at that, either. "Our plaything." And a young boa coiled around her handless arm.

Afreet-Jehanam picked her up, cradled her in the palm of his hand. He brought her closer to his face, but his stench did not bother her. "It pleases me that you finally submit to my desire."

She wanted to laugh. "We are not much of a match sexually."

"But we are, Sitt Fatima. Size is not everything."

The first scorpion stung her in the throat, and a cobra bit into her stump. The scorpions stung all over her body. Afreet-Jehanam laid Fatima down on a bed of shimmering snakes. And the demon began to shrink—half his size in a blink of an eye, another half in another blink, until he achieved the dimensions of a large, muscular man. But the transformation did not stop there. He removed the third eye from his forehead and made it disappear. His skin grew paler in color; the burning hair turned black, a human nose appeared. And a human hand reached out for her.

Fatima saw the most handsome of men bring his face close to hers. He kissed her. She kissed back. And life surged through her. She made love to him. In some moments she saw him as a man, in others as a demon. And she was being stung and bitten. She was a riverbed. She was a mere channel of life and its stories. She gained strength.

Fatima woke up. She felt refreshed and rejuvenated, filled with vigor. Afreet-Jehanam, no longer human, leaned on his elbow next to her. "You are beautiful," he said.

"I am without a hand," she replied.

"You are without much," the demon said, "and so you are beautiful."

She looked at her wound, saw it honestly for the first time: the lines of blood, the clots, scabs growing, the tissue attempting to heal itself out of grief and loss, the skin trying to forget what was once there. But the air about her missing hand began to shimmer in startling waves. A mass grew from her wrist, bubbled out like slow-boiling lava. She saw it swell, felt her blood pour into it. Stumps sprouted, and fingers began to form. And Fatima moved the fingers. Her hand was back. "This is unlike any hell I could have imagined," she said.

"Hell? I am insulted. Whatever possessed you to think of my realm as hell?"

"Well," she said, "you are a demon. This is the underworld. I just assumed."

"Ah, humans. Your ideas of hell are nothing more than the lees and dregs of unimaginative minds long since dead. Listen. Let me tell you a story."

Once there was and once there was not a devout, God-fearing man who lived his entire life according to stoic principles. He died on his fortieth birthday and woke up floating in nothing. Now, mind you, floating in nothing was comforting, lightless, airless, like a mother's womb. This man was grateful.

But then he decided he would love to have sturdy ground beneath his feet, so he would feel more solid himself. Lo and behold, he was standing on earth. He knew it to be earth, for he knew the feel of it.

Yet he wanted to see. I desire light, he thought, and light appeared. I want sunlight, not any light, and at night it shall be moonlight. His desires were granted. Let there be grass. I love the feel of grass beneath my feet. And so it was. I no longer wish to be naked. Only robes of the finest silk must touch my skin. And shelter, I need a grand palace whose entrance has double-sided stairs, and the floors must be marble and the carpets Persian. And food, the finest of food. His breakfast was English; his midmorning snack French. His lunch was Chinese. His afternoon tea was Indian. His supper was Italian, and his late-night snack was Lebanese. Libation? He had the best of wines, of course, and champagne. And company, the finest of company. He demanded poets and writers, thinkers and philosophers, hakawatis and musicians, fools and clowns.

And then he desired sex.

He asked for light-skinned women and dark-skinned, blondes and brunettes, Chinese, South Asian, African, Scandinavian. He asked for them singly and two at a time, and in the evenings he had orgies. He asked for younger girls, after which he asked for older women, just to try. Then he tried men, muscular men, skinny men. Then boys. Then boys and girls together.

Then he got bored. He tried sex with food. Boys with Chinese, girls with Indian. Redheads with ice cream. Then he tried sex with company. He fucked the poet. Everybody fucked the poet.

But again he got bored. The days were endless. Coming up with new ideas became tiring and tiresome. Every desire he could ever think of was satisfied.

He had had enough. He walked out of his house, looked up at the glorious sky, and said, "Dear God. I thank You for Your abundance, but I cannot stand it here anymore. I would rather be anywhere else. I would rather be in hell."

And the booming voice from above replied, "And where do you think you are?"

Fatima chuckled. Her hands touched her stomach, and suddenly she wondered if she was pregnant. She knew it was possible. History was filled with tales of half-demons. Would her child resemble Afreet-Jehanam, the ugly demon, or her lover, the most beautiful of men? And what if she was carrying a girl? An unattractive son might be one thing, but a daughter who looked like a demon? The potion. "I need my things."

"Needs, wants, desires," Afreet-Jehanam said. "I might as well be telling children's tales." He paused, looked into his beloved's eyes. "I can dress you in royal clothing, in silks and furs, in emeralds and pearls. What need you of past belongings?"

"One can never be free from the past and its pull."

Afreet-Jehanam waved his hand, and in a moment the red imp Ishmael came running with her clothes. "I collected everything," he said, "except for the robe. Ezra likes it quite a bit. He thought I wanted it for myself and would not give it up."

Fatima took the vial from the dress's pocket. "Has it been seven hours yet?"

"No," the grand demon said. Fatima drank the liquid. "But there was no need," he added. "Had you not panicked, you would have realized that it is a boy. Magic potions are redundant."

Ishmael looked stunned. "I am going to be an uncle?"

"I must leave," Fatima said. "I must complete my mission."

"Why?" Afreet-Jehanam asked. "You have ingested the potion you were to deliver."

"I am not free. I will return. As to the potion, I have another plan. I must continue. I am still far from the green city. The sooner I leave the better." Her lover opened his hand, and in his palm Fatima saw her decapitated hand. "That is my third hand," she said.

"And in it I will place my third eye," he said. "This will be the proof of our union. Place it upon your person and no demon will dare hurt you. Place it above the door of your house and evil will never enter."

She took the talisman, and it transformed in her hands. It became stone, turquoise, and the eye in the palm a slightly darker blue.

"Stay the night," the demon said. "You will be with your masters in the morning."

— *Four* —

According to my grandfather, I owed my existence, my special place in the world, to either of two things, the slaughter of a stud pigeon or the swallowing of matches. Depending on which story he was in the mood to tell, one of those two events forced him to escape Urfa, or, as he sometimes said, provided him with the opportunity of a lifetime.

There were always Armenian orphans living in the Twinings' household, but none stayed more than a year or so. The Twinings, being good missionaries, found homes for the various children. My grandfather, though, was a different story. Since Poor Anahid became the Twinings' maid and he was her charge, he lasted for eleven years. My grandfather claimed, and he was probably right, that the missionary doctor harbored some feeling toward him, his bastard offspring. My grandfather was an anomaly both in his length of stay at the house and in the timing of his escape to Lebanon. One can safely assume that all the orphans he grew up with, those who were not massacred during the Great War, escaped to Lebanon during the great Armenian orphan migration. My grandfather was ahead of his time. He survived the doctor's wife, and he didn't have to deal with the genocide and its consequences. He was blessed; hence, so was I.

In his early years, Ismail's father carried him everywhere, even after he learned to walk. But one day, after my grandfather's second birthday, the doctor's wife told her husband, "Shame on you. You treat this orphan better than you treat your own blood. Do you not love your daughters? Do they not deserve your attention?" The doctor was embarrassed. "This is Barbara," his wife added, "and this is Joan. Maybe you've forgotten who they are."

Simon Twining put my grandfather down and took his daughters for a walk.

When my grandfather was four, the doctor tried to teach him to read and write, but his wife said, "Don't be silly, my husband. English will be of little use to him. We'll send him to school with the other Armenians. He'll learn his language and be able to talk to his people."

However, when my grandfather, after services on Sundays, joined the other children for Bible study with the doctor, she did not object.

"I come from a time when ink was still liquid and lush." My grandfather broke silence as he stoked the fire. "None of this cheap Biro shit. My father's wife thought teaching me to write was money ill spent and time wasted." He performed the maté ritual—poured hot water from the kettle onto the metal straw, after which he ran a lemon peel across it. He replaced the now sanitized straw in the maté gourd and passed it to me. "You might think the doctor's wife was mean, and she was, but you'd be missing the point of the story. I wasn't allowed to learn to read, but Bible study is more valuable for a hakawati. Look at the great one, Umm Kalthoum. She was born into the poorest of families in a remote village of the Nile Delta in Lower Egypt. Umm Kalthoum should have been married off at twelve or thirteen. She would've remained unschooled and mothered a dozen kids: Muslim girls weren't allowed to be educated in that part of the world. But here's the gift, you see. At a very young age, girls are taught to read the Koran and nothing else. It gets hammered into them every day. For a singer, that's the greatest of gifts. She learned tone and rhythm, learned perfect enunciation and breath, voice projection, inflection—you name it. She never mumbles. One can understand every word she utters. She mastered the witchcraft of voice. When the time was right, she opened her mouth, unleashed her soul, and helped all of us get closer to God. It was a gift, I tell you. The doctor's wife may have been spiteful, but fate was on my side."

Poor Anahid and Zovik cared for the boy, treated him as their own, but they were servants in a house that desired constant labor. My grandfather followed them around, and the maids made sure he didn't interfere with their work.

It was at an early age that he learned to entertain himself. Sticks became his companions, and stones his toys. His inner world redecorated the outer one. His imaginary friends proved more loyal than any real ones, if only because, unlike the latter, they existed. He ate, slept, played, learned some, and avoided the Muslim boys and their Turkish insults. By the age of five, he was expected to do minor chores around the house. When he was six, the chores were no longer minor. Two years later, the doctor's wife decided the boy should learn a trade. "Who knows how long we'll be here to take care of him?" she said. "Better that he figures out a way to earn enough to fill his bottomless stomach." My grandfather was given to a pigeoneer to be trained.

That was how my grandfather got swept up in the great pigeon wars of Urfa.

Long before the one God, long before Abraham, long before the city was Muslim, before it was Ottoman or Turkish, pigeons used to carry the souls of Urfa's dead up to the heavens. Pigeons have had a special place in Urfa's heart ever since.

"It's not true what the Chileans say, that pigeons are rats with wings," my grandfather said. "What do they know in Chile? You know it was a pigeon that announced the presence of land to Noah on his ark, the European rock dove, the same pigeon you see in all the cities of the world. Chile? Pfflt, let them go sour with their undrinkable pisco."

Most homes in Urfa had ornately covered holes for the pigeons, but some had pigeon houses on their outside walls that were a diminutive replica of the original house, a clone birthed out of its forehead. In some neighborhoods, the birds had tiny palaces, with mini–crescent moons atop miniature minarets; the architectural designs of the pigeon palaces far surpassed those of the surrounding human houses.

"I hate pigeons," my grandfather added, "but it's not because they're rats."

My grandfather's mentor was an Armenian, Hagop Sarkisyan, who in turn worked for a Turk by the name of Mehmet Effendioglu. Though not a wealthy man, the latter was a pigeon fancier who owned over three hundred pigeons. Hagop trained the pigeons and had four boys to assist. Being the youngest, my grandfather had the worst job, cleaning the shit.

"Shit everywhere," he said. "Shit in the coops, on the terrace, on the roof. Do you have any idea what it's like to deal with so much shit? Of course you don't. You have a maid to pick up after you. I cleaned pigeon shit every minute of the day, and when I went home I had to wash it off me. My hair is as wild as it is today because I had to wash it so much when I was a boy."

Hagop, the pigeoneer, was the main flocker. His first assistant was in charge of feeding the pigeons, giving them the best seeds and the strongest vitamins. The pigeons had to be good-looking and sturdy. During the off-season, this assistant steered one or two of the pigeon flocks, though not the primary one, and never, ever, while the war raged. Mehmet, the master, sat on the roof and watched.

"It was only during the battles that I didn't have to clean," my grandfather said. "I was allowed to watch the birds fly. I have to admit, they were beautiful up in the skies, circling and circling around an imaginary drain, then shooting out, diving like an Israeli jet. In those moments, I forgave the pigeons their shit."

Ah, the wars, the wars. The pigeon wars of Urfa had been going on for over a thousand years. The war started every November and ended every April, which coincided, not by coincidence, with the worst weather for pigeons to roam, an aerial endurance test. In the afternoon, at four-thirty sharp, the warmongers of Urfa ascended to their roofs, where the cages were, and unleashed their flocks into the heavens. The fluttering cacophony of thousands upon thousands of wings and the jingling sounds of pigeon jewelry were heard in every corner of the city. Upon each roof, a pigeoneer steered his birds; his unblinking gaze never left his soaring flock. A long cane with a black ribbon at its end was his instrument. With each wave, he directed his birds' flight. And when he swung a large arc, his flock dived into the middle of another, disturbing the symmetry, confusing his adversary's pigeons.

"Hagop was good, but not outstanding. There was another pigeoneer, an Armenian by the name of Eshkhan, who was the prince of them all. He could direct his pigeons by simply whistling. Tweet, and his flock would circle; tweet, and it would come home. Eshkhan won the war more often than not, and it wasn't because he had the best pigeons. He could have sold his cocks for a fortune and bought better pigeons to train, but he never did. You see, everyone thinks it's about the money, but it isn't. It's about bragging rights. It's about manhood."

The war was won by him who had lost the fewest pigeons to either capture or death. He who ensured his pigeons didn't get lost or exhausted was a pigeoneer worth his salt, and not many were. Every day as the war raged, pigeons soared until fatigue seeped into their wings; oxygen rebelled and escaped their blood. Out of the sky, birds dropped, falling like bombs released by fighter squadrons, littering the earth with deformed corpses. Dazed, bewildered, and confused, some birds followed unfamiliar flocks and landed on alien rooftops, to be captured and paraded that evening at the local café, the spoils of war, the dishonor of their pigeoneers, the dilution of manliness.

"There are wars in the Lebanese cities," my grandfather said, "but they're not anything like those up north. It's done for fun here. It might get nasty in Beirut, but it's not a real war. If one of your cocks ends up with someone else's flock, you can get it back. The gentlemen's rule in Beirut is first time free. You see, in a warless zone, most of the cocks are mated, and a pigeon always wants to return home to its mate, so it's hard to keep a captured cock. You'd have to slay it. In a war zone, each team has about two hundred cocks and five hens. The flying teams consisted only of males, primarily Dewlaps. It's about the war, not pigeon fancying. The pigeoneers in Beirut have teams of all kinds of pigeons: Dewlaps, Tumblers, Apricots, Jews, Fava Flowers, you name it. The fanciers who were attached to their pigeons would never dare fly them during the war."

The pigeon keepers gathered at the Çardak Café, as they had for hundreds of years. They kept score of the previous afternoon's battles by counting the captured pigeons. Cages adorned all the walls of the café, and fanciers could admire or buy the caught birds. The original owner of a pigeon had first dibs, but only if the new owner wanted to sell.

"But you couldn't buy the peşenk," my grandfather said. "The peşenk was the leader of the team of pigeons. You can't win the war without a great one. All the other cocks follow him in flight. If a peşenk lands on another's roof and is captured, the original owner retires from the war. Checkmate. He has to get rid of his team and start a new one. The peşenk can never be bought. He's the chief of the clan, the mightiest of all."

My grandfather took a sip of maté, craned his neck, and spoke to the ceiling. "They say that talent skips a generation, which means that my father or my mother would have been a great pigeoneer, because, unlike my youngest, your uncle Jihad, I certainly wasn't. I have no idea where he got his talent from, and, thank God, he had the intelligence to stop when he did. He wouldn't listen to me, of course. Nobody does. But one day he finally understood that being a pigeoneer is a lowly vocation. Now, listen here. Just because I said I wasn't a good pigeoneer doesn't mean I didn't have other talents. Fate's schedule is not always naked and clear.

"One evening, I was bemoaning my luck. I was hungry and tired. I had been cleaning shit for about six weeks and seeing no way out of it. The damned doctor's wife said I whined a lot. She said there weren't that many options for a wayward boy like me. But she was mistaken, you see, only I didn't know it then. Remember, I was eight. So here I was, sweeping the main coop after a battle, and the stupid Mehmet calls. He hands me a fluffy, shiny black pigeon in a cage to take to the Çardak Café and give it to the owner.

"I went to the Çardak Café. Impressive, let me tell you, big and wide and busy. But then it was all pigeons. Pigeons, pigeons everywhere. Cages on the walls, on the counter, on the tables, under the tables. I began to get nervous. I thought maybe, if I lingered, the owner would ask me to clean the shit. I delivered the pigeon and ran out as fast as I could. I turned the corner, and there it was. I don't know what made me stop. I was running hard, and maybe I needed to catch my breath. Maybe God sent me a sign. Maybe it was written.

"What befuddled my young eyes was another café, the Masal, old but not historic, well lit but decrepit, smoky and dank. There were no doors, and the metal shutters were rolled up. There were tables outside, but the silent patrons had their backs turned to the street. Why be with people if you're going to be quiet? Why sit outside if you're not going to look at the world? And then I saw what enthralled everyone's attention. Inside, on a chair upon a small dais, sat the hakawati.

"He sat on his throne like a sovereign before his subjects. He wore a fez and Western clothing. A waxed black mustache two hands wide dominated his face. I couldn't see his mouth move. He held a book in his lap but hardly looked at it. I moved closer and heard his silky voice. Magic.

"He was a Turk, and, mind you, my Turkish wasn't very good at the time, but I heard him. I listened with my ears, my body, and my soul. He regaled us with the story of Antar, the great black warrior poet. He was in the middle of the tale, but my soles spread roots into the tiles of the pavement. I was enchanted.

"How can I describe the first time I encountered my destiny? A god's fire burned in my breast, my heart aglow. In comparison, my life before that moment had moved at a sad and sluggish pace. Ah, Osama, I wish I could make you feel what it is like when you finally align yourself with God's desires for you. I had received the call."

❧

By the light of a small bed lamp, I could see the curvy silhouette of Uncle Jihad's head and its replica, a larger shadow projected on the wall. He tucked me in a bit too tightly. As my father's younger brother, my number-one babysitter, and my favorite storyteller, he had the job of getting me to sleep, since my parents were having a dîner assis. My mother had told him to put me to bed and come right back, but he seemed distracted, lost in his thoughts. Though he said he wanted to make sure I slept by telling me a great bedtime tale, his heart didn't seem to be in it.

"Once, there lived a happy young prince," he began. He stared at the headboard.

"You said you'd tell me how I came to be." I rolled to one side and then the other to unsecure the sheets. "You promised."

"That's what I'm doing." He picked up the drink he had set on the nightstand, his fingers smearing the perfect outline of the dew that had gathered on the tall glass.

"I'm not a prince."

"I'm not starting the story with you." He took a sip of scotch, and his eyes sparkled for the first time. "Why would you think you're the prince?"

"You told me. You said you'd tell the story of how I became me."

"My dear Osama." He gulped more of his drink and grinned. "You should know better by now. The story of who you are is never about you. I'm starting from the beginning."

"If you do that, you'll barely be able to make dessert."

He laughed. "Let me worry about that. So where was I before I was ingloriously interrupted? There were two young princes."

"It was one happy young prince," I said.

"Well, now they're brothers, and I'm not sure how happy they were. Let's say they were content and loved each other. One day, the princes went hunting in the forest, but the younger brother didn't have the heart to kill any animals. They ended up shooting arrows into tree trunks. The younger prince asked his brother, 'Can you hit that flag over there?' and the older prince cocked his arrow and shot it and bored a hole in the flag. But it wasn't a flag. A very old and ugly woman admonished them, 'Why did you shoot my underwear? I'll teach you to respect other people's laundry.' She clapped her hands twice, and suddenly the princes found themselves in a forest they knew not. They walked in every direction but couldn't figure out how to get back home. Night fell. The following morning, they woke up and were still lost. 'We have to find food or we'll starve to death,' said the older prince. They found a pigeon in a tree. The older prince aimed his weapon, but the pigeon said, 'I implore you, noble prince. Don't shoot me. I have two sons at home, and they'll perish if I don't bring back food for them.'

"The older prince said, 'But we'll die, too, if we don't eat you.' And the younger prince said, 'We can feed on berries and root vegetables. Look, there are parsnips here, and rhubarb and radish.' The older prince felt pity and unstrung his bow. 'I'll repay your deed of mercy, my prince,' said the pigeon, and flew away. 'How can a pigeon repay a debt?' asked the older prince. 'We could have roasted him and served him with a berry-and-parsnip sauce.' "

"That sounds like an awful sauce," I said.

"Any sauce is good when you're hungry. The boys walked and walked and reached rushes that grew near a lake, and there they saw a wild duck. The older prince loved duck meat, confit with pearl potatoes, as did the younger. The older prince cocked his arrow, but the duck said, 'I implore you, noble prince. Don't shoot me. I have two sons at home, and they'll perish if I don't bring back food for them.' The older prince dropped his weapon, and the duck said, 'I'll repay your deed of mercy, my prince.' Farther along, the princes saw a stork standing on one leg and cleaning itself with its long beak. The older prince took careful aim, but the stork said, 'I implore you, noble prince. Don't shoot me. I have two sons at home,' and the prince unstrung his bow. 'We'll sleep hungry tonight,' he said, but the younger said he'd make a fabulous vegetable ratatouille, and he did, and it was sumptuous.

"The following morning, the boys walked and walked until they reached a castle where an old king was standing at the steps. 'You seem to be looking for something,' the king said.

"The older prince replied, 'We're looking for home, but we can't seem to find it.'

"The king said, 'What luck! I've lost my companions. Work for me, and I'll feed you and clothe you until you find your home.' The boys became the old king's companions and told him stories and entertained him. But not everything was wonderful: the king had a nasty vizier."

"There's always a nasty vizier," I interrupted.

"Someone has to be nasty. This vizier, who was envious of the princes, told the king, 'It's my duty to inform Your Majesty that these boys are up to no good. They mock the court. Why, just the other day they boasted that if they were your stewards not a single grain of rice would be lost from your storehouses. They must be shown their place. Mix a sack of rice with one of lentils, and have the boys separate the two in an hour's time. Show them where arrogance leads. Boasting must never be left unanswered.'

"The king was a good man, but he was nothing if not gullible. He gave the order to have the bags mixed and told the boys, 'When I come out of my diwan in an hour, I expect the lentils to be separated from the rice. If the job is done, you'll be my stewards, and if it's not, I'll cut off your heads.' The princes tried in vain to convince him that they hadn't been boastful. The king's servants led the boys to a room where the rice and lentils were strewn all over the floor.

"The boys fretted: this was a week's task for a thousand men. 'We are doomed,' said the older prince. They sat amid the rice and lentils and hugged each other. A pigeon appeared at the window and asked, 'Why are you sad, my princes?' and the older prince explained what the king had ordered them to do. 'Be not concerned,' said the good pigeon. 'I am the king of pigeons, whose life you spared when you were hungry. I will repay my debt as promised.' The king of pigeons flew away, and returned accompanied by a million pigeons, who set about separating the rice from the lentils. Uncountable wings flapped, the resulting air moving piles around the room, and thousands of beaks pecked at rice and lentils. Work, work, work—the pigeons made two large piles in minutes. The king couldn't believe his eyes. He asked his servants to look through the heaps, but not one grain of rice could be found among the lentils. He praised the boys' industriousness and talent and made them his stewards.

"The vizier was apoplectic. The next morning, he told the king,

'The boastful boys have been at it again, saying that if they were the keepers of your treasures not one ring would ever be lost or stolen. Put these vain boys to the proof, Your Majesty. Throw your daughter's ring into the river, and order them to find it.' The foolish king believed the vizier once more and ordered the ring thrown into the river."

"Why do people always believe liars?" I asked.

"We all need to believe. It's human nature. So the king told the princes, 'I understand that you boys are fond of boasting. I've thrown the princess's ring into the river. I'll be in my diwan for an hour, and when I come out, I expect you to have found the ring. If the task is done, you'll be the keepers of my treasures, and if it's not, I'll cut off your heads.' The princes sought the river. The younger prince walked up and down the bank, and the older prince waded in, but neither could find anything. A duck floated down the river and asked, 'Why are you sad, my princes?' and the older prince explained what the king had ordered them to do. 'Be not concerned,' said the good duck. "I am the king of ducks, whose life you spared. I'll repay my debt.' The duck flew away and returned with a million ducks. They swam up and down the river, diving underwater in teams, duck heads bobbing and weaving, until the ring was found. When the king returned from the diwan and saw the ring, he made the boys his keepers of the treasures.

"Seeing that his efforts had been foiled once more, the vizier hatched his master plan. He knew the king had tried to learn sorcery and necromancy and had failed and failed, so the vizier said, 'The boys have not ceased their boastful ways. They have said that an exceptional child shall be born in the palace this night, the brightest child in the universe, the most beautiful, the most delightful, but not only that. These vain boys were not satisfied with a child of such exceptional qualities. They said they asked the jinn to make the boy even more special and the jinn complied. They said the child will be the best oud player in the world, and boasted that if Your Majesty hears the child play the instrument, Your Majesty will weep. Such bluster will never do.' Since the king had never been able to communicate with the jinn, he boiled with rage upon hearing this news. 'If this miracle doesn't happen tonight,' he threatened the princes, 'I'll cut off both your heads, and I'll bury your bodies without prayers in unclean soil, and you'll meet those demons you're communing with.'

"In their rooms, the princes huddled and hugged. At least with the first two tasks they had known how to begin, even if they couldn't have accomplished much without help. But how could one find a child?"

"A stork."

"Of course. The stork tapped at the windowpane, and the princes opened the window. The older prince explained about the miracle. 'Be not concerned,' said the good stork. It flew away and returned carrying a bundle swaddled in white cotton. The stork gently placed the bundle on the floor, and out of it crawled the most beautiful baby in the world, and the princes fell in love with him right away and knew that they would cherish this boy forever and ever. The baby crawled over to the oud lying next to the bed and began to play an exquisite melody."

"A maqâm?"

"But of course. The melody was so charming that everyone in the palace began to wake, wanting to know where this music was coming from. They all rushed to the room and saw with their own eyes the miracle of this most special baby playing the oud. The king heard the song, and his heart expanded, and he wept. The beautiful princess loved the baby and she said, 'This boy will be my son, and this prince will be my husband.' The older prince married the princess, and their son was the most special boy in the world."

"What happened to the nasty vizier?"

"He went to France, where all the jealous people are."

"That's not a good story. I wasn't born playing the oud. I learned how to."

"You're simply remembering how to play, my dear boy." Uncle Jihad drained his glass completely. "You're claiming what you've always known."

"What about Lina?"

"Hers is a different story," he replied.

"How can that be? She's my sister. We can't have different stories."

"Who says?"

"It doesn't make sense," I said. "A family has one story."

❧

And my grandfather said, "The next evening, when the pigeon battle was over, I cleaned everything as fast as I could and ran back to the Masal. But I had arrived late. The hakawati was well into his story and had resolved the cliffhanger.

" 'Please,' I interrupted, calling to him from outside. 'How did Antar escape the deadly trap? It would seem impossible. I must know how,' I said in broken Turkish. I must have confounded him. He glared at me, unblinking. The owner of the café came at me. 'Get out of here, you dirty scoundrel,' he yelled. 'Get back to where you came from, you unbeliever.'

"Now, mind you, insults meant nothing to me. They bounced off me like iron bounces off a magnet. No, I mean like two magnets or something like that. After all, Barbara and Joan used to insult me every day, and the other assistants at work said horrible things. I felt bad that he thought I was dirty, so I said, 'I'm only dirty because I've been cleaning shit, and that's why I was late, and if I went home to clean up I'd miss more of the story.' It obviously didn't impress the owner, who waved a threatening cane in my direction. 'If you don't scram, I'm going to tan your behind,' and I said, 'That's not fair. It's not my fault I have to work. I want to hear the tale.' The owner raised his cane, and I was about to flee when I heard a horsy guffaw. A fat man, most respectable, in an expensive fez, suit, and tie, sat laughing at a table outside. Hookah smoke erupted out of his wide mouth. 'Why are you insulting a future customer, my man? Let the boy stay and listen to the tale,' he said, and the owner replied, 'His kind will never be a customer, effendi. He's a street boy.' Before I could contradict him, the effendi said, 'He's a working boy, not an urchin. How can you turn away a boy who wants to hear a story? Come, my boy. Sit at my table, and open your ears. I don't mind the smell of shit. And bring this boy some tea and something to eat. We have a story to listen to.'

"And that was how I was taken under the wing of Serhat Effendi.

"I was in paradise. I hardly spent any time at home anymore. Each day, as soon as the battle was over, I hurried to the Masal to hear the hakawati. I sat at Serhat Effendi's table every evening. I was served a highly sweetened glass of hot tea and a cheap sandwich, which was still better than anything I was getting at home. The effendi was nice to me. He didn't mind my stink, and he treated me with the utmost respect. Once, when I asked how I could repay him for the daily meal, he replied that my job was to keep him company, because he didn't like being by himself at the café. But we hardly ever talked, except for the times I arrived a bit late and he'd whisper in my ear what I had missed. On my ninth birthday, he bought me a delicious lokum.

"The hakawati enchanted me, that much I know. Yet I began to notice that the effendi wasn't as impressed. One night, after the story-teller had left us with another cliffhanger and Serhat Effendi was preparing to leave, I asked him whether he liked the story. You have to remember, he was showing up six nights a week to listen to this. He replied, 'The story I like very much.' I realized that what he had said was incomplete and hoped he would elaborate. 'I have heard it woven more lusciously.' He realized I didn't understand, because he went on, 'The story of Antar is one of the standards. This man tells it well, yet it seems that romance is not his forte. He does wonderfully with the travails and triumphs of the poet but seems to consider Abla, his enchantress and beloved, a trifle. We're getting half a story. Don't worry, though. It is very near the end, and we'll get someone else next week.'

"Do you know why I'm telling you this, Osama? It's because you should know that, no matter how good a story is, there is more at stake in the telling.

"And the effendi was right. The following week, we had a new hakawati, a much older man. At the designated time, he strode up to the dais and greeted his audience. He announced he would like to tell the story of Antar, the great black poet. I shouted, 'No,' and I was by no means the only one. The hakawati apologized and asked, 'Do you not like the story, gentlemen? I assure you it is the best tale ever told. Antar was the greatest of Muslim heroes, the most passionate of lovers, and most devoted to the faith. This story is one of the finest. Trust me. Even though I'm here for only two weeks and will have to resort to an abridged version, I will enchant you.' The listeners all as one yelled back, 'But we have just finished hearing it. The hakawati before you told the tale of Antar.'

"The hakawati paused and contemplated the situation for a brief moment. 'Shame. It's an uncalled-for shame that you were forced to listen to a pitiful version of the great story told by an incompetent dunce.' A man spoke up. 'It was a delightful version.' 'Never mind,' said the new hakawati. 'I'll bewitch you with my version, and you'll forget everything that came before me.'

"The audience still objected. A few were angry. It was then that I noticed that Serhat Effendi, wearing a bemused grin, wasn't participating in the impromptu discussion. 'We don't want to hear the same story,' the crowd shouted, and Serhat Effendi called out, 'Master Hakawati.' The room quieted as the hakawati acknowledged the effendi. 'Your reputation precedes you,' the effendi said. 'Your exquisite style is the talk of every connoisseur in our lands. We are blessed to have you here in our humble town, and we beseech you to treat us to your specialty, the tale of Majnoun and Layla. It is said that your rendition had the gracious princess weeping for two whole weeks.' 'Seventeen days,' corrected the hakawati. 'And that the Christian men of Istanbul who heard your version converted to the true faith.' 'That is true,' said the hakawati. And Serhat Effendi finished with, 'Is it, then, owing to our modesty that we are to hear the story of Antar instead of your masterpiece?' 'I beg your forgiveness, effendi,' the hakawati said. 'I would have been honored to tell you my signature tale. Unfortunately, I was instructed that under no circumstances am I to take longer than two weeks for my story. Two weeks, effendi. The only story I can tell in two weeks is that of Antar. I cannot insult my audience with a shorter version of my masterpiece. But please, dear audience, remove those sad masks from your faces. It pains me so. The happy news is that in a fortnight I'll be replaced by a young hakawati— a child, really, trying to make a name for himself. The owner says he's very good—for a Circassian, that is.' And here the hakawati paused before adding, 'And it seems the youngster is willing to work for a cup of unsorted and uncooked lentils.'

"The patrons had a fit; the café exploded. Men screamed at the owner, who tried to placate his customers. 'Yes, of course you deserve the best,' he repeated, until, finally, he had to apologize and promise the hakawati he could stay for as long as he needed. The hakawati smiled.

"After only the opening, Urfa realized it was in for a feast. Word of him and his words spread throughout the town. The next evening, the place was packed. Many couldn't find a seat. Twenty fully veiled women stood outside, refused seats, and didn't interact with any of the patrons. They listened, moved and unmoving. The following night, it was forty women on one side and more than a hundred men on the other. And when the masterly hakawati told of Majnoun's exile in the desert to avoid looking at the sweet face of his beloved, every veil turned moist, and every mustache as well. Zeki, the master storyteller of Istanbul, bewitched our little town for eight months straight.

"When I die and people begin to tell you that I wasn't a great hakawati, you tell them I studied with the best, Istez Zeki of Istanbul. Only Nazir of Damascus was as good as Zeki, and I studied with him as well. To find a better hakawati than those two, you'd have had to go to the lands of spices and Shahrazad, to Baghdad and Persia. Zeki was a master. The only reason he ventured into our backwater town was that he had to escape Istanbul for a few years. You see, even though he was in his eighties, he had seduced a vizier's wife. There was a price on his head. But he was so loved that other Ottoman officials helped him leave the capital. They told him to stay away for a couple of years, until they soothed the vizier's feelings. He never returned. He was asked by an affluent man to work in Baghdad, where he was killed.

"Well, maybe I didn't exactly study with Zeki, but I certainly studied him. Don't tell anybody that, because it's hard for people to discern the nuance. I heard him every evening and never missed a session. I studied his technique, his use of voice, tone, and inflection. When he paused, his audience held its breath. He was by far the best at silence. On my walk back home, I would practice saying the same words he did, in the same manner he did. I would move my hands in his way. As he reached a touching moment in the story, he had a habit of holding his hand out in front of him, palm toward God, as if offering Him that lovely moment or, better yet, offering Him the souls of all his listeners. When Zeki told us about the desert birds attempting to distract Majnoun from suicide, he had a different whistle for each bird. On the way home, I was able to whistle the way he did, and I became very good at it. His whistling birds broke open my heart. 'Oh, Majnoun,' the desert wren whistled, 'kill yourself not. Consider all pleasures life can offer,' and the quail whistled, 'Rediscover the enjoyment of eating. Do not forsake life.' Bewitching.

"Studying him wasn't as easy as it sounds, because I had to be two different people simultaneously. My first listened to the story and lived in its world, and my second studied the storyteller and lived in his.

"But, then, I didn't just learn from Zeki. God smiled upon my face and smote one of the pigeon assistants. I didn't see what happened, but I heard everything, because I was in the main coop, cleaning. It was peace season. The assistant, his name was Emre, was flying a flock. Mehmet and Hagop were on the roof with him, drinking their tea. It seemed Emre was unable to get the pigeons to fly higher. He kept swinging his stick wider and wider, but the pigeons flew in a low circle.

Hagop mocked the boy. My feelings were torn. I was happy, because Emre always mocked me, but I knew he would later take out his frustration on me.

"A troubled Emre couldn't understand what was happening. He cursed at the sky. One of the pigeons excreted, and, of all places, the shit fell right into Emre's eye. Mehmet screeched and said that was good luck. Temporarily blinded and befuddled, Emre covered both his eyes, cursed once more, and tried to walk away. He stumbled and fell off the roof and onto the pavement, headfirst. The building was just one story, and the ground was only hard sand. Mehmet and Hagop thought it was amusing. They roared with laughter before they considered that Emre could be hurt. When they looked over the ledge and witnessed the burgeoning pool of blood, their laughter stopped. The boy Emre became stupid and blind, and I was promoted.

"I no longer had to clean shit. Now I was responsible for feeding the pigeons. If it's not one hole it's another. I was also sent on errands and such. I had another boy, beneath me, to do all the shitty work. I wasn't paid more, because, after all, Mehmet was a Turk. But I was done with work much earlier, so I was able to leave and check other cafés in the city. At first I couldn't hear the other hakawatis, because they, too, told their tales in the evening, and I was committed to Zeki. But I would go into a café and ask the patrons to tell me stories. Most of them loved to do it, unless they were playing cards or backgammon. Someone would start a story. 'There was or there was not,' a man would say, and take it from there. His friends would help him tell it, correct him when he missed something, and take over if he faltered for even a second.

"Zeki ended his story when his audience ran out of tears. I felt bereft and alone when he left, but I wasn't alone, because all his audience felt the same way. I tested every hakawati in Urfa. I even saw a Kurd, and though I didn't understand any of the words he said, I liked the way he said them. But I didn't do that for long, because Serhat Effendi expected me at his table. He told me, 'You can search far and wide for the great stories, but in the end, the best ones come to you.'

"I practiced. I spun yarns for Zovik and Poor Anahid. I told stories to the uncaring pigeons as they mated. I spoke to trees, flowers, sticks, and stones. One morning, I began to tell a tale to Hagop, and he smacked me. 'I don't care about what you have to say,' he yelled.

"I practiced singing like Zeki. Whenever there was a song in the story, Zeki sang it. I was happy. I had a job. I had a passion. But I had no family, and that would be my curse. You see, the family I was part of was beginning to crumble like moldy Bulgarian cheese."

❧

The first time I saw a real hakawati perform was in the spring of 1971, after I had just turned ten. My grandfather had come down from the mountain unannounced to visit Uncle Jihad. Lina and I were in my uncle's living room with the two of them. Lina was there to study the paintings in Uncle Jihad's monographs, and I was there because I had nothing better to do. There were dozens of books and monographs strewn all over the place—on the coffee table, the floor—but I was more interested in the conversation between my uncle and his father.

"I don't want to go alone," my grandfather said, in a tone that was both pleading and astonished that he had to restate his wish. His fingers counted worry beads.

"I can't," Uncle Jihad said. "I have to look after the boy." That was a lie. I didn't need looking after.

"We'll bring him." My grandfather's gestures were becoming more expansive. "It'll be better that way." His hair seemed to shoot out in at least eleven different directions. "We can take Lina, too." He looked strange. He wore the traditional Druze trousers—black, with a billowing pouch below the crotch that could hold a small goat. The religious Druze wore them, and he certainly wasn't religious. I had never seen him dressed like that before.

"No," Lina declared, without removing her eyes from the pictures she was perusing on the coffee table. She had her arms crossed in front of her. "I'm not going to some cheap café in some ugly neighborhood. And you," she said to me, "stop staring at my breasts."

"I'm not," I replied too quickly.

Uncle Jihad grinned. "A girl after my own heart. My darling, you can't control the entire world."

"I'm not trying to control the world," she said, still not moving her head. "Just him. I get enough stares from other people. I don't need it from him, and he'll stop if he knows what's best for him." She contemplated a Brueghel painting of a woman who descends into hell and fills her basket with goodies. Uncle Jihad loved Brueghel.

"Sweetheart, it's because they're new," Uncle Jihad said. "In a couple of months, everyone will get used to them."

"Why are we talking about the girl's tits?" my grandfather yelled. "We were talking about me. I come down to the city to visit my children, but my children pay no attention to me."

Lina looked like a colorful statuette, immobile, trying hard to stifle a laugh.

"Goddamn it, Father," Uncle Jihad said. "Watch your mouth. Let's stop talking about the café. You know that Farid will be furious if you go there, more so if you take his children with you. Why don't we do something else? We can visit your in-laws. You haven't done that in ages."

"Damn my in-laws," my grandfather replied. Lina's lips curled into a full smile. "And damn Farid, too. Who's the father of whom here? He should be worried about my getting angry, not the other way round. I want to go. I'm seventy-one years old, and I'm dying soon. This could be my last chance. Don't you have any compassion?"

"What's the point, Father? You know they'll kick you out the minute they see you. They always do."

"No, no. Not this time. That's why you have to come with me. They'll think we're a family, and they won't recognize me, because I'll be going incognito." From his vest he took out a white Druze skull-cap and a large pair of eyeglasses that made his eyes balloon like the eyes of a goldfish in a tiny bowl. "See? I look like a peasant from the mountain."

Lina and I doubled over laughing. As I tumbled on the sofa, my head banged hers. My grandfather looked at his hysterical audience and began dancing and twirling around for us so we could admire him in full regalia. One of my hands rubbed the bump on my head, and the other wiped the funny tears from my eyes.

"Come on. Let's go," my grandfather said. "Please take me."

"I want to go," I said. I sat back up on the sofa. Lina studied me from her prone position. "I want to see the storyteller."

"That's my boy." My grandfather beamed.

"Oh, shit," Uncle Jihad said. "Fuck, fuck, fuck."

And on a clear April morning in Beirut, the four of us—my grandfather, Uncle Jihad, Lina, and I—drove to hear the hakawati.

"Time was much longer then," my grandfather said, "in the old days."

We drove in my uncle's Oldsmobile convertible. My father called it the problem car, but he couldn't convince Uncle Jihad to get rid of it. Since we owned the Middle East's exclusive Datsun and Toyota dealership, my father expected everyone in the family to drive one or the other. The business had begun as a Renault dealership, but the family had sold those rights to be the exclusive retailers of the Japanese cars.

"You could tell a story for a whole month then, but now who'd listen? Everyone wants it quick, as if life itself was quick."

My mother drove a Jaguar. My father overlooked it, because she'd always driven Jaguars. She complained that the Japanese cars were horrible, that the back ends slid sideways on mountain curves like a belly dancer's fat butt. She drove incredibly fast and claimed she needed a car that handled well. My father insisted the Japanese were consistently improving their cars, which would soon become the most reliable cars around, not simply the cheapest.

"Mind you, it's not that this hakawati isn't a fool," my grandfather said. "He's an incompetent dimwit who wouldn't be able to talk himself out of his execution, but we can't blame him in this case, can we? We're lost, I tell you."

My father persuaded Uncle Jihad not to drive the Olds to work, which wasn't a problem, since the dealership was a distance of four blocks from our apartment building. My father wasn't able to persuade him to stop calling the car Hedy, after an American actress my uncle considered "the most divinely beautiful creature on this blessed earth."

"And then there was radio," my grandfather said. "A curse."

"And television," my uncle added.

"Double curse. But who watches those ugly French and English stories?"

"I do," Lina said. Her condition for coming on this expedition was that she would get the front seat and the top would be down. My grandfather told her that princesses sat in the back, and she replied that princesses got assassinated if they did. Grandfather wasn't pleased about being relegated to the back seat. He had tried the age-before-beauty tactic, but my sister's stubbornness was famous. He got to glare at the back of my sister's hair for the trip, and I sat behind Uncle Jihad, the nape of his neck my primary view. Lina turned on the radio, moved the dial from an Arabic music station to one playing a strange beat. "Get up," the singer wailed. The second verse sounded French. The bass thump-thumped. The singer wanted to be a sex machine.

"Turn that off," my grandfather said. Lina didn't. Uncle Jihad did.

"What's the point of riding in a convertible if we can't have loud music?" Lina said. She had a red ribbon tied as a headband, and she moved away from the windshield so her hair would flow in the wind, but there wasn't much wind at the speed we were driving. "We should be driving on the freeways of America."

"The Autobahn is better," Uncle Jihad claimed.

"Why don't you just drive on the airport runway?" My grandfather imitated their tone of voice. "Just drive off and fly."

We were in a neighborhood I had never been to before. The streets narrowed, as did their buildings, and cars were parked helter-skelter. Gaudily hued laundry dripped water from balconies. Earthen pots of red geraniums and green herbs covered windowsills. Layers of posters desecrated every wall. Some were partially torn, revealing the poster underneath; the left eye of a politician appeared beneath the right arm of a scantily clad redhead smoking a cigarette, with the slogan shouting, "Experience the lush life."

Then the posters changed, became neater and less colorful. Pictures of Gamal Abd al-Nasser and Yasser Arafat, and pictures of others I didn't recognize. Photographs of Palestinian martyrs. The phrase "This generation shall see the sea" covered a map of the occupied lands. Ahead, three teenagers in army fatigues, with Palestinian kaffiyehs stylishly draped on their shoulders, waved their rifles at us to stop. One of the teenagers stared wide-eyed at the car. Another gawked at my sister's breasts. I wanted to warn him that she was sensitive. My grandfather moved forward in his seat and said firmly, "Look elsewhere, young man." The boy mumbled something apologetically and stared at the tire of the Olds.

"Now, why are such fine young men as you stopping our car?" Uncle Jihad asked. "We're not going anywhere near your camp."

The oldest of the three, who looked no more than fifteen, stood straighter. "Our orders are to check suspicious cars in the neighborhood. The Israelis are going to try something sneaky."

"True," my uncle said. "You can't be too careful. And I'm sure you boys are doing an exemplary job. You look like smart boys. Hold on. Are you the young lions? You're part of my friend Hawatmeh's Ashbal, aren't you?"

All three boys fell back half a step. In a quiet voice, the eldest asked, "You know the valiant leader?"

"But of course. Didn't you recognize the car? Who else but the valiant leader has such impeccable taste and magnificent manners as to offer such a wonderful gift to a lowly friend like me? I feel so overwhelmed whenever I think of him. May God show him the path to victory."

"Oh, sir, do not speak of yourself as lowly," the leader said. The other boys nodded in unison. They all stroked the car with their hands. "The valiant leader would never offer such a magnificent car to anyone who is not deserving. You're a great man, sir. Your modesty is a lesson for all of us."

"You're very kind, my boy," Uncle Jihad said. His bald head swayed as if he were being enchanted by a lovely melody. "I'm not deserving of adulation. But please give my regards to the valiant leader, and tell him—oh, I don't know, tell him that the car is a treasure and I'm ever so grateful." The boys cleared a path for us, and as we drove away, Uncle Jihad waved farewell to them like passing British royalty.

"My son," my grandfather said. Uncle Jihad bowed his head slightly in acknowledgment.

"You bought the car in Tehran, didn't you?" Lina said. "I remember. You had it driven here." She leaned back on the headrest and laughed, tried to imitate our mother. "Do you even know their stupid leader?"

"Yes," my uncle said, "that I do. He's a jackass. Every year he buys a few cars for his toadies. I charge him triple, and he thinks he's robbing me blind. Sad, really. Breaks my heart."

"You're wasting your talents, son," my grandfather said. "In a different era, you could have been the greatest, probably better than your silly father."

"You're very kind," Uncle Jihad said.

"Don't patronize me," my grandfather said.

"No, I mean it. But I'm not wasting the talent. I'm a car salesman, the modern storyteller. We're doing really well, Father. In the last year, we've made more money than in all the previous years combined. It seems that this is what I was born to do."

"Stop fooling yourself," my grandfather said. "Stupidity is unbecoming."

My father didn't like old Arabic cafés. According to him, only gamblers, drunkards, and swindlers patronized them. I assumed that everyone around us fit the description, because the café looked like every other one Uncle Jihad had taken me to. White paint peeled off the walls in sheets; cigarette and hookah smoke fumed the dank air. The customers sat on cheap wooden chairs with twine seats. The square tables were either Formica or white plastic. Greaseproof wraps and balls of foil speckled a few of the tables. Two kids roamed the room: a tea boy carried glasses filled with the scalding amber liquid, and a coal boy carried a brazier to replenish the hookah's embers. On a small wooden platform, a lonely chair was pushed back against the dirt-stained wall. This was where the hakawati would sit. This was where my grandfather's goldfish eyes remained fixed.

"I'm sure he'll use props," my grandfather sneered.

"I want to see how fast you'll get kicked out of here." Lina smiled at him, and he laughed.

My glass was too hot to hold, so I moved my lips toward it and slurped a bit of tea. It was too sweet. Lina leaned forward, too, laid her head on her crossed arms on the table, and looked up at my grandfather. "Do you think he is good at accents?" she asked.

"You're nothing but trouble," he replied. "He is awful at accents. You knew I'd say that, because it's true. He's Egyptian. They wouldn't know any accent other than theirs if it kicked them in the ass. But what's horrible about him is that he doesn't know how ghastly he is. Even his native accent is atrocious, and I don't think he's really Egyptian. He sounds like a foreigner in every accent."

"Like Dalida," I piped.

"But he must be good," Lina said. "They brought him all the way here."

"No one brought him here. He's probably getting paid two cups of tea for this. He's that bad. Just you wait. You'll see. Ah, look. Here comes the dimwit."

The hakawati, a man in his fifties or sixties, wearing a fez and an Egyptian jalabiya that was short and threadbare at the ankles, walked in from the boisterous kitchen. He carried a plastic sword in his right hand and a tattered book in his left. His gray mustache was waxed into glistening loops. My grandfather stared contemptuously, his nostrils flaring as if he smelled vomit. His tongue clucked. He muttered to himself. I heard only the word "book."

The hakawati lifted the jalabiya slightly and stepped onto the dais. He walked to the front and bowed, even though no one had clapped.

"Look at the silly peacock," my grandfather hissed.

"Don't, Father," Uncle Jihad said. "You're working yourself up."

"Good evening, ladies and gentlemen," the man announced. Lina and I both covered our mouths to hide our laughter. He cultivated his vowels, elongated them, and reaped a pretentious inflection.

"All the tra-la-la," my grandfather whispered. "Show-off." He turned away, and his elbow knocked his tea glass, almost tipping it over.

"In the name of God, the most compassionate, the merciful," the hakawati began.

"He's going religious on us," Grandfather snickered.

"Praise be to God, the Lord of justice, the Benefactor, the Faithful, and I state there is no god but God alone and He has no partners, a statement that saves whoever states it on the Day of Judgment, the Day of Religion, and I state that our master Muhammad is His slave and His prophet and His honest lover, may God pray on his soul, and on the souls of his honorable, decent, and virtuous relatives, and on the souls of his upright friends."

"Pfflt," Grandfather said to the table.

"And so," the hakawati proceeded, "God in all His glory made the stories of the early heroes a model to the faithful, a guide to the ignorant, a warning to the infidels, and I heeded God's wishes in choosing to tell this tale, for I saw that it contained the triumph of Islam and the humiliation of the mean infidels, and I looked up other stories but couldn't find one that was more truthful or offered better proof or was wiser than the story of al-Zaher Baybars, the hero of heroes, to whom God promised eternal victories as a reward for his unwavering faith, and what glorious and enchanting details I shall relate to you were told to me by my teachers—Sofian, the grand hakawati of Algeria, and Nazir, the Damascene hakawati of the Hamidieh—as they heard from their illustrious teachers, may God have mercy upon all of them."

And my grandfather stood up, his chair clank-clanking as it fell to the ground. Uncle Jihad quickly covered his face with both hands. My grandfather pointed a finger at his nemesis. "You," he bellowed. Behind the glasses, the red lines in his eyes looked like mighty rivers on a map. "You're a pretender. You've never met Nazir. You're not worthy of eating his shit."

The hakawati was speechless, his fez askew.

And my grandfather resumed his tale. "Just as the morning star out-shines all others, Murat's beauty surpassed any in the city of Urfa. His splendor was such as to make poets weep for not being able to describe it adequately or honorably. Yet this most obvious of traits was exceeded by his modesty. He was studious, honest, kind, and devout, which were amazing qualities for any man, but he was—what?—a boy of seventeen or so. Everyone wished him for a son, but the girls—the girls wished him for a husband. They prayed every night. They swore vows they could never keep, but in the end it didn't matter, for few of Urfa's girls could marry a dervish, and that was what he was.

"Like all dervish boys his age, Murat had to practice his religious rites and rituals relentlessly. But, unlike other boys, he took his duty of watching Abraham's pool seriously. No Narcissus he. Wearing his religious dervish uniform—a fez hat, short white skirt atop white breeches—he stood guard ceremoniously, didn't move, play, interact with the other boys or passersby. When not watched by an elder, the other boys broke loose, relaxed, and did what all boys do. Every dervish turned devilish. But Murat believed that God was always with him, and behaved accordingly. Like a statue sculpted by a master artist, the boy stood still before the pool, watched from atop his shoulder by God and from across the street by a gaggle of girls.

"Some of the girls were veiled, most were not. Muslims, Christians, Turks, Arabs, Armenians, Kurds, they came for a glimpse of heaven. But one kept coming back again and again. She knew his schedule. She wasn't allowed to get close to him, so she began to talk to him from across the pool, across the street, making a fool of herself. She didn't follow the well-worn laws of discretion. She arrived early and waited anxiously for him, standing as if her knees were unsure they could sup-port her weight. And when Murat appeared, dressed in his glorious dervish outfit, she yelled, 'Look at me!' The boy was so devout he didn't hear or see her. That is the greatest and deepest wound for a girl of fifteen, and that's how old my half-sister was.

"My father was the shah of his realm, and, like most shahs, he had no inkling that the realm was imploding. Did he notice the simmering stew of war? Did he feel the tension in the world? Did he hear the dying gasps of empire? Did he realize that the city's Turks had begun to regard him and his English family suspiciously? Obviously, he was on a mission. God had sent him to minister to the poor Christians in Urfa, and that was what he was doing. Did he notice that the people he was ministering to were getting poorer? The Armenians of the area were not being hired anymore. Did he notice that many more were having 'accidents'? He was spreading the word of God. He was ministering to a people but didn't realize how terrified they were growing. Did he feel the tension between the Turks and the Armenians?

"Did he feel the tensions at home? Did he see his daughters growing up? He didn't realize his elder daughter, Joan, was of marriageable age until she turned sixteen and his wife had to point out that there were no eligible husbands for her daughter in Urfa. He suggested she could wait for another year, and if not, he could send her to his wife's sister in Sussex. His wife didn't know what to do. She tried to point out that the world they knew was disappearing, that the Urfa they knew was disappearing, that the daughters they knew were disappearing. But the doctor had a job to do, a job that meant something, a job that defined who he was.

"And he paid no mind to Barbara the troubled. Barbara hated me, just like her sister and her mother did. She was closer to me in age, only five years' difference, so her insults were more humiliating. What still upsets me to this day is that every now and then a few Muslim boys would call her names—infidel, unbeliever—and she'd get melancholy, weep for days on end, but then she'd turn around and call me an orphan bastard. She wasn't always melancholy. Often she'd get excited about one thing or another—a game she'd played, a new dress she wanted. She would jump like a bunny while talking. She talked faster than anyone I've known.

"Once, I got stuck in the mulberry tree. I was young, maybe five, maybe six. I had climbed the tree for some fruit and ended up on a branch with my rear end higher than my head. My legs dangled from either side of the branch. I got scared and froze in place. I was relieved when Barbara saw me, because I thought she would get help, but instead she got a cane. I don't know why she did it. She whipped my bare feet and laughed. I couldn't lift my legs for fear of falling, and she didn't stop whipping my soles. I cried so hard that Zovik came out running. She tried to take the cane away, and Barbara turned on the maid. She caned Zovik. She hit Zovik over and over until she tired. She threw the cane at Zovik and went into the house.

"Of course, I avoided Barbara after that. I tried to be anywhere she was not. And once I began to work, that became less and less difficult. Before she finally turned to me for help, I probably hadn't spoken to her in over two years, and that's while living in the same pious house.

"She was in love, she told me, and I must help her. She said her heart was afire and she needed a go-between, a boy to inform her boy of the possibility of love. This wasn't some lovely fairy tale. Do you think I'm crazy? In the middle of her confession, I turned around and bolted. But where could I go? She was my half-sister. She came after me the second day. 'You must help me. I have no one else. I will die, and it will be your fault.' I scampered away again. I spent one night at the Masal; the next night I slept on Mehmet's roof. Poor Anahid was worried sick. She screamed at me when she saw me. Then Barbara screamed at me. I ran again and stayed away for about two weeks. But Barbara forgot about me the same way she remembered me. All of a sudden, I was no longer part of her grand scheme. I didn't try to find out what her new plans were, but by the time I returned to sleeping at home, Poor Anahid and Zovik had heard about Barbara and Murat. Now, you have to remember that Barbara was still only stalking Murat, and the poor boy hadn't yet acknowledged her existence. He must have known, I think, because the other boys must have told him. Whether it was so or not, he didn't look at her. And everybody began to talk. One day, a Turkish boy approached Barbara. If she was willing to love Murat, why could she not love him? He might not be as beautiful as Murat, but he could reciprocate, and he certainly could please her. Horrified, she slapped the boy and bolted home. The next day, another boy approached, and another. She stopped running away and ignored her new suitors.

"The city of Urfa had nothing but Barbara to talk about. Mehmet asked me if I had slept with the crazy English maiden. Hagop wondered if it was true that she walked around naked in the house. The boys wanted to know if her father had his way with her every Wednesday. The English, her mother and father, were of course the last to know.

"Barbara finally did the unthinkable. She waited until Murat finished his duties, and, in full view of all the other boys, she walked up to him and declared her eternal love. And he listened. Now, Barbara was not the most attractive of girls, but she wasn't ugly, either. It wasn't about beauty for the boy. I assume he was flattered: not many boys are chosen. Being the honorable person he was, he informed her that there was no hope for love. He was a Muslim and she a foreigner. She said he didn't have to do anything other than allow her to gaze at him. Even if she could not possess him, even if she only walked beside his shadow, she would die fulfilled.

"The following day, Barbara resumed her passion and her position. And now he paid attention. Soon they were seen walking together. Soon they were walking unseeing. They paid naught but each other any mind. Soon the tongues of Urfa walked as well, and the scandal of all scandals erupted. And so did our house. Her perplexed father tried to talk to her. When her mother found out, she caned Barbara and locked her in her room. Her mother left the rattan leaning outside the door to remind the household that Barbara was in for another round. But Barbara, crazy Barbara, wouldn't bend. She yelled and wept in her room. Apparently, that was nothing compared with what happened to Murat. He began to turn up at watch with black eyes and was unable to stand erect for the duration of the sacred guard shift. He neglected his studies of the Koran. He no longer had time for friends. He stopped twirling.

"What is it about unfulfilled love that turns its flames to infernos? No lock, no house, no rain, no sandstorm, no parent, and certainly no religion could keep the boy from being seen on certain nights atop the stone wall only paces away from her window, declaiming his obsessive love for Barbara in verse. She was seen in the streets not too far from her house, her mother dragging her back by any means at her disposal. 'Why?' Barbara was heard to wail. 'Why am I forbidden one glimpse of my beloved?'

"This went on for months and months. Barbara and Murat were seen holding hands in the ruins of the Crusader castle. They stared forlornly into each other's eyes behind the great mosque. I admit that I once carried a letter from Murat to Barbara. As I was leaving home to wash after feeding pigeons all day, he approached me and pleaded. I couldn't refuse. Barbara forgave me all my past sins.

" 'I can't keep her in chains,' her mother said. 'Begin packing,' her father replied. 'We'll leave by the end of the year.'

"The leaves of my familiar life had begun to yellow.

"That year—I was eleven—it became obvious early on that it was to be the year of the great pigeoneer Eshkhan again. He was dominating the war. His peşenk seemed invincible. Short orange feathers rose in odd angles on the top of his head—hence his name, Bsag, which means 'crown.' He led attacks into other flocks that caused chaos worthy of Judgment Day. Veterans of the wars lost more birds that year than in all ten previous seasons combined. Eshkhan's flock would ascend into the skies, and descend with twice their number. In one memorable battle, three pigeoneers lost their peşenks, which was a first as far as anyone could recall. Envy reared her poisonous head. How was he doing it? What was his secret? At the Çardak Café, the pigeoneers moaned and groaned. It wasn't fair. Half of them could no longer compete, and the other half had no chance of winning. And the great Eshkhan laughed at all of them.

"By the time March came along, Mehmet had lost almost half his team. He pretended that he wasn't upset, but he beat the assistants at the merest provocation. If one of his pigeons fell out of the sky, he beat me because I didn't feed it well. If the coop wasn't spotless every second of the day, he beat the shit-cleaner. One afternoon, Eshkhan's peşenk attacked Mehmet's team, and Mehmet flew into a rage. He began to scream across the roofs, 'How could you? I have nothing to fight you with. It's over. What's the point if not to humiliate me?' And, of course, that was the point—that was the point of any war.

"And Mehmet remembered that war is never meant to be fought fairly. The next day, he searched and searched and bought the comeliest hen in the land. It was an old trick, a very old trick, and Eshkhan's peşenk fell for it. When Eshkhan's team flew above Mehmet's roof, Hagop, grasping the hen by its tiny legs, raised his hands in the air. The pigeon fluttered its wings. Bsag saw the bait. He broke out of formation, circled above the roof, and landed on the ledge to investigate: Is this a beauty I see before me? Now, having a pigeon land on your roof and capturing it are two different things, especially a cock as wily as a peşenk. You can't allow him to see the net that will capture him, and since Bsag landed on the ledge, we couldn't approach him from behind. Still, the first assistant tried. He jumped clumsily and fell on his face, and the peşenk flew back up to the clouds. Of course, the boy received a beating.

"But—before Bsag escaped, I saw his secret. I discovered the source of his power. On the pigeon's white-feathered chest hung the most beautiful ornament I had ever seen: a tiny turquoise Fatima's hand that warded off any evil.

"There was a big fight at the café. Eshkhan called Mehmet a lowlife, among other things. Mehmet returned the insult. Eshkhan punched Mehmet and bloodied his nose. Mehmet was unable to return the blow, because he was held back. Eshkhan yelled, 'Let's see you try that again. Do you think my cock will fall for that old trick a second time?'

"He did. Bsag landed on the ledge, and the same thing happened. When the first assistant tried to capture it, the bird flew away. There was another brawl at the café. On the third night, three veterans with their own nets joined our group. Everybody wanted Eshkhan to lose. They waited for the peşenk to land. He did, on the ledge again. No one moved, for fear of frightening him. The veterans stalked. I whistled. I whistled exactly the way Eshkhan whistled, exactly the way he directed his peşenk. I didn't know what the signals were, but my whistling was enough to confuse the poor bird. Bsag looked at me, uncomprehending, and a net descended upon him. The veteran who captured him unleashed a victory cry up to the skies.

"Mehmet took Bsag out of the net, cut off his head with a serrated knife, and threw the still-shuddering body onto the street.

"Barbara had begun to calm down. She was sixteen now, and I figured she was becoming more mature. She asked me to bring home some matches from the Masal Café, saying she needed more than were available in the house. I couldn't refuse such a simple request. After all, there were enough matches in the house to burn it down, so I assumed she wanted them for something inconsequential.

"The evening Eshkhan lost the pigeon war and his peşenk was killed, I stole one hundred matches from the Masal and gave them to Barbara. She kissed me. That was the first time anybody other than Poor Anahid or Zovik had kissed me. I watched her break the phosphorus tip of each match and swallow it. After the fourth or fifth, I asked her what she was doing. She waved me away with a dismissive flick of the wrist. She swallowed the tips one by one.

"The house woke up to the sound of her crying and retching. Poor Anahid, Zovik, and I huddled in the doorway and watched as her father tried to examine her, as her sister tried to comfort her, as her mother tried to talk to her. Barbara had the yellowest skin I had ever seen.

"And Zovik whispered, 'You don't trample upon fate. Evil will close its circle.'

"Barbara vomited and vomited. Her sister was holding her. Her mother began to cry. She called out, 'Barbara, Barbara, talk to me. What's going on?' But she wouldn't touch her daughter. When the doctor noticed the broken matches on the ground and under the bed, he moaned, 'Oh, no.' Her mother saw, and the first word out of her mouth was a strident 'Whore.'

"Barbara vomited some more. Her father whimpered, 'You didn't have to take so many.' He looked vanquished. His eyes seemed to be melting. Her mother's eyes were afire. 'How could you do this? How could you be so disloyal? How could you betray your faith?' she hollered.

" 'If you had only told me,' the doctor said. 'You are my child. For you, I would have done it. For you, I would have gotten rid of the baby.'

"Barbara had trouble breathing. Her life evaporated before our eyes. She clutched her father's wrist. She said, 'I did not pleasure him enough,' and gasped her last breath.

"Of course, I didn't go to work that day. The doctor's wife went crazy. She went to her room and began to pack. 'I am leaving hell,' she said. Thank God, no one asked where Barbara had gotten the matches. But then the doctor's wife came up to me and yelled, 'You live while your better died. I want you out of this house.' She moved toward me, but Poor Anahid quickly shoved me behind her. The doctor's wife slapped Poor Anahid and retreated to her room.

"Poor Anahid sent me to our room and told me not to come out no matter what was happening. I stayed there for hours and heard all kinds of things going on in the house. Then one of the pigeoneer's assistants arrived. I thought he was going to ask me to go to work, but he told Zovik that Mehmet no longer had any need for my services. Mehmet also suggested that I leave town, because Eshkhan had vowed to kill me in front of four witnesses. He had been told that I whistled, captured his peşenk, and killed him with my own hands.

"It wasn't true, of course. But who would believe me? I wouldn't be able to convince Eshkhan. And if I did, then maybe Mehmet would kill me. I was in trouble. Zovik and Poor Anahid were crying in our room. The doctor's wife was crying in hers.

"Poor Anahid and Zovik decided that I should leave as soon as possible. They were at their wits' end and knew no one I could be sent to. I told them that I knew someone who might help. We left our room quietly, tiptoeing along the corridor, hoping not to be seen, and went to see Serhat Effendi. The effendi said I should go far away. He had a cousin stationed in Cairo. He had not written to him in a while, wasn't sure where he was exactly, but the effendi could find out his address in a month's time. Poor Anahid told him I didn't have a month. He said I should go to Cairo anyway. There should be no problem finding his cousin, since there couldn't be that many Turks in Cairo. He gave me a letter and money to buy train and boat tickets.

"The only thing I knew about Egypt was that Abraham and Moses and Hagar left it and were happy never to return. Back at home, Poor Anahid packed my few clothes. 'You can't go to Cairo,' she said. 'How will you find his cousin? That's just crazy.' 'And do you think a Turk will take in an Armenian orphan just because his cousin asked him to?' said Zovik. 'You must go somewhere safer,' said Poor Anahid. 'Beirut. Go to Beirut. Seek out the Christians. Go to a monastery. They will feed you and care for you.' I knew less about Beirut.

"I said my last goodbyes to Zovik and Poor Anahid. I didn't say goodbye to my father," my grandfather said to me. "I came to Beirut and created our story."

The cold made me shiver, and I huddled closer to the stove. My grandfather drank his bitter tea, a palliative for his digestive problems. "When I'm no longer in this world," Grandfather said, "and they ask whether you believed me, what will you say?"

I didn't think he expected a reply. He sat next to his stove, looking dejected. His pant legs were pulled up high enough that I could see his pale, hairless shins.

"You're eleven now," he said, "and I was eleven. . . ." His voice trailed into nothingness before he whispered, "You know now who I am." He removed the metal lid of the stove with the spatula and threw in his spent cigarette. He stood slowly, creakily, and stomped to his room. When he came out, he handed me an old white kerchief. "You are my blood," he said. "This is for you."

Inside the kerchief was a jewel, a tiny turquoise Fatima's hand with dark-brown and black blood encrusted in its grooves.

— Five —

The entire palace buzzed with stories of Fatima's arrival. Some said the slave girl had come back on a flying carpet, which rose back into the heavens after the traveler alighted. Fatima had returned with a herd of jeweled elephants. She was accompanied by a band of brigands or a thousand jinn. She wore a crown of rubies. She wore a robe of gold.

The emir and his wife interrupted their breakfast on the terrace and hurried into the palace. The vizier and the courtiers were gathered around Fatima in the throne room. Fatima greeted the emir and his wife with the requisite courtesy. The emir was oblivious to the change, but his wife realized, not without some weariness and concern, that the woman before them was no longer a slave. Fatima bowed too well. The emir insisted she regale them with stories of her adventures, and she did, albeit with a few omissions: adventures, yes; assignations, no.

"Will the healer be able to help us?" the emir's wife asked.

"Absolutely. She gave me the cure."

"And the underworld? You entered Afreet-Jehanam's domain and he gave you back your hand?" the emir asked.

"He felt I earned it."

"Preposterous," the vizier scoffed.

"It was as I said," Fatima replied.

"Are you certain?" the emir said. "No one can doubt your courage, Fatima. There is little need to salt and pepper the story."

"She arrived on a flying carpet," said one of the courtiers. "I saw her. She descended from the heavens."

"The underworld is not up there," the vizier said. "No man has ever descended to a demon's lair and made it back alive. This tale is a lie. I would suggest the slave girl offer some proof of her exotic journey."

"Would you be willing to place a wager?" Fatima asked. "If I produce proof, are you willing to surrender everything you have on you at this moment?"

And the vizier agreed. Fatima brought her left palm to her face and blew on it. Red dust appeared, multiplied, and formed a cloud that hovered before her. The imp Ishmael ran out of the dust. His brother Isaac followed, toward the vizier. "I claim all the gold," he said. Fatima's breath turned into orange dust upon touching her palm, and Ezra jumped out. Jacob ran out yelling, "The jewelry is all mine." Job disagreed. "It is mine, I tell you." The dust kept swirling above Fatima's palm, then turned blue, and Noah emerged, followed by Elijah. Violet Adam was last.

"I must catch my breath," Fatima said.

The eight little demons climbed all over the vizier, undressed him, relieved him of all possessions. They left him naked, mouth agape in shock. A mistake. "Help me, Ishmael," Isaac said, pointing at the vizier's mouth. The red brothers jumped back onto the vizier's head. Isaac and Ishmael came away with his gold teeth.

"Quite a reasonable return," Noah said.

"She bargains well," Isaac said. "She is from Alexandria. We shall be rich in no time. A most fortunate partnership."

"Next time, try to bet with someone wearing fur," Ezra said. "I love sable."

"You think as small as your mother's vagina," said Adam. "Next time, Sitt Fatima, have someone wager a harem."

Fatima blew into her palm again, and white dust appeared. The imps sauntered into the cloud and faded. "I think that was proof enough," she said, smiling lazily at the emir and smoothing the creases of her robe with the palms of her two hands.

❧

When I arrived at the hospital room the second morning, my father was sitting up in bed, pillows fluffed behind his back, white tabs attached to his chest, smiling, trying his hardest to appear jovial and nonchalant. Another brush with the unmentionable inevitable averted. His face was pale and fatigued, but his eyes darted about the room as if operating on a separate generator. Lina suppressed her wariness, and weariness, doing her best imitation of Auntie Mame. "It's going to be a glorious day," she chirped. "We should call the restaurant and order. They just might run out of lamb."

It was half past nine. Soon sunlight would begin to creep along the floor and fill the room, reducing the fluorescents to redundancy.

"I don't think that's necessary." Even though my father hadn't used his oxygen mask all morning, he held it in his hand.

"We can't break with tradition just because we're here. I'll ask the restaurant not to use salt, and if they can't, you'll only eat a little. We can't have Eid al-Adha without lamb."

"I don't think it's wise to order," my father said. "Samia will probably send us some of her meal when they're done. She'll be insulted if we order."

"She doesn't have to know," Lina said. "She may forget about us, and if she doesn't, do we really have to eat it? Can't we have good lamb for a change?"

"You're being mean. If anything is our tradition, it's that we celebrate together, with Samia's meal."

I walked to the glass sliding door, saw a sliver of the sun perched atop a building across the street. The newer building looked colossal next to the little house with rotted shutters, two incompatible siblings with different genes.

❧

The emir and his wife dragged Fatima into their private quarters to inquire about the cure. "The healer said it is about the stories," Fatima said, "the tales you choose to tell. Your lordship likes romance, which is why you have twelve daughters. Girls like love stories, whereas boys love adventure stories. The next time you make love, make sure to tell an adventure story and not one of romance."

"But I love stories of unrequited love," the emir said, "of exalted suffering. I love desire and the obstacles lovers have to overcome. I do not like tales of killing, maiming, and trying to prove who is stronger than whom. Those can be devastatingly boring."

"But adventure stories are the same as love stories," his wife argued. "And no matter, you must tell me an adventure story tonight. It has been prescribed. This is so exciting. I will hear a new tale. Do not take offense, my dear, but your stories have been getting stale for a while, the buzzing of listless houseflies and not the bites of mosquitoes. I have cravings for adventure."

That night, after coitus, the emir's wife demanded her tale. "No romance," she said. "No star-crossed lovers. I want a story that will engage a different organ, not my heart."

"A sexual story, then," the emir said.

"No, I want death and destruction. I want virile heroes who overcome evil. At least one city must be destroyed. I want a son and you want a son."

"Virile heroes? How about faithful heroes? Wait. Wait. I know which story. I know now. Listen." The emir began his story thus:

In the name of God, the most compassionate, the merciful.

Once, long before our age, the king of Egypt, ruler of the lands of Islam, was despondent because his realm was in disarray. The Crusaders thrived along the coast, behaved as if they owned the land. Corruption and perfidy dwelt in the hearts of the administrators of his realm. The foreigners were able to bribe, hoodwink, and deceive any official they chose. King Saleh wept in shame, for he knew that if he did not rule more wisely his great-grandfather Saladin, the great Kurdish hero who crushed the Crusaders and unified the lands, would not welcome him in paradise. King Saleh was watching that kingdom slowly crumble and putrefy.

One night, the honest king had a discomfiting dream. He called on the intelligentsia of the land, the philosophers, the judges, and the poets. "Hear me. I want to know whether last night was a propitious night for dreams."

The wise men replied, "By all means, Your Majesty. Last night offered a clear vision. It was the seventeenth of the month. The moon was not blighted."

"I was stranded in a desert, defenseless, surrounded by a thousand hyenas. But dust rose, and there appeared seventy-five magnificent lions. The lions attacked the hyenas, and, in a fierce battle, the grand ones annihilated their enemies and cleared the desert of the vermin. What can this dream mean?"

And the wise ones said, "Our lord, the hyenas are the nonbelievers and infidels who wish you harm. The lions are the righteous warriors who will protect you. It is imperative that you purchase seventy-five slaves to save the kingdom."

The king informed the most honest slave-trader in the city that he required seventy-five Muslim boys fit for a king and palace life, twenty-five of them to be Circassians, twenty-five Georgians, and twenty-five Azeris. The slaver said, "But, Your Majesty, we have nothing like this in the city. One would have to visit the big slave-markets closer to their lands for an order of that size. I have a keen eye for good slaves and a keener ear for differing tongues, but I am no longer the man who can go on this quest. The past years have been hard for my trade, and I have run up much debt. I would surely be arrested by my debtors on my travels, and my belongings, slaves or money, would be confiscated. I was famous and successful once, but my fortune drowned in the Red Sea and was overwhelmed in a sandstorm in the Sahara."

And the king's astute vizier asked, "Master slaver, may I test your ear? From my tongue, can you gather my origin?"

"Surely, my lord. Your father is a Turk and your mother is Moroccan."

The king knew he had the man for the job. He ordered his assistants to write a decree saying that the slaver worked for the king and should not be interfered with, and that any of his debts could be collected from the king's treasury. He ordered his treasurer to pay the man the price of the slaves, and set aside compensation for the slaver's labor to be paid upon delivery. He ordered his tailors to make the slaver a better outfit, and to bring forth seventy-six fancy slave-costumes. "For I have one more request," the king said. "I want one more boy." The king's audience looked puzzled, for he seemed to be speaking mechanically, as if he were reciting a godly lesson. "The boy must be intelligent, strong, precocious, and witty. He must have memorized the Koran. A beautiful face he must have. A lion's folds must appear between his eyes. A beauty mark, its color red, will be found on his left cheek. And he must answer to the name of Mahmoud. If you find him upon your travels, bring him to me, for he is the one."

❧

"My dear Salwa," my father called as my niece entered the hospital room, "why are you here? It's a holiday. Shouldn't you be relaxing at home with your husband?"

"For heaven's sake, where else will we be today?" Salwa said as her husband followed her in. My father's face brightened at Hovik's appearance. I wondered how long it would take my father to poke fun at his Armenianness. Not long. Hovik was fourth-generation Beiruti, and of the four languages he spoke he was least fluent in Armenian, but my father could never resist the temptation to mock his origins. My father always spoke to him in the grammatically incorrect Lebanese dialect the first immigrants were known for. And Hovik loved it.

After helping Salwa to the recliner, he kissed my father and replied to his questions in the bad dialect, mixing the gender of nouns and chuckling. He looked so young in contrast to my father, whose cross-hatched wrinkles, those not thrown into shadow by his enormous nose, multiplied as he laughed.

"Go home," my father told him, using the feminine.

"I am home," he replied.

❧

The emir of Bursa heard there was a slaver in town in possession of a decree from King Saleh. The emir asked the slaver the reason for his arrival, and the slaver explained King Saleh's request. The emir said, "You must be my guest for three days, to rest and recuperate. You can try the slave markets in the city, but I do not believe they will have all the boys you are looking for. After you have gathered your strength, you can try the markets farther north." The slaver thanked the emir for his generosity.

Upon finishing the morning prayers on his second day, the slaver heard a seductive sound. Was it the buzzing of early bees or the cooing of mourning doves? The faint sound flooded his heart. He followed it until he reached one of the palace's courtyards. Around a shimmering pool sat boys reading the Koran, and the sound bewitched the slaver. An Azeri boy called Aydmur broke the spell by asking, "What can we do for you, my lord?" And the slaver said he was the guest of the emir and wondered who they were. "We are slaves to the most honorable emir. We are Circassians, Georgians, and Azeris. We are all Muslims. Every one of the seventy-five of us is the scion of a king, a famous warrior, or an emir, but fate has determined to make us owned."

At lunch, the slaver said to the emir, "My lord, when I told you yesterday that King Saleh wished to purchase a group of slaves, you replied that such a group could not be found in this city. Yet I found exactly what I was searching for in your courtyard."

Light left the emir's face, and dark settled in. "I said you could not find such a group for sale. Those boys belong to me, and I do not wish to part with them. They are to become my personal guards."

The slaver felt his heart failing, for he could not argue.

That night, the emir was startled during a dream. He felt a hand touch his chest, and the face of fate appeared before him. The hand became a millstone, and his heart tightened. His breathing became labored. He could not muster the energy to twitch a muscle, and his soul wished to escape his body. And the face said, "Let my slaves go." The millstone turned back into the hand, and the emir could breathe again. The face disintegrated, and as it disappeared it said, "Do not accept any payment less than seventy-five thousand dinars. Demand eighty-five thousand first, and settle for seventy-five."

Before they could wear their new clothes, the boys were sent to the baths. While washing, the slave Aydmur noticed a sickly boy by himself in a corner, having trouble breathing the steam-laden air. Aydmur, the Azeri, asked, "Stranger, may I be of assistance?"

And the sickly boy said, "I am weak. My master is inside this room, and I must wait here even though the air is much too heavy."

Aydmur's heart ached as he watched the boy suffer, and he began to cry. When the slaver asked Aydmur why he was sad, the slave said, "The sight of this boy's suffering wounds my soul." The slaver asked the boy his name, and the boy said, "My name is Mahmoud." The slaver asked, "Do you know the Book of God?" and the boy replied, "I have memorized the Koran."

The boy had a beauty mark on his left cheek, but it was blue and not red. The slaver hesitated, then said, "You are a weak boy and not much use to anyone. Your owner must consider you a worthless burden." And life rushed through Mahmoud's face. "I am anything but worthless," he said. The lion's folds appeared at the bridge of his nose. "I am the son of kings." The blue beauty mark turned red. "I am worth more than a rude man can afford."

"Then I thank God, the merciful, that my king is not a rude man," the slaver said, and begged Mahmoud's forgiveness. The slaver asked to see Mahmoud's owner, a Persian, and paid him for the boy. He turned Mahmoud over to Aydmur and said, "Take your brother and wash him. When he is clean, dress him in this remaining suit. Our mission here is done. We will begin our journey home after the baths."

❧

Aunt Nazek and her daughters arrived next. My father asked why they were not at home celebrating, but he couldn't mask his glee. Aunt Nazek appeared surprised at his surprise. "We're here to wish you a Happy Eid," she told my father. "We're all coming. I thought you knew that."

"I'm not here to wish him a happy holiday." Her daughter May bent down to kiss my father. "I'm here for my quarter."

My father laughed. "If I had one, I would give it to no one but you."

"Well, then, you must have one." May opened her purse, took out some coins, and handed them to my father.

"By God. Where did you ever find them? I haven't seen these in twenty years."

Fatima swept into the room, all pomp and perfume, hugged me, and climbed on the bed next to my father. Having lost her father at an early age, she treated mine as hers, and he adored her like no other. She wiggled one arm under him, hugged him, and laid her head on his pillows, scrunching her coiffed hair. My sister joined them on the other side. She took one of the quarters, held it up to the light, and examined it as if it were a perfect diamond instead of a coin that had lost any value after the old currency's collapse. "You used to be able to buy so much with it," she told her daughter. "Not like today, when you can't buy anything for thousands of pounds."

"Don't listen to your mother," Fatima said. "Other people may have been able to buy things with a quarter, but it wasn't your mother. She just likes to pretend."

"In my time," my father added, "I used to be so proud if I earned a quarter in one day."

Aunt Samia knocked and walked in with her daughter, Little Mona. Lina held the quarter up. "Look."

"Oh my God." Mona grinned. "Blessed Eid al-Adha. Look, Mother. A quarter. Do you remember those?"

"Of course," responded Aunt Samia. "Do you think I'm brain-dead? Where are the boys?" She looked left and right, as if her sons could be hiding in the corners. "Listen," she said to Lina. "I already talked to the guard, so I don't want any problems from you. It's Eid al-Adha, and we're all going to be here. But where is everybody?"

At first, I didn't know what she was talking about. I thought she was just being her usual odd self. Even my father, who understood her better than anyone, missed what she said.

"Your boys are at your home, where they should be, waiting for the meal," my father said. "They're with their families, my dear."

"Don't be stupid, brother. We can't bring the kids here. This is a hospital. The in-laws are feeding them." Tin Can's wife came in and greeted everyone, then Mona's husband. Hafez, his wife, and their eldest son followed. It was when Aunt Samia said, "I need to sit. I'm not going to eat standing up," that my father understood. His face reddened. He looked ecstatic.

❧

The convoy entered Damascus, where its ruler, Issa al-Nasser, saw the Circassians and told the slaver, "Those boys look more like women than men," and when he saw the others added, "These are a little better," and when he saw Mahmoud, "This one is too ill. Why did you not discard him along the way and save yourself the burden?"

In the morning, when they were leaving Damascus, one of the slaver's debtors stopped him. "You owe me one hundred dinars," the man said, "and I will not let you leave without payment."

The slaver said, "Brother, let me pass this one time. I am on an urgent mission for the king. I have a royal decree. You will get paid, but let it not be now."

"Then I will take this boy until I get paid."

Mahmoud's new owner took him to his wife, whose name was Wasila, and who was the meanest of women, as mean as seven hives of African wasps. She examined the sickly lad. "He is not much of a boy, but he will do," and she began to assign him the difficult jobs: carrying the mortar from one room to the next, cleaning the outhouse, filing the corns and bunions on her feet. Mahmoud grew sicker, yet Wasila would not relent. "He is going to die soon anyway," she was heard to say, "so why should I not make use of his brief stay in the world?"

And the boy ran away. He walked into the desert. That night, the twenty-seventh of Ramadan, the holy month, Mahmoud lay down on the sand to die. He had been ill for too long. He was hungry, thirsty, and alone. But the hours passed and he neither slept nor died. When the night was two-thirds spent, by God's will the sky opened its doors and there appeared before Mahmoud's young eyes a dome of light so pure. From the heavens the light shone upon the land. He saw every-thing before him for leagues and leagues. He heard no sound, no rooster crow, no dog bark, no tree rustle. This was the true Night of Fate. The boy stood on his feet with difficulty and announced upward, "Hear me, O Lord. I beg Your forgiveness and plead for Your mercy. I beseech Thee, Almighty, in honor of this sacred, propitious night, to grant me this wish. Make me a king. Let me rule Egypt and the Levant and the rest of the lands of Islam. Bless me with victories over Your enemies and mine. Between my shoulders, plant the resolve of forty men, and I will sow Your will upon this earth. Make me Your king. Make me Your servant. You are the grantor. You are the powerful. You are the merciful. There is no God but You."

And the boy was healed.

The next morning, Mahmoud returned to his mistress, Wasila, and begged her forgiveness for running away. "Forgiveness is not mine to give," Wasila said, "and neither is mercy, so do not ask." She pulled the boy by the ear, dragged him to the backyard, and tied him to a pole. First she slapped his face, then she hit him. But she decided that was not enough of a punishment. She built a fire and raised a burning stick to flog him with. And God sent her sister-in-law, Latifah, to knock on her door. When Latifah entered, Mahmoud yelled, "I am at your mercy, my lady, for I am your neighbor."

Latifah saw the boy and pleaded with Wasila: "Forgive this boy, for my sake." And Wasila said, "I do not forgive, nor do I wish to, and who are you to interfere with my affairs?"

Sitt Latifah grew angry. She untied the boy and walked him over to her house. And she called for a judge and for two notaries.

When her brother arrived to claim the boy, Sitt Latifah asked in front of witnesses, "Have you bought this boy?" and her brother replied, "No. He is mine as security. His owner owes me one hundred dinars, and I will not let go of him until I receive my payment."

Sitt Latifah paid her brother one hundred dinars. "The boy is now mine." She turned to the judge and the notaries. "Ask this man, my brother, whether I have anything of his that belonged to our mother or father." They did, and her brother replied that nothing of hers was his. "Then note this down," Sitt Latifah said, "for I do not wish him or his to claim anything at a future date. And note this, and make it binding. All my money and all that is mine, all that I own and all that my hand grasps, belongs to this boy once I depart this world. If God will have me, I will leave with only a piece of cloth, and the rest will remain with the boy, whom I will take as my son. I will call him Baybars, the name of my deceased son, for he looks like him. To all I have said, you are witnesses."

※

Samia's son Anwar and Tin Can rolled in a gurney topped with crates of food, forcing everyone to move closer together. The aroma of roast lamb instantly vanquished the medicinal smells. Lina was about to say something, but she held back, overcome and overwhelmed.

"No, no," Aunt Samia said. "Take it outside. There's not enough space in the room. There's more family coming. We can serve ourselves."

"So much food," Aunt Nazek said.

"So much of us," Aunt Samia replied. "And what about the other patients? Who's going to bring them lamb on Eid al-Adha?"

"My lovely Samia," my father said, "what have you done? You're going to have Adha here? In a hospital room?"

Aunt Samia looked confused and unsure. "Of course she is," Lina piped in. "Since we can't take you to her house, she brings her house to you."

"Exactly," Aunt Samia said. "What did you think? I even brought my silverware and china. I'm not going to have my Adha meal on cheap plates. Do you know how long it took the boys to get everything up here? Two lambs I cooked. Not a smidgen of salt. You're my brother. For you, I won't put salt in my meal, but only for you. Now, where's everybody else?"

※

Baybars became Sitt Latifah's blessed son, and she doted on him. One day, as mother and son walked through the souk, Baybars admired a bow. The merchant asked if he liked it, and the boy told him it was magnificent. The merchant said the bow was made by a famous hero two hundred years earlier, had been used by none other than the great Saladin, and Baybars could have such a masterpiece for the measly sum of two dinars. Baybars said, "My dear man, that is a bargain. This is the most beautiful instrument I have seen." Sitt Latifah giggled. Baybars blushed and asked, "Are you laughing at me, dear lady?"

And Sitt Latifah replied, "No, my son, I am laughing at fate."

She removed her veil, and the merchant saw her face and bowed. "My lady," he said. "Please accept my apologies. I did not know."

Latifah ignored the seller and spoke to her son. "This is not a bow worthy of you. It is cheap, terribly crafted, and has a will of its own. No warrior has ever touched it or ever will. Come, allow me to show you your destiny." When she reached their house, Sitt Latifah led Baybars through the courtyard. She stood before a door, took a key from her cleavage, and opened the door. Baybars saw a hall with hundreds of bows and thousands of arrows, enough for an entire army. He picked the closest bow and realized he had been naïve. The merchant had lied. And his mother said, "I am called Latifah the bowmaker, because my father was a bowmaker, and my grandfather was before him, and his father was before that. All the heroes of our world had to visit Damascus to purchase bows from our workshop. And you, my glorious Baybars, stumble upon its hearth." Sitt Latifah gestured toward the entire room. "This is now yours. All of it belongs to you, but it may behoove you to pick one weapon and call it yours."

At first, Baybars considered the bows, but then he looked around and saw daggers, spears, bows, and swords that shone with a heavenly brilliance and beauty. One Damascene sword looked common, did not call attention to itself. He picked it up and noticed the exquisite workmanship. He placed it under his belt, and the sword radiated warmth to his belly.

One morning, Baybars watched another boy carry a pail up a ladder leaning against the barn. The boy entered an upper door, and Baybars followed him. Baybars saw the boy tying a rope around the pail's handle and asked him what he was doing. "I have to feed al-Awwar," the boy replied. "He will not let anybody into the barn, so the only way we can feed him is to lower his food from up here." Baybars looked over the edge and saw a great blue-black horse huffing and puffing, pawing at the ground. "Is he really one-eyed?" Baybars asked.

"No," the boy answered. "His eyes are as keen as a falcon's. He is called Awwar because he has a white patch over one eye only. Do you see it?"

"Yes, and he has a white mustache as well."

"True," the boy said, "but do not make fun or he will get very angry. He is terribly fond of his mustache. And do you see the curvy white lines between his shoulders? The mistress says these lines run exactly like the Euphrates and the Nile."

"Then this is my horse," Baybars said. "I will ride him."

The boy informed Baybars that no one could ride the horse, but Baybars untied the rope from the pail and knotted it around his waist. "Let me down and you will see." The boy held on to the rope, Baybars descended slowly, and al-Awwar stared. The horse snorted, retreated, and then attacked. Baybars began to climb the rope as it was being let down. Al-Awwar's head struck Baybars's buttocks, and he began to swing like the tongue of a church bell. He called for help. Al-Awwar watched with a bemused look. After Baybars was pulled back to the top, he leaned over the edge and spoke these words: "I shall return."

An army sergeant by the name of Lou'ai arrived at the house that afternoon and asked if he could speak to Baybars. The sergeant said, "My lord, I understand you wish to ride a great horse, and I have one for sale. Please, let me show you." And there, on the street, was a magnificent roan stallion. "You can have him for forty dinars only. He is worth a lot more, but I can no longer keep him. He has been my trustworthy companion, but I have not been paid for months. I cannot feed my children, let alone feed him. He deserves a good owner."

Baybars saw the horse's eyes follow every move of Sergeant Lou'ai. "This is your horse," Baybars said. "You should not be separated, for you have been faithful to each other." He asked the sergeant to wait. He went into the house and returned with fifty dinars. "I offer this for teaching me a lesson in loyalty. May your horse continue to be your honest companion for many years to come."

"Your generosity claims no boundaries," the sergeant said. "The doors of paradise will forever be open to you."

On the second day, back in the barn, the servant boy lowered Baybars, who held an apple in his hand. Al-Awwar approached and smelled the apple. He snorted, retreated, and attacked. He hit Baybars in the exact same spot as on the previous day, and Baybars went swinging again. This time, Baybars did not call for help. On the third day, Baybars was dropped with two pears. Al-Awwar approached, smelled the pears, and ate them. Baybars was pleased. When the horse finished his meal, he snorted, retreated, and attacked. Baybars swung happily. On the fourth day, Baybars was dropped with a bunch of grapes. Al-Awwar had him swinging after finishing off the fruit. On the fifth day, Baybars had seven figs, and al-Awwar ate to his heart's content and allowed the bearer to stay. But the horse would not let Baybars approach him. Whenever Baybars moved, the horse was sure to sidestep in the opposite direction. "Allow me on your back," Baybars pleaded. "Let me see the rivers and the land between your shoulders, for I will rule these lands one day. Be my horse, be my friend."

On the sixth day, Baybars descended with three sheets of amareddine, the dried-apricot paste. And this time, the horse loved the feast so much he licked Baybars's face, but when Baybars bent to pick up the saddle, al-Awwar attacked again.

That night, Baybars complained to Sitt Latifah, and she said, "No one has been able to ride al-Awwar, because he is a war stallion. He can only be ridden by a great warrior."

"But I will be a great warrior."

"So will every boy," Latifah said. "I cannot help you. I can, however, tell you a story about our great stallions. Listen, and hear me. Once, a long time ago, in an age long past, in a time of heroes and wars, there were three stallions. Heroes had ridden them during many battles, from one war to the next. The three horses grew old and weary. The heroes who had inherited them decided to set their steeds free as a reward for their years of faithful service. The horses were unbridled and unsaddled, unyoked into the wilds. The horses ran with the sand winds. Free at last. The heroes watched them gallop with an abandon that had not been seen in years. The horses ran toward a river to drink and wash themselves. Suddenly the sound of a bugle was heard, and the horses froze. The river lay before them, the bugle sound behind, and the great horses were torn. The heroes watched aghast as their stallions returned to them at a slow trot. A boy had amused himself by playing the bugle, and the horses returned for war. Those horses were the ancestors of all the great Arabians, which is why all warriors, from the far isles of Europe to the great mountains of China, have descendants of the three horses as their steeds."

Baybars kissed the top of Latifah's head and thanked her for the story. And on the seventh day, Baybars descended with three sheets of amareddine and a bugle. When al-Awwar finished eating, Baybars played "al-Khayal": "I am the rider, let us ride."

And Baybars rode al-Awwar out into the desert. He rode far from Damascus, rode until he reached the mountains west of the city, until both he and his horse were encapsuled in a sheen of sweat. Upon their return, as they neared the city, the sword shook. Baybars placed his hand upon it and felt it quiver once more. Al-Awwar stopped. Four men waited for Baybars to approach. He nudged his horse and rode slowly and warily forth.

"Greetings, traveler," the leader said. He was Damascene, but his three slaves were as dark as oak bark. They were muscular and huge; their horses looked like ponies beneath them. They were mighty warriors from the land of the rivers on the far coast of the enigmatic continent.

"Greetings, but I am not a traveler," Baybars said. "I am returning home."

"No matter," the man interrupted. "To continue on this road, you must pay a toll."

"This is a public road to Damascus. Does the ruler of the city know about this?"

"Commander Issa is my cousin. He suggested I earn a living, and I have taken his advice. Consider your payment a kindness tax. It is my generosity that allows you to breathe. Pay tribute to my benevolence or my African slaves will cut you and set free your captive soul."

Baybars bowed his head. "Then I fear I must repay your kindness," he said. When Baybars lifted his head back up, al-Awwar charged the men. The sword unsheathed itself, its action moving faster than its master's will. The leader quickly retreated behind his slaves and cowered. Al-Awwar understood which of the men was the target. The stallion squeezed between the slaves' horses and attacked the leader's stallion, causing its rider to fall off. Al-Awwar stomped the coward dead.

And then Baybars's sword had to parry the attacks of the three powerful warriors. With each blow, Baybars felt his bones rattle, yet his weapon would not give or break. One warrior attacked from the right, one from the left, and the last tried to get to Baybars from the front. Al-Awwar shoved the first horse and drove the second to the ground.

He frightened the third enough that it jerked back; Baybars's sword thrust forward, past the warrior's defenses, and stopped before his heart. A drop of blood appeared on the sword, but it did not pierce farther. The warrior looked down upon the weapon and saw his doom.

"A dishonorable cat plays with its prey before the kill. Finish this."

"I choose not to," Baybars said, "for I have no quarrel with you or your friends. I wish to return home. Leave me be and you are free to do as you please."

"If the situation were reversed, you would not be alive."

"Then I am happy it is not," Baybars replied. "If you wish to die, so be it. I am providing an alternative."

The warrior's chest inflated; Baybars's sword retreated but did not disengage. "If you do not kill us," the African said, "then we will become your slaves."

Baybars put his sword in its scabbard. "I cannot own you, for I myself am owned. Go," the future slave-king said. "May God guide your path."

"He has," the mighty warrior said. "We choose to serve you till our dying days."

The ruler of Damascus, Issa al-Nasser, called for Baybars and demanded information about his cousin. "He did not return to his house last night," said the commander, "and yesterday you entered the city with his slaves."

"The man sought to rob me," Baybars replied. The commander was horrified to hear the news. He called on his vizier to imprison and try Baybars for murder. The vizier explained that no crime had been committed: Baybars acted in self-defense, and there were witnesses. They could not arrest Baybars in daylight. Syrian justice needed to be meted out surreptitiously.

That evening, as Baybars walked through the yard toward the outhouse, six soldiers jumped over the wall and attacked him from behind. They covered him with a large burlap sack soaked in an anesthetic potion. They carried him over the wall and took him outside the city gate. The soldiers rode into the desert until they arrived at a Bedouin camp. One of them told the chief of the tribe, "Here is the boy, and here is the promised bag of gold. The commander wishes never to see this ugly boy's face again. Take him with you to the holy desert, and sell him to a ruthless owner. Or kill him. The commander does not care, as long as he gets rid of the troublemaker. The boy is wily. Do not let him escape."

"Escape?" the chief asked. "We have killed men for lesser insults. We have transported boys across the deserts for generations. Go. Return to your corrupt city, and tell your master the boy has vanished for all eternity."

The Bedouins did not have a full understanding of the concept of time. Eternity did not last the night. When Baybars did not appear for dinner, Sitt Latifah called her servants and asked if anyone had seen him. None knew the whereabouts of their master. The three African warriors announced that they would search for Baybars.

Baybars awoke to the feel of a hand covering his mouth. He could not move his roped arms. The face of a man coalesced before him, and the mouth said, "Be quiet." And the man untied Baybars. "Come with me," he said. "Quietly."

Baybars followed the man out of the tent. At the opening, a Bedouin lay on the ground. An ear-to-ear gash spoke of the Bedouin's immobility. The rescuer led him away. Shortly thereafter, Baybars heard the whinnying of al-Awwar, and he felt joy. The African warriors held the reins of Baybars's stallion. "I believe you should never be separated from this," one of the warriors said, handing Baybars his sword. Baybars thanked him and mounted al-Awwar.

Baybars's savior climbed into his saddle. "You may not have recognized me."

"I may not have recognized you at first," Baybars said, "but even in such poor light, no one can mistake the beauty of your glorious roan. I am grateful, Sergeant."

"The gratitude is mine," Sergeant Lou'ai said. "When your warriors inquired about you, I was thankful to be given the chance to be of service. Finding you could never be a problem. All I had to do was ask your horse."

Baybars suggested they return to the city, but the sergeant and the warriors objected. "These Bedouins are now your mortal enemies," one of the warriors said. "They will never rest until they avenge the dishonor of your escape. You do not leave enemies behind. There are only thirty of them."

"But we cannot kill them while they sleep," Baybars said. "Do we have to wait till morning?"

"Not at all," another warrior said. He struck a flint and lit a torch.

He unleashed a burning arrow high into the night. The warrior unshackled a ferocious war cry. "Wake up, cowards," he shouted. "You are about to die. Arise, heathens, and face your death."

Baybars led the mighty warriors into battle. As his sword killed its first victim, and the first drop of an enemy's blood stained his tunic, our hero banished the child he once was. The warriors massacred the Bedouins. Upon his return to the city, Baybars split the battle's spoils among the five of them, but he handed the bag of gold to the sergeant. "Would you please inform the ruler of Damascus that I believe he may have misplaced this?"

❦

We ate in all kinds of positions, standing, seated, kneeling, silverware clanking, shoulder to shoulder, back to back, crowded in a hospital room, as good an Adha meal as the family had ever had. Loud followed by sated quiet. My sister kept her eyes fixed on my father to gauge his condition. Tin Can, wiping lamb sheen off his black beard, announced that he had better get back to work. "I'm too stuffed to walk, but I have to," he said.

Everyone took this as an exit cue and began to leave. Finally, only Lina, Salwa, Hovik, and I remained with my father. He clutched the oxygen mask in his hand a little tighter. "Are you all right?" my sister asked him. She took the mask from his hand and placed it on his face. He wasn't. The panic in his eyes startled me.

Thirty minutes later, we had to call Tin Can back, because my father's breathing became labored, and water had resettled in the swamps of his lungs.

❦

Commander Issa lounged on a divan and contemplated the bag of gold on the brass table. He gulped his wine. He was entertaining the king's emissary, who had arrived from Egypt to collect taxes. A feast of delicacies lay before them. "I do not understand why you are allowing an inconsequential matter of an errant boy to trouble you," his guest said.

"Inconsequential?" the commander huffed. "The damned boy killed my cousin."

"But you were about to kill your cousin," the taxman mumbled with his mouth full. "You said he was an embarrassment to manhood. The boy did you a favor."

"I can kill my cousin if I wish, because he's family. This boy, Baybars, is impudent."

"Why not do what everyone does with impudent boys? Send him to Cairo. Let him become the king's problem. Invite him for lunch, and I will impress him with the glory of Cairo and its court. I have yet to meet a boy who does not wish to be king."

Every cook in the palace worked on the following day's luncheon. Baybars could not believe his eyes or his nose or his tongue. The king's emissary said the feast was nothing compared with the grandness of the king's meals. He talked of the excitement of the holy court and regaled Baybars with tales of honor and glory. "The riches of Cairo," the emissary said, "are beyond a mere boy's imagination. Every hero from across the seas sails for the city to prove his mettle. It is the only home for men of worth."

"I must visit," Baybars said.

"You must."

"I must ask my mother's permission."

"You must."

Sitt Latifah was not happy to have her son leave, but she realized that he was smitten. "You have an aunt in Cairo," she told him. "Her husband is an important vizier. I will write my sister so she may care for you. Ask all those who believe in you to follow you there, so you will not be alone. I will pack enough so you will want for nothing in Egypt. And ask God, the merciful, to watch over you."

And Baybars prepared to meet his destiny.

BOOK TWO

Please tell my story. It is surely as weird as the story of Moses's staff, the resurrection of Jesus, and the election of the husband of a lady bird to the presidency of the United States.

Emile Habibi, The Secret Life of Saeed, the Pessoptimist

. . . stories do not belong only to those who were present or to those who invent them, once a story has been told, it's anyone's, it becomes common currency, it gets twisted and distorted, no story is told the same way twice or in quite the same words, not even if the same person tells the story twice, not even if there is only ever one storyteller . . .

Javier Marías, Tomorrow in the Battle Think on Me

All sorrows can be borne if you put them into a story or tell a story about them.

Isak Dinesen, cited by Hannah Arendt in The Human Condition

— Six —

So—what do you think of the emir's story?" Fatima asked Afreet-Jehanam. She was lying in her lover's arms, on the bed of slithering snakes, relaxing and unwinding. She could feel the changes in her body, but she still did not look pregnant.

The jinni, stroking her sensuously, said, "The emir is a good story-teller."

She shifted her naked weight onto her elbow so she could face him. The snakes released by her movement rearranged themselves. "Is it a good adventure story?"

Afreet-Jehanam stretched and yawned. "The story of Baybars is many lifetimes old. There are numerous versions."

"I am loving it," said Ishmael, who was on his knees scrubbing the floor. The imps busied themselves with their chores. Hither and thither they ran.

"Me, too," Noah chimed in. "It is a delightful story."

"True," said Fatima, "but it sounds to me like many of his other stories, without the sentimental romance. Is this tale adventuresome enough? Will this story, unlike his earlier ones, produce the desired effect, a son to inherit his throne?"

"That was your rule," said the jinni. "I thought you made it up."

"I did, but I know it to be true."

"Maybe fate does not wish them to have a son."

"Ah, fate," she said. "Is fate anything more than what man chooses to do? Is fate not our expectations of ourselves?"

"If it is true, they will have a son," Afreet-Jehanam said, "but since the tale being told is not the most traditional of adventure stories, not enough killing and pillaging, he will not grow to be the greatest of warriors."

"Then he will grow to be wise," she said. "But the emir's tale and its hero are young yet. Let us be patient and see what transpires."

"Whatever may transpire, we can be sure the son will be different," said the jinni.

"Wonderful." Ishmael jumped up and down gleefully. "He will be able to decorate that horror of a castle."

"Oh, great," said Isaac. "Just what the world needs, another accessorizer."

Suddenly all the snakes hissed as one, and the scorpions raised their tails and readied their stingers. The crows and bats descended in droves from above. Afreet-Jehanam sat up, a snarl upon his face. But the snarl remained frozen like that of a once-feared predator after a visit to the taxidermist. A magician in white robes and a long white beard materialized out of nothingness. His hand unleashed a white beam that froze the jinni stock-still. The crows attacked first, but hit an invisible shield around the magician and fell stunned to the floor. The bats followed. The snakes spat their venom from below, but it hit the shield and dripped down slowly to the ground. The traces left by the viscous poisons showed the shield to be egg-shaped. With his other hand, the magician let loose a force upon each imp and sent them all crashing into the walls. And his eyes turned to naked Fatima. He waved his arm and waved it again. Fatima felt the talisman, the turquoise hand with its inlaid eye, grow warm between her breasts. Regaining her senses after the initial shock, she bent down, picked up her sword, and charged the magician. Before she reached him, he began to fade. "Whore," he called before he completely disappeared. She turned around to find her lover gone.

On a Monday morning in June 1967, near the end of term, Madame Shammas entered our class without knocking, not allowing us time to stand up and greet her respectfully. Businesslike, she marched swiftly to Nabeel Ayoub and announced, "Please get your things, son. Your father is here to take you home." Voice gentle yet authoritative.

Nabeel stood up, bewildered initially, then looked slyly at his classmates, his seated nonspecial friends. He hurriedly packed his things and left the room behind Madame Shammas.

Our teacher, Madame Saleh, stared at the closing door, outside which a muffled rush of high heels echoed. "I want you to behave

yourselves, children," she said. "I'll be back in a few minutes." She
walked to the door, stopped, turned around, almost caught me stuffing
a piece of paper in my mouth. She addressed the bespectacled girl two
seats to my right. "Mira, I'm leaving you in charge."

My spitball missed Mira's back. Her chestnut pigtail swung like a
pendulum as she walked to the front. The class was atwitter, nervous
with pent-up energy. We knew we were supposed to misbehave
because Madame Saleh was out, but we didn't know exactly what to do.
We settled on throwing crumpled paper at Mira and hissing every time
she yelled, "Shut up."

Ten minutes later, the class was in an uproar. Madame Shammas
announced on the intercom that we all should get our things ready to
be picked up. The Israelis had begun the war.

Traffic congealed as parents came to collect their children. Some of the
adults were nervous, some angry, a few nonchalant. I saw a tiny bump
of an accident and two almosts, because the cars were in a hurry. I
waited, but no one came for me. The maid had told Madame Shammas
that my mother was at her weekly visit to the hairdresser.

One of my favorite programs was *Lost in Space*. I thought of the
Israelis as space aliens. They're not like us, people said. They come
from all over the place and keep coming. They're foreigners, people
said. Godless.

Finally. "There you are, champ," Uncle Jihad said. He had walked
from his apartment, which was right next to ours, not too far from
school—five streets, four turns, three jasmine vines, two jacarandas,
and one white-oleander bush away.

"There's a war," I yelled, jumping up and down.

"Don't worry." Uncle Jihad's belly shook as he laughed, his bald
head glittered in the sun. "It's very far from here." I hadn't thought of
worrying.

Uncle Jihad walked in a manner that suggested all was proper in the
world. I trotted behind him, my eyes unable to stray from the back of
his turquoise jacket. He wore his clothes the way a peacock fanned his
tail. "Keep up with me," he said cheerfully.

I grasped the offered hand. I loved his well-manicured fingers and
the light smell of lotion emanating from them. We walked hand in
hand down the street, a spring in our step.

A radio from a coffee shop across the street screamed that we must dig trenches with our fingernails. "The Palestinian Resistance can be so delightfully melodramatic," Uncle Jihad said.

♣?

The beasts of the underworld looked to Fatima for guidance. The snakes coiled about themselves, holding their heads high, waiting. They looked like thousands of miniature minarets, tiny lighthouses in an infinite sea without a shore. The bats and crows, too stunned to fly, began to gather in groups of their own kind. Fatima sought the imps. One by one she found them, shocked and woozy.

Adam wept. Ezra wailed. "My brother," Job cried. Each imp shed tears of skin-matching color. "Our brother is gone," Elijah moaned. "We'll never see him again," Noah added. And the scorpions and spiders and the beasts of the underworld joined in mourning.

"Wait," interrupted Fatima. "What happened? Who was that white son of a whore? Where has he taken Afreet-Jehanam?"

"Do not mention the name of the departed to the bereaved," Isaac said. "It grates our hearts." He shook his head in dismay.

"The name of the magician is King Kade, the master of light," Ishmael said.

"He loathes the underworld and its inhabitants," Ezra said.

"Considers us parasites," added Noah.

"His mission is to rid the world of dark," said Jacob. "That is his vow. Are we dark? Look at me. I am yellow."

"He is obsessed with jinn," Ishmael said, "but he does not attempt to use our power. He kidnaps the powerful jinn and tortures them. He chains and whips them, forces them to work on his palaces before he kills them. He had Mithras, the mighty demon, paint a giant mural of bucolic scenes. As he painted, King Kade's angels threw darts at him and they touched up the mural with dabs of white, dab, dab, dart, dab, dab, dart. And then King Kade sucked the life out of Mithras. Oh, Afreet-Jehanam, my poor brother. What tragedy awaits you."

"Stop this," Fatima yelled. "What has become of you? Why are you bemoaning your brother's fate already? First, we will find that white idiot and kill him; we will annihilate him for coming into our realm without an invitation. After that, we will bring my lover home."

"No," said the imps, all eight of them in one voice. "We cannot."

"Then I will go alone," Fatima said. "You sit here and cower if you choose. I will fight the bastard myself."

"There is no hope," said Ishmael. "He wove a potent spell eons ago. Nothing from the underworld, living or not, can harm him. The most powerful jinn have tried to no avail. Creatures mightier than all of us combined have declared war upon him. The spell he wove cannot be undone. He cannot be conquered by anyone from the underworld."

"But I am not from here," announced Fatima. "I will defeat him."

One by one, the little imps' facial expressions changed, their demeanor transformed. Ishmael stood up first. "I may not be of any use at the great encounter, but I will make sure you get there."

"And I will confound his armies," Job said.

"I will get the carpet," said Noah.

"Get a few," said Elijah. "It is a long trip—why be cramped?"

"Come, my lovelies," Jacob said. He raised his arms and created a yellow orb of mist above his head. The bats flew into it and disappeared. Elijah invited the crows into his sphere, and Adam brought the snakes, the scorpions, and the spiders.

"Let us be on our way," commanded Fatima, sitting on one of the carpets.

"Upon thy head, King Kade," said Isaac, "we declare war."

"North," said Ishmael. "We go to the land of fog and rain, the land of ice and snow, the land of infinite skies."

"No, not yet," said Fatima. "First, I go home."

❧

Once upon a time, the oud was my instrument, my companion, my lover. I played it between the two wars, started taking lessons during the Six-Day War and gave them up during the Yom Kippur War, a period of seven years.

My mother had wanted me to take piano lessons. "The lessons will be good for you," she said one evening, when I was sitting on her lap out on the balcony of our apartment. The railing was a whorly arabesque of metal roses sprouting wherever the lines changed angles. My mother's raised feet rested on one of the few unrosed spots. She attempted to tidy my hair while staring at the swirl of stars in the dark summer sky. "I think you're talented. I hear you singing all the time." She pulled my head to her bosom. I felt the softness of her silk housedress on my cheek, my eyes focusing on a print marigold as it heaved and contracted with each breath. The tireless scrapings of cicadas saturated the air. "Never once off-key. You're my gifted baby."

I squirmed, pushed myself off her chest with both hands. "I don't like piano," I said.

My sister, Lina, had been taking piano lessons for the past four years, ever since she was six, my age now. Her teacher was Mademoiselle Finkelstein, a white-haired, dowdy, bespectacled spinster who smelled of mothballs and vanilla. Whenever Lina slipped, made a mistake as she played the "Méthode Rose," Mademoiselle Finkelstein would smack her knuckles with a wooden ruler that she used to tap a beat on the top of the piano. I asked Lina why she never complained about being hit. She said that the ruler wasn't painful, that Mademoiselle Finkelstein only tapped her gently, that she loved her teacher. Her crimson knuckles told a different story. When I asked my father why Mademoiselle Finkelstein was such a cruel woman, he said it was because she was unmarried, which caused women to become bitter, harsh, and unforgiving after they reached the age of thirty. Of course, he explained, they made wonderful teachers, because they had the unfettered time to dedicate to their profession and they knew how to instill discipline. On the other hand, unmarried men, like his younger brother, Uncle Jihad, were simply eccentrics and did not suffer accordingly. The difference, he elaborated, was that men chose to be unmarried, whereas women had to live with never having been chosen.

✤

For Fatima, the bogs of the Nile Delta were a welcoming sight, though the imps held their noses. She bade the carpets descend as they approached Bast's cottage. "I beg you," Bast said the instant she saw Fatima. "Do not talk to me of King Kade. I am not having a happy day. Cleopatra wants to mate, and I am in a foul mood. When I bleed, that so-called holy magician of light is not what I want to talk about." The healer turned around and walked into her cottage.

Fatima and her entourage followed. "Stop being childish and churlish. You are needed."

"Leave me," Bast said, trying to stare Fatima down.

"No." Fatima sat upon one of the barrels in the room, as she had once before.

"At least tell your companions to disappear. They are so colorful they sour my eyes."

"Self-centered witch," Elijah harrumphed, and he vanished, leaving a barely discernible indigo cloud that dissipated quickly.

"What is wrong with color?" Ezra asked. "Are you some big-city artist? Oh, never mind." And he, too, disappeared into his orange cloud, followed by Jacob, Job, Noah, and Adam.

Isaac looked at Ishmael and shrugged. Ishmael grinned. They turned into cats. Isaac became a red Abyssinian and Ishmael an Egyptian Mau with dark eyes. And the Alexandrian healer laughed. "Still too red," Bast said. Isaac wined his red and meowed.

⁂

Istez Camil, the oud teacher, was a widower. I met him at our concierge's apartment, a small, sparsely furnished two-bedroom unit on the ground floor. I was visiting the concierge's son, Elie, who was thirteen, seven years older than me. Everybody was gathered around the blue-gray transistor radio, listening to a scratchy news report. The beige waxed-paper shade of a small lamp sitting atop the radio vibrated each time the announcer pronounced an "s." The concierge sat in the main chair of the living room, his wife next to him on the chair's arm, Istez Camil in the other chair, and the five children, including Elie, huddled on the floor around the crackling radio.

The perfidious enemy attacked. The mighty Arab army. By the grace of God. We shall conquer. The evil imperialist forces will be crushed, spat the radio.

I noticed an oud leaning against the wall. I bent down, traced my fingers across the delectable wood, along the intricate designs of the mother-of-pearl encrustations, the delicately carved inlaid ivory. The instrument felt bigger than I was. For a moment, I felt lost in its magic.

"Do you like it?" asked Istez Camil, kneeling on one knee, his hand centered on my back.

"It's beautiful," I said.

"My father made it a long time ago." Istez Camil lifted the oud gently, bringing the front close to my eyes. "Would you like to learn to play?"

"There's a war going on," snapped the concierge, looking up at the ceiling. "Can we concentrate a little?" He leaned over and pumped up the volume of the transistor.

We shall get rid of the occupying forces once and for all, liberate all of Jerusalem.

"Ask your parents if they're willing to pay for lessons." Istez Camil's shirt buttons were fastened incorrectly, making his collar look oddly skewed. "And don't worry about him," he whispered, discreetly pointing at the concierge. "He's just a crusty old man who thinks politics is important."

Elie stood up, stretched languidly, and gestured with his head for me to follow. I heard the concierge mutter as we left the room. Elie didn't speak, and I tried to keep pace with his long strides. His faded orange jumpsuit, a couple of sizes too big, billowed between his legs with each step. Slim and athletic, he moved with a cocky assurance. He descended the stairs to the garage, entered his father's tool shed, and handed me a toolbox to carry for him. I almost dropped it, had to lift it with both hands. The toolbox made it difficult to walk. By the time he noticed I wasn't behind him, he was already up the ramp and on the street. He came back down and took the toolbox with one hand; I followed him unencumbered. We entered the garage of a building around the corner from ours. He stopped in front of an old, rusty motorcycle, put the toolbox down. I broke the silence. "Is that yours?"

Elie nodded. His permanently serious face appeared to be concentrating on the machine in front of him, his lower lip completely hidden behind his jutting upper one.

"Your father lets you have a motorcycle?" I asked.

"He doesn't know, does he? And he won't know, because you won't say anything to anyone about this, will you?"

I raised my eyebrows, but Elie paid no attention. He was on his knees. His wide eyes, their whites gleaming, looked intently at the engine. A vaccination scar on his arm looked like an old, frayed button. He opened the toolbox, handed me two screwdrivers, a box wrench, a monkey wrench, and two pairs of pliers. I held them close to my chest to ensure their safety.

"I got this for free because it doesn't run," Elie said, "but I'm going to fix it." He put his palm out, extending his long, tapered fingers. "Screwdriver." I carefully placed one in his hand.

"No, not that one. The other one." Elie tinkered with the engine. "We're going to win the war," he said, keeping his gaze on his task, his aquiline nose glued to the motor. "We're going to annihilate the Israelis, throw them back into the sea."

"Are you going to fight?"

"I can't join the army yet. But they don't need me. We'll humiliate them. Pliers."

"Who's we?" I asked.

"We," Elie said dismissively. "We, the Arabs."

"We're Arabs?"

"Of course we are. Don't you know anything?"

"I thought we're Lebanese."

"We're that, too," Elie said. "The Lebanese haven't started fighting yet, but we will. The Israelis didn't attack us, but we're not going to wait. We'll crush them. And we have a secret weapon. You see, there are five strong countries." He looked up at me, held up the five greasy fingers of his left hand. "We have two and the Israelis have two. We have Russia and China on our side, and they have America and England on theirs." His right forefinger pushed down two fingers on each side, leaving his middle finger pointing upward. "So we're even. But then there's still France. The Israelis think France is on their side, but she's not. France will be ours, because France loves Lebanon. France is our secret weapon. We'll trounce the Israelis for sure." He brought the last finger down into a clenched fist.

I stared at him with renewed admiration.

"Monkey wrench."

❧

"King Kade is such a troublemaker," Bast said, "but he does serve a purpose. A while ago, when I was even more ill tempered than I am today, I considered fighting him, but I came to realize that the warrior shield did not suit me. I was always meant to fight internal battles, not external ones. King Kade was my test."

"You failed?" Fatima asked.

"Not at all. I won, if you wish to call it that. I prefer to think of it as transcendence. He no longer bothers me."

"He bothers me."

"Then you must conquer him, or conquer yourself, whichever is harder."

"I will defeat him," Fatima said.

"Of that I am certain."

"Teach me how."

"First, you must find him."

"I think it's time for Osama to take music lessons," my mother told my father as she sat on a taboret in front of her dressing table. She was applying makeup, one eye closed, a finger delicately powdering the eyelid with color. I stood to the side, watching her reflection in the mirror. Her thick lashes were as dark as a starless night. She inspected her image, took out her lipstick, applied a coat of red, her mouth forming a demure O. She blotted her lips with a tissue.

"I'm not sure that's a good idea," my father said, examining his appearance in the armoire's long antique mirror. "Our boy is too smart for music." He winked, then turned his head back to the mirror, continued knotting his tie. "He's already a year younger than his class. We shouldn't waste his time with music. He should concentrate on academics. If anything, we should get him into sports to toughen him up a bit." He stroked two fingers along the deep grooves that ran from his nostrils to the corners of his mouth.

"I don't think music lessons will interfere with his studies." She bobby-pinned the final strands into her beehive, applied so much hairspray my eyes watered. "If they do, we'll just stop them. I'll talk to Mademoiselle Finkelstein next week and see what she thinks."

"I want to play the oud," I said.

"The oud? Why? It's so limited. You can play anything you want on a piano." The diamond necklace glittered as she turned around to face me. "With the oud, you can only play Arabic music. You don't see anyone playing the oud among the great orchestras."

"It's beautiful," I said. She shrugged, turned back to the mirror. "Why aren't we listening to the news?" I asked. "How come we're not following the war?"

"Because we have to get ready for dinner," my mother said. "Don't worry, dear. The war is far away."

"Are you going to fight?" I asked my father.

"Me?" He laughed. "Why would I do a thing like that? This war doesn't concern us at all, has nothing to do with us. We're a peaceful country." He ran a hand across his perfectly trimmed hair, used both palms to check for any stubble on his freshly shaved face.

"Don't we want to crush our imperialist enemy?"

"Not tonight, dear." My mother stood up, towered over me. She smoothed her dress, examined the mirror once more. "Now, tell me, don't I look beautiful?"

"You're beautiful," I said, dazzled by her blue lamé evening dress.

"Does your father think so?" She picked up her small silver handbag and stuffed her lipstick inside.

"I do," my father said. He held her in his arms and kissed her cheek. "You're stunning."

"Let's just try not to make fools of ourselves tonight. Can we keep our hands off our hostess? I know it's difficult, but we can try, can't we?"

"It's just flirting, dear," he said as he walked out the bedroom door. "Only flirting. All women love it. It's a compliment."

My mother rolled her eyes to the ceiling lights. She patted my head and left the room, the clack of her high heels on smooth marble reverberating in the foyer, out the door, until she reached the elevator.

The following day, the concierge painted the windows of our apartment blue so the Israelis could not see the lights at night.

"Why would the Israelis want to bomb us?" I asked my mother.

"They don't. It's just a precaution. Everyone's doing it."

"How will we get the paint off?"

"Nail-polish remover, I think."

❧

"The army of light—the white army, or whatever they call themselves these days—will lead you to him," Bast said. "But be careful. Like all bright things, he is deceiving. I doubt you will find him in his first house or his second."

"The third," Fatima said, "it is always the third."

"Seek the highest, for that is where his power lies, in the skies, in the air, up north."

"How will I defeat him?"

"That I cannot tell you. Each warrior must find her own way."

"How would you defeat him?"

"Easily," Bast cackled. "I would entice him into my world. In my mud and muck, he would be lost. But you cannot do that."

"I have no means to entice him."

"Be not obtuse," the healer said. "You have enticed males more powerful. You seduced the one you want to rescue, which is why you have to meet King Kade in his realm, not yours."

"I need your wisdom. Help me crush him. How can I do it?"

"By opening your eyes. I will offer you a final bit of advice. King Kade is unbalanced."

"I gathered that from our brief interaction. He called me a whore."

"There you have it," Bast said, "and you still refuse to see. Although that is not the kind of unbalanced I meant. King Kade is very strong, much stronger than you or I. Strength, however, is misleading. Anything extreme is unbalanced and must turn into its opposite." Bast began to search her pantry. With her back to the seeker, she added, "I can see you are disappointed. You were hoping for something else. I will give you this."

An ecstatic Noah appeared next to Fatima, accompanied by a tiny popping sound. "Take it," he yelled. "Take them."

"You have a bright one here," Bast said. "Too bright. Can you turn a darker shade of blue?" And Noah changed into a dark-blue tabby and jumped onto Fatima's lap. "Much better," Bast remarked. She handed Fatima three leather pouches. "This is mud: holy mud, sublime mud, and profane. You have to determine which is which and when to use it. One is from a source in France, one is from a spring between the two hills Safa and Marwa, and the third is from one of the seven mouths of the Nile."

A meowing Cleopatra appeared at the door. Noah's hair bristled under Fatima's hand. Cleopatra jumped onto the table and coyly approached Isaac and Ishmael, who scampered off and out of the cottage. The shocked eyes of Cleopatra followed their trail, then turned toward an obviously frightened Noah, who disappeared in a puff of smoke.

"Oh, Cleo," Bast said, "they are the wrong species for you, and you are the wrong gender for them." She studied Cleopatra's hackled fur. "And on this note, my dear Fatima, kindly emulate your helpers and vanish."

Istez Camil's liver-spotted hand shook as he puffed on his cigarette. He seemed uncertain how to sit on the burgundy divan in the living room, didn't know where to put his arms. From his seat, he could easily see the upright piano in our dining room, and his eyes darted between my mother and the instrument. My mother stood up, took a cup of Turkish coffee from the silver tray brought in by the maid. "You said you wanted it sweet?" she asked as she placed the cup on the coffee table before him and moved aside a vase overflowing with a profusion of cut flowers—lilacs, lilies, and tuberoses.

He nodded, stuttered, a nervous smile on his face. My mother moved an ashtray toward him. She retrieved the other cup from the tray, dismissed the maid, and sat down. She crossed her legs, right knee on left, adjusted her skirt to make sure it fell evenly. She waited until he had had a couple of sips of coffee. "So how long have you been teaching the oud, Mr. Halabi?" She smiled. "Should I call you Istez Halabi? Is that more respectful?"

"No, madame, there is no need," Istez Camil said. "I've been teaching for over twenty-five years." His gray hair had been recently trimmed; his neck mottled raw from shaving. "I've backed up a number of singers and have played professionally since I was thirteen years old. I haven't been playing much lately. Semi-retired, you see. I'm concentrating more on teaching."

"That's nice," she said. She placed a cigarette in a silver filigreed holder and lit it. "I've never really considered the oud for my son. I was thinking piano. Such a delightful instrument. If not that, then I thought the violin. But he seems to be infatuated with the oud." She looked at me, her eyes gleaming, then back at Istez Camil. "I don't understand it, really. Don't you think piano is better at his age? If he plays the piano, he can shift to oud easily if he cares to. But vice versa would be difficult. Don't you agree?"

"The piano is a wonderful instrument." Istez Camil stubbed out his cigarette in the ashtray, his hand no longer shaking. "I'm not sure I'm the right person to answer your questions, though, madame. I would always choose the oud over the piano. Always."

"Me, too," I chirped.

"Oh, you." My mother laughed and slapped the air in front of her, pretending it was me. "Tell me, Istez Camil, why would you not choose the piano?"

Istez Camil looked at the floor, his face flushed like a peony. "It is cold, madame. It's a cold instrument. Distant, no soul. Whereas the oud—the oud becomes part of you, your body. You engulf it, and it engulfs you." He lifted his head. "There's also the idea of tarab to consider."

"See, that I never understood. I always thought tarab was overrated."

"What's tarab?" I asked.

"Hmm, let's see," my mother said. She scrunched her face. "I'm not sure I can explain it. It has to do with Arabic music. How would you describe it?"

"Is my boy asking about tarab?" Uncle Jihad entered the room, his voice booming. He wore a dark suit and a linden-green paisley ascot. He lifted me by the waist and kept me up until I kissed the top of his bald head. "Tarab is musical enchantment. It's when both musician and listener are bewitched by the music."

Uncle Jihad noticed Istez Camil standing up. "I'm sorry," he said, putting me down. "I didn't know you had guests. How rude of me." He walked over to shake Istez Camil's hand, but stopped midway. "My God. What an honor." He gestured wildly, looked toward my mother. "Layla, do you know who this man is? This man is a master."

"You exaggerate, sir," Istez Camil said. He remained standing.

"Exaggerate? Let me shake your hand, please. Layla, this man has played with Umm Kalthoum!"

*

They flew higher and higher, Fatima with the wind in her hair and the imps beside her, three carpets with three passengers each. North they went. "Was the healer helpful?" Jacob yelled, to be heard above the whooshing of air. "I could not tell."

"It is always riddles," Job replied. "I hate riddles. I do not test well."

"She was very helpful," Noah said. "She gave us mud."

Elijah groaned. The air grew cooler and clearer, the sun subtler.

"We are about to find out how helpful," Fatima said. "Look ahead."

Before them, a distance away, a band of white eagles appeared from behind a snowy mountain peak, and more eagles, and more. "A thousand," said Ezra.

"Coming for us," said Elijah.

"A pox upon the son of a whore King Kade," said Adam. "Our first trial."

"Do not say that," moaned Job. "I hate trials more than I hate riddles."

"How insulting," Isaac said. "We travel all this way for this. A magician of his stature, and he sends us feathered trifles? I expected so much more. I am grievously disappointed."

"The magician means to try us with symbols," said Ishmael. "How childish."

Job put his hand on his brow and shook his head. "Allow me." Still cross-legged on the carpet, he raised his arms to the sky and announced, "Try this." And between Job's arms formed a cloud from which countless mosquitoes shot out. "A thousand for each of your birds," he announced. "A thousand upon each of your thousand. A million for you."

"Mosquitoes?" asked Fatima.

"Hush," answered Job. "You think me a beginner. Just watch."

It seemed to Fatima that the mosquitoes traveled faster than any insects she had encountered before, a rushing, rolling, buzzing wave of beige. The white eagles headed directly into the cloud of pests. "I hope they are all females," Fatima said.

"Please," he replied. "They are lesbians."

"Ouch," exclaimed Ezra.

The mosquitoes did not slow the flight of the eagles instantaneously. It took the predatory birds a minute to reduce their speed, after which they began to fly in circles. Beaks snapped on air, and feathers ruffled. The eagles seemed agitated and confused.

"Not enough," said Isaac. "The birds are too pristine. Let them suffer."

Job pointed his hand, and fleas rocketed toward the eagles. Then he sent gnats, mites, and ticks. The lice he saved for last. Splotches of red bubbled on the eagles' white. "A much better color," said Isaac. The eagles were overwhelmed and vanquished. Feathers were released from bodies and floated toward the ground. Within a short time, no eagle remained aloft.

Fatima looked below at the carnage. "Sad," she said.

"Why?" asked Elijah. "They were too pretty."

"I hate white," said Isaac. "It is drab and colorless."

♣

Elie watched the burgeoning yellow-and-blue flames of the bonfire he'd built in an empty lot far from our building, hoping to lure Israeli fighter planes to waste their bombs there. The pop of the burning wood interrupted the eerie silence. The side of my sister's face was lit by the fire, a flicker in her eye as she stared at Elie. I watched the passing cars, all their headlights painted blue, with only a tiny sliver of a cross to allow white light through. Elie yelled at the sky, a war cry. The hollow at the base of his throat expanded. The ridge of his collarbone vibrated. Lina opened her mouth, but didn't scream. She was staring at Elie, as if in a rapture.

That night, the Egyptian army downed forty-four Israeli planes over the Sinai. Gamal Abd al-Nasser's boys are fighting for their motherland, the radio intoned. I sat by the window, illuminated by the soft light of the morning sun. "That's all lies," Uncle Jihad said. He switched to BBC Radio: The Israelis are advancing easily. Jerusalem is theirs.

The concierge, Elie's father, yelled at Madame Daoud on the third floor. "Talk to my husband when he comes in," she yelled back. "I'm not going to stand here and listen to this."

"Traitors," he shouted. "You want the Israelis to destroy our homes."

"Eat shit." She slammed the door.

My father bent over the banister and bellowed, "What's all the shouting about?"

"They haven't painted their windows," the concierge said, his voice quieter, meeker. "They want the Israelis to kill us."

"Don't be stupid," my father chided. "You think they want to die? Probably no one told them to until you just started yelling. I don't appreciate you pestering the tenants. Now, go back downstairs and I'll talk to them about painting their windows." He returned to our apartment, muttering, "Nobody knows his place anymore."

The Daouds were strange in that they rarely opened a window in their apartment. At first, I assumed it was because they were Jewish, but my mother, who was a friend of Madame Daoud's, told me otherwise. She said that many Jewish families opened their windows. She thought the Daouds kept theirs closed because they had lived for a time in Bologna and everyone knew that Italians were terrified of drafts.

. . .

"It's those fucking Americans," Elie said. He lit a Marlboro, flicked the match with middle finger and thumb. "We can crush the Israelis, but we can't fight the Americans. All the planes are being flown by American pilots." He took a long drag, banged the worn leather seat of the motorcycle. "Fuck all of them. All the damn American imperialists."

"Are we losing?" I asked.

He turned, shoved me. I stepped backward, frantically trying to keep my balance. "We'll never lose. We'll win the war. God is on our side." Elie turned back to the motorcycle. I ran out of the garage, up to the apartment, and hoped he wouldn't notice I was gone.

❦

Behind the first mountain peak stood a huge palace of majestic silver splendor. Three tall towers stabbed virginal white clouds. From above, the palace shone with unearthly brilliance, its silver reflecting the sun's glory. A large, glittering pool was centered in the courtyard.

"Look at the beautiful women," Elijah said when they landed in the courtyard. "They have such perfectly formed breasts."

Seventy-two virgins, beauties with big round eyes and hair of various shades of blond, appeared perplexed at the sight of the colorful imps. As did twenty-eight strikingly white prepubescent boys. "Welcome, travelers," said one of the girls.

"I think they were expecting only one warrior," Fatima said. One large divan faced one hundred couches arranged in rows. The surrounding verdant garden soothed the senses. "This must be someone's idea of paradise."

"Come," another houri said. The women and boys wore dresses of sheer silver silk that revealed more than if they were naked. "Join us. Let us ease the weariness of your journey. Allow us to rejuvenate you." Ten of the seminude and smiling boys carried large jugs of wine. Each resident of the garden carried a cup filled with the burgundy liquid. "Come," said a boy. "Relax. We can sing tales for you and entertain you."

A houri stroked the top of Isaac's head. "Are you truly pure?" he asked.

"We are as chaste as the sheltered eggs of ostriches."

"How dull," Isaac replied. "I am going to look around."

The stunned houri burst into a magical melody, and her sisters joined her. One of the virgins took Fatima's hand, but she shook it off. "I never lie with a woman whose breasts are more pronounced than mine."

The song began to falter. "But we are chaste," said one.

"We are bashful," said another.

"Neither man nor jinn have touched us," said another.

"You can have intercourse with us," said another.

"We have wine," said another.

"We have song," said another.

"A truly overflowing cup," said another.

"Do you not possess desire?" asked another, and Ishmael said, "No."

"Nothing here of interest," said a returning Isaac. "The song is in a minor key."

And the company took to their carpets and flew.

❧

The following day, they sat in our living room looking out of place, three men all the way from Syria. My mother had to serve them coffee, since the maid was packing.

"Are you sure this is necessary?" my mother asked. "It's not as if anything is happening here. Lebanon will not get involved in the war."

"The Israelis are coming, madame," the maid's father said. His hairy wrist extended three finger widths past the frayed sleeve of his shirt. He would not look directly at my mother. He seemed very tired, with drooping eyelids and a slack jaw. "We can hear them. The girl should be at home."

"Fine. Fine. I'll go see that she's packed." Lina and I followed her out of the room. "Last time I'm hiring an Arab girl," my mother said as she walked into the maid's room.

The girl wore her best dress, chlorophyll-patterned, front-buttoned, hemmed an inch below her knees, showing white calves. A canary-yellow headscarf covered her hair, her worst feature. Standing there, gazing at her open suitcase, she looked much older than thirteen.

"Let me see how you're doing," my mother said. She unpacked the top layer, looked underneath. "Anything else going in this suitcase?"

The girl shook her head. My mother rearranged the clothes.

Lina gave me her "I'm about to tell you something you don't know because you don't know anything" look. "Mom's checking to see if she's stealing anything," she said in French.

"Tais-toi!" my mother snapped. She reached into her pocket, took out a hundred-dollar bill. "Listen," she said to the girl. "I want you to have this. You've been very good to us. I know it's a lot of money, but I want you to promise me something. You will hide it. It is only for you. Under no circumstances are you to show it to your father or your brothers. Not even to your husband if they marry you off. This is for you. Only for you. Do you understand?"

"Yes, madame." She hid the bill in her brassiere. "Thank you, madame."

"Now get the hell out of here."

The radio moaned about betrayals, a defeated voice. The air seemed thick. I stood in the concierge's living room looking at a family of strangers. The concierge's wife hovered around her guests, concerned. There were four of them: a husbandless woman, a tattered version of the concierge's wife, and her three children. The woman's lips were pursed, her eyes blurry. She seemed not to inhabit her ghostlike face. A lethargic fan stirred the air.

"They had so many planes," said her eldest son, almost a man. "They kept coming and coming. They lit up the skies at night and bombed everything. We didn't have a chance. Everyone ran away."

Elie stared. "Did you fight, cousin?"

"Fight? We didn't have a chance to breathe. They came across so fast we barely had time to run. They used napalm. It burns your skin down to the bone before it kills you. How can we fight that with rifles?"

"We're lost," another cousin said. Elie walked out in a huff. I followed quietly.

I tried not to be noticed. My mother refused to look at Uncle Jihad, stilled her gaze upon the ceiling. Both sat on the divan, their legs resting on the glass coffee table. My mother's morning demitasse remained untouched, no longer steaming.

"She's gone, Jihad," she said softly. "She's gone." My mother had found out that Madame Daoud had left in the dark of night, gone to Italy to visit family, her husband said.

"No word, no note, nothing." My mother closed her eyes and sighed.

"Why do you think she's not coming back?" Uncle Jihad asked. "Her husband is still here."

My mother slowly lowered her head, opened her eyes, and gave him a "let's-be-serious" look. "He needs to take care of things before he joins her."

"You're being morose." My uncle laid his hand upon her shoulder. "She'll always be your friend."

"Nothing remains," my mother said, shaking her head. "All is lost."

"I've lost my childhood innocence," Lina sighed. She was sitting on the piano stool, the upright to her back, its top lid open as if it were letting out a sigh of its own. Forlorn, she showed me her profile like a dejected Egyptian film star. She kept smoothing her skirt without looking down, a practiced, automatic gesture.

"What do you mean?" I asked.

"How can I witness the suffering of the Palestinian children and remain childhood-innocent?" She exhaled loudly. "I suffer with them. I'm no longer a child."

"But you're ten, stupid."

"No longer. Because of what I've seen, I am now a woman."

I shoved her off the stool and ran. She came after me.

"It's over," my mother said, "and our army didn't fire a single bullet."

"It's not our government's fault the war ended so quickly," Uncle Jihad said. "They're probably still in session, contemplating action."

We watched the news on television in the family room, thousands of Palestinian refugees arriving in Lebanon, like the rolling, rolling, rolling cattle on *Rawhide*.

"This chaos is disconcerting. There are so many of them," my mother said. "What will they do?"

"They'll wait," my father said.

"What's Lebanon? Some kind of purgatory?"

"What's purgatory?" I asked.

"Come here and I'll tell you," Uncle Jihad said, patting his thigh. My legs dangled over the edge of his lap. "According to Dante, there's paradise above, inferno below, and purgatory, which is like a hospital waiting room or train station until it is decided where one will go."

"Who gets to decide, God?"

His grin widened. His head shuddered, a noncommittal nod. "Anyone but us."

And King Kade sent the faithless wind against them. "Now, that is more like it," said Isaac. Thick white clouds approached. The passengers held on to the carpet hems as the winds grew stronger. A cold, swirling gust blew Jacob off. He fell a few lengths, vanished, and popped back into place. The carpets turned fractious and began to misbehave.

The company was forced to alight in a green meadow with shin-high grass. Noah folded the three carpets into wallet-sized squares and swallowed them.

"This is a lovely meadow," said Job, "and its color perfect."

Fatima and the imps walked north. "This is exhausting," Elijah said. "By the time we get where we are going, I will be too tired to do anything. My hooves are sore. I think we should fly again and risk the winds." Below them was a deep valley they had to cross to get to the second mountain.

"The next wave comes," announced Ishmael, pointing his tiny hand. White horses with white warriors atop them galloped toward the imps from below. The riders brandished silver swords above their heads. "I count a hundred, twenty rows of five."

"Look behind the wave of attackers," Ezra said. "There are another hundred, and more waiting. They are over a thousand at least."

"Why are they lined up that way?" asked Fatima.

"Fanatics are not imaginative," replied Isaac. "Metaphor becomes more important than substance."

In the center of the valley, a giant white-leaved oak birthed both horses and riders. A leaf would fall to the ground and would change into either man or beast. "May I?" said Adam.

"No," replied Noah. "Allow me. Sister, may I have one of the bags?"

"Which one?" asked Fatima, hand holding out Bast's three gifts.

"Methinks it matters not," the blue imp answered. "I will take this one. It smells of the sacred Nile." He opened the bag and emptied its contents on the meadow in front of him. "Stand back and admire." The mud fell upon the abundant grass, divesting it of its fastidiousness and sanctity. The mud spread and burbled. A tiny spring erupted. "Let me help." Noah brought his hands together. The tiny spring exploded into a river, and the water coursed toward the riders.

"More," said Isaac. "Teach them suffering."

Noah brought his hands together once again, and the river water rose. "And it shall be," Noah said, and unleashed a flood.

The valley basin was soon covered with blue. The horses panicked, and their riders attempted to calm them. When the water covered the bark of the giant tree, the horses had to swim. The spring gushed forth more water, and a lake formed, grew monstrously large. Warriors and steeds drowned. The water reached the top of the white-oak tree. Blue swallowed white.

"Plop goes the white army," Isaac said.

"Will the oak survive?" asked Jacob.

"Yes," said Adam, "but it needs protection." With his arms held high, he formed an orb of dust out of which a giant violet serpent with a golden crest and fiery eyes thrust its head. The snake hissed, flicked its tri-forked tongue. "Come out, Thebes," Adam said. "This is your new home." The snake uncoiled its body, swollen and plump. Out of the orb it slithered and slithered and slithered, and into the lake it entered, its scales glittering beneath the water. Thebes devoured the straggling riders one by one. Once sated, it wound its body around the giant white oak below the surface of the lake and rested its head atop the highest branches.

"A snake fit for such a magnificent tree," Adam said.

🦋

In November 1968, the Farouks moved into our building, into the Daouds' apartment. It had been over a year since the latter had left.

The doorbell was shrill. "Buon giorno, signora," Uncle Jihad said to Mrs. Farouk when she opened the door. Those were the only words I understood as he rattled hundreds more in Italian. He had the opportunity to practice his Italian quite a bit, because there was one Milanese family in the neighborhood, and one Genovese bachelor, a pilot.

Mrs. Farouk blushed, opened the door wider. She had reddish-brown hair and a complexion that easily flushed. She spoke in Italian, gestured grandly, inviting us in. We followed her into the living room, my white tennis shoes squeaking on the polished blond wood. Her husband sat reading an Arabic novel. Oud music wafted from hidden speakers. Mrs. Farouk introduced Uncle Jihad, Lina, and me to Mr. Farouk, who stood up to greet us.

"We're the welcome wagon," Uncle Jihad said, his face bright and beaming. When he was excited, his voice slipped into a higher register. "And I brought the kids to meet yours."

I felt Lina stiffen before I saw the Farouk girls walk in. Fatima was eight, a year older than I, pretty, skinny, but not the cause of my sister's consternation. Mariella, thirteen, was the most beautiful girl I had ever seen. Long, light-brown hair, green eyes, full lips, and a large mouth. She strolled in, knowing her effect on a room.

"Che belle," Uncle Jihad said, looking at her father. "They seem to have inherited the best features of both of you. A delectable mix of Iraq and Italy. How wonderful."

She ignored Lina, approached me, offered her creamy hand. "Hello, I'm Mariella," she said in a fully adult voice. "This is my little sister."

Mrs. Farouk cleared her throat. "We were so happy to find this place," she said. Her accent was funny, an amalgam of numerous Arabic dialects. "We weren't sure about moving to Beirut. We got tired of Amman, and I thought maybe Rome, but then we decided Beirut offers the best of both worlds, don't you think? And then we found this apartment. How gorgeous, a sign from heaven. It was in such good shape. Do you know who was living here? I intend to send them a note of thanks."

"You'd have to send it to Israel," I chirped.

"The Daouds emigrated to Israel," Uncle Jihad said. "They retired, sold their chocolate factory, and left."

"Israel?" Mrs. Farouk asked. "Why would they do that? It's such a dull country. The people are so serious."

"They're Jewish," Uncle Jihad said. "I think they felt safer."

"I'm Jewish, too. You don't see me packing to go live on a kibbutz."

I checked the windows, saw that they were open, a soft, cold breeze rippling the muslin curtains. The oud music was still playing as we all got to know each other. Even Lina asked questions, animated, chattering. "You'll love the neighborhood. Lots of people of all ages."

I tuned everyone out and concentrated on the exquisite melody. I had no idea who the musician was, but he was a magnificent oud player. Uncle Jihad laughed loudly. I strained to hear the soft music. Madame Farouk laughed. Noise. I shushed them.

The room turned quiet. Shocked faces stared back at me as I realized what I had done. Quiet seconds elapsed. My heart beat faster; I was about to cry. Uncle Jihad laughed nervously. "I apologize for the boy," he said. "Sometimes he lives in a world all his own." He looked at me with a worried expression. Everyone seemed to wait for me to say something.

The oud player took his maqâm into a different key. "I'm sorry." My voice much softer than usual. "I'm very sorry. I was listening to the music and forgot where I was." I paused. No one said anything. "I was lost in the music and my lack of manners."

They broke out in laughter. Fatima was the only one who didn't. She regarded me with an unwavering, measuring gaze. Uncle Jihad, his arm around my shoulders, said, "This boy is a treasure. Always says the most amazing things."

"This boy is a jackass," Lina said.

"How charming that a boy his age can get lost in this music," Mrs. Farouk said. "My husband will probably want to adopt him."

Mr. Farouk was smiling, looking intently at me. "This is music from my home."

"This is Maqâm Râst," I said, and sat on the palms of my hands.

"How did you know that?" Mr. Farouk asked, surprise registering on his face. I shrugged.

"The boy here is very talented," Uncle Jihad said. "He plays the oud beautifully, plays day and night. He can play maqâms. He's studying with Camil Halabi."

"I can play one maqâm only."

"I'd love to hear you play," Mr. Farouk said. "I can play for you, and you can play for me. Would you like that? Your teacher is a great musician. I always thought he was dead. I heard him once, when he came to Baghdad, a long time ago, when the city was still alive, when we still cared about beauty." He looked up at the ceiling. "Why don't you let him borrow the album, dear?" he said to his wife. "He can listen to it without anyone disturbing him."

Fatima appeared in my class two days later. She wore white stockings and a short, lace-trimmed blue dress littered with white daisies. Fragile and wispy, she walked over to Nabeel, who was sitting next to me. "I want to sit here." Nabeel shrugged, and moved from the seat he had occupied for weeks. She sat down, kept her head lowered, but looked up at me with her brown eyes, appearing both nervous and confident. "You have to be my friend," she said.

❧

The crystal palace lay atop the second mountain peak. Its size, architecture, and translucence dazzled the eyes. Everything inside—stairs, columns, balustrades; tables, chairs, bookshelves—was made of clear crystal without any obvious imperfection. Sunlight refracted within the great hall, producing shards of fiery color. It was eerily quiet, devoid of life. "I could live here," said Jacob. "I would want to redecorate a bit, but the lighting is stupendous."

"It is too sterile," huffed Isaac. He jumped on one of the lounges, dropped his loincloth, and peed. "You cannot stain the furniture. I could not live here."

"We might have to," said Fatima. "The door just closed by itself."

The eight little demons scampered about the hall in every direction. Ishmael tried the door, which was locked and bolted tight. Ezra and Elijah checked the windows.

"The trials are getting more difficult," said Job. "I hate that."

"Cumbersome," said Isaac, "but not difficult." He hiccupped, burped, and regurgitated a seed out of his mouth. "Sweet," he said. "Sister, allow me to have one of the remaining bags."

"Pick," said Fatima.

"This one," Isaac said. "It smells of rich earth." He spilled the mud onto a spot in the center of the hall and planted the seed. "Watch," he said. He stood back and admired his handiwork. "Grow," he commanded, and the ivy crept gradually. Each small vine sprouted another and another.

"Poison ivy?" asked Fatima.

"A variant," replied Isaac. "Worry not. You are one of us. Poisons are your lifeblood."

The ivy twined around ankles, covered the floor, and began to ascend the walls. Greenish flowers erupted on the branches as the ivy snaked its way to the ceiling.

"Dull flowers, though," said Ishmael. He threw morning glories upon the ivy.

"My damned turn," announced Adam. He changed the floor cover into ground ivy with blue-purple flowers. Noah threw in hyacinth beans. Ezra added cypress vines.

"Xanthous," said Jacob, and a canary-bird vine flowered in yellow effulgence.

"Xanthous?" snapped Isaac. "Do you make these things up?"

"Let him be," said Ishmael. "He is a little different, harmlessly so."

"Sweet," commanded Elijah, and sweet peas burst forth. "Oh my. I meant jasmine."

"Stop it," said Isaac. "If you are going to do this, do it right." Deep-red bougainvillea covered walls, floor, and ceiling. "I could live here now." He stepped gingerly across the vine until he reached the door, which was entirely covered. He pushed through the ivy, and the door tumbled and crumbled. "Hurry," he said. "The palace will not remain erect much longer."

❧

"The word 'maqâm' means 'place' or 'situation,' " Istez Camil said. "It also means 'shrine.' In music, it's about scale, but also mood. Do you know what that is?"

"No." My fingers mechanically ascended and descended the oud's neck. I had been doing scales for forty-five minutes.

"Each maqâm is related to a specific mood through its structure and modality. When you play a maqâm, the technique should become invisible, so that all that remains is pure emotion. The intent is to induce a certain mood in the listener and yourself. The intended mood will determine what maqâm and what kind of improvisation you will play. For example, if you want to induce a sad mood, you can pick one that's very microtonal, like Maqâm Saba."

He nodded, hoping to elicit some form of acknowledgment. I shook my head. Istez Camil stood up, was about to say something, but stopped. He lit a cigarette. "You're tired," he said. "We'll finish this next time."

I put down my instrument, stretched my fingers. "Why do people think you're dead?"

"Dead? Maybe because I've stopped playing publicly." Istez Camil looked out the window, his back to me.

"Why did you stop?"

"I played the wrong note," he said. "I played the wrong mood." I didn't say anything, waited for my teacher to elaborate. "My wife had died. I bored my audience. There was only one maqâm I could bear to hear—or play. The audience couldn't hear the variations of the maqâm I was playing. They grew weary of hearing the same maqâm over and over."

"Maqâm Saba," I said. "I love how slowly it moves, how infinitely tender, like teardrops descending along cheeks, a cascade of grace."

"See? You do understand." Istez Camil wouldn't turn around. "A cascade of grace. That's so wonderful. It describes all the great oud playing from Shah-Kuli or even earlier. It is said that he was the greatest musician that ever lived."

"Tell me."

"When the Turks defeated the Persians and reconquered Baghdad in 1638, eight hundred janissaries were killed in an ambush, so the Turks launched a general massacre. They cut the heads of thirty thousand Persians, but the sultan still needed his entertainment. A Persian musician, scheduled to be executed, was brought to the diwan. As his countrymen, friends, and family were being decapitated one by one, the great Shah-Kuli played a maqâm for the pitiless Sultan Murat. He sang so sweetly, played the oud so gently, ended his performance with a dirge that brought every listener to tears." He turned away from the window, smiled at me. "The listeners' teardrops descended along the cheeks to the beat of the maqâm. A cascade of grace. And the weeping sultan commanded a halt to the killings."

꙳

There was no palace behind the third mountain peak. The company flew from top to bottom and back, scanned every nook in the steep landscape, but found nothing.

Elijah unleashed the crows. "With thine eyes," he said, "find."

Jacob unleashed the bats. "With thine ears," he said, "find."

"Could it be inside the mountain?" Adam asked. "I can send the scorpions."

"Could it be farther ahead?" asked Noah.

"Wait," ordered Fatima.

Bats and crows scudded over the land. Fatima followed as many as she could with her eyes. "Higher," she said. "He must be higher." She unhooked a black ribbon from her hair and held it at arm's length. She raised it high above her head. A group of seven crows followed her direction and flew above the mountain peak. She jerked her ribbon once more, and the crows flew higher still. Higher, and the crows would reach the clouds. Before she could jerk her ribbon again, one of the crows folded its wings and dropped. Elijah sent its siblings to break its fall and return it to him. The indigo imp held the suffering crow in his hands. "The bird speaks."

"Call the crows and bats back," Fatima announced. "I know where King Kade is."

"Where?" Ishmael asked. Elijah and Fatima both replied, "He is in the clouds."

❧

The first Thursday of December found Uncle Jihad and me in a small café in Msaitbeh. We'd gotten permission from my parents, since it was a school night. The whitewash was peeling off the walls, which were unadorned, not one picture or painting. We sat at a Formica table that was too high for me. Uncle Jihad greeted all the men, although it was quite apparent that he didn't fit in this environment. He was by far the most colorful thing to have walked through the doors. There were no women. Not one chin on any man in the full café had seen a razor in at least twenty-four hours, whereas Uncle Jihad's hairless face and head shone a warm blue from the reflected fluorescents.

By the time my tea—strong, sweet, served in a glass—arrived, the café had grown quiet. A boy, a couple of years older than I, turned the transistor on, and the music began. "You are about to hear the goddess," Uncle Jihad whispered, and placed his forefinger on his lips.

The introduction began as a simple melody played by violins. The percussion, one derbakeh and two daffs, provided a steady rhythm. The violins repeated the melody, over and over, inducing a hypnotic effect. Most of the men had their eyes closed. Ten minutes passed before the band began to wind the melody down. Applause could be heard from the radio. "She's onstage," Uncle Jihad whispered. "She has arrived." Silence. I could hear some of the men in the room breathing. One second. Two seconds. Ten seconds.

Her voice came on, clear, strong, powerful. The room sighed in unison at her first utterance, then quieted again. A man wearing dark eyeglasses held together with a gray piece of tape leaned back on his chair as if he were about to be showered with rose petals. Another man conducted an imaginary orchestra with both hands, exhibiting a grace that belied his big frame. Gentle pulsations were visible around his temple, large veins following the beat of their own metronome. Umm Kalthoum carried the melody, sang of love in Egyptian dialect, and the words of longing made sense. I had heard the band repeat the melody many times, yet now it seemed the tune was created only for her delivery of these words. She repeated each line, once, twice, three times, more, until it vibrated within me. I listened, ears open, mouth open, eyes wide. When she finished the melody, the room shook. Men applauded, stood up, yelled at the radio.

"Long may you live!" "Again. One more time." "May God keep you!"

"It didn't happen," a man said to the radio. "You have to do it again."

She did. She began the song again, from the beginning. Now the men talked to the radio after each line. Over the radio, I could hear the men in her audience shouting encouragement to the singer. The leader of the imaginary orchestra repeated an elongated "Ya Allah" after each verse; his eyes rolled up, looking at the tobacco-stained ceiling as if asking Him to come down and listen. Each line became a tease. Will she repeat it? Will she take it further?

When she finished the melody the second time, the audience erupted, the room was in an uproar. A short man stood on a table and shouted, "Allah-u-akbar." Uncle Jihad looked radiantly happy. She began the same melody again. I was in ecstasy. The room shook in delight.

When she finished, and her audience and the café went still, she waited a little and then launched into a new melody. Same song, same key, a slightly different track, further elaboration of her longing. She repeated this version only twice, then went back to the first, after which she launched into a third melody, did not repeat it. Then first melody again, third, first, second, first. By the time she was done, a full hour into the song, the room was utterly exhausted and hoarse.

We drove home in slow traffic, Uncle Jihad excited, tapping on the steering wheel.

" 'Umm Kalthoum' is a stupid name to call someone," I said. " 'Mother of Kalthoum'—what does that mean? And how could they call her that when she was a girl? She'd have been too young to be a mother."

"Umm Kalthoum is the quintessential Arab," Uncle Jihad said. "She's probably the one person whom all Arabs can agree to love. Ever since they lost the last war, she's been on a never-ending tour trying to raise Arab morale. Not that it will do any good, but I think it's wonderful she's so dedicated. I love people who are passionate about lost causes."

❦

"Rest for a minute," Isaac said. "You will be fighting him alone, and you will need your strength. As long as King Kade is alive, we cannot break the spell. We cannot accompany you."

The imps sat cross-legged in a circle around her, shoulder to shoulder. They had folded two carpets, and were floating below the clouds on the remaining one.

"The most powerful weapon you have is your courage," Ishmael said. "Yet the line between courageous and foolhardy is hazy at best."

"Be patient," said Job.

"Be wary," said Jacob.

"Be amazing," said Adam.

The imps stood. Each placed his left hand upon his brother's shoulder and his right upon Fatima's body. "We are with you," they said in unison. "Once and forever." And they vanished.

❦

"Come sit next to me," Mariella said, laughing, mischievous, and coquettish. She sat on the faded yellow concrete wall that surrounded the building next to ours. Her legs dangled above the seven tiles in a single pile. She crossed her legs, which hiked her skirt a little higher.

Lina bristled. "Aren't you going to hit the damn tiles?" she asked Hafez, who held the tennis ball and stared agog at Mariella.

"It's a stupid game," Mariella said. "Come sit here and let the children play." She leaned back, tried to look as adult as possible.

"Can't you sit somewhere else?" Fatima said. "We're playing here. You're right above the tiles."

"I sit where I please."

"Go sit with her," Fatima told me. "If that's what you want, just go."

"We don't need you," Lina said. "And you're too slow anyway."

I joined Mariella on the wall. "Aren't you going to come and play the oud for us?" she said. "My father keeps asking about you. You should visit." The ball came hurtling six times in a row, but the tiles remained standing. Mariella pretended to be completely unaware there was a game anywhere in our vicinity. Then the tennis ball, seemingly from out of nowhere, smacked her left thigh. She shrieked.

"Sorry," Fatima said. "I didn't mean to do that."

"Good shot," Lina said. The other kids were all laughing.

"You're a whore, Fatima," Mariella said. "You're nothing but a whore."

I heard the roar of Elie's motorcycle before it appeared. He turned the corner onto our street, his sunglasses reflecting the afternoon sun. All the kids stopped to stare. Dressed in militia fatigues, he looked much older than he was but still much too young to be driving a motorcycle. He stormed by us without a glance, got off his bike in front of our building. His mother ran out of their apartment to greet him. She hesitated, then slowly, wordlessly, stroked his hair with her right hand, and held it out gently, as if pointing out to him that it was a bit long.

I slid forward to jump off the wall and run over to Elie. Mariella gripped my arm and dug her fingernails into my skin, almost drawing blood. I looked back at her, but she was watching Elie. His father came out, shouting. "Where've you been, you son of a dog?" Elie strode past him into the building. His mother stared at their backs.

❧

She felt him. Of that, at least, she was sure. Fatima steered her carpet into the thick clouds. Inside, blinded by white, she ascended slowly, through viscous sky instead of moist, through oleaginous instead of damp. As she approached the topmost layer, as sunlight began to seep in, she felt as if she was slogging through mud. Her progress slowed to a crawl. Breaking through, she saw the castle of mist in the distance. It seemed solid at first glance, but it changed its shape unhurriedly. A tower would shrink, a window appear, a ramp vanish, the whole ever shifting, with a mind of its own. She alit at the gate. As she had expected, she was able to walk on the clouds. The gate slid open for her, and she entered King Kade's domain. Inside the unfurnished castle, she felt vulnerable, unable to get her bearings. The hall changed with every step. Warily, she moved toward the door, which disappeared when she attempted to open it.

"King Kade, King Kade," she called to the cavernous space. "Are you not tired of these silly games?" She unsheathed her sword from its scabbard, slashed the wall in front of her. The blade met no resistance. Walls of cloud. She walked through.

❧

Fatima tried on lipstick in front of Mrs. Farouk's vanity mirror. "I think dark reds suit me better, don't you?"

"Why's your name Fatima?" I asked.

"There's nothing wrong with my name." Her face creased up in anger, which made her look like a younger replica of her mother, particularly with the weird lipstick.

"I didn't say there's anything wrong with it. I just asked why. Don't yell at me."

I stood up, but she pushed me back onto the bed. "Then don't ask stupid questions."

"It's not stupid. You can't have two sisters and one is called an Italian name and the other an Arabic name."

"Of course you can. What a dumb thing to say. My mom named her, and my dad named me." She picked up a perfume bottle, turned it upside down on her index finger. It smelled like chemical flowers. She dabbed some behind her ears and lifted her arms toward the ceiling and smeared perfume under each.

"My parents named both of us," I said. "That's the normal way. They discussed it for a long time. Osama is my mother's favorite name."

"But your sister is Christian and you're Druze, so don't talk to me about strange. Did your parents discuss that?"

"Of course. My mom gets the girl, and my dad gets the boy."

"That's weird," she said, then wiped off the lipstick and threw the used tissue in the basket. I did not point out that her mother would guess Fatima had been in her bedroom if she saw the discarded tissue. I followed her out of the room. Outside her apartment, my cousin Anwar sat on the stairs, looking uncomfortable. He stood up quickly and asked if Mariella was home. Without slowing down, Fatima punched him hard in the stomach. I watched my cousin double over. Fatima descended the stairs. Her lips still had a tinge of red. Anwar's lips were glassy with snot. I ran after Fatima. I didn't want my cousin to worry about my seeing him cry.

❧

Across the room, King Kade sat atop a massive, ephemeral throne whose color blended with the floor, the walls, and his garments. His hands and face seemed to float in space because of the uniformity of color surrounding them. And King Kade asked, "Have you come to burn incense at my altar?"

"I have come to shatter it. I have vanquished your armies. It is now your turn."

King Kade laughed, a bubbly and breezy sound. "You amuse me. I can see why the devil kept you. Maybe I will choose to keep you for myself. I shall place you in a gilded cage instead of an engaging parrot and have you entertain me with witty remarks. Approach me, warrior."

"Prepare to die, fool," Fatima replied.

King Kade laughed again. "Attempt to say that phrase in a deeper voice, for it does not yet strike fear in its listener's soul."

"Then why do you tremble?"

The color of King Kade's cheeks changed from ashen to bright pink, and a scowl visited his face. He raised his hand and unleashed a beam of fiery light. The talisman between her breasts sucked it in. Fatima's hand, her ward against evil, turned warmer and bluer the stronger the beam became. "And you think me amusing?" she asked.

"No longer," King Kade replied. "You have become tiresome."

He directed his beam toward her sword, which flew across the room, clanging and settling in the corner. She turned to retrieve it and was struck by a heavy blow that felled her.

"You are a fool as well as a whore," King Kade said. "You may be immune to magic, but you will always be frail. I need no witchcraft to destroy you."

Two immense albinos with long silver-white hair and large wings sprouting out of their backs towered over the crouching Fatima. The first kicked her and sent her tumbling. The other lifted her above him and threw her against the wall, which seemed to turn solid on impact.

"Fool, fool, fool," muttered King Kade to himself.

Fatima tried to crawl toward her sword, but the albino picked her up again and threw her against the other wall.

"Who should prepare to die?" King Kade asked.

"He who plays with angels," Fatima said. "Thy doom arrives."

When the second albino lifted her, Fatima took a match from her robe. "Fire," she whispered, and a flame burst forth. She lit the angel's wings, which burned immediately. He released Fatima and wailed in pain and grief. She whispered, "Fire," again and burned the second albino's wings. The albinos bent over in agony, burned and melted until nothing of them was left. She turned to King Kade and sent a flame in his direction.

He extinguished it with a flick of his wrist. "You cannot harm me with trivial magic," he said. "I have defeated warriors much more powerful than you."

"But none wilier," she said. "And none, I am sure, as beautiful."

And she threw the last of the mud at the magician's tunic.

♣

I recognized Uncle Jihad's broad, meaty face behind the silly white beard. His wet laugh was identifiable. He had stuffed at least two pillows under his red coat. I walked up to him, pointed at his beard, and said, "You spoke Italian to Mariella, then to Fatima. You're no Santa."

He puffed out his chest, and the corners of his mouth disappeared into a smile behind his lifeless beard. "I hear someone speaking," he said in English, "but I can't tell where it's coming from. Is there a poor, helpless child who doesn't know that I fly across the world and speak to all children in their native language? Where's this child who doubts who I am? Let him come forward." He swiftly picked me up before I could escape his grasp.

"Speak Congolese, then," I challenged.

"Blah, blah, blah, blah, naughty little boys, blah, blah, blah."

"That's not a language. You're making it up."

"What? You understand Congolese now? I've spoken the language since the beginning of time. It's primitive, you know, but it's delightful, because each 'blah' has a different meaning, depending on intonation. Want me to tell you a Congolese story?"

"No," I said. "No story. Not now. Can I have my present, please?"

The Christmas party was at Uncle Halim and Aunt Nazek's apartment. Santa Claus had come to our flat the year before. That gathering had been so successful, and the children had had so much fun, that the family decided to repeat it at Aunt Nazek's, even though no one other than my mother had ever put up a Christmas tree before. To ensure that the party took place in her home, Aunt Nazek had bought a colossal fir tree. It didn't fit in her living room. My mother couldn't take her eyes off it. She'd be talking to someone, and her gaze would inadvertently flip back to the giant tree. The ceiling should have been at least a meter higher. The top of the tree had broken in two places; one segment ran along the ceiling, and the tip angled toward the floor. The silver star on top pointed down at a wooden footrest in the corner. From behind us, we heard a woman's voice whisper, "Is the footrest supposed to be the barn or the crib?"

My mother and I turned toward Mrs. Farouk, who was leaning over the sofa. I didn't understand what she meant, but my mother's eyes suddenly lit up, her left hand landed on her heart, and she burst out with a laugh so loud the entire room went still. Her laugh, a noisy, sharp aspiration, wasn't at all ladylike, but she didn't stop. I nudged her. "What? Tell me," I said.

"Come sit next to me, my dear friend," my mother said, "and allow me to discover your entire life story. I know we've met, but we haven't been properly introduced."

Mrs. Farouk sat on the arm of my mother's chair, and they began a whispery discussion of décor. "Do tell me about the coffee table," Mrs. Farouk said. "Where do you think she got it? A reject from a low-end department store in Lahore?"

"Ah, precious. No, no. She had it handmade. She'd seen it in a magazine."

"Car magazine, no doubt."

The laugh, the noisy, sharp aspiration.

Lina came and sat next to me. She held her presents, a Monopoly game and a Clue. She asked me what was so funny. I had no idea. My mom winked across the room at Santa, whose whole body vibrated with glee and giggles.

"Do you think the coved ceiling is good or bad for the tree?" Mrs. Farouk asked. "You'd think the curves would refer back to the new angles of the tree, but they don't somehow. One has to applaud risk takers, though. Brava."

And my mother exploded again. Lina shrugged. I felt better that I was no longer the only one not getting the jokes. I looked longingly at her board games and then diverted my gaze to the dining room, where I had left my presents—two play guns and a set of exotic matchbox cars with a loopy plastic road. Lina placed her trove on my lap.

"By the way, I hear you're a friend of Mrs. Daoud," Mrs. Farouk said.

"She was my best friend," my mother said. "I miss her terribly."

"She must be wonderful. The apartment is in such great shape. I didn't have to change anything. I find it incredible that, out of all the apartments in Beirut, we'd get hers." She straightened her back, smoothed her hair with the palm of her hand. Her eyes flicked sideways and back. "An Italian woman, so to speak. She lived in Bologna. I'm from Rome. Amazing."

My mother sighed, and gloom revisited her face. "I can't forgive her," she said. "I can't forgive Israel for taking her from me."

I woke up to an Israeli gift. They had landed at Beirut Airport, blew up all fourteen planes, and left. "The Israelis called it Operation Gift," Fatima said. We were sitting under our bush in the gated garden across the street from our building. Fatima and I had a few hiding places, not all hidden, where we separated ourselves from the world. Under the bush, behind the red Rambler that hadn't moved in years, under the fountain in our building's lobby, all protected us from Israeli bombings or the infernal company of my cousins.

"My dad said they didn't just bomb airplanes," she added. "They broke into offices and wrote all kinds of curse words on the blackboards. They wrote that Arabs are donkeys. They did that. And then someone went to the bathroom on a desk. That's disgusting."

"Yuck," I said. "Number one or number two?"

"Number two."

Elie came out of the building, glaring ahead, seeing nothing in his path. He cursed the sky as he walked by, his shock of black hair looking like a woodpecker's crest. Fatima shot him hateful glares. I tried not to blink. "He's mean," Fatima said.

The motorcycle roared past us. Mariella held on to a smiling Elie, her hands cozy around his waist. She looked delighted. He had a large gun in a holster around his thigh.

❦

"You mean to defeat me with a mud stain?" King Kade asked sarcastically. "I can calm the raging flood and enrage the dormant sea. I drive clouds away and call them back. I make mountains and forests quake. And you mean to vanquish me with this?" He looked down at the dirty blotch on his tunic. His eyes twinkled as he pointed toward the dark spot and chuckled. He arched his eyebrows and covered his mirthful mouth. He pointed his finger at her, then back at the stain, and broke into a fit of hysterical laughter. The laughing magician was no longer all white, no longer uncontaminated. He laughed and laughed, and his laughter changed gradually, almost imperceptibly, from breezy to throaty and phlegmy, until finally even he noticed the metamorphosis. The stain on his robe spread. His long beard grew shorter in length.

Aghast, King Kade said, "But it is not yet darkness. Night has not fallen."

The robe grew ragged, shrank. The cloth turned threadbare and tattered before it disappeared, leaving the magician naked. His body released its hairs, and his skin darkened and shriveled. His penis and scrotum withdrew inward, and a vagina began to form. The stomach shrank, and the hips expanded. Sparse black hair sprouted out of the creature's bald head. Every other tooth in the monster's snarling mouth dropped to the floor, charring a small circle around it, and the teeth that remained turned as black as soot. The creature's breath turned vile. Her breasts drooped below her sternum, and her dark nipples elongated and dripped poisonous green bile upon her leathery skin. And the eight imps appeared beside Fatima.

"Envy," cried Ishmael. "Thy end hath come."

"Too late," the monster spat. She backed into the corner, tried to cower behind the throne of clouds. She hissed at the imps. "Vengeance is mine, for your brother has departed our world."

"And you shall join him," Ishmael said. He jumped onto the monster and bit into her flesh. Isaac joined him, and his bite produced cries and wails and the sound of breaking bone. Ezra's sharp teeth descended upon her thigh. Jacob and Job ate her fingers, Noah her knees. Elijah swallowed her breasts. And Adam—Adam received the blood of her neck. They tore flesh, gnawed gristle, and sucked marrow. They crunched bone and chewed sinewy muscle. Their lips and cheeks turned slick and waxy red. The imps feasted until she was no more.

♣

Sneaking out of the apartment with my oud, I ran the twenty-three paces to Uncle Jihad's door, and knocked. I scurried inside when he opened the door and quickly shut it behind me. I always managed to make Uncle Jihad laugh, even if I hadn't intended to.

"And which evil organization are you hiding from? The American government? Dr. No? Nixon? The Mossad? The PLO? Just tell me who's after you and I'll annihilate the lot of them."

"I'm not hiding." I went into his living room to make sure no other family member was there. "I'm being discreet."

"Ah, discretion," he said. "The privilege of youth."

I sat on a chair and said, "Sit, sit," pointing to the sofa in front of me. "You have to be my audience."

"My God," he gushed. He sat down, dog-eared the paperback novel he was holding, and put it aside. "I'm so flattered. I'm overwhelmed. I'm not used to being chosen by genius."

"Stop it. You have to behave yourself. I've learned a new maqâm, and Istez Camil said I should play it in front of an audience for practice. He thinks I play too much by myself and don't involve others. You're my practice. Act like an audience, all right?"

He began clapping and cheering. I beamed. "The special one is here. Hurrah. Take a bow." I bowed from the chair, and he continued clapping. He hooted and whistled until I picked up my oud. He quieted down when I plucked the strings to make sure it was tuned. I limbered up my fingers. "That was amazing," he said. "More, more."

"More of what? That was just a scale." I began to play the maqâm, which I thought was the most beautiful melody in the world. Istez Camil had said that it was hundreds of years old and all music derived from it. I didn't care, because I didn't want to play any other music. I wished I were Iraqi and lived in Baghdad, in a house with an enclosed courtyard with a fountain and a pool of water, and I could have guests over all day and all night to hear me play this wonderful maqâm.

Uncle Jihad came over and kissed my brow. "That was beautiful," he said. He bent his knees to be level with me. "I can't believe how good you've gotten."

"Istez Camil says I have a hundred more years to go before I can play well."

"He's right. But I can say, and I'm sure he'll agree with me, that you play wonderfully, and with passion. You just need the hundred years of ripening." I hugged him. He stroked the back of my head. "You should play for your father," he added. "It might look like he wouldn't want you to, but he does. Our grandmother, your great-grandmother, played the oud. I bet you didn't know that. But she stopped playing after she married your great-grandfather. It was the great love story. Let me tell you the story."

"No, no," I said. "Tell me a story about the oud."

"The story of the greatest musician that ever lived," Uncle Jihad said.

"Did he play the oud?" I asked.

"He played the lyre, which was the ancestor of the oud."

"Was he Lebanese?" I asked.

"No," Uncle Jihad replied. "He was Italian. His name was Orpheus. He lived a long, long time ago. Before he came into being, the best musician was his father, the god Apollo. He played better than any mortal since he was a god, and that's saying a lot. But one day Apollo and the eldest muse, Calliope, had a son called Orpheus. His father gave him his first lyre and taught him to play it. And the son overtook his father, the pupil became better than the teacher, for he was the son of the god of music and the muse of poetry. With each note, he could seduce gods, humans, and beasts. Even trees and plants were still when he played. His music was powerful enough to silence the Sirens. Orpheus was human, but he played like a god, and in doing so, he lost track of his humanity, becoming godlike. All that mattered was the perfect tone, the ultimate note. And then, as all gods must do, he fell— fell in love and became human again.

"Orpheus met Eurydice and married her, but Hymenaeus, the god of marriage, wasn't able to bless the wedding, and the wedding torches didn't burst into flames but fizzled instead, and the smoke brought tears to the eyes. Not too long after her marriage, Eurydice was wandering in the meadows and was spotted by the shepherd Aristaeus. Bewitched by her beauty, he whistled his appreciation, whistled low, long, and slow."

"That's not right," I said.

"No," he replied, "no, it wasn't. Eurydice got scared and fled. While running away, she was bitten in the ankle by a white scorpion. Eurydice died. And Orpheus was devastated. He sang his song of grief for all to hear. Up in the skies, the gods wept. They wept so much their clothes turned all soppy and shrank. That's why the gods are depicted seminaked in the great paintings. They cried so much it rained for forty days and forty nights. For as long as Orpheus sang, his eyelids, and the world's, were forbidden sleep. On the fortieth night, he realized that he couldn't retrieve his wife by singing to the heavens. He was looking in the wrong direction. He must descend to the under-world and reclaim her.

"His song was his protection against the denizens of the nether-world. The lyre enchanted Cerberus, the giant three-headed dog who guarded the underworld. As Orpheus descended, the ghosts heard his song and shed their dry tears, for they remembered what it was like to breathe. Sisyphus sat on his stone and listened. The three Furies stopped their tortures, joined their victims in the enchantment. Tanta-lus forgot his eternal thirst for an instant.

"And the song squeezed Proserpine's heart. 'Take her,' said the god-dess of the underworld. She called on the god Mercury to bring forth limping Eurydice. 'Follow Orpheus with his wife,' Proserpine com-manded Mercury. 'Set her free in his world. But listen, Orpheus, and hear this. Your wife will live again on one condition. You will lead her out of my realm, but you may not look back. If you fail this task, I'll retrieve her forever.' Orpheus set out, walked out of the underworld. He heard the god's winged footsteps behind him, sometimes faint, sometimes not. He trusted and walked forth through passages dark and steep, through dank tunnels and tortuous paths. He believed his love would follow him. Light changed. He could see the gate before him. He looked back and saw his wife dragged back down to the underworld. 'A last farewell,' he heard her say, but the sound reached him after she had vanished. And he lost her."

"That was not a happily ever after," I said. "You promised to only tell me stories with happy endings."

"You're right, but that's easy to fix. Orpheus died and descended into the underworld and was able to look at Eurydice as much as he wanted."

"And they lived happily ever after."

"That they did."

"How come it's always bad to look back?" I asked. "What if some-thing is going to hit you from behind? What about rearview mirrors?"

"I don't really know," he replied.

I paused. "Would you have tried to retrieve Grandmother from the underworld?"

"Hmm." He hesitated, cast his eyes upward as if contemplating. "I don't think she would've wanted me to. It was the right time for her to leave. Eurydice died before her time, which was why Orpheus went down to get her."

"If I die," I said, "will you come for me?"

"I'll turn the world upside down and inside out. I'll find you wherever you are. I'll not only come for you, I'll bring an entire army. You're my little hero. That's what you are."

Who will raise the dead again? Fatima found her lover, Afreet-Jehanam, human-sized and demonlike, lying prone and lifeless on the white altar of King Kade. The imps jumped atop the altar. Weeping, Ishmael said, "Our brother is dead." Fatima ran her fingers through the demon's hair, which was no longer yellow and fiery, just unresponsive blue strings of air. She kissed his inert lips. "Wake," she said, but he remained dead. She kissed his palm, pressed his hand to her chest. She used his swordlike fingernail to cut her lip. She kissed him again. "Wake," she said, "drink my blood," but he remained dead. She removed the loincloth of rhinoceros hide and held his listless penis. She put the penis in her mouth and licked. "Wake," she said. "I am not done with you yet." And the penis grew rigid, but the jinni did not breathe. She climbed on the altar. "Wake," she said. "I am Fatima, tamer of Afreet-Jehanam, vanquisher of King Kade. I am master of light and dark. Wake." She straddled her lover, descended upon him until he was inside her. She felt the force of life tremble within her. And his hair was enflamed. She bent down and kissed him. A streak of blood dripped from her lip to his, down across the convex curve of his cheek. It transformed into a young mud snake upon touching the altar.

"Wake," she said, and he opened his three red eyes.

Elie leaned on his motorcycle, looking ruffled and agitated. He didn't notice me until I was right in front of his face. He was now sixteen, and my mother always said that was a horrible age, because you were mean, unhappy, and uncharitable most of the time, and you ended up listening to American music. Elie was moving up in the militia. He already commanded a troop of boys who were older than he was, and, more important, he now carried two guns. He stared at his shoes. I stared at him until a sudden flutter flashed in the corner of my eye. Mariella walked out of the lobby, wearing a drunken smile and a sweater so tight her breasts looked like a high shelf. She whistled a Beatles melody. She strolled by, pretended not to see us. She was a bad actress, but Elie was fooled. "I'm here," he called.

"Oh," she sighed. "I didn't see you." She kept walking, laughed coquettishly. "I want something to drink." She entered the store on the ground level of the adjacent building, then stuck her head back out. "I'll be right back."

"I need to find a place," he said. I nodded, unsure what to say. "She's upset because I can't find a place. She no longer wants to come with me to any of my friends' places. She thinks it's beneath her." He paused, eyed me to make sure I was following. "You're my friend, right? I've always taken care of you, so you're my friend." I nodded, still silent. "I have to use your room. Your mom takes bridge classes Mondays and Thursdays. We can go up there then."

"Why do you want to visit me when she's not there?" I asked.

"Don't be silly. I want to use your room. You're not going to be there."

"You want to be alone with Mariella?"

"Yes. What the hell do you think I'm talking about?"

"What about Lina?" I didn't think she'd be happy if she knew he wanted to be with Mariella. My sister liked him.

"Get rid of her."

Mariella came over and greeted me by bumping me with her hip. "How's my little boyfriend doing?" She held her Pepsi bottle with both hands, and her lips played with the straw.

"We're going to use his room," Elie said.

She didn't reply, didn't even look at him. She concentrated on my eyes. I blushed. "I don't understand why you play the oud for my sister but not for me," she said. "Don't you like me?" I blushed again.

I waited in the building's lobby on Thursday afternoon. Elie had said he'd come down as soon as he was done being alone with Mariella. I waited for a long time. Finally, he came out of the elevator, walked by me, smiled, and grabbed his crotch.

My bed was a mess. The duvet was on the floor, and so was one of the two pillows. The other was crumpled. I tried to make the bed presentable. I smoothed the damp sheets, fluffed the pillows, and covered everything with the duvet. I sat on the bed to make it look less strange.

Istez Camil asked me to repeat the maqâm. My fingers hurt. I was dripping sweat like hanging laundry. I was happy, though. Istez Camil wouldn't admit it openly, but I knew he was impressed. I could tell because he sat up straight in his chair and his eyes turned into slim slits of brown, unmoving, unwavering, staring at the well-instructed fingers of my left hand.

"Again." He clapped his hands for a beat. One, clap, clap, one, clap, clap. I finished, and he wanted me to start over again. Sweat dropped into my eyes. I asked him to wait a minute. I wiped my brow, took a sip of water, and scratched my itchy head. "Let me see," he said. He stood up and held my head. He ran his callused fingers through my clammy hair. He told me to take a break and left the room. My mother rushed in a few seconds later. Anxiety paralyzed my tongue. She held my head down and searched my hair. "Oh my God," she exclaimed. "Don't move." She dashed out of the room. I heard her on the phone but couldn't discern what she said.

The whole family had to wash their hair with anti-lice shampoo. My mother called everyone in the building and demanded that they all use the medicine. The household linen was boiled and disinfected, and so was my entire wardrobe.

My sister glared every time she walked by me. I worried that she would figure out that Elie had been in my room. All my cousins avoided me. I ended up sitting under the bush in the gated garden, huddled close to Fatima. At one point, my cousins Hafez and Anwar ran toward me and started mussing up each other's hair and screaming, "Yuck, yuck, yuck!"

At dinner that night, in front of the television news, my mother wouldn't stop talking about the lice. I remained silent. Uncle Jihad nudged me with his elbow. "See." He ran his palm over his smooth scalp. "Sometimes it's good to be bald."

It seemed every time I saw my grandfather now he was noticeably older and weaker.

He combed my hair and I wept. "I knew you'd need me." His voice was gentle and soft, elderly and frail. After every stroke of his fine comb, he would dip it into a bowl of scalding, soapy water. "I knew they wouldn't understand. Your parents are too modern." He ran his left hand over my eyes, onto my forehead, all the way back to my hair and neck. "These days no one understands feelings, and when I leave this world—soon, probably—who will understand yours?" I cried, couldn't stop my body from shaking. He combed. "You're my boy, my blood."

— Seven —

In Cairo, Baybars and his followers were housed by his aunt. "You are the son of my sister," she told him. "You are as dear to me as you are to her. This house is your family home." She arranged for his belongings to be moved into private chambers. She introduced him to her husband, Najem, one of the king's viziers. That night, she laid out a wonderful feast. "Tell me about my sister," she said. "I would love to hear her stories." And Baybars told her how Sitt Latifah had saved his life and adopted him, how she taught him archery. His aunt's face flushed with affection.

The next morning, Baybars wanted to breathe the fresh Cairene air. He and his warriors rode into the city. Al-Awwar was not in a good mood and made sure that his rider knew it. What was supposed to be a delightful exercise turned into a battle of wills between horse and rider. "None of our horses are happy," the warriors said. "The vizier's stable hands tend the vizier's horses and not ours. We hired some help, but al-Awwar may require a stableman all to himself."

Baybars saw that his stallion was not well groomed, his mane was not combed. Baybars apologized to his horse. Al-Awwar arched his neck and snorted.

That night, Baybars asked his uncle Najem if he knew where he could find a capable and worthy groom. The vizier said, "The stablemen's shop is in the Rumaillah quarter, and you are sure to find a good man there. However, under no circumstance should you hire a young man by the name of Othman. The ruffian is about your age, but he has the criminal experience of an old man. He is a thief and a scofflaw who can only be controlled with a branding iron. The king has issued warrants for his arrest, but he continues to evade the law and find naïve folk to defraud."

At the stablemen's shop, Baybars met an old man with a beard as white as swan feathers. Baybars told the chief of the stablemen he was looking for a groom, someone who was clever and strong, honest and guileless. The chief presented a groom, but Baybars did not like him, or the second, the third, or the fourth.

An ostentatiously dressed young man with the face of a rodent entered the shop. Upon seeing him, everyone cleared out except Baybars and the chief, who ran toward the young man and prostrated himself and kissed the offered hand. Othman asked, "Did you get any money in today?" and the chief replied that he had not. "And what is he looking for?"

"He is looking for a groom, but he did not like the ones I showed him," the chief said. "He must want a special one."

"Do you like me?" Othman asked. And Baybars said yes.

Othman thought the young man an easy mark: he would work for him that day and rob him that night. Baybars thought, "Either that young man will obey me, or I will kill him and rid the world of a parasite." Baybars paid the chief stableman five dinars. The chief was about to put the coins in his pocket, but Othman glared at him, and he handed the money over.

Baybars and his groom arrived at Najem's stable. The instant the other stable hands laid eyes upon Othman, they scattered in every direction. Baybars said, "This is al-Awwar. I can see that he likes you, which is an excellent indication of your good nature. Take care of him, wash him, and feed him."

Alone in the stable, Othman thanked God for His glorious gift. Equestrian equipment, more valuable than anything he had stolen before, hung from hooks on the wall; beautiful, intricately stitched leather saddles lay in order on a wooden bar. What would he take first? He filled his coat pockets with golden bridles and silver bits. He found a large sack, in which he placed two saddles and five silver reins. He mounted his horse and rode out of the stable.

"Where are you going?" asked Baybars, leaning against the side of the stable.

"I am going to wash the equipment," Othman replied. "It is the groom's job. I do not yet trust the servants here. I shall hire people I have used before."

"But I cannot have you spending your own money on my equipment," Baybars said. "I will give you ten dinars, and you can pay your cleaners with that."

Greed forced Othman off his horse, and Baybars hit his new groom with the hilt of his sword. He dragged the rascal back into the barn by the hair. "You will learn your lesson, you lying ingrate." Baybars tied Othman up and hung him from a pole. He noticed that the thief's belt was a whip. "You wear this to inflict pain," Baybars said. "Now, then, you will be pained by my righteous anger." And Baybars whipped Othman until the groom fainted.

Othman awoke to find a multitude of eyes upon him. "Help me down, brothers," he said, "for I suffer." The other grooms did not move. "You," Othman called to the youngest groom. "Come help me down. Let me rest for the night, and in the morning you can hang me up again." The groom untied Othman and helped him down. Othman hit the boy, tied him up, and hung him in his place. All the other grooms hid. "Fools." He climbed back on his horse and escaped.

In the morning, Baybars found the young groom hanging instead of Othman. He untied the boy and saddled al-Awwar. He called the grooms and asked if any knew where Othman lived. One said, "He lives in the Rumaillah quarter, in the Sharbeel neighborhood, next to the long well. I do not know the house. He has threatened to kill anyone who says where it is."

Baybars rode out, and the African warriors emerged behind him. When he reached the neighborhood, Baybars asked a passerby if he knew Othman's house, and the man ran in the other direction. A second man shouted, "Beware the evil eye," and he, too, scurried away. A third refused to answer, and a fourth wet his pants and fainted. Baybars walked into the neighborhood bakery. He yelled at the baker, "My master Othman claims you cheated him out of a dozen loaves of bread, and unless you clear this up, he will burn your store down."

"That is not possible," the baker replied. "It was only yesterday that I sent a dozen loaves with the boy here."

"You had better explain it to my master, then, because he is furious."

The baker told the boy to go to Othman's house and find out what happened. The boy said to Baybars, "You can ride ahead. I will walk there. It is a shame to make your horse trot at my pace." But Baybars said, "I have a better idea. Since you like my horse so much, ride him, and we will follow you." The baker boy could not believe his good fortune. Al-Awwar allowed him to ride, and the boy led the men to Othman's house. He was about to knock on Othman's door when Baybars stopped him. The boy realized he had been tricked into revealing the house, and his mind flew in panic. "I will not tell," Baybars whispered. "Go now." The boy raced back to the shop. Othman's mother opened the door and asked Baybars what he wanted. He said he wanted Othman. "And who is looking for him?" she asked, and Baybars replied, "His master. He works for me. I intend to make an honest man of him, to lead him onto a path of righteousness."

Othman's mother glared at Baybars and said, "It is about time. I have been waiting so long. My son is in one of the caves of the imam. He is with his men, planning their revenge upon your family, I presume. Find him, and inspire him to virtue."

"Where do I find these caves?"

"They are near the tomb of the imam, of course. Ask someone. I cannot do everything for you."

No one would tell Baybars and his companions where the caves of the imam were. From a vendor, he bought ten watermelons and asked that they be delivered to the tomb of the imam. The vendor called an old porter with a donkey. The porter put the watermelons on the donkey's back and began to march toward the tomb. "Where exactly is your house, sire?" the porter asked.

"I need to go to the caves. I shall pay you double if you lead me there."

The porter trembled and shook. The donkey, his companion of many years, stopped and moved closer to his master to comfort him. "I cannot take you there," the porter said. "My soul would be forfeit. Only thugs and murderers roam the caves."

"If you do not take me to the caves," Baybars said, "I will claim your life myself."

The old man took a couple of steps and then whispered into his donkey's ear, "My penis is bigger than yours, friend." And the donkey laughed so hard that his knees buckled under him. His stomach reached the ground, and his braying reached the sky. "Look, master," the porter exclaimed. "My poor donkey is in pain. He cannot go any farther. Please, I must unload him and let him rest here." He pointed east and added, "The caves are there. You will not miss them. Let my miserable donkey rest."

Baybars and his companions moved on, leaving the porter and his donkey behind. "He has gone, has he not?" asked Baybars, and one of his warriors, looking back, replied, "Yes, he is riding his donkey toward the city as swiftly as he can."

There were numerous caves in the hill, and Baybars did not want to search every one of them. One of his warriors unbridled a threatening cry. "Othman, groom of Baybars the bold," the warrior yelled, "your master demands your presence."

Othman appeared at the mouth of a cave with eighty men backing him up. "Why did you follow me here?" he asked.

"You are my groom," Baybars said, "and I am your master. You will either serve me or die."

"Begone," Othman shouted. "Leave, or I will have my men tear you into tiny pieces and cook you in unclean water over a slow-burning fire." The warriors trotted slowly toward the brigands, and, just as slowly, the brigands began to disperse. "Stay here and fight," Othman commanded. "We outnumber them twenty to one. They only look frightening." And Othman unsheathed his sword and yelled, "Follow me," and ran unfollowed toward his nemesis. "May I?" asked one of the warriors. He jumped off his horse, did not take out his sword. He waited for the running Othman and unleashed a slap like fire upon the groom's face, knocking him to the ground. The warrior tied Othman's hands and threw him onto the back of the stallion.

When they reached the gates of Cairo, Othman began to whimper. "Please," he begged, "do not take me into the city with my hands tied and my head uncovered. It is not becoming."

"You are afraid of being mocked," Baybars said, "and I am afraid you will run away and break your promise of service."

Othman vowed to serve his master. The African warrior untied him and offered him a headdress. They reached Cairo, and Othman said, "Please, wait. I pray at the Lady Zainab's Shrine for good luck each time I enter the city." And Baybars allowed him.

Othman entered the shrine, knelt on the ground, and prayed, "Dear Lady, mother of us all. I place myself in your protection. Save me from this man." Othman felt Baybars's hand on his shoulder. "Smite him, mother of faith. Clobber him now."

Othman heard Baybars kneel beside him. "You followed me," Othman whined.

"I will follow you wherever you go," Baybars said. "My soul will leave me before I leave you."

"Smite him," Othman screamed. "Crush him, my Lady. This insane man will not leave me alone. Help your servant."

And before them appeared the Lady in all her magnificent glory. She shimmered in blue, shone in silver. And her bewitching voice said, "I am happy with you, Prince Baybars. This groom is one of mine, and I will watch over him forever." The Lady paused, laughed. "The groom has been serving God for years. Let him now serve and obey you." She placed her hand upon Othman's head. "I will make sure he follows the virtuous path and fulfills his destiny."

And a weeping Othman said, "On my honor, I now repent." He reached for his master's hand. "I will be your servant." And a weeping Baybars returned, "And I yours."

The vizier Najem was livid when he saw Othman on his property. He drew his sword. "Stay your hand, Uncle," Baybars said, "while I explain. This man has repented. He swore obedience to God. I have taught him proper ablutions and prayers."

The vizier studied Othman and witnessed faith in his eyes. He congratulated Othman on achieving wisdom and Baybars on finding an honest groom. He then said, "The king hunts in Giza every spring, and all the honorable men follow him. The season is upon us. Our house will begin to make preparations. You are welcome to stay in our tent or bring one of your own."

Baybars wanted to go, and he wanted his own tent. "I want a big one," he told Othman. "I want a pavilion worthy of a king. Go and buy me one." Othman said that a tent that size had to be ordered in advance and there was no time. A disappointed Baybars said, "Well, then, procure me the best you can find. I do not wish to be mocked."

Othman decided that the best place to find a pavilion worthy of a king was in a king's court, so that was where he went. He found the servant in charge of the king's tents, introduced himself, and asked how many tents the king owned.

"Only the chamberlain would know something like that," the servant said. "There must be hundreds. We have only used ten since I have been here."

"Well," Othman said, "if they have been stored for so long, how do you know they are still usable? How do you keep moths away? Are they fresh, or do they smell? Our glorious king should not have flawed tents. I will examine every one of your tents and make sure they are worthy. It will be my duty and honor to serve my king."

"But there are so many of them," the servant said.

"True," Othman replied. "I might be doing this for the rest of my inoffensive life, but I feel it is what I was born to do. Let me start with the biggest pavilion you have."

"The biggest one is immense. We cannot open it within the palace."

"That is surely the one I must start with," Othman said.

And Othman led twenty of the king's servants out of the palace, carrying a large, bundled pavilion, which could not be unfurled except in pieces.

Baybars exclaimed, "You have outdone yourself, Othman. This is fit for a king."

"For an old-fashioned king," Othman said. "Tan is too bland a color. We must change it." He did not add that, unless the color was turned, the king's chamberlain might recognize the tent.

"Well," Baybars said, "do with it what you will. Take it to Giza, and have it set up before I arrive. I am happy to have a tent of my own." And he left his servants.

Othman told the African warriors, "You three should paint the canvas. Your lands are known for their opulent and bright colors. You would do a much better job than I."

"A mule would do a much better job than you would," the first warrior said.

The second added, "So would a dog."

And the third, "But that does not mean we should do it. It is middling work."

"Brothers, you insult me," Othman said, "and I will not defend myself. Yet you swore to serve Baybars as I did, and if his social standing is improved by the painting of this tent, then it is not middling work. I will have the servants of the house do it. We will dye it."

"Dye?" the first warrior said. "You might as well put up a sign that says the owner of this pavilion is a cheap fool."

"We need pigment," said the first. "We need limestone," said the second. "We need gum arabic," said the third.

"We have all that," said Othman.

"Yes," they said, "but we do not have elephant dung."

"Will horse dung do?" Othman asked.

Othman and the warriors had to recruit servants and men on the street to help them carry the folded tent to the ship. He asked his mother to join them. "How long has it been since you had a holiday?" he asked her. "I will ask Baybars to hire you. You are the best cook in Cairo."

At Giza, Othman enlisted every able man to raise the pavilion. He needed a hundred. Once it was erected, he realized that they had nowhere near the furnishings or lamps for a tent that size. "We did not think about that," one of the warriors said.

"No matter," said Othman. He walked to the river, where he saw the king's servants unloading the rugs, pillows, and oil lamps for the royal tent. "My dear fellows," he said, "the king has commanded that you deliver all the furniture to Baybars's tent because he wishes to have dinner there." And then he saw the servants of the king's judge and told them the same thing. He spoke to all the viziers' servants. By the time everything was delivered, Baybars's tent looked as full and beautiful as a golden peacock's tail.

Baybars arrived the next day and was furious that Othman had commandeered the entire council's furnishings. "You have made a fool of me," he yelled. "By God, I will skin you alive for this." He picked up a stick, and Othman took off with Baybars behind him.

Othman reached the king's procession. He prostrated himself before his king and said, "Your Majesty, I am under your protection. My master wishes my doom, and he said I could never serve him again unless I extended an invitation to King Saleh."

"Your deliverance is in hand," the king said. "Lead us to your master's tent."

The processioners had to rub their eyes to be sure that what they saw was not a desert mirage. Before them, Baybars's pavilion stood as big as a city. Its colors and design were utterly new to them. White lines divided the tent like a quilt. Abstract shapes ran amok in some sections—triangles in olive green, squares in burnt umber, cones in pale lilac, circles in sky blue, ellipses in brown, swoops of yellow ocher. Other sections showed images of the great hunt—russet lions brought down by golden spears, black warriors on white stallions encircling a herd of wildebeest. And the guests looked on in stunned silence. The guests sat in the pavilion, and it still looked unpeopled. Baybars welcomed them all and ran outside and called for Othman. "Who told you to invite all these gentlemen, and how will we be able to feed and honor them?"

And Othman promised to take care of everything. He ran to the king's cooks. "The king is having dinner at Baybars's tent but is unsure of the quality of Baybars's cooks. The king does not wish to insult Baybars, so he commands that you cater the dinner secretly." He went to each of the viziers' cooks and repeated the story. To his mother he said, "The entire court is coming to dinner. Please make my favorite dishes. These nobles will think the food their poor subjects eat is a delicacy."

Within an hour, a feast of immense proportions was served to the king and his nobles. The king said, "In the name of God, the most merciful," and took the first bite.

"One of my cooks makes a dish very similar to this," one of the viziers said, "except this is much better. Its flavors are more subtle."

"And I have the same carpet as this," another vizier said, "but you can tell that this is of finer silk."

The king said, "This lentil-and-rice dish is so simple, yet so delicious. Can you find out from your cooks what the secret ingredient is?"

Baybars ran to Othman and asked. Othman asked his mother. "Salt and pepper," she said.

Everyone ate and was merry, and the king said, "May God bless the host of this feast."

Back at the court in Cairo, Baybars knelt before his king, who did not recognize the boy his dream had once asked for, since Baybars was no longer Mahmoud. And the king announced, "A gracious host and a possessor of immaculate taste should be rewarded. I hereby offer the suit of prince of protocol to Baybars. He will be responsible for all invitations and events of this court."

And that was how Baybars became the king's prince of protocol.

❧

The sound of rolling dice on the backgammon board echoed in the living room. When my father and Uncle Jihad played, the noise was as loud as a demon battle. With every move, they smacked the ivory chips on the board with a bang. They teased each other mercilessly, yelled and screamed in jest. They both liked to gamble and were good at the game. When they played other people, they were more subdued, because money was involved, but they played each other only for quarters, so they could resort to the clamor and the teasing. Manhood, not money, was at stake. I was always afraid that they would break the glass table under the board.

I was lying in bed reading, with the door closed, when the phone rang. I picked up the handset and heard my mother's voice. She asked me if Uncle Jihad was there. There was no hello, no how are you. She said she'd been trying to get hold of him and figured he must be with my father. "Tell him to come to the phone, but don't tell him or your father who it is."

"Why?" I asked.

"Just do what I tell you for once."

Uncle Jihad left his game and picked up the phone in the foyer. All he said was "Hello," and then his face seemed to twitch and tighten. He hung up the receiver without saying anything. Before I had a chance to ask what was going on, he put his finger to his lips and smiled, asked me silently to join in his conspiracy. "I have to leave," he announced to my father. "Clients."

"On Sunday?" my father said from the living room. "Come finish this game. I'm trouncing you. You can't deny me that pleasure. My luck will change if we stop. Don't leave now. Curse you and your ancestors, you insensitive lout. Stay."

My mother came home carrying a German-shepherd puppy in her arms. The puppy was so cute even my father smiled when he saw her. "What's this?" he said, and my mother replied that it was time. She gave the puppy to me. I looked at Lina to see if she was jealous, but she wasn't even looking at the dog. She scrutinized my mother. My mother removed her high heels in the anteroom, something I had never seen her do before.

"You're right," my father said. "It's time the boy learned some responsibility."

"I'm going to take a bath," my mother said. "I need it." She walked by, and I saw a bruise on her instep.

Uncle Jihad came in a few moments later. He went into the living room to finish the game with my father. I carried the puppy in so he could see her. Uncle Jihad asked what I was going to call her. I hadn't thought of that. The puppy slobbered all over my face as I carried her to my mother's room. She was still in the bath. I stood outside her bathroom door, felt the change in the moistness of the air. I asked what was the name of my dog.

"Not now, darling." Her voice always sounded hollow when she was in her bathroom. "I'm resting."

"The dog needs a name," I insisted.

"Call her Tulip. That's the name of a famous Alsatian."

We didn't find out about the accident until the following day. My father read about it in the morning paper at work. I heard about it at school. Fatima told me what little she knew; her details were sketchy. My mother had been in a car accident, a four-vehicle pileup. A number of people had died, but my mother was unhurt. I knew that because I had seen her. Other boys in our class began to add details. A big accident. A truck coming from Damascus had careered off at the steep curves of Araya as it descended toward Beirut. It ran over and crushed several cars. My mother's Jaguar was in the way. She saved herself by flying off a cliff. "Like a magic carpet," a boy said. "The Jaguar took off into the skies."

"I meant to tell you," my mother said when my father came home, "but I was too tired." When she lay on the burgundy divan, it seemed that the living room's furniture—the divan, the small Léger hanging above it, the smaller Moghul paintings on the side wall, the glass coffee and side tables—was handcrafted with her in mind.

"I don't understand why you didn't," my father said. "You could have died, and you didn't think it was important to tell me? Why? Why would you do such a thing?"

My mother held a cigarette and stared at the smoke floating toward the ceiling. "I was going to tell you. I was tired, shocked. I needed a bath. And time passed."

"But you had time to stop and get a puppy?"

"Yes," she said. "Isn't she sweet?"

Everyone in the family used to say that Jaguar should donate their cars to my mother. She was their best advertisement. Elie said she drove like a warrior. Aunt Samia said she drove like a man. Uncle Halim said she drove like a taxi driver. Uncle Wajih said she drove like an Italian. And Uncle Jihad said she drove with élan. It was the way she handled the car that attracted attention. Her left hand hardly touched the steering wheel. She leaned to the left, her side against the door, her elbow jutting out the window, her head propped against her hand. She drove as if the world and its roads belonged to her.

My father sighed. He stopped his pacing. "Why don't you go to your rooms, children? I need to talk to your mother."

Both my mother and my sister said, "No."

"I'm not a child," Lina added.

"I don't want to do this now," my mother said. "I'm all right. The car is totaled, but I'm fine. It happened quickly. I reacted. It turned out I did the right thing."

"How fast were you driving?" my father asked.

"What difference does it make? The truck lost control. It rolled into our lane. If I'd slowed down, I'd have been crushed like the other cars."

"You take too many risks when you drive," my father said. "I've told you that a hundred times. You never listen to me."

My mother inhaled deeply and kept staring at the ceiling.

"This is the third accident," he said softly. "And you don't seem to take it seriously." He looked at her, shook his head, and walked out of the living room, mumbling the word "husband."

Aunt Samia poured herself another glass of arak. We sat around her dining table. Most of the family was on the terrace. "Why don't you just hire a driver?" she asked my father. "That would solve all your problems."

I had eaten too much. My stomach rumbled and rebelled. I didn't want to leave the table, though, because I wanted my aunt to stop talking about my mother, who had stayed home.

"Stop it, Samia," Uncle Jihad said. "There's no way she'll use a driver."

"She could've been killed," she said.

"If someone else had been driving," Uncle Jihad said, "everyone in the car would have been killed. It's a miracle she survived, but having a driver wouldn't have saved anybody in this case." His small towel worked overtime. He sweated profusely and kept wiping his bald head.

"You always take her side," my aunt said. "You refuse to see, for some reason."

"He's not taking anyone's side," my father interrupted. He looked weary and drawn. To me he said, "Why don't you go outside and play with the boys?"

I shrugged.

"Go," Aunt Samia said. "You can't stay here. Your father wants you outside." I shrugged. "See?" she said to my father. "You're not strict with your family. They're undisciplined. How will you be able to control them if you let things like this slide?"

"Samia." Uncle Jihad sighed. "Don't start. This was a wonderful meal. Don't ruin it."

"I'm just thinking of his family."

"You should think of his family a little less," Lina said, materializing as if by sorcery. She leaned against the doorjamb. She wore a light dress and short heels and had her hair pulled back, which made her look adult and sophisticated. "After all," she added, "thinking was never your strong suit."

My eyes felt hot in their sockets. Aunt Samia wrung the glass of arak with both hands.

My father stood up, livid. I thought he was about to slap Lina, but he controlled himself. "How dare you?" he yelled. "You never speak to your elders in that tone." His fingers coiled and uncoiled. His hand muscles twitched. "She's your aunt. How could you? I know we've taught you better manners than this."

Lina hesitated. I could almost see her eyes parsing out all the possible outcomes. In an unemotional voice betraying no inflection, she said, "You're right, Father. I don't know what came over me." She smiled. "I'm really sorry," she said to my aunt. "I don't know why I'd say such a thing. Please forgive me." She turned around and began to walk away.

"You will be punished for this," my father called to her disappearing back.

They were both lying.

My mother did punish Lina. She had to. "You're making me do this," she repeated. "I'll not allow bad manners in my house." My father tried to intervene on Lina's behalf, but my mother would have none of it. My sister was grounded for a week. She was allowed out only to go to school, and would have to have all her meals in her room. I sneaked in the grated-fresh-coconut-and-chocolate balls she liked so much. Then

I saw my father sneaking her treats. Uncle Jihad brought her main dishes, all kinds of stews and rice. I thought they were doing it behind my mother's back, but on the third day, I saw her give Lina a whole plate of cheese desserts.

At the end, Lina was grounded for only four days, because my mother thought she had gained too much weight staying in her room. She spent that time listening to a kind of music I knew little about, hard sounds, harsh chords. This was not the Beatles. This wasn't the Monkees or the Partridge Family. I peeked through her keyhole to see how one listened to such jarring noise: erratic jumping, jerky hand movements, and head movements bouncy enough to ensure maximum wild hair. I didn't understand the thump-thump of the bass.

❦

King Saleh of Egypt had a judge who was as evil as his countenance. If one examined his features clearly, one could ascertain that he was touched by Satan: his ears stuck out, and the top of his left had a jagged rip, as if he were a feral cat that had lost a fight. This man, one of the king's council members, had grown in power through duplicity and treachery. Mischief-making was the sweet his heart craved, and perfidy the air he breathed. He was known by the name Mustapha al-Kallaj, but that was not the one he was born with. He was Arbusto. He was born in Faro, Portugal, the nephew of a king. He was raised in opulence, educated by masters, loved by his parents, but the richest soil and deepest well water cannot turn an evil seed into a fruitful tree.

A sister was born, two years his junior. Even as a young girl, she was as wise as a sage, as beautiful as a perfect emerald. She sat at the feet of her teachers, quenched her thirst for knowledge. She was called the Rose of Portugal, carried herself with the grace of a cypress.

Her iniquitous brother stole her honor on her fourteenth birthday. He impressed himself upon her in her chambers. As soon as her handmaidens heard her shrieks, they rushed to her rescue, only to be slain by his sword. When the foul Arbusto left, his sister crawled to the butchered corpses of her friends and covered her hands in their still-warm blood.

"The sacrifices you have offered will never be in vain," she said. "We will walk the Garden together." She stabbed her heart with a dagger.

In the morning, the girl's mother wailed, "I have lost two children to the night." The king ordered Arbusto's arrest, but none could find him. He sailed to Cairo, and used his scholarship and cunning to masquerade as a learned Muslim.

Arbusto became King Saleh's judge, and the king relied on his counsel.

Arbusto's heart filled with hatred and scorn when he saw Baybars in his new suit standing at the diwan's door as the prince of protocol. He wrote a letter to a man by the name of Azkoul, a malicious soul who delighted in murder, massacre, and mayhem. "As soon as you finish reading this note," it said, "you should be riding toward Cairo. Come to the diwan, and the man who asks what it is you need is the one I want not breathing. Tell him you have a proposal for the diwan, and offer him a folded piece of paper. When he turns his back to you, strike him dead. I will ensure that you are not punished." Azkoul flushed with joy at the prospect of a killing.

At the court, Prince Baybars received the paper from Azkoul and turned his back to open the diwan's door. Azkoul took out his sword and raised it to strike. As Baybars swung the doors open, Azkoul's bloodied head rolled into the diwan, and his body collapsed behind the prince.

"What manner of murder is this?" bellowed the king's judge. "How can the prince of protocol kill a seeker of the diwan?"

Two men entered the diwan and bowed before the king. "No one but us killed the seeker," the fierce Uzbeks confessed. To an astonished council they relayed the story. "The man is named Azkoul; he is an infamous killer. We saw him enter the city and recognized him. We trailed him, knowing that where he travels treachery follows. We saw him raise his sword to kill the prince, who had his back turned, and we struck, cutting a cankerous blight from a devout world."

And the king said, "Justice prevails again."

Baybars thanked the Uzbeks for saving his life and invited them to be his guests. The Uzbeks rode with Baybars out of the palace. When they arrived at Najem's, they asked if this was his home, and the prince replied that it belonged to his uncle. Baybars could not own a house, since he himself was owned. "But that is not true," one of the Uzbeks said. "We will present our case to the king tomorrow."

In the morning, the prince and the fighters knelt before the king.

The Uzbeks said, "Your Majesty, Prince Baybars is not a slave. He is naught but a son of kings. We have proof of his history and his genealogy."

The king said, "I would like to hear about Prince Baybars. How did he come about? Who is he? What happened? Tell me his story."

❧

My grandfather died in April 1973. I had just gotten home from school when Aunt Samia's panicked Filipina maid called on my mother, saying that my grandfather, who was visiting his daughter, wasn't doing well. My mother ran up the stairs in her housedress and clogs.

My grandfather lay shivering on the couch, Aunt Samia on her knees before him. She shivered as well, but it was an altogether different kind. "I don't understand," she said. "What can I do?" My grandfather clutched his chest with his right hand. When Aunt Samia saw my mother, she begged, "Help me, please." My mother knelt beside my aunt. Shoulder to shoulder, they seemed to be praying before my grandfather, the altar. I was the only witness.

"His heart," my aunt said. She had called an ambulance. "He wants to know his name." Her voice sounded like cheap plastic. "He doesn't know who he is?"

My grandfather had trouble breathing. He shook his head. "No," he uttered.

"Hold on, Father," Aunt Samia said. "Help is on the way."

"Your name is Ismail al-Kharrat," my mother said.

"We know you," Aunt Samia said. "You'll be fine. We know who you are."

His eyelids fluttered; his eyes seemed to scream in pain. "He doesn't know my name."

"Who doesn't?" my mother asked. "Osama? He knows your name. We all do."

"No," he said. "He knows not." His tremors subsided.

"Calm down, Father," Aunt Samia said. "Just breathe. In, out. Don't worry."

And he shook again, an unearthly quiver. "No." His hand tightened. Aunt Samia whimpered. My mother teared. "He knows your name," she said. "He always knew your name."

"No," he said. "He knows not my name."

"Say your name," my mother said. "Whisper in my ears and He will hear it." Aunt Samia stared at my mother. She grasped her arm. "In my ears," my mother said. "From mine to His."

She moved her head to my grandfather's lips. And my grandfather spoke.

"The Saviour knows your name," my mother said. "He knows."

The paramedics arrived five minutes later. They rolled him on the gurney into the elevator. "You drive." Aunt Samia handed my mother the keys. "You'll get us there before they do." They trampled down the stairs. The clamor of my mother's clogs slapping the stone echoed off the walls. He died on the way.

I knew his names. I knew his story.

My mother didn't want me to attend his funeral. I was too young, she insisted. I'd be scarred. At first, my father agreed with her. I would attend the consolations but not the burial.

But then Aunt Samia had a fit. And Uncle Wajih had a fit. And Uncle Halim had a fit. I was twelve, a man, and this was family. I became the cutoff: any cousin older than I was (Anwar, Hafez) would attend; younger ones (Munir, etc.) wouldn't.

My mother wept continuously and didn't leave her room. By early evening, when the rest of the family and guests began to stream in, she was called out. She wore mourning black, which accentuated the redness of her puffy eyes. Upon seeing her, Aunt Nazek bellowed, "Look. Look and see the grief your leaving has caused." Aunt Samia beat her chest and yelled, "Why, Father, why? Why did you leave me?"

My father's cousins, the Arisseddines, took over logistics. They began to send their children out with the death announcement to all the Druze villages. They seemed so efficient and meticulous. The sons of Jalal Arisseddine divvied up the important families, government officials, and parliamentarians. The sons of my father's uncle Ma'an divided up the villages and the religious communities. Every time my father approached his cousins, he forgot what he was about to say, and was led back to his chair by Lina, who didn't leave his side. He seemed shrouded in fog. The Arisseddine women greeted arriving mourners and guided them toward the family. They moved chairs from Uncle Jihad's apartment into ours. Cups of coffee were in constant rotation.

My mother seemed lost and despondent. She slumped in her chair, back bent, head down, staring at her shoes. More of the ladies cried, and Aunt Samia wailed. The wail woke my mother up. She stood up straight, looked at me, then at Lina across the room, next to my father. She arched her eyebrows when she caught Lina's eye. My mother wiped her mouth, and Lina took out a tissue and wiped her lipstick off hers. My mother walked over to my father and began whispering in his ear. He nodded once, twice. He shook his head no. He nodded again. And life revisited his face.

It wasn't an accident that Aladdin was Chinese.

"Once, a long, long time ago, in the land of China," my grandfather used to start his tale, "there was a mischievous boy called Ala'eddine."

"Why China?" I would ask.

"The Druze and the Chinese are related," he would reply.

I didn't look Chinese. I once asked my father if it was true, and he dismissed it as one of my grandfather's ramblings. So did my mother. "Well, you see," my grandfather had said, "the Druze believe that when someone dies the soul instantly jumps into the body of a baby being born. So we're supposed to be able to figure out who was reincarnated into whom. There aren't that many Druze. The wise men of the Druze, and you know they're not that wise, realized there was a problem. A Druze would die, and there'd be no one who was born at that same instant. They had to be born somewhere, you see. The dead were sometimes born in China, the land of a thousand dawns. The Chinese believe in reincarnation, which could mean they're related to the Druze. And, most important, China is far enough away so that no one can check. The Chinese get born over here, and we're reborn in China."

When I repeated that to my mother, she thought it was ridiculous.

Yet, as we sat in the living room the day my grandfather died, Ghassan Arisseddine, one of my father's older cousins, announced quietly to the room, "Lucky are the gentle people in China for receiving you in their midst at this hour." Neither my mother nor my father flinched.

The family met at eight in the morning to accompany the coffin from the morgue to the village, to the bey's mansion, where the funeral was being held. The hearse led a motorcade of thirty cars on an agonizingly slow drive up the mountain.

I sat behind my mother in our car—an unhurried, hushed, uphill ride. At a donkey's pace, the journey's markers strolled by unfamiliarly, the orange orchard, the three banana groves in a row, the unmarked turnoff, the protruding rock that looked like a detrunked elephant. The lush blue shore that should have danced only shimmied. The change from the green of pines to that of oaks took longer; the shades of ocher lingered, imprinted strange blends onto my retinas.

My mother broke the silence once. "It's not a good idea to have an open casket."

My father guided me toward a pavilion where the men gathered. Hundreds of white plastic chairs were set in rows facing another row of chairs with faded russet cushions. The bey, his brother, and his two sons approached our family; all exchanged kisses and condolences. My father had told me to reply with "May you be compensated with your health" to anything that was said to me. There was discussion and insincere protestation about seating arrangements. As the eldest male, Uncle Wajih had the main seat, and the bey sat next to him. Uncle Jihad took the end chair, and I the next one. My father maneuvered himself next to me. The bey's brother ran up to my father and offered to exchange seats. My father begged off. "I'm sure the seating will be rearranged when others begin to arrive."

And we sat in silence. My father didn't bat an eyelash. He gazed at the rows of empty chairs facing him. Uncle Jihad stared to his right, down the hill, at the undulating olive orchards beneath us. A damp, cold gust brushed and licked my face. Uncle Jihad pulled his jacket across his chest. He wept silently. My father didn't. "Are you warm enough?" Uncle Jihad asked me.

As if planned and coordinated, the residents of three villages arrived at the same time. The men and women separated at the gate of the bey's mansion and marched up the delicate incline. The women nodded toward us as they ambled by. Before us, the men arranged themselves in a line, whose order, who stood where and next to whom, seemed predetermined. They covered their hearts with the palms of their hands, uttered in unison something I couldn't understand. My father and uncle and all the men in our line made the same gesture and replied in a different incomprehensible sentence. Their line snaked toward ours; their hands shook our hands. Most of the men kissed the bey's hand.

The Christian families didn't perform the same ritual. Neither did the Muslims. All paid their respects. Friends kissed in greeting. Whenever a man of some import appeared, he was given a seat in the family line: You are family. The special men accepted condolences for a couple of rounds before moving into the anonymity of the guests. The Ajaweed, the Druze religious, sat in the first row facing us, fully decked in their traditional outfits.

The bey moved next to my father. He was much older than my father and looked it. He wore an English-cut suit and an awkward-looking fez. "My father loved yours," he said, twirling his white mustache with thumb and forefinger. A man from a lost era.

"And for that," my father replied, "we are eternally grateful."

"If you need anything in these trying times, our family will do whatever it takes."

"And your generosity is boundless," my father said to the bey.

They both stood up to greet the new arrivals, the ritual beginning again. As if it were a magician's trick, Uncle Jihad now sat next to the bey, and my father was on my other side.

"We were so happy to hear the news," Uncle Jihad said, covering his eyes with dark sunglasses. "A worthy grandson at last. Our family was overjoyed for yours."

"A birth is always happy news," the bey said. He flushed, and his eyelashes fluttered spastically in my uncle's direction.

"The birth made us happy," my uncle said, "but it wasn't what brought joy to our hearts. The miraculous news is that the boy looks exactly like you. God smiled upon us."

The bey giggled and jiggled, tried to stifle his mirth. "Yes, the little bey takes after me."

"And God raised the degree of difficulty for the ladies of his generation. How will they be able to resist the little rascal's charms?"

The bey slapped his thigh, and his Jell-O–mold paunch shivered in glee. "How will they indeed?"

We stood up for the next batch. When we sat down, my father's seat was empty. He sat between his two older brothers. Already bored, Anwar and Hafez elbowed each other. I spent my time counting suits, sports jackets, and religious Druze dress. I counted three fez hats, twenty-three Ajaweed hats, one Borsalino, and seventeen bald heads. The sky lowered, and a spring fog ascended. From the valley below, the thin mist rose languorously toward us, obstructing our view of Beirut. Normally, the whole city could be seen, the multistory buildings along the coast, the old Mediterranean houses, the airport with its crisscrossing beachfront runways. All went blank. I concentrated on the fog, now a translucent layer covering the olive groves. It would rise and cover, in order, the loquat trees, the lemons, the mulberries, and the fig trees. The fog made the village appear to be wobbly, wavering atop a precipice.

Upon seeing a skinny man in an ill-fitting suit walking to a jerrybuilt podium, the cliques of chatterers hushed. He began to recite poetry in a nasal voice, sang beautifully, like a goldfinch with a slight cold. The mood shifted. The poet recalled my grandfather, sang about his family and those left behind. When the poet brought up the years of service to the bey, he called my grandfather the bey's friend, not his servant. The bey's face molded into sad at the mention of his own deceased father's name. A few seats away, Uncle Wajih coughed and cleared his throat in an unsubtle attempt at disguising tears. My father remained stoic.

The poet paused, took a deep breath, and lowered his eyes. The air bristled with a tense silence. The poet began a new verse, raised his voice to the proud skies. He stepped off the podium, and all the men stood up. I felt Uncle Jihad's hand on my back, guiding me. The family men marched behind the song, and the remaining male mourners followed us. Into the house we went, without a pause in the incandescent song.

The women, all in black with white mandeels, sat in a semicircle around the open coffin, rows and rows. My grandfather looked like a wax model sculpted by an incompetent artist. His hair was combed, forced under control for the first time. His face looked like a composite drawing. The model hadn't sat for the artist.

The women wailed. Aunt Samia called upon her brothers to resuscitate her father, to breathe the fire of life into his lungs. Village women bemoaned the bey's misfortune. My sister could only look shocked and dumbfounded. My mother stared at the floor. Behind her sat a silent Mrs. Farouk. The poet sang of my grandfather's sense of humor. The men stroked the coffin. Uncle Jihad closed his eyes and mouthed words of piety. I placed my palm on the wood, and the coffin shook as if in anger, rejecting my touch. I clasped my hands behind my back. My cousins looked petrified. My mother tried to catch my eye. Calm down, her hands mimed.

The women began their ultimate laments. "Who will replace him?"

"How will we live with such sorrow?" "O Lord, be gentle with his journey." Aunt Nazek draped herself across the coffin, shouting, "Don't take him away." Aunt Samia cleared a path for herself by moving two men aside. She held her father's face with her hands, but withdrew them quickly upon first touch. "You can't go without me." She lifted her left leg off the floor and raised her knee, but it wouldn't reach the coffin. She tried pushing herself up with her trembling arms. "I'm going with you," she announced.

The men lifted the coffin, raised it above their shoulders. It floated out of the hall. And after prayers, the men carried it to the cemetery. I watched the coffin drown, sink into the mist.

"Are you feeling bad?" asked Uncle Jihad. "Was it the funeral?"

"Why did everybody have to shout so much?" I asked. Tulip lay at my feet, and I used her body as a footstool, the way she liked. "Aren't we Druze supposed to have silent funerals?"

He sipped his drink slowly, seemed to be having a conversation with the ceiling and not me. "In principle, but not in practice, for how will the dead know that we love them?" he said. "You know, darling, funerals used to be much more dramatic when I was your age. Believe it or not, they are quieter now, more sedate." He hummed, took another sip. "Why, I can just imagine what they'll be like when you're my age now. Probably no one will show up. Bang, bang, bang, and it's over. Mourners will arrive only if alcohol is being served, like at Irish funerals." He ran a washrag over his head. "It's only the funeral, my sweet. You know, some people flagellate themselves on the first day, the third day, the week, and the fortieth. It's a never-ending process. We have crazy funerals, and that's it. We're much more sane, don't you think?" I assumed the question was rhetorical. "You're not buying any of this, are you?" I shook my head. "Well, listen. A long, long time ago," he began, "when the Mongol hordes ran amok in our world, when Genghis Khan scorched the deserts of China and plundered the rest of the world, after the barbarian king had burned Baghdad to its final ember, after he massacred one hundred thousand in Damascus and watched the city's streets covered in rivers of blood, after the Mongol general descended upon our fertile lands, my story begins. The general's brother Tu Khan was bored."

"Tu Khan?" I asked. "That's a bad pun. That's not even Syrian good."

"Don't interrupt, my boy," he replied. His eyes, aloft still, were wide-set, dark, and revivified. "I'm on a roll. Tu Khan was bored."

"Bored, not bird."

"Acch, now, that's bad. Listen. Tu Khan decided to have a feast. He brought the seven best cooks in the region and demanded that they create the greatest meal that had ever been served. The cooks toiled and slaved and came up with seven courses. The first course was exquisite, one oyster on a bed of lemon purée. Tu Khan ate it in one bite and wept, for the taste was glorious. To ensure that no one else would share the taste and thereby dilute his experience, Tu Khan had the cook beheaded. The second course was soup, a pork-and-apple consommé. So thin, so clear, so delectable, and its creator was beheaded. Third was sautéed sand dabs, fourth was grilled pheasant, fifth was filet mignon. Off with all their heads. The sixth was rack of lamb, of course. Tu Khan could not believe his tongue. His jaws extended farther, moved toward the plate. Within minutes, his mouth was a hand's width in front of his face."

"Ah, Tu Khan," I said.

"Precisely," Uncle Jihad went on. "And we kill the penultimate cook. Now, the seventh cook was Beiruti. He was no fool and was in no mood to be killed. He made crème brûlée, using the milk of cows that had drunk their water from the Litani River. Tu Khan had his first bite and wept again. Creamy, smooth, impeccable. But before his second bite, his stomach rumbled. He licked the spoon and his stomach yiked. He had a bowel movement before the third bite, and it wouldn't relent, the never-ending stool. Plop, plop, diarrhea, dysentery, Tu Khan didn't have time to move; he soiled his pants and the glorious paisley-infected textile he'd been sitting on. 'I'm quite all right,' Tu Khan said, but he really wasn't. He lost five kilos within the first hour, three more in the second, and another three in the third. Rumble, rumble, his stomach wouldn't stop self-evacuating. He refused to sleep sitting up and had his slaves place him on the edge of his bed with his ankles in stirrups, so his stool could fire out unencumbered. Boom, boom, all night; his diarrhea was so explosive he was hitting the wall across the room, painting an abstract-expressionist mural. Nothing great, mind you, mediocre painting informed by Lee Krasner. By morning, Tu Khan was dead, wasted away into a stick man.

"The bereaved Genghis refused to have his brother buried in exile, for his soul would remain on earth, eternally searching for home. Genghis would bury him among their ancestors. Grief, sadness, sorrow. A Mongol funeral march began. But grief, sadness, and sorrow weren't enough to commemorate a man as great as Tu Khan." And my uncle's voice grew deeper, more serious. "No. It wasn't enough. Along the way, the funeral procession killed every living thing it encountered: entire villages, cities; men, women, children, generations of babies not yet born; animals, birds, trees, shrubs, flowers, forests. Everything was smashed along the path, from Beirut to Ulan Bator, a viscous trail of death and devastation to mark the funereal journey."

He gulped the rest of his scotch. I waited for him to say something.

"I guess we have it better now," I said. He smiled, nodded. I laughed, nervously. "So when did he marry Rita Hayworth?"

"Stop that." My uncle laughed. "That's another story."

"Now you're telling me that Genghis Khan destroyed Beirut as well? I thought it was Hulagu who conquered the Middle East. Should I trust you?"

"Never trust the teller," he said. "Trust the tale."

♣

The Uzbeks began to tell the king Baybars's story:

Baybars's grandfather had three sons, Talak, Lamak, and Jamak. He was old and wanted to test his sons and assess who was fit to succeed him as king. He sat Talak on the throne and told him to rule for one day. That evening, the king asked his eldest how he ruled, and the prince replied, "I was a fierce leopard, and my subjects were sheep." The second day was Lamak's turn, and he told his father, "I was a ferocious hawk, and the people were pigeons." At the end of the third day, the youngest said, "I decided fairly between parties. I helped the persecuted against the persecutors. I tried my best to rule such that when it came time for me to meet God I would not feel a twinge of guilt or remorse." Much to the consternation of his older sons, the king declared Jamak his heir.

After the king died, Shah Jamak assumed the throne and made his brothers viziers and declared that they would rule the land together. But his brothers plotted to kill him, because the twins, evil and envy, had taken root in their hearts. In the middle of the night, the brothers tied Jamak up while he slept and put him in a large bag. They gave the bag to a warrior slave and commanded him to carry it to the desert and stab it twenty-one times, until it was drenched in red.

The warrior followed orders. In the desert he took out his sword. The voice in the bag said, "Who are you?" to which the warrior replied, "I am your death."

"That cannot be," said Jamak, "for my death should be honorable and require to see its victim's face." The honest warrior felt shame. He let the king out of the bag. "I have never killed an unarmed man before," he admitted.

"And you should not start now." Jamak turned and walked into the desert.

Jamak walked and walked, across flatlands and hills, until, one day, not far from the city of Samarkand, he saw a lion attacking an old man on a horse. The old man called out for help, for he no longer had the strength to fight off the beast. Jamak said to the lion, "Come meet your conqueror." Unarmed, Jamak held his ground as the lion veered toward him. Just when the beast was about to pounce, the old man, with his last remaining strength, threw his sword to the young savior. With one movement, Jamak caught the sword, drew it from its scabbard, struck the lion's skull, and killed it. Jamak wiped the blood from the sword onto the lion's red mane, returned the weapon to its master, and said, "You live another day, Father."

The old man thanked Jamak and begged him to stay with him so he could honor him as his guest. The two men rode into Samarkand, and a large procession greeted them. Jamak realized he was sharing a horse with the city's king. "My lord," Jamak asked, "why were you riding alone when you could have had an army accompany you?"

And the king replied, "I was hunting with my friends, and I saw a doe and stalked it, but I could not get close enough. I followed it until I got lost, and that was when you showed up, at the perfect moment." The king asked Jamak for his story. The old man admired the shah's courage, nobility, and wherewithal. He made Jamak a vizier and married him to his daughter, Heather.

The king of Samarkand died, and Jamak ascended to the throne. He ruled justly and honored the heroes who in turn loved him and obeyed him. God blessed him with five sons, the youngest, Mahmoud, being his favorite. One day, the shah went to Friday prayers and saw his brothers, Talak and Lamak, begging outside the mosque. He called his servants and said, "Take these men to the baths, wash them, dress them in the finest clothes, and bring them back to me." Back at the palace, when Jamak's eyes fell upon his brothers, who now appeared as he remembered them, he hugged them. He sat them beside him and inquired after their health. The brothers said, "We are here because we missed you so much. We left our lands and lost everything trying to find you. We thank God that you are alive and safe and prosperous." And Jamak welcomed them and made them viziers. Yet, before long, envy and evil grew even mightier in their hearts.

The brothers had fallen upon hard times. Once Jamak was out of the way, they had ruled the land with darkness and contempt. After much abuse, the people had rebelled and captured the two fake kings, intending to execute them. The brothers begged desperately and dishonorably for their lives. The people released them into exile and found an honest man to rule.

Now the brothers noticed how much Jamak loved Mahmoud, and they formed a plan. They would kidnap Mahmoud and demand the king's treasury in return. During the night, the brothers tied up the young prince and rode away with him while everyone slept. When the shah discovered that his brothers had disappeared with his son, he cursed his brothers and berated himself for his foolishness. Queen Heather cried and dressed in mourning black.

The brothers took their nephew to a cave and kept him roped, intending to slay him after they received the ransom. They left Mahmoud by himself while they went out to hunt and forage for food. Once they were gone, the prince cried for help. A Persian dervish happened to be passing by, and he rescued the boy. The Persian decided to take Mahmoud to Bursa, where he could sell him for a good price. The prince grew very sick, and the Persian took him to the baths and sold him to a slave-trader who happened to be there because of the fine management of fate.

The king thanked the Uzbeks for their story. He turned to the prince and said, "My son Baybars, you are not a slave." And Baybars said, "Praise be to the Almighty."

And that was how Prince Baybars became a free man.

It was the first time I had seen Istez Camil since my grandfather's funeral. He had shown up for the first day of condolences, but I had been at school. No music was played during the mourning period. Istez Camil seemed more jittery than normal, tired and haggard. He was dressed in a white shirt with moon-shaped sweat stains under his arms, and a pair of thin gray cotton slacks, short at the ankles and chafed at the knees.

Whatever I played seemed easy. Notes flowed from my fingers with a newfound skill. Istez Camil shook his head. His lips were pale, the whites of his eyes unusually flat. "You're not getting it," he huffed.

"Not getting what?" I stopped playing, stared at him. "I think I'm playing well, very well, no mistakes."

"Cascade of grace, remember? This is a cascade of grace no more." He wouldn't look at me. "You're hitting the right notes, but there's more to this than that."

"It, this, that," I snapped. "I'm playing well." I refused to look at him, too, now. Shocked at my fledgling audacity, I lowered my voice. "You say I'm not but won't tell me exactly what it is you want, what it is I'm supposed to do. More feeling, more feeling. I'm feeling it now. How can you tell whether I'm playing with feeling or not?"

"I can tell," he said slowly, "and you can tell." He stood up, turned his back to me again, and stared out the picture window. "You have to be more honest with yourself. You have to."

"I'm playing well," I insisted. I whispered to my shoes, "This is who I am."

The resumption of my oud lessons wasn't enough for my sister. She waited for the day when my father began whistling again while shaving in the morning. That afternoon, she shut the door to her room and resumed blasting her *insufferable music at full throttle*, as my father called it. He would ask her to lower the volume, and she would for a few minutes, before reclaiming the air.

Except I no longer found the music insufferable. I began to discern its simple charms. I also began to discern Jimmy Page's solos, to guess at Eric Clapton's peculiar handiwork.

One afternoon, I opened her door without knocking, and found her experimenting with colored eyeliners. She glared at me through her vanity mirror. The space was pregnant with tension and the acidic scent of many perfumes. I lay on her bed and stared at the ceiling. She didn't say anything. The rustle of my blood coursing through its veins echoed the rhythm of the base. My head buzzed. "Play something weird," I said when the song ended.

"Kiss my ass, stupid," she said over her shoulders. "Be like furniture and shut up." When she stood, I noticed she was wearing tight mauve shorts that clung to her curves like a wet bathing suit.

"I don't know if that's a good idea." My head was propped up on her pillows, and I followed her with my eyes. "You know your father won't like it."

"I'm not going to wear this to school. It'll be all right."

I didn't argue. She walked to the closet. For the previous few years, it seemed to me she had been growing taller with each step she took. I remained uncomfortable with the size and shape of her shorts, which made her look unnatural and unfamily. On the floor, next to her feet (in laced-up knee-high black boots), was an album with the face of a man wearing more makeup than she was. "Play that," I said.

"Shut up," she replied. "If you want to be in here, you can't talk."

The next afternoon, I was back on her bed. She played David Bowie. I was like furniture.

The October War started a few months later. We were winning, yet few seemed to believe it. The Syrians and the Egyptians surprised the Israelis. Radios once again unequivocally blared the Arab victory. "Wait," my father said. "The Americans won't let this happen."

At school, the Palestinian boys beamed, a manifest bounce in their step. They believed it. The student council called for a strike in support of the war. There were supposed to be speeches, but I went home. I saw Lina smoking a cigarette at the mouth of the building's garage. Elie straddled his idle motorcycle and talked to her. I wondered whether the mauve shorts were to impress him. From afar, Elie, like the Palestinian boys, looked as if he believed.

I lay on Lina's bed and listened to Deep Purple. She arrived angry, carrying a guitar. "I need you to learn to play."

"There's a war going on," I replied because I had to say something.

"Who cares?" she said. She handed me the guitar as she stormed to her album rack. "You have to play, and you have to play well, and you have to make it look easy, and you have to do it by Saturday night. We have two days. Two days to figure out what you're going to play and how you're going to play it impeccably." She rifled through her collection and picked out *Abbey Road*. She scratched the Deep Purple album as she quickly removed it from the turntable without replacing it in its cover. "This is what you have to learn. It's impressive."

The opening notes of "Here Comes the Sun."

I had to take the guitar to school. While various student leaders gave speeches, I played in a corner of the cafeteria's outdoor terrace. Oblivious to anything else, I didn't hear the Israeli plane until it was right above me, flying low, its noise deafening.

Two seniors sat on the floor next to me, startling me. "Don't mind us," one of them said. I knew of him, but never imagined that he'd talk to me. He was the son of a Lebanese woman and a Kuwaiti prince, although he didn't look it. He was never seen in anything but dirty T-shirts, sweats, and jeans. He had only one pair of sneakers. I guess he desperately wanted to look more like an American than an Arab prince. He didn't smell as awful as his friend, though.

"Go on," his friend said. "We can listen."

"Better than those dumb speeches," the first added.

I replayed the opening. The Kuwaiti started to sing, and his friend joined him. I was surprised, since I hadn't considered vocals. I had memorized the song, but hadn't thought of actually singing it. I wasn't sure I wanted the song enunciated. I stopped playing. The Kuwaiti raised his eyebrow. "I'm not very good yet," I said. "I'm just learning."

"I can tell," he said. I paused. "That's not a guitar pick."

"It's for the oud. That's what I play."

"The oud is for old-fashioned Arabs," he said. I no longer wished to be an old-fashioned Arab. He extended his hand toward my modern guitar. "Here, let me play."

He didn't use a pick, sang a folk song in an American or Australian accent. His playing was bad, and his friend shook his head to an inconsistent beat. The Kuwaiti prince asked me if I liked the song as he handed me the guitar. I told him I did, and his face relaxed, looked grateful.

"I wonder if the speeches are done," his friend said as they stood up.

"Can you imagine what would happen if we win a war?"

"We almost won. Maybe next time we will."

I didn't think they believed. I resumed playing.

·   ·   ·

On Saturday, I played "Here Comes the Sun" for Lina. She was impressed, though not as surprised as I thought she'd be. "Aren't you going to sing?" she asked. I told her that would require more practice, since I had never sung before. She didn't seem to mind.

That afternoon, we left home sans guitar. Lina wore wild makeup and her mauve shorts. She looked like she'd fit better on Carnaby Street than in Beirut. We rode the bus four stops, and ended up at a coterie of buildings similar to ours, but much more upscale, seven buildings of nothing but marble and glass. She led me into one whose lobby was enclosed, air-conditioned, and stark. In the elevator she suggested that I not talk too much.

A girl my sister's age opened the door. She had two pigtails that began at the top of her head and descended ungracefully to her shoulders. "You brought your little brother?" The left corner of her mouth crunched up to meet her eye. "Yes," my sister replied and walked by her into the apartment. I hurriedly followed. I didn't need to be told that Pigtail Girl was the reason I had to play the guitar, that she had done something to offend Lina.

A dozen boys and girls milled about the large glass-enclosed balcony, chatting noisily and ignoring the rock music. "Try this," Lina said, pointing to an orange beanbag, and she joined two other girls.

All the teenagers ignored me. They seemed preoccupied with looking modern, cool, and Western. I concentrated on the music, helped myself to a bottle of Pepsi. My sister kept throwing glances at a tall blond boy across the room from her. He seemed too sure of himself, used to being the center of attention, and welcomed it with a modicum of disdain. With Lina, there was no modicum; her disdain was unequivocal and unfettered. Her glances grew less subtle and more hateful. I wondered where he fit in the unfolding drama. I didn't wonder for long.

Pigtail Girl walked into the room with a guitar. The instant the blond guy saw her, he lifted his arms as if warding off evil. "You have to play for us," she said, turning the music off.

"No, no," he said. "I don't want to ruin the mood."

"Please," the girl insisted. "For me."

My sister struck as quickly as a famished cobra. She snatched the guitar out of Pigtail's hand. "He doesn't have to," she said, as she walked toward me. "The little shrimp here can play. He's not bad." She handed me the instrument and plopped herself next to me on the beanbag. "Play," she ordered, nudging me with her elbow.

I played. My sister began to sing. Her two girlfriends joined in after the second verse. I didn't look up from the guitar, too nervous. The singing wasn't very good, but by the last verse, half the company had unleashed their voices.

"That was great," one of the girls said. "Let's do it again."

My sister wouldn't have been able to contain her glee had she cared to. She looked as if she'd eaten a whole jar of fresh honey. She wasn't the only one; her two friends were laughing.

"Let's not," Pigtail said. "Let's go back to real music now."

"Let's have your boyfriend try to play," Lina said.

"No," he snapped.

"Play another song," one of Lina's friends shouted to me. "You're good."

"I'm learning how to play," I said quietly. "I don't know many songs."

"Another song, please."

"It's okay," my sister said. "One song is enough for now."

"I can play another song if you can sing it," I told her. She looked puzzled. I opened "Something." Her eyes grew wide and their whites glimmered. She began to sing, too loudly, too happily.

I stopped my oud lessons.

— Eight —

And they all believed in fate. Do you think my grandmother would have married my grandfather were it not for fate? Do you not wonder how he won her?

It was destined. The tale was already told. Everything had been written.

He first saw her at the end of the Great War, in 1918, during the plagues, the lean times, when the infantilizing French occupation replaced the malicious Ottoman one. My grandmother was walking to school with a cousin. Najla wore a mandeel, but she didn't cover her features. She draped it upon her delicate shoulders. There was a lot of talk at the time about mandeels, sheer or opaque, and whether women should wear them, but I don't think she was making a statement. She enjoyed showing her face, her luxuriant hair, and my grandfather was lucky enough to catch sight of her. He was besotted. She was a mere fourteen. He was eighteen. He had seen pretty girls before. Yet she was beautiful and ever so graceful. He asked himself how he could make her remember him, and he thought, English. She was walking to the missionary school in the village. He said, in English, mind you, "Hello, my beautiful princess."

She laughed and said she was a sheikha, not a princess, and the cheeky boy should have known that. She left him standing bewildered on the hilly path. She had said "cheeky" in English, and he had no idea what it meant. He didn't know whom to ask. Because of his father, the doctor, he could speak some English, but because of the doctor's wife, he couldn't read that cursed language. He considered asking the bey, but my grandfather couldn't risk embarrassing him if he didn't know. He had to find an Englishman.

There were two of them trying to convert the village. My grandfather hung around the missionary school for two hours before he saw a foreigner exiting a building. My grandfather was polite but insistent. He said, "Pardon me, sir," over and over, but the man paid no attention; the English never listened. Finally, he shouted, and the missionary stopped. My grandfather asked him what the word meant, and the missionary shooed him away.

Waiting for Najla the next morning, my grandfather sat on a rise above the street, for he did not wish to appear improper. When she approached, he confessed, in Lebanese Druze dialect, "I don't know what the word 'cheeky' means. I don't think my English is very good."

My grandmother's cousin kept pulling at her sleeve, trying to get her to move along. My grandmother replied, looking at her feet, "I don't speak it well, either. I don't know what that word means. Last week, they taught us a story about the problem of cheeky boys talking to nice girls in the city of London."

And he knew she was the one for him.

You'd think there was no way. You might say, granted, this man was the bey's hakawati, and the bey loved him, but he had no family. The story of his origins was murky. People knew that he was born in some village in the Matn, but no one had heard of the Kharrats. The discovery that the Kharrats didn't exist wouldn't happen till much later. How would my grandfather be able to marry a nice Druze girl—a sheikha, no less? Why would a respected family consent to such a marriage?

Well, my grandmother was not as nice as she appeared. Her family had issues.

You know that my father's paternal grandfather was an English doctor, a missionary, and his paternal grandmother was the missionary's Armenian servant. My father's maternal grandparents were almost a carbon copy. My great-grandfather was a Druze doctor who many believed had become an English missionary, and my great-grandmother was his Albanian servant. Yes, it's true.

Settle down. There are differences, and that's what makes for a good story.

❦

At five in the morning three days after my arrival, I received the dreaded call. Lina said my father was critical and I should come straight to the hospital. I was shocked and unnerved by the call, but not surprised. My father's condition had been worsening. Yet, when the phone rang in the dark and I answered, the bed felt much too big.

My sister and her daughter stood weeping in the doorway, their arms intertwined. A multitude of doctors, interns, and nurses hovered above my father in his bed. They looked like seagulls hovering above food. I craned my head to look in, but a seagull closed the door. My sister gasped. One of the flimsy hospital fluorescents hiccupped. Salwa nudged me gently and pointed to the gurney along the corridor. I guided my sister to it and sat her down. Lina stared at an imaginary spot on the opposite wall. My feet felt unmoored, and the ground beneath felt soft. And yet I couldn't move from my spot leaning against the gurney. I had to remain motionless, as if my soul could get seasick. "They think his lungs might have collapsed." Lina wasn't talking to me. She was staring ahead, speaking softly, as if in confession. Her priest, I didn't look at her, either. "He had trouble breathing the whole night." She sighed. "It got worse, until he couldn't get any air in. He looked so scared. He's probably terrified out of his mind right now." The groans of a patient two doors away marked time. They were oddly comforting; I imagined their slow pace calming the frantic doctors behind the closed door. With every breath, fear seared my lungs.

❦

Around the year 1880, the sultan pasha left Istanbul on the advice of his viziers. The effete Ottoman Empire had been gasping and wheezing for breath, and it was thought that a goodwill tour of his lands might remind his no longer so loyal subjects to pay their taxes promptly. During his stay in Lebanon, he spent one night in my great-grandfather's village as the guest of the bey. The sultan was so impressed with the bey's generosity that he decided to offer his host a remarkable gift, one of his own servants.

"Why is that brother of a whore offering me a maid?" the bey yelled the next morning. "Does he mean my service was lacking? Is he saying my mansion needs cleaning? And he expects me to send someone all the way to Tripoli to get her." He fumed throughout the morning open-house. The daily visitors and supplicants drank their Turkish coffee in silence, too afraid to speak. It was at that inauspicious moment that my great-grandfather, the young Sheikh Mahdallah Arisseddine, arrived to pay his respects. The bey greeted him with

"And you, my boy, will reward my faith by going to Tripoli and bringing me this girl."

Mahdallah came from a titled family of sheikhs, not princes or beys, not even important sheikhs, but, still, an eminent, respected family of some consequence. He was the youngest of seven, and the first in the family, the first in the entire village, to attend university. His father, not well off to begin with, couldn't afford to pay for Mahdallah's college education after raising seven offspring. Wanting to have a Druze doctor in the village, the bey had stepped in. At the time that my great-grandfather was unceremoniously dispatched to fetch the servant, he was one year away from a medical degree from the Syrian Protestant College. He lived in a small hellhole of a room in Beirut; he visited his family—and paid his respects to the bey—in the mountain village whenever he had the chance.

There were many other reasons for the bey to fend for the Arisseddine family. The beys, in all their history and incarnations, were never altruistic. It was obvious while my great-grandfather was still in school with the missionaries that he was brighter than the other village boys. The bey wanted the most intelligent man beholden to him, so he paid for his medical schooling. The bey also hated the fact that someone was smarter than he was, which was why he never tired of having the young man run menial errands for him.

The beys were uniformly unintelligent, probably because of inbreeding—there were only two other families that the men were allowed to marry from. According to my grandfather, inbreeding negatively affected the males, but the women in the family were exceptionally quick. Therefore, my grandfather insisted, the bey's wife would have recognized that changes were afoot. The politics of the land would not remain the same, and, to maintain their power, the beys couldn't rely solely on the blind support of the ignorant. They would need a new source of loyalty. Mahdallah Arisseddine and his family, particularly his second son, Jalal, would prove to be the bey's boon in later years. But now I'm ahead of myself.

❧

My father was drugged unconscious, his head slightly raised. He looked unfamiliar, his nose now enormous, the only part of him that hadn't shrunk. The ventilator's thick accordion tube forced its way inside his mouth to his lungs, coercing his chest into expansion and contraction. His chest, sparsely haired, dry, taut, looked like an Indian medicine drum. Thin, translucent ocher-colored tubes drew blood from his side into a dialysis machine, which pumped the cleansed blood back into his system. A catheter attached to a suction machine went up his penis, through the urethra, sucking out his urine.

Effusions of sound. My sister weeping in the corner, her sharp intakes of breath in discord with those of the ventilator. The chugalug of dialysis, the technician in charge of the machine seeming mesmerized by its churning liquid sounds. The metronomic beats of the monitor. Jagged Richter line in red, loopy one in white, a wavy yellow, and a green on a screen above my father's head. Could Mesmer have ever envisioned the hypnotic movement and sound of these modern contraptions? I needed to slap myself, remind myself this wasn't a dream, nor was it a repeat of an earlier scene. We'd huddled around a hospital bed for my mother years earlier, and now my father.

I stood at the foot of the bed, staring at him, my left hand touching his foot. My niece entered the room and waddled toward me, looking as if she might give birth then and there. She stood beside me and stroked my back. My sister turned around, wiped her tears with the back of her forefingers.

"One of you has to go out there," Salwa said. "I need a break. There are a lot of people, and your aunt is driving me crazy."

"I'll do it," Lina said. She moved to my father's bedside, kissed his forehead. "Everything will be all right," she told him, her voice breaking again. She covered her mouth, turned around, took out tissues from her bra. "Talk to him," she said. "Tin Can says he can still hear us. Comfort him. You know how frightened he gets."

Salwa took my father's hand and squeezed it. "It's me, Grandfather." She looked at me, motioned with her head to the chair. I moved it for her, and she lowered her weight onto it. "Are you in pain?" she asked him. She sounded so mature, confident. "Can you hear me? If you can, squeeze my hand."

He squeezed. My fingers twitched with a mind of their own.

"Are you in pain? Squeeze my hand if yes." He squeezed again. "Is it the pillows?" Squeeze. On either side of the bed, Salwa and I raised him a bit by his shoulders. We fluffed the pillows beneath him. "Is this better? Do you need water?" Salwa dipped gauze in a cup and wiped it across his mouth, above and below the ventilator tube. He pressed his lips together, holding the gauze in place for a brief moment. "Your lips look very dry. Would you like me to run moisturizer on them?" He didn't squeeze. "Do you still hear me?" She stroked his forehead. "Sleep now. I know the dialysis hurts, but it won't last long. You'll have new blood. The kidneys aren't working, and that's why you've been feeling awful. Don't be afraid. We're all here."

She reached out to me. I moved to her side, took her offered hand. She directed me to her shoulders, and I massaged them. "The anesthesiologist said the drugs make him forget everything," she told me. "I don't think he's really awake, do you? It's probably better that way."

❧

The story of how my great-grandfather fell in love is relatively well known, so I won't get into it here. Just think Tristan and Isolde on a train from Tripoli to Beirut, without the deaths or whale weights. There was singing, though, of a different kind.

Who am I kidding? I have to tell you the story, at least the highlights. I can't help myself. Besides, you might be one of the few people who haven't heard it.

The Ottoman sultan must have been trying to impress the bey, for the gift was notable, even though it went unappreciated by its recipient. My great-grandmother Mona was more than a maid, not simply a housekeeper. She was an entertainer; she played the oud, had a delightfully soft voice, and knew more than one hundred songs, including some folk melodies from her native Albania. Because she performed the songs of praise well, she was one of the sultan's favorites, which was why she had remained a virgin in his harem.

I believe she lost her virginity on the train trip.

My great-grandfather must have cursed his luck and the bey's entire family while he made the long and tiring journey to the northern city. But then he arrived at the sultan's ship to claim her. He stopped cursing his luck when he saw her walk down the plank with her small oud and her belongings in a satchel. And he thanked God when, four hours later, she sang a story of love that night on the train, sweet chords, dulcet tones. As for my great-grandmother: she had never met a soul who looked at her so adoringly. Hope flowered in her heart, hope of being seen as someone different, someone better, hope of being seen.

"I can't let you clean house for the bey," he told her. "I just can't."

"I do what I must."

"I'll not have you sing for another man."

At the village, my great-grandfather didn't go directly to the bey's mansion. He stopped at his parents' house, dropped off the oud, and walked to the mansion, with my great-grandmother a step behind. He made the introductions and said, "I beg your indulgence, O Bey. This maid would be of great value to me. I live alone, with no one to take care of me. My room needs a woman's touch. I can't have guests since I don't know how to brew coffee. If you can spare her, I'd love to own her."

The bey laughed. "You think me a fool. She'll be doing more than brewing coffee for you. She's not much to look at, but she'll do. I don't need her. Take her. We can't have the village's future doctor remain inexperienced in the ways of the world."

My great-grandparents walked out together with the bey's blessing.

And my great-grandfather said, "I wish to spend my life with you."

My great-grandmother said, "I will be your family and you will be my man."

And my great-grandmother never played the oud for anyone else again.

Years earlier, when the bey married, twenty-one village women cooked for two whole weeks, and the wedding lasted six days. When Mahdallah's brother married, his wedding lasted three days. My great-grandparents' wedding lasted all of one hour.

Mahdallah had to state the Shahada and convert to Islam. His first conversion.

Mona brewed coffee for his guests in the small room. They were happy and content, took care of each other, and began to consider a family. Their first son, my great-uncle Aref, was born in Beirut before my great-grandfather returned to assume his rightful duties as the doctor of his home village.

But before I forget, I want to tell you why all Mahdallah's sons, my great-uncles, have short names (Aref, Jalal, Ma'an).

On his first day of school, when my great-grandfather, a not very tall eight-year-old boy, met his teacher, she, in her prim, proper British manner, asked if he could speak English.

"Yes, madame. I can."

She had her doubts, it seemed. She asked if he could read and write the language.

"Yes, madame. I can."

In a firm, clipped voice, she demanded that he go up to the board and write his name.

He did:

MAHDALLAH ARISSEDDINE

"My dear young man," the teacher said, "your name is longer than you are."

And my great-grandfather was so shamed that he swore none of his descendants would ever endure such ignominy.

❧

My niece was crying. My father had stopped responding to her. The technician nodded off next to the dialysis machine. The blood in the tubes looked more black than red, and it re-entered my father no redder. The ventilator inhaled and my father exhaled; he breathed in when it expired. Was that an inversely proportional relationship, or a direct relationship? My math failed me.

I wanted to pray but didn't know to whom I should direct my pleading. There was no map to follow. My left hand caressed my father's foot, came across moistureless crags. Lines forming unreal countries along his instep and sole. I walked to the nightstand and poured the verbena-scented lotion onto my hands. I massaged the moisturizer onto the arid skin of his foot. I loved the scent, my mother's favorite. It made sense that he'd continue to use it. The miniature frame was still next to his bed. Her picture. She retained the same ageless look in every photograph, a regal amalgam of severity and benevolence. I wondered whether I was truly seeing the undersized photo or my memory was filling gaps where my eyesight failed.

Help me, Mother. He was your husband.

The technician opened his eyes. He looked dazed for a moment, stupefied. "Only a few minutes left," he announced officially.

My niece and I could clearly see the time blinking two minutes, thirty-seven seconds, in big red digits. Thirty-six. Thirty-five.

Salwa gripped my father's hand. "Everything will be all right, Grandfather."

The machine beeped: a continuous high pitch that was surprisingly comforting. Pleased with himself, the technician restated the obvious: "It's over." He slid aside the single cotton sheet that was my father's cover. He unhooked tubes from tubes, re-coiled the machine's, opened a small trapdoor in the front, and put them in. He clamped shut the lonely tubes sprouting from the bloodstained, iodine-blotched skin of my father's side. Medicinal smells.

"Are we going to remove the tubes?" I asked.

He stared back with confused and tarnished eyes. I wanted to relieve my father of some intrusion. If only I could pull out one tube—one single tube—we would all feel better.

The technician packed his machine more quickly. My niece watched everything in bafflement. We were strangers in a land where the natives spoke an incomprehensible language.

Mahdallah worked as a doctor for a year before he was approached by one of his old teachers. The Englishman made my great-grandfather a sweet offer. The Anglicans would send him to England to study further, to practice and learn in superior hospitals. The mission would pay for everything, for his entire family's stay in England. The mission, however, could only make this offer to a member of its own congregation. To accept, Mahdallah had to be baptized.

My great-grandfather wasn't religious. It was just that you didn't change your religion. It wasn't done. He may have become a Muslim, but he didn't practice, didn't take it seriously. He did it to get married. As a Druze, he couldn't marry a Muslim or any non-Druze. All he did was state the Shahada, testify that there is no God but God and Muhammad is the Prophet of God. That was it. No big deal. Just a formality.

Baptism. Now, that's a commitment.

The Anglicans had been trying to baptize Druze for years. The two groups were stuck with each other, like Nile crocodiles and plovers. Most of the infrastructure of the Ottoman Empire was in the cities and Muslim villages. The Catholic French and their charities directed their work at the Christian villages. The English and their missionaries couldn't set up shop except in the Druze areas. The conversion rate was not very high.

An Englishwoman had pitched camp in the village in 1843. Her name was Helen Kitchen. With a seemingly endless supply of funds, she had a compound built, consisting of three impressive buildings, the first in the village with tiled roofs. There was already a school for boys, so she started one for girls. She made conversion a condition of entry. Girls wanted to learn. They made the sign of the cross, did their homework, left school, got married, and had kids, and no one remembered they were no longer supposed to be Druze.

After a few years, Mrs. Kitchen realized that the girls studied their Bibles and could sing hymns with the best of them but didn't consider this a religion. When she attempted to make the ritual more serious (baptism?), the girls were shocked and embarrassed. Mrs. Kitchen stopped making conversion a requirement for enrollment. The girls still studied the Bible, sang hymns and Christmas carols, but there was no pretense anymore. Once, when a missionary confronted her, accusing, "But these girls aren't Christians," she replied, "Neither was Jesus."

She educated thousands of girls, many from neighboring villages. She actually became a local. When she died, she was buried in a Druze cemetery. To this day, many Lebanese women, Druze and Christian, visit her grave and keep the site clean.

Mahdallah converted. He was watered. Secretly, though. He refused to baptize his son, Aref. No one suggested his wife convert. He would spend the rest of his life denying that deed.

The family spent four or five years in London. The gray weather didn't suit them. They didn't mind the cold—their village was colder—but the lack of sunshine ensured they would never settle in that city.

The village gossips said: The gray weather is making the harem girl barren.

The village gossips said: And God will never bless the betrayer again.

The village gossips were wrong on both counts. My great-grandparents had other children, but it took time—not as long as Abraham and Sarah, but long enough for gossip.

But here are two facts, documented and checked:

My great-grandparents Dr. Mahdallah and Mona Arisseddine and their son, Aref, around five years old at the time, boarded a Belgian-registered ship, the *Leopold II*, from England to the port city of Beirut, in June 1889.

My other great-grandfather, the esteemed missionary Dr. Simon Twining, accompanied by his recently betrothed, the heart of darkness, sailed from England to Beirut on the identical ship, the *Leopold II*, in June 1890.

The doctors would surely have met had they been on the same crossing. What would they have talked about, standing on deck, holding on to the railing, looking at the sun drowning in the golden Mediterranean? They wore similar cotton suits of Western cut, white shirts, ties. Their hats were also similar. Mahdallah would not wear his fez until he reached the village. They had countless things in common, or would have in times to come, and the conversation would not lag until, finally, Ah, sir, what say you we blend the seed of my loins with your seed and produce some exasperatingly strange characters: the wicked hag of the mountains, the naïve and haughty villager, the parsimonious simpleton, the talented, frustrated homosexual, and the sexual Sisyphus, who would betray his family over and over and over and over again?

Then there was the evil Sitt Hawwar.

Upon deciding to return to the village of his birth, Mahdallah, while he was still in London, commissioned the village builder, a man by the name of Hawwar, to put up a house. Hawwar charged the young doctor an exorbitant amount of money. One of Mahdallah's brothers was supposed to oversee the building and its financing, but he must have been distracted, for when the young doctor returned, he found a windowless skeleton of a house with patchy cement floors and only an undercoat of paint.

Mahdallah complained. Hawwar promised to finish the job quickly, before the winter snows. Mahdallah and his family could wait out the house at his parents'. But the wife, the harem girl, the Albanian, insisted the bare-bones house was her home. She moved her family in, shaming the builder into working harder and faster.

That was a mistake. And she compounded the mistake. She didn't know any better—she was a foreigner. Mona Arisseddine told her neighbors the truth. She said they could have built three houses for what they paid. She mentioned how much her husband paid for each material. The stove wasn't even new: you could see it was used. "Look," she kept saying, "look."

Sitt Hawwar, the builder's much younger wife, became Mona Arisseddine's enemy.

Mona Arisseddine told people the builder was a crook.

Sitt Hawwar told people the doctor was a Christian.

Three Druze men showed up at Mahdallah's clinic one morning to kill the good doctor. The only thing that saved him was a heavy patient load that day. The men walked into the clinic and asked to see him. They were told they would be next. A parent with a sick child entered, and the men decided to let the doctor help the child before they murdered him. Then came an elderly woman, a man with a broken foot, another sick child, and so on. At the end of the day, the sister-in-law of one of the would-be slayers arrived with her ill daughter. She asked her relative what he was doing there, and he replied that he was waiting to exterminate the doctor.

"Are you crazy?" she yelled. "This man is treating my daughter and you want to kill him? Why don't you go kill a government official or something?"

The three embarrassed killers left, and a village story was born. And the bey warned that he would personally torture and kill anyone who attempted to injure the *Druze* doctor.

"If that woman hadn't shown up," my grandfather said, "you kids wouldn't be here. Think about that. It was fate. Mahdallah had converted, so he had insulted their faith. Neighbors had killed neighbors before. Why wasn't your great-grandfather killed? You ask me and I'll tell you. It was because I was meant to marry your grandmother, of course. Do you see that?"

"No," I said. The other kids didn't even hear him. Anwar was too busy pummeling Hafez. Lina, who had been sitting next to me, had disappeared with my other cousins. Little Mona was in Aunt Samia's arms, fidgeting.

"Stop it, Baba," Aunt Samia said. "It's Eid al-Adha, no time for your crazy stories. You've no idea what a bad example you set." She stood up, put her daughter down. "And you," she admonished me, "why do you just sit there and listen? Why don't you get into a fight with your cousins? You want people to think you're a coward? Get in there and smack one of them."

I jumped off the sofa and ran out of the room, looking for my mother. She wasn't in the dining room, where the rest of the family was yelling. I sprinted to the terrace. Every apartment in the building had a large balcony, but Aunt Samia's penthouse had a terrace encircling it. I envied Anwar and Hafez for being able to run around whenever they felt like it.

My father said Aunt Samia got the biggest apartment because she was the eldest.

My mother said Aunt Samia got it by whining for ten whole days that she deserved it because she was married to the most helpless man in the world.

I ran almost all the way around the terrace before I found my mother leaning against a wall, smoking a cigarette. My father was talking, gazing warily at her. She stared out toward Beirut's dappled rooftops, distracted, as if counting the tines of each television antenna on every roof in the city.

"You've been spending too much time alone," my father said, "and that makes it harder for you to tolerate other people. It's a family get-together, Layla. You can't leave before lunch."

After each drag on her cigarette, my mother moved her hand to cup the bun at the back of her head, as if doubting its existence. The smoke would circle the bun for an instant before dying.

"If those children were mine," she said, "I would short-circuit them. Poof. Clack. Everything tumbles. The motor sputters, rumble-rumble, dies. No more noise."

My father's face tightened in shock. "That's an awful thing to say, even for you. How could you?"

My mother noticed me. Her lips curled into a smile. "Osama, I don't want you hanging around your cousins too much. Too many bad habits."

I knew she'd want me to ask this now, at this moment. "Is it true they kill Christians in the village?"

My father looked at me in horror. "Of course it's not true. Who told you that?"

"Grandfather said the village men almost killed your grandfather because he was a Christian."

"How many times have I told you not to believe any of my father's stories? He's a hakawati. He makes things up. My grandfather wasn't

Christian. He was a Druze. You know that. If anyone tried to kill him, it was about something else."

"Yes," my mother said. The sun struck her face, and she looked brighter. "It was probably about something like an elevator. You know how the Druze are. They're hospitable, and they take care of their own. Mind your seventh neighbor and all that."

"Don't do this," my father said. "The old man's tales are more than enough. Let's not confuse the boy with more, I beg you."

My mother straightened. "You're right." Her crisp voice melded with the sound of approaching steps. "No one tried to kill any Christians in the village. Your grandfather makes things up."

Lina turned the corner, followed by Anwar, who was always trying to engage her in some convoluted game. "They kill Christians in the village?" she asked.

"No," my father said. "No, they don't." He turned around and faced the railing.

"If it's true," Anwar told Lina, "I'll have to slit your throat with a knife."

"And before you do," Lina replied without missing a beat, "I'll take that knife and shove it up a place that will surprise you."

Anwar gasped. My parents both yelled Lina's name. "I have to go talk to that loon," my father said. "Things can't go on like this. He's a menace."

"Don't." My mother held out her hand. "You'll only upset yourself, and you'll regret it later. Let it go. Nothing can be done. Not now. Not here." He took her hand. "Family," she said, and pulled him to her. She dropped her spent cigarette.

"Oh, no," Anwar said. "Mother gets upset if anyone leaves cigarettes on the terrace."

"I'm sure she does." My mother stepped on the cigarette with her stiletto heel, her calf tensing. She twisted the ball of her foot to the right, to the left, to the right. She took my father's arm and walked away, leaving a trivial stain of ash, mashed filter, and loose tobacco in her wake.

About the elevator. When Mahdallah returned from London, he was asked by the villagers what he had seen in the great land of abroad.

Many wonders. Strange inhabitants. There were buildings in London where people did not use stairs. A room moved, carried passengers from floor to floor. Moved up and down. Buildings had many floors. Visitors didn't have to tire themselves by walking up stairs. Why, in the great city of New York, buildings were even higher. Twenty stories or more.

The villagers went away shaking their heads. Should such a foolish man be allowed to walk the streets of the village? Was he dangerous? Should a madman be allowed to mingle with the innocent? A committee was sent to interview the doctor subtly. Luckily for our family, Mona was there. The committee said some villagers had the notion that buildings in the land of the foreign had mobile rooms within them. How exactly did Londoners move between floors?

Before the doctor could reply, his wife jumped in. Why, they ascended and descended stairs, of course. Climbed the stairs when they wanted to go up. Most stairs were made of cement and stone, some of wood, and the latter were often rickety. The doctor stared at his wife, uncomprehending. The committee waited for him to add something. There were great banisters, he said. Beautifully carved. Some staircases were marvelously ornate. Some buildings had a flight of imposing stairs on each side, complete with balustrades and carved mythical animals.

The committee apologized to the doctor. The villagers were simple folk, they said. They always misheard or misunderstood what was being said. The committee begged forgiveness and left the well-grounded doctor to his own devices.

Finally, my great-grandparents had their second child. Jalal Arisseddine was born in 1891. His brother, Aref, was eight then. Mona might have hoped that with Jalal's arrival people would stop referring to her as the harem girl, since she was now the mother of two sheikhs.

Jalal would grow up to be an important personality in Lebanese history. He was an attorney, a keen student of letters, possessor of a piercing intellect, a man worthy of admiration. Even his critics, and he had many because of his writings rejecting pan-Arabism, respected him. He was jailed three times by the French colonial government. His last internment coincided with the end of Vichy rule in Lebanon. He was released in November 1943, on Independence Day.

Every day he spent in prison, his aged mother brought him food, though she fasted in protest. She could barely walk, but she refused to have anyone carry the meals for her. She waited outside the prison doors on the day of his release.

He came out a hero. She remained that harem girl.

My great-uncle Ma'an Arisseddine was born in 1894. My father loved him deeply, for he was the man who gave him his early breaks. In the grand scheme of stories, he was nothing, almost an unmentionable, for he was not an odd character or an interesting one. He was a thread, one of many, without which the tapestry would crumble, the yarn fray, and the tale unravel.

But I know of another thread.

Even though the evil Sitt Hawwar loathed my great-grandmother, or probably because of it, she showed up to congratulate the new mother when baby Ma'an was born. She dragged along her husband, the builder, who was wearing a robe of Chinese silk. She made her husband walk around the small living room. The villagers oohed and aahed, admiring their first view of foreign silk, ignoring the newborn. Now, the proverb was that one should look after one's seventh neighbor, and Sitt Hawwar was Mona Arisseddine's second neighbor on the right, so Mona should have treated her even better, or at least been more circumspect. But, then, there was history. And Mona Arisseddine asked her neighbor how much that robe cost.

This story about neighbors arrives from far away, so listen. The parable is Iraqi, all the way from the ancient city of Baghdad; it flew here on waves of air, needing to alight in cavernous ears. Long ago, in a time long past, there lived an honorable Bedouin who was so hospitable and charitable that he was known as Abou al-Karam, Father of Generosity. One day, a poor man raised his tent pole next to the Bedouin's, and of course Abou al-Karam made sure his neighbor lacked nothing, offering him food, water, and clothing. For seven years, whenever the tribe traveled, their tents remained adjacent. The neighbor became known as Bin al-Kareem, Son of the Generous One. After each of the tribe's raids, Abou al-Karam would share the spoils with his neighbor: horses, mares, camels, food, slaves, the enemy tribe's possessions.

By the end of those seven years, Bin al-Kareem and his sons had become wealthy. By the end of those seven years, Abou al-Karam's youngest daughter had become a desert beauty, lithe and tall as a poplar, graceful as a doe. And Bin al-Kareem's younger son wanted her. He courted her. He sang verses for her, followed her when she went to the well, knelt outside her tent when she tried to sleep, whispering endearments. The beautiful girl refused him. He stalked her wherever she went, made it impossible for her to move freely. And the girl told her father, who said, "One night more and you will not have to worry about this nefarious boy."

That night, when the girl went to bed, the boy appeared outside her tent and began whispering to her. "Wait but one more night," she said, "and you shall receive your just reward."

At dawn, Abou al-Karam gave the order to break camp. Later that morning, the camels and pack animals were laden and the tribe began to march. For all of the previous seven years, wherever Abou al-Karam pitched his tent in a new camp, Bin al-Kareem pitched his right next to it. That day, arriving at a suitable pasture, Abou al-Karam searched until he found a spot next to a teeming anthill. There he made his home. When Bin al-Kareem arrived to pitch his tent, he said, "O dear neighbor, there is an anthill on my site."

"So there is," replied Abou al-Karam, "and God's earth is wide."

Bin al-Kareem said nothing further. He drove his family and his belongings away from the tribe, up north, far away from his once-beloved neighbor. But his heart ached, and his mind was troubled. He relived the insult over and over in his head. Why? he asked himself. Why did his friend betray him? One night, he had a dream. He saw Abou al-Karam's daughter walking in the desert, followed by wisps of clouds, and he divined what might have happened. The next morning, while hunting with his elder son, he said, "What a shame we had to leave our good neighbor. And that daughter. What a beautiful girl. Our family is inferior to hers and there was no hope of matrimony between us, but, still, what a gorgeous lass. A shame we left before you had a chance with her."

"Shame?" the son yelled. "You call that a shame? Shame on you for uttering such words. Was she not my sister? Did we not eat of the same food? Did we not share the same honor for seven years? Only sons of whores and sons of shame would consider what you're thinking."

"Forgive me, my son," the father said. "The sorrow of parting must have clouded my judgment. Let us return to our tent and forget we had this conversation."

The next day, while hunting, Bin al-Kareem said to his younger son, "What a shame about that adorable girl."

"Shame?" sighed the boy. "One night more, Father, and she would have been mine. One night more."

And the father unsheathed his sword and cut off his son's head.

And the father wound woolen thread around his son's head, and wound, and wound, until he had a large ball of yarn. He waited until he met a traveler heading south, and he asked, "Will you carry this gift to my friend Abou al-Karam?"

When the traveler arrived at Abou al-Karam's camp, he found him in his tent, sitting with guests. The traveler placed the gift before Abou al-Karam, who asked, "Who sends this gift?"

"A man who called you his friend and brother," said the traveler.

Abou al-Karam summoned his slaves to unwind the yarn. As they unraveled it, they uncovered the son's head. And Abou al-Karam beat his chest in sorrow, sighed the breath of remorse. He understood that his neighbor of seven years was as true as a brother and as jealous of his name. The guests demanded the tale, and Abou al-Karam told it. The guests all said in one voice that he must marry his daughter to his neighbor's elder son, which would make Abou al-Karam and Bin al-Kareem brothers.

And so it was. Two neighbors, one superior and one inferior, but equals in honor and pride, became one family, and lived long to take pleasure in their children.

And Mahdallah Arisseddine worked hard. He became a well-respected doctor in the region. Patients arrived from all over. Yet he couldn't increase the size of his family by much.

Finally, ten years after his third son was born, Mona got pregnant again. This time, everyone knew it was a girl. They had waited long enough. The eldest, Aref, was already twenty-one years old. When Mona was in her eighth month, the doctor was asked to trek to Aleppo to heal a man from the al-Atrash family, a prince from Jabal al-Druze in Syria who had fallen gravely ill while traveling. Mona objected, but Mahdallah said he would be back before she gave birth. She said she didn't believe him. He said he had never lied to her. She let him go.

Her last words to him were "I'm calling her Najla, after my mother."

For, although the doctor healed the prince, the doctor died. He spent his last few days away from his family, wasting away in a strange bed, trying to medicate himself, alone, in a city farther north than Tripoli, where he met his wife, a much longer journey.

Like my great-grandmother Lucine Guiragossian, my great-grandfather Mahdallah Arisseddine died of amoebic dysentery. His death in 1904 came four years after hers; his was in the city of Aleppo, a little bit farther south than Urfa, the city where she died.

He died a Druze, but he was buried in a Christian cemetery, since there were no Druze cemeteries in Aleppo. God rest his soul.

This would not be Mona's only tragedy. My great-uncle Aref was a wild young man. While his father was still alive, he managed to keep himself under some semblance of control. His father's influence was such that the boy graduated at the top of his class and enrolled in medical school at his father's alma mater. Mahdallah rented him a small room in Beirut. Aref studied hard, but he also played hard. Rumors of his mad conquests trickled to the village.

To his impressionable teenage brother, Jalal, he said, "All women are different. A Druze woman tastes like half-cooked lamb with rosemary and peppers, a Maronite tastes like beef marinated in olive oil, a Sunni girl like calf's liver cooked in white wine, a Shiite like chicken in vinegar with pine nuts, an Orthodox like fish in tahini sauce, a Jewish woman like baked kibbeh, a Melchite like semolina stew, a Protestant like chicken soup, and an Alawite like okra in beef stock."

And Aref tasted them all and more. He wanted a bite of each sect of his land, and that desire developed into a gastronomical obsession. The Sunni (university girl), Maronite (housewife in Sinn el-Fil), Orthodox (housewife in Ain el-Rumaneh), and Druze (maid in Beiteddine) were not difficult to obtain. The Jewish wife of Mr. Salim Kuhin wasn't hard, either; he met her outside the downtown synagogue. For the Melchite, he had to travel all the way to the Bekaa Valley, to Zahlé, and find Mrs. Ballat, the manager of the pension where he stayed. The Shiite was difficult. He traveled to the south and met a number of girls, but Sidon didn't open its gates for him. Tyre resisted him as it did Alexander the Great. He had Alexander's moxie and cunning, but he lacked Two-Horned's patience and resources. Tyre defeated Aref. He was lucky enough to find a Shiite prostitute in a nightclub near the port of Beirut.

Three days after Aref's twenty-first birthday, his father died. Aref shook off whatever constraints he may have had. The Protestant was his biology professor, an Englishwoman, but then he decided that, as a nonnational, she wasn't a representative morsel of the delicious sectarian spectrum. He had to search for three months, fail one class, and barely pass another before he found an appropriate Lebanese Protestant. He rode the train north to Tripoli to savor an Alawite, had to live there for two months before the seduction was complete. He made love to an Armenian in Bourj Hammoud on the way back to Beirut.

When he finished the entire menu, he celebrated with a drunken, boastful evening with friends, and then he returned to the village for a few days, his medical education all but forgotten. Those days dragged into a few more, and those into a few more still, as he grew fond of a married woman, Sitt Yasmine, whose husband was a farmhand for the bey.

Every morning, Aref hid behind the village's great oak tree, waiting for the farmhand to leave. Then my great-uncle would ride his horse to the house, tie the reins to the window shutter, and entertain himself with Sitt Yasmine. If only he had tied the horse to the back window. The neighbors told the husband he was being cuckolded, but he didn't believe at first. One morning, a friend took the farmhand by the arm and brought him back to his house. "See," his friend said, "there's the horse." The farmhand yelled, screamed, "O Sheikh, get out of my house now or I will commit murder." Aref escaped out the back. The farmhand and his friend gave chase, intending to do him harm with a rake, a hoe, and an empty bucket between them. Aref laughed, tried to tie his belt while running. He reached a cascade of olive orchards, the silver-green trees in rows that stretched to the bottom of the hill. He jumped across into the lower orchard, landed on the soft earth, ran a little more, and jumped again, but this time his foot caught in an olive branch. He spun in midair like a tetherball and shot headfirst to the ground. He died on impact.

The farmhand returned the horse to my great-grandmother. She must have opened the door for him with my grandmother Najla in her arms.

Miraculously, Sitt Yasmine remained unharmed. It is said the farmhand was so shocked by witnessing the demise of a sheikh that he forgot his wife's betrayal and didn't remember to beat her.

When my grandfather decided he wanted my grandmother for a wife, he sent word to her brother Jalal, already a respected family man at twenty-seven. Jalal had left the confines of the village for a more cosmopolitan life in Beirut. Since Ismail al-Kharrat didn't have a family to represent him, he sent one of his admirers, a charming but not very gifted fellow, a sheikh himself, and the first cousin of the bey on his mother's side. My great-uncle received him as a good host should, but when the guest requested his sister's hand for the hakawati, Jalal said a simple no. My great-uncle would have laughed, but, as an Arab intellectual, he lacked a sense of humor.

"And that bastard just said no," my grandfather said. "He didn't elaborate, felt no need to explain his position. I had my guy prepared with all kinds of wonderful things to say about me and why I'd make a good husband for your grandmother, but the bastard didn't have the courtesy to let my guy speak. Just no."

"You can't call him a bastard, Baba," Aunt Samia said. "He's my uncle. He's the children's great-uncle. You can't just curse him like that."

"The man was a bastard," Uncle Halim insisted. Already drunk, he sipped his arak delicately. He took another sip and then gulped down the rest. "It's not like Baba is adding anything new to the equation."

"You're taking his side?" Aunt Samia said. She stood up, handed Little Mona to her bewildered husband. "Of all people, you have the gall to say something like that?" Uncle Akram held the girl with his arms straight and outstretched, as if she were smelly locker-room laundry. "In *my* house?" Mona's legs dangled in midair. Her father turned his head left and right, hoping someone would rescue him. "You choose to do this in front of all these kids? Do you care if they all grow up to be gypsies with no morals? Maybe you want them to grow up to be Kurds?" She walked toward the kitchen, pivoted, returned to take her daughter. "And you," she admonished her husband, "you sit here and listen to him insult the family and you do nothing."

"But it's not my family." Uncle Akram looked to my father for support.

"You always resort to that, don't you? Whenever I need you, you hide." She took a deep breath, raised her voice. "Uncle Jalal was called a bastard. What are you going to do about it?"

"But he's not my uncle," her husband said.

"And he is a bastard," Uncle Halim said, snickering.

"No," Aunt Samia said. "No, no, no." Her daughter began to pout and whimper.

Lina grinned. My mother looked at her and winked. Uncle Jihad, who was sitting on the corner couch, entered the winking fest. Then he nodded at my mother, as if agreeing to something, and threw his contribution into the ring.

"Osama," he called loudly, "what happened to the money you borrowed from me?" I didn't understand. "Did you spend all of it?" His voice didn't match his face. My mother was trying to catch his attention. She nodded to Little Mona and raised her eyebrows. "Samia, my dear," he said, "why don't you give me the precious darling?" Aunt Samia, still staring at Uncle Halim, handed her daughter over distractedly. With the little girl in his arms, Uncle Jihad returned to me. "Did you think I'd forget the money, Osama?" He waited a few breaths before adding, "Did you waste the money"—breath—"or did you hide"—breath—"the money?"

My mother grinned, shook her head slowly from side to side in admiration, as if telling Uncle Jihad she was in awe. He shrugged, as if replying it was nothing.

You could count. One. Two. And the jinn of hell broke their chains.

"You stole my money," Aunt Samia shouted at Uncle Halim, who recoiled visibly. Her face was as red as if dunked in tomato paste, and her eyes were as white and wide as saucers.

"Samia, no," my father yelled, but she was off in her outraged world.

"It was my money. It was mine. My mother wanted to give it to me. To me. My money."

"Samia," my grandfather pleaded, "stop it."

"The neighbors, Samia," my father added. "The neighbors will hear."

Anwar and Hafez pushed all the way back in their chairs. Lina sat forward. Uncle Jihad seemed to have lost interest. He tried to distract Little Mona, who was staring at her livid mother.

"You hate Jalal because he wanted you to give the money back to Mama. But you hid it. He isn't the bastard. You are. You're a lowlife."

"If it weren't for the children," Uncle Halim yelled back, "I'd smack you from here to the village, you big-mouthed idiot." Aunt Nazek moved closer to him, tried to calm him, but he stood up. "I returned the money. I didn't hide it. You're a big fat liar." He shook his finger at her. "You're lucky the children are here."

"This is unreal," my grandfather said.

"I'm not a liar. You hid it. You hid the money."

My father stood up. From the look on his face, you could see it was over. He seethed. "Everybody just eat shit and shut up," he screamed. Quiet. My father sighed. "Samia. He was eight years old. You were—what?—twelve? What's the matter with you? You were children. What the hell does it matter what he did then? How much did he hide? Was it one quarter or two?"

"I don't care," she said, but we all heard the defeated whine creep back into her voice. "He stole my money." Her rapid breathing slowed. "He stole my money again. I can prove it."

"Eight?" my mother asked Uncle Jihad.

"Yes." He nodded, stroked Little Mona's hair. "I was about as old as this one here. I was traumatized, I tell you." He blinked once, twice. Looked up to the ceiling in mock sorrow. "That incident scarred my life."

"And you." My father turned to his. "Why do you keep telling my kids these stories?"

"They're not just your kids," my grandfather replied. "And don't blame me for this one. I was telling how I married your mother. An old man has a right to reminisce, and children need to know where they came from." He refused to look at my father.

"Every time you tell one of your stories, something horrible happens."

"There's nothing wrong with the story of how I met your mother."

My mother sat up, stretched lazily, smiled beatifically at my grandfather. "You know, Uncle Ismail, the story might not be appropriate for the children. You see, if you tell the story, they'll grow up believing that the whole family, almost everyone in this room, wouldn't be here if it weren't for the bey."

"That's not true," both my father and grandfather said.

"And we wouldn't want that, would we?" she asked.

❧

The hospital kept to a Mediterranean schedule: visiting hours after siesta were from four till eight. Evening had blued the room. I was tired, yet an orderly was just beginning the dinner round. He wouldn't enter my father's room. I nestled next to Fatima on the recliner; her arm swallowed me up. "I'm scared," I whispered.

"You know, grief feels very much like fear, almost interchangeable," she said. "You'd think we'd get used to grief, but we never do." She stroked my hair gently, scratched my hair, clicked her fingernails together. We called that "cleaning lice." Fatima's Italian mother used to do that. I'd loved it as a child, and I loved it now.

Lina trudged into the room, looking like she was about to disintegrate—eyes puffy, skin dark beneath them. She acknowledged Fatima and me but went directly to my father's bed.

"Have they all left?" Fatima asked. My sister nodded in between heaves and tears. Fatima waited. "What about Salwa?"

"Hovik took her home," Lina replied.

"Good. She looked exhausted. Not as exhausted as you, though. You're going home. Sleep in your bed tonight."

"No. It's quite all right. I'll stay here."

"No, I'll stay. You go home. You can't keep sleeping on the recliner. I'll take over."

"I'm not going home," my sister said. "He wants me here. I'm used to the recliner. If he wakes up and doesn't see me here, he freaks. I have to."

The sound of the machine—inhale, exhale—echoed inside my skull. Aspiration, beep, beep, expiration. My head seemed to melt upon itself. I heard myself say, "No, you both go home. I'm staying." They gawked as if I were a poltergeist. "I need time with him, and you need the rest."

Fatima blew kisses my way. She hurriedly collected my sister's belongings.

Lina wouldn't take her eyes from mine. I blinked. "You sure?" she asked.

Fatima picked up my sister's overnight bag, kissed me, and dragged my sister toward the door. Lina disentangled herself and came over. "Go to the nurses' desk and they'll give you a pillow and blanket." She hugged me. "Call me if anything happens." She squeezed me tight. "It was always just you and me, stupid. Always was, always will be." And she kissed the top of my head. The sound of the kiss echoed in my skull.

When my grandfather discovered he'd been rejected, he pleaded his case to the bey. This was the girl for him, he said. He loved her. No other would do. If Najla wouldn't marry him, who else would? Could the bey intercede on his behalf? And the bey did. He called Jalal Arisseddine, asked him to reconsider. The hakawati was his protégé, a decent fellow. The bey himself would make sure the girl was taken care of. The girl wouldn't find a better husband, after all. She was an orphan of impure parentage, and had a disreputable deceased brother—three strikes.

The girl's brother agreed to marry her to the bey's hakawati. The girl's mother did not.

And the bey called Mona Arisseddine. She put on her mandeel and trudged up the hill to the mansion. The bey gave her the same spiel, and she said no. He repeated the same words, and she said no again. He repeated them once more, and she rejected his offer a third time. She left the befuddled bey and returned home.

The bey called *his* mother. His mother said, "I am ashamed to have raised such a fool."

And the bey's mother put on her mandeel and trudged down to visit Mona Arisseddine in her home. The mothers discussed the hakawati. Mona said he had no family. The bey's mother reminded Mona that she didn't, either, and she'd turned out to be a wonderful mother. Mona said the man was an entertainer. The bey's mother ruminated on how quickly we forgot.

Could he make her happy? The bey's mother told Mona to ask her daughter.

The mothers asked Najla if she thought the hakawati could make her happy.

Najla looked at both women and said he made her laugh.

Wedding torches would flare.

Mountain weddings were known for many things: the feast and the accompanying feeding frenzy; the dancing, the Lebanese dabké and the dances of the swords and shields; the rites of riding to collect the bride; and most of all the zajal, the poetry duels.

At weddings, poets competed in praising the bride, the groom, luminaries attending the wedding, and matrimonial traditions in general. They also dueled, entertained the crowds by engaging in boasts and insults, composing verses on the spot. A poet was guaranteed an invitation to every wedding. A good one was even paid. At some weddings, amateurs joined in, tried their luck in verse. My grandparents' wedding became famous for a verse.

A tasteless, reprehensible quatrain uttered by none other than the evil Sitt Hawwar.

> *A groom with a huge mouth filled with many needless words,*
> *Yet no incisor and no molar,*
> *Married a girl with a bigger mouth,*
> *Whose teeth entered a room before her.*

I followed the aromas emanating from the kitchen, but knew better than to go in. I stopped in the prep room. Aunt Samia was complaining to someone, most probably Aunt Nazek. "I can't take it anymore," she was saying. I grabbed a piece of bread from the table and bit into it. "I don't know why she thinks she needs to keep her nose so high up in the air," I heard her say. "It's not like she produced a bushel of sons, just a toad of a girl and a gnat of a boy." I bit into the bread again and again.

My grandfather came up from behind and covered my eyes. I knew it was him because of his smell, but I couldn't tell him I knew, because my mouth was too full. "It's only me," he said, chuckling. "And don't eat the bread by itself when there's so much food around."

As noiselessly as possible, he moved a chair next to the table, motioned for me to stand on it. He uncovered a deep bowl in the middle of the table, moved it closer. I could see the stew inside. "The secret," he whispered. He tilted his head, and I did the same. I saw soft steam churning upon itself, imagining a porcelain cover no longer there. "The bowl has lips," he said, "and can tell you stories, if only you allow your ears to hear or your nose to smell."

"Or my lips to kiss," I said softly. I bent, and the steam caressed my lashes, licked my lips. I stuck out my tongue and licked right back.

Aunt Samia walked in. "Put that filthy tongue back where it came from."

I jumped off the chair and ran out as fast as I could. I heard her ask, "How could you let him do that, Baba?" but I didn't hear his response.

He found me on the terrace, leaning over the railing, staring at the rosebushes in the gated garden below. "That was fun," he said. "I bet you don't know what was in the pot. I know you think it's chicken stew, but it most certainly is not. It's imp stew. You have to catch those little devils, no bigger than chickens but very hard to trap. Killing the imps is never easy. You have to find them at the right time of the year and freeze them. That's how you do it. Not easy."

"Oh, come on."

"It's true. And you have to blanch them to get rid of their red color, so no one can tell that it's imp stew. You don't want your guests to throw up, now, do you?"

"But the guests would taste them."

"Oh, no, imps taste like chicken. Samia is just trying to trick us."

I didn't say anything. I heard his breath.

"Does your father still like his meat?" my grandfather asked.

"Ask him," I said.

"He's not here, is he? So—I'm asking you. Does he still sneak into the kitchen and eat the aliyeh when no one is looking?"

"What's aliyeh?"

"It's the fried lamb and onions and garlic and salt and pepper. What you need to prepare to add flavor to the stew. When your grandmother would cook, she'd have the best aliyeh—well, she had the best everything. She was the best cook ever to walk this cursed earth."

"Our cook is probably better. That's what everyone says."

"Don't be ridiculous. No one will ever be as good as your grandmother. Her cooking woke the dead and the gods. Where was I? Your father. Well, your devious father would crawl into the kitchen on his hands and knees, holding a piece of bread between his teeth so it wouldn't touch the floor. He'd get to the stove, stand up quickly, and dip his bread into the aliyeh while it was still frying, pick up as much as he could in that morsel, and run out before his mother caught him. He'd run, blowing on the food in his hand to cool it. Blow, and duck to avoid your grandmother, who ran after him. It was a game they played, and he had to stuff the bread in his mouth or she'd take it from him. He must have been your age, or maybe a little older. We couldn't afford much meat when he was younger. We couldn't afford imps, either."

— Nine —

B elow, in the underworld, Fatima said, "I must rise."

"Why?" said Afreet-Jehanam. "You should deliver here."

"My child shall be born aboveground. He will master this world but must be a citizen of the one above."

"You *do* treat me like a plaything," her lover harrumphed. "I am the father. I should have some say."

"But you do, dear, you do. Now, get me a carpet, please. I must be going. I do not wish my water to break in midair."

In the castle, the emir's wife felt her first pain the same instant Fatima felt hers in the underworld. She held her stomach, smiled at her husband.

"Should I stop the story?" the emir asked. "Should I call someone? Should I boil water? Where's the midwife? What—"

"No, husband, go on. This Othman fellow begins to amuse me. Just help me with more pillows." She pushed her body farther up on the bed and adjusted herself with a groan. "The troublemaker comes," she said. "Pray continue, husband. Distract me."

❧

Prince Baybars, Othman, the Africans, and the Uzbeks attended Friday prayers at the mosque. The faithful eyed Othman with a mixture of awe, concern, and fear. Othman yelled, "Stop the staring. I have repented to God, who forgives all sins, and now I pray like you do." The faithful welcomed him to their bosom. Leaving the mosque after prayers, the group heard a barker announcing the availability of the house of Prince Ahmad al-Sabaki, which ran the length of the farmers' market on one side to the dyers' market on the other. Baybars asked who owned the house, and the barker answered that it was the four granddaughters of Prince Ahmad.

The barker led the group to one of the four doors of the house, where he said, "Forgive me, lord, but the ladies asked that anyone who wished to inquire about the house must enter through the green door, which no one has been able to open for generations." Baybars turned the key in the lock, and the door swung open, the hinges sliding silently, as if they had been oiled that morning. The interior of the house was opulent. Othman's fingers twitched, and he had to clasp his hands together. The barker disappeared and returned a few minutes later to announce that the ladies were ready to greet them.

The men entered a large hall where the four ladies lounged on colorful divans. With one voice the four said, "Which of you opened the door?" and the prince identified himself. "What is your name, young man?" their voice asked. Prince Baybars told them.

"No," they said. "What is your birth name?"

"I was born with the name Mahmoud."

"And where are you from?"

"I am from Damascus."

"No," their voice said. "Where were you born?"

"I was born in Samarkand."

"And who are you?" asked the ladies.

And Prince Baybars told the stories of his grandfather and his father, and those of his mother, and those of his uncles. "This is who I am," he finally said.

The women asked if he could afford the price of the house, and Prince Baybars assured them he could. And their voice said, "You claim wealth but carry no sign of it. You are a dissembler." Baybars grew angry; the lion's folds appeared at the bridge of his nose, and his beauty mark turned red. "You are the one," the ladies' voice said. "We have been waiting for you for far too long. The house is yours if you can pass a test and make a promise." Baybars inquired about the test. "That monolith there must be moved." The ladies pointed to a prehistoric menhir in the corner. "The house was built around it because no one has been able to relocate it. It is known that only its master can lift it."

Baybars's men gathered around the monolith. "This should be easy," one of the Africans said. The Africans and the Uzbeks tried to lift the stone, but it would not budge. Baybars moved in to help, and, lo and behold, the instant he put his hands around the monolith, he lifted it right out. "It is cumbersome but not heavy," he told his servants. He took a couple of steps, and from behind the menhir he asked the ladies, "And where would you like me to put this?"

"Down," they said, "so you can make your promise. You must build each one of us a mosque named after her. Promise that and claim your home."

And that was how Baybars became a homeowner.

❦

My aunt arrived first, in 1920, when my grandmother was sixteen. Najla began labor in the morning. At six in the evening, while she was still in pain, the bey sent one of his attendants to fetch my grandfather. The bey had begun his drinking early and needed entertainment.

"Run," Great-Grandmother Mona told him. "You're not needed here."

The midwife, on her way back home after the delivery, informed the night watchman at the mansion's gate that the bey's hakawati had a healthy baby girl. The watchman told one of the servants, who waited to make the announcement until there was a break in the evening's tale. Had it been a baby boy, the servant would have interrupted.

"It's a good thing you're here," the bey told my grandfather. "No woman wants to announce right after delivery that she had a girl. Wives are very emotional. You should call your baby Samira, after my dear mother."

Najla called her Samia.

Najla decided she wanted meghli, the sweet made of spices. It was supposed to be served after a boy was born, but Najla said, "If it helps me make milk, then isn't it just as good for a girl?"

The midwife agreed that all new mothers should eat meghli, but she advised the new mother not to serve it to guests. "Nonsense," Mona said. "My daughter can't eat meghli by herself and not serve the guests. I will make the first batch."

"I want my daughter to be queen of the village," Najla told her mother, who agreed wholeheartedly. She was almost successful. Aunt Samia blossomed into a queen manquée.

❦

One day, King Saleh was riding through the city when he came to Lady Zainab Street. There were wooden planks spanning a small gulf, and his subjects crossed with difficulty. He felt ashamed that the maqâm of Lady Zainab was not in a more fortunate quarter of the city. He said, "A bridge must be built here, and a small neighborhood, with decent shops and adequate housing." He put Baybars in charge, and Baybars was honored by the responsibility.

The prince had Othman summon engineers to build the bridge. They hired carpenters and artisans and built a neighborhood so lovely it was as if the Lady watched over it. A marvelous gate protected it, and clean streets invited people in. The prince said to Othman, "Bring me grocers, butchers, perfumers, tailors, oil merchants, coffee traders, and other honest brokers."

Othman brought the shopkeepers, and they moved into the neighborhood within a couple of months, transforming it into the most popular in the city.

Evil Arbusto, the king's judge, heard of the miracle, and his blood coursed with envy. He called on his close friend the mayor of Cairo. The mayor inquired why the judge looked sad and was told, "There is a sight in the city that breaks my heart. The slave Baybars has built a lively neighborhood that I would love to see reduced to cinders and ash."

"I know the neighborhood," the mayor said. "It will be a pleasure to be rid of it. That scoundrel Othman has bested me a few times, and now I will get him back." The mayor called on a rogue by the name of Harhash and told him of his wish to burn the neighborhood. Harhash asked where the neighborhood was. The mayor said, "Next to the maqâm of Lady Zainab."

Harhash recoiled. "I cannot do this. I will burn any other neighborhood, but not the Lady's neighborhood. That is blasphemy."

The mayor screamed, "That is not blasphemy, you jackass. You do not even know what the word means. You and your men will burn what I command you to, or I will have you in prison, and you will never see the light of day for the rest of your life."

And Harhash agreed to commit arson, for he had no other choice. He and two of his men went to study the neighborhood. The men told Harhash, "This neighborhood can only be burned in the middle of the night, when there are no witnesses." Lady Zainab, the neighborhood's protector, had made sure the weather was hot enough that a tailor was taking his siesta on the floor of his shop and not his house, and so was able to hear the conversation of the men standing nearby. When they left, the tailor sought Othman and informed him of what he had heard.

Othman and the Uzbek and African warriors rode to the neighborhood. Othman told the gatekeepers to close the gate but keep its portal open. He ordered the residents not to light their night lamps that evening. And the prince's servants waited for night to fall.

Harhash and his twelve men arrived with barrels of oil and found the neighborhood dark and the gate closed. "This is a blessing," Harhash whispered. "We can do our job and no one will witness." He sent one of his men ahead through the portal. As soon as the man entered, one of the Africans banged him on top of the head with his closed fist, and the rogue collapsed unconscious. Othman waited a little and then whistled. Another man walked in and got thumped by another African. Othman whistled again. A third man entered, and this time Othman hit him on the head, but the man did not collapse. He stared wide-eyed at the Africans, and one of them thumped him quickly. Othman sulked. The warriors took turns whistling the rogues in, until Harhash was the last one to be knocked unconscious. The arsonists woke and found themselves tied and lined up before the fiercest-looking men they had ever seen. Harhash began to weep.

"Oh, Harhash," Othman said, "have times been so tough that you have resorted to playing with fire?" And Harhash replied, "Be not cruel, friend. Do you think me impious enough to commit a dastardly crime with the Lady so close were I not forced to? That these warriors stand here to protect this neighborhood is the only proof I need that the Lady still watches. Now I will never taste the fruits of paradise."

And Othman joined Harhash in weeping. He sat down on the ground and said, "Oh, Harhash, you are not damned. If you repent before the Lady, as I did, God will listen and forgive." Harhash and his men gave up their wayward ways and swore allegiance to God. Othman said, "Now you and your men can work for me," and one of the Uzbeks said, "But you are a servant yourself." And Othman replied, "True, but I am moving up in the world. Soon Harhash here will be able to afford his own servants. It is an ever-shifting multilevel process."

❦

Fatima's room was across the hall from the royal chambers, and the second stab of pain forced a sigh that echoed that of the emir's wife.

Fatima asked her attendants to leave her, but when she was alone, she no longer wanted to be.

"Ishmael," she said, "come." And Ishmael popped up next to her in bed. "What an awful-looking room," he said. "You want your child to grow up to be a scholar?"

"Do something, then."

"With pleasure," Ishmael replied gleefully.

"Hold on," said a materializing Isaac.

"I will do it," said Elijah. "You have no taste."

"Go home," said Ishmael. "She asked me to do it."

His seven brothers ignored him. Adam turned the drapes violet and Noah changed them to blue. Ezra and Elijah had a wrestling match over the carpet. Fatima's bedspread had four competing pattern designs. By the time she yelled, "Stop," the room was a disaster, clashing gaudiness in every corner. She looked around. "This is truly awful. I love it."

Aunt Samia loved and idolized her mother. For her, my grandmother could do no wrong. God, in all His great bounty, created the world in six days, and on the seventh, He concentrated on Najla. She was the most virtuous woman who had ever lived, the most devout, the most intelligent, the most fill-in-the-blank-with-an-ideal-trait. My poor, poor grandmother Najla, born an orphan, married to a ne'er-do-well hakawati, still managed to raise the perfect family and provide her children with a loving environment. Aunt Samia mimicked her mother's every movement, modeled her entire personality after her. She learned to cook the same meals, weave the same textiles, cross-stitch the same patterns. Whenever she remembered, Aunt Samia pronounced her "s" the same way my grandmother did, spitting saliva upon the listener. Luckily, she didn't often remember, and she never did it after her mother passed away.

And Aunt Samia had the same adversary as my grandmother and my great-grandmother: none other than the evil Sitt Hawwar, the builder's wife, who would commit the most egregious of acts against her. Aunt Samia had thought that she would end up spending her life with her mother, since she remained a spinster long past marriage-able age.

"We'll grow old together," she used to say to Grandmother.
"No, we won't," Najla would reply. "You will get married."

❧

In the morning, the mayor and his men rode into Lady Zainab's neighborhood. Surprised to find it still standing, the mayor asked the first shopkeeper if he had seen or heard anything during the night. The shopkeeper replied that he had not, because he had turned off the lanterns and fallen asleep. The mayor yelled, "It is against the law to extinguish the lamps," and he had his men take the shopkeeper out and beat him. He moved to the next shop and asked that shopkeeper if he had had his lamp extinguished last night. The man replied that Othman had ordered him to, which angered the mayor even more, and he had his men beat the second shopkeeper. The mayor went into the next shop, a perfumery, and told the shopkeeper, "Show me your dried carnations." The perfumer opened a box, and the mayor said, "This carnation is crooked." The puzzled shopkeeper said, "Find me a carnation that is not," and received a terrible thrashing for his insolence. The mayor then asked the dairyman, "Why is cow's milk white but your butter is yellow?" and he replied, "It is always so," and he, too, received a whipping. The mayor moved from one store to the next, meting out severe beatings.

The shopkeepers sought Othman, who said, "I will solve your problem, but you must pay me." The men asked what he wanted, and Othman said, "A tub of your yellowest butter and one crooked carnation and one lamb sandwich and one cup of coffee and one comb of honey."

The shopkeepers laughed and said, "You help us with the mayor and we will give you two of each." And Othman added, "Oh, and a dessert as well. One must have sweets. And tomorrow, if anyone sees the mayor in the neighborhood, he must shout, 'Baklava, baklava,' to remind me of my sweet reward."

When the oil merchant saw the mayor at his shop the following day, he yelled, "Baklava, baklava," and every boy in the neighborhood followed suit. The other shopkeepers began to yell, "Baklava, baklava," as well. The confused mayor asked, "Who wants sweets at an oil shop?" and he heard the voice of Othman say, "A man like you should think only of bitters, never sweets." Othman, Harhash, and the warriors surrounded the mayor and his men, disarmed them, and relieved them of their clothes, leaving them all utterly naked. The mayor said, "I am going to arrest you and throw away the key." Othman laughed. "You cannot arrest me. I work for a prince now. If the king knew what you were up to, he would throw you in jail."

The warriors carried the naked mayor to the tanner and dunked him in a vat of black dye. "Now he is darker than I," said one of the Africans. They put the naked mayor on his horse backward and rode him out of town. The neighborhood boys ran after him, jeering and whistling.

And the mayor swore revenge against Othman and Baybars. He had his men buy him a coffin, take him to the diwan in it, and inform the king that Othman had killed him.

Upon seeing his murdered mayor, the king called for Baybars and Othman and asked them what happened. Othman said, "I wish I had killed him, but I did not. Had I not sworn to follow the righteous path, I would surely have slain him." The king asked him to elaborate, and Othman did, calling his witnesses: the shopkeepers, the warriors, and Harhash.

And Arbusto said, "But you beat up a government official, and here he lies in his coffin before us. This is murder, and you deserve death for it."

Othman said, "No, I do not. If I am to be killed for killing him, then I should at least have had the pleasure of doing the deed. Now that I think of it, I do not believe God would mind if I killed a dead man anyway." Othman drew his sword and stabbed the mayor in his coffin. The mayor sat up and died again. "Lazarus?" Othman exclaimed.

The angry king said, "This man was not dead. It was a ruse. My own mayor attempted to deceive his king. It is a good thing he is well and truly deceased. I call on you, honest Baybars, to wear the mayor's suit."

And that was how Baybars became mayor of the great city of Cairo.

"Distract me," Fatima said.

"Let us decorate the room again," said Job. The imps were lounging around her bed.

"No," she replied. "Tell me a story, a tale so strange, a tale so true, so wonderful and engrossing that it will seduce my mind."

"Demon tales," cried Ezra.

"No," Fatima said. "I know those too well."

"Parrot tales," said Isaac. "Those are the best."

"I will tell them," said Ishmael.

"No, I will," said Elijah.

"Me, me, me."

And Fatima decided that Ishmael would begin and the imps would take turns. "However, if one of the servant girls comes in here, she is going to be confounded by your presence. Make yourselves less shocking." Ishmael and Isaac turned into red parrots. The rest followed suit in their different colors. The rainbow-hued parrots perched atop the bed's backrest, the curtain rods, the lamps, and the short column at the foot of the bed.

❧

My uncle Wajih was born two years after Samia. He arrived with little fuss. "He's going to grow up wise," the midwife said. His arrival was the cause of many a celebration. The bey himself blessed my uncle. "He'll become the head of an illustrious family, a reaper of honor, an amasser of wealth, and a man of substance." My grandfather offered cigars to all the men in the village. My grandmother offered sweets. Evil Sitt Hawwar had to keep quiet for a while.

My uncle Halim made his first appearance in our world in 1925. There were no delivery complications; the umbilical cord did not accidentally strangle him. Yet my grandmother recognized that something was off the instant she held him in her arms. His head seemed just a tad too warm, and his eyes seemed to flutter jerkily when closed. "He's going to be a dreamer," said the midwife.

My father came next, in 1930, and two years later came Uncle Jihad. They were their parents' favorites. "We were too young," my grandfather told me once. "It's not that we didn't love all our children. We did. But then your father, Farid, was born. We had been married for eleven years. We were—I don't know—more mature. There was a difference, but it wasn't intentional."

I didn't care. I was busy watching a lizard stand utterly still.

"Your grandmother loved Farid. He was special, much smarter than his siblings. If you placed all three other children on one scale and your father on the other, his intelligence would outweigh all of theirs. And then Jihad—he spoke before he was nine months old. He was brilliant.

He made me so proud. How can you blame your grandmother for treating them differently? How can you blame her for loving them more? They were the chosen ones."

❧

Upon returning to his house, Baybars found the old mayor's intendants and attendants waiting for him. He inquired how he could help them, and they said, "We offer condolences on the death of the mayor, congratulations on your promotion, and our services." Baybars asked that each inform him of his duty and salary with the previous administration.

"There were no salaries, sire. The previous mayor slurped any government money that appeared in his bowl. We earned our keep from the duties and taxes paid by Cairo's cadres of thieves, gamblers, wine merchants, and criminals."

"And how do you collect those duties?"

"Each cadre has a head, and the head of heads is Commander Khanjar, chief of the city's gates." Baybars ordered his new staff to give up their wayward ways. "I will pay your salaries, enough to feed and clothe your families. You may not collect funds from anywhere else. Renounce your past misdeeds, swear vows of honesty, pray, and fast. If I hear of any of you committing a deed that would anger God, I, the mayor of Cairo, will seek revenge." And his staff swore allegiance to God and Baybars. "Get me Othman," Baybars demanded.

That night, Baybars and Othman paid the commander a visit at his headquarters. Surrounded by his men, he sat on his chair like a prideful tiger wearing clothes that were much too fancy. Khanjar did not stand to greet his visitors, nor did he ask after their health, because he possessed a head swelled with self-importance.

Baybars greeted the commander with "Peace be upon you."

Khanjar replied, "I know not peace. State your need, boy. Are you the one who was given the mayor's suit? Are you the one who fooled Othman and Harhash onto the path of virtue? Follow me, be my boy, and I will reward you. I will take care of all your needs, all your wants, and more." Othman chimed in, "We have come here to ask for your blessing."

The commander beamed. Joy and greed burst from his eyes. "Then your presence here is most welcome. If you capture one of my artisans, release him and I will remunerate you. Obey me and acquire wealth, but cross me and you will regret it for the rest of your shortened life."

"We aim only to please you, my father," Othman said. "But how will I know if I catch one of your people?"

Khanjar thought. "Maybe if they gave you a secret word. You must punish anyone who does not work for me and spare those who do."

Othman objected. "No word remains secret in the criminal world for long. It would be better if you introduced us to the members of the cadres. Inform the clans that the new mayor wishes to know them one and all."

※

Quawk, began the parrot Ishmael. A quawk here, a quawk there. Let us embark on the tales of the wise parrot. There was once a wealthy merchant who married a young woman of exquisite beauty. On their wedding night, he informed his lovely wife that he would be leaving on an extended journey the following day. His wife asked him not to go. She would be lonely. He said, "My business demands that I travel. I buy my silk in China, my cotton in Egypt. Spice I procure from India, and perfume from Persia. My shops need merchandise," and she replied, "But I need you. I have no need for money with you by my side."

Her husband glowed with pride and said, "A moneyless man is a fatherless one, and a home without money is haunted. The sun never shines on an indigent." But, as the saying goes, a man who is given to much traveling does not deserve to be married.

The following day, the merchant walked to the bazaar and bought a magnificent parrot and a magpie. He charged his wife to obtain the sanction of both birds whenever she had to make a decision. Then he threatened the birds with a horrifying death if they allowed his wife to betray him. And off on his journey he went. Weeks passed, and then months, and the merchant extended his expedition longer and longer. One day, as the winsome wife hung laundry on the roof, she noticed a royal procession below. She saw a handsome prince astride a steed, and her heart was filled with love and lust. The prince chanced to glance up and was dazzled by the fair lady's loveliness. Upon returning to his castle, he sent an old woman to the lady's home with an invitation to his palace for that evening, which she duly accepted. Arraying herself in the finest apparel and donning her best jewels, she faced the birds.

"Dear magpie," she said. "What thinkest thou of the propriety of my purpose?"

"I like it not," said the magpie. "I forbid thee to leave."

The lovely lady opened the cage door and wrung the magpie's neck. She turned to the parrot. "My dear parrot. What thinkest thou of the propriety of my purpose?"

And the prudent parrot said, "My lady. You are most fair tonight. You are lovelier than the new moon, which weeps in shame and quivers with envy at the mere mention of your name. Sit, my lady. Let me entertain you for a while. I am a hakawati, and your gloriousness inspires me to tell a great tale. Allow me to begin."

❧

Three nights after his meeting with Khanjar, Baybars played host to him; the chief of the gates was to introduce all of Cairo's thieves and criminals. "Shall we begin the introductions?" Baybars said. "Othman, bring in the first cadre." Into the hall walked thirty black-robed women, each with her manservant. All bowed before Baybars. "Commander," Baybars asked, "who are these women?"

"They are the cadre of savage doves, pretty and lethal. They live in all the neighborhoods of Cairo. They approach men and persuade them to join them at their houses. The savage dove plies her victim with wine until he is drunk, and then the manservant covers the man's face with a pillow and sits on it until the man loses his breath. They confiscate his possessions, bury the body in the yard, and start over again."

Othman led that group out into a different hall and brought in another, twenty brown-robed women. "This is the cadre of roaming doves," the commander said. "They are docile and timid until a foolish man believes he has a willing victim. When the man invites the woman to his house, she asks to share some wine. Then she laces his cup with opium, strips him of his wealth, and leaves him unconscious."

The third group of women wore robes of red. "These are the luscious doves, the most beautiful doves of all, and the most proficient; they trick men into assuming compromising positions and proceed to purloin the house's belongings as their powerless prey watch. Every man wishes to drink from a luscious dove's beauty cup, even when he knows it could be lethal." The fourth group was ten white-robed women. "The cooing doves," the commander said. "Pickpockets and shoplifters." The fifth group was twenty-five boys. "The baby porcupines are thieves." The sixth was ten younger boys. "The hedgehogs are specialized pickpockets. A hedgehog works with a baby porcupine. When they see a possible victim, the porcupine hits the hedgehog, who runs to the man and begs to be saved. While the man comforts the hedgehog, his pockets get emptied." The seventh cadre was the old doves. "These crones pretend to be sages, seers, and fortune-tellers. They are invited into houses and rarely leave empty-handed." The eighth, ninth, tenth, and eleventh cadres were all porcupines: the burglars, the gamblers, the highway robbers, and the murderers.

"The twelfth?" Baybars asked, and the commander replied, "That would be me."

Baybars left Khanjar in the hall and sought out the assembled horde of criminals. He faced them with Othman and said, "I command you to give up your wicked ways and seek solace in God's love. Vow to live an honest life and swear not to sin again. He who makes the vow will be set free, but he who does not will be enchained." And the women said, "But how can we live an honest life if we owe money to the commander? He forces us to work in order to pay him."

Baybars said, "If you make the vow to God, your debts will be forgiven. Is there anyone here who will not make the vow and give up the life of crime?" There were no raised hands.

Othman lit a fire and with a branding iron marked the left wrist of every reformed criminal, dove, porcupine, and hedgehog in the room. Right after he branded one of the luscious doves, she whispered, "I know thirty-seven distinctly different pleasurable ways of using this branding iron," causing Othman to flush and blush and rush to the next.

"If anyone wearing this brand is caught committing a crime, the penalty of death will be imposed," Baybars said. "So it shall be."

And Baybars returned to Khanjar and said, "My father, I have turned your workers into honest men and women. I will place the children in schools. It is now your turn. You are over eighty years old. Have you not worshipped God in all this time? Have you not prayed or fasted?"

Khanjar replied, "I have never set foot in a mosque. For seventy years, I have stolen from men, betrayed them, and killed them. Do you think I am as easy to convert as my minions? You are a fool, a little mind and a light head." And he unsheathed his sword and struck, but Baybars's sword parried the commander's blow with one smooth motion, its hilt knocking him out. Othman tied him up and dragged the commander to jail, where he spent the rest of his life.

❧

A quawk here, said the parrot Isaac, and a quawk there.

And the hakawati parrot began telling the lovely wife this story:

Four men—a tailor, a jeweler, a carpenter, and a dervish—traveled together on a long journey. They camped for the night and took turns guarding their belongings. The carpenter stood guard first, while the others slept. He saw a big log lying on the ground, and to pass the time he carved a statue of a beautiful woman out of it. The tailor woke up, and as the rest snored, he admired the lovely form and decided to sew a glorious outfit for the lady. Out of divine cloth, he fashioned raiment fit for a queen. It was the jeweler's turn next, and he created wonderful adornments for the statue with the most precious of gems. And the dervish saw the creation and was so enamored that he prayed to God with all his heart to make her real. When light rose, the four men beheld a breathing woman of such comeliness their hearts were infatuated. Each man claimed her as his wife. They fought, they argued, but they could not arrive at a mutually acceptable decision.

Finally, they saw a Bedouin riding by on his camel and asked him to arbitrate.

"I sculpted her out of wood," the carpenter said.

"I clothed her."

"I gave her brilliance."

"And I gave her breath," said the dervish.

The Bedouin said, "All four of you have a rightful claim, and I see no way of dividing this woman. I therefore claim her for myself. She was created in the desert, and these are my lands. She will be my wife."

The five men quarreled and quarreled, but could find no solution to their dilemma. They rode into town, and asked the first policeman they came across to be arbiter. After each man laid his claim, the policeman said, "Each of you has a point, and I cannot decide for any of you, so I claim this charming woman as my own."

The six men went to a judge and regaled him with their stories. The judge said, "We have a problem here. For the sake of fairness and impartiality, I claim this woman myself. She will be my wife so you can cease your fighting."

The men squabbled into the night. Finally, the dervish said, "We can come to no resolution, because no man can arbitrate. None can resist the charm of our beloved. We must resort to an inhuman referee, the Tree of Knowledge."

The seven suitors and the woman marched to the wise tree in the center of town. As soon as they approached the giant oak, its bark split open and the woman ran inside and the trunk closed back upon itself. The Tree of Knowledge said, "Everything returns to its first principles," and the seven men were shamed.

♣

Aunt Samia was twelve when Uncle Jihad was born. She attended the English missionary school in the mornings and helped her mother with household chores in the afternoon. Since my grandmother was busy with her newborn, Aunt Samia took a daily walk to the bakery of the neighboring Christian village, which the family felt was superior to the one in ours. The baker's daughter was my aunt's age, and they struck up a friendship. My aunt began to take the bread walk a bit earlier, visit with the baker's daughter, and chat. My aunt taught her a song she'd learned at school, "There's a Beautiful Land Far, Far Away," and her friend taught her the "Marseillaise." One day, after spending a week in song, Aunt Samia felt feverish and had problems urinating. My grandmother took her to a doctor in Beirut, and she spent two nights in the hospital. It was a minor infection. She returned to the village and spent a fortnight in enforced bedrest. She lost track of the baker's daughter.

Unbeknownst to the family at the time, evil Sitt Hawwar started a rumor that my aunt had to have her uterus removed and that she could no longer bear children. Evil Sitt Hawwar didn't exactly say that my aunt had had an abortion, but she left the suggestion dangling. Not one suitor approached when my aunt matured to marriageable age. As time passed, when a family or a man would ask about my aunt, the rumor would surface. She waited and waited for someone to choose her, wondered what was so awful about her that not one was willing to test a fish hook in her waters. She would not get married for a long,

long time: not till three of her younger brothers had married, not till she had to live the ignominy of being a spinster, not till she was thirty-eight and had been lying about her age for some while, not till my grandfather finally intervened and found her the most inappropriate husband in history.

My aunt didn't tell anyone about her friendship with the baker's daughter for years. It seemed that, since the timing of her friendship and the ugly rumors seemed to coincide, she felt they were intimately related. She believed she was being made to pay for the crime of fraternizing outside of the alliance of family. She finally came clean to her youngest brother, Jihad, on a night in early 1976, when the war still raged but hadn't yet forced the family to abandon the building. She confessed in the garage, which acted as our shelter when missiles cried havoc in our skies. Uncle Jihad tried to tell her that what she'd done was not a sin. He said that what happened to her was simply a common medical condition, and that she was a victim of the nastiness and naïveté of mountain people.

"Do you really think you're being punished for singing songs with a nice girl?"

"It wasn't about singing."

"What? Did you do something else—maybe something inappropriate?"

"Of course not. How dare you? She was just my friend. We talked."

"How's that wrong? What did you talk about?"

"I don't remember. We talked about our families, about our villages. We talked about the French and whether they would leave. I don't really remember specifics."

"You think you're being punished with a horrible life because you talked to a girl for a week? That's irrational and naïve. It doesn't make sense."

"You don't understand."

Uncle Jihad did not. After trying to reassure her for about a month, he called in the cavalry, my mother. At first, Aunt Samia was horrified that her secret was out. My mother told her she was being silly, something my mother told her on a regular basis. "How can you think that making friends with someone is wrong?" my mother said. "What happened to you was the work of a sinister woman and had nothing to do with any sins. Sitt Hawwar was an evil, despicable person. It wasn't your fault. And look at you. You life isn't miserable. You're rich, you're the matriarch of a great family, and, most important, your mother would be proud of you if she saw how successful you are. And you know who was punished? Don't you remember how horribly Sitt Hawwar died? Who was at her bedside when she left this world? No one. Her children were nowhere to be found. Don't you remember the gossip? She was in the hospital, and guests would pay a visit, and there were no family members around. Could there be a life worse than that? She died alone, and no one cared. Samia, you stupid, stupid girl. Sitt Hawwar lost. Her soul left this world unlamented."

Aunt Samia felt better. After that day, she began to wear higher heels.

❧

And when the hakawati parrot's tale was over, Ezra the parrot said, the merchant's wife retired to her chambers for the night, because it was too late to meet the prince. The following evening, she put on her best robe and demanded the parrot's permission to leave. Let me tell you a story, the parrot said.

Once, in a land far away, there lived an old king who was terrified of dying. He sequestered himself in his chambers, refusing to see his viziers. He neglected affairs of state. His subjects worried. His attendants wept in private. The viziers had exhausted all options and plans to entice their king out of bed. The king's glorious parrot spread his emerald wings and flew up to the skies. Higher and higher, into the heavens he soared. He reached paradise and descended into its garden. He picked a fruit that had fallen from the Tree of Immortality. He returned to his master and said, "Take the seed of this fruit and plant it in fertile earth. Feed it love and wisdom and the sapling will turn into a fruit-bearing tree. Old age will forsake whoever eats from the tree's fruit, and vigor will revisit him." And the king's servants were surprised when their master called: "Plant this fruit's seed in my garden. I wish to glimpse its crop in my lifetime."

The sagacious bird said, "Remember the legend of the wise King Solomon and the Fount of Immortality. He refused to quench his thirst, for he wished not to outlive his loved ones."

"Bah!" uttered the king. Life coursed through his veins, hope revived him, and he woke every morning to witness the incremental growth of his tree. "Love it more," he told his gardeners. "Faster, quicker, it must rise." The tree grew, and buds burst into flowers, from which small fruit appeared. Finally, the day arrived when the fruit was ripe and ready. "Pick that one," the vivacious king said. "It looks the most succulent."

The gardener carried a small ladder to the tree. At the same instant, an eagle high in the clouds saw a slithering snake not too far from the king's garden. The eagle lunged and clutched the snake, lifting it into the skies. With its final breath, the snake spat out its venom, and one drop fell upon the fruit as it was being presented to the king.

"Bring me an old fakir," the king demanded. When his servants found one, the king commanded that he taste the fruit. The fakir took one bite, keeled over, and died.

The king raged. "Is that horrible parrot trying to hasten my demise?" He seized the bird by the feet, twirled the parrot above his head, and threw him against the tree. The parrot broke his neck and met his end. The tree became known as the Tree of Poison, and none approached it.

As hope left him, the king grew sickly. He retired to his chambers once more and spent his time cursing the tree from his window. Soon he saw the specter of death approaching.

While things were thus, a vicious young wife quarreled with her old mother-in-law. The girl raised her voice at her elder and cursed. Shocked, the mother-in-law informed her son, and the ingrate took his wife's side. His mother was so livid and distraught that she resolved to kill herself so her son would be blamed for her death. She sought the garden, bit into a fruit from the Tree of Poison, and was instantly transformed into a youthful beauty.

"What miracle is this?" the lovely girl asked.

The king witnessed the transformation from his window. "How guilty am I?" he said to himself. "I have killed a true friend." He called his servants in a faint voice. "Pick me a fruit," he whispered. But wicked death reached him before the picking.

❧

Pictures from Uncle Wajih's wedding show a young, somewhat distraught Aunt Samia. She didn't particularly approve of her brother's marriage to Aunt Wasila. She had on a ridiculous dress, bad makeup; her hair fell long and straight to the shoulder. At Uncle Halim's wedding, she looked older and not unhappy. At my parents' wedding, she looked miserable, the effects of Lebanese spinsterhood. One day, my grandfather seemed to wake up from a stupor and realize that his thirty-eight-year-old daughter was still unmarried. My father denied the veracity of this version of the story. He said that the whole family discussed the lack of suitors for my aunt's hand all the time. My grandmother must have talked to my grandfather about it often, but my grandfather said he'd never paid attention, he was too busy, until, one day, the scales fell from his eyes. "If no man has shown up at our door," he told my grandmother, "then we must find one."

From that moment of epiphany onward, my grandfather divided men into two categories: possible future sons-in-law and not. Into the former fell only one man, barely.

Uncle Akram was another entertainer hired by the bey, a percussionist, to be precise. He played the Lebanese derbakeh, and he played it well. But it wasn't his drumming talent that earned him a job with the bey. After all, percussionists were as common as asses in the mountains. Uncle Akram's real talent was his narcolepsy, which the bey found comical. The takht—an oud, a violin, maybe a recorder, and the derbakeh—would be playing, someone might be singing, and in the middle of the song, the beat would stop. Uncle Akram's head would drop to his chest, and he would swim in his sea of dreams. The band would either stop playing or go on without him, taking their cue from the bey's mood and his level of sobriety. But whether they stopped or not, when Uncle Akram came to, he would pick up the exact beat he had been playing as he fell asleep. That never ceased to send the bey into a fit of laughter. Uncle Akram never figured out he was the object of a joke, and the bey forbade anyone to enlighten him.

My grandfather approached Uncle Akram and asked him to marry Aunt Samia, who was much older than he. My grandfather sweetened the deal by promising to talk to his son Farid about a possible job: my father had just opened the car dealership. My grandfather suggested drumming was not a profession that provided consistent earnings.

My grandmother didn't think Uncle Akram was a good match for her daughter. Neither did her daughter nor any of my uncles. Yet they all agreed that Uncle Akram was a decent man.

By the time I came along, Uncle Akram had been employed at the dealership for years, and Aunt Samia was nothing like the down-to-earth, austere, hardworking housewives I associated with the mountains. None of my aunts were. I always wondered when the transformation occurred. When did my aunts shed their dry mountain skins and evolve into shiny Beirutis, albeit rough around the edges? None of them had finished high school, and they didn't read books, so I assumed that money or location was the catalyst of the metamorphosis, but sometimes I wondered if it was just their singular personalities.

In 1985, my father had to be flown to London for an emergency triple bypass. My mother and sister accompanied him, of course, and I flew in from Los Angeles, where I was living. My mother rented an apartment on South Street, off Park Lane. Deciding that neither of my father's women could care for him—or me, for that matter—Aunt Samia insisted on coming along to take care of all of us. "What will Layla do without her maids? She can't cook, she can't clean. She doesn't know a frying pan from a Crock-Pot. Her daughter is worse. How's she going to take care of my brother? Balance his books?"

She didn't understand any language but Lebanese and had completely forgotten what few English songs and words she'd learned in school. This was her first trip outside the Arab world. Yet, when she arrived in London, all she asked of me was to write down the apartment's address on a piece of paper so she could show the taxi driver where she needed to go.

She was a robust, well-shod, plump sixty-five at the time. The first forty-eight hours, while my father was being prepped for surgery, she stocked the kitchen. She found a supermarket, bought everything we needed all on her own. "There was a butcher in the middle of the market," she said, telling my father of her first shopping expedition, "but everything was packaged. I couldn't buy plastic meats. I whistled to get the butcher's attention, but I didn't know how to say lamb, so I went, 'Baa, baa,' and he understood. I held up one finger and said, 'Kilo.' But then he cut a nice piece of meat and covered it as if I were some dog going to chew it. I told him, 'No, no,' and gestured with both hands that I wanted it in smaller pieces. He asked, 'Chop?' and showed me his knife. I smiled at him, and he chopped the kilo into smaller pieces, but he didn't understand that it was for cooking. So I call him and say, 'Chop, chop, chop, chop, chop, chop, chop, chop,' and his brains finally worked, and I got my finely chopped lamb. They don't understand cooking over here."

When my father was wheeled in for the operation, my mother asked me to take my aunt out to lunch, since the procedure was going to last for at least four hours. Three hours later, we returned. From the window of the cab, I saw my mother crying behind the hospital's glass door, her hands covering her face, her body shaking. My sister had her arms wrapped around my mother. My heart dropped to my testicles. Aunt Samia bounced out of the black cab before it came to a stop, jiggling muscles and fat on heels. "My brother," she wailed. "They killed you, my brother." I flew out of the taxi behind her. My mother, her face still wet, was tying to calm my aunt, who was sitting on the floor in the hospital entrance, her legs splayed before her. "Samia," my mother said, "he's going to be fine. I'm crying with relief, not grief. The operation was a great success. The doctors just came out. We'll be able to see him within the hour."

It took a moment for Aunt Samia to register the information and change the expression on her face to one of unbridled fury. "You scared me," she hissed. "You've just taken ten years off my life." My mother shrank back as if slapped. It was rare to see her at a loss. Lina stepped in front of her, steely eyes glaring down at my aunt. Aunt Samia looked appalled. "I'm so sorry," she said, tilting her head to look at my mother's face behind my sister. "Forgive me. Please forgive me. I shouldn't have said that." She tried to stand up, and Lina didn't help her. My mother moved forward and lifted her by the elbow. "That was inexcusable." Aunt Samia began to weep. "I was frightened."

My father had to recover in the London apartment for two weeks. My aunt cooked and was in charge of the household. My father felt guilty that she had to work so hard and asked me to take her to the Playboy casino, using his membership card. Like most Lebanese, my aunt loved to gamble, and her face sparkled at the news. My father thought I could easily pass as him, since no one ever asked to see anything but the card whenever he went to the club. He was wrong. I handed the card to the receptionist, and he asked if I was Farid al-Kharrat. Realizing that there was a problem, my aunt bounded off like a tiny tank, through the swinging doors and into the casino. When I was allowed in after explaining who I was, I found her already at the blackjack table, sipping a gin and tonic, pointing with her finger for the dealer to hit her.

❧

"And so," Jacob began, "by the time the parrot had finished his story, the hour was late and the lady could not meet the prince."

Fatima felt a contraction and heard the scream of the emir's wife in the other room. She held her palm up and interrupted the story. An excited servant rushed into the room. "The emir wishes to inform you that the mistress is giving birth," she said. She halted, marveled at the wonder of eight colorful parrots in the room.

"My nephew arrives," said the parrot Ishmael.

"Wait," said Fatima. "Wait. There is still time. Tell me how the story ends."

"The master comes," announced the parrot Isaac.

"Yes, yes, I know," said Fatima. "The story. The story."

"I wanted to tell the story of the dervish and the three coins," said the parrot Job. "It is most exquisite."

"For me," said the parrot Noah, "I would have told my favorite, about Aladdin and the lamp. It is most sublime."

The parrot Adam said, "I would have told the story of Abraham entering cursed Egypt, how he hid his beautiful Sarah in a chest."

"Behold the wonder," said the parrot Elijah. "The master comes."

"No," said Fatima, "I have time. Finish."

"The parrot tells ninety tales," said Ishmael.

"Maybe more," said Isaac, "maybe less. And the merchant finally returns home. He notices that the magpie is no more and asks the parrot what happened. The parrot tells him about the prince, about his wife, and about the stories."

Jacob said, "The merchant, in a fit of temper, slays his wife for her duplicity, and wrings the parrot's neck for being a witness to his shame."

"Ooof," said Fatima.

"Observe the marvel," said the parrot Job.

"Behold the wonder," said the parrot Elijah.

"The lord arrives," said the parrot Isaac.

"Tremble," said the parrot Ishmael.

"Aiee," said Fatima.

BOOK THREE

And as to poets, those who go astray follow them.

Koran

If you cannot climb a tree that your father has climbed, at least place your hands upon its trunk.

Ahmadou Kourouma, *Waiting for the Wild Beasts to Vote*

A life in which the gods are not invited is not worth living.

Roberto Calasso, *The Marriage of Cadmus and Harmony*

Ten

The *Los Angeles Times* announced that Elvis was dead. Below the main headline, NEW FLOODS BATTER DESERT, stood a smaller one, ELVIS PRESLEY DIES AT 42; LEGEND OF ROCK 'N' ROLL ERA. I was reading the paper of the man standing before me in the customs line at the Los Angeles airport. The line was moving quickly as the customs official gave passports a cursory glance and let everyone through. When it was my turn, he didn't even look at mine, but directed me to two other customs officials, a man and woman, who stood behind a gleaming metal table. The man, a red-haired, mustached guy with an uncanny resemblance to Porky Pig, demanded that I put my bags on the table. The woman, more obese than her partner, pointed to my carry-on. I smiled, careful not to show my teeth. My two front teeth did not match. Porky began poking through my belongings, sniffing around. I wanted to joke that I had no food in there, but I didn't think he'd find it funny.

"What's the purpose of your visit?" the female agent asked.

"Just a vacation. I've never been to America before." Anticipating the next question, I answered it. "I'll be here for ten days." I hated lying.

Porky was jumbling up what my mother had meticulously packed. Another fat customs official approached with a German shepherd at his side. The dog began sniffing me. He reminded me of my Tulip, who had recently died of a heart attack. I bent down to pet him. "Don't touch the dog," Porky snapped from behind the table. "Please put your bags back on the cart and follow me."

My left eyelid fluttered sporadically. I discreetly covered it with my left hand and followed Porky to a small, windowless office with only a metal table and a wooden chair. The customs official with the leashed dog followed us. The German shepherd sniffed my bags.

"I don't have anything to declare," I said nervously as Porky closed the door. "I swear." I shifted my weight from one foot to the other. The back of my shirt was wet. The white walls had cement gray showing through the many chips in the paint.

"Please empty your pockets on the table," Porky said harshly. He used the word "please" often, but his tone suggested otherwise. My hands shook. Out came a packet of cigarettes, a lighter, my wallet, my keys to our apartment in Beirut, two guitar picks, and some Chiclets gum. The German shepherd sniffed my crotch. His owner stood back, lips curled. "Please take off your jacket," Porky said, taking me by surprise. I handed him my brown leather jacket. He squeezed it and had the dog smell it. "Take off your shoes, please."

"They're boots," I said, "not shoes." The distinction was important. They were cowboy boots I had bought expressly for this trip. Handmade boots, no less. Handmade in Texas, it said on the tag. I bought them for seventy-five dollars from a street vendor in Beirut. The boots were brown and had a serpent sewn in blue thread. I didn't want just any old shoes for living in America.

"Please take off your shirt," he said. Sweat dripped down my chest. I wished that I were bigger, that my chest were more impressive. "And your pants." Porky and his compatriot went through my jeans, turning out the front pockets, feeling into the back ones, fingering the coin pocket. The dog sniffed the jeans. "Please turn around and face the wall." I put my hands on the wall and spread my legs as if Starsky and Hutch were arresting me. "No, you don't have to do that. Just pull down your underwear." Porky's tone was nicer all of a sudden. His voice had a touch of discomfort. "Could you please spread your cheeks?"

It took me a minute to realize what he meant by "cheeks." I figured it out, but I was embarrassed that I hadn't known *that* use of the word. I sensed his face approach my anus.

"Thank you," Porky said, his tone now hesitant. "You can get dressed now."

Outside, I looked for a taxi. The early-evening light was even, the sky mildly cloudy. The air was heavy, particle-filled. I took shallow breaths as the taxi driver loaded my bags into the trunk. His left hand was darker than his right, and the tops of his ears were sunburned. He drove me on my first American freeway, the 405. I noticed the roads were wet.

We exited on Wilshire Boulevard, straight into heavy traffic. The cabbie cursed. I looked at the car next to me, a black Alfa Romeo Spider with the top down. The driver, in a colorful shirt and Porsche sunglasses, was singing along loudly to the Beatles' "Oh! Darling," bopping his head up and down, drumming on the steering wheel. "Please believe me," I sang along, regretting that I hadn't brought my guitar.

I wasn't some hick from the mountains. I had seen hotels before. I had stayed at the Plaza Athénée in Paris and the Dorchester in London, but neither had prepared me for the extravagent sumptuousness of the Beverly Wilshire. The desk clerk, a boy not much older than I, stood behind the counter, with hair the color of desert sand and a glint in his blue eyes, smiling, showing his excellent teeth. "My name is Osama al-Kharrat," I said. "My father's already here."

"Ah, Mr. al-Kharrat. We've been expecting you." His voice was sweet, confident. "Your father left a message saying his party will be back around nine."

The "party" was my father and Uncle Jihad, who had both wanted to try gambling in Las Vegas. They had decided I should meet them in Los Angeles, where I could look for a school to attend. Beirut was becoming more harrowing. The civil war that everyone had thought would last only a few months had been going on for a couple of years, with no end in sight.

The desk clerk handed me the keys. "Don't you want to see my passport?" I asked.

"No, I trust you." His smile widened. "If you're not Mr. al-Kharrat, then I'll be in big trouble." He wore a dark suit and a white shirt, but his tie was bright yellow, with tiny Daffy Ducks running all over the place.

I grinned back at him. "I am who I said I am."

"The suite is two floors," the bellboy said, opening the door. I walked in ahead of him, trying my best not to appear overwhelmed. "There are two bedrooms on this floor, and a master bedroom below." He carried my bags to one of the rooms. I stood by the banister and stared down at the living room. A spherical crystal chandelier hung from the cathedral ceiling to the lower level. The drapes, as heavy as theater curtains, covering windows two stories high, were the same color and pattern as the wallpaper, gold with stylized metallic gray-blue paisley peacocks. The wall-to-wall carpeting was inches deep and avocado green. I was taking it all in when I noticed that the bellboy was still waiting behind me.

"Oh, sorry," I said, taking out my wallet. My smallest bill was a five. He thanked me and left. One point against this hotel. At the Plaza Athénée in Paris, the bellboys and waiters deliver and leave before you have a chance to tip them. Much classier. I walked into the first room, with the same avocado carpet, the wallpaper in dark rose with a big white floral pattern, matching the bedspread and curtains. The bellboy had put my bags in this room. The bathroom was cream and yellow ocher, with two doors, each opening to one of the upstairs rooms. I walked through the bathroom to the second room, which I assumed to be my father's, but on the nightstand was a Patek Philippe, rather than one of the Baume et Mercier watches that he wore. The cologne was the black Paco Rabanne, definitely Uncle Jihad's, too strong for my father. I descended the stairs to the living room and master bedroom. I sat on the bed, caressed the pillow, laid my head down. I usually loved smelling the scents of my parents on their bed, but something here was peculiar. I stood up, looked around, and saw one of my father's watches.

I went out to my room's balcony with the newspaper and smoked a cigarette, figuring my father would never come out there and catch me. I saw Beverly Hills and America, the parade of cars along an endless boulevard. Dusk. The clouds in the sky had become more ominous, pewter-colored. I was excited, about to see a summer storm. A neon sign on the building across the street said seventy-eight degrees in bright red. In Celsius, 25.555 into infinity, I thought.

Again I wished I had brought my guitar, but I couldn't risk immigration officials' figuring out I was not here for a short tourist visit. In any case, I hoped to buy a better guitar for my new life in America. The *Los Angeles Times* said Thursday's weather forecast was more rain, and highs in the mid-eighties. There was an advertisement for chambray "work shirts" with a touch of class. Why only a touch? A bus hijacker had released the seventy hostages he was holding at a Baha'i retreat not too far from Los Angeles. I felt the moistness of the air, a hot, light-smeared night. I stubbed the cigarette out in the ashtray.

❧

The hospital's fluorescent light emitted a tiresome buzz. I'd grown inured to it in my father's first room, but once Tin Can had him moved to the second room, with all the monitors, at my sister's insistence, I found the interminable hum annoying. I turned off the main lights and switched on a small lamp with a pleated shade that my sister had brought in. I sat on the bed next to my father, focused my eyes on him. I forced myself to look at him, to see him as he was. The image of a younger version kept superimposing itself upon his face. I wasn't sure that the younger image was accurate, either. My father used to say he looked like Robert Mitchum—the hair, the nose, the mouth. "I'm his brother," he'd tell us. Of course, he looked nothing like the actor—not the hair, the nose, or the mouth—but you couldn't argue him out of the resemblance.

Now his skin was slack and spongy. His nose didn't flare, nostrils no longer nervous: another ineffectual organ added to his collection. His eyelids sagged, unmoving. His hair was all white now, even his eyebrows, and his lips had practically disappeared. I kissed his brow.

How black your hair was.

I should feed his hungry ears, but instead I wept, immodestly and noiselessly.

Guilt, that little demon, gnawing and debilitating, voice thief.

I awoke to the pain of a pinched nerve in my shoulder and the sound of Lina entering the room. "You should have used a pillow and blanket." The light seemed fuzzy, as if I were looking at the world through grubby contact lenses. Lina walked over to my father. Her hair was matted, sleep-flattened. The strange early light made her seem acutely lonely. "How is he?"

He's dying, I wanted to say. He seemed fine two days ago, or was it three days ago? I hadn't wanted to sleep. I'd wanted to spend the night by his side, available. I'd wanted to enchant him. I had wanted so much.

❧

I heard the key turning on the lower floor, made sure the balcony doors were closed, and descended the winding stairs to greet my father. Uncle Jihad was pouring drinks at the bar.

"Osama," he said loudly. His eyes sparkled, and his lips broke into a delicious smile. He topped his tall scotch with water and managed to take a sip before I reached him. I stood on my toes to kiss his cheek. He wasn't particularly tall, but at five feet four, I had to stretch to kiss practically anybody. Jolly creases appeared on his chubby face. He looked dapper in a blue suit, jacket unbuttoned, showing his distended stomach, as if he had swallowed a basketball. I heard my father moving about in his room. "Want me to make you a drink?" Uncle Jihad asked.

"I'll take a Coke," I said, walking toward my father's room.

A young blonde woman stood in front of my father's mirror applying lipstick, burgundy red, on full lips. She smiled, put her lipstick in the handbag on the dresser. "Hello," she said, extending her hand. "I'm Melanie." My father came out of the bathroom, zipping his pants.

I felt Uncle Jihad's hand on my shoulder. "Here's your Coke," he said.

"Elvis is dead," my father announced in Arabic. He sat on the large sofa, sipping his scotch. He was his brother's follicular opposite: he had a full head of wavy, thick black hair that you could lose quarters in. He'd changed into brown shorts and a green Lacoste shirt—a concession to Melanie, the stranger among us. Had she not been here, he would be in boxer shorts and T-shirt.

I glanced at Melanie and hesitated before I replied in Arabic, "I know. I read about it."

Even in Western getup, my father didn't look American—too short, too dumpy. When I was younger, my father always wanted me to watch wrestling with him on television. Before the match began, he'd pick a wrestler to root for, and I was left with the other. He wouldn't let me pick first, or choose the same wrestler he did. His man always won. "Pick the one who looks like a decent man," he said. "Decent men never lose." Since I got stuck with the eventual loser, I passed the time comparing my father, in boxers and T-shirt, with the wrestlers in tight trunks. My father had the loose calves of a sedentary man.

"I thought you'd be more upset," he said. "Rock and roll is dead and all that."

"I'm not upset." My voice rose. "I don't care if Elvis is dead. I don't like him. He was old and fat and stupid. It's about time he died."

My father snorted. "We have an appointment tomorrow with the dean of engineering at UCLA." He was still speaking in Arabic, completely ignoring Melanie, who sat across the room. "He says that admission is closed for this fall, but he was impressed with your youth and your grades."

Melanie was reading *Time* magazine, pursing her lips.

"This isn't a child's game," my father said. "It's an interview that will determine your future. Do you understand that?"

"Yes, yes. I'm ready."

"The appointment is tomorrow afternoon at three," he said, picking up the barricading newspaper, a signal ending the conversation.

Melanie sat serenely in her chair. She looked young, couldn't be more than twenty-three, but she had a confident manner. She was like a prettier Nancy Sinatra, with full breasts that were about to burst from her décolleté black dress. Her bleached-blond hair fell below her shoulders. Her eyebrows were plucked. I wanted to inspect them and see if they'd been shaved and drawn in with brown pencil. Her nose was dainty, her chin tiny. The most prominent aspect of her face was the makeup. Her thickly applied lipstick was too dark against her skin. Her eyeliner seemed to cover her lids, and the eye shadow was three-toned, mauve, purple, and light blue. She was the opposite of my mother, who applied her makeup judiciously. I knew Melanie was taking my measure as much as I was hers, but she was more subtle about it.

Uncle Jihad was nursing his drink. He still wore his suit, his tie slightly askew. "Why engineering?" he asked me. "You told me a month ago you wanted to study math."

I looked at the dents and ridges of his bald head. Sweat collected in them, forming miniature pools. Every few minutes he ran his handkerchief over his scalp, momentarily reducing the sheen. Whenever he and my father went gambling, my father kissed the top of Uncle Jihad's head for good luck.

"I like math, Uncle. It's what I'm good at. Engineering is applied math, basically."

"Are you sure that's what you want?"

"Of course he is," my father interrupted from behind the paper. "He can't make a living with a math degree."

It was almost one in the morning, eleven in the morning Beirut time, and I had been up for more than thirty-six hours, but I wasn't ready to sleep yet. I slumped in my chair, my mind racing. "It's raining a lot," I said in English, hoping to engage Melanie in conversation.

"It's been raining all over," Uncle Jihad said.

"This isn't normal," Melanie said. A smooth, melodic voice. "It's unseasonable. The California deserts are having major floods. It even rained in Vegas."

"Is that where you met?" I asked.

In the large bed, with the lights out, I lay thinking. My father had gone into his room with her, closing the door. The night was humid.

❧

The dialysis machine chugalugged my father's blood and regurgitated it back into him. Could a scene be déjà vu if it was truly repeating itself? This was another day. Salwa sat on the bed and held my father's hand. "This won't take long," she told him. "Only another forty-five minutes." My sister, on the rust recliner, leaned back and covered her eyes with her forearm. The narcoleptic technician's head rested on his chest. I stood at the foot of the bed, counting off red time with the dialysis machine.

There was a knock on the open door. I was the only one who could see out, and my sister waved for me to send whoever it was away. A beautiful woman of indeterminate age stood in the doorway in an extravagant sable coat and stiletto heels. She wore stylish, heavy makeup, which made her face look as white and pure as a cake of halloumi. Her short bouffant hair was dyed a chestnut brown with precisely equidistant blond streaks. I recognized her after she smiled a childlike smile yet terribly saucy. I hadn't seen her in over twenty years.

"Nisrine," I said softly as I walked toward her. I surprised myself by using her first name. How old was she? She kissed me, cheek to cheek, three times. "I don't think it's a good idea for you to go in," I said. "He doesn't like to be seen when he's sick."

She kept her hand on my cheek. "I knocked only to make sure he's decent." She strolled in and stopped as if she had encountered an invisible electric fence, as if she were face to face with death's scythe. A tiny cry escaped her lips, and her face crumpled. Her first tear carved a furrow in her foundation. Nisrine's hand went to her left eye, and her finger removed one contact lens, then the other. She cried, holding her tiny lenses in the palm of her hand as an offering to the gods of grief.

Nisrine and Jamil Sadek moved into the third floor of the building behind ours in 1967. In no time, they had established themselves as the most popular couple in the neighborhood. She was beautiful, witty, and flirtatious, and he was a delightful drunk. Few remembered she was a mother of three, for she was rarely seen with her children in public. Fewer still could help enjoying the misshapen, congenital liar she was married to. Captain Jamil was the only man in the neighborhood I was able to look down on, literally and figuratively. He was shorter than many children, but not exactly a dwarf. His huge paunch always seemed about to topple him. He canted his side hair like a sheaf over the top of his bald head. And he was no captain.

Stories about him were legion, but none were as famous as the one about his repeated failures at being promoted to full-fledged pilot. He made sure that all called him Captain Jamil. He was the oldest copilot at the airline and flunked every captain exam, but you'd never know it from talking to him. He told tall tales of saving flights from sure disasters, of passengers writing him sheaves of letters detailing their gratitude. He told of the other captains' looking up to him and pleading with him for flying lessons. None of his listeners believed him, and all pretended they did.

One day, he arrived at our house for lunch. As a gift, he brought a bottle of blended scotch whisky in a yellow box sporting pictures of affluent, well-dressed men. "This whisky is called House of Lords," he announced. "It's specifically made for English royalty and nobles. A member of the British Parliament who happens to be the queen's best friend presented it to me on my last trip to London." This was the only time anyone unraveled his lie publicly. Uncle Jihad drove to Spinneys, the supermarket, while lunch was being served, and returned within half an hour with another yellow box of the cheap brand. He placed it on the table and announced that the queen herself had given it to him, but on one condition. "The queen told me, in her perfect British accent, of course, that she loved me and considered me worthy of such a perfect bottle of whisky, but that this magnificent brew should be served only to the best of men, to the greatest of friends." And he poured a glass for Captain Jamil.

It was the captain's young wife, though, who ensured that the couple received an invitation to every event. She was a bon vivant, and bright, if not too cultured or sophisticated; an uneducated Sunni from Tripoli who realized that she had to rely on her piercing wit and charm to overcome being married to a parody and get ahead in life. And did she ever get ahead. At every gathering, men roamed her summers like fire-flies. She amused them, teased and cajoled them. Told the best dirty jokes and the funniest bawdy tales. She was the only woman who could turn our neighborhood militiaman, Elie, into an ogling, trembling teenage boy who desperately tried to cover his excitement every time she walked by. She and Uncle Jihad formed a mutual-admiration soci-ety. They would sit in the corner and make fun of everybody else. He once asked her why she married her husband when she could have done so much better. She replied that she'd been young. Captain Jamil had appeared at her doorstep in his sports car. She was blinded by the pilot's uniform. He spoke to her of flying, what it felt like to be up in the air, the freedom, the glory, the escape from the mundane. She dreamed of magic carpets.

One day, Uncle Akram made the mistake of hinting to my father and Uncle Jihad that he had slept with Nisrine. At an evening gather-ing on our balcony, as Nisrine delicately puffed her hookah, my father said to her, "Nisrine, my dear, Akram is telling quite a few people that he has bedded you." She cracked up and crackled, smoke sprouting from her mouth like the sudden eruption of a mountain hot spring. I could see the unadulterated glee in Uncle Jihad's brown eyes. "Hey, Akram," she shouted across the balcony. "Come over here and enter-tain me for a minute." He hurried over like a child called by his favorite teacher to the blackboard. "Tell me, dear," she cooed. "I hear you have a wonderful story, and I love stories." She smiled, batted her eyelashes a few times, and took a long drag from the hookah. She blew the smoke seductively into his eager face. "I hear that you fucked me, and I want to know whether I was good."

I poured myself a glass of fresh grapefruit juice as my father read the morning paper. Melanie was already dressed in a light-green summer suit. She was standing by the tall windows. "Looks like it's letting up," she said. "Might turn out to be a nice day. We can probably walk."

"Where are we going?" I asked.

"Shopping," my father said. "I should get your mother something."

My father went to his room to get dressed, and I sat down and phoned my mother. I had forgotten to call when I first arrived, as I had promised. She wanted to talk. "I miss you already." I grunted acknowledgment. "Will you make sure to take care of yourself?" I looked around the room. "You will call me once a week?" I watched Melanie light a filtered Kool cigarette and drink her coffee. I used the word "mama" to make sure she knew who I was talking to. Melanie turned around in her chair, crossed her legs. "I don't care how old you are, you'll always be my baby." A lipstick stain appeared on the filter. Melanie used her forefinger to flick the ash dramatically. "I don't know what I'll do without you here." Smoke curled out of her mouth. The lipstick was pink this morning. "You're your mother's only son."

When I hung up, Melanie smiled at me tentatively. "Aren't you a little young to be going to college?"

"I'm terribly smart."

"I can see that." Her laugh included an unattractive snort.

My father wanted to take our rented Cadillac to Rodeo Drive. Uncle Jihad wanted to walk, since it was only across the street from the hotel. The doorman suggested we take the hotel's car, which dropped us off at Giorgio's, two blocks away. The four of us must have appeared quite a tableau to passersby, a hodgepodge family of sorts.

The salesman zeroed in on my father, ignoring the rest of us. It must have been the Brioni suit. My father explained what he wanted. The salesman, an attractive young man, looked normal below the belt, but his torso leaned back at an almost unnatural angle, his left arm draped across it, and his right hand seemed to tweak an imaginary string of pearls. All of a sudden, both forefingers pointed at my father. "I have something that may be just perfect," he said, and scampered across the floor, disappearing from sight. He returned with bundles of cloth in delectable colors, reds, variegated greens, yellows from lemon to ocher. He put them on the counter and spread one out. "Cashmere shawls," he said. "No woman can resist." His hand smoothed the fabric in a wide arc. "You just have to pick the color."

"What do you think?" my father asked. I wasn't sure which of us he was asking, Melanie or me.

I stepped forward, touching the fabric in the same wide arc. "This is beautiful."

"I think so, too," Melanie said.

My father went through the pile, picked a deep-sienna shawl. "You think your mom will like this?" I nodded. He handed the shawl to the salesman. My father kept looking, picked up a blue-green shawl, and held it next to Melanie's eyes. "And this one, too," he told the salesman. Melanie blushed.

"I want you to know something," my father said in Arabic. "She's not a prostitute."

I stammered something unintelligible. I didn't know what to say.

"I'm not paying her." He was staring at a far corner of the store.

"Okay." I stared at the other corner.

"She wants to be a singer. I can't tell if she's any good. I don't understand this music. She sings a lot, so listen and tell me."

It began to rain softly. Uncle Jihad carried a bottle of cologne and whistled a Lebanese tune. He picked up a loud yellow scarf, flicked one end over his left shoulder, examining the effect in a full-length mirror. Melanie looked at a dress on a hanger, fingered the material. "Why don't you try it on?" my father suggested.

"He is loved," I said above the dins of the room.

My sister had taken Nisrine to the visitors' room. Fatima had returned and claimed my sister's seat. The diminishing red numbers of the dialysis machine entranced her, as they did me. Twenty-two minutes, thirteen seconds. Salwa held my father's hand.

"What do you mean?" she asked.

"It's so obvious Nisrine loves him," I replied. "You can't fake that reaction. It broke my heart watching her."

"Yes," she said. "They were lovers once."

"No," I blurted. "No. It only seemed that way because they both loved to flirt." My niece just looked at me, her eyebrows forming the top halves of question marks. "How would you know anyway?" I said. "You weren't even born." My voice faltered. "It can't be. He flirted with her in front of my mother. He wouldn't have done that if it were for real. They were friends."

Fatima raised her arms in despair and sighed.

Salwa looked at me with my mother's eyes, brown and wide. In a steady voice, she said, "She was one of his many mistresses."

"How can you be sure?" I asked, my voice much weaker than hers.

"I'm not saying I don't believe you, but all you're going by is what Lina tells you."

"He paid for her eldest son's schooling. You know that."

"Of course," I replied. "They were friends of the family."

"Stop, Osama," Fatima ordered, loud enough to shock the technician awake. "Take our word for it. If you want me to list all his mistresses, I will. Maybe it's time you talked to your sister and compared notes."

Lina filled her lungs with smoke on the balcony. I studied the straight lines of building rooftops. "How could you not know they had an affair?" Lina asked. We both looked out at the calm Mediterranean, which could be seen through a large gap between two buildings.

"God, Osama. You know he slept with other women. You couldn't have been that blind. Why do you think she finally left him?"

"Please. I'm not stupid. He didn't hide his womanizing from me. He was proud of it. I just didn't think he'd do it with Nisrine. I don't know why. Not her."

She leaned forward on the railing and took another drag. "Why not her?"

"Oh, I don't know," I huffed. "Maybe because she was a friend of the family. Maybe because my mother knew her. Maybe because we all knew her. I don't know."

She reached out and pulled me to her. I took the cigarette from her hand and noisily smoked half of it. "Bad form," she said.

"Yes, that's it," I snapped. "It's fucking bad form. That's what it is."

I felt her shake before I heard her laugh, a staccato outburst. It took a few seconds for me to join in. I tapped the cigarette ash too hard, and the glowing cinder dropped toward the street below. "I can't fucking believe it," I said.

"Fuck yes."

"But you're wrong. She didn't just leave him because of his philandering. You know that. It wasn't just the women." I gripped the balcony's rail, took a loud breath. "He had this way of looking at women he was flirting with, an expressive quality—humorous, even. It was as if his eyes asked them to confide in him, to tell him their stories."

"His eyes never invited me to share with him," she said.

"Me, neither."

❧

We sat at the burnt-orange dinette set, my father, Melanie, and I, wait-ing for Uncle Jihad to finish his shower. My sister had called and teased me as usual. She said my mother missed me so much she went out and bought a pot of hydrangea, and now no one could tell I was gone. My father smoked, read the paper, and drank his coffee. He made a gur-gling sound with each sip. "We have to ask about residence," he said. "Where will you stay?"

"Don't know. Maybe the dorms." I looked around the suite. "Maybe I'll stay here. This is grand enough for me."

"It's nothing compared with the suite in Las Vegas. We had a swim-ming pool in the room."

"It's true," said Melanie.

"In a hotel room? Why? Did you swim in it?"

"No," my father replied. "Why should I swim in a pool?"

"I don't know. You have a pool in your room, you should swim in it."

"That's silly." He crushed the cigarette in the ashtray and picked up the paper.

"Oh, Dad, you just have no imagination."

Melanie had to stop herself from laughing.

My father folded his paper. "Why don't you two go out dancing tomorrow night? You two should go to a dance club and have fun. What's the name of the place you told us about?"

"My Place," Melanie said. "It's the *in* club."

"You want us to go dancing?" I asked, to make sure I'd understood correctly.

"Yes. Go out and have fun. I don't want to go to a dance club. My ears won't be able to handle it. You two kids like music. Go out and have fun."

Uncle Jihad came down whistling a polka, his feet keeping time on the stairs. He hesitated for a moment, appearing concerned, and his face blanched. He seemed to lose his breath, but it was only a brief interruption of the polka, a musical hiccup. He descended the stairs happily. My father stood up. "Let's go," he said. "We don't want to be late to the interview."

❧

In the waiting room, my cousin Hafez leaned over and whispered into my ear, "I must see him. I must." His moist eyes pleaded, regarded me with such ardor, as if I were a saint and my blessing was what he lived for. Or was it my father's?

"I'll ask Lina."

"Please, don't. You know she wouldn't let me." His hand fell on my knee, like my father's used to whenever he wanted me to pay attention. "I'm asking you."

It was as if I were seeing him for the first time. Hello, I'm your cousin Hafez. We grew up together and spent hours and days and weeks and months and years in each other's company, but you have no clue who I am. Let me introduce myself. I was supposed to be your twin, but . . .

Hafez hesitated slightly at the door before entering the room with me. My sister smiled at him. I cocked my head toward the balcony, and Lina understood. She gestured a need for a cigarette and stood up. She slid the balcony's door silently and glided out.

Hafez and I were a study in contrasts, I in Nikes, jeans, and a UCLA sweatshirt, and he in suit and tie and Italian moccasins. My disheveled hair was badly in need of a trim, and his was gelled and styled. He looked more like my father in his prime than I ever did. He was a family man with three teenage children, and I was nothing more than an unkempt teenager, even though only six weeks separated us. He was always more our family than I was.

He stood at the foot of the bed, what had been my space in the room. He looked as if he was about to cry but still wasn't used to the idea. He stared at my father as if he wanted to tell him something, or wanted my father to make things right. "I guess his heart is tired," he whispered. He inhaled deeply. He was standing as close as possible without our touching. "I hadn't expected him to fall before my mother. She has been all right this week, with all the family here for Eid al-Adha, but she'll begin to get worse when Mona returns to Dubai and Munir to Kuwait. They—" He stopped. His face flushed, and he shut his eyes. The only reason his brother and sister hadn't flown back to their homes in the Gulf was that they would have to return to Lebanon for my father's funeral.

❧

The UCLA campus was as big as a whole city. School hadn't started yet, but the campus was busy nonetheless. My father gave Melanie a couple of hundred dollars to shop at the student store. The engineering department was an entire building. The size of the dean of engineering was proportional. He was six feet six and round, with a ruffle of double chins draped over his starched white collar. He introduced himself as "Dean Johnson, but call me Fred."

"I understand you're quite the intelligent young man," the dean said. He seemed jovial and pleasant, a nice person, with a cheerful, impish expression on his fleshy face.

"I test well." I had the right instincts for multiple-choice questions.

"Have you taken the SATs yet?" He leaned back in his chair.

"Yes, I have. Everything is in the folder."

He reached for the folder and perused the papers. "You scored sixteen hundred?" he asked—rhetorically, I presumed.

"We had to have him take the GCE with the British Council," my father said. "We weren't sure there would be any baccalaureates this year, because of the war."

"This is very impressive," Fred said, shaking his head. "I wish you had come to me a little earlier. Admissions have been closed for a while." He kept looking at all my scores. "Are you considering any other university?" he asked, not removing his eyes from my papers. "Wait. Don't answer that. Let me make a phone call." He stood up and left his office.

Neither my father nor Uncle Jihad nor I spoke a single word while the dean was out, as if any syllable would bring down a jinni's curse upon the proceedings. But then Uncle Jihad stood up, went over to my father, and bent his head. I heard the sound of my father's lips meeting Uncle Jihad's head. A good-luck kiss.

The dean re-entered the office, obviously excited. He leaned on his desk in front of me. "I may have been able to do something, but I have to ask you some questions. Are you sure UCLA is the right school for you? Have you thought about what we have to offer?"

"Yes. I like the school. I like Los Angeles."

"And there's a war back in your country, right?"

"Yes," I replied, unsure where that was going.

"And UCLA is your only chance right now for an uninterrupted education, right? UCLA will provide you a peaceful setting where you can pursue a degree and continue your record of academic excellence.

Isn't that so?" I nodded. "Good. Then that's settled." He laughed
heartily. "Here's what I need you to do, young man. I'd like you to fill
out an application for admission to the university. It has to be done
right away, so I can take it to the admissions office before they close.
That also includes an essay. Do you think you can do that now?" I
nodded once more. "Good. Josephine outside will put you in an empty
office, and you can get to work. I'll talk to your father here about
logistics."

"Can I also take music classes?" I asked. I heard my father sigh.

The dean looked at me quizzically. "It's not the norm for engineering students to take music classes."

"Shouldn't it be?" I asked. "In the Middle Ages, the music and
mathematics departments were one and the same. You couldn't study
one without the other. They're complements, really. It stayed that way
until the last century. The separation of music from mathematics is
recent."

"You don't need to study music," my father said sternly. "You've
already studied enough music. We won't discuss this anymore."

"Filling out the application may take some time," the dean told my
father. "You can wait, or I can send him to the hotel by taxi, whichever
is more convenient."

"Are you sure you can get him in?" my father asked.

"No, I'm not sure. The dean of admissions is willing to look at his
records. That's a very good sign. I'll find out soon. In any case, here's
the application." He handed me some forms. "Just take it outside to
Josephine, and she'll find you a quiet place to fill it out."

I thanked him and got up to leave. "Remember," he said, "put everything we talked about in the essay. And don't mention the music-and-
math theory, okay?"

As I closed the door, I heard my father say quietly, "He's just a little
immature sometimes. Not always."

Before she led me to the office, I asked Josephine where the men's
room was. I went in, peed, masturbated, and sneaked a couple of puffs
from a cigarette. The essay I wrote elaborated on my theory of com-
bining math and music, and I included a timeline graph as well.

I had just stepped out of the shower when Uncle Jihad opened the
bathroom door on his side. I covered myself with the towel. I was starting to hate the idea of a bathroom with doors connecting two rooms.

"It's not like I haven't seen you naked before," he said as I wrapped the towel around my waist. He tilted his bottle of cologne and dabbed a few drops on his scalp.

"I see you broke the perfume bottles as well," I said. He laughed.

Uncle Jihad used to tell a story about a parrot, the pet of an oil-and-perfume merchant. For years, the parrot entertained customers with tales and anecdotes. One night, a cat chased a mouse into the shop, which frightened the parrot. She flew from shelf to shelf, breaking bottles in her wake. When the merchant returned, he hit the parrot with a blow that knocked off her head feathers. The bald parrot was upset for days, until, one morning, a man with no hair entered the shop, and the bird yelled in joy, "Did you break the perfume bottles as well?"

Uncle Jihad washed his hands, building layers of lather. "I think the dean really wants you." He talked to my image in the mirror.

"Yes. I think I'm in." I dried myself with a second towel. "My father wants me to take Melanie dancing."

"He told me. I think it's a good idea. He thinks you spend too much time studying and reading. Melanie will have fun, and it'll be good for you."

"*He* should take her dancing."

"He's not the dancing type."

He stared at my chest, probably wondering why I hadn't filled out yet. I went into my room and put on a UCLA T-shirt Melanie had bought for me.

"Where did they meet?" I asked.

"At the baccarat table."

"Did he stop to think she's almost as young as Lina?"

"Hey," he said, shaking an admonishing finger, "I don't want you to say anything like that. You can't even think that." He stood before me in my room, his face an angry red. He looked exhausted, for some reason.

♣

Chain-smoking, Lina had finished three cigarettes on the balcony. She gestured for me to get rid of Hafez, running her forefinger across her throat. She may have left the room, but her specter hadn't. "I hear you went to the old neighborhood," Hafez said. "I go there quite a bit these days so I don't forget. I can take you into your apartment if you want."

"That might be interesting."

"Why don't you play the oud for him?"

I hesitated, surprised. "Hafez, I haven't played the oud in about thirty years."

It was his turn to look stunned. "Why? You were so good. What happened?"

"I switched to guitar a long time ago, and then I stopped playing that. I got bored."

"I don't understand." His voice rose to more than just a whisper. He seemed more animated. "Everyone was so envious of you. The family used to talk about your playing. How can you get bored with music? I wouldn't have." He smiled at me, and his eyes regained a bit of luster. "I guess I should go now, look in on my mother. Call me if you want to go to the old neighborhood." I walked with him to the door, four steps. "I would have kept on playing if I had your talent," he said. "Yes, I would."

That night, my sister and I were in my father's room. The lights of the ward had dimmed. She cuddled herself in the recliner, and I sat on the floor, leaning against the bed. She poked me with her foot, once, twice. Go home. Go home. I held her foot with both hands, pressed my thumbs along the heel.

"Hafez isn't the only one who was disappointed you stopped playing," she said. "I don't think I've ever forgiven you. No one has. When Salwa was a child, I used to regale her with stories of how amazing you were. She never got to hear you. She tried to take up the oud, but she wasn't any good. I should blame you for that as well."

"Blame me." I pinched her foot. "I only played when I was a child."

"And I have to admit that I wasn't as fond of your guitar."

"You're the one who made me learn to play."

She reached for the water bottle on the side table. "I can tell you a strange story about Hafez. If you want, that is."

"Of course I do. Gossip stokes the fire of my soul."

"Hah. Well, where do I start? For the last six or seven years, Hafez has been disappearing a few afternoons every week. You know that, right? He swore to his wife that he wasn't cheating, but he wouldn't tell her or anyone what he was doing. I knew Hafez wasn't cheating—it's Anwar who's the asshole philanderer. It was just that no one knew what Hafez had been up to. Anyway, a few years ago, Fatima decided she wanted to go to the souk in Tripoli, do the tourist thing, mix with the common people. She dragged me along, and there we were, in the gold market, when we saw him. He was carrying a tourist guide to Lebanon, in English, holding it front side out, so everyone could see. He tried to look bewildered and engrossed, gazing around as if he were seeing everything for the first time. Just as I was about to call him, a woman walked by him and said in English, 'Welcome to Lebanon.' His face lit up as if he had swallowed the sun, the moon, and all the stars. Then he saw us and turned as red as a ripe summer tomato. He swore us to secrecy and explained. It turned out his favorite pastime was to stroll around various places pretending to be a tourist. He did it mostly in Beirut, but he hit all the other major hot spots of Lebanon, too. He walked all over the place with a guidebook, desperately trying to be seen as someone other."

*

Shavings of light were strewn on the avocado carpet. I had slept late. I heard nothing downstairs. I drew open the curtains on a glorious day, the light clear and merciless. I put on shorts and sunglasses, went out on the balcony for my morning smoke. I lay back on the chair, soaking up sunlight, and hummed "California Dreaming."

"All the leaves are brown." A cold gust of panic. I jumped out of my seat and hid my cigarette behind my back. Melanie stood at the balcony door in shorts, her sunglasses hooked into her bikini bra; she carried a tray with a coffeepot and two cups. "Sorry about startling you, but I thought you might want a cup of coffee up here. They went shopping." She had a touch of roguishness to her smile. "You can take the cigarette out of your butt." I had to laugh. She sat down, poured us coffee. Her bikini top covered nothing but her nipples. "We don't have to go dancing if you don't want. We can go to a movie and tell them we went dancing."

"It's just that I hate disco," I said. "I never go to dance clubs."

"That's settled, then." She lit a cigarette. "What do you like to do? What did you do in Beirut on Friday nights?"

"Planted explosives, shot at pedestrians from balconies, that sort of thing." She almost choked on her coffee, gave her weird snort. "Mostly stayed home or hung out with a friend," I said. "Played music. Got stoned."

"You want to get high tonight?" She gauged me with her eyes.

"Absolutely."

"I have a friend in town we can go see. He's got a great record collection and killer weed. We'll spend the evening there. He's an honest dealer. Every college student needs one of those."

I settled back in my chair, drank the coffee. I looked at her hands, perfectly manicured. She was wearing much less makeup. I admired her attractive profile, the chin small yet angular, the European nose, small and tilted up. My mother couldn't compete with that nose; hers was thin, though long and curved like a bird's beak. My mother was known for her beauty, but it was an altogether different kind. "Do you ever think of my mother?" I asked.

"I don't know your mother."

I looked at the clear sky, a much different blue than in Lebanon.

When my father and Uncle Jihad walked into the living room, Melanie almost spoiled the surprise. She flitted about like a three-year-old girl on a sugar high, unable to keep the smile off her face. She wore black hot pants and a sleeveless denim jacket that reached her calves. I sat on the big sofa, facing the door, my right foot across my left knee, looking all too important. My father began to guess at something peculiar. "You're looking at a UCLA student," I announced.

My father's face broke out in unadulterated joy. He leapt across the room, picked me up, and hauled me over his shoulders. I squealed, unable to control my delight. Melanie was jumping up and down. She was about to embrace Uncle Jihad but pulled back at the last moment.

"I'm so proud of you," my father said from below.

"Well, put me down," I said, chuckling. He did, but with a bear hug. I had to push him away, because I couldn't breathe. "Dean Johnson called. They want me. I can check in to the dorms on Monday, and classes start on Wednesday."

"Did you call your mother?"

"Yes, I told her. We have to pay tuition on Monday, Dad."

"Okay. Let's go open up a bank account for you. And here." He gave me an American Express card with my name on it. "This is a company account. Use it only in case of an emergency. Do you understand? I'll give you a monthly stipend. I want you to write down every expense you incur. I want to see a monthly report. Every single penny."

I hesitated, but this had to be the best possible time to broach the subject. "I want to buy a guitar, Dad."

"No, absolutely not. No more guitars. I told you that in Beirut.

You're here to study. I don't want to hear another word about guitars anymore. Find another hobby."

"But, Dad, I'm really good. I need to practice."

"No whining and no guitar."

Melanie's friend Mike lived in a small apartment on Pico Boulevard in West Los Angeles. As we walked along an open corridor, I saw the blue light of televisions flickering behind drawn curtains, heard the canned laughter of sitcoms. Fonzie on the tube delivered his bon mot, "Aaay!" The apartments all faced a glittering swimming pool. Melanie knocked on a door with the number seven in tarnished brass. Mike opened the door, wearing gray swim trunks, blue T-shirt, and red flipflops. He was tall and muscular, with wavy black hair, a heavy mustache, long wiry sideburns, and small yellow wire-rims atop a predatory nose. A scar as white as marble ran down his neck. "You must be Osama." His voice was twice the size of mine. "Melanie has told me a lot about you."

A light-brown mutt jumped up on Melanie the instant she walked through the door. She shrieked, almost stumbled, and hugged the dog. "Bobsie," she said in baby talk, "you're still the cutest dog, aren't you?"

The apartment had an avocado-green carpet, a cheaper version of the hotel's. An elaborately framed Patrick Nagel print hung on one wall. I sat on a yellow-green Herculon sofa next to Melanie. Small talk ensued. How did I like America? Land of the big and tall and perfect teeth. Was I looking forward to living in Los Angeles? Better than spending every evening in the bomb shelters of Beirut.

Melanie opened a shoebox on the cable-spool coffee table. "Smell," she said, holding a sprig of marijuana under my nose. "It's great stuff."

"It smells great, but I'm sure it's not as good as hash. In Lebanon, we throw this out. Hash is the pollen." I sat back and almost knocked a chrome lamp over.

"I don't think I want to throw out *this* grass." Mike smiled as he walked to his entertainment center and put an Al Di Meola record on. Melanie rolled a joint using a contraption with a Stars and Stripes motif. She lit the joint and passed it to me. "This is good shit."

The first hit went straight to my head. I petted the dog, who jumped up on the sofa and put his head on my lap. "He likes you," Mike said.

"I had a wonderful dog called Tulip who died of a heart attack over a year ago."

"Your dad told me the dog was run over by a car," Melanie said.

"No, no. She had a heart attack. I was in the mountains, and Tulip was with my parents in Beirut. There was a lot of fighting, and all the noise scared her so much it caused the heart attack. I was really upset that I wasn't there when she died. But my dad took care of everything."

I took another hit, feeling high yet slightly unsettled. Loose change nestled in the sofa. Mike poured a bag of tortilla chips into a blue crystal bowl—my first taste of Mexican food. "Were you living in Beirut itself?" Mike asked between tokes. "In the middle of the war?"

"Yes. I was even shot at a couple of times. It's crazy. You can't imagine what it's like."

He smiled as he rolled another joint. "I can imagine. I did three tours in Vietnam."

I wasn't sure I heard him correctly. I was already stoned, feeling wonderful. "Did you say you were drafted three times?" Melanie was looking at me with a shit-eating grin. She passed me the second joint, stood up, and danced seductively to the music.

"No, drafted once." He lay back in his chair, legs wide apart. "I re-upped a couple of times." He looked as stoned as I felt. I stared at his muscled calves.

"Why did you do that?" I slurred my question.

"I really don't know." He put his glasses back on, took them off, breathed on his lenses, and polished them with his T-shirt. Melanie walked through the beaded curtain into the kitchen and reappeared with a beer and a Coke in either hand, showing me both. I pointed at the Coke. Mike took the beer. "Who knows why we choose what we choose," he said, reaching over to open my can of Coke. "Maybe because life in-country seemed to be more real than it was back in the world." He smiled gently. "You doing okay? You need anything?"

"Tubular Bells" was playing, but I couldn't figure out when the music had changed. Mike was saying something that sounded like "Plei Me Special Forces Camp." I wasn't sure I liked the music, even though I'd heard it numerous times before. "Battle of Ia Drang." Mike's left hand massaged my neck. "Beirut must have been horrifying, too." Minuscule creases appeared on his forehead. "Sex and death, death and sex, or vice versa." He held another joint to my lips with his right hand, and I took more drags. "M-60 machine guns gung ho." I started seeing Linda Blair's head rotating, and I couldn't stop giggling.

I tried to apologize to Mike but was unable to stifle my laughter. How could my father forget how Tulip died? My father told me he held Tulip in his arms as she had a heart attack. Now my father didn't remember how she died. I wondered if I could forgive my father for that. The Nagel print was ugly. I wondered if anybody in the world had a Nagel original. I took a sip of Coke and stuffed my face with tortilla chips. One of the throw pillows had a honeycomb pattern that made me dizzy. I kept attempting to figure out whether it was a black pattern on a white background or vice versa. I laid my head back on the chair, looked up at the cottage-cheese ceiling. I snapped my head back quickly. "I just thought of Hendrix and got scared," I said loudly. I was alone in the room.

"Tubular Bells" repeated itself. Crumbs of tortilla chips remained in the crystal bowl. I pushed the bowl until it fell off the table and cracked.

Melanie emerged from the bedroom adjusting her skirt, hobbling on one shoe, the other in her hand. "It's midnight," she said cheerfully. "We don't want to be too late." Mike followed her out, wearing only boxer shorts.

I stood up while Melanie applied her lipstick, fixed her hair at the mirror. "It was nice meeting you," Mike said. I walked out the door without replying.

Melanie drove the Cadillac back to the hotel. I pulled down the visor and looked at myself in the mirror. "Are you okay?" she asked.

"I'm fine," I lied. "Do you think I have ugly teeth?"

"No, they're not ugly. If you think they are, they can be fixed, but I think they're cute—sexy, even."

"Not sexy enough for you to have sex with me," I said, staring straight ahead. I felt her hesitation. "Don't worry," I added. "I don't want to have sex with you anyway."

"I know," she said, shyly and evenly. "I didn't think you did."

❧

One minute my sister was talking to me, whispering quietly about nothing in particular, and the next her voice faded. Even in sleep, she seemed tense, her breathing more hamsterish than restful. I slowly lifted myself off the floor. The muscles of my lower back and hamstrings groaned and objected. I walked around the bed toward my father. He seemed to be incrementally imploding, as if his wan skin were unhurriedly devouring his insides, and his body would soon collapse upon itself once the meal was finished.

When it would get to be my time to leave, I hoped I'd go quickly, suddenly and unexpectedly, like Uncle Jihad, not like my father, and not like my mother.

I held my father's hand and stroked his dry hair, willing myself to imagine a reflex, an indication of responsiveness to my touch. I wanted to believe. I bent down and kissed his forehead, and my shirt grazed the ventilator tube. I felt an urge to take an iron bar, smite the machine, crush it. The pathetic rage of the impotent.

I kept praying for some form of movement from my father. I bent my face into the slit of his line of sight, hoping my dimly lit familiar and familial face would comfort him.

Once, when I was eight or nine, my parents took me to London, my first visit to the brooding city. My mother had wanted to walk in Hyde Park. My father, who never understood why people still walked, decades after the automobile had been invented, said he'd come along because he didn't want to stay in the hotel by himself. We left the lobby through the revolving doors and were inundated by a weaving multitude of people. My mother turned back into the hotel, but my father stood his ground, mesmerized. He held my hand and watched as a sea of pale skin engulfed him. He looked confused for a moment, and then he smiled and said good morning in Lebanese to a passerby in a suit. The man smiled and replied in Lebanese as well. He bowed his head, and his palm sought his heart in an exaggerated gesture. He nodded toward me in acknowledgment and continued on his way. The Lebanese face, unknown yet familiar, had moored my father. Happy again, he led me back into the hotel.

❧

Uncle Jihad didn't answer my knock on the locked bathroom door. I walked around to his room, still early-morning groggy. He wasn't there. I knocked on his bathroom door, then tried it. It was unlocked. Uncle Jihad sat on the toilet, his pajama pants around his ankles, his head slumped, his eyes staring at a spot on the carpet. The bathroom smelled of shit. I suppressed an urge to scream. I rushed over, shook him by the shoulder. His skin felt cold. I recoiled. I bent down to look at his face. His eyes were lifeless. I searched for a pulse on his wrist. None. I broke into silent tears. Shaking, I walked out of the bathroom into the orange corridor, held on to the metal railing for support. My father sat at the dinette table, drinking his coffee and reading the paper. Melanie sat opposite, already dressed and made up.

"Dad," I said, my voice distorted. "Uncle Jihad is dead in the bathroom."

He looked up at me disbelievingly. I watched his face gradually change; his eyes grew whiter, his jaw dropped. He ran up the stairs, followed by Melanie. I let them pass me. I heard my father wail. I had never seen my father cry before, never seen him so distraught. He knelt on the floor and rocked Uncle Jihad in his arms. I couldn't understand a word my father said. I stood in the doorway in shock. My father wouldn't stop. He wept, the bathroom reverberating with the sound. In between sobs, my father kissed Uncle Jihad's bald head. Melanie, tears flowing down her face, tried unsuccessfully to calm him. I no longer recognized the man in front of me. I called my mother. "Listen to me," she said. "Put your father on the phone. Then you go to his room and get his travel pack. In it, you'll find a pillbox. Take out a Valium and give it to him. Do you understand?"

In the bathroom, Melanie held my father, who held Uncle Jihad. I gave my father the bathroom phone and watched his face as he began to calm down. I ran downstairs and came back up with the tranquilizer. I watched him nod in acquiescence to my mother's instructions. He handed me the phone. My mother told me to put him to bed and said she would call back in ten minutes, after she called the hotel management.

Melanie and I helped my father down the stairs, his arms draped over both of us. I put him in bed, under the covers. Melanie drew the curtains, darkening the room. I stroked his head, just as I had seen my mother do many times before. He promptly drifted into sleep.

I went back up to check on Uncle Jihad. I didn't want anybody to see him naked with his pajama bottoms down. When I entered the bathroom, I held my nose and flushed the toilet.

"Do you want to carry him to his bed?" Melanie asked.

I nodded. I was pulling his pants up when I realized his bottom was soiled. I wiped his behind with a damp washcloth. My stomach felt queasy again.

I tried to lift Uncle Jihad from his shoulders while Melanie took his feet, but he was too heavy. We ended up dragging him slowly. The carpet kept pulling his pants down, exposing his genitals. By the time we got him onto the bed, I was dripping sweat. I covered him with the comforter and closed his eyes. His skin already felt leathery.

Uncle Jihad used to tell me an Iraqi story about whom to mourn.

It seems the great Caliph Haroun al-Rashid was traveling among his people when he came across a woman weeping. He asked the cause of her immense sorrow, and she replied that she was mourning her beloved son, who had just died. He asked her what her son did while he was alive. She said he worked for her. She was poor, and her son kept her alive. She no longer had anyone to take care of her and no one to make her a living. "Cry no more," said the caliph. "I will give you a sturdy mule. He will work hard for you and help you earn a living. You shall not miss your son. You will be as comfortable as you were before."

Haroun al-Rashid moved on. He came across another woman crying next to the grave of her son. The caliph asked her the same question, "What did your son do while he was alive?"

"My son? He used to gather honest nobles and men of good repute to his feasts. He would serve them the most delicious of meals. He would entertain them with the most ambrosial of music, regale them with the greatest of tales. When these men left his feasts, he would ride with them, keeping them company until they lost sight of his tent."

"Weep on, O mother of a most gracious son," said the caliph. "Cry and shed more tears, for no one, certainly not I, can comfort you or make good such a great loss."

And Haroun al-Rashid wept.

I sat on the bed, crying and stroking Uncle Jihad's head. My mother called. Just as she said that someone from the hotel would be coming to the room, I heard a knock on the door. My mother had talked to Air France and booked my father on a flight to Beirut. Melanie led three men in suits to Uncle Jihad's room. "All I want from you is to put your father on the flight this afternoon," my mother said. "That's all. Everything else will be taken care of. Once he's on the flight, Air France will make sure he gets here, but I need you to get him on the plane. After the doctor and coroner do their work, the hotel will ship Jihad to

Beirut. Just take care of your father. You can stay in the room till you go to the dorms. It's dealt with."

"I'll get him on the plane," I promised. I watched more men walk into Uncle Jihad's room.

"One more thing," she said. "Make sure she leaves. I don't want her using the suite after your father's gone. Don't let your father know that I know. But remember, after your father's gone, she's gone. I don't want her with you."

❧

The muffled footsteps sounded odd, quieter than nurses' rubber soles. Fatima's tilted head appeared in the doorway, peering into the room. Her hair was loose and framed her face. She grinned and tiptoed in, cradling two pillows and a blanket in one arm and her high-heeled pumps in the other. "How did you get in?" I whispered.

"What do you mean? I just walked in. I waited for you at home and then decided, fuck you, I'm not letting you sleep on the floor."

"But we're not supposed to be here. We can't get a bed in here or anything."

"Then you should've returned home. Lina, too," she whispered, setting the heels and bedding down by the recliner, where my sister was snoring softly.

Fatima disappeared into the hallway and returned with a gurney. "If we serve food on it, we can sleep on it. I'm certainly not going to sleep on the floor." Fatima picked up the pillows, fluffed them, and lay down on the gurney. "Come here," she said.

I lifted myself onto the gurney and squeezed next to her. She wrapped her arms around me and nuzzled my neck. "Your necklace is imprinting itself on my back," I whispered.

She rotated it around one hundred and eighty. "Is that better?"

"Wearing an emerald necklace to come here doesn't make sense."

"I know, but it's your father's favorite necklace of mine. He was always complimenting me on it. I thought maybe, you know, if . . ."

❧

I folded Uncle Jihad's clothes, put them in his suitcase. I went over his room inch by inch, combing every nook, making sure I forgot nothing.

Melanie and I packed my father's things while he sat cataleptically in the corner. I knelt before him, held his hand. It took him a while to look at me.

"I have to get you dressed," I said. "You're going home."

I made sure he wore a light cotton shirt. I debated whether to give him his favorite wingtips or his moccasins, which would be easier to take off during the flight. I chose the wingtips, appearance being paramount to my father. He had his best tie on, double-knotted.

"You know where to get hold of me," Melanie said. "All you have to do is call Mike. He'll always know where to reach me. If you ever need anything . . ." Her voice trailed off.

I took my father to the airport in the hotel's limousine. I waited till an Air France representative arrived to escort him. When she tried to walk him through the metal detector, he refused to let go of my hand. "I want to come along," I said. "Until he gets on the plane."

A stewardess came out to escort him to his seat. I stood up and hugged him. He swayed gently back and forth on his heels, but his arms remained at his side. I watched the jumbo jet lift into the shimmering air, taking my father home.

I went to the Guitar Center on Sunset before returning to my suite at the Beverly Wilshire. With my American Express card I bought a Gibson J200, the most expensive guitar I could think of, the same kind that Elvis played.

— Eleven —

Fatima sweated and the parrots squawked. A servant poured hot water from a ewer into a porcelain basin. Fatima concentrated on the steam rising out of the bowl as it melded into the arabesque turquoise design of the ewer. "Quawk," bellowed Ishmael.

"Enough," cried Fatima, gripping the damp sheets. "Be quiet or begone."

"Breathe," said Elijah. "Concentrate on your breathing."

"I am in too much pain."

Elijah began to breathe loudly, with a military cadence. The other parrots followed suit. "Inhale," said Job. "Exhale." And Fatima's breathing matched that of cockswain Job.

She screamed again. "My back hurts."

"Turn around," said Isaac. "It will relieve the pressure."

The frantic, disheveled midwife's assistant rushed into the room. She staggered upon seeing Fatima on all fours with three parrots walking along her lower back and the other five breathing in unison. "My mistress asks if you can hold off for a while," the assistant said. "The emir's child arrives, and his mother is having trouble. My mistress cannot come right now."

In spite of the pain and discomfort, Fatima wanted to laugh. "Hold off? Can day hold off night? Tell your mistress she need not worry about me."

The assistant ran out. The parrots stared anxiously at Fatima. She glanced back at the remaining servant and said, "Leave. You are not needed here." Fatima winced in pain.

"Should you not return to our world?" asked Adam. "This fornicating palace is not a good place to give birth."

The assistant re-entered the room. "My mistress says I should deliver your child."

"No, you imbecile," yelled Fatima. "I am the one delivering my child."

The two wails echoed simultaneously. The midwife cut the cord of the emir's son at the same moment as her assistant cut the cord in the other room.

"It is a boy," announced the midwife's assistant.

"I know," replied Fatima.

"It is a boy," announced the midwife.

"He is dark," said the emir.

"He will surely lighten when we wash him." The midwife handed the boy to a servant, who took him to the assistant to be bathed.

The servant and the assistant opened the doors in unison, wailing bundles in hand. They walked down the corridor to the baths. The boys quieted as soon as they lay side by side. The assistant washed them with light soap and water, rubbed them in olive oil and lavender. She reached for the cotton cloths to wrap them with and stopped midway, astounded by the babies before her. She had been a midwife's assistant for two years, had seen many babies delivered, but she had yet to see anything resembling this pair. One was the most beautiful child. His hair was the color of yellow fire, of sun-drenched fields of wheat. His skin was as white as calcite, his features tiny perfections. The other was the ugliest child. His hair was the color of soot, and his skin even darker. Big ears, big nose, big mouth, beady eyes, a horrible concoction of humanity.

The assistant wrapped both boys and handed the light boy to the servant and walked out with the dark one. "Here is your boy," the assistant said. "He seems very healthy."

Fatima held the baby, and all eight parrots squawked loudly.

"This is not our boy," said Isaac as soon as the assistant left.

"This is not my nephew," said Noah.

"This is not your son," said Ishmael.

"He is my son," replied Fatima. "Both boys are." She kissed the baby's forehead.

The emir's face brightened when he saw his light-faced heir. His wife extended her arms to take the baby. "He is so beautiful, my husband. The most perfect boy."

"Yes, it is all my doing. My tale of Baybars worked its magic, and I shall delight in regaling him with the rest of it." The emir leaned over the mother and child. "He is indeed a worthy son," he said. "Bright like the day, glorious like the sun, after which he will be named. Welcome into what will soon be your world, Shams."

In the other room, the imp Ishmael held the baby. "What shall your name be?" He kissed the boy and passed him to Isaac, who said, "Welcome, my master," and kissed the boy as well.

"In darkness and in light," said Ezra.

"In devotion and in fickleness," said Jacob.

"In obscurity and in clarity," said Job.

"In sun and in rain," said Noah.

"In sorrow and in rapture," said Elijah.

"In profusion and in paucity," said Adam. "We will follow you and stand by your side."

"We are family," said Isaac.

And Fatima whispered to her boy, "As beautiful as an onyx, as dark as the darkest night, after which I name you. Welcome to what has always been your world, Layl."

"Rise, son," said Ishmael, "and greet your own."

And Layl opened his eyes, and in the emir's room, Shams opened his.

❧

The king's judge, Arbusto, sent a letter to Khodr al-Bohairi in Giza. "My dear fellow, I wish to inform you of the appearance of a king's favorite, a much-hated slave who goes by the accursed name of Baybars, upon whom the king has bestowed much power and honor. I ask you, my son, to help me do away with the usurper and rid the people of this slave's rule. Send your Arabs out to cause trouble, to steal from the people of Giza, to rob travelers and elicit havoc in your area. I will advise the king to send out the slave boy to control the situation, and you will kill him once he arrives. As a reward, I will recommend that you become the mayor of Giza." Upon reading the note, Khodr al-Bohairi saw bright gold in his future.

That evening, he and his men waylaid the mayor of Giza and killed him. Within a fortnight, the king received news of chaos and upheaval in Giza—a mayor murdered, officials slain, tax collectors ambushed, merchants burgled. Arbusto said, "The only man who can purify Giza and exorcise its evil is the man who purified our Cairo, its mayor, Prince Baybars."

Giza's high judge cried, "Help me, Prince Baybars. Khodr al-Bohairi has kidnapped my virgin daughter with the intent of selling her. We have no heroes in Giza who can face him but you. No one has been able to find the criminal or his hideout." Baybars said, "I cannot rescue her or kill Khodr al-Bohairi if I do not know where they are," and the high judge moaned, "Ah, my daughter, if we do not find you tonight, your life will be forfeit."

"We will find her tonight," Othman said, and Harhash added, "Before the sun rises."

This story comes from the Bedouin tribes of Arabia. Pay attention.

Once there was a wise and important Bedouin who took his young son with him to the camel market. While the man haggled with a merchant, his boy was abducted. The Bedouin searched everywhere, but could not find his son. He hired a crier, who walked up and down the market shouting, "My patron will pay one hundred rials for the safe return of his son." Greed blossomed in the kidnapper's heart. He decided to wait for the price to rise. But the next day, the crier shouted, "My patron will pay fifty rials for the safe return of his son." The abductor assumed it was a mistake. The third day, the announcement was "My patron will pay ten rials for the safe return of his son." The kidnapper quickly returned the boy and claimed the reward. He asked the Bedouin why the price had dropped so drastically, and the father said, "On the first day, my son was angry and refused your food. On the second day, he ate a little of what you offered to assuage his hunger. On the third day, he probably asked for the food. On the first day, my boy had his honor and pride, and on the second, hunger bargained with honor. By the third day, when he humbly had to beg his captor for food, his pride was lost and his worth was less."

By the time the moon rose in Giza, Othman and Harhash had burgled eight houses, broken into five stores, and relieved a money merchant of a large bundle of cash as he returned home with two incompetent guards. They turned the loot over to the high judge and went back at it. By midnight, they had attacked three more stores, including a wine shop, where they tied the owner upside down from the ceiling by his ankles.

"This is ridiculous," said Othman. "These people are inept."

"They are bunglers," replied Harhash. "We have to make more mistakes. I am losing interest." And Othman said, "Women. The women must be smarter." They broke into a brothel. Through the window they entered, avoiding the busy main hall, and ascended the back stairs. Half-naked women with drawn scimitars and daggers awaited them inside an upstairs room.

"Most men come in through the front," said the leader of the women.

"But that is not always satisfying," replied Othman. "We are finally captured, and stand helplessly before you."

"News of your exploits this evening has preceded you," she said. "I certainly did not expect only two of you."

"We are ambidextrous," said Harhash.

"And much too clever by half," she said. "Still, I must play my part in the drama and turn you over to Khodr al-Bohairi. Come visit after you are done with the fool. I am sure we can come up with many mutually beneficial arrangements."

Khodr stomped and ranted. "I should cut off both your heads right this instant. How dare you come into my city without permission? What made you think you could steal from me?"

"We assumed no one was running the city since the mayor got himself killed," said Othman. "We have just arrived from Cairo, and had we known you were the chief, we would have come and paid our respects first."

"You are from Cairo?" Khodr al-Bohairi asked. "What luck. Can you recognize a slave who goes by the name of Baybars?"

"But of course," said Othman. "He is a mere boy. I have stolen his allowance many times, yet he still trusts me. If you wish, I can deliver him in less than an hour."

"This is most fortunate," Khodr al-Bohairi said. "Bring me the boy."

Othman and Harhash returned to the hideout accompanied by Baybars, the Africans, and the Uzbeks. The ensuing melee lasted all of minutes. The warriors killed forty-three bandits but kept the vanquished Khodr al-Bohairi alive briefly. "Where are you holding the daughter of the high judge?" asked Baybars. The bandit chief pointed to a door, and Harhash escorted the unharmed girl out. "You must pay for the heinous crimes you have committed," announced Baybars, and cut off the bandit's head.

Baybars returned the girl to her father the next day, and the high judge restored all the stolen goods to their rightful owners. And the heroic deeds were celebrated.

✤

Fatima felt stronger. She got out of bed, picked up her baby, and visited the emir and his wife. The emir's twelve daughters made way for her to see their pristine brother, a boy who more than matched their famous beauty. "You look divine," the emir told Fatima, "as if you had just returned from the baths and had never been pregnant."

His wife, fatigued, disheveled, and in pain, asked, "How did you lose that weight in a matter of hours?" She felt awkward at being envious of an inferior.

"To you," the emir said, "we are ever so grateful for our great fortune, and a great fortune shall be bestowed upon you. You are now a free woman. Allow your son to be raised with mine. He shall receive the same training and the same opportunities. Most important, I will regale the both of them with the grand tale of King Baybars."

"Dear Fatima," the emir's wife said, "show us your son."

Fatima held out her boy, and audible gasps escaped all the lips in the room.

"He is so . . . hmm . . . ," said the emir's wife. "Dark. Yes, dark. What an interesting color. Let me see him. Let me hold the two young warriors. What did you call him?"

"He is named Layl," Fatima said.

The emir's wife held Shams in the crook of her right arm and Layl in the left. The boys held each other's eyes. "Let us make sure they are friends forever."

"Shams and Layl," the emir said. "What glorious names. Such sturdy boys."

The emir's wife was unable to produce suckling milk, whereas Fatima's breasts had ballooned to a ridiculous size. "I can feed both," Fatima said.

Eight imps gazed enraptured at the immaculate scene. Violet Adam, blue Noah, and orange Ezra knelt on the floor, hands and heads resting on the majestic divan. Green Job, indigo Elijah, and yellow Jacob sat on its backrest, their eyes unwavering, looking down at the odalisque. Red Isaac and his brother red Ishmael lounged on either side of a naked Fatima cradling the twins. Shams suckled her right breast and Layl her left.

When the well-wishers began to arrive at the palace, the emir's wife tried to separate her baby from Layl. The little prince would wail if he did not have Layl's dark face within eyesight.

"You know me," the emir's wife said to her husband. "I am not prejudiced. I do not mind that Shams's playmate is the son of a servant. But the boy is so repulsive. Kings and emirs, sultans and lords are lining up to pay their respects to my son. I cannot present him to his equals while he is in the company of the monstrosity. I cannot bear it."

"Oh, my dear," her husband replied, "how delightful that you are so sensitive. Fear not. Everyone will know the ugly one is our boy's slave. It will give our son a bit of cachet to have a servant at such a young age. The boys will be good for each other."

On a glorious, cloudless morning, in the palace's great hall, all the royalty of the land, all the wise men and judges and poets congratulated the emir and his wife on the arrival of the heir. They offered gifts to the newborn, gold and silver, swords and spears, crowns and jewels, sandalwood and musk, frankincense and myrrh. The baby emir ignored all his suitors and their gifts, for he only had eyes for Layl.

"Praise be to God," the kings said. "Our master has arrived."

"Such a beautiful boy," the queens said. "What lovely parrots, and so colorful. Where on earth did you find them?"

At night, the parrots were imps and circled the family—Fatima, Afreet-Jehanam, Shams, and Layl—as the kings and queens and lords and beasts of the underworld arrived to pay their respects. The jinn of the seven circles, the gondoliers of the rivers of death, the sirens, the harpies, and all the demons and devils bowed before Layl. An ebony column rose from the ground and rose and rose, and it was a giant jinni carrying two chests upon his broad shoulders. The first, a camphor-wood chest, the jinni opened and presented to the dark prince; full of gems and gold and incense it was. The second he opened and out shot his gorgeous human wife; like a dazzling sun she was. She genuflected and, from a purse dangling between her creamy breasts, extracted a ring and tucked it in the baby's swaddling clothes. She whispered so her husband could not hear, "This is one of five hundred and seventy-two I own, but it is my favorite, for it belonged to Shahzaman, the best of all lovers, even under duress. Forget me not when you are older."

Afreet-Jehanam held Layl up for all to see, and the crowd gasped in reverence. "Such a beautiful child," the imps sang. Scorpions descended upon the babies from all around and stung them over and over, and the boys cooed. Snakes followed the scorpions, and then mosquitoes bit into their skin. Finally, Fatima held one boy in each arm, and a hush fell over the denizens of the underworld. Her eight imps beamed.

"I think the boys are hungry," Fatima said. "We thank you for your gifts."

As if on cue, Layl pursed his lips. Shams mimicked him. Layl opened his toothless mouth and yawned. Soon his gaping mouth almost hid his face. It opened wider, and a mewl escaped and grew in volume, until it reached an uninterrupted crescendo of a roar no human can reproduce. Shams joined in, same tone, same pitch. Fatima looked about her. Isaac and Ishmael had begun their bellow. Noah, Job, and Adam. Afreet-Jehanam growled more loudly still. All the devils, all the demons howled in one voice, and all stopped at the same time. Silence.

Layl and Shams slept.

"Our master has arrived," cried the demons. "Now our story begins."

❧

Harhash approached Baybars and said, "My prince, as you know, I have no family to speak for me. I have dedicated my life to your service and consider you my brother. I wish to marry the high judge's daughter. She is a beauty and an untouched virgin. I would be honored if you spoke to him and proclaimed my wishes."

Baybars agreed. He met with the high judge and asked for his daughter's hand for his companion. The high judge replied, "It would be an honor." And so it was. The company returned to Cairo, and an exultant Harhash rode with his lovely new wife. Othman was envious. "I, too, want to marry a virgin," he told Baybars. "I want to be happy as well." And Baybars said, "I want you to be happy. Have your mother find a wife for you. She is your family."

Back in Cairo, Othman asked his mother to find him a wife, and she agreed to look for one. She put on her robe and walked to the maqâm of Lady Zainab. She entered the shrine, knelt, and prayed to the great lady for guidance in selecting the perfect bride for her once-prodigal son. She opened her eyes, and there, not far from her, knelt a young woman of exquisite beauty. Othman's mother rubbed her eyes, for she assumed that the kneeling supplicant was an apparition of Lady Zainab, but it was not so. The girl was praying. Her devotion and supplication rendered her face angelic in appearance. Othman's mother asked, "What is your name, my daughter?" and the young woman told her it was Layla. "And the night, your namesake, struggles to match your beauty. I pray you, tell me to whose family you belong, for I wish to ask your hand for my son."

Layla said, "I have no family but my brother, and he is the high judge of Giza."

Othman ran to Baybars. "My mother has found me a wife. She is none other than the sister of the high judge. Will you please speak for me as you have for Harhash?"

Baybars agreed wholeheartedly and sent a letter to the high judge of Giza, telling him of the happy news and asking for his sister's hand for Othman. The high judge's reply said, "My lord. I cannot deny you any wish. I will gladly offer my young sister in marriage to your companion. However, I have not seen or heard from her in years. Are you sure she is worthy of such an honorable man? Would he not prefer to marry a woman more devoted to our faith?"

Baybars read the letter to Othman. "More devoted?" he yelled furiously. "My future wife was praying at Lady Zainab's Shrine. The Lady chose her for me. My wife is most faithful and committed. Write and tell him."

The high judge's next letter said only, "My sister?"

Othman's wedding lasted three days, with King Saleh and his entire court attending. Baybars set up a feast to end all feasts for his friend, and even the Africans and Uzbeks celebrated and congratulated their companion. Finally, when the wedding night arrived, the couple retired to their room, leaving behind a heckling party.

"Reveal yourself to me." Othman knelt before his wife on one knee.

"Show your beauty, my life." Layla took off her marriage veil, and a dazzled Othman wept. "If I prayed to Lady Zainab every second of my life, I would not be able to show how grateful I am. If I offered my life in gratitude, it would not suffice. You are the most lovely being ever to have graced my miserable life. I am humbled by your charms."

"And you, my husband, are most eloquent," Layla said. "Come."

She pulled him to her and kissed him with a passion that surprised him. She undressed him while he fumbled with her knots. She laid him on the bed, his head on the pillow, and continued kissing him. He tried to remove her robe. "Relax," she whispered from above. Soon she descended upon him. He unleashed a cry of ecstasy that mingled with the laughter in the halls outside their room. "You are my husband," she said. "Mine." And she poked and pinched places he did not know existed. His next cry was of joy mixed with pain.

"Wait," he shouted, but she did not.

"No," he said, but he did not mean it.

"But," Othman said, "you are not a virgin."

Her face registered surprise. "I never claimed to be."

"No," he said. "No. That cannot be. Lady Zainab picked you for me."

"So?"

"Only the devout pray at the shrine."

"Do not be foolish," she said. "I have been praying all my life. What has virginity got to do with it? Do you not remember me?" She pulled up her left sleeve and showed him the brand. "I thought that was why you married me."

"Oh, no," he moaned. "What kind of dove were you?"

"Luscious," she said, affronted. "Please."

"My life is over. I will be the mockery of every man in Egypt."

"You will be the envy of every man in Egypt."

"I was supposed to marry a virgin."

"And you were not supposed to be one."

"Do not whisper of it to anyone," he pleaded.

"You are my husband," she said. "Your shame is my shame, and mine is yours. I will never betray you, and you will never betray me. We share honor."

Othman covered his eyes. "I am being punished for all the wrongs I have committed."

"Punished?" Layla asked, aghast. "You think marrying me is punishment? Keep thinking that and I will show you what actual punishment is. If you ever consider that I am not your ideal partner, even if the thought only crosses your mind, I will turn your life into a nightmare. You will think you are in the seventh circle of hell, married to Afreet-Jehanam. Punishment, bah. I am Layla, your ideal wife, your perfect love. Practice saying it every moment of your life. Lady Zainab offered you to me. She is never wrong. You are the perfect man for me."

"But you are not what I asked for," Othman objected.

"What you asked for? Has it occurred to you that the Lady was answering my prayers, not yours? I did not ask for a husband. I prayed for a companion, a partner, someone to share my joy. I had given up my profession, and I was bored. I asked Lady Zainab to point out a friend who could make me laugh, who could tell me stories, who could take me on an adventure. And she appeared before me. 'Listen to me, my daughter,' she said. 'You have served me well and brought me joy. I will reward you with your ideal husband. He is God's servant, and was one long before his vows to me. He is a trickster and serves to bring a smile to His face. If your future husband can polish the dust off God's heart, surely yours will glimmer for eternity.' "

"She said that?"

"And your mother approached me as the Lady ended her speech. You are the answer to my prayers. I do not know whether I am the answer to yours, but you had better believe that I am, for my prayers require that you love me and make me happy, and it shall be so."

Othman's smile appeared slowly, and then the frown returned.

"How can I face the morning with a clean sheet?" he asked.

She closed her cinnamon eyes and shook her head. "You are childish and have much to learn." She took his left hand. She kissed it, drew her dagger, and held it before him. "They want to witness the blood of a virgin. We can give it to them." He nodded, gave her permission. She made a shallow cut in his wrist. She kissed him. "Bleed for me, my husband." She kissed him again. "I mark you as you have marked me."

❦

The emir's wife threw a tantrum. She threw every glass item in the chamber at the wall. The emir tried to mollify her. Whiz went a perfume bottle flying across the room.

"Calm down, my dear," the emir said. "You are not being rational."

Splash, as another perfume bottle shattered against the scented wall. "Rational?" his wife shrieked. "You expect me to be rational when my son is involved?"

"Well, break something besides perfume bottles. It is suffocating in here. You are overreacting, my dear."

"He called that woman mama. His first words, and he directed them not to me but to her. My son thinks the servant is his mother. I will not have it."

"Trouble yourself not, my dear. It is only temporary. Do you think our boy—or anyone, for that matter—could believe that he, a divine creature, sprang forth from a slave? She spends more time with him. Do you want to be the one changing his diaper? Be patient. It will not be long before he begins to understand the way of the world and a servant's place in it."

"Even his sisters cannot play with him. He howls whenever one of them approaches. He prefers to play with those infernal parrots. I am going to pluck each one of those birds feather by feather—pluck, pluck, pluck, pluck, pluck."

"Not yet, darling. You tried to keep them apart for a while, and what happened?"

"He crawled right back to that woman and her baby, shrieking his lungs out until he reached them."

"And no one could hold the little devil back," the emir said. "My son takes after me, so strong and powerful."

"I am going to poison that ungrateful wench and watch her die. A lingering, deliberate poison I shall use, until suffering seeps out of her pores."

"No, my dear. Wait another year, until Shams is more independent, and then poison her."

"Pluck me?" screeched Job. "I will pluck her eyes out."

Shams crawled behind Layl on the carpet, his head almost attached to his twin's behind.

"Pluck," said Jacob. "Pluck, pluck. That is what she said."

Fatima rested. She lounged on the divan, her head settled on three fluffy pillows of ostrich feathers.

"Listen, listen," said Ishmael. "That was not the best part of the tantrum."

"She means to poison Fatima," said Isaac.

Fatima laughed into her pillows. All eight parrots cackled, Job so hard he fell off the backrest onto the floor, his two feet sticking up in the air and his feathers shaking in mirth. The cacophony of merriment surprised and amused the twin boys. They looked around them and joined the laughter.

"I will get rid of her," said Ezra. "I will transport her to another domain."

"No need," said Adam. "An asp will pay her fornicating whoriness a visit tonight. She boasts about poison, and it will be delivered."

"We will have none of that," commanded Fatima. "This woman is the mother of my son."

❧

King Saleh was sitting on his throne in the diwan when a messenger approached, carrying a letter from the mayor of Aleppo to the leader of the Muslim world: "Rescue us, Your Majesty. The evil King Halawoon has raised an army, which at the time of this writing is laying siege a spear's throw away from the walls of our city. Halawoon and his fire-worshipping army must be defeated. Call your armies, and let the true faith raise its banners in victory once more."

And Arbusto said, "Send Prince Baybars. Give him an army of fifty slaves. With God to guide his swords, he will vanquish Halawoon in no time and return to Cairo within a fortnight."

"Fifty?" the king asked. "To fight Halawoon's army? Is that not unwise?"

"Well, then, make it one hundred. Surely a warrior of Baybars's caliber could destroy Halawoon by breathing on him. Let us try out the new slaves. They have been trained well and will easily dispatch an army of unbelievers."

"True. But how big is Halawoon's army?"

"The letter does not say. Personally, I doubt it can be more than a few hundred or they would have walked through Aleppo. Our slave army will massacre them, and we can keep our main forces in Egypt."

The king considered this and said, "One hundred slaves will not be enough. Give our Prince Baybars two hundred men."

"One hundred and fifty."

"Done," said the king. "One hundred and fifty. Prince Baybars and his slave army will liberate Aleppo and report back to us."

Othman's wife kept repeating, "Are you sure?" Othman kept nodding his head. "The king wants to send one hundred and fifty men to fight an army?" she asked. "Has he gone mad?"

"Who can tell?" Othman replied. "When Prince Baybars asked for more men, the king said they were not needed. The prince thinks we will do just fine. I am calling on my old gang, and so is Harhash. We should be able to raise seventy more men or so."

"I will call on the doves," Layla said.

"Absolutely not. I will have enough trouble when I tell the men that my insane wife wants to experience the adventure of war. We do not need more women."

Baybars, the Uzbeks, and the three African warriors rode to inspect the slave troops on the day they were set to march. Harhash stood with his men, and Othman with his. The ex-brigands were well armed but looked less like an army than a ragtag group of dangerous lunatics. The slaves, on the other hand, were impeccable in manner and appearance. Baybars was pleased.

He decided to divide the leadership of the slaves among the Africans and Uzbeks, but one of the slave warriors interjected, "I beg an audience, my lord," and Baybars permitted him to speak. "We are two cadres of slaves, my lord," he said. "Each cadre has trained together for years. Dividing them haphazardly might not be best."

Prince Baybars stared at the regal slave warrior and said, "We meet again, friend."

"Yes, my lord," Aydmur replied. "Our destinies cross once more. This is the cadre I have trained with. We are twenty-five Circassians, twenty-five Georgians, and twenty-five Azeris. We were brought here to be the king's guard, but we have been forgotten."

"I, my dear Aydmur, have never forgotten you or your kindness at the baths in Bursa. Without your help, I might still be the Persian's slave. At one point, I was meant to be a member of your group."

"In our hearts, my lord, you will always be one of us."

"Are you fit to lead both cadres?"

"I would be honored, my lord," replied Aydmur the Azeri.

"This is a most fortunate sign," the prince announced. "Aydmur, my brother, I ask you to lead the slave army. Let us ride."

"Who is this man?" Othman whispered to Harhash. "He seems arrogant and pompous."

"Ask your wife," said Harhash, trying to stifle a laugh. "She knows everyone."

Othman attacked Harhash. Layla could not help smiling.

Behold. The reign of the slave kings approaches.

♣

On the day of his second birthday, naked Shams walked up to Fatima, extended his hand, and said, "Look, Mama." The imps exploded in laughter at the sight. Layl joined in. Proud and beaming, Shams held a turd in his hand.

"Ah," said Fatima. "I am happy that you are able to do that on your own. However, we do not hold such things on our birthday. The world is here to celebrate. We must be as clean as we can be." And, as swiftly as a hummingbird's wing fluttering, Fatima extended her finger, her fingernail elongated into a sharp sword, and she cut her son's hand off. She bade his arm to replace the hand with a new one. "Now, that is better. Let us get you ready for the feast."

"I will do their hair," cried Elijah.

"I do the shoes," said Ishmael.

Noah conjured a fountain of warm water in the middle of the chamber, and the imps bathed the twins of light and dark. Adam garlanded them with scents. Jacob and Job dressed them in silk and satins. Ezra studded their outfits with jewels, and Isaac crowned them with gold.

Fatima led the glorious twins into the grand hall. The royalty of the land oohed at Shams's exquisite beauty and aahed at the sight of the colorful parrots circling above him. The emir's wife snatched Shams and carried him to the center of the room. She held him up for admiration. "Behold my son." The notables lined up to pay their respects. One by one, they bowed before the baby emir and kissed his hand. And on this day of his second birthday, Shams performed his first miracle. The turban of the seventh person in the receiving line, a prince from a far-off land, intrigued Shams. As the man bowed, Shams removed his turban. Embarrassed, the prince tried to cover his bald head, but Shams was even more intrigued with the scalp. The boy touched it, and the prince jumped back in pain. The emir's wife began to apologize, though suddenly the prince was no longer listening. He brought his hands before his eyes. Surely he had felt something tickling them. He felt his head, and there it was. The entire room saw a full head of hair growing on the once-bald prince.

A man ran to the front of the line, pointing to his bald spot. "Touch me," he called. "Touch me." Another bald man joined him, and then there were three and four. The line was no more. A woman shoved through. "Can you do moles?" she yelled. Another held her infant son and shouted, "Cleft lip."

The emir's wife tried to retreat, but she had no place to go. The mob of notables surrounded her on all sides. Shams began to wail.

"Everyone will have his turn," pleaded the emir's wife.

"No, they will not." Fatima held her hand up, and the green parrot, Job, flew above the melee. She raised her hand again, to stop the violet parrot, Adam, from joining his brother. Suddenly, the royalty of the land were frantically scratching their skins. Fleas gorged themselves on noble blood. Elijah descended from above and lifted Shams. As soon as Shams joined Layl in Fatima's arms, the fleas disappeared.

"Be not afraid," the emir's wife said, still scratching her arms. "Please stay. The fleas are gone, and we will burn sage to make sure they remain away." Her arms turned redder and redder. "Do not leave. My son will heal you all. He will perform the great miracles. He is the chosen one. I am his mother."

"I think we have had enough excitement for the day." Fatima led her sons and her parrots out of the hall.

♣

Al-Awwar whinnied, pranced, and quickened his trot. "Yes," Baybars told his horse. "We approach home."

When Commander Issa, the ruler of Damascus, heard the news of the approaching slave army, he was forced to march his troops out of the city to greet the new leader of the king's army, his nemesis, Prince Baybars. Issa paid his respects, but his heart was engulfed by flames of hatred and envy. "And when will the rest of the troops arrive?" the commander asked, and Baybars replied that none were forthcoming. Joy cleared a place for itself in the commander's heart. "I am much impressed. The king must consider you a great hero, Prince Baybars, to assign you so few warriors to battle Halawoon's thousands of men."

Prince Baybars said, "Perchance, my commander, you will be so generous as to lend us troops to help us defeat the fire-worshippers." Commander Issa said he would be more than happy to oblige the prince, but his men were needed to police his city.

Sitt Latifah waited at the gates of the city for her much-loved son to arrive. As her eyes alit on the prince astride his warhorse, she ran to him. Baybars jumped off his horse, knelt before his mother, and kissed her hand, which had two tiny age spots that had not been there when he last kissed it. She kissed his hair. "Look," she announced to the city's denizens. "See my glorious son, the great warrior Baybars. My child returns home leading an army, just as my dream foretold. Bask in his brilliance." Sitt Latifah held a banquet that night for Baybars's army. "My son," she said, "in my dream you led a powerful army and vanquished God's enemy, Halawoon. It is bound to happen. I do not doubt the courage and valor of your fighters, but I expected a larger number of men to be under your command." Prince Baybars explained that the king felt more troops were unnecessary. "I do not wish to disagree with kings," Sitt Latifah said, "but I refuse to send my son into battle lacking. I will call the archers. From far and wide they will come to pay their debts to our family. A thousand of the finest bowmen you will have."

Othman and Harhash excused themselves from the feast. They kissed Sitt Latifah's hand and said, "Pardon our rudeness, but the moon is high. It is our time."

The following day, Othman and Harhash returned accompanied by one hundred disreputable-looking men. Othman told Baybars, "These men will fight for you, my lord." Baybars asked if they had repented. "Surely, one and all," Othman replied. "They agreed to repent if I performed a miracle. Yesterday I showed them the way into Issa's secret coffers. They were duly impressed, and all have repented this morning."

All one hundred said, "God be praised," and patted the bags of gold on their belts.

"And so our army grows," said Baybars.

One thousand archers on horseback arrived to join the slave army. Sitt Latifah greeted them. "You are men of honor. This is my son. Follow him and I will continue to provide your sons with the finest bows for generations to come. We are grateful."

Baybars bade Sitt Latifah farewell, and the slave army marched out of the city. They were scarcely a league away when they noticed dust rising behind them. A Damascene troop of a thousand men was trying to catch up. Their leader rode a glorious roan. "I will follow you, my prince," said Sergeant Lou'ai. "My men and I will fight the infidels."

Baybars said, "Your honor knows no limits, my sergeant. By saving my life once before, you paid your debt to me a thousand times."

"We are almost twenty-five hundred men," Othman said to Harhash. "I am now an honest man, but the blood of greed still runs through my veins. The more we have, the more I want."

Harhash replied, "Greed for a just cause is justified. I ride with you."

"Greed?" exclaimed Layla. "Wanting more men is a sign of sanity. The women in Damascus are knitting mourning shawls. Halawoon's army is thought to be at least thirty thousand strong."

The slave army stopped in Hamah for a rest. Layla told Othman, "I do not wish to spend the night here. It is much too hot and the accommodations are lacking. Take me to the shore. We can spend the night in the Fort of Marqab near Latakia."

"Fort of Marqab?" cried Othman. "That is out of our way. We are heading to war."

"Accommodations?" scoffed Harhash.

"I am glad you approve, dear Harhash," Layla said. "Tell our master we will rejoin you in two days, before you reach Aleppo, after I have had a good rest and breathed gentle sea breezes."

Aleppo rose before the slave army. Baybars saw Halawoon's troops laying siege to the great city, one division on each side, east, west, north, and south.

"That is a large army," said Baybars.

"Too large," added Othman.

"It behooves us not to fight them in the plains," said Aydmur. "We must enter the city. Attack the southern division ahead of us, break their ranks, and clear a path to the gates. The other divisions will not have time to come to their rescue. Once inside, we choose when and whom to fight, and our archers will have more luck from the towers."

"We do not need luck, sire," one of the archers said. "God guides the flight of our arrows."

"Pardon me for interrupting," said a refreshed Layla, "but this one division is approximately eight thousand men. By what means do you plan to defeat them?"

"The slaves will create a wedge," said Aydmur.

"And this slave will be the wedge's foremost point," said Baybars.

"And these slaves will be with you," said the Africans.

"I will ride the second wave," said Layla. "I prefer my death less certain."

"And I must protect my wife," said Othman.

And when the historians sat down to write the story of the great reign of the Mamlukes, the slave kings, before they could elaborate on the rule of two hundred and fifty years, before they could talk about the first defeat of the Mongol hordes, before they could tell how the slave kings crushed the Crusaders, they had to record the first battle, what became known in the books as the Battle of al-Awwar, the greatest warhorse that ever was.

❦

The tales of Shams's healing powers spread across the land, from east to west, from deserts to mountains, and hopeful believers trekked for leagues and leagues to witness and partake of the miracles. After his second birthday, he began to heal many complaints of his supplicants, but his specialty remained primarily hair-related. His ability to seduce bald heads into growing hair became legendary. There were some logistical restrictions to his powers, though. His constant companion, Layl, and at least one of the parrots had to be present. Best results— soft, smooth, and untangled—were achieved when the two red ones were around. Timing was essential as well; Shams could only cure for an hour before naptime.

The emir's wife wished her baby were more pliant. If only she could make him comprehend the magnitude and importance of his talents. If only she could separate him from his dark attendant. The time limitations were hard on the attendees as well. The waiting line to be touched by the One was interminable—and constantly changing as titled devotees went ahead of commoners. After an hour of touching, Shams would close his eyes to nap, and the parrots would instantly fly him out of the hall.

When he reached the age of three, Shams's powers were still chiefly cosmetic. The emir's wife preferred to call his new specialty "breast perfection" instead of "breast enhancement," because "When he touches a pair of unnaturally small breasts, they inflate to an ideal size. The Chosen One does nothing haphazardly, but is guided by the Infallible Wisdom of the Divine." Later that year, he developed the ability to adjust people's weight: his touch increased a thin man's heft and reduced that of a fat man. Tailors were ecstatic, their work made much easier by the miracles, for almost all the residents of the emir's land soon had the same measurements, and all began to wear no color but ecru following the trend set by Shams's mother. "My son inspires me to seek simplicity," the emir's wife said. "I have no more need for the spices of life."

By his fourth birthday, Shams was able to cure the common cold and sexual impotence. The last increased his devout following a hundred-fold, from thousands to uncountable.

"My son the body-enhancement specialist," Afreet-Jehanam snorted to his lover as she watched the two boys happily playing with slick, slithering snakes. "His devotees are imbeciles, and the ecru woman is insane." He squeezed Fatima's shoulder, his arm around her. "And it is not good for him to be called a prophet." Layl stood up, covered in asps, and reached for the crows flying playfully above him. "I have always had trouble with prophets. They never understand nuance or subtlety. They cannot grasp irony if it slaps them in the face."

Shams grabbed a black scorpion with both hands and tried to bite its glistening tail off.

"No, darling," said Afreet-Jehanam. "You must not do that." He kissed Fatima's hair. "I would like to see more of them. I miss the boys, and I miss you even more. Promise me you will bring them below more often."

At the age of five, Shams cured two of the major illnesses, insanity and leprosy. The names Shams and Guruji—the epithet bestowed upon Shams by a small group that had traveled all the way from Calcutta—blossomed on praying lips throughout the known world, from the backwaters of Ireland to the steppes of Siberia to the swamps of China.

And rivers of ecru rushed toward the prophet.

❧

Al-Awwar surveyed the scene before him, gauging the best point of attack. He raised his head, shook it, and snorted. He neighed loudly, announced his intentions to his surprised enemies, and charged. The infidels rushed to take up defensive positions. A giant melee erupted.

And before al-Awwar reached the first disorganized line, a thousand arrows soared above him and landed in the hearts of a thousand infidels. And when al-Awwar trampled the first soldier, another thousand arrows felled another thousand. Steel arrow-tips projected from the throats of Halawoon's soldiers, and the feathered shafts stood quivering in the soldiers' napes. And the slave army entered the fray, and a great wedge was formed.

"Leave some for us," cried Lou'ai as he led the second wave through. Othman rode close to his wife in order to protect her, but she shoved him away. From her belt she whisked out a leather whip with multiple strands, each with a sharp metal hook at its end, and unleashed her fury against the enemy. Skin and blood burst forth along her path.

"You frighten me," exclaimed Othman.

"I would never wish to don your robes," Harhash bellowed.

When al-Awwar reached the walls, the gates opened to welcome him, but he did not enter. He turned in mid-stride and returned to battle. Like rushing water hitting a wall, the wedge separated at the gate in two directions and rejoined the fray. And in less time than it takes a master archer to shoot an arrow into the sky above him and wait for its return, the slave army had massacred one division of Halawoon's army and entered Aleppo's gates as glorious heroes. The city's populace poured out of their homes, garlanded the warriors with jasmine and roses, and bowed before their rescuer, Prince Baybars.

From the city's eastern parapet, the mayor of Aleppo showed Baybars and his companions the enemy's lines and positions.

"See Halawoon there," Othman said. "He doesn't seem too happy."

"The sight of his flag of fire burns my heart," said Baybars.

One of the archers cocked an arrow and unleashed it; the flag was torn in two. The stunned mayor applauded the archer and asked how he could shoot so much farther than any of the city's archers. "We have Sitt Latifah's bows," the archer said, "and none are better."

Othman's wife climbed the stairs to the parapet, carrying a swaddled bundle. "If your arrow can hit the flag," she said, "should you not aim for a few of the fire-worshippers before they figure it out?"

"Get the archers up here," Baybars ordered. "Hit them before they retreat." The archers hurried forth, and the first hail of arrows descended upon Halawoon's troops. A hasty retreat was called, and disarray ensued. Halawoon could be seen cowering behind one of his officers. Slaves picked up the royal red tent, and he ran beneath it out of the line of fire. The archer shot his arrow and snapped the main pole. The tent collapsed upon its occupant, and Halawoon scuttled like a scarlet ghost. Aleppo's people cheered. "That hit the mark," exclaimed Prince Baybars.

Saadi, the great Persian poet, once told a story that went like this: Not long ago, a king in the divine city of Shiraz held an archery competition for the amusement of his friends. He had a jeweler forge a ring of pure loveliness, upon which was set an emerald of inestimable value. The king caused the ring to be fixed high on the dome of Asad. A barker announced that whoever sent an arrow through the ring could claim it as a reward for his impeccable skills. One thousand of the best archers in the land shot at the ring with no success. It so happened that a young boy on a roof was amusing himself with a small bow. One of his arrows, shot at random, penetrated the jeweled ring. A great cheer erupted from the rapt audience. The ecstatic king offered the ring to the young boy, who took his great prize and wisely hurried home to burn his bow, so that the reputation of his immaculate feat should never be impaired.

Layla uncovered her bundle, a small gilded cage within which a red dove cooed at the sight of her owner. She opened the door, and the pigeon perched on her finger. Her husband said, "You carried a pigeon all the way from Cairo?" and she replied, "Two."

"Where is the other?" Othman asked.

"We are calling him now. He will join us soon."

Baybars told his companions, "We have to decide when to attack our enemy. It is true they outnumber us, but we have courage in our hearts. With the city's troops, we now number five thousand men." And Aydmur added, "Our enemy has twenty-five thousand men left. Determination and the right plan of attack will compensate for the unevenness in numbers."

Layla raised her hands in the air, and the dove fluttered its wings in joy. "He comes," Layla said. A splendid red cock appeared in the sky, circled, and landed upon Layla's outstretched arm.

"Where did he come from?" asked Othman.

"Not from too far, I hope." She set both doves upon the cage and removed a message from the cock's foot. "Forsake your planning," Layla told Baybars and the warriors. "The army of the sons of Ishmael arrives and seeks to redeem the kingdom's honor. They number five thousand men as well, and they lust after infidel flesh. If you desire a taste of your enemy's blood, tarry not, for Halawoon's army will not last much longer." On the far horizon, a large swirl of sand bloomed.

"Get the horses," commanded Prince Baybars.

❧

The emir's wife paced her chambers, irate. "There are too many of them. They are coming from all over, and the line gets longer every day. I cannot get to our garden anymore without passing through the reeking rabble. Not only that, but some of our friends no longer wish to be healed, because they do not wish to mingle."

"If you do not want the people to see our son," the emir said, "we can deny access. We will make an announcement, and the seekers will return home soon enough. Frankly, I am not happy with the situation, either. It was grand and entertaining to help the needy, but years and years of incessant lines is enough. So much pleading, so much begging, does a soul no good. I thought it made you happy, but now that I know, we will stop the insanity."

"No, we will not. We will move the people away from our home. We will build a shrine, a glorious building with columns the thickness of twenty men and soaring arches and at least two minarets that reach the sky. Shams will receive visitors in the temple, and the masses will pray for him while they wait. Will that not be lovely?"

❧

The slave army rode out of the western gate with Baybars at its head, reached the enemy lines before the army of the sons of Ishmael. The ringing of swords, the war cries of heroes, rose on the battlefield. Fire-worshippers fell and were felled. Al-Awwar paid them no mind; he searched for the red specter of the fire king. The coward cowered behind his slaves. Al-Awwar lurched forward, pushed one steed out of his way, then another.

The sons of Ishmael crossed the battle's threshold. Upon hearing

their war cries, Halawoon the vile mounted a horse and bade his minions protect him. He ran away with his royal slaves and a squadron of
his guards. Al-Awwar trotted after him, but the battle lay behind. He
turned around, angry with himself for allowing the cowardly escape,
and bulldozed his enemies, trampled them with the ferocity of a lion
mauling an oryx. The slave warriors triumphed. Their enemies were
slain or enslaved. The victorious fighters met in the field, amid the
dead and defeated. Prince Baybars congratulated his troops on the victory. "A most valiant triumph it was," said the leader of the sons of Ishmael. "I am called Ma'rouf ben Jamr. I am the kingdom's chief of forts
and battlements. My people and I are at your service."

"I thank you, my chief. Your arrival was most opportune. How did
fate encourage you to meet our enemies on this auspicious occasion?"

"We were inspired by an eloquent letter from one of your subjects, a
staunch dispatch which called us to arms to stand by loyal Prince Baybars, the defender of the faith."

Othman cried, "Where does the chief of forts reside? Pray tell me it
is not the Fort of Marqab." And Ma'rouf replied, "It is precisely there."

"Where is my faithless wife?" Othman demanded.

"Faithless?" his wife asked, as she penetrated the circle of men. "You
call the writer of that letter faithless? I play my part in God's theater.
Do not revile what you do not understand."

"You asked my leave to visit lady friends in the fort, not the chief of
forts."

"But I did visit my lady friends. They happened to dwell in the
harem."

"You mock me," Othman said. "I am bereft of honor, naught but a
shell of a man."

"Judge not your wife, or yourself, too harshly," Ma'rouf interrupted.
"I long ago made the acquaintance of your lovely dove. The kingdom
was in need, and your wife's actions were heroic. A wife's valor
demeans not the honor of a husband."

"I do not know how to live with such shame," said Othman.

"Practice," replied Layla.

The army began its journey back to Cairo. "Ride with us to Damascus," Baybars told Ma'rouf. "You will be my guest. Allow my mother's
eyes the glorious sight of our army. It will please her to find her dream

come true." And so the great army arrived in Damascus and was fêted. Sitt Latifah was elated. The army celebrated for three days, and separated. The sons of Ishmael returned to their homes, and the slave army left for Cairo, where they were fêted once more as the liberators of Aleppo and the great defenders of the kingdom. The king gifted Baybars with new robes.

And that was how Baybars became the commander of the king's army.

❧

The first public kiss occurred on their seventh birthday during the ceremony at the temple of the sun with the two minarets. The emir's wife had planned the event for months, and worshippers had begun lining up, laden with presents, at the same time. The emir's wife had hoped that Shams, the sun prophet, would behave in a more prophetlike manner on his birthday. The eight parrots had been noisier than normal, giving the emir's wife a terrible migraine.

The light and dark twins sat shoulder to shoulder on the ostrich-feather cushion, and Shams touched the head of each worshipper genuflecting before him. When the worshipper offered a gift, Shams in turn offered it to Layl, who tore into the package. When Layl found a delightful miniature wood carving of a horse, he showed it to a thrilled Shams, who kissed him. Not a friendly kiss, not a brotherly kiss, but a full mouth-to-mouth, indecently lasting kiss.

And the emir's wife's face turned as red as the color of the chuckling parrots, Ishmael and Isaac, perched atop the throne.

"He kissed him," the emir's wife said. "In front of all, a shameful kiss. I would not have been surprised if they had undressed each other right then and there."

"They are only seven, my dear," the emir said. "Boys are expressive at that age. It is nothing. He is a prince and can do as he pleases. Most do worse things with their slaves."

"Not kissing. I do not understand why the dark one has to be around him at all times. I cannot see my son alone. And what is with the damn parrots? They hover over him perpetually, as if our guards are not good enough. That Fatima woman has ruined my son. Why can I see him for only an hour a day? I demand to visit with him, but if it is not my allotted time, my own son refuses, throws a tantrum until I relent and allow him back to his rooms. I hired a tutor, but he told me he could teach Shams nothing. He told me my son was born educated."

"Are you complaining that our son already knows how to read and write?"

"No, of course not. He has inherited our finest qualities. What I cannot stand is the company he keeps. That woman runs her own fiefdom within mine. I cannot bear it."

"Then get rid of her."

"I tried. I told her I would not be needing her services, and she laughed. I sent the guards to kick her out, and Shams threw a hysterical fit. He thinks she is his mother, not I. Oh, my husband, I am at a loss."

"What can I do to ease your suffering? Would you like me to continue the tale of Baybars?"

Twelve

I woke up confused, unsure where I was. It had been two months since I moved into the dorm room, but I still couldn't envision it as my home. Each morning I woke up feeling anxious. I had expected to be ecstatic finally living on my own, independent, away from family, but that was not to be. I had a roommate the first week, which at the time I had considered to be bad luck—I had asked for a single. He was morose, rarely said a word or listened to any, and was so homesick that he packed his bags and dropped out of school the second week. I missed him.

I wished I could pack my bags as well, but there was nowhere for me to return to.

The phone rang, and I hesitated before picking it up. I had paid extra to have my own phone in the room, but still wasn't used to receiving calls on it. It was from Rome. "I wasn't sure you'd be in," Fatima said. "I thought you might be in class." She had moved there with her mother in 1975, when the war in Lebanon started. When we were in Beirut, not one day passed without our talking, but we were unable to keep the schedule since we separated. We tried to call each other at least once a week.

"I should be," I said, "but"—I couldn't think fast enough; was there a good reason for missing classes?—"I'm tired, so I took the morning off." I stared at the small bouquet of silk ocher lilies strewn haphazardly under the couch, waiting to be thrown out. They belonged to the old roommate, who forgot to take them with him when he returned to Fresno. I should also throw out the chair, itchy brown plaid upholstery atop fake wood.

She asked if I was still unhappy. I rattled off my grievances. I told her how I didn't understand anyone who lived on my floor, and there were so many of them, how hard I tried to get to know these Americans, and how amicably impenetrable they were. The Lebanese students weren't any better. I didn't belong with them, either. I told her how much I hated my room. "But you know," I went on, "I've seen the places of some of the other Lebanese boys here, and they're much worse." I imagined her in her splendidly lit apartment in Rome, probably lying on her stomach, as she usually did, legs bent at the knees, her ankles crossed in the air. Her phone would be nothing like the cheap Princess I was using.

"You'll get used to being alone," she said. "We all do." She told me how much she missed the neighborhood; she even admitted to missing her vain, self-centered, irresponsible, and uncaring sister, who had refused to leave Beirut. "With Mariella not being here, I have no one to hate on a daily basis," she added. "She's having sex with every militia leader in Beirut, but I can no longer call her a whore. I miss that. I'm worried about her." I heard her pause and hesitate. "Your sister is fooling around with a militia leader as well."

"What are you talking about?"

"Lina is enjoying Elie's company," Fatima said. "She had always fancied him. I don't know why. I mean, he was a lowlife before the war, and now he's a killer."

We all knew Elie would grow to be a military man; he moved up quickly in the militia when he was a boy. Since none of us had considered there would be a civil war, no one ever thought he would someday actually matter. "She didn't mention it to me," I said.

The joint in the ashtray had extinguished itself. I had a deep-boned urge to relight it and inhale for a long time. I reached for the pack of Gauloises.

"Of course she wouldn't," Fatima said. "You're her family. I'm her friend."

❧

The story goes like this.

A day of great beauty; snow covered the entire village, and a sky of unequivocal blue towered above. It was January 1938, and Uncle Jihad, all of five years old, vied for his mother's attention. He poked her thigh with his finger, until she finally slapped his hand.

"Put your coat on and go play with the other boys," my grand-mother said. "Don't interrupt adult conversation."

"I'm not interrupting your conversation," Uncle Jihad said. "I'm interrupting your work." My great-grandmother Mona, my grand-mother Najla, and my seventeen-year-old aunt Samia were knitting around the iron stove. "I don't think my sister should be working on my sweater," he added. "She doesn't know how."

"Stop meddling in what doesn't concern you," my grandmother said. She was the only one among the three without a mandeel. My great-grandmother wore hers around her hair; Aunt Samia's was on the coffee table in front of them.

"It does concern me." Uncle Jihad poked his mother again. "I'm going to be wearing it."

"Shhhh, my boy." My great-grandmother covered my uncle's mouth. "So much energy. Settle down. First, you're not going to be wearing it. This one is for Farid. And your sister may not be as good as your mother and me, but we weren't as good as she is when we were her age. That's the point. She's learning. She's only doing one sleeve. So be quiet and let us work."

"Why do you always explain things to him?" Aunt Samia asked. "Why is he treated differently from other children? Tell him to sit still and be quiet."

"Sit still and be quiet," my grandmother said.

The women resumed their task and their conversation. My great-grandmother expressed her concern for her son Jalal. "He's causing trouble. I can't understand why he's doing it. He writes these awful things in the newspaper, and the French warn him to stop or face the consequences. Everyone is giving him bad advice. The bey goads him on, but he's not the one who's being threatened. He's always kissing European hands, yet he wants Jalal to stir the pot. The French want to put Jalal in you-know-what."

"What's you-know-what?" asked Aunt Samia.

"Prison," Uncle Jihad replied. "The French think Uncle Jalal is a bad man because his writings are provocative."

"Provocative?" asked Aunt Samia. "What does that mean?"

My great-grandmother and grandmother looked at each other. My great-grandmother smiled. My grandmother shook her head and bun-dled Uncle Jihad in wool: coat, hat, scarf, and gloves. She walked him out the door. "Play." She pointed toward the sloping hill at the edge of the pines. "Farid is there. You can't stay indoors all the time. Go."

"It's cold," Uncle Jihad replied.

"It's not that cold." She gestured to her long black skirt and black sweater. "Look. I'm not even wearing a coat."

"You're going to talk about a husband for Samia."

"That's none of your concern," my grandmother said. "Go play, and don't come back until it's time for lunch."

Ah, so many stories begin with three women knitting and talking. My favorite . . .

One evening, a king explored his city, walked the alleys, and listened to his subjects through the open arched windows. He passed by a house where three sisters knitted around a fire.

The eldest said, "I wish I would marry a baker. I would be able to eat fresh bread every day. And cakes—I would be able to eat wonderful cakes." The middle sister said, "I wish I would marry a butcher. I would be able to eat meat any time I wanted." The youngest said, "I wish I could marry our king. I would love and cherish him, take care of him, ease his worries so he can govern even more fairly."

The king appreciated what he heard. He sent for the three girls, and when he saw the youngest girl, he decided to make her wish come true. He married the eldest to his baker and the middle sister to his butcher. He commanded the two bridegrooms, "Treat your wives with utmost respect, and feed them whatever they desire." And, in a grand ceremony that lasted many a day and night, he married the youngest sister. The king lavished his wife with gifts and luxuries, which planted the seeds of envy in her sisters' hearts. The new queen grew with child, and the king was ecstatic. The eldest sister said to the second, "If our sister provides her husband with an heir, the king will love her forever. We cannot allow that to happen." They offered the midwife gold if she would get rid of the queen's child. The young queen delivered a healthy baby boy, but before anyone could see him, the midwife sprinkled magic water and spoke an incantation. The baby turned into a puppy. The king asked to see his child.

"This is what your wife gave birth to." The midwife held the puppy up. The apoplectic king said, "I refuse to be the father of this," and with his own sword he cut off his son's head.

The queen became pregnant once more, and when she delivered, the midwife changed the boy into a piglet. "This is what your wife gave birth to," the midwife said. The livid king said, "I refuse to be the father of this," and killed his son.

The midwife changed the third son into a white calf. The calf looked up at his father just as the sword was about to fall, and the king held his hand. "I refuse to be the father of this," the king said. "Inform the butcher I want this calf's heart for dinner."

The queen wept and asked, "What happened to my children?" The king spoke to her. "I have offered you everything and received pain and disdain in return. I can bear no more. I refuse to be a husband to you." He forbade his queen to leave her chambers, and he stopped visiting.

The butcher received the calf and thought to himself, "This is a majestic specimen. It would be a shame to kill it for a fleeting meal. I will kill another calf and save this regal animal for breeding." The calf proved that the butcher understood his beasts, for he grew to become a white bull of unparalleled size and beauty. The great bull matured among the rest of the king's cattle until, one day, a new milkmaid appeared, and he fell in love. The young maiden flinched and blanched when the great white bull approached her. She ran away from him, and he did not chase her, for he did not wish to frighten his beloved. She joined the other girls as they milked the cows, but her eyes kept surreptitiously moving back to the magnificent beast.

The following morning, the white bull led the cows to a meadow where a profusion of spring flowers bloomed. Joy blossomed on the milkmaids' faces upon seeing the flowers, and they set forth picking narcissi, roses, hyacinths, violets, and thyme. The bull cooed a lover's call, and the maiden went up to him, garlanded his broad neck with gardenias, his silver horns with violets, hyacinths, and thyme. The bull sighed in pleasure and slumped down on the grass before his beloved. The maiden climbed astride the great bull, and he rose and carried her away. The other milkmaids blushed at the sight of a virgin astraddle the great bull. He carried her for leagues and they came across an old crone resting on a large rock. The maiden greeted the crone who asked, "Is he your husband?" The girl said he was not, and the crone asked, "Is he your brother?" The maiden swore that he was not. "Then why are you not veiled?" the crone wondered.

"He is but a beast." The maiden stroked her bull's neck.

"He is a boy in love. A witch had changed him into a bull."

"That is awful," cried the maiden. "He would have been such a handsome man. Is there anything we can do?"

"There always is. Changing one species to another is difficult, requiring magic, skill, and elaborate potions. Regaining its original form is easy, requiring nothing more than the pure, true love of one of its kind."

The maiden asked, "Are you suggesting—" But when she glanced up, the crone was no more. The bull lay on the grass once again, and the maiden climbed off his back. "I will love you," she told him, and kissed him. They made love in the meadow, and when the maiden finally opened her eyes, fulfilled and filled, she saw above her the perfect prince.

The milkmaids heard of the miracle and informed the butcher, who wanted to see for himself. The butcher told the boy, "You look familiar, almost as if you are family." His wife trembled, and her face flushed, so the butcher beat her until she told the truth.

The king listened to the story and ordered the two sisters and the midwife beheaded in the public square. He visited his queen for the first time in years and apologized, but she said, "I had offered you everything and received pain and disdain in return. I will bear no more. You have killed my sons. I refuse to be your wife."

The king said, "I was wrong. How can I make up for it?"

"Die," the queen replied.

And so it was. Guilt and sorrow did the disloyal king in. The queen witnessed her son's rise to the throne, and the milkmaid wore the crown of the betrothed.

I was trying to stop crying. My knee hurt, my elbow hurt, and the bruise on my left upper arm was turning darker by the second. Uncle Jihad knelt before me, calming and shushing me. He had put his first-aid kit on the dining-room table and me on one of its chairs.

"They were older than me, too," he said. "They were Wajih's friends. That's what drove my mother crazy. Wajih didn't do anything, but he didn't stop his friends. He was too scared. He just watched. That's what I'm trying to tell you. These boys don't hate you. They're scared of you. You're much smarter, more talented."

"And much smaller," I snapped. "And there are a lot of them."

"I know that." He swabbed mercurochrome on my knee. "But this won't last long. Soon you'll be running these stupid boys in circles. Soon they'll be shining your shoes and picking up after you." He tickle-poked my stomach. "You'd like that, right?"

"But what'll I do now? I can't wait till soon."

"I'll take care of things now. Don't worry."

"You won't tell my father?"

He mimed running a needle and thread through his lips. He covered my knee with a Band-Aid and began to examine my elbow.

"What'll I tell them when they see me like this?" I asked.

"Tell them you fell."

"You're telling me to lie to my parents?" I stared at him.

"I'd never do such a thing," Uncle Jihad replied in mock seriousness. "Never, ever lie to anyone, let alone your parents; lying is bad. But being discreet is good. You fell, right? Maybe they pushed you, but still, you fell. That's what we'll say. We're not going to tell your parents everything, for their own good. We don't want them to worry unnecessarily." I flinched as he dabbed hydrogen peroxide on my elbow. "Wait here," he said. "I think we've earned some fruit juice." He went to his kitchen and returned with two tall half-filled glasses of pomegranate juice.

"Are you going to tell me what happened to you that day?" I asked.

"I was watching the village boys. It was cold but clear, so all the boys that weren't working were sledding down the hill. Snow had fallen for three straight days, so it was perfect. They didn't really have sleds, of course, only broken wooden boxes. I saw Farid with his friends, but before I could reach them, four or five big boys jumped me. They were Wajih's friends, so they couldn't have been less than fifteen or so. They lifted me up and put me in a box and pushed it downhill. They were amusing themselves. I was too frightened to scream and had no idea what to do. My feet and hands were inside the box. The sled picked up speed. Even the laughter of the other boys stopped. I finally heard Farid screaming for me to use my hands to slow the box. I tried but couldn't. Farid was running down the hill, but I was sliding too fast and toward a cliff. It was a small cliff, mind you, but a huge drop to fly over in a wooden box. Everyone, including me, thought I was a goner. And I was. I hit the edge and flew with my box, higher and higher, until a large pine tree bent its hand and picked me up out of the sky."

"The hand of a pine tree?"

"Imagination, my boy. Cum grano salo. The branch of a pine tree, it was. It felt like a hand because the tree caught me while I was flying. The hand of God came down and took the form of a pine branch. By my coat it caught me, while the box kept soaring higher and shattered when it hit the ground. I was saved."

"How did you get down from the tree?"

"It took forever."

❧

The Chinese magnolia trees were covered with divine pink-and-white blossoms, practically the only beautiful sight anywhere near my classes. Unlike the rest of the university, the science campus was unsightly, mostly built in the ugly sixties: large cubes of concrete whose windows opened upward, as if the buildings were sticking their collective tongues out at the world and saying, "We're ugly and we don't care."

A voice shouted, "Hey, champ." I walked over to a table occupied by my fellow Lebanese. Four of the six were playing cards, and one was eating a hamburger even though it was still morning. No matter what time of day you arrived at the Bombshelter, the burger bar in the Court of Sciences, you were almost guaranteed to find at least one of the Lebanese students there. A card game was sure to sprout as soon as there were two. I was probably the only Lebanese at UCLA who didn't care for cards.

"Where've you been?" cried Sharbel. He was by far the oldest and biggest guy in the group, towering over everyone. He was in three of my classes.

"Where is it?" he asked. He was trying to sound jovial, but his voice betrayed his anxiety.

I handed him my folder, and he immediately began copying the math assignment into his own notebook. He was so large he took up almost half the table by himself, and the other boys had to adjust their card game to accommodate.

"How can you live in the dorms?" Iyad asked. "Isn't it too crowded?"

"You have to live with strangers," Joseph said. He was in two of my classes. All the Lebanese students at UCLA were in engineering school, no exceptions. The only variation was which discipline within engineering; mine was computers.

"I'm not living with strangers," I objected. "I have my own room."

"Well," Sharbel said, "it's not like you're living with a friend. That makes a difference."

Iyad banged his hand on the table and yelled triumphantly. All the Americans stared at our table with disapproving eyes. I turned my back, moved my chair slightly, hoping that anyone who looked our way would think I wasn't part of the group.

Two Americans, engineering students, nodded at Iyad as they passed by. He completely ignored them. When he was with the group, which was more often than not, he showed disdain toward all non-Lebanese. He had once called his American girlfriend his sperm depository while she was sitting in his lap as he played cards. The group spoke Lebanese, even or maybe especially around people who didn't understand the language. They would have been speaking English or French had they been in Lebanon, but in America, they spoke Arabic. We were all misfits.

❧

The morning after God, the miraculous tree, saved her youngest, my grandmother put on two black sweaters and covered her head and torso with a diaphanous mandeel that dropped almost to the ground in back. In Druze white and black, she left her house and trudged up the hill through the snow to the bey's mansion. It was official visiting hours. Petitioners and supplicants were going in and out of the main entrance, so my grandmother went in from the side. She greeted everyone in the women's hall, sat down, and inquired whether she could have an audience with the bey. Yes, the bey himself, not his wonderful wife. She knew he was busy, very busy, but if he could spare a few minutes, she would be grateful. No, she would not mind waiting. She had all day. She drank coffee with the other visitors, chatted with the women. She had the chance to have a second cup of coffee. "I know he will see you," the bey's wife said. "Forgive him, but he's very busy, what with the world preparing for its next big war."

"His generosity knows no bounds," my grandmother replied.

Finally, one of the attendants whispered that the bey would see my grandmother. She and the bey's wife went to a smaller room, where the bey was deep in discussion with another man. The bey used my grandmother as an excuse to terminate the conversation. "A delicate matter," he told the man. "I'm afraid it can't wait."

Alone with the bey and his wife, my grandmother had to ask after the children, the grandchildren, the cousins, the house, the meals, the vacations, before the bey inquired what she wanted. "You've been very generous to our family," she said. "May God keep you above us to guide us, protect us, and be the shining example for us to follow. Your father educated my father and uncles, and your kindness extended to my brothers. We are ever in your debt."

"You are most kind," the bey's wife said, and the bey added, "You are most eloquent."

"Our family is thriving because of your liberality, and I am embarrassed to bring this up. As you probably know, my two youngest sons are going to the local school. They are doing very well, too well. I'm not sure the school is providing them with enough opportunities."

The bey's wife coughed. "Are you saying the school isn't good enough for your boys?"

"No, of course not. It's a good school. My other boys went there, but the young ones are special. My youngest loves to read, and there aren't any books at the school."

"Have you talked to your husband about this?" The bey leaned back in his chair, no longer feeling the need to listen. "You want them in a better school?"

"That would be ideal, but it would cost a lot more money. I'm willing to work. My older children no longer need me in the house. I'll pay everything back."

"The best schools are very expensive. Have you asked your brothers for help?"

"They have children and worries of their own."

"As do I, and a lot more children, and more charities and more obligations," the bey said. "The greatest happiness is accepting one's life for what it is."

Stories of the beys abound—their origin, valor, heroism, gallantry, generosity, wit or lack thereof. Uncle Jihad's favorite origin story:

In the thirteenth century, maybe the fourteenth, maybe the fifteenth, a brigand, an escaped black slave from Egypt, wreaked havoc in the Bekaa Valley and Mount Lebanon, and neither the local authorities nor the Ottoman government could do anything to stop him. A bounty was placed on the brigand's head. The man killed the innocents, raped the virgins. The Ottomans declared that anyone who captured or killed the slave would be given the title of bey. (In some versions of the story, the title offered was pasha, and a further heroic act was needed to receive a full bey's worth of plot and adventure.) The brigand passed through the village and raped two women, one of them the sister of the first bey-to-be and the other his betrothed, his first cousin. After slaying his sister and ensuring that his fiancée was honorably killed by her brother, the soon-to-be-bey searched the village and mountainside for the nefarious slave, but to no avail. That evening, despondent and intending to drown his sorrows, he descended to his basement to partake heavily of his secret cache of red wine. Lo and behold, he found the black slave prostrate, facedown in a shallow pool of spilled wine. Livid, he cudgeled the limp slave's head and split his skull, causing blood to pour into the wine puddle.

He was honored and glorified and became our bey.

Wait. One more. Not a story of origin, but one of wit. On a night in the eighteenth century, maybe the beginning of the nineteenth, the bey commanded one of his minions to deliver a letter to a sheikh in Hasbayya, a town a few hours' ride by horseback. The man asked if he might wait till daylight to ride. The bey wanted him to leave instantly, saying, "Do not fret, for the moon is bright, and I will command it to follow you and light your way."

The man set off on his horse, and every few minutes he looked up at the sky and the moon was still there. No matter how far from the village he rode, the moon followed. He entered Hasbayya and woke all its citizens. "Long live our wise bey," he shouted. "He bade the moon follow me, and it surely did. Look upon the sky and admire the wonder, the bey's gift to your village. Rise, rise, and behold the mystery."

The townsfolk rose and beat him and went back to sleep.

"You know," my grandmother said, "it's not as if I brought up whether any of his grandchildren attended the local school." She was slicing white cheese for sandwiches.

Uncle Jihad held a book in front of his face and pretended not to listen. My great-grandmother clucked her tongue. She waited for the kettle to boil.

"Why did you approach him?" my great-grandmother asked.

"What did you expect the simpleton to say? 'Take my money, because I care about your problems'?"

"He helps other people. Why not our family?" My grandmother stopped slicing, sighed. "I had no choice."

"Of course you did. We'll ask Ma'an."

"He has enough to worry about."

"Everyone has enough to worry about. This is family."

One more story from the lore of the beys. This one was about a woman.

In the late eighteenth century, the bey married a woman of great prominence. As usual, she was much smarter than he was. Her name was Amira, which means "princess," and it was a most appropriate name, not in the sense of a pretty girl waiting to be rescued, but in that of a woman destined to rule directly and not by proxy. Her husband was a fair bey, as fair as a feudal lord could be in those days, but there was never any doubt as to who governed. Internecine fights were all but eliminated during his years in power, taxes were paid on time, bandits disappeared from the mountain, all because he had begun executing people who didn't follow his commands. His wife was merciless. The bey died suspiciously early, leaving behind three sons. Sitt Amira informed the elders and sheikhs that she would rule until her sons were of age. The elders and sheikhs judiciously agreed, even though records showed that her eldest son was nineteen. Sitt Amira was the bey for twenty years. She sat with the sheikhs and village officials and commanded them, though when supplicants paid her a visit she followed tradition, more or less: she sat behind a gossamer curtain and settled disputes with her voice alone.

She was not well liked. It is said that half the people dislike their ruler, and that's when the ruler is just. She was not just. She played the various factions in Lebanon off against each other. She lured the Ottomans into a war with the pasha of Egypt. She allied herself with the winner of every battle, but only after the battle was won. She disposed of anyone who displeased her. By 1820, she had become so powerful that the Ottoman Empire had to take action, sending an army to depose her. Sitt Amira was a superb politician and as wily as a jackal, but she couldn't fight a whole army. She fled into the mountains and disguised herself as a shepherdess to await the army's departure. Unfortunately for her, shepherdesses of the mountains walked around barefoot. On the first day, a shepherd boy saw her creamy white feet, returned to his village, and boasted of having seen the most beautiful feet in the whole world, not one callus. The Ottomans arrested her on the spot, and she was never heard from again.

My grandmother and great-grandmother rode a jitney to Beirut and arrived at Ma'an's house unannounced, as usual. For my grandmother, the choice of which brother to approach wasn't complicated. Neither of the two was terribly well off, so that wasn't an issue. Jalal was the more respected, the better educated, but he was also more aloof. My grandmother also felt that his household was less stable, because his writings were creating a stir. Since the French were losing control over events in Europe, they were exerting it on their colonies, and Jalal was paying the price. She was closer to Ma'an. She trusted him.

My grandmother laid out her tale. Briefly, sticking to the essential points, she informed her brother that her youngest sons needed to attend a better school. If they remained in the village, they would have no future. It wasn't because they were her sons that they deserved better. It was because they had potential. My great-uncle agreed without equivocation, allowing her to keep the rest of her practiced arguments in her breast. "Do not come seeking aid, my sister," he said. "Assume it. I should have suggested it myself. That scamp of yours, the youngest, should be sent to the best schools. He's much too smart for his own good."

And my grandmother broke into fountains of tears.

Within two weeks, my father and uncle were separated from their parents and siblings. Ma'an had the boys move in with his family and attend a boarding school in Beirut. The agreement at first was that the boys would go up to the village on Saturday afternoons, after school, and return on Sundays, but it was honored less and less as the boys found more and more excuses to stay in the city. My father and Uncle Jihad would never again consider the village their home. They spent a week or a month there from time to time. During the civil war, when Beirut flayed itself, my father even stayed in his summer home in the village for a while. And Uncle Jihad—Uncle Jihad considered the village "quaint and authentic, without any of the usual tourist traps. Or even tourists, for that matter."

The bedroom was dark and quiet, except for the desultory sounds of cars passing below and the momentary reflection of their headlights on the window curtain. I lay in bed staring at the ceiling. I had smoked a joint and was delightfully numb.

There was a whispery knock on my door, so quiet I wasn't sure I heard correctly.

"Are you asleep?" A voice asked softly from behind the door.

"Everybody is asleep," I replied, "but Jardown is awake."

"Say what?"

I jumped off the bed. I recognized the inquisitor when I opened the door, acne-faced Jake or Jack or John or Jim from three rooms to my right. He said he had noticed the ephemeral yet distinctive smell seeping from under my door. He and his roommate had run out of dope, and they wondered whether I was willing to share. I was invited to their room, to hang, as he called it, and they would return the favor somehow.

Their cramped and cluttered room was lit by a desk lamp only, and they must have run out of dope recently, because the room reeked. The stoned roommates, in identical jeans and T-shirts, sat on one bed, their backs leaning on the wall, against a poster of the three Charlie's Angels and one of a tall basketball player. Jake or Jack or John or Jim lit the joint I gave him. They were both smiling stupidly, and I probably was as well. We couldn't start a conversation successfully. Jake's roommate asked if I wanted to listen to any music. I shook my head and picked up the guitar lying on the second bed. I played "Stairway to Heaven."

"He's good," Jake told his roommate, who took another drag. In the dark, the joint seemed ablaze.

"He plays so well, but it's cold and distant," his roommate said, in a voice that seemed to emanate from a haze. "It's as if the playing is there, but he's not."

I sat up. "What was that?" I asked, but I couldn't get either one of them to repeat what was said. Their eyes were glazed, far away lost. They did not seem to recognize I was there at all.

❦

"I was born in a time when lands had fewer borders," Uncle Jihad said. "There were many nationalities in Beirut, and boys came to our school from all over the world. The change was almost too much for me, but your father, he took to the school like a gourmet to foie gras. He befriended three other boys, and they became inseparable. They're still friends to this day. Me? I was lost for a long time. I didn't make any friends for a few years. You can say I made friends with two trees, two big trees in the middle of the school, a carob and a Kermes oak that couldn't have been any less than four hundred years old. I spent all my free time up in those trees. Everyone called me Tree Boy for the longest time. I called the carob tree Chacha and the oak Charlemagne. I preferred trees to people. After that I preferred pigeons, but it was trees first.

"My father has his pigeon stories and I have mine, for life, like a good tale, repeats itself. I noticed my first flock of pigeons in the skies of Beirut when I was a boy of thirteen. They were always there, but, like most people, I'd been oblivious. Notice their existence once and you begin to see them everywhere, all the time. I had no idea at the time that my father had been a pigeoneer when he was young, and apparently a terrible one. My father told us very little about his growing up. I guess he was embarrassed about his background, or maybe he was saving his best stories for you. I saw my first flock, and ten minutes later I saw my second, and then my third and fourth, and all of a sudden my skies brimmed with pigeons. One afternoon, atop Charlemagne, while admiring a flock in flight, I began to guess at the presence of magic. I was able to discern the art, as well as the logic, of flight patterns. The realization was both gradual and instantaneous. Magic. And as soon as I had my epiphany, my eyes understood where to look for the locus of the sorcery. Though I couldn't see him, the wizard himself must have been on the roof of the old three-story building below the school.

"The following afternoon, I ran to the building and asked about the pigeons. The shopkeeper on the ground floor told me to go up to the roof. The pigeon fancier, an aged man, realized I was a smitten boy. He allowed me to walk around and look at his prize collection.

"There were five cages on the roof, each of them bigger than my bedroom. One cage had young pigeons of different breeds, another had only coupled pigeons. One was empty because the birds were being flown. I walked around and fell in love. I wanted to say something clever, so that the pigeoneer would like me and I'd be able to visit again, but my mind was numb. He was obviously a gentleman, but I wondered whether he'd let me come up a second time, or a third.

Wouldn't he quickly tire of a young boy who wanted to spend time with pigeons? I got scared and stuttered, 'Can I work for you?'

"The pigeoneer looked me up and down. He smiled and shook his head no. He said I was too young and obviously from too good a family to work for him. I went from taciturn to loquacious in less than a second. I told him that I could come every day after classes, he was only a few meters from the school, and I was a fast learner, and would do whatever he asked and never complain, and that I looked like I was from a good family because I was going to a good school, but I was from the mountains, and my family was still up there, and I really wanted to make the pigeons fly, and he should try me out. It became obvious that he was trying his best not to laugh out loud. He said he could only afford one lira a week—which was a fortune, and he knew it. Had I walked away when he told me he wouldn't hire me, I would have failed the first test of a pigeoneer. He always said he knew the instant I came to the roof that I would end up a pigeoneer, that he saw it in the obsessive twinkle of my eyes.

"The man's name was Ali Itani. He was a Shiite, and he owned the old building—which had no elevator, I should add. I showed up to work the following afternoon and found him arguing vociferously with Kamal Hourani, a man who looked like his identical twin except he was a Catholic. 'You brother of a whore wouldn't know what honor was if it smacked you on the side of the head,' one would say, and the other would reply, 'Honor? You lowlife want to talk to me about honor?' They were both seventy-one at the time, and they wore the exact same clothes, except for the shoes: checkered navy-blue shirts, and tailored pants that were worn and frayed. Ali's shoes were black moccasins, whereas Kamal's were burgundy, both pairs comfortably kneaded by years of wear. Though their insults were getting worse and worse, they were standing close to each other in a relaxed posture. My Sherlock Holmes mind reasoned that their arguing was a common occurrence. It turned out that Ali Itani and Kamal Hourani had been best friends since they were six years old. They both swore to me that they had been insulting each other nonstop since 1898. They had lived through schooling, work, marriage, family rearing, widowhood, two occupying powers, one Great War, numerous small wars, religious conflicts, and independence, without ever thinking of ceasing their rude insults. I felt I had entered the Garden.

"That was my first interaction with the great city of Beirut. Of course, I had been living there for over seven years, since I was five, but it seemed that I had only been a tourist. Like all cities, Beirut has many layers, and I had been familiar with one or two. What I was introduced to that day with Ali and Kamal was the Beirut of its people. You take different groups, put them on top of each other, simmer for a thousand years, keep adding more and more strange tribes, simmer for another few thousand years, salt and pepper with religion, and what you get is a delightful mess of a stew that still tastes delectable and exotic, no matter how many times you partake of it. Those men seemed to have been together for eons, and since they'd run out of conversation long ago, all that was left was ribbing and mockery and repeating the great tales to each other.

"At the first lull in the faux shouting match, Ali noticed me standing there, pointed at me, and said, 'This is the young man I told you about.' Without even allowing him to finish the sentence, Kamal yelled, 'Run away, young pup. Run as fast as your legs can take you. Stay away from this invertebrate of a man, whose only intention is to worm his way into the life of his betters and feed on their loves, for he has none of his own.' See? I told you I had found home.

"Of course, Ali told me to ignore Kamal and began to explain my duties. I had assumed I'd be cleaning up after the pigeons and feeding them, but he already had another boy for that. No, he surprised me. He wanted me to seduce the birds. A confounding task, if I say so myself. 'Make them fall in love with you,' Ali said. 'I want the pigeons to want to return home for you.' I had no idea what he was talking about. I must have stood there staring at him like a fool, which elicited gales of laughter from the two old coots. 'Don't worry, young pup,' Kamal said. 'You'll soon understand Lazy Brain's speech. He wants you to go into the cages with the birds and get them used to you. It's another one of those easy tasks that Lazy Brain can't master.'

"So my job was to be with the pigeons, spend time in the cages, hold them and pet them if they let me. That's what I understood, and that's what I did for the first few days. I'd show up after school. The elderly twins would be chatting up a storm and arguing about little things and big things. I thought at first that there was nothing they could agree on, but I was wrong, of course. They could both agree that it was a lot of fun to tease me.

" 'Are you loving those two Tumblers enough?' Kamal would ask, and Ali would add, 'Look at that Lemon. She seems to be moping because you're not paying attention to her.' I'd get so flustered that I'd walk to the pigeons they were talking about, and the pigeons would move out of my reach. I thought I could never get them to love me. Yes, I was that gullible.

"There was a wonderful pair of Istanbuls that I admired a great deal. Beautiful to look at, dark-gray feathers speckled with white, and an orange chest that seemed to have been inflated with an air pump. They'd grown to an immense size, as big as chickens. They were inseparable, and the cock seemed totally smitten with his mate. He'd coo to her, and she loved it. Four or five days after I had started, I was watching them, and my world seemed to shrink to the size of those lovers. She strolled on the ground, jerkily pecking at seeds, and he followed her every step, cooing and engrossed. She stopped and turned toward him, and he nuzzled her neck. Then he started to stroll, and she followed. 'You're beautiful,' I said to them. I realized that I had spoken out loud to a pair of birds. I looked around, and the twins seemed bemused. 'You do know how to pick your boys,' Kamal said to Ali. It was the first time I'd heard one address the other without a slur.

"After that, the volcano released its pressure, and I began to talk to the pigeons incessantly. I talked to them about everything. I told them how lovely they were. I warned them of the dangers of the world, complimented them on their choice of partners. I talked and talked, and Ali and Kamal had found the boy who was going to entertain them for a long time. The pigeons did respond. They may not have understood a word I said, but they began to enjoy the sound of my voice. When I ran out of things to say, I'd just prattle. And you can probably figure out what happened. I talked and talked, and one day I started on what I do best. For my audience, pigeons and humans, I began to tell stories."

❦

Sharbel sat on my right and Ziad on his, third row from the front, far enough from the proctor, but not back in the suspicious rows. As I received the exam from the student in front of me, my hand shook so hard that I had trouble separating my sheets and passing the rest. I put the exam on my desk but didn't look at it. That was my ritual. I had to calm myself before every test. If I didn't settle my nerves, my handwriting would be illegible. Once I had myself under control, I rolled quickly, so I never worried about the time it took me to relax, though today I needed more time, because of the cheating. Sharbel had assured me I wouldn't get in trouble, because I could swear that I didn't know someone was copying off me, but I knew he lied. If I made a mistake, Sharbel, and then Ziad, would copy it. I didn't think any of us could use innocence as an excuse, and I also didn't think either of them would be gallant enough not to finger me if they got caught. They were Lebanese, after all.

I closed my eyes, breathed in and out. I concentrated on moving my breath to my arms and then to my knees. I imagined myself writing smoothly. As I visualized myself smiling triumphantly, walking outside, lighting a victory cigarette, a hard poke on my right shoulder almost knocked me off my chair. Sharbel's eyes were those of a lamb about to be slaughtered. He raised questioning eyebrows, terrified because I wasn't even reading the exam.

I began the first problem. I glanced Sharbel's way. He was pretending to work, his unmoving pen to the paper, but he did nothing until I finished the first sheet and slid it aside. Then he began writing furiously. I finished another sheet, and he nudged me. I looked up. I'd covered the previous sheet before he was ready. When I tried to move it, I was slammed forward. The American student sitting behind me saw us cheating and kicked my chair violently. I looked around and pretended blamelessness. Why did he kick my chair and not Sharbel's? Size, it was always size. Sharbel was at least one foot taller and eighty pounds heavier. I tried to collect my papers about me, but Sharbel nudged me again. I was sure the kicker would rat on us. I began to shiver. I worked fast, struggling to control my pen, submitted my exam, and ran out. I had twenty-five more minutes to spare. I could feel Sharbel's glare boring into the back of my neck.

🔹

"Not to brag," Uncle Jihad said, "but I was good even then. I remember the first story I told the pigeons. I was in one of the two better cages, where all the Rashidis, Sharabis, and black Bayumis were. Those were some of the birds that Ali would hate to lose, so I told them this story from the *Tales of the Homing Heart*.

"There was once a poor shepherd from a village in the mountains. He was so poor he couldn't feed his children, and the family slept hungry more often than not. One night, he was so hungry that he dreamed of Beirut, the city of prosperity and bread. He decided he'd go to the city and make his fortune. He didn't even wait a minute, but packed a small satchel and walked all the way to Beirut. He looked for work, talked to every merchant, builder, baker, cook, and watchmaker in the city. He begged to be hired, but no one wanted him. He tried the following day, and the following, but he couldn't find any work. How was he to make his fortune? A week later, and he still had found nothing. He was hungrier than he had ever been, and lonelier than he could have imagined. He was tired, and when night fell, he went into a mosque and lay down on the carpet to sleep. But in the middle of the night, policemen woke him up and beat him and took him to jail. He stood before a judge, who asked why he broke into the mosque. The shepherd told about the dream, but the judge was not impressed and sentenced him to three days in jail. 'Dreams are for fools,' the judge said. 'Only last night, I dreamed of a treasure buried in the mountains, in a field where two sycamores, two oaks, and a poplar cast shadows that moved like dancing men. Do you see me leaving my job to chase after the treasure of dreams?' The shepherd spent three nights in jail. When released, he ran all the way back home and sought the familiar field where two sycamores, two oaks, and a poplar cast shadows that moved like dancing men—the field where he had been allowing his sheep to graze for all those years. He dug out the treasure and became rich and fed his family and was able to sleep every night sated and content."

※

Jake or Jack or John or Jim and his roommate asked me over a week later. They brought the weed, I brought my guitar. We smoked so much, so quickly, we were floating in bliss in minutes. "Let me see your guitar," Jake said.

I was so stoned that I could barely stand up, but I managed. I sat next to him with my guitar, and he looked at the instrument with awe, stroked the neck with his hand.

"That's so beautiful," he cooed.

"It's a J200."

"What's that?" Blank eyes looked up at me.

I wanted to tell him it was a brand, a name, but words wouldn't leave my lips. I played a note; it plunked, because his hand was still on the neck. I moved away from him and played a few chords. The roommate asked to borrow my guitar. He held it briefly, and then strange sounds shot out: fast strums of inexplicable chords that had no rhythm or reason. He shook his head punkishly, like a pendulum on methamphetamine. He sang hoarsely, off-key. "I like to play with passion," he said. "And I love your guitar. I felt great playing it. I felt real."

"Real," I repeated. I tried to think of something to add, to make an impression.

"Where are you from?" said Jake.

I wondered if he was making fun of me, but he was too stoned. "I'm from Beirut," I said.

"Beirut." Jake closed his eyes. "That's in Latin America, right?"

"Right," I said.

"Can you play something from your country?"

"Tango or salsa?" I chuckled at my own joke. I took a long drag and allowed the smoke to percolate in my lungs. My brain was grateful. "How about something from Baghdad?" I began a maqâm for the first time in years, clumsily in the first few bars. The guitar's sound proved awkward, and my pick had to strum harder. My fingers still remembered how to play, but the frets got in the way. I had to improvise. I slowed down, allowing myself more time to adjust. Count Basie and not Oscar Peterson. I switched to Maqâm Bayati, which had the fewest half- or quarter-notes. Images of the great desert seared the back of my eyelids. The notes seemed so naturally logical. My fingers played with a tarantulan languor.

I opened my eyes to see Jake gawping, his expression tinged with shock and wonder. His roommate looked dazed. "That was different," Jake said.

"You shouldn't play anything but that," the roommate said. "It had soul."

The hairs on my arms rose for an instant. I began another maqâm, trying to lose myself in the essence of the music, in its passion. Played for about ten minutes before I paused and noticed that my discriminating audience had passed out. I resumed the maqâm, but I couldn't make the guitar produce the sounds I was hearing in my head. Finally, it came to me. I knew what was wrong. I walked out of the room and into the common kitchen. I unstrung my guitar and put it on the

Formica counter. I searched the drawers for the right tool, but could come up with nothing better than a steak knife to defret my J200. The steak knife was too flimsy, so I tried a bread knife. Without its frets, my guitar would sound better, more me. The bread knife didn't work, either. I plugged in the carving knife, and the current jerked it into life. I went to work. The sound of the knife's tiny motor grew deafening, but I persisted. I went too deep with the first fret, not so much with the second. I'd figured out how to operate by the third and fourth, but I stopped at the fifth. I stared at the dying instrument before me and left it. I returned to my dorm room and lay down, my head buzzing.

❧

"I was with Ali for years, through school, through college," Uncle Jihad went on. "And you should know, those wonderful pigeoneers had a lot to do with our family being where it is today. There was another one as well. Let me explain. Ali abhorred this one pigeoneer, Moham-mad Beʿaini. They were mortal enemies, and not simply because the Beʿainis were Sunni and the Itanis were Shiite. It seemed that Ali's father had once insulted Mohammad's, and the bad blood festered. Ali and Mohammad had never actually spoken to each other. They grew up with the feud, and each assumed the other was evil. One day, two or three years after I started with Ali—maybe it was 1948—one of Mohammad's pigeons landed on our roof. Ali recognized it immedi-ately and held his tongue. The bird seemed lost, so I approached it from behind, netted it, and carried it to the small cage, but Ali said, 'No. Wring its neck. Mohammad won't ask for it, and I won't return it.' I was flabbergasted. I refused to do it. 'It's for the bird's own good,' Ali said. 'It'll suffer away from home. We can't keep it. It's the humane thing to do.' I held it out to him. If he wanted it dead, then he'd have to kill it. Kamal came to my rescue. 'You can't make the young man do your work. Either kill it yourself or return it.'

" 'I won't return it,' insisted Ali. I told him I would, and he replied, 'He knows you work for me. I won't have it.' Well, I knew about saving face. 'I'll take it back and tell him you weren't here when it landed.' And relief blushed Ali's face. Even Kamal smiled. I walked the bird to Mohammad Beʿaini's. The look on his face was priceless when he rec-ognized me. I told him that Ali hadn't been there, but he didn't believe me. He took the bird back and thanked me.

"Now, in a great story, Ali and Mohammad would become great friends, and their grandchildren would marry each other, and they would have offspring that were family, but that wasn't the case. Mohammad simply stopped talking badly about Ali and refused to be anywhere near anyone who would. And whenever someone complimented Ali on his magnificent coop, he said, 'I wish my pigeons were as lovely as Be'aini's.' They both passed away without having spoken a word to each other. So, you ask, why am I telling you a story without a great ending? Because, as in all great stories, the end is never where you expect it to be.

"Mohammad Be'aini didn't become a close friend of mine, either. But when I graduated from college and Uncle Ma'an put your father and me up in our first apartment, I started a small coop on our balcony. Ali offered me three pairs, a Rashidi, a Turkish, and a Zahr al-Fool. Two days after my coop was up, a young boy knocked on my door with a priceless gift from Mohammad, a pair of gorgeous Yehudis. We hadn't seen each other since that first day, so I paid him a visit and thanked him.

"I was able to repay him quickly. Pigeons loved me, you see. They bred for me. At one time, I was probably the best pigeon breeder in all of Beirut. My Yehudis were all prize pigeons. I gifted Mohammad with a wonderful pair. I also gave him a stunning pair of speckled Zahr al-Fool. Of course, I gave Ali similar mates. So, you see, Mohammad and Ali did end up having offspring that were family after all. I had become a well-known pigeoneer. By then my father knew, and he wanted me to stop, because he hated pigeons. He considered the profession demeaning. Did you know that a pigeoneer's testimony isn't accepted in a court of law? You know why? By law, a pigeoneer's word can't be trusted, because he spends his time on roofs and is therefore a Peeping Tom. People are naïve. Of course, that's why most muezzins are blind. They may be high up, but they can't see.

"Your father wanted me to quit, too. Fairly or unfairly, society considered pigeoneers contemptible, and he wanted reputable men to respect him. More important, what decent woman would marry him if his brother was a pigeoneer? Your mother certainly wouldn't have. I had to quit and start a company with him. When it came time for me to give everything up, I sold my pigeons for a tidy sum, the seed for our corporation, but we still needed a lot more money. Both Ali Itani and Kamal Hourani gave me everything they could spare. Neither was rich, but they held nothing back. They were in their eighties by then. They both passed away before I could repay them. Kamal died first, and of course Ali couldn't bear it and followed him not ten days later. I can tell you, I spent those ten days with Ali. His grief was unbearable, and death surely rescued him. I repaid my debt to their families.

"But since I was desperate, I had also asked Mohammad Be'aini, and he didn't hesitate, either. It turned out he was wealthier than anyone I knew. He ended up being the biggest contributor of the army of angels."

♣

I was lucky that I was sober when my mother called. She asked about school. How was I doing with finals? Was everything going as well as it should? Yet I could hear the anxiety in her voice. "Listen," she said, "I wanted to tell you this before you heard it from someone else. Your sister's getting married next week. It's not going to be a big wedding, just the family and close friends. We're not making a big deal out of it."

I watched my hand clench the phone. My mouth felt dry and cottony. My head hurt. "What do you mean?" I asked.

"What do you mean what do I mean? Wedding, marriage, your sister."

"Who's she marrying?"

"Elie, of course. The wedding's next week. They're in love. They're happy. They're getting married."

"I don't understand. Why does she want to marry him? Why so quickly?"

I heard her sigh on the other end. "Listen, darling," she said, "you have to be an adult now. You don't need to have everything explained. Think about it." She paused for an instant. "Why would there be a wedding so soon after Jihad passed away? It's not a shotgun wedding, but an AK-47 one." She paused again. "Why would I allow her to marry that fucking bastard with half a brain?" Another pause, a long breath, quieter. "Now, darling, don't ask me any more questions. I'm just telling you that Lina is getting married and then I'm going to kill her."

She hung up without saying goodbye. I figured there were many reasons for her to be angry in this situation, but, knowing her, the fact that she was going to be a grandmother at her age might top the list.

I decided I would leave for Lebanon on the Saturday after finals. I could get a plane to New York, then Rome, then Beirut, and arrive just in time. Civil war or not. It had been calm for about six days. I could go to the wedding, spend some time with the family, and return before classes began again. The wedding would be in the mountains. Nothing was happening there. There had been no bombs, no shootings, at least for the last little while.

— Thirteen —

One day, a messenger entered the diwan carrying a letter from the mayor of Alexandria: "A majestic galleon waving the flag of peace entered our port and dropped anchor. A nobleman emerged and announced that he is the vizier of the king of Genoa and brings a letter to the sultan of Islam and bears many gifts for Your Majesty. He wishes an audience at the diwan." King Saleh dispatched a reply asking the mayor to allow the vizier entry. The vizier of Genoa sailed the Nile and sought the diwan upon arrival in Cairo. He genuflected before the king and offered a letter from his liege. King Saleh asked his judge, Arbusto, to read the letter, which stated that the king of Genoa had made a vow when his daughter, Maria, was sick. He had promised God that if He healed his daughter he would send her on a pilgrimage to Holy Jerusalem. Now his daughter was well again, and the monarch wished to fulfill his vow. He begged permission for Maria's pilgrimage, and asked King Saleh to ensure her safety by assigning loyal and courageous soldiers to protect her. The king of Genoa would pay the guards five thousand dinars.

The customs of protection were under the jurisdiction of the chief of forts and battlements, Ma'rouf ben Jamr, and so King Saleh commanded Prince Baybars to carry a letter asking the chief of forts to assume responsibility for the princess's protection.

Prince Baybars traveled to the Fort of Marqab and was greeted effusively by Ma'rouf. After Ma'rouf read the letter, he kissed it and touched his forehead. "For you, my loyal friend, and for the sultan, I will protect the princess myself. I do not require payment. Distribute the money among the needy, among the widows and orphans."

Ma'rouf waited for five days in Jaffa before the Genovese ship dropped anchor in port. The princess and her companions disembarked and set up camp. Ma'rouf paid the princess a visit. When Maria saw her protector enter, she stood up and greeted him. His demeanor and grace impressed her eyes, and love tumbled into her heart. Maria asked, "Are you my escort, dear sir?" and he answered in the affirmative. She bade him sit and join her. She asked her attendants to serve her guest. The following day, Ma'rouf led the convoy to the Holy City. The princess rode on a litter borne by slaves, and the chief of forts and his men surrounded it on all sides. The princess entered the city with Ma'rouf. She visited the holy sites of Jerusalem, distributed alms to the poor, admired the wonders. The Mosque of al-Aqsa astonished her. She asked Ma'rouf if she could enter, and he replied that she could if she went in with him, unaccompanied by her servants and attendants. Maria and Ma'rouf marveled at the Aqsa's architecture. As she wandered inside the mosque, she saw a wise imam reading to young students. Maria asked Ma'rouf, "Would this exalted teacher be able to interpret a dream?" and Ma'rouf asked the imam, who said, "Tell me your dreams, young maiden, and God will guide my interpretation."

And Maria began, "In a desolate valley, I thirsted. I walked until I reached a river whose water was as white as milk and as sweet as honey. I cupped my hand and took a sip that quenched the heat of my thirst and cooled the aching fire in my heart. A black fly fell out of my lips onto the ground. A white fly entered my mouth and settled in my throat. Upon the river sailed a boat, and I rode it until I reached new land, another valley, which was verdant, filled with springs and brooks, resplendent with songbirds and fruit trees. I slept under a willow, and a white bird pecked my head, from which escaped a small bird that I loved very much. A black bird attacked the small bird and carried it away. I wept for my kidnapped little bird and woke up."

And the wise imam said, "The desolate valley is where you came from, and God guided you to the verdant valley that is Islam. The black fly was the darkness, and the white fly that nestled in your throat is the Shahada, the Muslim profession of faith—I witness that there is no god but God, and that Muhammad is the Prophet of God. The boat is the vessel of life. The white bird is the honorable man who will marry you and love you. Your joining shall produce a viable seed that will flower away from you. God has shown you the way. Surrender to His will."

"I will become a Muslim," Maria said, and she uttered the Shahada in faith. She kissed the imam's hand, and he blessed her. She told the imam, "I cannot return to Genoa as a Muslim. I must marry a valiant man of faith to protect and defend me in my new life." The imam asked her to bring him the man of her choice, and he would marry them. "The man of my choice is here," Maria said. "There is no one more worthy." Ma'rouf's heart blinked and fluttered.

"And what would be her dowry?" asked the imam.

"I will offer ten thousand dinars," answered Ma'rouf, "on my honor, upon my return to the Fort of Marqab."

"So be it." The imam married the ardent couple, signed the documents. He wrote a fatwa stating that the girl had surrendered to the faith and married of her own choice. "God be with you, my daughter. Wrap your shawl about you. Do not exit as you entered."

Boarding hadn't been announced yet. From a phone booth, I called Fatima to shock her. I was in Rome—Da Vinci Airport in Fiumicino, to be precise—and I wasn't going to see her. I was flying to Beirut, surprising everyone. "Why is your stupid sister marrying that idiot?" she spoke loudly into the phone. "She won't talk to me. She's avoiding everybody. It doesn't make sense."

"They're in love," I said lamely.

"Don't be stupid. That bastard doesn't know what the word means, and Lina is just being brainless. He'll ruin her life. Your mother wants her to get an abortion. Your sister won't listen. She wants his child and doesn't want to raise a bastard. She's nuts."

I didn't say anything. The receiver felt heavy. "They're boarding," I said.

"And if you ever come here again without visiting me, I swear I'll roast you in a big Italian oven."

On the journey out of Jerusalem, Maria lay within her litter, but she relaxed the curtains and smiled at her husband, who was riding beside her. Happiness made Ma'rouf sit up in his saddle. He rode close to his bride and beamed. Ma'rouf led the entourage past the turnoff toward Jaffa, and the vizier of Genoa inquired where they were going. "To the Fort of Marqab," Ma'rouf replied, "so you can be my honored guests."

A feast was held in the Fort of Marqab upon their return. And on the wedding night, Ma'rouf visited his princess. The following morning, he left her chambers and took his usual seat among his men. The Genovese vizier said to Ma'rouf, "You have been most kind and generous to us. We are grateful. And now we must be on our way."

"Return to your home, and tell the king of Genoa that his daughter has become a Muslim and has married Ma'rouf, the chief of forts and battlements."

The vizier blanched. "Have you entered her chambers?"

"I surely have. She is my wife."

The vizier moaned, slapped his face, and beat his breast. "Kill me now, sire. I cannot return to Genoa without her."

The king of Genoa heard the wails and lamentations of Maria's attendants before they walked into the court. The vizier, haggard and pale, announced, "Your Majesty, the princess has given up her faith and married a Muslim. She did not wish to return."

The king turned wrathful. "Send a letter to King Saleh and kill this messenger."

Back at the diwan, King Saleh's judge read him the letter. "This cannot be, Your Majesty," Arbusto said. "The king of Genoa trusted God and you with protecting his daughter's honor. You entrusted Baybars, and he and his good friend Ma'rouf betrayed you. A scandal of this magnitude I have never witnessed." The king called Baybars to the diwan and demanded an explanation. Baybars said, "I have received a letter from Ma'rouf saying that the princess chose the true faith and was not forced into it. God gifted her. Ma'rouf has a fatwa from the imam of al-Aqsa confirming the gift of God and the princess's choice of Ma'rouf for a husband."

King Saleh said, "That is a true story. Islam is a bequest from the Almighty. My judge, send a letter to the king of Genoa explaining what happened. Be gentle. His daughter's choice to live so far from him will surely be difficult to hear and bear."

The king's judge was not gentle. "King Saleh has allowed his protégé, Prince Baybars, to kidnap your daughter," the letter said, "and sell her to Ma'rouf's harem. If you send me a ship to Jaffa, a full money chest, and a battalion of men in disguise, I will return your daughter to Genoa myself. The king is ill in the mind, and I do not wish to remain here and witness the realm's demise under his successors." The king's judge sent the letter to Genoa by messenger. He packed his belongings and all the goods he had stolen through the years. Arbusto discarded the robes of judge and abandoned the fair city of Cairo.

Maria woke up ill, and Ma'rouf called in the doctor. "Heal my wife, surgeon," he said. "I beg of you. Make her well." The doctor examined Maria and said, "The change in climate is not doing her good. Take her to Deir ash-Shakeef, and have her rest for three months. I cannot identify the symptoms, but a three-month rest should cure whatever ails her."

Ma'rouf took his wife, accompanied by one squadron, and sought the healing air of Deir ash-Shakeef. Within a few weeks, she began to feel better, if slightly heavier. "My husband," she said. "I am not ill, unless being with child is a disease." Ma'rouf jumped with joy.

Some while later, Arbusto paid a visit to Ma'rouf in Deir ash-Shakeef. The villain presented himself as a rich merchant and offered Ma'rouf a number of opulent textiles for his wife. "A glorious gift, honest merchant," said Ma'rouf, "but what have I done to deserve such generosity?" Arbusto said he only wished for one thing, a letter from the chief of forts and battlements authorizing the bearer to travel the lands without interference. "Your reputation for honesty and valor is well known," Arbusto said. "If I have such a letter, no one will dare accost me." Ma'rouf obliged.

Arbusto slept the night outside Deir ash-Shakeef. In the morning, he tore his garments, washed his hair with sand, and hit his face with rocks. He called on Ma'rouf, who exclaimed in shock, "What has become of you, honest merchant?" Arbusto said, "Twenty leagues north of town, I was waylaid by a band of ruffians. I showed them your letter, and they spat on it. 'The chief of forts and battlements is a limp braggart and a toothless house-cat that professes to be a lion,' the scofflaws said. They overwhelmed me and stole all my belongings."

The hero stood up and yelled at the ceiling, "I, a house-cat?" He stormed off to retrieve his sword. "Stay here," he told the merchant. "I will return with your valuables and the valueless heads of your attackers." He and his men headed north, leaving his wife with two guards.

Arbusto paced before the soldiers, pretending to be anxious. He removed bonbons from his left pocket and stuffed them in his mouth. One of the guards asked what he was eating. "Date bonbons," Arbusto replied. "Would you like some?" Out of his right pocket, he retrieved a bunch and gave them to the guards. Within a half hour, the sedative had coursed through their veins and the guards lay unconscious. Arbusto broke into the princess's chambers, covered dormant Maria in a large burlap bag, and bore her away.

❧

Beirut Airport's arrival lounge seemed fuzzy, like the imprecision of settings in dreams. The space itself hadn't changed, but the air was off-kilter, reeking of camphor, cigarettes, and humanity. Dust motes scurried across the stone floor, terrified of being stepped on. The ubiquitous posters of the unsmiling Syrian president forced me to stare ahead. His secret-service men, in polyester civilian, were only slightly less numerous than his pictures.

I negotiated the fare with the taxi driver, a man as old as my father. He asked for an exorbitant sum. His Mercedes was restored and revamped. Look. See? Not a scratch, not one bullet hole. "Look at me," I said. "Do I look like a guy who cares what kind of car I get in?" He came down twenty. I went up two. He said our village was far, at least forty minutes. I said I could find another taxi.

Banks of ominous slate clouds hovered as we drove along the mountain road. Trees seemed sparser. "Kindling," the driver explained. The car spasmed with every pothole. "At least this area is safe for now," the driver said. "For your people at least. You're Druze, right?"

"Half," I said.

He turned to me questioningly, as if the concept was utterly foreign. He waited for me to elaborate, and I didn't. "Why did you come back? People don't return anymore."

"Wedding."

"And you're arriving empty-handed?"

"My bag will be here tomorrow."

"It used to be that emigrants returned with sacks and sacks of beautiful things, money and jewelry. They struck gold abroad and returned home to be men. Everyone leaves now, but no one returns. If I were you, I wouldn't have come back, not even for a wedding."

"I've only been gone a few months."

He shook his head in disbelief. "It sure looks like you've been away longer."

I wanted to look in a mirror, examine my face. Did I look like a foreigner?

❦

King Saleh breathed the ill winds of infirmity. The doctors advised a month's rest in a moderate climate. The king and his courtiers moved to al-Mansoura, where the fresh breezes had healed many a disorder. He regained his health and returned to Cairo, only to relapse. He heard the knells.

"Bring me my son," the king said. Baybars rushed to his king's bedside. "You built a neighborhood for me once, my son," the king whispered. "Give me a mosque that will bear my name for eternity."

Baybars called on the architects, builders, and artisans. "I will not know sleep and neither will you until this stately mosque stands in honor of our sultan. Begin." A mosque of unequaled grandeur was erected in one month. On the Friday after it was finished, the king visited the mosque, helped by his attendants. "I am a happy man," he said. He returned to the diwan and tried to sit, but was unable. He was carried to his bed. "Turn me toward the Qibla," the king said. "We belong to God, and to Him we return." He lay facing east. "I witness that there is no god but God and that Muhammad is the Prophet of God." The king died.

❦

Our village sparkled at sunset. A guard in a dark suit and frayed white shirt, with a machine gun hanging on his shoulder, stopped the taxi at the gate to my father's house. He bent his head to peer through the driver's window. "Who're you?" he asked.

"Who're you?" I replied.

He cracked up. "Who're you? You're not dressed for a wedding." Another machine-gun-toting, cheap-suited man joined him and bent to check me out. He grinned, obviously having begun his libations early.

"If the groom was worthy," I said, "I'd have dressed better, but since he's no more than a silly communist betraying the great cause, I can't be bothered."

Both men broke into tipsy laughing fits. The second man exclaimed, "I know you."

I tried to sound grave. "Go tell your leader that such frivolities are beneath him. I'm here to give him a tongue-lashing."

"Spare the poor man," joked the first. "He doesn't know the trouble he's getting into."

More men gathered around. The floodlit house was about twenty yards from the gate, and the entire front garden was overfilled with fighters desperately trying to pass for wedding guests. The bey's guards alone numbered more than thirty. Ever since the civil war started, he'd begun to pick up protection the way a stray bitch in heat picked up studs.

"I know you," the second guard repeated. "We met a year ago. You're not here."

"I certainly am not. I'm a figment of everyone's imagination. Now, make way. Don't make me get out of the car."

The men guffawed. One shouted, "The brother of the bride is here." Another corrected, "The brother of the new boss has arrived." A machine gun was fired into the air, momentarily shocking any merriment out of my system. It was followed by another and another. A few yards away, the bey's guards followed suit, joining Elie's militia in an ecstatic firing orgasm.

After the machine guns stilled, the diesel generator took over, an old one that sounded like the chugalug of a steam train. The electricity in the village was off. My father had built this house as a summer home, but the fighting had forced the family to move into it temporarily. Though it was comfortable enough as a vacation house, it was neither spacious nor adequate for full-time family living. It was definitely not grand enough for a wedding.

My father came out of the house when he heard the machine-gun welcome. Guests hadn't begun to arrive yet. When he saw me emerge from the taxi, he looked as if someone were speaking to him in a language he couldn't grasp. The expression on his face was worth all the trouble I had gone to. I could see him wanting to move toward me. I imagined the muscles beneath his suit tensing, waiting for a release that had been long in coming. I climbed the five steps toward him. His eyes wore a moist film of my face. As soon as my lips kissed his cheeks, his arms engulfed me. I allowed myself to melt in his arms.

Another round of machine-gun fire shocked us apart. The men, touched by the unfolding scene before them, father and son brought together again, expressed their appreciation by firing at the sky.

My father led me into the house. A cursory glance showed the family and close friends getting set for the arrival of guests, a raucous flurry of activity. My cousin Hafez was the first to notice me, from across the hall. He was sipping a scotch as he pushed a table to one side with his thigh. Shock bloomed on his face, then a smile. He mouthed, "What, my brother?" I smiled back.

My mother emerged from the corridor that led to the bedrooms. Whenever she felt pressured, whenever she felt she was fighting alone against the world, the first thing she did was make sure she looked her best. Even had I not known much about the reasons for this wedding, I would have guessed she didn't approve, because she looked striking. Farah Diba would have killed the shah to look like her. My mother wore a high chignon, pinned randomly with a number of single cream pearls. The front of her black hair was pulled tight, with a part in the middle. Her ears wore four pearls each, a black surrounded by two creams and a large teardrop cream dropping below the others. Her strapless dress was cream-colored as well, fitted and tight, studded randomly with the same pearls. "Tell the idiots to stop shooting," she snapped at my father. "It's a wedding, not a bacchanal." She stopped, stared at me, aghast. I smiled. Her hand covered her mouth. She shivered, swayed, and dropped to one knee. I heard the faint rip of material. My father rushed to her. Soon practically everyone in the house surrounded her.

"Make room," yelled Aunt Wasila, rudely pushing people aside. "Don't crowd her. She needs to breathe." The bey, who was bending to help my mother, was unceremoniously shoved aside with the others. "Clear out. Guests will be arriving soon."

"I thought he was a ghost," my mother told my father.

"He's not, my dear. He's all real." His concern made his smile seem wistful. "Are you all right?" He helped her stand.

"She'll be fine. Just give her a few minutes." Aunt Wasila took my mother by the hand and led her back toward the corridor. "You," she called to me, "come in and speak to your mother while she recovers." On the floor, a fallen pearl gleamed in her wake.

❧

Maria awoke in dimness. She felt woozy and disoriented until she realized that the bed was swaying gently. She asked, "Where am I?" and Arbusto, covered in darkness, said, "At sea. Toward Genoa." Maria tried to guess at what had happened. She considered what had befallen her, such humiliation after such glory. She wept in silence and surrendered her fate to God. For three days and three nights, tears were her lovers, her intimates. And on the third day, a storm erupted.

The sky unleashed its waters, filling the sea beyond its brim. The only light to lead the way was lightning, and thunder called the boat in every direction. A fateful gale broke the mast. Storms and squalls battered the lonely ship for days and weeks and months and months. Sailors lost their sanity, and their captain lost control of his vessel. On the day the storms abated, Arbusto climbed to the deck of the ship, which was moored on the shallow shores of an island.

"Where are we?" Arbusto asked the captain, who replied that the island was called Tabish. A neglected monastery peeked above the woods blanketing the island. The captain sent the passengers ashore with his men, who had to cut wood to repair the ship's battered ribs of oak.

Upon the deserted island, Maria felt even weaker, and labor overwhelmed her. "I must relieve myself," she informed her kidnapper, and walked into the woods. Arbusto did not object, nor did he accompany her, for he knew the island presented no possible escape. Into the forest she marched and marched, concentrated on one step followed by another, did not dwell on her hopelessness. She reached the monastery and climbed upon the abandoned altar, where she delivered a baby boy as beautiful as the new moon. Maria covered her son in her robe, kissed him, and said, "Your fate, food to hungry fish, is certain if you accompany me. I leave you in God's house, to His mercy." She closed her wet eyes, knelt on her weary knees, and prayed. "Promise me, O servant of this holy site, in the name of God and all His illustrious prophets. Guard this boy, and protect him from any evil that may prey upon his soul."

She left her boy and returned to the ship. A week later, she was brought before her father in Genoa. Arbusto realized that, if he could pass as a king's judge, why not as a priest. He donned the apparel of a man of God and led Maria to an audience with the king, who asked his daughter, "Have you abandoned your faith?"

"I have abandoned more than that."

"You must be punished for marrying a Muslim," her father said. "You will be a prisoner in your quarters for the rest of time." And a weeping Maria spent her days gazing out her window, waiting for God's redemption.

❦

The tear was on the left hip of my mother's dress, minor but conspicuous. Aunt Wasila knelt and examined it. My mother swiveled sideways before the full-length mirror, her hand smoothing the rent fabric. "Let's try to tape it from the back," she said.

I wondered why Aunt Wasila was being so helpful. She had always kept her distance from the family, and all the more since Uncle Wajih had passed away four years earlier.

"Tape is tacky," Aunt Wasila said. "It's a small tear. Where's your sewing kit?"

"You look great," I murmured.

"You don't," my mother said. "Go change."

I explained that my bag hadn't arrived yet. She asked if I was having any problems in Los Angeles. Dissatisfied with my simple no, she asked about school. Aunt Wasila pulled a long thread through the rip.

"I thought you'd need me," I said.

My mother relaxed visibly. "That's sweet. Now, comb your hair. You're wearing jeans to your sister's wedding. What's this world coming to?"

My cousin Mona knocked and entered, paying Aunt Wasila no mind. "Lina wants to know why her brother hasn't gone in to see her," Mona said, and laughed. "Although she didn't exactly call him her brother."

Lina kicked out all our girl cousins when I entered her room. "They fuss so much that I end up trying to soothe their nerves instead of the other way round." She sat on a taboret, gazing at her reflection in the mirror. Her makeup was done, and she already had on her wedding dress. All that was left was pinning the veil. "Are you trying to steal my thunder?" she asked.

"When have I ever been able to do that?" I sat down on the bed. My feet hurt. "How can I compete when you look so grand?"

"You're being so nice. How come? Are you sober?"

I stretched out on her bed, sank my head into her pillow, breathed in her perfumes. I fervently wished that we could lie there and listen to

David Bowie or be howled and moaned at by Led Zeppelin, the two of us. She stood up, and I tried to see if she'd gained weight. She stood taller than anyone in the family. My mother was tall as well, but she was thin and bony. Lina wasn't fat, but she could fill a dress, which made it difficult to gauge her weight. She sat on the bed, leaned back on her arms. "I wish I could lie down, but my hair would be a disaster if I did."

I got on my knees, crushed two pillows together, and placed them at the foot of the bed. "Lie this way," I said. "Trust me."

She lay back gently, her neck held up by the pillows, and her hair floating in air. She patted the bottom half of her dress, which seemed to rise like a soufflé once she was prone. "Take my shoes off. Ah, that's much better."

I lay back down and had a close encounter with her white-stockinged feet. I scrunched my nose. She wiggled her toes. "I can't believe you're here," she said. "And I'm so happy that you're not asking me stupid questions."

"There are too many. I didn't know where to begin. Where are you going to live?"

"Don't start," she said.

"I'm not asking why, I'm just being practical. I'm not asking if you love him or anything like that. Where are you going to live? You can't go to the barracks, or wherever he's holed up these days. He certainly can't live here with you as long as he's fighting."

"We'll buy a place when the war is over. Until then, we'll keep going like this. It won't be for long. We'll make do."

"How will he support you? You quit school. Why? You're the smartest person I know."

"I'll finish later. Look, I'll make it work. Shut up. I'm resting."

❧

Ma'rouf and his men could not find any bandits or brigands. He inquired at every village along the way whether anyone knew of a band of scoundrels who had waylaid an innocent merchant. Soon he began to guess at the merchant's mendacity. Ma'rouf returned to Deir ash-Shakeef to discover his wife gone. "I am a vain and daft man," he declared.

He sent out parties to search for the deceitful villain. One party followed Arbusto's trail to the city of Jaffa, where it was discovered that he had sailed on a ship bound for Genoa. Ma'rouf called his men. "I will set sail and retrieve my wife and butcher everyone involved in this perfidy. Return to the Fort of Marqab, and perform my duties until I return."

In Genoa, Ma'rouf set forth toward the king's palace. He unsheathed his sword and prepared to attack the gate, but a fork-tailed swallow circled his weapon twice and flew before him. Ma'rouf followed the swallow's flight and reached one of the palace's towers, which was covered with a blooming canary vine. He heard faint weeping, which pinched his heart, for he recognized the sounds of his beloved. "I hear you," he called.

He climbed the vine, clinging to nooks and fissures in the stones, until he reached the topmost window. Inside, he saw his wife sitting before a still loom.

"Who goes there?" Maria asked.

"I am Ma'rouf, your husband."

Maria whimpered and mewled. "You, Ma'rouf, search for me, but you will not find me yet. I am as alive as this wrecked loom, and as empty as this dispirited yarn. Without my son, I do not exist, and without your son, you are not a man. He is on an island called Tabish. Bring me my son or I will not leave this mausoleum."

Ma'rouf joined his wife in weeping. He climbed down the tower, returned to the port, and sailed for Tabish. He searched the island. He scaled its hills, unseated its rocks, uprooted its trees. He tore up its monastery brick by brick, log by log. He could not find his son. Ma'rouf knelt before the uncompromising sea and cried again, bemoaning the capriciousness of fate. "By the life of my father, and his father before him, and his father before all, I swear upon their blood that pulses through my veins, I will find my son, my blood, my life."

"It's almost time," my mother said. She made Lina stand up and display herself. My mother, Aunt Samia, and the girls made sure that nothing was left to chance. No one seemed satisfied with the dress. It wasn't store-bought, but it was definitely designer-rushed.

"You're so beautiful," Aunt Samia said. "You make us proud." Lina looked perplexed, as if she weren't sure the conversation was about her.

"Look at her," Aunt Samia told Mona. "Look how she carries herself. This is how a bride should be on her wedding night." What I had never thought I would see, a blushing Lina, manifested itself before my eyes. "Learn from her, my daughter. Her head always high, beaming, full of confidence. If only my mother could see you now. She would be proud, just as I am."

My mother took my sister's hand, brought it to her lips, and kissed it.

"Get the veil," Aunt Samia said. "You don't want your father to have to wait when he gets here." She held the fabric in her hand and examined it like a tester at a textile factory. "Are you using it as a train? Come on, girls. Make yourselves busy." She turned to me. "What are you doing in this room, my boy? Get out of here. We have to talk about the honeymoon, and you shouldn't be hearing this."

"There won't be a honeymoon yet," Lina said. "He doesn't have time. We'll do it when the war ends."

Aunt Samia's face twitched. It seemed for an instant that her energy was about to crumble, but she caught herself in time. "That's a great thing, if you ask me. Why go on a honeymoon and leave your loved ones behind while a war is going on? I didn't have a good time on my honeymoon, so I don't recommend them. My husband slept for the whole week in Cairo. You don't believe me? Go out and ask him what was the best thing he saw in Cairo and he'll tell you the pillow at the Hilton. You'll probably have to wake him up to ask him, but he'll tell you. Honeymoons—honeymoons are not for our family."

"Are you ready?" my mother asked. She shooed everyone from the room. "If you want to see the bride come out, you had better be out yourselves."

I looked at Lina, and she shook her head for me to stay. At the door, my mother announced, "I'll send your father in a minute."

"Mother," Lina called. My mother stopped and turned around. She waited for Lina to say something, but Lina couldn't speak. My mother closed the door and walked toward her.

"I want to kiss you," my mother said, "but it's not a good idea. Air kisses, however, won't harm the makeup." My mother held both of Lina's hands, and they air-kissed three times. My mother walked toward the door. "You'd better be ready."

My father, dapper and lordly, held his hand out to my sister. Lina hesitated, snatched one last glance at her reflection, and moved toward him. Arm in arm, they took one step and faltered. "I'm leading," my father joked. They recommenced, but the march still looked off-kilter, as if my father had practiced for this moment all his life and life decided not to cooperate.

I had expected my father to be more subdued, but I had underestimated his resilience. He didn't appear to be a man who had just survived the death of a second brother, his best friend at that. I lagged behind, stopped, and watched them as they passed down the darkened corridor into the light of the living room. Cheering, applause, whistles, and ululations broke out loud enough to obliterate Mendelssohn's "Wedding March" piping out of the speakers. Someone, I assumed Uncle Akram, began drumming the derbakeh. A woman burst into the mountain wedding song, a paean to the beautiful bride. By the time I reached the end of the corridor, my father had handed his daughter to Elie, who was desperately trying to look confident in a suit instead of his usual fatigues. Elie looked around at the crowd before quickly kissing Lina—a brief peck to signify eternal commitment. Uncle Akram, visibly upset with Mendelssohn's discordant competition, knocked the record player with his thigh. A scratch was heard, and then the strings stopped, and Uncle Akram banged the drum harder, with a faster syncopation.

The newlyweds carved the cake. Elie tried to put his arm through Lina's, but the fork kept getting in the way. A piece of cake fell on her sleeve and to the floor. She laughed. My mother shook her head. A couple of kids reached for the fallen morsel. The bey's grandson, bundled up in two sweaters despite the room's heat, stuffed the cake into his mouth. Our future bey looked up to Lina, opened his mouth wide, extended his tongue, and showed her the piece of extra-moist cake in his mouth.

Everyone seemed in a festive mood, but it wasn't just the wedding. Wartime parties are always inhibition-loosening, euphoric affairs. I tried to talk to Elie, but he seemed to be avoiding me—and the rest of the family, for that matter. It was disconcerting to see a militiaman with dozens of fighters under his command, a killer of men, desperately avoid making eye contact. When I cornered him to offer best wishes, he interrupted by blurting, "It's not my fault. It was supposed to be just fun," sounding like a terrified four-year-old, his eyes expanding to encompass the top half of his face.

·   ·   ·

My feet were sore, my arches throbbed. The last of the guests were filing out, but it wasn't yet time to break up the receiving line. Lina
looked the most tired of all, whereas Elie seemed to be gaining
strength as the festivities wore on. Aunt Wasila and her children left
with the guests, as did Uncle Halim and his family. Aunt Samia took
off her heels and began to help the servants clear the tables, until my
mother asked her to stop.

"Give me twenty minutes to freshen up and I'll be ready to go,"
Lina told Elie.

He cleared his throat. "It's probably best if I go back to Beirut with
my men." He could not lift his gaze from his shoes. "They have to be
there just in case, and—uhmm—I don't think it's right if there's a fight
and I'm not there. We might get attacked."

"On your wedding night?"

"Well, the enemy bastards don't care about my wedding night," he
stammered.

"I guess you should go, then," Lina said.

"Yes, I guess I should." He backed away with slow, irresolute steps.
"Thank you, everyone. That was a great wedding." He looked briefly
at my mother. "I wish my family could have been here. Thank you."
He walked out, hollered at his inebriated men. They got in three battered Range Rovers and sped down the hill toward the city. In the distance, Beirut, enveloped in utter darkness, swallowed the red rear
lights whole.

"I guess I should change anyway," Lina said.

"Yes," my mother replied. She sat on the sofa and propped her feet
on the small ottoman. "Change into something more comfortable, and
I'll make you a good scotch."

As soon as Lina went into her room, my father allowed his rage to
conquer his face. He dumped his body next to my mother. His heat
and intensity radiated across the room. I knew that if he said one thing
he would explode.

"I'll make you a good scotch, too," my mother said.

"Maybe we'll get lucky," Aunt Samia said. "Maybe they *will* get
attacked tonight."

"Ha," my mother snorted. "You shouldn't have said that." She shook
her head. "Ha." She asked my father, "Is there anyone we can call?"
My father chuckled.

You might have asked yourself what happened to the boy. You might
have wondered why his father did not find him. Listen. Another storm
brewed the waters of the Mediterranean and forced a ship carrying
Kinyar, the king of Thessaly, to the island of Tabish. The king and his
crew explored the island and discovered the monastery. "This is the
cuddliest child my royal eyes have ever seen," announced Kinyar. He
reached out to pick up the son of Ma'rouf and Maria, but a powerful
slap knocked him on his behind. He looked around in terror. His men
drew their weapons. They saw nothing. "Why do you smite me?" Kinyar asked the monastery. "I am the father of this boy, come to deliver
him to his mother." He reached for the infant again, and this time he
was not felled. He ran out with the boy, and his men rushed after him,
fumbling and stumbling. They stole away on their ship.

The galleon from Thessaly stopped a pilgrim ship heading toward
the Holy City. The king boarded the captured ship and declared, "I
seek a volunteer, a wet nurse to feed my child. I will slay you all unless
you give me what I want."

A young nun said, "I have given my life before and I will give it once
more. There is no need for all of us to die." Kinyar took her to his ship
and allowed her companions to go their way. The nun exposed her
breast to the hungry boy, and milk miraculously flowed. "The baby
will live," the nun said, and Kinyar said, "I will call him Taboush, after
the island that offered him to me."

We had an early breakfast the morning following the wedding. My
father had a piece of bread stuck in his throat. He coughed, smacked
his chest, and reached for his glass of water. My mother kept watch,
with a mild concern, from across the table. He cleared his throat, lit a
cigarette, and sipped his coffee. "I'm going to check on our home," he
announced.

"There's nothing to check on." My mother spread butter on her
toast. She was the only one in the family who buttered her bread. "We
took everything that's of any value."

"I have to check on the building. Unless we make our presence felt,
we'll have squatters moving in."

"The reason we don't have squatters is that the neighborhood is still dangerous. Be reasonable. It's not worth the risk, and your showing up once a month isn't going to stop refugees from taking over."

"I'll be careful," he said.

A bit later, I told my mother I was taking a long walk and sneaked into the car with him. If my mother didn't approve of my father's going to the old neighborhood, she certainly wouldn't have wanted me to tag along. "Onward to our next adventure," he said. We passed many checkpoints along the way, crossing from one militia zone into the next, and none gave us any trouble. You could probably encounter every militia and every denomination driving from our mountain village to the neighborhood in Beirut.

We arrived, and I felt off-balance. Our neighborhood hadn't been hit as badly as others, but it was scarred. It was also *Twilight Zone* uninhabited.

My father checked each apartment. In ours, the furniture was shrouded with dusty linen, but anything that would fit into a car had been moved. Only one window was broken. I went to my room. My bed, bookshelf, and dresser looked like giant misshapen children dressed as ghosts for Halloween. My father gave Uncle Jihad's apartment a cursory inspection. He didn't wish to tarry there. I lingered. I walked around the living room and dining room. The coverings in this apartment had a palpable finality.

Uncle Jihad's numerous obsessions were notorious. He was a devoted Italophile, a Brueghel aficionado, a film buff, a lover of folktales, and a collector of rare stamps, movie magazines, miniature crystal sculptures, matchboxes, restaurant menus, and Lebanese earthenware. His apartment used to be full of his essence, knickknacks and whatnots all over the place. Everything had been cleared out. Almost everything. Discarded on the floor I found a postcard of a Brueghel painting, *Mad Meg*, one of his favorites. Two things I could never forget about the painting, the determined look of Mad Meg herself, the I-will-get-what-is-rightfully-mine-in-this-hellhole attitude, and the giant freak using a poker to empty his butt of its contents while the crowd below him eagerly waited for the about-to-fall treasure. I picked up the card and examined the browns and ochers and reds, the weird creatures in hell, the spears and shields and misplaced heads, the animals and half-ships and battlements, and the woman, seemingly the only full human, an unsheathed sword in her right hand, a basket of goodies in her left, a filled bag tucked in at her waist, walking with a helmet and a steely determination. She got what she came for and it was time to leave. Just as I remembered. I pocketed it.

I walked into the den, and the movie wall was still up. It could not be moved. Through the years, Uncle Jihad had cut out images from movie magazines, particularly Italian ones, and had pasted a collage onto the whole wall. A window had been broken in the den, and a piece of glass had embedded itself in a picture of the Ferris wheel in *The Third Man*. I pulled it out and cut my index finger. I shoved my finger in my mouth and sucked on my wound.

I began to see the wall with Zen eyes. Movie stars stared back. At least three Marilyns, one in which she sat in a director's chair, looking back. Jane Fonda in *Klute* and *Barbarella*, Bette Davis in *Jezebel* and *Now, Voyager*, Audrey Hepburn in *Roman Holiday* and *Breakfast at Tiffany's*. Warren Beatty as Clyde lay on top of Faye Dunaway as Bonnie. Marlon Brando sat next to Jack Nicholson. Sophia Loren broke down on her knees in *Two Women*, Anna Magnani broke down in any one of her movies. Catherine Deneuve in *Belle de Jour*, Julie Christie in *Doctor Zhivago*. Hedy Lamarr in a long evening gown, her left arm behind her back, the hand encircling the right elbow, the poster saying "Il piu grande film per la stagione 1948–49, *Disonorata*." Katharine Hepburn shared a scene with John Wayne, Glenda Jackson got off a train, Shirley MacLaine looked astonished. Julie Andrews and Christopher Plummer performed with the von Trapp kids. A horrified Joan Crawford, subtitled *So che mi uccidrerai!* Shirley Temple, Cary Grant, Clark Gable, Jimmy Stewart. Three-quarter view of Sissy Spacek and Shelley Duvall. A shirtless James Dean. A shirtless Sean Connery. Three versions of a mustached Burt Reynolds. Natalie Wood running joyfully toward her youth-gang boyfriend. Maria Callas sitting in an alcove in Pasolini's *Medea*. Olivia de Havilland, Twiggy, and Ingrid Bergman. All the colors faded except for Marlene Dietrich's lipstick, which seemed to have been touched up, her cigarette interrupting the red. A shark, Robert Shaw, Roy Scheider, and Richard Dreyfuss advertised the film *Lo squalo*. Gene Kelly dancing, Johnny Weissmuller as Tarzan. Beach scenes from *Dr. No* and *From Here to Eternity*. Dustin Hoffman with a woman's thigh and on a horse surrounded by Indians. The Oscar in multiples. The delicious underarm of Rita Hayworth in *Gilda*, the sumptuous eyes of Elizabeth Taylor in *A Place in the Sun*. Mae West, belle of the nineties. Franco Nero, gorgeous with a five-o'clock shadow, Robert Redford and Paul Newman, Steve McQueen in *Tom Horn*, William Holden and Kim Novak, Dean Martin and Jerry Lewis. Ursula Andress, Romy Schneider, and Dalida. Judy Garland, Judy Garland, Judy Garland.

But in the lower right corner, one image was scraped away, with the wall's plaster showing through. I didn't have to be told who scraped it off or what picture it was. After Uncle Jihad's death, my father wouldn't have wanted anyone to see the image of Alan Bates and Oliver Reed kissing fiercely. My father must have spent quite a bit of time scraping.

My finger still bled. I dabbed the blood around my lips and kissed the forlorn space. The red imprint of my lips matched Marlene's.

Fourteen

Adam was bored. The Garden was lovely, but he wanted someone to talk to. "Dear God," he prayed, "I need company." God gave him a mate. Out of his tail, a woman was created, but Marwa turned out to be as mischievous as a monkey. Adam was not happy. "Dear God, I need better company." Eve was brought forth from the thirteenth rib of his right side. Decent women can claim Eve as their ancestor. All giddy girls are descendants of Marwa.

This legend has a Jewish counterpart in that of Lilith, who was created at the same time as Adam, of the same dust. "I am your equal," she said. "I will not lie helpless beneath you. I, too, seek fulfillment." Adam was not happy. God made Eve from his side, to stand by him, to support him, to submit to him.

And Lilith? Lilith coupled with demons on the shores of the Red Sea. God forsook her.

I cannot tell you whether Fatima is a descendant of Lilith or Marwa, but I can tell you she had little to do with Eve.

In her part of the world, Fatima was famous—infamous, if you prefer, but not in the Western sense. She wasn't a film star, her face didn't appear in magazines, her name wasn't bandied about in professional journals. She was famous in Arab terms, in discreet terms: she was talked about. No story was juicy enough if Fatima wasn't on the gossiper's tongue. Fatima didn't couple with demons. She preferred short, filthy-wealthy Gulf Arabs, and "coupling" wouldn't be the right word to use. Her reputation was solidified with her first marriage—solidified, mind you, for she'd already developed one by simply being Mariella's little sister.

Story of her first marriage: June 1981, I had just graduated from

UCLA and was hired as a computer engineer and programmer by Ellisen Engineering, the only company I'd ever work for. Fatima was studying psychology at the University of Rome and was due to graduate. She didn't. Like my sister before her, she got married. Unlike my sister's, her marriage lasted longer than her wedding, but not by much. He was an inordinately rich Saudi prince, a young one, one of numerous siblings, not in any line to rule, maybe a ministry one day. He met her in Rome and was besotted. He had never known anyone like her, he claimed, and probably would never again. "I liked him all right" was what Fatima would always say. His family wasn't too happy but didn't disapprove. The boy was Saudi, after all, and he had at least three more chances to improve his selection. The trouble began at the wedding, which I couldn't attend because of work. It seemed the prince's mother and his homely sisters kept good-naturedly pestering the bride, joking and demanding that she get pregnant. "Shouldn't we finish the wedding first?" she replied. Two months later, when her mother-in-law inquired if Fatima might be pregnant, Fatima rolled up a newspaper—a Lebanese *Al-Nahar*—and smacked the princess on the nose three times: Don't—smack—put your nose—smack—in my business—smack. As horrifying as that was, puppy-training her mother-in-law wasn't the reason for the divorce. Horror of horrors, the prince took his wife's side. When, finally, the prince's father asked his son if Fatima had ever laid a hand on him, the prince turned crimson, and the nature of the couple's sexual relationship was discovered. Even that could have been hushed up—this was the Arab world, after all—if the prince hadn't admitted, much to his humiliation, that, even though they had been having sex since they met, he had yet to earn coitus. Straw, meet camel.

During his eighth-birthday celebration, Shams and his disciple were having laughing fits. It began innocently enough. The royalty and notables of the land lined up to offer the young prophet gifts and receive his blessing in return. Shams would whisper into Layl's ear, and the two of them would giggle. The emir's wife could hear what they were whispering, and she realized that the worshippers could as well: This one had a big nose. That one had body odor. The two red parrots were perched atop the throne, and the violet parrot, the one the emir's wife hated most for his frequent use of obscenities, had settled atop the sun altar. All three were chuckling. But then the dark slave boy began to whisper into the prophet's ear, and the prophet blushed and covered his mouth.

"Give us a funny face," Shams commanded the genuflecting matronly princess.

"Funny face?" the confused princess asked. She nervously adjusted the sheer scarf covering her hair.

"Yes," said the prophet, grinning. "Give us a funny face. A good one."

"Now, dear," the emir's wife interjected, trying to appear calm, "you cannot ask such things of your wonderful supplicants. It is not mannerly."

"What is the point of being a fornicating prophet," Adam said, "if you can't command the faithful?"

"No funny face, no blessing," decreed the prophet.

"I do not understand, my lord," said the princess. "I will offer any gift that pleases you. I do not know what a funny face is, or else I would gladly offer it."

"This is a funny face." Layl stuck his tongue out and pushed his nose up.

"This is better." Shams pulled his mouth wide and stretched his eyelids with his fingers. "You better give us your funniest face. No blessing if it is not your best face."

"You desire and I obey, my lord." The princess jammed two fingers up her nose, stuck her tongue all the way out to the left, and surprised everyone by crossing her eyes. The boys screeched and buried their heads in the throne's big pillow, their legs scissoring the air in delight. The princess smiled, proud of herself.

"Wait," said the beautiful prophet, settling down. He placed his palm atop the princess's head, squashed the scarf into her jewel-adorned hair. The whole room saw her body shudder with ecstasy and glow with joy. After she kissed the prophet's hand and stood up, everyone gasped. Ten years had disappeared from her face. The emir's wife thrust a mirror at her, and the princess yelped. She turned back to the prophet and kissed his feet over and over. "Thank you, thank you, thank you," she mumbled.

.　　.　　.

On his eleventh birthday, the beautiful prophet and his faithful companion faced the adoring horde. Every year, the number of pilgrims had increased, and when the emir's wife spread the word that the prophet would be giving his first sermon, thousands upon thousands of devotees arrived from the four corners of the earth. They sat, they stood, they covered the land to the horizon, buzzing with anticipation and good cheer.

"Blessed are you, my people," Shams began. "Blessed are those of you who have traveled for weeks on your pilgrimage. I am grateful and not worthy of such devotion." Shams hesitated, and Layl whispered into his ear. "Blessed are you who pray to God, but He demands more. From now on, you must pray eight times a day at least." He nodded at his audience. "Yes, it is true. You must pray every three hours. Worry not. You will get used to sleeping in two-hour shifts. It is much healthier. Rejoice and be exceedingly glad. Oh, and bathing. You must bathe before each prayer, eight times a day. If we bathed more often, we would not smell so bad when there are a lot of us. Exult." Layl nudged his twin, who rambled on. "And no farting." Layl turned his head to hide his snickering. "I decree that if you have to fart you must fart downwind. Before you fart, make sure to gauge the wind's direction. I decree further that silent farts are to be banned. Others must know who the guilty party is. And hear this, for I have a warning. If you fart silently upwind, a double transgression, there will be no absolution. You will not be able to wear my colors."

"Unless you get a doctor's note," chimed Layl.

It took one devotee to laugh heartily before a few others hesitantly joined him. The emir's wife chided her son: "You promised to stick to the script."

"Blessed are the poor," Shams announced. "They do not have much."

The laughter rippled through the crowd. Devotees cheered and applauded. "What about marital decrees?" someone shouted.

"Well, you cannot marry your mother—or your father, for that matter. A wife must be no taller than her husband, and no more than a hand shorter. You must never use the word 'ambidextrous' when your spouse is in the room, or 'hair.' That is much more challenging. You can use the word 'hair' with strangers or with friends, but never with your wife."

"What about diet restrictions?" another devotee yelled.

"Yes. You cannot cook a lamb in its mother's milk. You cannot mix fruits in savory dishes, only in dessert."

"And no broccoli," said Layl.

"I am the prophet of these lands, and I am not going to eat any more broccoli."

As the masses cheered, the emir's wife pleaded with the prophet to end his sermon.

※

What was the reputation of Fatima's sister? Who was Mariella, the great Mariella?

Rewind to January 1975, a few months before the civil war erupted. My class and the senior class took a ski trip to The Cedars. To break the monotony of the three-hour drive from Beirut, our bus stopped at Hilmi's, a lemonade shop in the town of Batroun. It was a Sunday at six in the evening, and the shop was busy, filled with skiers on the way back to the city. With the influx of all the students, there was hardly a place to stand.

A threesome of seniors, the most popular boys in school, cut in before Fatima and me. One of the boys was the captain of the varsity soccer team. Fatima decided that maneuvering around a crowd for lemonade was too much trouble, and she walked outside. Her exit was fortunate, because she missed running into her sister. I heard Mariella's laugh before I saw her. She held a translucent cup of lemonade with a lipstick-smeared straw sticking out. "If this place was such a secret," she said loudly, "how come there's an infestation of people?"

Her companion didn't look amused. Tall and dark, he wore a grim face and a soldier's uniform, but it was not that of the regular army. "So it's not a secret, but it's the best lemonade."

"You obviously haven't been to Rome." Mariella walked toward the exit; she didn't have to squeeze through the mob, which parted like Moses's sea to make way for her. Her red wool dress would have been short on a ten-year-old. She noticed me in the crowd, and her eyes smiled an instant before her lips spread into an unequivocal grin. "Osama," she squealed. "My darling."

She tousled my hair and kissed my astonished lips. Esmeralda stunned Quasimodo. She winked to let me in on the silly game.

"Where have you been hiding, you pretty thing?" she asked. I doubted anyone would believe her charade, but I assumed that wasn't the point. "Will you come see me soon?" Her voice was coy and disarming. "I miss you terribly." She walked away, still looking at me, and blew me a kiss once she reached the door. "Call me," she yelled. Her companion glared. He was a good head and a half taller than I.

The soccer captain quickly positioned himself beside me. "You know Mariella Farouk?" His voice was surprisingly low and hesitant. "She's hot, isn't she?" His eyes were a light brown, possibly hazel, with three random flecks of maroon stationed differently in each. "Do you know her well?" he asked. "Umm, are you good friends? Have you known each other for a while? She's going to compete for Miss Lebanon. I'm sure she'll win."

One of his friends jumped in. "They say she gives the best head, which is remarkable in a way. You'd think a girl who looks like her wouldn't have to. You know, an ugly girl should try harder and all that, but, no, she's gorgeous and she likes it. You can't beat that."

I shuddered and felt my face flush. "She's Fatima's sister," I exclaimed.

The soccer captain shoved his friend. "Don't mind him. He doesn't know what he's talking about. Let's get some lemonade."

As the bus climbed the mountain to the ski resort, a confused Fatima, in the aisle seat next to me, tried to make sense of why the soccer captain had rushed to a seat across from her and was trying to engage her in small talk. It took all of two minutes for her to grow bored and feign sleep, her head nestled on my shoulder.

A few months later, when the battles erupted in Lebanon, Mr. Farouk asked his wife to take their two daughters back to Rome, where she was from, to remain until the events in Beirut stabilized. Mariella refused to leave. She was having too good a time. She was an adult at nineteen. She had a life. No silly skirmishes were going to interfere with her plans.

Mr. Farouk was killed first, in 1976. He was kidnapped by one of the militias, tortured, and slain. His mangled body was found in a ditch on Mazra Street. He was the first person I knew who died because of the civil war. His death completely overwhelmed Fatima, but not Mariella. He was well loved and respected, which meant that quite a few people, including my father, worked for many a day and sleepless night to get him released, but it was for naught, since no one could figure out which militia had kidnapped him and for what reason. He was ostensibly an apolitical Iraqi Christian with no known enemies. Fear of the irrational, of the random, caused stories to bubble up in explanation. Mr. Farouk was actually a CIA operative. He was an Israeli spy. He was a Syrian spy. He was a journalist writing the only true story exposing the conspiracy of the great nations against Lebanon. He was an Iraqi royal. He was a once-famous Latvian actor who ran afoul of the Soviet propaganda machine. His death had meaning.

Even though her father's murder should have offered Mariella an inkling of the dangers that could befall her, she was too involved to notice. Mariella would never have seen herself as a victim; she was a player. Like a lesser-stage Evita, she moved up the ranks, from one militiaman to another (Elie had been a practice run, a steppingstone). She was able to switch sides and back again a few times. The insignia on the uniform didn't matter, the size of the gun did. Any other woman would have been terminated, but her talent made her untouchable, at least for a while.

Mrs. Farouk called my mother daily from Rome. She begged, whimpered, and pleaded with my mother to help Mariella, make her call Rome, make her stop the lunacy. Mariella didn't want or need my mother's help. In fact, she helped us. Once, when our family got trapped in Beirut, Mariella sent a jeep to pick us up and ferry us to the safety of the mountains—safe for us, but risky for the driver and the accompanying bodyguard. Fatima would call her sister constantly, but Mariella had stopped listening to anyone.

The soccer captain was right—she was crowned Miss Lebanon, but she was shot before she could make it to the Miss Universe contest. By the time she entered the Miss Lebanon competition, her reputation was such that a vote against her meant a judicious end to a judge's life. She won even though she wasn't a Lebanese citizen. More astonishing, she won even though she had bypassed the talent competition.

It is said that she retained her temper and her tantrums. The story of her death became infamous. She had survived dumping power-hungry militia leaders; she had survived crossing from east to west and vice versa; she had survived a lover's discovering her in bed with his underling. (The underling was more respected and promptly replaced the jilted man. Was Mariella an expert at leadership assessment, or was the mere fact that the underling bedded his superior's girlfriend a cause for immediate respect? One wonders.) What proved fatal was accusing her last lover in front of other fighters of having an inadequate dick.

Over the years, Fatima had expended great energy in debunking theories that she was who she was in response to her older sister. She called all such talk psychoanalytic psychobabble, and irrelevant to boot.

But once, when we were kids, Mariella showed me a pendant she'd received for her birthday. "It's a real emerald. My birthstone, and it matches my eyes."

Brown-eyed Fatima had an indecent fondness for emeralds.

❧

The boys began to spend more time in the world. They played in the grand garden, accompanied and watched over by the colorful parrots. The emir's wife could see them throwing stones at an old elm tree's trunk. She called to Shams from her balcony, but he pretended not to hear. She, on the other hand, could hear their joyous shrieks quite well. She called again, but her son only glanced up at her and returned to his playing. He threw a stone at the trunk, and from out of nowhere, a devotee jumped in front of the target and the stone struck her forehead. She covered her wound with both hands, bowed down before her prophet, and repeated, "Thank you, thank you," before running away with the injurious stone in her possession.

The green parrot squawked a warning, and the boys left the garden quickly. Three ecru-clothed devotees popped out from behind the hedges, too late to catch a glimpse of their adored.

And, for the seventh time that morning, the emir's wife wished her son's dark slave an ignominious death. Tear him into a hundred pieces and roast the parrots and eat them all. One of the handmaids cleared her throat, interrupting the sumptuous reverie, and offered a letter once her presence was acknowledged. "Who is this from?" asked the emir's wife.

"I do not know, mistress," the servant replied. "The letter appeared on a silver tray placed upon your bed."

The emir's wife blanched upon reading the unsigned note: "What you desire can be accomplished with patience and my help. If you wish annihilation of the dark one, seat yourself beneath the third willow at midnight of the seventh night of the moon's pregnancy."

. .

Under the third willow, the emir's wife sat anxiously, her head covered with her cape. She glanced at the moon for the umpteenth time to make sure this was the proper night. Why was she always early? Royalty should make others wait. The night was still, not a breath of wind, yet the willow's leaves rustled with a will of their own. She inhaled deeply and felt faint. The world shimmered, and a cloaked woman of manly size sat facing her beneath the second willow. Though the mooned night was bright, the cloak's shadows hid the stranger's features.

"Royalty deigns not to speak to a supplicant with a hidden face," the emir's wife said.

The woman chuckled and released her cloak, revealing a head and face wrapped in an unnatural haze. "What are you?" the emir's wife asked. "Trickery does not impress me. I command you to show me your face."

"Which face would you like to see?" The woman's voice was as deep as her laugh, throaty and rough. She snapped her fingers and the haze thinned. Her face was atrociously ugly and deformed.

"Do I have a choice?"

"Of course you do." The woman snapped her fingers once more and her face transformed into that of the emir's wife.

"You are a witch." Horrified, the emir's wife covered her own face. "Remove that visage at once."

"As you please." The woman changed her face into that of an ordinary peasant with unexceptional features.

"Are you a witch?"

"Of a kind. Are you interested in what I am or what I have to offer? I can help you get rid of your nemesis and mine, in time."

"I do not see how. I have tried everything. I have tried poisoning him, at least a hundred times, used every poison known to man, but the boy does not get so much as an upset stomach. I have hired killers to get rid of him and his mother, bird catchers for the parrots. They mock me. Last month, I had ten archers shoot at Fatima, and the arrows fell short of their target, who simply laughed."

"Mortal schemes will not injure her, and none will wound him, for he is a demon."

"Oh, come, come," the emir's wife scoffed. "He is an ugly brat, but a demon?"

"He is not just a demon; he will rule their world. He is the king of jinn. Killing him will not be easy, but it can be done. Is it what you desire?"

"Of course it is. Kill him and I will reward you with whatever you wish. My son must be freed from his shadow."

"I cannot kill the dark one without your help. Throughout the ages, it has been so. To obliterate a demon king, his mother must destroy his life organs."

"Fatima could never hurt him."

The woman stared at the emir's wife and hesitated. "But you can. Consider this: since he and your prophet are inseparable, fate considers him your son. When the time comes, will you have the courage to follow through?"

"Yes. I will destroy his heart."

"Not his heart. He is a jinni. To kill him, his mother must destroy his testicles."

"Oh my." The emir's wife turned ashen. "He is still only eleven. They are not even functioning yet."

"Then we must wait until they are."

❦

More on Fatima: Fast-forward to October 1990, I was twenty-nine, employed, a productive member of society, and Fatima was thirty, on her third marriage, a citizen of the world. Comparing her with my sister once more: After Elie, Lina gave up on marriage, or, really, never thought about it. She actually never thought about Elie, either, never saw him again after the wedding, which she claimed woke her up. On the other hand, after her first marriage, Fatima chose a different track. She upgraded, traded husbands in for better models.

That October, Fatima and my sister decided to visit me in Los Angeles at an inopportune time. Four of us from work were scheduled to attend a self-improvement workshop at the Asilomar Conference, near Carmel. Our boss, a devotee of the seminar's facilitator, suggested that our attendance would help team-building. I would have been away from Los Angeles for only four days, but neither Fatima nor Lina wished to remain in the city without me.

Lina said she'd come along and stay nearby. The coast was gorgeous. She could take walks on the Asilomar grounds, hike in the rolling hills, shop in Carmel. Fatima—Fatima decided she had to attend the workshop. She would stay in the same hotel as Lina but would spend her days observing the strange rituals of lost souls.

Fatima unclasped her hair, and it bubbled like an inchoate oil well, gushing and falling behind her head. She leaned back in her Adirondack chair, covered her eyes with sunglasses, and adjusted her necklace, making sure that every passerby noticed both the necklace and her bust.

"Why are we here?" she said. "I'm bored. Have you seen the people in that workshop? They're all healthy as mutts and they're all complaining. Oh, help me, great fucking guru, I have a hangnail, and I don't sleep well on nights with a full moon."

"You keep pushing your bust out like that," I said, "and everyone will know you're a tramp."

My sister, unsure what to make of the California fall weather, walked toward us in a soft cotton dress and a wool cardigan. Her hair was held atop her head with a childish barrette. She seemed fully contained, without needs or trouble, her step light and buoyant.

I found myself between the women, a position I had grown accustomed to.

"Your brother thinks I'm a tramp," Fatima announced.

"That's not exactly true," Lina said. "You're a whore."

"I'm not," she said, distracted and bemused. "I may not be the most virtuous of maidens, but whores do it for money."

"Oh God," huffed Lina. "You've gotten a hundred times richer with each marriage. Have you ever fucked a guy who wasn't wealthy?"

"Fucked?" Fatima sat up in her chair, looked around her, pretending shock. "Moi?" Her fingers touched her chest. "You really do think I'm a cheap whore. I don't fuck my men."

"And you certainly aren't cheap. Have you told the boy about your emerald necklace?"

"Not yet. I haven't had the chance, with all the meditations and healings."

"She hasn't told me," I said, "but she has been brandishing that thing all day."

"That's not the one, silly boy," Fatima said. "Can't you tell one emerald necklace from another? That one is exquisite."

"Gaudy," added Lina.

"Stunning," said Fatima. "Should I tell him the story?"

"Do," said Lina.

"Okay. Listen. This is how I found out I liked my husband. He's ever so sweet. This was in April. We'd been married for a few months. I was in Riyadh because he couldn't get away and couldn't be without me. I'm bored and antsy. I get a call from my ex-husband in Doha. He misses me. Tough, I say. He must see me. Boring. He can't live without me. Practice, I say."

"Sensitivity is part of her charm," interrupted Lina.

"Shut up," Fatima went on. "So he says he regrets running away from me."

"And leaving behind just a few millions in change," added Lina.

"It's my story. Let me tell it. Anyway, I'm not impressed. But he begins to whimper, and you know what hearing a man whimper does to me. He says he's been to New York, to London, to Berlin, he even went to Thailand, but no one understood his needs the way I did."

"That would have touched me deeply as well," Lina said.

"I think why not. I told him to get his ass on a plane and meet me in Rome."

"But she's not a whore, mind you."

"I tell my husband I need a break and I'm going home. He says that's a wonderful idea, he'll join me. What could I do? I remind my husband of my rules. No one stays in my house in Rome. It's my sanctuary in this horrible world. He says he'll rent a hotel suite. I figure I can leave him in the hotel every now and then and tell him I need to be at home. We're in Rome. I meet my ex at the Spanish Steps. Not my fault. He's a tourist. He begins to whimper again: Take me to my room. Take me to my room. I decide to take a walk. Make him beg some more. We go down Via Condotti, a pleasant spring day."

"You get a full-fledged weather report gratis."

"Shut up. I'm enjoying this. We're walking, and it's not my fault that Bulgari has a great store there, with the most magnificent picture window display. I stop. What woman wouldn't?"

"Yo," Lina answered.

"What intelligent woman wouldn't? In the window, calling my name loudly and repeatedly, is a lovely emerald necklace. My jaw drops. My ex asks me if I like it. Of course I do. He walks into the store. I have to follow him; I can't stand in the street by myself. He asks to see the necklace, places it on my neck—a match made in heaven."

"Otherwise known in the holy books as Bulgari in Rome."

"He buys it for me. One hundred and seventy-five thousand dollars. So, of course, I take him to his room."

"And he's still in the hospital recovering."

"He had fun. Anyway, I'm back in my husband's suite, and I've forgotten that I'm wearing the necklace. He asks me about it. I tell him I was taking a walk and saw it in the window and just had to have it. He asks how much it was, and I tell him. And he says no wife of his will ever pay for her own jewelry. He takes out his checkbook and writes me a check for one hundred and seventy-five thousand dollars. Isn't he sweet?"

"You know, you're right," said Lina. " 'Whore' is not the right word. It sounds trite."

"True," Fatima said. "It says little about talent."

"Demimondaine," I said.

"Yes," Fatima exclaimed. "That sounds so much more encompassing. I've found myself. And here I thought this workshop was a puerile assignment in psychological masturbation. I didn't even have to endure a dark night of the soul. It's a bargain. I stared deep into my being and saw my true self. This is who I am. I'm a demimondaine."

A doe appeared, and two others followed her. Slow, hesitant steps.

My sister yawned and stretched. "You didn't tell me what she did today."

"Let her tell you," I said. "I'm sure she'll enjoy bragging." Fatima only smiled. I sighed. "One of the women in the workshop showed up with a lot of different crystals, and this one over here asked what they were for. The woman said one was for healing, another was for dreaming, and so on. The grande dame said, 'Oh, how sweet. My people have quite a bit in common with your people. You collect crystals, and I collect emeralds.' "

Lina guffawed, and the startled does ran away terrified.

"Are you getting anything out of the seminar?" my sister asked me. "It doesn't seem to be work-related, so I can't figure why your boss is asking his employees to do this."

"It's okay," I said. "Misguided, perhaps. If nothing else, it's a social event, something for us to do outside work. It would have been easier without Fatima giving grief to so many."

Fatima sat up and faced my sister. "Can you imagine if you asked any of your workers to do something like this? You're the president of al-Kharrat. Send a memo to all your dealerships. I, Lina al-Kharrat, capo di capi, ask that you attend a self-improvement seminar and meditate. Bring your tarot cards."

"Shut up." My sister smiled at me. "Is there something I can do to make up for this one's behavior?"

I sat up. "You can tell the big whore not to seduce the workshop leader. Everyone was aghast."

"Me?" Fatima said. "I didn't do anything. Is it my fault if he spent the entire morning ogling me and showing excitement? No, no, no, shorty. You can't pin that one on me."

"Excitement, you say?" Lina asked.

"The whole morning session," I said. "You know her. Three hours of stretching lazily, readjusting her butt every few minutes. In the middle of the session, she interrupted to suggest that the floor wasn't very comfortable and asked for a fauteuil. The guy was a goner. The group couldn't concentrate on anything but the bulge."

"Was the guru gargantuan?" Lina asked.

"Please," Fatima replied. "God, when are we leaving?"

❧

A lovely spring day, and nightingales sang in the bushes, and golden finches competed from trees. Gardenias tossed their scent into the air, and narcissi preened. And from her balcony the emir's wife was shocked at the scene in the garden before her. Her twelve-year-old son lying on his stomach without a stitch of clothing, his white behind saluting the sky, his head nestled between his dark twin's spread thighs. The dark one, naked and hairless, lying on his back, his head cradled in one hand and his other hand curled into the prophet's golden strands as Shams licked his testicles, an effortless indulgence. The boys formed a calm, sinewy interlacing of alabaster and onyx. When Layl opened his eyes and noticed the emir's wife aghast, a devilish grin appeared on his face.

❧

Last Fatima story: Fast forward once more to March 1996. I was depressed; my mother had passed away two years earlier. Fatima took me on a vacation of sorts to lift my spirits.

Liquid heat rose off the asphalt in waves. It was springtime, but the temperature in Riyadh hovered in the hellish. Buildings shimmered and swayed as our car sped by. The tinted glass made them appear sickly and subdued, about to faint from fatigue. The air-conditioning slapped my face and made me shiver. Fatima began putting on her black abayeh, covering an obscene amount of flesh. She didn't struggle, concealed her body with professional experience. Her head and face remained revealed.

"You're fucked up," I said.

"Blah, blather, blah. You're here, so stop your complaining." She took a compact from her purse, applied scarlet lipstick, and winked. "Can I help it if you still trust me?"

I floated in the back seat of the Mercedes, its black interior luxurious and gloomy. "You're fucked up," I said again.

"Mind your language." She put away the compact, extricated a brush, and ran it through her hair. "He doesn't speak English, but I'm sure he knows the word 'fuck.' "

The driver was in full Saudi uniform—headdress and Gucci sunglasses. He intermittently glanced back in the rearview mirror, but we didn't sustain his interest.

"Tell me you're not getting married again," I said. "Please."

"Oh, no. Fuck that. Enough is enough."

"Then why are you back here?"

"Diddling," she said.

"And I'm here as your Sancho Panza."

"Ta-da! You're wising up." She leaned over and impressed a moist kiss on my cheek. I moved my hand to wipe it away, but she held my wrist. "Don't. Leave it." She replaced everything in her handbag and zipped it. "Don't be so petulant. Have I ever failed you? You've been sitting alone in that godforsaken joke of a country, grieving your losses and moping. I know it's hard, but you've been at it for too long. I couldn't cheer you up over there. I thought a real change in scenery would do you good. This is a great place to spend your vacation. It may look ever so dull on the outside, but the stories, darling—the hidden stories are fucking incredible. Watch, listen, and learn. Trust me."

On cue, the car stopped at the entrance of a grand shopping mall. I grabbed the door handle, but she stopped me. She covered her head, and the veil dribbled over her face. A mysterious woman was birthed before my eyes. The driver opened the door, and I exited. Fatima slid over on the seat and held out her hand, the only skin exposed. Two emerald rings bewitched my eyes. She gently pulled on my hand, helped herself out of the car, and strolled ahead of me, a billowing, flapping black ghost. The clack of her high heels on the pavement, the head held aloft, made her seem like royalty traveling incognito.

A group of three veiled women turned their heads as she passed them. Two men ran to check the license plate of the car, and one of them dialed his cell phone. Fatima walked through the glass doors of the mall seemingly oblivious, but I knew better. I hurried in after her.

She didn't slow her step inside, didn't look right or left. The black abayeh was not as formless as it first appeared, its finely sewn lines and folds accentuating her buxom and indolent body. Shoppers whispered in hushed tones as she passed. Men looked utterly confused, their faces showing naked lust and fear. They had no means to approach her. Faltering and off-balance, they ogled. She got on the escalator.

"Am I just supposed to follow you?" I asked.

"Of course, dear, if it makes you happy, but you can walk alongside me, too. I do provide options." She entered a record store, looked around, moseyed from section to section, and finally headed toward the Arabic compact-disc racks. "Come along." She ran her graceful fingers through a stack of discs, some of traditional Arabic vocalists, others more contemporary.

"I didn't know you liked that stuff," I said.

"I certainly don't. I'm here for you, dear. This is all for you." She held up an Umm Kalthoum disc. "Look." The top of the plastic wrap had been sliced delicately with an X-acto knife. She tore through the wrap with her impeccably manicured fingernails, extracted a handwritten note from the disc box, and read it to me. " 'If you like the music of Umm Kalthoum as much as I do, we probably have even more things in common. I'm a good man, twenty-four, gentle, educated, and very respectful of ladies. Let's talk. Here's my cell phone number.' "

"You've got to be kidding me." I could only imagine her face as she looked at me, smug, bemused, probably laughing.

"There are others. Look. Kazem al-Saher. Three different discs have notes. These boys are so desperate. So many of them." She took out another note, different boy, same request.

"That's sad."

"It is," she replied quietly, and sighed. "Damn. Once upon a time, I thought it was amusing." She chucked the discs onto the rack, crumpled the love notes, and turned around. "Let's go." She took out her phone. "I'm ready," she told her driver.

I followed her down the escalator. "Whenever I feel blue," she said, "which is not very often, I try to come to Riyadh. I feel so wanted." She paused. "I'm inspired by the braves." She marched toward the exit. The automatic doors burped in noxious heat. No fewer than twenty men, Saudis clad in expensive desert robes, waited in the scalding temperature. As soon as the identifying Mercedes reached the curb, they twittered; she was the bell to Pavlov's dogs.

A tall, handsome man walked quickly toward her. He slipped between us, and his hand touched her ebony abayeh, leaving a small yellow Post-it note on her back, with a handwritten phone number. I squinted, trying to read it, but another man blocked my view as he stuck on another note. Only two braves.

The Post-it notes glimmered in the sun as she walked toward the open door of the Mercedes. Two lonely gold islands in a sea of oil black.

♣

The emir's wife had an ominous premonition that the prophet's thirteenth-birthday celebration was going to be a disaster. It was not an unqualified premonition, for she had been witnessing the horrific changes in her son for the previous month. He had become moodier and crankier. His healing powers seemed to be fading, if not disappearing completely. His rebellious heart no longer cared. He would touch the supplicants and no change occurred. He could only pretend to heal for about ten minutes before giving up in a huff and returning to his room.

The emir's wife could no longer lie to herself about what the twins were doing in that room. She had caught them frolicking in the garden on more than one occasion. And when she tried to reason with him, Shams told her to perform unnatural sexual acts upon herself.

At her wit's end, she tried to talk to Fatima, her nemesis, who only said, "All boys go through this stage. Leave him be. He is no longer the same person he was as a child. The powers he possessed then have transformed. Guruji has died. Mourn for him, but let him go. None of us is the same person in each stage of our life." And the emir's wife hated Fatima even more and promised to dedicate her life to the eradication of that woman.

The largest crowd of all appeared on the morning of the thirteenth-birthday celebration to witness Shams becoming a man. Their prophet and his companion stood before them, drunk on wine, and laughed. And the prophet yelled, "Eat my shit, you dimwitted bastards. Have you nothing better to do? Go home."

The horrified emir's wife heard the woman's voice echo in her head. "It is time."

— *Fifteen* —

I stood before the hospital vending machine and contemplated the latest existential crisis: Was drinking insultingly horrible coffee better or worse than spending the morning decaffeinated? I allowed the machine to slurp my money. Dark, viscous liquid poured out of a crooked funnel. I picked up the paper cup and almost spilled the coffee on Aunt Wasila and her daughter, Dida. My free hand settled above my heart to calm its startled beat. Dida kissed me. I tried not to stare at her nose, which she had recently had cut and reshaped to Anglo-Saxon.

"I won't kiss you," Aunt Wasila said. "I know you hate fake sentimentality." She shoved a baker's box into my chest, and I could feel it was still warm. "Fresh croissants. And better yet." She took out a thermos out of her Prada handbag. "Better than that gunk in your hand." I could have kissed the tiles beneath her feet. "I was hoping that if I arrived early I'd get a chance to see him briefly," she said. "I know he doesn't like anyone to see him infirm, but he won't know I'm there." I looked from mother to daughter. "Just me," Aunt Wasila said.

I showed Aunt Wasila to my father's room, and she stood rigid before his bed, examining and measuring. It was impossible to believe she was his age. Her look, posture, and demeanor did not speak the language of the aged. A momentary fear startled me; I was afraid the aroma of fresh croissants would disturb my unconscious father. My sister poured three cups of coffee out of the thermos. She handed one to Fatima and took a sip. Aunt Wasila nodded at them and turned to leave. I walked her back to the visitor's room.

Aunt Wasila was our family's lightning rod. She was to our family what Israel was to the Arab world, the one who could unite everyone in hating her. As soon as she married Uncle Wajih, she embarked on a prolonged war against the family, at times clandestine, at other times overt. Only my mother was spared. Aunt Wasila didn't consider her an enemy, because she figured out early on that my mother cared not one whit about the family—or about her, for that matter. Both women were outsiders. My mother cherished the role, for she had no wish to belong. Aunt Wasila did, and sought revenge for her exclusion.

On August 6, 1945, the day the Americans dropped the bomb on Hiroshima, our family—my grandfather, my grandmother, their five children, my great-grandmother, and even my great-uncles Jalal and Ma'an—walked to Aunt Wasila's village, literally a stone's throw away, to inquire about the availability of her hand in marriage. According to Uncle Jihad, who was thirteen at the time, everything ran smoothly. Aunt Wasila was surrounded by her mother and numerous aunts. It became obvious that Uncle Wajih was impressed with Aunt Wasila, and the feeling was mutual, because she began to smile, converse, and engage with our family. She would suddenly stand up, grab a tray of refreshments, and run up to the guests, her head snapping right and left, depending on whom she was talking to. Aunt Samia, already twenty-five, wasn't forgiving of the sixteen-year-old girl. "What does he see in her?" she asked her mother softly. "She moves like a cornered lizard." Unfortunately, Aunt Wasila's nephew, who was too young to welcome the guests, was hiding behind the old couch. He heard Aunt Samia's comment. The next day, our family was informed that Aunt Wasila had chosen another suitor.

It's hard for me to envision Aunt Wasila as that young village girl. By the time I came into the world, my father's siblings had all relocated to Beirut, the company was up and running, and Aunt Wasila was never seen in anything but pants except at funerals and weddings. The idea that she was once quasi-innocent, forced to be demure and wear traditional Druze dress, was incomprehensible to anyone who knew her. Compared with her, Margaret Thatcher and Golda Meir were blushing maidens.

Aunt Wasila eventually changed her mind about Uncle Wajih, and they were married in 1946. She moved into my grandparents' house. That was an arrant family mistake. Aunt Samia believed it was Aunt Wasila who persuaded her husband to ask his parents to move out of their bedroom, which was bigger than the newlyweds'. The bitter internecine war between my aunts erupted. In years to come, many would try to broker a peace between the two women. All attempts were unsuccessful. Aunt Samia felt that her nemesis had committed the most dastardly of sins: she had treated my saintly grandmother with disrespect. As for Aunt Wasila, she could never forgive because she was a congenitally hateful woman.

When I was born, Aunt Wasila had been married for fifteen years and had had enough of the family. Though she lived in the same building, she and her children hardly interacted with us, much to the consternation of my father and Uncle Wajih. By 1974, when Uncle Wajih passed away, the breach was complete, and that shook my father. He tried rapprochement many times and failed abysmally. Once, in 1996, he dragged himself to her house and begged her to relent.

"I'm an old man," he told her. "I don't want to go to my grave with my family scattered. I'm not asking that you fall in love with the family, only that we don't remain so distant. People mock us."

"I show up to the important functions. I haven't abandoned the family."

"I'm asking you to forgive," my father said.

"Some things can never be forgiven."

"It was so long ago," my father pleaded. "It's almost fifty years now."

"Some things can never be forgiven."

❧

On the fortieth day after King Saleh's death, the king's council met at the diwan to elect a new leader of the faith. "I should be king," said many a council member. King Saleh's widow, Shajarat al-Durr, sent a note with one of her attendants that said, "I am fit to rule." Some demanded, "The new king must be Arab," but others came back with "The king should be Turkoman." The Kurds refused any such suggestion. "There shall be no king who is not a descendant of the king. King Saleh has a son in the city of Tikrit called Issa Touran Shah. He must be king." The council agreed and dispatched Kurdish envoys with a letter informing their kinsman Issa Touran Shah that he was the new sultan of Islam.

The envoys found the new king drunk in Tikrit, his face buried in the generous breasts of an Ethiopian slave girl, his lips devouring her supple skin. "What can I do for you?" he muttered in between grunts.

The messenger handed him the letter, and Issa Touran Shah in turn gave the letter to his girl. "Read it to me," he said. "My eyes have a higher priority."

"The world is not everlasting," read the slave girl. "Your father has passed away."

"That is bad," followed by what sounded like the squeal of a piglet.

"You are now king."

"That is better," followed by what sounded like the snore of a sated glutton.

King Issa Touran Shah left Tikrit and headed toward the great city of Cairo. In the great city, the king visited the tomb of his father, where he kissed the ground, read the Fatiha, and asked God to guide His servant. God may have guided the king, but wine complicated the directions. In the diwan, he teetered upon his chair, and Prince Baybars whispered in his ear, "Fear God and cease your drinking. Your subjects deserve a sober ruler." The king promised to drink no more, but he appeared sheepish and even more inebriated the following day.

Prince Baybars complained to Othman, "Alcohol should not influence the decisions of the ruler of Islam. We must open his eyes."

"My wife believes she can persuade him to stop drinking," Othman said, "but I do not trust him. I have seen the way he looks at women. It is not natural."

"If she can inspire him to wisdom," Baybars said, "we must seek her help."

Layla informed Othman that she needed to get into the king's chambers. "I will not have you in his room," Othman objected. "No respectable woman enters a man's chambers unless they are her husband's." Layla replied, "I will take some friends."

Layla and three companions, retired luscious doves, waited for the king to fall asleep. They hid behind the largest curtain, joined by Harhash and Othman, who refused to have his wife in the room without him. When the muezzin called the faithful for the prayers of dawn, Layla shook King Issa Touran Shah out of his slumbering stupor. "Wake," she said sternly. "It is time for prayers."

The king rubbed his heavy eyes and sat up. "My prayers have been answered. Show me your breasts."

Layla slapped the king so hard his neck almost swiveled full-circle. Behind the curtain, Harhash whispered, "I do not think you have to worry about your honor."

"Why did you hit me?" cried the king. "You are my subject. Behave accordingly." Layla double-slapped him, palm out and back of the hand. "Stop that," he yelped. She raised her hand to strike him again, and he cowered. "I am the king."

"You are a dog." Layla threw the terrified king to the floor and pulled his hair. He tried to move away but recoiled when he saw the other doves emerge from behind the curtain. They slapped him in order, one by one.

"You are an embarrassment," the first admonished.

"You are lower than human waste," said the second.

"Your father is suffering in heaven."

"Who are you?" asked the king.

"Remove the drapes of drink from your eyes," yelled Layla. "Can you not see?"

"You are the leader of the kingdom of Islam." The first dove kicked him.

"We are here to protect our faith." The second dove threw him at the wall.

"No," whined the king. "This cannot be. God's women are gentle and kind."

"Be quiet." Slap.

"God is rarely kind," said the third dove.

"And neither are we," added Layla. "We are here to guard our own. Follow the word of God, Issa Touran Shah. Do not equivocate. Our eyes follow you. Falter and we will return. If you have even one sip of wine, you will think we were kind on this visit."

"Not one sip. Do not fail us."

"Fear us."

"Tremble." Each luscious dove smacked the sobered king before leaving the room.

In Paris, King Louis IX saw sparkles and glitter in his dreams and decided to invade the kingdom of the faithful, following in the footsteps of many a foreign king before him. "The Muslim king is an inept drunkard," King Louis said. "My dreams speak of untold treasures in the fool's coffers. I will be wealthy beyond my wildest imaginings, all for the glory of God. And God, ever so benevolent, does not require that I pay for His army out of my assets. Inform the faithful that donations are needed to pay for the soldiers of God, troops to force Arab tongues to speak His name. We ask for money to spread His word in the inhospitable desert. Praise be."

Louis raised a great army and promised them riches. They sailed across the Mediterranean and landed in Egypt, where they laid siege to Damietta. Greed coursed through King Louis's veins, and he split his army in two. He kept the siege going and sent half his army to al-Mansoura. Need I remind you that greed is always fatal?

The day after the doves' visitation, King Issa Touran Shah appeared in his diwan weary and clearheaded. Baybars and the kingdom's viziers were pleased. The king whispered in Baybars's ear, "I have followed your counsel and have eschewed vice." The king ruled justly for seven days. On the eighth, a messenger arrived with a missive from the mayor of Damietta: "O Prince of believers, morning prayers were interrupted on this day and the air darkened. A king of the foreigners has landed on our shore and crawled inland with his army. Help us and guide us, leader of the faith, and may God guide you in eternal victories."

"What am I to do?" asked the king.

"I will lead the first wave of your army into battle," said Baybars. "The infidels are attacking us. Declare jihad and call on all the armies of Islam. Follow me with the second wave, and together we will destroy the army of foreign locusts."

"Brilliant," exclaimed the king.

Baybars had the peasants of Egypt divert the waters of the Nile toward King Louis's army. The foreign horses drowned, and the exhausted soldiers struggled to extricate themselves from the great river. This time, al-Awwar wasted no time, heading straight for King Louis. The hilt of Baybars's sword struck the foreigner, and he fell unconscious. Baybars marched toward Damietta, where he met King Issa Touran Shah and the army of Islam, led by the slave general, Qutuz the indefatigable. The army of believers attacked, and the foreigners were killed left and right. Touran Shah watched the battle from a promontory. Prince Baybars rode up the hill to inform the king of his glorious victory. Our hero saw the king bringing a cup of wine to his lips.

Baybars chided, "Shame on you, my king. You had repented."

The king replied, "Forgive me. In the joy of victory, I forgot my oath."

He dumped the contents onto the rock before him and threw the goblet up into the sky. But fortune was not with him that day. The cup hit a solitary falcon in flight. Dazed, the bird fell and touched down on the back of the unsuspecting king's turbaned head. When the frightened king tried to shoo the falcon off, the bird dug its claws in. Fluttering wings obstructed the king's view. He tumbled forward, and flew off the hill to his inglorious death.

♣

My niece's belly left the elevator before her. She waddled toward the patient rooms, not looking in our direction. I waved my arm. She saw me and smiled. She had a much better poker face than I did, not registering any surprise at the sight of Aunt Wasila and Dida so early in the morning. "My feet are killing me," she said.

I told my aunt I'd be back and walked Salwa to the room. "You don't have to stay with them," she said. "Hovik is parking the car and will be right up. He actually likes them. You don't want to be there when Aunt Samia arrives and realizes she's not early enough to beat her rival."

"You want to spare me the stress but force it on your husband?"

"Hovik finds the family fascinating. He'd want to be there. He considers being around our family an anthropological study." She stopped and looked at me. "You enjoy it as well, don't you? You're like Hovik, an inveterate watcher." I shrugged, smiling. She resumed her waddle.

"I got you something," she said. "Hovik is bringing it up. Don't argue with me, and I don't want any shit from my mother, either. I'm warning you."

"Argue with you about what?"

Salwa went up to my father and touched his hand. "Grandfather," she said, "I saw Aunt Wasila outside, and she was asking about you. Isn't it funny that she's here? Can you hear me?"

Hovik and Salwa met in February 2000. She had a stomachache and was running a high fever. She went to the emergency room and was seen by the resident, Hovik. The diagnosis was simple, since a few cases of *Helicobacter pylori* had been reported recently, but it took long enough for the young doctor to fall in love while taking her case history. Cupid struck Hovik's heart with the gold-tipped arrow, whereas it was the one with a tip of dull, blunt lead that pierced my niece to the marrow. He was smitten at first sight, and she recoiled in disgust. She was, after all, her mother's daughter, weaned on the bitter stews of love's folly.

When asked why she was repelled at that first meeting, my niece said, "Well, look at me. What the hell did he see? I'm not that pretty under normal circumstances, and at the time I looked and felt horrible. I had been throwing up all morning and had severe diarrhea to boot. Fever was burning me up while the fool's heart caught fire. I thought the man was a pervert. I had no doubt. I felt nauseated and nauseating, and the doctor asked me for a date? A yucky, weirdo pervert, unprofessional, and too handsome for his own good."

Yes, he was handsome—terribly handsome. He was so handsome that women would develop imaginary aches and pains, palpitations, colic, and severe distress, yet he was captivated by the only one who had no interest in him whatsoever. He called her on her mobile phone; she yelled at him and hung up. He called again to apologize, she threatened to call the hospital and get him fired. He sent a note of flowery apology with a dozen roses. My niece told her mother, who drove to the hospital and announced in front of everyone that she would dissect his internal organs one by one if he didn't leave her daughter alone. Hovik came to his senses. He stopped.

But you don't trample upon fate. In May, my father had to have an updated pacemaker installed. As my sister and niece were returning to the hospital from lunch, Lina noticed a couple of young doctors in the lobby. One appeared stunned, rooted, mouth agape, eyes following Salwa's path. My niece walked on, oblivious, and Hovik remained oblivious to anything but my niece. Maybe it was the look of despair upon his face, maybe it was the look of adoration, but it certainly was a look my sister recognized well. She saw herself in the young doctor. He'd won a silent convert. My niece was smack back in his narrative.

"I can see your problem," the other young resident told Hovik. And that young resident, trying to impress, told the doctor in the cardiac unit that Hovik was infatuated with a relative of one of his patients. He had no idea that Tin Can was family. Tin Can told my father, who of course demanded a confrontation with the ill-bred lackey. Tin Can informed him that the lackey had done nothing wrong and that he would talk to the young man himself.

Hovik was embarrassed when Tin Can confronted him. He waited until my father was alone and paid him a visit in his hospital room, that fateful day a few years ago. Hovik introduced himself, asked about my father's health, and finally begged my father's forgiveness. "I've made a grave mistake," Hovik said. He made my father promise to listen to his whole story. He would appear the cad, he was guilty, but if my father listened to his entire tale, he might understand.

Hovik explained how he met my niece. He admitted how badly he had behaved. He was possessed by the demon of love. How else could he explain it? He could have destroyed his career. How could he have called her when she specifically warned him not to? But he had stopped. He was in control. It was the shock of seeing her once more that had confounded him. He would disturb her no more. He was not wanted.

"You mean to take my granddaughter away from me?" my father asked.

"Meant," Hovik replied. "That is no longer the case, I assure you."

"Fool." And my father told Hovik how he had won my mother, how much he loved her, how he had wooed her, how much he missed her. "Fool," he repeated. "You tried to win Salwa with clichés? Who sends roses anymore? My granddaughter hates roses. It's spring. Send her crocuses, hyacinths, and narcissi. Her favorite color is yellow. Daffodils. You'll have to woo her with her poetry—not yours. Polish up on your R's, Rimbaud and Rilke—they're her favorites. She hates movies. Don't even try. And you're too pretty. Get a bad haircut. Wear clothes that don't match. And don't, and I mean don't ever, suggest a walk on the beach or a candlelit dinner. She would as soon slit your throat. Listen to her. Always listen to her."

❧

The mourning army returned to Cairo with little fanfare. Forty days after the burial of the king, the council met to elect the new prince of the faithful. The Kurds still argued for the king's lineage. The Turkomans nominated a vizier by the name of Aybak. They fought the entire day and drew their weapons three times before Shajarat al-Durr, King Saleh's widow, sent her servant to the diwan once more to announce that she was fit to rule. The Kurds and Turkomans decided she would be an acceptable compromise.

The coronation of Shajarat al-Durr, an exquisite affair, lasted only a little less time than her reign. Once the news of her ascent to the throne reached the land of Hijaz, the sharif of Mecca wrote to the council berating them for not following the traditions of the faith. He warned that if the queen's reign continued, the tribes of Hijaz would no longer heed the calls of Cairo. The queen read the letter and announced, "I will step down, for the good of the kingdom."

The diwan reconvened. Every side argued. Antipodal positions were assumed. The council was exhausted. Finally, the vizier Aybak was elected in a straw vote. To ensure that his reign would last longer than Shajarat al-Durr's, he married her.

Aybak's plan, joining the lines of two claimants to the throne, worked, but only briefly. All supported his rule and heeded his commands. Not everything, however, was aligned with Aybak's ambition. Fate had no use for him, could not bear him, and dismissed him rather cruelly, by gifting him with the source of every man's fall from grace: the great desire.

He saw her while promenading with his courtiers. She was a young Bedouin girl of a beauty that pierced his heart. He called to her, "O most glorious, whose daughter are you?"

The king sought out her father, received his permission, returned to the diwan, and called on his engineers to build a magnificent palace for his new betrothed. The king spent one month in bed with his beloved. He did not show up at the diwan, and he never once visited Shajarat al-Durr or his first wife, Umm Ahmad. Prince Baybars paid the king a visit and said, "You have been neglecting your duties. You must return to the diwan and handle the affairs of state."

The king replied, "Queen Shajarat al-Durr is furious with me, and unless someone calms her down, I will not venture out of these chambers to be nagged and berated by that harpy."

Baybars went to the queen and begged her to forgive her king. He spoke honeyed words to her, he lauded her generosity, he praised, until she finally relented. "Tell him to pay me a visit," the queen said. Baybars sent a message to the king that the great queen had forgiven him.

The following morning, the king made his appearance at the diwan, and that evening, he visited Shajarat al-Durr. She greeted him warmly and fawned over him, and the happy king said, "Let us relive the good times. Bathe me." Shajarat al-Durr led her husband to the bath. She undressed him and began to undress herself.

"Does your Bedouin girl have hair more luxurious than mine?" The queen smiled flirtatiously. "Skin more white? Lips more full?"

"My wife, you are beautiful, tribes from the deserts to the seas sing of your loveliness, but you are old. The girl is fourteen. Do you expect to compete with that?"

Shajarat al-Durr, who once ruled the world, knelt down and washed her husband's hair. She soaped it thoroughly, until lather built. She took out a dagger and slit the king's throat from carotid to carotid. She watched disloyal blood flow upon the bath's marble before she plunged the dagger into her own heart.

And the Kurds said, "The kingdom should return to the line of true kings. King Issa Touran Shah had a boy. He is seven and goes by the name of Ala'eddine. He shall be king."

The boy was made king and one of his Kurdish cousins was elected regent. Fate had no use for this king, either, and sent him the Mongols.

⁂

Hovik's face was that of a man who hadn't had a good night's sleep in quite a while. His mustache needed a trim. His distress was comforting. Apparently, he genuinely loved my father; then again, perhaps his concern was for his pregnant wife and coming son. He tiptoed into the room, carrying Salwa's handbag, her coat, and a gray chamois sack that might seem amorphous to an untrained eye. Mine recognized the danger. Nothing was in that bag if not a small oud.

I felt the veins in the back of my hand pulse.

My sister recognized the bag and raised questioning eyebrows.

"I don't want it," my niece said softly. "I couldn't play it. I tried so many times."

"But it's a memento," my sister replied.

"It's a constant reminder of how talentless I am."

My sister asked Hovik to stay in the room and led her daughter and me to the balcony. She lit a cigarette, expelled the smoke toward the sky. My niece took the cigarette from her mother's lips and threw it over the balcony. "I'll get you a patch," Salwa said.

"This isn't the right time," my sister said.

"This is nothing if not the right time."

"Listen. Are you sure you want to give Osama the oud? It's not as if he's going to pick it up and start playing after all this time. I'm not sure the instrument is playable. We all have a family heirloom, and this one is yours. She wanted you to have it."

"Who wanted her to have it?" I asked.

"Our grandmother," Lina replied. "I thought you knew that. She gave it to me on her deathbed to give to my daughter. How old was I then, seven—eight? I couldn't even conceive of the idea that I'd have a daughter. This is our great-grandmother's oud."

"My god," I gasped. "I didn't know this thing existed. Does it still play?"

"Check it out," Salwa said. "I had it restrung. It plays adequately, considering that no one has played it in over a hundred and twenty years."

"A hundred and fourteen," my sister and I said in unison.

I delicately removed the oud from the chamois bag. The workmanship was beyond anything I had seen in years and years—the inlaid ivory carved in miniature arabesque detail, wood of invaluable cedar, splendid tear-shaped mother-of-pearl (genuine, not sister-of-polystyrene) lining the neck. And my great-grandmother gave up this exquisiteness for the love of her husband. "A sultan's gift," I said.

"Literally," my sister said. "From a sultan to us."

"I can't take it," I told my niece. "You could send your son through college with it."

"I'd trade it for a foot massage right now." She tried to lift her foot off the floor as Exhibit A, but could barely get it high enough to slip a sheet of paper underneath. "Look, if I ever need it, I'll take it back. I was just hoping you'd play for him."

"I can't play. I haven't played in so long." I plucked a string, and then another. The oud's sound was disappointingly bad. "You don't just pick up an instrument after all these years and start strumming. This isn't a fairy tale."

"He always talked about how well you played," Salwa said. She stared at the balcony's glass door, at my father's bed behind it.

"He didn't like my playing," I objected. "He never did."

"You're crazy," my sister snapped. "Did you just say that?"

"It would take me months to be able to play a simple maqâm. Should I force him to go through the torture of listening to me practicing scales again?"

The oud was out of tune. I tightened the top string, and my fingers hurt. The sound was actually atrocious, the wood having aged beyond repair. I pressed my ring finger for an easy note, and the skin at the tip felt like it was about to break. Would my fingers ever relearn what they had forgotten? Would my hands remember what had been consciously erased? My fingers asked questions I had no answer for. They ached. My whole body ached; my eyes felt as if they were about to shoot out of my head. I slid along the railing and sat on the floor and cried. My sister hesitated, but then slid next to me and burst into tears. Together, side by side, shoulder to shoulder, we bawled. If only the gorgeous oud didn't sound like a ukulele.

✣

A letter arrived from the mayor of Aleppo, announcing that an army had appeared on the horizon, Mongols, as numerous as locusts, as destructive as termites, as methodical as ants, as cruel as African wasps. A few days later came a letter from Damascus saying that the locust army had conquered Aleppo, Hamah, and Homs and was heading toward Damascus. From the refugees that poured into Egypt the council discovered that the land of Islam was being completely overrun by the foreign hordes. The Mongols reached Gaza.

"They have conquered the cities of my people," said a Persian. "Shiraz fell, as well as Isfahan."

"The barbarians burned Baghdad to the ground," cried an Abassid. "The armies either surrendered or dispersed."

"King Hethum of Armenia helped the Mongol Hulagu," said a Syrian. "The Armenian set the great mosque of Aleppo afire himself, and the Mongols encouraged him."

"Ah, a pox upon Armenia," said a Turk.

The counsel deliberated for hours. The only army left in the lands was the army of Egypt. The Franks had either sided with the Mongols or chosen to remain neutral. From Baku to Edessa, from Basra to Damascus, the Mongols ruled.

"I will never surrender," Layla told Othman. "I am Egypt."

"We will not surrender," announced the African and Uzbek warriors. "We are Egypt."

"Why are they deliberating?" asked Aydmur the slave warrior. "Our course is clear," said the twenty-five Circassians, the twenty-five Georgians, and the twenty-five Azeris.

"I will choose death before surrendering to the fire-worshippers," Baybars told the diwan. "You have heard the reports of what has happened to our lands. Our enemies kill those who fight and those who surrender indiscriminately. You cannot willingly give Egypt up to this. I will not allow it, and I am Egypt."

The king's regent said, "We cannot fight them. Even God cannot count their numbers."

"If you cannot trust God to count, you are not fit to rule," Qutuz the indefatigable spat out. "I will fight even if I am the only one on the battlefield. Shame on any man who chooses life without God over death with Him."

"You will not fight alone," Prince Baybars said. "I will follow you."

"We will follow you," cried the council.

"I will not serve a baby king," said the slave warrior Qutuz. "Dethrone him."

The diwan stripped the boy of his title and elected the great General Qutuz the indefatigable as sultan of Islam, prince of the faithful, the first Mamluke.

Behold. The reign of the magnificent slave kings has begun. Rejoice.

The great jihad was called. The high sheikh of Azhar University wrote a fatwa. Anyone who could wield a weapon and did not fight the enemy was an infidel whose burial would not be in a Muslim cemetery. Anyone who had money and did not spend it to ensure the victory of the army of God was an unbeliever.

And the grand army coalesced, the Berbers from the Sahara, the Africans from Sudan, the tribes from Hijaz, and the Arabs from Tunis. The infidel Mongols were celebrating in Gaza, drinking, whoring, and carousing. Having never lost a battle, they were not expecting anyone to be foolish enough to attack. And attack them the army of innocents did. The Mongols had their first taste of fear. The slave army hit with ferocious force, shattering the Mongol illusion of a conquered world at their feet. The barbarians retreated, and the slave army followed, killing more and more of the straggling invaders. The Mongols stood their ground in the plains of Bissan; they dug in and waited for the attack, but they were in for another surprise. From Anatolia to Persia, from the Caucasus to Andalusia, soldiers and armies arrived heeding the fatwa. The archers of Damascus, the horsemen of Kandahar, the pikers of Baghdad, and the swordsmen of Shiraz joined the slave army. The war of all wars erupted. Dust storms swirled. Swords clashed with shields, spears pierced armor, and many a hero fell. The Mongols were hit from all sides, but amid all the chaos, Hulagu Khan and his generals noticed that certain of the battalions of Islam never broke rank, never faltered. The Mongols, who had nurtured bedlam and anarchy in war, were encountering their opposite, an army of impeccably trained slaves. Order vanquished disorder. The barbarians had sown fear wherever they trod, and now fearless slaves trod on them. The invaders ran away in terror and were cut down, their dead and dying discarded on the battlefield as feast for the hyenas of the plains.

The slave army suffered great losses, and none as great as the loss of the king. An errant Mongol arrow killed Qutuz the indefatigable. Prince Baybars took command of the slave army and routed the Mongols at Ain Jalut (the Spring of Goliath). He killed scores of the invaders, and their blood dried on his hands and fingers, causing them to stiffen and ache with the pain of triumph. Othman, ever his servant, heated a bowl of water for the hero, who soaked his hands and released the blood and pain.

Prince Baybars led the victorious army back to Cairo. The entire population of the city poured out of the gates to greet the hero before he entered. Feasts were served in every hall, every house, every corner. The celebration lasted for three sleepless days.

At the diwan, everyone nominated the only truly worthy king. He was crowned al-Zaher Baybars. Finally, fate aligned with history, fact shook hands with storytelling. The great one had reached his destiny. The hero of a thousand tales, the shining example to all the faithful, the lord of lords, had become sultan at long last.

You have before you the greatest hero the world will ever know. This is the famous tale of King al-Zaher Baybars. Now our story begins.

Listen.

BOOK FOUR

Man is eminently a storyteller. His search for a purpose, a cause, an ideal, a mission and the like is largely a search for a plot and a pattern in the development of his life story— a story that is basically without meaning or pattern.

Eric Hoffer, *The Passionate State of Mind*

Nay, say they, these are but muddled dreams;
Nay, he hath but invented it;
Nay, he is but a poet.

Koran

Literature is the most agreeable way of ignoring life.

Fernando Pessoa, *The Book of Disquiet*

— *Sixteen* —

The best stories always begin with the appearance of a woman. The story of the family corporation does, and the woman in question is, of course, my mother. What did my father tell Hovik that day? How *did* he win my mother?

He saw her for the first time while she was walking with a friend on Bliss Street. He was twenty, working as a clerk in an import-export company on Bliss, and my mother was eighteen, attending the American University. He'd been hearing about the two girls, the blonde and the brunette, from his co-workers, who wouldn't stop blathering about the pair of pretty university girls. The brunette was lovely, but the blonde was so lusciously sexy. My father had to endure his co-workers' descriptions, in full, striking detail and with gestures, of what they'd like to do to the blonde. He heard how the rascally wind had blown her blouse open to reveal a spectacular cleavage. The brunette was pretty, really pretty, but the blonde showed mind-bending curves.

My father saw my mother, the brunette, and was smitten.

But wait. This is not that kind of fairy tale. He was smitten. Of that, there could be no doubt, but was it love at first sight? Was it love at all? Cynics dismiss love at first sight, saying that one person cannot possibly know another in an instant.

My father knew a number of things when he saw my mother. He knew she was a classic Lebanese beauty. That was obvious. He knew she was from an upper-class family—the way she dressed and carried herself was a giveaway. He knew that if he married her he would gain access to a world he could only dream about. He also knew that she would never give him a second look, not unless he became someone else, someone better, someone important.

My father also understood that my mother was smarter than all his co-workers combined. He instinctively knew that she wasn't a woman who relied on accident or luck. Her choice of companion was well thought out. She and her blonde friend would certainly attract attention, and a lot of it. One of my father's co-workers actually felt sorry for my mother because her beauty couldn't match the blonde's. He was terribly stupid.

The blonde's beauty made you want to bed her. My mother's beauty made you want to introduce her to your mother. That was precisely the contrast that my mother intended. The blonde distracted the riffraff and took them out of my mother's way.

Years later, in 1992, one of the major newspapers ran various historical pictures of Beirut in hopes of inspiring readers to remember how good things were before the war. One picture was of the blonde and the brunette, wide smiles on their young faces, eyes brimming with dreams and curiosity, buns high atop their heads, stepping in unison. The caption said: "Madame Layla al-Kharrat (nee Khoury) in 1950 with unidentified woman."

Upon seeing my mother that first time, my father became intoxicated.

The poet Saadi, my mother's favorite, once told a charming personal tale of love and intoxication.

When Saadi was young, he cast his eyes on a beautiful girl who appeared briefly on a balcony as he was walking down her street. The day was torrid, dried the mouth, boiled the marrow in the bone. Unable to withstand the sun's harsh rays, Saadi took shelter in the shade of a wall. Suddenly, from the portico of her house, the girl appeared. No tongue could describe her loveliness: an impossibility, like the dawn rising in the obscurity of deep night. In her hand she held a cup of snow water sprinkled with sugar and mixed with the juice of a grape. Saadi caught the scent of roses but was unsure whether she had infused the drink with the blossoms of the flower or those of her cheeks. He received the cup from her comely hand, drank from it, and was restored to healthy life. Yet the thirst of the poet's soul was not such that it could be allayed with a cup of water—the streams of whole rivers would not satisfy it.

> *He who is intoxicated with wine*
> *Will be sober again in the course of the night;*

But he who is intoxicated by the cupbearer
Will not recover his senses till the Day of Judgment.

Alas for poor Saadi, the winsome cupbearer was not destined to be his wife. Fate would never permit happiness to a man of such talent— a content poet is a mediocre one, a happy poet insufferable. Saadi married a Xanthippe, one who would make the original blush in shame for falling so short in shrewishness. And Saadi was forced to lay down the most exquisite poems bemoaning his matrimonial misfortunes and compose even greater lines insulting his wife.

✤

The humble King al-Zaher Baybars entered his first diwan to the cheers of the adoring nobles and wise men of the land. He listened attentively to news of his kingdom and began to bestow titles and responsibilities upon his people. Aydmur became a prince and the leader of the kingdom's army; Sergeant Lou'ai, the emir of the lands of the Levant. Baybars called on the Turks, the Kurds, the Turkomans, the Circassians, the Arabs, the Persians, and all the other nationalities to present heroes who were worthy of leading them, and he made these men the emirs of their tribes. The Uzbeks and the African warriors became his official companions and bodyguards. And all rejoiced—all except for Othman, who sat glum and morose. Baybars asked his friend why he was not in a happy mood, and Othman replied, "You gave all these men new robes and bestowed titles upon friends and strangers, yet you forgot your own brother."

A shamefaced Baybars declared before the world that Othman was now an emir, and a smile crept over the new emir's face. Othman returned home to Layla, who greeted him with "Welcome, my emir. I am glad it is only a minor title, because I would not want to deal with your big head had he given you a title of note."

Othman said, "Emir is a title of great worth."

"Of course it is, dear. How many men were made emirs today? And how many emirs were there before today? These are the lands of Islam. Kings, sultans, and caliphs are as common as camels. Emirs? There are as many emirs as there are males in these parts."

The following day, Othman was even more glum and morose in the diwan, and King Baybars asked, "Why are you unhappy, my brother?"

"Because I am a trite emir."

. . .

And what of Ma'rouf? Have you forgotten him? Ma'arouf, who had been searching for weeks and months and years for his son all over the Mediterranean?

The nun—the nun raised the infant Taboush for two years in the palace of Thessaly. While carrying a large gift for Taboush's second birthday, she slipped in descending the stairs, and her soul ascended to the Garden. "Oh well," said King Kinyar. "I must assign someone to raise the boy now that the nun has betrayed us." He picked one of his men at random. "You will be the boy's guardian. Raise him and care for him. Teach him to be a man. If you fail, you and your descendants will be tortured to death." The guardian raised Taboush and cared for him. Every day he took the boy for walks outside the palace, to the lovely hills and meadows of Thessaly.

One day, Ma'rouf came across Taboush along the road, and the father's heart fluttered and raced. Ma'rouf greeted Taboush's guardian and asked if the boy was his son, and the guardian informed him that the boy was the king's son. And Ma'rouf looked into the boy's eyes and saw his father's eyes and his grandfather's eyes, and he said to himself, "This is my son. I know him as I know myself." Ma'rouf began to show up on the same road every day so he could play with Taboush. He brought him gifts and sweets, and Taboush began to love him. Ma'rouf had a plan to take the boy with him off the island, back to Maria, and was waiting for the right opportunity. Ma'rouf would whisper into his boy's ears, "You are honor descended from honor. You are my son and the light of my eyes."

The guardian grew suspicious and informed the king about the man who was befriending his son. The king ordered the guardian not to take the boy on his walk the following day and instead sent a full squadron of a hundred men. The soldiers attacked Ma'rouf, beat him, and brought him to the king, who shackled Ma'rouf and jailed him in an isolated cell of iron. "You thought you could take my son away from me," the king said, "but I will take your liberty and pride. You will live here, beneath our royal feet, until you rot and decay. Meditate upon your folly, for you now have the time." And when he was left alone, Ma'rouf wondered what was to become of him, the chief of forts and battlements, without son, without wife, without honor.

To say that there was a class difference between my mother's family and my father's would be like saying that a Rolls-Royce is a slightly better car than a Lada. Even my grandmother's family, the Arisseddines, sheikhs though they might be, were no match for the Khourys. Luckily for my father, she was from a small branch of the family that was not closely related to the first president of the republic. Still, a sensible man wouldn't have undertaken to woo a woman who had the same last name as the man who was running the entire country.

Aunt Samia considered my mother's family cursed. "It's not your mother's fault," she'd say. "She never had a chance to understand family. The curse began long before your poor mother was born." My mother's father was an only child—probably the biggest curse, according to my aunt. He was both orphaned and widowed. My maternal grandmother died when my mother was only three, and my grandfather remarried a Belgian. "Could you have worse luck?"

My mother had two half-siblings. "But they don't really count, do they?" my aunt would ask. "They visit the ruins of the Roman temples during a trip to Lebanon, and that makes them Lebanese? That's not family."

My grandfather was intelligent, educated, and successful, but if you pointed out to my aunt that he couldn't have been cursed, what with having all those qualities and being an ambassador to boot, she replied, "True, but we're talking an ambassador to Belgium."

My mother grew up in Belgium, where her father emigrated. When she was fourteen, a cousin suggested that my mother should return with her to Beirut. My grandfather and his Belgian family stayed in Brussels, and my mother went with the cousin—my grandfather in essence admitting that his daughter would have a better chance of finding a suitable husband in Lebanon. My mother's separation from her immediate family was fortunate. My father would have to persuade her to marry him—a ridiculous task to be sure, but not as impossible as persuading the rest of her family as well.

However, my grandfather the hakawati always said that my father and mother were fated to be married, and, of course, there was a story, one concerning an improbable nocturnal meeting between an Arisseddine and a Khoury in late June 1838 during the Battle of Wadi Baka.

In 1831, Ibrahim Pasha, the ruler of Egypt, temporarily liberated Greater Syria, including Lebanon, from the yoke of the Ottomans. At first the populace was happy to be rid of the corrupt and unjust

Ottomans. But Ibrahim Pasha proved no better, and in 1838 the Druze revolted. At Hawran, site of the first battle, fewer than fifteen hundred Druze fighters defeated some fifteen thousand Egyptians. The Egyptians kept replenishing their forces, however, and the Druze couldn't. What was left of the rebels retreated down to Wadi al-Taym, until only four hundred bunkered in Wadi Baka. Ibrahim Pasha himself led his army of thousands against those four hundred.

With the help of Emir Bashir of Lebanon, Ibrahim Pasha had forced Maronite fighters to help him against the Druze. Most refused the call and hid in the mountains. Those unable to disappear joined the battle but never took their swords out of their scabbards. One was a Khoury, my mother's great-great-grandfather.

When the Druze rebels realized they could hold out no longer, they decided to wait for nightfall and attack. They would kill as many as they could before dying, and perhaps a few of them would be able to escape. One was an Arisseddine, my father's great-great-grandfather.

The Druze attacked at night. Almost all of them were killed. Khoury saw a couple of riderless stallions trotting away from the battle and caught up to them and took their reins. Beneath the belly of one of the horses, a badly injured Arisseddine was holding on for dear life. Khoury unsheathed his sword for the first time, handed it to the rebel, and sent him on his way.

Their descendants were married one hundred and eighteen years later.

❧

One day, a man walked into the diwan saying, "I have been victimized, O Prince of believers. I have been violated. Redeem my honor, my lord, I beg of you." Baybars asked the man to tell him the story. "I am a merchant from Syria, and every year I travel to Egypt to trade. Usually, I avoid al-Areesh, because King Franjeel demands high toll taxes, as if the roads belonged to him and his foreign friends. This year, I was carrying perishables and had to travel the shortest route. I set money aside for the unfair toll, but when my caravan passed by al-Areesh, the king's army confiscated my entire merchandise, including my camels, my horses, and my voluptuous Kazak slave, whom I had just bought only two days earlier. It is not fair."

The story angered Baybars, who said, "I am not happy with these alien kings who do not respect treaties that they themselves forced upon us. Al-Areesh is Egypt. It is time we reclaimed our city. Prepare the armies."

"No, no, no, no," cried Emir Othman, and Layla said, "Of course I am coming."

In the Crusader fort of al-Areesh, King Franjeel berated Arbusto. "Were it not for your holy robes, I would cut off your head right now. This is your fault. You tempted me with riches, and now Baybars the barbarian is coming for me."

The unperturbed Arbusto replied, "Do not fret. You know this fort is impenetrable. Shut the gates and I will take care of the rest. I will call on the other coastal kings for help. I will speak first to the king of Askalan. Hold the fort and the slave army will be defeated."

"I will come with you," announced the cowardly king. "I will leave the commander of the fort in charge. Shut the gates."

"There," said Aydmur, pointing to the offending edifice a short distance away. "The fort of al-Areesh is secure and sturdy. Unless we get into the fort, we will lose many men. So far, no general has discovered a way of breaking into the fort of al-Areesh."

"I am tired of this endless equestrian journey," announced Layla. "Let us rest. When night falls, I will open the gates." She dismounted from her mare and rubbed her sore behind. "I will give you a signal with my torch when it is accomplished. I have been talking to my people on the inside. It will not be difficult."

"People on the inside?" Othman glared at his wife. "You will not be going. I will not allow it. No wife of mine opens gates. I will open them."

That evening, with the help of his wife, Othman dressed in a priest's robe, combed his hair in Arbusto's manner, held a jingling censer in his hand, and walked to the gates. The guards, believing he was Arbusto, rushed to let him in. They bowed before him. Othman extended his hand and waited until each man had kissed it. "I am grateful for such a courteous reception," he said. "In return, I offer my blessings." He lit the incense—myrrh mixed with opium—and said, "Inhale my blessings, deeper and deeper." Soon the guards were traveling on a different plane. Othman opened the gate and signaled the slave army. The fort of al-Areesh was vanquished before its defenders realized they were being attacked.

"Well done," Layla told Othman, and Harhash said, "You inspire him to new heights."

"The coward Franjeel is not here," huffed Baybars, "and neither is Arbusto."

"They left for Askalan," Layla said. "They meant to raise an army to assail us while we laid siege to al-Areesh."

"Their plan was foiled," said Aydmur, "and the next will fail."

"While you raze this fort," said Layla, "I will ride ahead and uncover their next plan."

"No, no, no, no, no." Othman stomped his foot.

⁂

My mother's first admirer was her second cousin Karim—his father and her deceased mother were first cousins. She was fifteen and enrolled at a Carmelite boarding school when he decided that she would make him a suitable wife. Karim had everything going for him, or at least he seemed to think so. He was twenty-three, the eldest son of a prosperous man, and had surprised everyone, himself most of all, by passing the baccalaureate. And since he graduated high school, his father began to groom him for a career in Lebanese politics.

He met my mother at a family gathering. My mother swore she didn't say a word to him and he never noticed. She was busy eating while he regaled her with his stories and future plans. Since she proved to be a first-rate listener, Karim began to woo her in earnest by sending a single red rose and a box of Harlequin chocolates stuffed with almonds to her school every Wednesday. She didn't care for him one way or the other, but her girlfriends loved the chocolates.

He wrote to her father in Brussels, who in turn wrote to my mother wondering what was going on. My mother put his mind at ease by saying she had no intention of marrying before getting a university degree. The young man courted my mother for four and a half months, during which she barely had to utter a single syllable. He visited her once and brought her a potted succulent, an asclepiad that had impressed him mightily. It was after his remarkable second visit that he received a call from Brussels telling him that my mother never wanted to see his face again, under any circumstances. It wasn't the asclepiad.

He had arrived for the second visit, their third meeting, in his best gabardine suit, his mustache soldered with wax, his face flushed with pride. He showed my mother off to the woman accompanying him, a lady in her thirties, whom he introduced as his father's first cousin's young wife, a new aunt. "Isn't she pretty?" he said of my mother. "And she's smart, too. She'll finish school." My mother was about to tell him that she didn't wish to be anyone's exhibit, to be shown off like some antique carpet or fine embroidery, when she suddenly realized that she was the one he was trying to impress. The gloating smile, the studied placement of the hand around his *aunt's* waist, and the forced coziness were meant to convey to the young beloved that her suitor was a man of the world, a man who had mistresses, a man who was desired. He wasn't just anybody. He wanted to impart the idea that she, too, could aspire to be special because someone special wanted her.

My mother called her father. Karim stopped sending her Harlequin chocolates stuffed with almonds. Her girlfriends were miffed, and one actually wondered aloud why my mother couldn't have waited till the end of term to break her suitor's heart.

⁂

"I would have preferred to stay and watch the fort being pulverized," Harhash said. "It is not as if one can witness total destruction every day."

"Be quiet," Othman said. "A friend would not complain. A good friend would support a man whose wife keeps shaming him in public. A good man would not concern himself with a fort when it is his friend's honor that is being pulverized."

"Will one of you wake me when this tired diatribe is over?" Layla said. "My husband is beginning to sound like a muezzin, repeating the same words five times a day. Shame, if you ask me. Whereas the blind muezzins are uniformly dull, my husband was once interesting, but he has been reduced to a single-whine conversationalist."

After twilight, Layla knocked on the gate of Askalan. "Who's there?" asked a voice.

"A luscious dove," answered Layla.

The gatekeeper slid open the peek hole, and his mouselike face appeared in the aperture. "The luscious doves have repented and retired. Everyone knows that."

"Do I look retired to your ugly eyes?"

"I have never seen a luscious dove before. Why should I believe you? Why would a luscious dove come to this city? I think—"

Quicker than the strike of an asp, Layla's hand slipped through the viewer. Her fingers poked the gatekeeper's eyes, squeezed his nose, and jerked his face forward, slamming it into the gate. She held on to the gatekeeper's nose, and he screeched, "Ouch, ouch, ouch, ouch. I believe you. I will open the face—I mean the gate. I will open the gate. I swear."

The three travelers entered the city. Layla spoke to the gatekeeper. "These two men are my personal physicians. Inform the working women of the city that I have arrived, and that I expect them to pay their respects in the morning." The gatekeeper's eyes were filled with lust and desire. She used only her third-best smile on him. "We need a place to sleep. Lead the way, and make sure my mare is fed and groomed tonight."

Baybars and his slave army raised the kingdom's flags outside Askalan. One of the African warriors asked permission to assume the duties of crier. "Hear me, foreigners," the African bellowed. "The king of kings has arrived, and he demands your capitulation. Inform Brigitte, the usurper king of this city, that he is to abdicate. Surrender all and we will allow you to return to your countries. Resist and we will drop these walls upon your heads. Give up your arms or this fort will become a mausoleum interring your bodies for all time."

"Well said," Baybars cheered, and Aydmur added, "I am in awe."

"I am dying, Egypt, dying of boredom," cried Layla from the city's parapet. "Will you not come in and conquer already?" As the gigantic metal gate slowly lifted, Othman appeared at the entrance, gesturing for the mighty army to invade. Baybars's army entered Askalan, whose soldiers were surprised to find themselves fighting within the city walls. Swords hit their marks, and maces descended upon the heads of infidels, and Askalan fell quickly.

Baybars asked Othman where Arbusto and the kings were, and Othman said, "We are late. Arbusto decided to travel to King Diafil of Jaffa and ask for his assistance. King Franjeel of al-Areesh told King Brigitte about the size of our army, and both decided to join Arbusto in Jaffa."

The victorious King Baybars said, "After razing this fort, we will head to Jaffa, the den of sin." And Othman asked his wife, "Does that mean we ride ahead?"

The beautiful city of Jaffa had three glorious lighthouses, three anxious kings—Franjeel, Brigitte, and Diafil—three lust-stricken guards at the eastern gate swearing unwavering fealty to the luscious dove, but no Arbusto, who had left by sea, allegedly to fetch reinforcements from Europe. As the three kings prepared for a siege of their city, Layla prepared the three porters at the gate. "No, no, no," she said. "Touch without permission and you lose the offending hand. I will come back one evening soon, and when I do, you will open the gate when I tell you. You will do whatever it is I tell you. Is that understood?"

King Baybars destroyed Askalan, and to this day, the city by the sea remains in ruins. He crushed the walls and led his army to Jaffa, where he received a missive from Othman. "The lettering is delicate," said the king, "and the parchment is sweetly perfumed. He says the three kings are inside the city and advises us to approach the gate at nightfall and knock."

"What kind of silly names are those?" asked Lou'ai. "Franjeel, Brigitte, and Diafil?"

When the sun had set in the Mediterranean, the king of Islam stood outside Jaffa's gate with his hushed army, and knocked, and the gate opened to let him in. In the morning, Diafil's soldiers woke to find Jaffa overwhelmed, swords upon their necks, and the city restored to its rightful ruler, King Baybars, who liberated the lands from foreigners.

Two days after my father noticed my mother and decided she was the woman he wanted to marry, she fell in love. Yes, it was love at first sight. His name was Khoury as well, Nicholas Khoury, though he wasn't from the same family, not even Maronite, but Greek Orthodox. My mother was pleased that she wouldn't have to change her name. They saw each other at a political youth meeting at the university, she a freshman, he a medical student. He dominated the gathering. He wanted to change the world. He wanted the new republic to be a beacon of liberty and justice to the rest of the Arabs. He wanted to spread literacy throughout Lebanon and the Middle East. He considered improving the plight of women the most important undertaking for a

Lebanese man, and in keeping with that credo, he would specialize as a gynecologist.

My mother was impressed with his dedication, his earnest moral stance, and his height. In her, he saw an audience, a fan, and a pretty one at that. He was pleased to be the first man, other than her father, whom she looked up to. He believed she would be his perfect partner; she would help him soar. They began dating in earnest three weeks after they met. Within four months, he had formally proposed and she'd accepted. He wrote to her father for his blessing and introduced her to his family, and in the summer they flew to Europe together and visited her family in Brussels. They agreed on a long engagement, three years at least, until both graduated.

He couldn't suffer being away from her, and involved her in all his social and civic activities. She attended political lectures, activist meetings, and long-winded café discussions. She volunteered once for a Palestinian relief organization but gave it up after about ten minutes and made him promise to stop working with organizations that dealt with suffering hands-on.

My poor father was crushed. Even though he had never spoken to my mother and she had yet to notice him, he firmly believed that she was to be his wife. He had already claimed her. But here was this other man who never left her side, who breathed her air, invaded her intimate space, and clamored for her attention. Although my father wouldn't see her alone for a few years, he didn't surrender. He formulated bigger plans.

Laylat al-Qadr, the Night of Fate, is better than a thousand months. It is said that the Holy Koran was sent down on the Night of Fate and was revealed to the Prophet Muhammad over a period of twenty-three years. During the Night of Fate, God listens to sincere supplicants, grants prayers, and forgives sins. The Night falls during Ramadan, the holiest of months, but God has not revealed its exact date, because He wants believers to worship Him during the entire month. Some say it falls on the night when the moon's horns refill the circle, yet it is also said that the Prophet hinted that believers should seek it on the odd nights of the last ten days of Ramadan.

On an evening in 1953, Jalal Arisseddine had a dinner party—casual, forty guests or so. A few politicians were invited, some writers, friends. Nicholas Khoury had been begging a common acquaintance to introduce him to my well-known great-uncle and had finagled an invitation. And of course my great-uncle invited his brother Ma'an and his two nephews. Few of the guests were Muslim, and those that were wouldn't have been considered observant. It was an evening in Ramadan, and none of the guests had been fasting or celebrating or praying. Still, considering the events that sprouted, we can safely assume it was an odd night.

It was undoubtedly the Night of Fate, because God heard my father's pleas.

That evening, my mother met the man who would sweep her off her feet, dazzle her, bewitch and charm her. She met the man who would love her and adore her, who would become her steadfast partner. A man whose wit and light would dim her fiancé's star, stub and extinguish it by the time dessert was served. Love at first barb. That night, my mother met Uncle Jihad.

A Swiss man with a ponytail who claimed to be Jean-Paul Sartre's good friend offended almost everyone at the dinner party. The ponytail alone was shocking enough, but because of Sartre-said-this, Sartre-would-have-done-that, the party broke up into smaller groups to avoid him. Uncle Jihad inched slowly from group to group until he sat next to the bewitching girl who had been pretending not to notice his advance. Looking at the Swiss, whose audience had been systematically reduced to her earnest fiancé, she leaned toward my uncle and whispered, "I wonder why that braggart has to wear his hair like that."

"So they can pull his head out of Sartre's ass," Uncle Jihad said.

My mother had found her soulmate.

He had no idea she was my father's infatuation, and, surprisingly, they hadn't met before, although they attended the same university, were in the same department, and were the same age. They had similar interests but took classes at different times. Uncle Jihad didn't mix in her social circle. He wouldn't have had the time in any case, since he still managed both his and Ali's pigeon coops. My mother and uncle talked and talked, and grew so engrossed that my father's heart filled with hope and her fiancé's filled with panic. Nick sidled to my mother, put his arm around her. My mother closed her eyes for a moment so as not to show her frustration. When she opened them, she noticed Uncle Jihad's face momentarily and impolitically express shock.

"This is my fiancé," my mother said.

"I figured," Uncle Jihad replied.

My mother, knowing that his smile belied his disapproval, shuddered. She tried to banish the color of embarrassment from her cheeks.

That was one story my mother loved to tell, but her version of the events of the evening was slightly different from Uncle Jihad's. According to Uncle Jihad, my mother fell in love with him, but he knew instantly that she would be a wonderful wife for his brother. My mother would smile and shake her head when the story was told in her presence. She said that she adored him that evening but she wasn't in love. She didn't believe in love at first sight.

The last time the subject came up, I was with my mother during a healthy respite about six months before she died. She lay propped against her pillows, and I was sitting on her bed. She had been quite ill for a week, but suddenly she looked rejuvenated. Gauntness and pallor had temporarily departed, and the wrinkles of strain had been filled with new flesh. Hope, the great deceiver, seduced her that morning. "I remember that evening as if it were yesterday," she said. "The candles, the guests, the foreigner with a horrible ponytail. Can you imagine how appalling that was in those days? How insufferable that man was, and how embarrassing that the only one who fell for his asinine chatter was poor Nick. That evening, I was horrified that I didn't know who this man I was supposed to marry was. The scrim that had been hanging before my eyes was raised. The look on Jihad's face when he realized that I was with Nick rattled me. He probably would've been less surprised had I told him I was engaged to the water closet. He disapproved of my choice, and I realized I did as well. What was even more terrifying was that I didn't have the courage to admit my mistake. I knew that night that I'd never go through with the marriage, but I couldn't bring myself to admit it to anyone, not even poor Nick. But my epiphany had nothing to do with being in love. Do you think for a moment that Jihad fell in love with me or I fell in love with him? Please. No matter what Farid and Jihad might have ardently wished to believe, no one was ever fooled. I recognized—oh, what shall we call it?—his special ability to be best friends with women, the instant I saw his impish grin from across the room. My God, how could I not, given the way he crossed his legs or what he did with his hands? No one would talk about it, but that didn't mean anyone was fooled."

Nick wouldn't leave my mother's side for the rest of the evening, and the Swiss was forced to follow his remaining audience across the room. The two men's discussion bored my mother and uncle until the Swiss asked a question: "Will there ever be an Arab Sartre?" My mother rolled her eyes, and Uncle Jihad tried to control his chuckling. Nick commenced a monologue explaining the impossibility of such a phenomenon: the subordination of content to the aesthetics of language in Arabic literature, the dominance of panegyrics and eulogies as an art form, etc. "All you have to look at," said Nick, "is the deification of a loser like al-Mutanabbi. Writers try to emulate him, penning pretty little verses that mean nothing and affect nothing. He sold his services to the highest bidder, and his poems ended up being paeans to corrupt rulers. Things haven't changed much. Until the day arrives when we're no longer dazzled by glitter, we're stuck with the banal beauty of al-Mutanabbi."

My mother's groan startled her fiancé. Confounded, he stared at her, mouth agape.

"Beauty is never banal," my mother said.

"Al-Mutanabbi is one of my heroes," Uncle Jihad said. "Such a romantic fool."

"Romantic?" my mother said. "Are you sure you're not thinking of Antar? I've never heard of a love story associated with al-Mutanabbi."

"No, no. It isn't a love story. It's a death story. A glorious death story."

"Do tell," my mother exhorted.

"You want me to tell you the story? Here? Now? I'm not sure I can." My mother arched her eyebrows. "You must ask again." My uncle cracked a grin. "Please, make me feel important."

My mother's hand went to her chest. She batted her eyelashes. "Please, sahib. Tell me a story and enliven my evening." She smiled. "How was that?"

"Just the right touch," Uncle Jihad said. "Let's see. In the glorious days when poets were heroes and men were valiant, when the sun shone brighter and lies were never spoken, there lived, and died, the greatest of all poets. I'll leave the stories of his tragic life for another sitting, for tonight I'll relay the story of his death. Al-Mutanabbi died on his way to Baghdad, but he didn't die alone. He wasn't what one would call a well-adjusted individual. He knew he was a genius and was obsessed with his immortality. Few put anything down on paper in those days. All poems were memorized, all stories, even the Koran. Well, al-Mutanabbi would have none of that. He wasn't going to rely on others' memories when it came to his work. He wrote everything down, every single word, leaving nothing to chance. We're talking papyrus, large rolls of papyrus. He rode to Baghdad with his son, two slaves, and eight camels loaded with his life's work. Of course, you cross the desert with laden camels and you'll attract the attention of brigands. Thieves attacked the convoy thinking they were about to strike the mother lode and would soon be in possession of treasures. The poet died defending his work, and with his last breath begged his killers not to destroy it. The only one who escaped was the poet's son. He saw his father expire and rode away, but he didn't get far. Guilt over abandoning his father's poetry overpowered him, and he returned to the scene to fight. But the robbers were enraged at finding nothing of value, and they tortured the son and killed him."

"Ah," my mother sighed. "To die for banal beauty. What happened to the manuscripts?"

"Funny you should ask. Al-Mutanabbi was of course a penniless poet."

"Is there any other kind?" My mother clapped her hands once and laughed.

"They unloaded the camels and discarded the valueless poetry, but, as it happened, one of the nasty brigands had an unexplored sensitive nature."

"And he just happened to be able to read?"

"Of course. He read and was entranced and bewitched. He repacked the poems and kept them for years, had them copied and distributed. One would hope he was able to repack all the poems without losing any to the harsh desert winds."

"But what if he wasn't able to," my mother said, "and some of the papyrus flew away?"

"Imagine. Poetry still hovering over the skies of Baghdad."

"Or buried under the desert sands," my mother said. "Someone drills a well in Iraq, and out gushes poetry instead of oil."

"But will the discoverers understand Arabic or appreciate poetry, for that matter?"

"Al-Mutanabbi's basic problem to begin with."

Nick shook his head. "I know that sounds romantic, but what

was the point of al-Mutanabbi's death? Has his poetry saved a single
life?"

My mother sank into a chair, closed her eyes, and sighed softly.

"Let me introduce you to my brother," Uncle Jihad said.

So what happened to Nick, and how did my mother end up not marrying him if she was unable to say no? My sister, who had met Nicholas
Khoury, believed that he and my mother didn't marry because a voice
inside her must have been issuing warnings, if not outright curses, the
whole time. Lina couldn't imagine my mother ever caring for anything
political. That my mother would have committed herself to a man who
believed that opposing Zionism was not just a worthy goal but a way of
life, a prerequisite for being human, was unthinkable to Lina. My
mother, who had transformed being apolitical into an art form, could
never have completely submerged who she was for the sake of a man.
"I know that a discussion about art and poetry was the puff that
brought down the house of cards," Lina once told me, "but how could
the house have stood for so long, given his views? This was a man who
believed in didactic art, for heaven's sake. Novels should uplift the people and guide them to a better understanding of how persecuted they
were. He saw Trotsky, Sartre, Lenin, Orwell, and Huxley as models to
emulate and wasn't bright enough to perceive a contradiction. Mother
was getting a degree in liberal arts while she was with him. This was a
woman who wore mourning black for forty days when Calvino died.
Everyone kept asking her which member of the family had passed
away. She went to her deathbed sincerely believing *Anna Karenina* was
mankind's greatest achievement. That idiot told her that Tolstoy was
the epitome of the spoiled bourgeoisie. He told her not to listen to violin concertos because the best violinists were Jews and therefore probably supporters of the terrible policies of Israel. Told that to my
mother? She mentioned it to me in passing, and I practically fainted.
She may have agreed to marry him, but even if he hadn't spun right
into disaster head-on, she wouldn't have. She knew he was a tragedy."

The disaster occurred on the day of Nick's commencement. My
mother attended his ceremony, sat in the audience with his family.
Nick's mother couldn't contain her pride. His father had desperately
wanted to see his son's graduation but was unable to leave his sickbed.
At the end of the ceremony, my mother faked a headache and left the
happy party to be on her own. She didn't want to discuss the future.

Nick, wearing his cap and gown, returned home to check on his father, who felt such pride that he volunteered to be Nick's first patient. Nick's father had been complaining that day of dizziness, lethargy, and digestive problems. Nick treated him by setting up a glucose intravenous tube. His father died before he had a chance to sneeze, a tragedy and a scandal. Nick locked himself in his room for two weeks after the funeral. His entire family grieved.

The human soul is resilient; Nick did recover emotionally and psychologically.

Human societies are less resilient; the dishonor would not be easily forgotten.

Two months after he had killed his first patient, Nick understood that he wouldn't be able to work in Beirut. No one would consent to be his second patient. He would have to go far away, to a place where no one had heard of his misdeed. Nick asked my mother to go with him to Kirkuk. She refused, of course. And my father began his wooing in earnest.

My father set out to make himself someone else, someone better, someone important. He persuaded his brother to give up his pigeons so they could set up a business. To do that, they needed money. Following their mother's footsteps of long ago, my father and Uncle Jihad walked the same hill to the mansion of the bey, who was always claiming to be our family's benefactor. The bey greeted my father and uncle warmly and called for coffee to be served, but he also called his servant, my grandfather. What insidious thought could have been going through the bey's head no one knew, and this was one story that neither my grandfather nor my uncle nor my father wished to provide theories for or elaborate on.

Before his own father, my father had to ask the bey for financial help. The bey said, "Isn't that too grand a project for you? You don't know the first thing about automobiles. How can you sell cars when you don't even have one of your own?"

Dispirited, my father returned to a rainy Beirut, and for the first time it was Uncle Jihad who had to remind him of the dream. "You'll see," Uncle Jihad said. "In every story, when things are at their most dire, an angel comes and helps the hero."

"But this is no story," replied my father.

"Of course it isn't. This is life. In real life you get more than one angel. You get two or three. Hell, you get an army of angels."

My grandfather quit that day. He was so embarrassed for his sons he told the bey he could no longer work for him. The bey asked how he would survive without his entertainment, and my grandfather said, "All you have to do is ask, my lord, and I will come running to entertain you. Yet I've worked for you for so long that my stories have become aged and corroded. I cannot in good faith take your money and pretend I'm offering anything in return."

That night, my grandmother berated her husband. How would they be able to support themselves? They still had an unmarried daughter. The bey gave my grandfather two days of rest before calling him to the mansion. "Tell me a story," the bey commanded, and my grandfather did. "You have served my family well," the bey said, and resumed paying him his weekly salary. And my grandfather remained at his master's beck and call until the day he died—my grandfather, that is, not the bey, for when the master dies his son takes over his possessions.

The al-Kharrat Corporation was birthed officially in 1955. Like most newborns, it began life small and odd-looking. My father had asked his old Iraqi school friend Khaled Mathaher, an up-and-coming businessman—or, as Uncle Jihad used to call himself when he started out, a businessboy—for advice. The reply had come in a letter from Baghdad that became a family keepsake. "Automobiles!" it shouted. "Sell automobiles. Cars are the future." The Mathaher family had a Renault dealership in Baghdad, and Khaled would help my father obtain one for Lebanon. And the story began.

Listening to the advice of my grandmother and not my grandfather, my father registered the corporation as a family business, with the four brothers, Wajih, Halim, Farid, and Jihad, as partners. The fact that my father listened to his mother and not his father wasn't surprising—my father didn't get along with his father, was embarrassed by him, and rarely if ever listened to him. He should have on this occasion, because my grandfather's counsel proved to be prescient. My grandfather told my father that his two older brothers shouldn't be part of the corporation. My father could hire them or help them, but if they were partners, he and Uncle Jihad would have to work around their incompetence for years to follow. My father not only ignored the advice, he convinced

Uncle Jihad that Uncle Wajih should be president of the company, since he was the eldest. My grandmother brimmed with joy as she saw her family reunite.

My great-uncle Ma'an offered his two charges a final gift, two small plots of land in Beirut. One would become the family workplace, the first dealership, and the other the family home, the building that would be erected not long after as one of the pledges my father made my mother if she married him. The army of angels, friends of my father and Uncle Jihad, provided loans—with no interest, of course. The dealership building was one shoddily built room that barely had space for six clean desks. In its lot, the company opened its doors with three cars, which were sold the first day. "A bang," Uncle Jihad used to say. "We opened with a bang."

Within a year, they added the Fiat dealership, and then the exclusive Arab-world Toyota and Datsun dealership a few years later. On the day the Japanese contracts were signed, my father and Uncle Jihad bought their first custom-made Brioni suits, and my mother received a diamond necklace whose price no one talked about publicly.

My father did accept my grandfather's advice on one thing, the poetic choice. Yes, my mother was seduced with poetry. My mother was a romantic but not a fool. In the two years during which my father pursued her, after he had declared his intentions to Uncle Jihad and her, she had made a point of objectively gauging whether he would make her a good husband. She studied him, found out almost everything there was to know about him: where his career was going, how he treated his family, his level of education or lack thereof, his womanizing. She claimed to have kept a notebook of checks and balances. She tested him. She misbehaved in public to observe his reaction. She made him wait when he picked her up. She interviewed him endlessly.

For his part, my father interviewed Uncle Jihad. What would she like? He never bought flowers that weren't approved by my uncle. My mother kept no secrets from Uncle Jihad, and she soon found out that he kept none from my father. My mother would point out a wonderful dress to Uncle Jihad, and the next day a package would arrive at her house. My father knew who her favorite singers were, what her favorite food was, and of course, who her favorite poets were. My father sent her poems, and my mother adored that. He sent her poetry she knew well. Whether it was Rilke, Dickinson, or Barrett Browning, she knew the Westerners. She loved the old Arabs, al-Mutanabbi or the *Muallaqat*—Amru al-Qais and Zuhair in particular. My father worked hard.

One day, my grandmother asked him when he intended to marry, and he told her about my mother even though she hadn't consented to marry him yet. He confessed his entire seduction scheme. And my grandfather, in his usual obstreperous manner, interrupted, "But you're no poet." When no one understood what he meant, he elaborated. "Only a poet can sing a familiar poem and make it sound as if it has never been uttered before. Only a hakawati can bewitch with a tale twice-told. You have to dazzle her with something she doesn't know, a poet like Saadi. Lovers flock to lesser poets, but few are better than him."

When my grandfather recited some lines from Saadi, my father wasn't impressed, but later, when my mother sat him down to talk, he could come up with nothing else.

"I know you could make me happy," she said. "I know you would take care of me, but we're such different people. That could be hell for the both of us."

And my father replied, "It is better to burn with you in hell than to be in paradise with another. The scent of onions from a beautiful mouth is more fragrant than that of a rose held by an ugly hand." Stunned, my mother searched for a translation of Saadi seemingly forever. He became one of her favorites. Even on her deathbed, she quoted him to the nurses.

My mother agreed to marry my father if he pledged three things: to become more successful, to buy her a better home, and to stop his womanizing. Two out of three.

❧

Back in Cairo, Othman lay on the sofa and admired his wife as she undressed. By the light of a dozen candles, she rubbed a concoction of olive oil and verbena onto her arms. Othman said, "I am pleased that bedtime modesty is not something you insist upon."

She raised her gaze slowly, looked into his eyes to gauge his meaning, but he lowered his quickly in embarrassment. Though she returned to applying the lotion, pretending nonchalance, they knew each other too well. He saw her ears were pricked. "I have been thinking," he said.

In the glow of candles, she massaged the lotion onto the two expansive worlds of her breasts. She discreetly made sure he had the appropriate reaction before moving to her neck. He blinked rapidly. "I have been thinking that we cannot go on like this. A pre-emptive strike is needed." He tried to clear his retinas of the delicious impression, tried to clean up his mind so he could complete a lucid thought. "I have been remiss, my wife. I have not been myself lately. Arbusto has been allowed to roam free, creating trouble, for much too long. He is my enemy, and I have not dealt with him. It is time."

"Yes, he is a rogue worthy of your time."

"I will capture him and drag him on his knees before the king."

"A most noble goal, to be sure."

"Will you help me?"

She did not look up from the task at hand, but it was of no avail. He had seen surprise and delight flush her face. "You never have to ask, my husband."

"I want to hunt the villain, who must be causing trouble somewhere in the coastal cities. We will not return to Cairo without Arbusto enchained and on a leash."

"We?"

"I need your help." He smiled at his wife. "You do have so many leashes."

"You and I?"

"Partners."

"And my husband's enemies will rue the day they were born."

Naked, she climbed atop Othman, and kissed him. "Say it."

"We leave tomorrow," he said, laughing.

She kissed him again. "Say it."

"We should start packing." His eyes sparkled like diamonds along a riverbed.

She kissed him once more. "Say it."

"You are my wife." He took a deep breath and returned her kiss. "I would rather live for eternity as your slave than spend a single moment without you."

— Seventeen —

The first bullet bored through the passenger door of one of the dealership's cars, a blue Toyota, in April 1976. The war—or "skirmishes," as everyone called it then—had begun a year earlier, but the company still hadn't been severely affected, since its customers, like the rest of the Lebanese, foolishly assumed that the trouble wouldn't last long, the Palestinians and the militias involved were simply letting off steam. As a matter of fact, some in the family considered the war further proof of the blessed luck of the corporation and my father's inspired business acumen. Hadn't my worrywart father bought insurance coverage for almost every conceivable disaster, including war? Blind luck wasn't responsible for this decision. My father had imagined that he would one day be so successful that the Israelis would blow up his company in a fit of pique. (They actually did, in 1982, but it wasn't in a fit of pique.) Uncle Jihad drove the blue Toyota home as a keepsake. Insurance would pay for it.

Until the day of his death in 1974, Uncle Wajih was president of the corporation, with the problems predicted by my grandfather. Uncle Halim was not a problem, though. He worked for the company from the beginning, did whatever he was asked, and didn't care to make decisions. As a brother and a full partner, he was included in most discussions and was happy to go along with whatever was happening. He bragged to anyone who listened that he was the company's dynamo, but even he didn't believe himself. Uncle Wajih, on the other hand, believed himself. My father and Uncle Jihad must have forgotten to mention he was supposed to be president in name only.

The bigger the company grew, the bigger his head. By the seventies, when the company was outselling all other Lebanese dealerships combined, he had become so arrogant in his dealings with strangers as to be unbearable. Uncle Jihad and my father had to work around him. He was agreeable most of the time, but every now and then, he made sure to stand against his younger brothers to prove his worth. My father and Uncle Jihad had to find ways of outmaneuvering him. In the early days, they sought my grandmother's intervention. They had to drive up to the village and persuade her to drive down with them and talk to her eldest.

When the Japanese arrived, all were ecstatic except for Uncle Wajih. In order to raise the money to sign the Japanese contract, the company had to sell its rights to Fiat. He decided to put his foot down and refused to budge. He even insulted the Japanese executive visiting Beirut. My grandmother wasn't able to persuade him to change his mind. Uncle Wajih insulted her as well, by suggesting that she knew nothing about the corporate world. Of course, my grandmother was horrified. Everyone assumed Aunt Wasila was pulling his strings. Aunt Samia swore it was so. No brother of hers would ever insult his mother unless his wife put him up to it.

At their wits' end, Uncle Jihad and my father sought Aunt Wasila's help. They explained the situation and were able to convince her easily. She took care of the rest. Uncle Wajih left the office for home, and returned the following morning to yell at everyone to work harder so they wouldn't wreck his Japanese contract.

While Uncle Wajih was alive, not one Lebanese—or Arab, for that matter—ever thought twice about having an incompetent man as president of a successful family company. Whenever buyers or suppliers needed anything, they asked Uncle Jihad or my father. It was the non-Lebanese who had trouble understanding. The baffled foreigners considered the time spent listening to Uncle Wajih a waste.

The business went from success to success under my father and Uncle Jihad. It would take a couple of years of war for the Lebanese division of the company to grind to a temporary halt, but even then there was hardly a financial ripple, because the company had dealerships doing good business in twelve other countries. There was more than a ripple emotionally, though, since by then the Lebanese dealership was essential to how my family defined itself.

It was in 1977, after the death of Uncle Jihad, that the company began to lose focus. His loss was demoralizing, and particularly devastating to my father, who would never really care about the company again. Neither he nor Uncle Jihad had prepared anyone to take over. After all, in 1977, my father was only forty-seven. No one else could do his job, so he showed up at the office when the bombs took a rest, but he didn't do much.

Again, however, the corporation was blessed. Ten days after my sister's wedding, when Lina finally grasped that her life wasn't going to be anything like she'd imagined, that she was probably never going to see Elie again, nor did she want to, she decided to reinvent herself. She would get her first job. Pregnant and feeling slightly bloated, she showed up at the dealership and began her conquest. Within a couple of years, she was running the corporation.

&

Othman, holding the reins of two horses, scanned the vast skies. "Where is he?" he asked his wife.

"There." She pointed toward the north. "You will see him as soon as he crosses below the white cloud." The pigeon's red color deepened under the cloud. The bird circled twice before landing on her hand. He cooed to his mate and entered his cage. " 'We have a destination,' " Layla announced, reading the pigeon's message. " 'The nasty one is in Antioch.' " After receiving the message, the couple ran across an envoy from Aleppo carrying a letter to the sultan in Cairo. The messenger refused to divulge the content of the missive, even to an emir.

"Trouble in Antioch?" Othman asked the messenger.

"How did you know? The mayor of Aleppo is begging the king to send an army to help him fight King Fartakamous of Antioch, who is laying siege to Aleppo as we speak."

"Our army will soon be on the move," Othman said to his wife. "Where do you think we should go, Aleppo or Antioch?"

"Antioch. Combat is not the best use for our talents. Let us leave that to the warriors."

Othman and Layla entered Antioch easily. The city was almost empty—armyless, kingless, and Arbustoless. "Now to work," Othman said.

That evening, a pretty boy from Shiraz visited the couple. He stood by the door and bowed before Layla. "A luscious dove commands and I obey. I understand you seek information. This humble yellow rump is at your service."

Noticing Othman's confusion, Layla explained, " 'Yellow rump' is what unscrupulous men call the boys they abuse for pleasure, an insult referring to the use of saffron as lubricant. In some cities, the boys have begun to form cadres and are claiming the name." She returned to the boy. "Sit, sit. Tell us what happened here."

The boy nodded and said, "The priest Arbusto tried to persuade our king to declare war upon the sultanate. Fartakamous declined, saying that the great sultan had been collecting Crusader kings like a child collects insects. He had no wish to be crushed."

"A wise king," interjected Othman.

"But not as wily as Arbusto, who befriended the king's son, Kafrous, my master and owner. A few days ago, Arbusto accompanied Kafrous on a ride and returned bedraggled with a corpse. He claimed to have been attacked by a garrison from Aleppo. The king led an army to crush Aleppo while Arbusto went to get reinforcements from King Francis of Sis."

"For your help," Layla said, "we will free you once our army liberates Antioch," and she sent the boy on his way. "Let us be off to Sis."

Naturally, the great slave army defeated King Fartakamous of Antioch, and he joined his brethren, Kings Louis IX, Franjeel, Brigitte, and Diafil, as Baybars's prisoners. And Baybars crushed the walls of Antioch. The hero of a thousand tales received another flowery letter from his friend Othman. "Lead your army to Sis," it began, "and may its fort crumble upon your magnificent arrival. The mellifluous evil one convinced King Francis of the lie that the sultanate wished to murder the innocent monarchs. The gullible king shut the gates of Sis and declared war upon you. That was his last decree, for he soon found himself unable to forswear slumber. He will continue to sleep until your advent, because his wakefulness bores my charming wife. His guards have been searching the fort; they seem to have misplaced the king. My dutiful wife, and not I, will greet you and open the gates. The unhappy news is that Arbusto fled before our arrival, and therefore I have gone south to Tripoli. King Francis and a dozen of his sleeping officers await you with bated breath. Do hurry, for my wife wishes to rejoin me as quickly as possible."

A few weeks later, Layla and Harhash rode through the Lebanese mountains above Tripoli. As the city's fort came into view below, twelve mean-looking riders blocked their way.

"Usually, I kill my victims instantly and relieve the corpses of their possessions," said the leader, "but I have never encountered beauty unprotected on these roads before. I could be persuaded to delay your death."

"Oh, how silly." Layla unleashed her nail-studded whip, striking from nine paces away, and the brigand flew forward off his horse and landed dead at her horse's hooves. She turned to one of his men, who looked less stunned than the rest. "What are you doing here?"

"What? How did you recognize me? I am in disguise. I just infiltrated this group."

"Infiltrated?" asked one of the brigands, but that was the last word he uttered, for Othman struck him down. Harhash shook his head in confusion. "Why would you want to infiltrate an incompetent band of amateurs?"

"Amateurs?" asked another of the brigands, but Layla had only to feign a whipping motion and the brigand turned and fled in terror, followed by his companions.

"I had to," Othman said. "Arbusto could not persuade King Bohemond of Tripoli to declare war, so he is recruiting brigands to cause trouble and force the sultan to attack. I hoped to come across Arbusto if I joined them. But why did you ride with my wife?"

"She needed protection," Harhash said. Layla and Othman stared at him. "Well, I was bored. One battle, two battles, they all begin to look the same. I prefer your adventure. I was crushed that you left Cairo without me. Shame. I thought I meant something to you; I thought I was your friend."

"We wanted to be together," Othman said, and Layla added, "This is our honeymoon."

❧

We wished for a bigger storm, more powerful, more destructive, strong enough to get the combatants to take a break from the fighting. In the winter of 1976, the rain was soft, the shelling wasn't. The underground garage muted the sound of the bombardment. The fighting was in a different part of town, but my mother was worried enough to take us to the shelter. Light from a couple of kerosene lamps and infinite candles threw flickering shadows across the unwashed walls. My mother lit a cigarette. "I'm dying, Jihad, dying of boredom." She turned off the transistor radio, interrupting the voice of the BBC anchorwoman in mid-sentence. "Entertain me or suffer the consequences."

"Me?" Uncle Jihad said. "Why don't you tell us a story? Tell your children about the greatest love, how you picked their father out of all your suitors."

Lina picked up the transistor and moved two plastic chairs away to Uncle Akram's parking space. His car must have been leaking for quite a while, since there was a large oil stain resembling the dark continent of Africa. Lina sat down, tuned the radio to a rock station, and put her legs on the second chair. Her butt hovered over Libya and Tunis, and her feet dangled over the southern tip of the horn. "Lina seems to be entertaining herself," said Uncle Jihad. "Wouldn't it be nice to tell your son about you?"

"You're supposed to entertain me," my mother said. "Don't fail me, mister."

"Relentless woman." Uncle Jihad laughed. "All right. I'll tell you a story about my mischievous youth, but I don't want you to get any ideas, Osama. Let's see. Where does one start? In the early days, before I was born, that's when we'll start." He tapped out a cigarette and took his time lighting it, had two long puffs before beginning a third. "During the early 1900s, there was a Druze brigand, Yassin al-Jawahiri, who terrorized the mountains. Well, 'terrorize' might be too harsh a word. He was a card who fancied himself a Druze Robin Hood. He stole from the Ottoman Empire and its officials and shared some of his bounty with the Druze villages, and in return the villagers sheltered him, even against the wishes of their leaders, the princes and sheikhs of the mountains. He was a hero to the Druze, this Yassin al-Jawahiri."

"Al-Jawahiri?" my mother interrupted.

"One and the same."

"This isn't fair," I said. "I don't know what you're talking about."

"You know the Jawahiri family," my mother said. "Jihad is going to tell us how they became our friends."

"Why?" I asked.

"Because it's a great story," Uncle Jihad said. "Now, let me tell it. This Yassin was a clever fellow and became so popular that there was a song written about him. It went like this:

Ya Yassin, Ya Jawahiri
Your rifle slung on your shoulder,
becomes snug on that shoulder
Before your enemy blinks.
Vultures and foreigners behind you
Turn, turn, and shoot them.
Ya Yassin, Ya Jawahiri
Return to us our hero.

"That's a stupid song," I said.

"I learned it as a little boy. You know my father. He probably knew every song sung in the mountains. When he told the Yassin story, I remembered the song. Anyway, Yassin caused havoc for many years, but then the First World War started and the French arrived. Well, the French were more ruthless than the Ottomans. They caught Yassin and executed him."

❦

"How does one capture a villain as wily as Arbusto?" asked Harhash.

"How does one woo evil?" asked Layla.

"We set a trap," said Othman. "We seduce his greed."

"We seduce his ego," added Harhash.

"And top it with lust," said Layla. "A powerful brew indeed. We send a message that a luscious dove has arrived in Tripoli, enamored of his infamous reputation, infatuated by his power. She wishes to be his slave and answer his bidding, do anything he desires."

"She will help him bring the sultanate to its knees," said Othman. "She is able to seduce any man, including the virtuous King Baybars."

"She is able to relieve men of their reason," said Harhash. "She can open any door."

"He will come running. I will spread the rumor among the city's thieves."

"I will inform the pleasure-givers," said Layla.

"I will take the bandits and highway robbers," said Harhash.

And Layla vowed, "I will drain him dry as hay. Sleep shall neither night nor day hang upon his penthouse lid. He shall live a man forbid."

"Let us begin," said Othman. "When shall we three meet again?"

Layla waited in her room. When the knock came, she lay on the divan while Othman and Harhash hid behind the curtains. "Come in," Layla called. "Come sit next to me. I have admired you from afar for so long, and I yearn to see you up close."

Arbusto entered the room wearing his best robe and a scent of jasmine, trying to appear magisterial, but his nerve failed him. He sat at the end of the divan, beside her bare feet. "I thought your kind had repented." He pulled his miter to make sure his clipped ear was covered.

"I retired from public service, not private."

"That is a good distinction in your profession," Arbusto said.

"I have waited for this moment." Layla kept her eyes fastened on her prey, whose gaze darted about to avoid hers. "Every time I heard stories of your exploits, I shuddered in secret joy. I was first intrigued, then enchanted, then infatuated. I kept hearing more and more stories. You have done some terrible things." She winked, and he flushed. "You have been a bad boy." She rose from the divan slowly, making sure her curves were highlighted. "Have you not?"

"Yes, I have." A nervous laugh escaped his lips.

"And you must be punished. Give me your hands."

Arbusto extended his hands meekly. She tied them and secured him to the divan. His lustful eyes followed her every movement. She turned her back on him, and an astonished Arbusto heard her talk to the draperies, "Do you want him awake or unconscious?"

"Is that it?" asked Harhash, coming out. "The evil Arbusto captured so easily? I had expected more twists and turns, more excitement."

"I would have dragged it out had I known," said Layla.

Harhash slapped Arbusto's face. "You disappoint me. You are a bad boy? You need to be punished? You fell for that?" Smack. "You did not even make her work. Come sit on my divan and let me tie you up? Shame on you. I had expected so much more."

"The important thing," said Othman, "is that we have captured this villain."

"True, but there are conventions," replied Harhash. Slap. "This thief has stolen the thrill of capture from me."

"Oh well," said Othman. "Reality never meets our wants, and adjusting both is why we tell stories."

❧

"Hmm, so I was ten," Uncle Jihad said. "I know it's difficult to believe, but I was still a fairly reticent child. Beirut and the school proved to be overwhelming. I wasn't unhappy by any means, but I was a lonely boy. I spent all my time reading books and watching the world. Uncle Ma'an and his family tried to draw me out at first, but their hearts weren't in it. And after all, they had enough troubles of their own. Uncle Jalal was spending more time in jail than out of it. In 1942, the war was raging in Europe, and the streets of Beirut were boiling. The Arisseddines had time for nothing but Uncle Jalal's problems with French rule. My grandmother was spending most of her time in Beirut, but I hardly ever saw her. I rarely saw any of the family. Only after independence, the following year, did the family return to anything resembling normal.

"My blossoming began one day when I was standing under the oak tree Charlemagne, trying to understand how a yo-yo worked and singing the Yassin al-Jawahiri song to myself. A boy asked me how I knew the song, and I replied that I'd known it since I was born. I boasted that I knew everything there was to know about the man."

"Was that boy Nasser al-Jawahiri?" asked my mother.

"The one and the same. Nasser went home for the weekend, and on Monday a horde of Jawahiris descended upon the school. There were about a hundred of them, men and women, geriatrics and children, religious and secular, all one family. It was a big commotion, and I was surprised to discover they had come to talk to me. I was taken to a hall and interviewed. They asked if I was Druze and were very happy to find out my mother was an Arisseddine. They asked me about Yassin al-Jawahiri, and I answered. My father had told me the story, so I knew quite a bit, and I could see the astonishment on their faces with each of my responses."

"Tell me you didn't," my mother said.

"I was as innocent as a lamb of God. I swear. In any case, it took me a while to figure out what was happening. I didn't understand, so you can't blame me for the beginning. I was answering their questions. I loved the attention. I knew each correct answer would get more."

"Oh, Jihad," my mother said. "You bad boy."

"What happened?" I asked. "Tell me."

"The Jawahiris would have come to the conclusion that your uncle was the reincarnation of Yassin al-Jawahiri," my mother said. "The family had come to investigate, and Jihad was a very bad boy."

"And your mother is a harsh judge," Uncle Jihad said. "They didn't come to investigate, but to confirm. If it had been an investigation, a much smaller number would have come. They wanted to meet the great Yassin. I simply answered their questions."

"You could have told them where you got the information," my mother said.

"They didn't ask. They never once asked how I came to know. They believed."

"What would they ask? Hey, do you have a crazy hakawati for a father, and does he know the most minute detail of every story ever told, and has he repeated them all to you over and over and over?"

"Harsh woman. Harsh, unforgiving woman. I didn't do anything wrong. I was lonely. When they told me I was Yassin al-Jawahiri, I couldn't have been happier. They introduced themselves one by one. 'I'm your nephew so-and-so, but of course I'm much older now than when you left.' What did you expect me to do? I was the centerpiece of a magnificent epic. Stories swirled around me. More, I became what I'd always daydreamed of being, a hero whom people looked up to, and I did it without having to display a smidgen of courage. In one instant, I had acquired a new story, a new family, a new identity, and gifts, many gifts. Nothing expensive, but nice things like hand-knit vests and caps, and lots and lots of food. I was invited to their houses for meals. I never had to eat school food. They sent morning pies, savory pastries. They created a space for me in their hearts."

"And you created a space in your stomach," my mother said as Uncle Jihad patted his ample belly. "I presume you didn't horribly abuse their gullibility, since Nasser is still a friend."

"Abuse? Sweetheart, I was the joy of their lives. Nasser did become a good friend. The Jawahiris loved me. As I said, our family was busy. No one paid much attention to my comings and goings even though I was so young. Things went on like that for about a year and some, until the day Uncle Ma'an discovered what was going on. He was very angry. He put on his best suit and his fez and took me to the Jawahiris to apologize for my bad behavior. I had to sit there and look contrite, head bent, while everyone glared. Uncle Ma'an went on about what a scamp I was. He told them I wasn't Yassin and there was no way I could be. He explained that I had been born many years after Yassin died— reincarnation is instantaneous. If they could find it in their hearts to forgive me, he would make sure I'd never disturb them again. I wasn't a bad boy. I was from a good family. I just didn't know any better. He actually said I was his favorite nephew, that this was his fault: he'd been busy and hadn't been paying proper attention to my upbringing. It was Nasser's mother who saved me. She said that, even though I wasn't Yassin al-Jawahiri, she'd grown to cherish me, and I was welcome at her house at any time. Things settled down a bit, and a fortnight later, Nasser said that his mother wanted me to come to a big lunch for a nephew who had just gotten engaged. I couldn't say no. After all, she was an astonishing cook. At the lunch, I felt awkward, and so did most of the Jawahiris. It was a celebratory feast, yet the mood was somewhat gloomy. I missed what we had before. I was among the Jawahiris, but I missed them. I longed for the way I had felt when I was around them, how special I was. I didn't know how to make things better or what to say. Nasser's mother served the lamb, and it was almost eerily quiet. There were people talking, but it was relatively hushed. When Nasser's mother, bless her, offered me dessert, she patted my head and told me not to be too upset with Uncle Ma'an. She said he was a great man but he could be a bit rigid. And this was where I was bad."

My mother gasped and broke into a wide grin. "No. You didn't?"

"I'm afraid I did."

"What?" I demanded.

"Al-Jawahiri is a common family, not titled," my mother explained. "Ma'an Arisseddine was a sheikh."

"I wanted to make everyone happy. I told Nasser's mother that Uncle Ma'an was a great man, honest and honorable. Just as she had said, he was also rigid about principles when it came to his family's social position and obligations."

"You didn't leave it at that," my mother said. "That would have been too subtle."

"I didn't. I added that I'd heard him say that a sheikh should guard his position in society at all costs, that one's family name is all one ever has. I didn't make that up, he'd said it often. I just made sure to mention it at the right time. Nasser's mother stood up straight. Her face lit up. She yelled to the entire room, 'Of course. That makes sense. The sheikh would never want to admit that his nephew was reincarnated from a commoner. The fact that the boy's father isn't a sheikh would make the man even more insistent that his nephew had nothing to do with us.' The family exploded into a cacophony of joy. Even Nasser's cousin, the future groom, stood up and shouted, 'I knew you were one of us. I always knew. My heart never lies.' The feast turned raucous. Everyone began to sing. Everyone was happy."

The cigarette in Uncle Jihad's hand was more ash than filter. He dropped it on the ground and stomped on it. He had been carpeting the floor with cigarette butts. He lit another, signaling the end of the tale.

"How long did it go on?" my mother asked.

"Quite a while, I'm afraid."

"You never told them?"

"No, there was never any need. For a couple of years after that lunch, I was back to being family. Then I started to work, and I also got more serious about studying. I didn't get to see them as much, and I drifted away, but then the relationship changed, and we became friends. Our families are very close. You know that. Hell, they came with us to pick you up for your wedding. We've been together for so long that I don't think anybody remembers who Yassin was, let alone that I'm supposed to be him. We owe them much, and we try to pay our debt."

I looked at my mother, and she saw I was confused.

"More than half the people who work for the corporation are Jawahiris," she explained. "Whenever a Jawahiri needed a job, your father found a place for him. Now we know why. I always assumed it was because they were friends of the family."

"It's a bit more than that," Uncle Jihad said. "We don't usually like to talk about this. We had no money to start the company, and we had to borrow. A lot of people helped. Quite a few, but not the people you would have expected."

"I know," my mother said. "Farid calls them the army of angels."

"Yes, I do, too." He chuckled, then sighed. "The Jawahiris were part of the army of angels. They didn't have much money, but I had to ask. I was desperate. If we hadn't come up with the money, Farid would have killed himself. I went to them, and they all loaned me money, they dug into their savings. I didn't know at the time, but Nasser's mother sold her jewelry to loan me the money. I was family. They believed in me. We paid them back, of course. We paid everybody back a lot more than they gave us. If that delightful buffoon Nasser came down these steps right now and said he needed a heart, I would tear mine out and gift it."

♣

Cairo's jails were crowded with Crusader kings, and the Crusader cities were returned to the people. The great Baybars had liberated the lands.

The queens of the captured Crusader kings begged King Flavio of Rome to intercede on behalf of their husbands. King Flavio sent an emissary to Baybars offering two treasure chests for each of the released kings. He also asked for Arbusto's release. "No," said Baybars. "I agree to release the kings, for they are of royal blood and were deceived into treachery. Arbusto, however, is the father of lies. When he lies, he speaks his native tongue. I will not let him go."

"Your Majesty," said the Roman emissary, "King Flavio will free six thousand Muslim slaves in good faith if you can find it in your heart to release the priest."

And Baybars searched his heart, nodded his assent.

That evening, Layla asked her husband, "Arbusto released? What kind of an exchange rate is that? Is one European life worth six thousand of ours?"

♣

"Will they ever stop?" my mother said. The shelling had been going on and on, and we were all getting tired. "This infernal night is never ending. Make it pass, Jihad. Make it pass or make those bombs stop. Those are your options."

"Shall we play cards?" Uncle Jihad asked.

"No. Tell me another story. Entertain me once more."

Uncle Jihad turned to me and winked. "Why don't you tell us a story, Osama? It's time you contributed to our lore."

"Yours are so much better," I said, "and she asked you."

My mother stretched her back. "I'd love to hear a story, Osama. Really, my dear, any story is good. Anything is better than this boredom."

"I can tell the story of Baybars," I said. "It used to be one of Grandfather's favorites."

"Baybars?" My mother turned to Uncle Jihad. "The Mamluke? Is there a story about him that I don't know about?"

"The story is a classic," Uncle Jihad said. "One of the standards."

"Why?"

Uncle Jihad laughed, and I said, "Because he's a hero."

"Actually, Osama, that's a great question," Uncle Jihad said. He took a deep breath, searched his pockets for a cigarette, which basically meant that he was going to tell a tale, not I. "I'm laughing because your mother has a talent for getting to the crux of an issue. I'm assuming she knows who the man is."

"Of course I do."

"What she's asking is why there's a story about him. You see, the story of the story of Baybars is in some ways more interesting. Listen. Contrary to what my father and most people believe, the only true event in that whole story, in all its versions, is that the man existed. Everything else has been distorted beyond recognition. Al-Malik al-Zahir Rukn al-Din Baybars al-Bunduq-dari al-Salihi owes his fame to his talent for public relations, without which his reign might have been reduced to a historical footnote."

"Wait," I said. "At Ain Jalut he—"

"Listen and learn, Osama," my uncle interrupted. "Though it's true that Baybars defeated both the Mongols and the Crusaders, it actually was a victory for the Mamlukes. He wasn't the best general among them by any means. And his victories over the Crusaders, like Saladin's, were temporary, for whenever ferment spread in Europe, nervous kings and popes called for new crusades. There were so many crusades. You know, when the knights of the First Crusade landed on our shores, they massacred the entire population of Beirut without showing mercy on a single soul before heading toward Jerusalem—all of Beirut, every citizen was killed. And after the Great War, in 1918, when the French arrived with their fleet of innumerable warships, the first governor, General Henri Gouraud, announced upon landing in Beirut, 'Saladin, we have returned.' Believe me, Baybars did not defeat the Crusaders. No one did. But he also wasn't a decent ruler. His subjects despised him, because he was a ruthless, fork-tongued megalomaniac who rose to power through treachery and murder. Quite a few sultans followed his mentor, al-Saleh, but their reigns were shortened when the ambitious slave killed them. He murdered two openly, Touran Shah and Qutuz; the death of Qutuz was Baybars's springboard to power, since he insisted on applying an old law of the Turks stipulating that he who killed the ruler should take his place. He was also despised because he was born with blue eyes and developed cataracts in one. One blue and one white meant an evil eye."

"So he wasn't a hero?"

"He was in a way," Uncle Jihad went on. He laughed when he saw my face. "Don't be so disappointed. He was definitely a marketing hero. Baybars consolidated his power and created a cult of personality by paying, bribing, and forcing an army of hakawatis to promulgate tales of his valor and piety. These days, few can discern historical accounts from the stories of the hakawatis. He was the precursor to all the Arab presidents we have today." He reached out and stroked my chin, lifted it up so my mouth closed. "Here's a fun fact, in almost all the remaining versions of the story, none of them are about Baybars. You see, the hakawatis' audience is the common man who couldn't really identify with a royal, almost infallible hero, so early on the hakawatis began to introduce characters that their audience could empathize with. The tale, even during its inchoate years, was never about Baybars, but those around him. The story of the king is the story of the people, and unfortunately, to this day, no king has learned that lesson."

In 1982, a couple of months after the infernal Israelis blew up the dealership during an aerial bombardment, and after their siege of Beirut, I went home for Christmas. The city was mired in civil war and occupied by Israeli troops, but that didn't stop my mother from asking me to take four-year-old Salwa for a walk while she got a manicure and pedicure. A week of calm had inspired courage in the city's denizens, but not in me. Whether that was because courage was never my forte or because I was no longer a denizen of Beirut, I couldn't tell. A few months earlier, the Israelis had bombed the city incessantly. A few months earlier, the Syrians had assassinated the Lebanese president. A few months before that, the militias had massacred thousands of Palestinian civilians in the camps. Today, my mother wanted a manicure.

"At least the PLO is gone," she said. "It's safer now, in principle." The Israeli invasion had incapacitated her for quite some time, but recently she'd been reclaiming her normal life.

It wasn't as if my mother were the only crazy one. The Lebanese took advantage of every lull. The blare of car horns as I pushed Salwa's stroller along was deafening. Military jeeps drove by and honked their way past civilian automobiles. The Corniche was filled with prome-naders.

I stood in front of the building where my mother was having her nails done. She was somewhere on the second floor. The manicurist usually came to the apartment, but today my mother had wanted an excuse to go out. I considered pushing the stroller across the boulevard to the Corniche, but I felt paralyzed. The people enjoying their walks didn't inspire any confidence in me. I felt safer standing close to the building, and my napping niece didn't seem to mind.

In the midst of my passive panic attack, I heard a hissing sound com-ing from behind the war-damaged green wall separating the building from its neighbor: "Psst, psst." I began to back away slowly, pulling the stroller. My blood was rushing so fast I almost blacked out. I was twenty-one, too young to die, much too young. "Over here," the voice behind the wall said, quietly and urgently. I couldn't tell who was stu-pider: the man who was hiding and expecting someone to respond to his call, or me for not running into the building screaming my terror out. "Osama," the man called. A bearded face appeared from behind the wall. "It's me, Elie."

I barely recognized my brother-in-law, although he had the same features, the same nose and mouth and brow. It wasn't the beard or the gauntness that made him unrecognizable and disturbing. It was the eyes, brimming with the brilliance of insanity. Elie's most distinctive feature had been his swagger, but he wasn't able to exhibit any as a dis-connected head.

"Hey. You look different." I backed up another step. "I can't stay, because I have to take Salwa inside."

"No, wait," he pleaded. He didn't move from behind the wall. Only his angled head with its crown of untrimmed hair showed. "I can't stay, either—too many traitors around—but I want to talk to you. I saw you from two buildings away and ducked over here; it's too dangerous. We must meet at a secure location."

"A secure location?"

"Where no one will kill me. Meet me at Trader Vic's tonight at eight. I have many things to tell you. Don't stand me up, I beg you. Promise me." He withdrew his head without waiting for my agree-ment. I looked around, wondered why the air didn't feel different, why there wasn't some form of proof that Elie had been there. Salwa stirred in the pram. I checked, but she was still napping. Elie hadn't even asked who she was.

The dank fog of smoke forced what dim light there was to scatter randomly. Elie was sitting on a high stool at the bar, and seemed about to tip over. The bartender, a bald, muscular man in a colored polyester shirt, leaned across the bar surface and whispered something into Elie's ear. When the bartender pulled his head back, I could see that he wasn't exactly sober, either. The room groaned and sweated, feverish amid an infestation of bamboo. I shuddered. The bartender noticed me and arched his eyebrows. I sat next to Elie and ordered a beer.

Elie discovered my existence when the bartender placed the bottle in front of me. "My mother won't talk to me anymore," he said.

He exhaled a dragon's worth of smoke. I wiped the irritation from my eyes and took a sip of beer. "How are you doing?" I asked.

"My mother won't talk to me," he repeated. "I've been trying to get in touch, but she won't even open the door. I might get murdered any minute and she doesn't care."

I felt as if I were stuck in a portentous Godard movie. "Tell him why," the bartender said as he cleaned glasses with a dingy towel. He looked like a wrestler flexing before a match.

"I threw an ashtray at her."

"And he's surprised she doesn't talk to him," said the bartender.

"I didn't hit her, did I? I threw the glass ashtray at the door to get her to move. She didn't want me to leave. She argued and argued and then threw herself in front of the door, as if that was going to stop me. She can't tell me what to do."

Not a Godard movie, a Hollywood B-movie. An abrasive Don Ho was actually singing in the background. "She can't tell you what to do," said the bartender, "and now she won't talk to you. You can't have it both ways."

"Hey," called Elie, "whose side are you on?"

"Your mother's. I'm always on a mother's side. She raised you better than this. And you know she'd do anything for you. Tell him." The bartender jerked his head toward me and flicked his towel at Elie, who turned his back and almost fell off the stool.

The bartender sighed and told me the story himself. When the

Israelis laid siege to Beirut, the Palestinians and the Lebanese leftist militias hunkered in for the last stand. The city was shelled by battleships in the west, tanks and rocket launchers from the mountains in the east, north, and south, and jets from above. Elie didn't return home for two weeks, remaining in the bunker and dozing whenever he could on the beach, where he was launching ineffective rockets at Israeli gunboats. For a fortnight, his mother, the concierge's wife, worried to the point where she pricked her arms with darning needles in order not to think of her son. Finally, after midnight on a night of heavy shelling, she left her house and walked the two miles to the bunker. Her son was sleeping on a raffia mat, shoeless but fully clothed under a single blanket.

He opened his eyes and saw his mother glaring at him. "I only wanted to make sure you're all right," she said, turning around to go home.

Elie's gaze was fastened on the label of his beer bottle, which he was systematically tearing to shreds. "It's the Christians," he said out of nowhere. "They betrayed us all."

I wished he would look at me when he talked, but, then again, it was probably just as well that he didn't. "But you're Christian," I said.

"I mean the Maronites. Don't pretend you're a foreigner with me."

"Elie. My mother is a Maronite."

"I don't mean all of them, just most of them. You can't deny it. They're going to kill all of us. If they don't shoot us, they'll slit our throats. If they don't slit our throats, they'll poison us. If they don't poison us, they'll run us over with their Range Rovers one by one and break our bones and watch us bleed to death on the road."

"Elie. My sister—your wife—is a Maronite."

"No, she's not. I don't care what she thinks. She's not. She would take after your father, not your crazy mother. You don't get to choose. And she was baptized Orthodox to marry, so she can't fool me. I know better now, and I knew better then. I'm in control. Did I tell you my mother isn't talking to me? Can your mother talk to her?"

"Elie." I repeated his name in hopes of calming him. "Have you been sleeping all right?"

"What a stupid question. I haven't had a good night's sleep in years. Do you think it's easy? You escaped. You ran away. The rest of us can't. We're not all like your family. When things get rough, they go to the mountains—or, better, they go to Paris. Your house gets destroyed, you buy another, or two. All I can do is kill, kill, kill."

I drank the rest of my Heineken in one long gulp. "Have you run over someone with a Range Rover lately?"

"Two of them, ran over them twice, but I wish I had a Range Rover, because then they'd be dead instead of in the hospital. If I had a four-wheeler, everything would run smoother."

I slid off my barstool and started to leave, but Elie grabbed my arm. "Wait," he said, "I have a good story for you," and he plunged off into uninterruptible jabber territory. "We weren't ready. In principle, we should have been. We used to use it as a threat: The Israelis are going to invade. The Israelis are going to invade. We didn't really believe it. We also thought that if they did the Syrians would stand in their way. After all, that was why they were here. But the second the invasion began, the Syrians started running and hiding like the dogs they are. It was left to the Palestinians and us to fight. The glory of the left. For Trotsky, Che, and all that. My men ended up on the beach trying to stop the Israelis from landing troops there. There were so few of us compared with them. We had to do it in six-hour shifts. It was exhausting. Having to be one hundred percent on your guard for six hours was deadly." I pulled my arm away, and he panicked. "Wait, wait, I'm getting to the strange part of the story. So, one day—we've been doing this for about a month, everyone was exhausted and psychotic—I finished my shift at noon and was going to take a shower and force myself to sleep, but then a jeep full of Palestinian commandos stopped next to me, and a friend of mine tells me to get in. I tried to tell him that I wanted to shower and sleep, but he wasn't buying it. They were going to see a movie, and I was coming with them. A movie.

"Well, the only working movie theater, running on generators, is the Pavilion, which was showing nothing but porno. My friend even bought my ticket. We walked in, and the theater was completely full of guys with rifles and machine guns. The ones in the seats had theirs leaning against the seats in front of them, and there were probably a hundred guys standing with their weapons propped against the walls. There must have been more than six hundred fighters in that theater, all completely engrossed in four couples fucking around a pool in Beverly Hills. All of them, and I mean all, had their pants open, their dicks out, whacking off to the unfolding American dream on the screen."

I closed my eyes and shook my head.

"I need money," Elie said.

"I figured," I replied, but he wasn't listening.

"I want to get out of here. I want to have a family, kids. You know, the normal life. I can't do it in Beirut now, so I have to go away, maybe the Gulf or Brazil or Sweden, somewhere nice. I need money. Can you get me some? Ask your father. Tell him for old times' sake."

"For old times' sake?"

"Yes," he said. "I always respected him."

"It wouldn't do any good. I'd have to ask Lina. She's the one who's in charge now."

"Oh."

"She's the one who runs the company."

"Oh."

"Do you want me to ask her?"

"No. I don't think that's a good idea, definitely not. I'm not crazy."

By the time my sister began work, the dealership had moved to the safer suburbs—safer, but not safe. The danger was not a physical one. The company was apolitical, and even militias needed cars every so often. What was unsafe was that the company was profitable, maybe not as much as it was in the years before the war, but enough to tempt a few unscrupulous mafiosi, otherwise known as Lebanese political leaders. For a while, cuts had to be paid to various powerbrokers for every car that was sold. During one of the numerous peaks of the war, the bey walked into the company's offices and offered protection. In exchange, he would buy into the firm for 20 percent of the net profits. Of course, he couldn't pay anywhere near full price for his share, what with the country's precarious financial situation and all. The bey became a partner in the Lebanese dealership. Had my father still cared about his company, that fact alone would have killed him. Unfortunately for the bey, it wasn't a successful investment. By the time the current bey succeeded his father, he was the main shareholder in a company that wasn't the cash cow it used to be. Their family had spent a fortune investing in the corporation, and our family had long ago sold out of it. A bad deal.

My sister was a good businesswoman, but her true talent lay in understanding human hunger. Everyone in the family had become rich, which meant there was no one left who had the drive to keep the company successful. Slowly, she began to disinvest, breaking up the various dealerships and selling them. She sold the last dealership, the one in Kuwait, four months before the Iraqis invaded. There were many good reasons for selling off the company bit by bit. My sister correctly understood that other companies would mimic the Nissan and Toyota plan, and the market would soon be glutted with competition. The gold mine of my father's day had turned silver in hers. And she quickly got tired of constantly having to pay people off so she could do her job. In essence, she had to bribe partners to let her make money for them. It wasn't just the bey. She considered him small change. In every country, the company had to have a local partner who did nothing but sit back and rake in money.

"Look," she once said, "I'm not averse to bribing, but after a while, you have to say enough is enough. I decided that when I turned forty I wanted to look in the mirror and not feel any guilt or remorse about the way I'd lived my life. I know it sounds silly, but I felt that running the company was nibbling at my soul. I waited for the right time for each division and found the buyers. On my fortieth, I'd been free for years, and I ran to the mirror to check. And you know, I wish I'd seen guilt or remorse. They would have distracted me. On my fortieth birthday, looking in the mirror, I couldn't see anything but goddamn wrinkles."

— Eighteen —

Two days after her arrival and my mother still looked tired; jet lag did not become her. To the uninitiated eye, she looked well enough, maybe needing a bit of rest, but one had only to look at the weary eyes, the dollop of extra foundation under them, to see that she wasn't as robust. My father's gaze fixed upon her as she poured herself a glass of water. And we had a dinner to go to.

"You don't have to come if you're tired," I told her. We sat in my kitchen, midafternoon. "It's a casual dinner. Clark only wants to meet you. I can ask that we do it later."

In the fifteen years since I'd lived in Los Angeles, my parents had visited me three times, but this, in 1992, was the first since I had bought my new house. My father had met Clark, my supervisor. He had wanted to. Since he didn't understand much about computers, he equated programming them with magic, and he wanted to meet the arch-magician, the high priest of binaries. And now Clark had suggested he give a dinner for my parents in order to meet my mother, whom he had heard so much about.

"Don't be silly," she said. "I'll be fine after a nap. He's your boss. It can't be that casual."

I chuckled. "It's different over here, very laid-back. They don't take their dinners that seriously. I'm not sure they take anything seriously."

She finished her coffee. "Well, we have to." She stood up and began walking to the bedroom. "After all, I'm getting old, and I want to spend more time with my son. So I'm going to insist that your boss, what's-his-name, give you more time off. You'll visit Beirut more often. We'll do all that after my nap."

I expected my father, who watched her get up, either to mention his concern for her or to make a quip about my infrequent visits, but he did neither. He followed her into the room.

While my parents napped, I stayed in the kitchen reading *The Handmaid's Tale*. I noticed a sputter of movement outside. A second glance showed a brown falcon on one of the branches of my avocado tree. Its beak was a striking, unnatural red, but then it bent its expressive head and tore off a sliver of flesh and feathers. The falcon had caught a city pigeon. Blood dripped from the carcass onto a lower branch. Momentary bright red streaked before the wood sucked the color in, turning it into a darker brown. A few drops fell on a leaf—poinsettias and Christmas.

I didn't know what to do. Wake my parents? I wanted to call someone, Fatima or Lina: Look. I can see a falcon having a pigeon feast in Los Angeles. Who would have thought? I called Animal Control. "Hi," I said. "This might sound strange, but I have a falcon in my yard."

"So?" replied the Animal Control operator.

"I don't know. Doesn't it seem strange that there's a falcon in my yard?"

"There are hundreds of falcons in L.A.," she said.

Once, when I was a young boy—I must have been six or seven—my father took me on a business trip to the United Arab Emirates, where the corporation's partner was one of the ruling princes. On the third and last day, the prince drove us out of the city for an excursion. That was my first encounter with the desert. Sand dunes everywhere; no plant could survive, no living thing should in that barrenness. Giant oil fires billowed black smoke that mocked the heavens. We rode for a few hours, until we reached a cluster of tents that had been set up to host us. An impressive meal was served, and my father glared at me to ensure that I wouldn't slip and ask for utensils. I didn't eat much, because I couldn't figure out how to scoop the rice into my mouth with just my fingers, much to the amusement of our hosts. After lunch, as the scorching sun cooled, the prince decided to show off his falconry skills. He perched one of his three falcons on his leather-laden arm. Even blindfolded, it looked proud and regal. His servants unleashed a pigeon into the skies, and the prince unhooded his falcon. The predator took off and majestically dived into his prey's path. Claws dug into the helpless pigeon. The prince asked me, "Would you like to feel what it is like to have a bird of such magnificence on your arm?"

I was frightened. My father suggested I was too young. The prince boasted that he was younger when he flew his first falcon. One of his servants put a long, fingerless leather glove on my right hand. It was much too big and loose. The prince coaxed the falcon onto my forearm. The falcon's eyes were mean and menacing. I shivered. The falcon dug in his claws, and the glove offered scant protection. I felt a sharp pain. The falcon jerked and flew off, screeching as it ascended. The prince couldn't catch the leather leash in time. The falcon soared high and far.

The servants panicked, running around on the desolate sand with no apparent purpose. The prince shouted loudly and incomprehensibly. My father bent on one knee and removed the ineffective glove. Bright red bubbled from three punctures in my arm.

"Your son frightened my falcon," the prince said.

"Damn your falcon to eternal hell," my father replied. "My son bleeds."

When my father woke up from his nap, I told him about the falcon and wondered whether he remembered the one in the Emirates all those years ago. He couldn't recall a thing. I brought up all my markers—the desert drive, the grandiose flames of oil rigs, hands forming rice balls and flipping them into open mouths—but he dismissed my recollection. "I'd have remembered something like that," he said. "Your arm was hurt?"

Uncle Jihad used to say that what happens is of little significance compared with the stories we tell ourselves about what happens. Events matter little, only stories of those events affect us. My father and I may have shared numerous experiences, but, as I was constantly finding out, we rarely shared their stories; we didn't know how to listen to one another.

❧

"It is time." The woman sat under the second willow. "We must act without delay. Are you ready?" The emir's wife lowered her voice so she would sound serious and resolute. "Of course I am. The dark one and his evil mother must disappear."

"So they shall. Tomorrow, when the sun extinguishes itself in the sea, invite Fatima to tea. If you are able to remove the amulet from her person for a moment, I will make sure she never plagues your life again."

"What about the boy?"

"The boy will be no trouble. I can handle him easily."

"All you ask of me is to invite Fatima to tea and remove her amulet?"

"You must invite me as well."

"I do not understand."

"Invite me."

"Will you join me for tea tomorrow evening?"

The woman smiled, and even though her face looked like that of an ordinary peasant, the emir's wife was frightened.

I was wrong. The dinner party wasn't exactly casual. Joyce and Clark had invited three other Ellisen employees and their spouses for dinner in their yard. Joyce, a good chef, had gone overboard. When she told us we were to sit outdoors, my mother announced, "Dinner in the garden. How lovely!" After which everyone referred to the yard as the garden.

A damp warmth soaked the evening air. Clark wiped his brow and moved his chair next to my mother's. Usually, at any social event with my co-workers, we relied on Joyce and the other spouses to provide a spark. We, programmers all, weren't known for our conversational charm. Tonight, though, my mother, still dazzling at sixty, held court. My parents' aging had shifted their party roles. My mother, who used to be more reserved at social gatherings, had become more vivacious; my father, more reticent. Women used to fawn over him at get-togethers; he showered them with attention and listened rapturously to their concerns. He no longer listened as much. At some point, my mother had decided to make this evening memorable, and she was well on her way. As it had always been, gay men—in this case, Luis and his boyfriend— fluttered about her radiance like moths, and she basked. The women fawned over her now, while their husbands pretended to hold themselves back. I gave them until the third glass of wine before they unleashed their adulation.

The evening light dropped an octave lower, and my mother went into high gear, without budging from her throne. Her idiosyncratic laugh—a noisy, sharp aspiration—filled the night.

Megan, one of my co-workers, was thrilled when she tasted the soup. "Potato-and-leek," she exclaimed. "My favorite."

"Vichyssoise," corrected Luis. "You know how the Eskimos have a million words for snow. Well, Joyce has a million words for potato-and-leek soup."

"That's an urban legend," my mother said. "English probably has as many lexemes for the word 'snow' as Inuit. French has more."

"Really?" said Luis. "I always thought it was true."

"We all do, because it has a nice ring to it." My mother put her soupspoon down. "The legend began in 1911, when the anthropologist Franz Boas—aren't they always the troublemakers?—wrote that the Inuit had four words for snow. In each retelling, as with any good story, the number increased, until one newspaper mentioned four hundred."

"Speaking of four hundred," Clark said. "Now that I have you here, Mrs. Kharrat, I have to ask. Is it true that Osama has hundreds and hundreds of cousins? It's always 'my cousin did this' or 'my cousin said that.' He's always talking about some cousin or other."

"I don't think he has that many," my mother said. "He certainly doesn't have many on my side of the family." She held my father's hand. "He does have a few on his father's side. But I can see why it can be confusing for you, because in English they're all cousins. You can't even differentiate by gender. In Lebanese we have different words for each kind of cousin, pinpointing each family relationship." She chuckled. "This isn't urban legend. You can say that Lebanese has hundreds of lexemes for family relations. Family to the Lebanese is as snow to the Inuit."

Carol, another of my co-workers, had been quiet for a while, staring at my mother. Finally, she said, "I'm so envious. I don't know how you European women do it. You're always elegant without even trying."

"I work hard at it," my mother replied. "It only looks like I don't."

"No, please. Just look at you right now. I couldn't carry that off in a million years, and neither could any of my friends." She looked at Megan, who nodded in agreement. "You have very little makeup on. If I wore your blue dress, it would look silly on me. I think it's the way you carry yourself. I wish I knew how. I'm just a fuddy-duddy."

I could see my mother hesitate, surprised by the illusory intimacy. She glanced at my father and then at me, and I discreetly shook my head no. "You're not a fuddy-duddy, darling, whatever that means," my mother said. "You're very pretty, very pretty."

Carol lowered her head, as if talking to herself. The wine had infected both her diction and her loquacity. "I'm not talking about that. It's class. It's the look. It doesn't matter how expensive a dress I wear or how I do my hair. I bet you look stylish and chic in a night-gown." She paused, sank even lower in her chair, and whispered, "I want that."

Her husband swallowed a bountiful gulp of Cabernet. "Well, how about if you stopped looking like a girl? She's a woman, a lady." His third glass of wine?

The look of horror on Carol's face was no match for the ones on the hosts'. My father couldn't mask his surprise.

"Now, now. That was rude." My mother turned her full attention to Carol. "Now, dear, do you really want to hear some advice?" My mother must have had three glasses of wine, but her eyes were alert, and her gaze was ever devoted and fixed.

"Yes, definitely." Carol slapped her husband's hand.

"Do you want practical or philosophical suggestions?"

"Both."

"Get your colors done. You have to know what looks good on you."

"But I have," whined Carol.

"Oh, heavens. That's surprising." My mother put her palms on her thighs. "Well, get them done again, dear, and not at a department store this time. The Versace sweater doesn't suit you. You only wear him if you want the greasy gutter boys of Milano to hoot and whistle when you walk by. The color is wrong, wrong, wrong. You can't carry off that orange; few people could. Frankly, I don't see why anyone would want to. It's such a repulsive color, so Dutch. Get your colors done, darling. Promise me."

I knew what was coming next and could probably have repeated it verbatim.

"Now, when my son was younger—when was it, darling, ten years ago?"

"Twelve." I closed my eyes.

"Well, we got together in Paris. He was still at university and he arrived looking so bedraggled and shabby. I wanted to buy him something nice, so I took him to Boss. He loved a lot of the things, but he refused to try on most of them. I kept pestering him, and finally he said, 'It doesn't matter what I wear, I'll never look like him,' and he pointed to the delicious blond Boss model. So I told him, 'Big deal. I don't look like Catherine Deneuve, either, but that doesn't mean I have to look like that dead singer'—what's her name?"

"Janis Joplin," I said.

"Yes, her. So my boy comes up with the wisest thing. He said, 'Everything here is too big for me. I couldn't grow into it.' At first, I thought he was talking about his physical size, so I tried to reassure him—it can't be easy being small. But then I realized he was talking about something else. He really couldn't make those clothes fit him. In his mind, the Boss suit was made for that blond model, not him. And that's the secret. Never wear clothes that are bigger than you are unless you intend to grow into them. If you want to wear a great suit, either you believe it belongs to you or you'll look like you're thirteen and wearing your mother's clothes. Doesn't that make sense? It's the same in life. Never live a life too big for you. You either grow bigger to encompass it or shrink it to fit you. I wonder which country invented shrink-to-fit. Oh boy, I'm not making sense, waxing philosophical. Just call me Nietzsche—no, not him. Who's the one who wrote about aesthetics?"

"Hegel," I said, knowing full well that she knew the answer to every question she had asked me.

"Yes, call me him."

The emir's wife poured a cup of tea for Fatima, who was leery of her hostess's intentions. "Why am I here?" Fatima asked.

"I thought we should start afresh," replied the emir's wife. "I know we have not always seen eye to eye, but I was hoping we could work on our issues, woman to woman."

"How do you propose we do that?"

"By being civil first. We get to know each other as friends, no longer mistress and slave, but equals."

"But I have not been your slave for years."

"See?" The emir's wife poured herself a cup. "Our relationship is already improving. We can do what civilized women everywhere do, drink tea, chat, gossip, discuss important topics."

"If you are trying to make peace, there is no need to work so hard. I have nothing against you. I am willing to give you what you want without having to drink tea."

"I want us to be friends. We can talk about what friends talk about, the weather, fashion."

"But you only wear one thing."

"I can compromise. I can also admire beautiful things. You wear the nicest robes, and that amulet on your neck is utterly wonderful. May I see it?"

Fatima hesitated and tried to gauge what the emir's wife was up to, but she figured she was aboveground and indoors. She unclasped the necklace and handed it to the emir's wife. And the room rocked and filled with smoke and the stench of rotted flesh. A giant blue monster with three red eyes and four arms held a sword, a cudgel, a cup, and the head of a man by its hair. A necklace of skulls was her naked body's only adornment. "Fool, what have you done?" Fatima screamed at the emir's wife. "You invited a demon into your home?" She reached out to grab her talisman but was too slow. The monster unleashed a fire upon her, and she disappeared.

"You can give humans many gifts," the demon Hannya said, "but they never seem to be willing to give up their naïve humanity. One should never be allowed to be invulnerable. It is unhealthy." She extended her sword and used it to move Fatima's hand along the emir's wife's trembling lap. "This is useless now. You can wear it since you think it lovely. You had better be ready for tonight. I will not have you fail me."

✤

One day in February 1993, my mother developed a severe backache and then even worse abdominal pains. Her symptoms were difficult to diagnose in the first two days, but when jaundice made its portentous appearance, a histopathology was performed. She was offered a diagnosis: pancreatic cancer, stage IV B, and a life expectancy of two months at best. When the doctors told her, my mother didn't cry; she did what absolutely no one had expected. She walked out on my father.

After thirty-seven years of marriage, she packed a small bag—a very small bag; "I won't be needing much," she told Lina—and left. It didn't occur to her until she stood on the doorstep to wonder where she would go. She had no close family in Lebanon, and no friends, either, since they had all left during the war and had yet to return. On the spot, she made another decision that shocked everyone who knew her. She took a cab to Aunt Samia's apartment and moved into her guest room. One could say that no one was more surprised than the hostess herself.

My mother's parting words were "Let him get used to my not being there."

Was it a scandal? Not as much as one would have thought. Few people outside of family knew about it, and for those who did, Aunt Samia had her lines prepared. "But Layla is at her own home, of course," she would say. "I can take care of my sister better than anyone. It was easier to move her than for me to move in. The whole family is at my house now anyway."

To this day, none of us can figure out why my mother did it. The assumption at first was that she meant to punish my father, and her leaving did overwhelm him, but that was much too simplistic. He rarely left her side while she was at my aunt's. In the first few days, he pleaded with her to come back home, but soon yielded to her obstinacy. In some ways, she allowed him more access to her than she ever had, but she refused to return. He became her manservant in an unfamiliar home. Early on, while she was still mobile, but doped up on painkillers and exhausted from chemotherapy, he wouldn't allow anyone else to help her get around. He arrived every morning at seven, waited for my aunt's maid to bring the tray of coffee, and took it in himself and woke her. He would stay with her until she kicked him out, which she apparently did only when she thought he needed a break. Even when she became completely infirm and a nurse was brought in, he remained her primary caretaker. She triumphantly exceeded the doctors' expectations by living for nine and a half months. And she died in the hospital with her family around her, and her husband crying and kissing her hand, swearing upon his mother's grave that she was the only woman he had ever loved.

While the twins slept in their bed, millions of black ants crept into the room and carried the dark boy out the window and onto the balcony, whence he was flown off by fifteen young jinn. Still asleep, Layl was delivered to the monster sitting under the second willow.

Much to the emir's wife's horror, the monster did not hesitate. Hannya raised the arm carrying the sword and cut off Layl's head. She proceeded to cut off his arms and legs, then dug out his heart and cut off his testicles.

The head she gave to ten hyenas. "Take this to your den. Guard and protect it, for by its power you will produce the sturdiest of offspring."

Twenty eagles received the arms. "Take these to your nest. Guard and protect them, for by their power your wings will increase in strength and your feathers will decrease in weight."

The legs she gave to thirty monkeys. "Take these to your trees. Guard and protect them, for by their power you will grow more nimble."

The torso she gave to the lions. "Take this to your lair. Guard and protect it, for by its power you will be the most powerful of beasts."

The heart she kept for herself. The testicles she gave to the emir's wife. "Destroy these, for as long as they exist the demon king can resurrect himself."

The emir's wife stared aghast at the bloodied testicles in her hand. "How can I destroy them? I have no experience with such things. I am naught but simple royalty."

"Destroy them as you wish," hissed the monster, "but do not fail me."

The emir's wife swallowed the testicles in one gulp. The monster smiled.

And the scream of Shams was heard round the world.

❧

I stood at the door of the hospital room with my carry-on strapped on my shoulder, hesitating as if I needed permission to enter. On the plane, I had visualized many different scenes, but none matched the sight of my dying mother unconscious, or the despair planted on my father's face. Reality always flabbergasted me.

My father moved from despair to fury as soon as he caught sight of me. He couldn't speak, simply glared, angry and teary. Now, that was a scenario I had pictured. He considered it egregious that I would be anywhere but at his side during troubled times. When I saw Fatima in the visitors' lounge, she told me to be strong, and I knew she wasn't only speaking of my mother's decline. He sat on my mother's left side and Lina on the right. When she looked at me, I realized I was late. My sister's face was the tuning fork that forced induction. My knees buckled and I stumbled like a newborn foal. The metronomic beats of the monitor, the jagged peaks of colored lines on the monitor nauseated me. My mother's timed breathing.

I wanted to say that it wasn't my fault, that I'd taken the first flight out and made good time. Nothing would escape my lips. My sister hugged me, and my head nestled in her bosom. I squeezed my eyelids shut so I wouldn't have to look at her breasts, at my father, or at my mother.

My father hadn't shaved in at least four days, and his face seemed to grow a fresh wrinkle with each beep of the monitor. He stooped over the bed, sheltering my mother.

"She won't make it through the night," Lina whispered in my ear. When she felt me shudder, she added, "She knew it. She said goodbye." She massaged my shaking shoulders, and then led me out to the balcony for her cigarette. "She knew you were coming," she said, raising her voice a bit to contend with the traffic below. "Don't worry. It wouldn't have mattered. She's been on heavy morphine for a week, didn't understand much, and didn't really try to make sense. But she knew, so she kept saying goodbye while reciting stanzas."

A cleansing breeze whipped around the small veranda. I could hear the distinctive whooshing and popping sounds of two plastic bags being kited by the wind. "I should go back in," I said.

"Wait," Lina said. "Give him a minute."

"I didn't do anything wrong." I couldn't look at her, but heard her tears. I stared through the picture window at my Hermès-turbaned mother and my father at her side. "What did she say?" I asked.

Lina put her arm around me. "She hasn't been able to speak clearly for a while."

"You should've called me earlier."

"Don't do that," she said. "I've kept you updated. It just happened quicker than I'd expected."

"What did she say?"

"How much she loved us, how much she loved you."

"Be more specific." I shook my head. "Please."

"I don't know, she was rambling in three languages. It wasn't clear or uplifting or anything. She recited poetry that made little sense. She mixed lines and made some up, I think. She was smiling the whole time. She said she loved you, I swear."

My body slumped. "I want to go back in."

"She thought the male nurse was our father. I didn't know whether to laugh or cry. She looked at the nurse and offered him the Saadi line 'I'd rather be shackled to you in hell than stroll in the Garden with another.' Well, our father tried to get her to repeat it to him."

A graceless laugh escaped her lips.

Shams's sorrow was so deep that his wail of lament lasted one incessant week. He did not sleep or eat, and none could console him or interrupt the howl. His cry of sadness forced every creature that heard it to shed tears. The imps tried in vain to comfort him, pleading with him to help them search for his twin, but he could not hear them. They wept and begged, but Shams wailed on and on.

"Go," Isaac told his brothers, his cherubic cheeks waxy wet. "Ishmael and I will watch over him. The rest of you must find our sister and nephew. Ask every human, every jinni, every beast and insect. North, south, east, and west, search every crevice of the world. Find them."

The emir's wife knocked on her son's door, knocked again and again. The wailing broke her heart, and she wanted to mother him. She opened the door, gingerly and shyly, and entered. In the middle of the room, her prophet hugged himself, formed an orb upon a chair, his face buried in his thighs. The howl poured from his body. Isaac and Ishmael—brother demons, not parrots—each on one knee, each redder than blood, stroked Shams's head and kissed it.

She waited, crying, hoping Shams would acknowledge her. She took a deep breath to calm her soul. She cleared her throat, but the sound she made could not compete with that emanating from her prophet. "Shams," she called. "My son."

Isaac and Ishmael glared at her, but Shams—Shams looked at her with loathing, his eyes redder than the two demons. He raised his arm, his palm facing her. "Blood be upon you."

Out of nothing, out of the immediate air, blood soaked her. First her hands dripped; strings of blood fell from her fingers to the floor. She thought she was wounded, but it was not so. Her hair felt sticky. She looked at the floor, where a large puddle of blood had formed. Ecru turned to red, and her robe became soaked and clung to her body. Her legs felt viscous and clammy, and her vagina felt full. She desperately wanted to lift her robe and examine her privates but was unable to do anything other than scream and run for help.

❧

By the time my mother's funeral ended, my father looked as if he had been through wash, rinse, and spin-dry cycles in one of those tiny washing machines that fit under the kitchen counter. Still, he had to find the energy to be with all who came to offer him obsequies. He was so tired by the end of the day that he fell asleep as soon as his head hit the pillow. In the morning, we had to prepare for visitors. The day following the funeral, our house was full of people, hundreds, until bedtime—the post-death rituals meant to exhaust one out of grief. The second day, repeat.

I walked into his room the third day after the funeral. My sister was fixing his tie, getting him ready for another day of condolences. My father looked up and saw me, and his face clouded once more, a confusion of ire and despondency. "Happy you could join us," he said, as if I had been somewhere else for the previous three days.

"I'm sorry." I waited, then decided to put everything on the table. "I'm going to leave this morning. I have to get back to work."

"But you just got here," my sister said.

"You're not leaving," my father fumed.

"I have to." I clasped my hands behind my back. "I really have to."

"Why did you even bother to come?" my father snapped.

"Look. I'm very sorry, but I have to leave. I'm needed at work. You don't need me for the condolences."

"We need you," my father said. "Your place is here."

"I was here. But I also have commitments."

"If you leave, I'll never speak to you again. I'll disown you."

"No, you won't," Lina interrupted. "You'll not do that. You don't mean that."

"If you leave now," my father said, "you are not my son."

"I am your son," I said.

"No son of mine abandons his father."

— Nineteen —

One day, a bizarrely dressed man walked into the diwan. He spoke a language that the court's translator did not understand. Surprising everyone, Baybars replied to the stranger in his language and treated him with the utmost respect and hospitality. The sultan read the letter the messenger had brought and began to weep. Othman rushed to his friend's side. "What is it, my lord? Tell me and I will realign the sun and the moon to ease your sorrow."

Baybars handed the letter to Othman, who could not read it. "I can barely read Arabic, my king. Why would anyone send you a letter in this strange language?"

"To test if I am the one," Baybars said, "and this is not strange. It is my native tongue."

One of the Uzbeks took the letter. "Shall I translate? This is one of the many languages of the vast province of Khorasan, which means where the sun rises, where bakhshis play the oud and sing the great glory of God. The letter is from Shah Jamak of Samarkand, addressed, he hopes, to his lost son: 'In the name of God, the compassionate and the merciful. To our son, the prince of believers, sultan of Egypt and Syria, whose name is Mahmoud ben Jamak and whose mother is the Lady Heather. Know, my son, that, from the moment God decreed that you leave us, your mother and I have been unable to enjoy food or slumber. Your mother grieves, and I comfort her and tell her God cannot allow her suffering to go on forever. A few days before this writing, your mother found a coin embossed with your image on the obverse, and she fainted, knowing that her son lived and had become the sultan of Islam. I write to inquire whether this is true. Tell me, I beg you. Are you my son?' "

Baybars wept, and his friends joined him. "Deliver a letter to my parents. Inform them that I will be arriving soon." He stood up, holding the royal scepter close to his heart. "Tell my father who I am."

❧

It took me a few minutes to realize what my sister was up to. She wanted me to understand, but I was missing the clues she was throwing out. Breadcrumbs are harder to see along phone lines. She was entertaining herself at my expense and my father's. We had our trivial talk—I was doing fine, she was as well—before the vicarious seduction began.

"Come home for Christmas," she said. "We miss you."

"I don't think that's a good idea." It had been eleven months since I had been to Beirut, since my mother's death.

"Don't be silly. Of course it's a good idea. It's always a good idea."

She went on to tell me about all the crazy family goings-on: how Uncle Halim had flipped completely, the stories he was telling, the scandals he was unleashing; how Aunt Samia hadn't talked to her youngest son for a month because she told him she didn't want a birthday present, and he believed her. "You don't know what you're missing," she added.

"Well," I said, "you always keep me informed."

"It's not the same as being here. Come home."

"I can't. I'm too depressed." I sighed, and, as usual, the instant I uttered those words, gloom filled me.

"We'll take care of you. You need to be with us."

"I don't think I can deal with things now."

"Yes, you can," she insisted. "Hold on a minute." She didn't cover the mouthpiece, and I heard my father pleading in the background. All I could decipher was "Tell him. Tell him."

I felt the eight tentacles of an octopus squeeze my marrow.

"I'm not taking no for an answer," my sister said. "We'll even pay for the ticket. You're coming home."

"He's telling you what to say."

"The weather has been wonderful. We're thinking of going to the mountains for a few days."

"He's furious with me." I heard the embarrassing whine in my voice, but I couldn't stop. "He hasn't been able to speak to me for almost a year. The last words he said to me were that I'm not his son. I know he didn't mean it, but still, he shouldn't have said it."

"We miss you terribly," she said. "I'm glad you're coming."

"Why is he doing this? This is going to be hell."

"Oh, yes," she said, laughing. "It most certainly will be fun. And I'm going to enjoy it."

&

Baybars prepared for the trip to Khorasan and Turkmenistan. "It behooves us," said Layla, "to ask your mother, Sitt Latifah, to join us, my king. Family should meet family."

"Of course," cried Baybars. "Brilliant." He turned to Sergeant Lou'ai. "Ride forth to your hometown, and inform my mother that I am in need of her wisdom."

The convoy set forth. An impeccably outfitted battalion of the slave army rode the best Arabians of the lands, and a thousand slaves in most exquisite dress accompanied them. The king had filled a hundred treasure chests with textiles from Egypt and Syria, some embroidered with silver and gold, others of pure silk. He brought with him trays of silver, antiques of gold, and brilliant jewels from the southern lands of Africa. They left the land of the Nile and crossed the Jordan, the Euphrates, and the Tigris. They reached the lands of Persia and the mountains of Khorasan. Baybars rested in the holy city of Mashhad and sent Othman ahead to Samarkand. "Ride ahead, my friend, and inform my father that his son is near."

And when the shah heard of his son's arrival, he said, "What glorious news. Let us ride out and greet the sultan. Announce to my wife that her son arrives."

When Baybars saw his father's convoy approach, he and his companions climbed on their horses and set out to meet it. The great warhorse al-Awwar trotted toward the shah, and father and son hugged while still atop their steeds. The men in both convoys were touched by the unfolding scene before them, father and son brought together again, and expressed their appreciation by raising their swords, shouting, and cheering at the sky.

&

My father didn't stand up to greet me, nor did he utter a word. He simply nodded in acknowledgment. I said hello and asked how he was doing. He nodded once more. He slouched a bit and extended his fingers to stare at them. "Hope you're feeling better," I said.

He nodded. I looked at my sister and arched my eyebrows. She led me into my room, where my suitcase was already open on the settee but not yet unpacked.

"He's very happy to see you," Lina said. "He's just sleepy."

"He couldn't even look at me," I said.

"Don't be daft. Of course he looked at you. He doesn't want you to know he did."

❧

In the palace of Samarkand, Queen Heather ran to Baybars and nearly toppled him. She kept hugging him and squeezing him and kissing him. "You are Mahmoud, my son. I would swear to it on Judgment Day, before God the Divine." She kissed him so many times that she grew dizzy. "Wait. Let me rest." She sat on her cushions. "My eyes have seen the impossible sublime. My son, the sultan of Islam. While I carried you, I knew God had great plans for you." Baybars knelt before her and kissed her hands. "A mother knows," she added. "The king of kings even I did not imagine, but I knew you were chosen. I was pregnant with destiny."

"Be joyful, Mother. Your son bows before you. To help assuage your past sorrows, I offer you this." And Baybars opened the chests of dazzling gifts. "More important, this is the honorable Sitt Latifah. She adopted me when I had nothing and offered me all that is hers. She raised me and taught me to care for God."

The queen leapt to her feet and kissed Sitt Latifah. "My son has two mothers, further proof that he is blessed. Come sit beside me and regale me with stories of what he was like away from me." The two women talked of their son and told stories of former times.

"I, too, had two mommies," said Queen Heather. "My mother had a twin sister, and no one could tell them apart, not even my father. They raised me as one."

❧

I tried to force myself back to sleep. Not a dash of light penetrated the rolled-down shutters. The nightstand clock read four-eleven. I shut my eyes and hoped. I rolled over, but the mattress didn't seem to want to readjust, as if it knew what was best for me and was waiting for the end of my silly experiment. I resigned myself to its will. In the silent apartment, I could hear the movement of warm air within the heating system. The vents would expel the air with a sound like the long har-rumph of an ogre. I could also hear my niece's aged hamster running its wheel in her room—a hamster that had been around forever, appar-ently immortal.

I rose with the emergence of first light and had to remind myself to put on shorts and an undershirt. I left my room, not having to tiptoe—bare feet on marble barely made any noise—and walked through the corridor, the den, the main living room, and into the kitchen. I opened the fridge and couldn't figure out how anything was arranged. Soft light suddenly seeped from under the maid's door. I heard faint rustling before Fely opened the door, still adjusting her uniform, which looked like polyester pajamas.

"Please, sir," she said in Filipina English, smiling as if her life depended on it.

I smiled back. "I'm trying to get juice."

"Please, sir," she repeated, and turned on the kitchen lights. "Orange juice, coffee, every morning, five minutes." She brushed past me and reached for an untouched crate of freshly picked blood oranges, her fingers navigating the fleshy globes, choosing the best ones. The air burst with orange perfume. "Please, sir."

Fely had been the family maid for at least ten years, trained by my mother. The soft, smiling exterior belied a willful, controlling woman who ruled her domain, exactly the kind of maid my mother, and my sister, grew to love. The kitchen belonged to her. She would do all the work. I was to return to my place and would be taken care of. I went back to the den, turned the television to the satellite news, and waited. Fely came in with a silver tray, Turkish coffee, kettle and cup, large glass of red juice, and two madeleines. "Good morning, sir," she said, and retreated before I could reply. I heard the toilet flush in my father's bathroom.

He walked out of his room in morning attire, pajama bottoms and his plaid dressing gown, which didn't cover his undershirt or the dozens of chest hairs poking through the fine cotton. He stopped briefly when he saw me. "Good morning," I said.

He only grunted. He sat on the other sofa—he, CNN, and I formed an equilateral triangle. He wouldn't look at me. I stared at the televi-sion, as did he. Fely brought him his coffee and newspaper. He surreptitiously sneaked a look before unfolding the newspaper and burying his face in it. I stood and went back to my room. I didn't re-emerge until Lina woke up.

❧

Jamak and Heather held a weeklong feast to honor their son, the sultan. Samarkand rejoiced in the royal happiness. There was an archery competition on the first day, a horse race on the second. And on the eve of the return to Cairo, a dream appeared.

Layla sat up in bed in the middle of the night. "Wake up." She nudged her husband. "Wake up. I had an awful dream." Othman sat up beside her and hugged her and eased her shuddering. "The dream began wonderfully. You and I were in a bucolic meadow in a flowering springtime when, all of a sudden, an ugly crone appeared and announced that I had forsaken a friend. 'His time is up,' she said."

"Worry not, my wife. Return to sleep; perchance your dream will unfurl further."

And she did. In her dream, she looked out toward a sickle-shaped bay with two arms extending out to sea. She stood on a solid shore where footprints left no trace; the sand was free of seaweed and firm to walk on. She was thirsty, standing by a well. "Have you forgotten me already?" a voice said. "Has it been so long?" She turned around but saw no one. "You were my friend, and my sword was yours. Whenever you called, I ran to you. I have been calling for fifteen years and no one has heard. I have been erased from the stories of my friends."

"Ma'rouf," Layla cried. "Forgive me, for I thought you were dead. Show yourself, and I will ride the stormy clouds to bring you home."

She gasped as a naked Ma'rouf, emaciated and riddled with disease, appeared before her, shackled to the wall of a dark cell, his unkempt white beard almost reaching the floor. "Save me," he said. "I am about to fade away."

"Wait for me," she said. "I am coming."

And in the morning, husband and wife prepared for travel. "Are you sure we know where to find him?" asked Othman. "Hundreds of his relatives from the sons of Ishmael have been searching unsuccessfully."

"He is in Thessaly," Layla replied. "I described my dream to various seamen. All agreed that I saw Thessaly and its sickle-shaped bay, and that is where we are bound."

"So it shall be."

"I told you we should have left quickly and more quietly," said Othman.

"I did not think it necessary," said Layla. "I assumed that men have some dignity. If someone told me he did not wish my company, my dignity would forbid me to tag along. I thought dignity was a common human trait."

"Not so, my darling. Dignity is the rarest of man's characteristics."

"Funny that you should be talking of dignity," Harhash said. "Need I remind you of your previous adventures? Does anyone recall being strung up in a stable and whipped? Does anyone remember being brought into town without a headdress, tied up with his butt in the air?"

"Does anyone recall being bonked on the head as he walked through a gate?"

"I never claimed to possess any dignity," Harhash said. "I will do anything for a good story, including befriending ingrates like you two. One day, when I am old and weathered, I will be able to sit down with my friends and tell our great tales. A good storyteller can never afford the luxury of being dignified."

"Well said, my Harhash," Layla replied. "Now, what of those stories you mentioned? We have days left before we reach Thessaly. Tell me more about my husband tied up."

"What is our plan?" asked Harhash once the three friends landed in Thessaly.

"Wait," said Layla. "Look."

An ornery-looking old lady was walking along the street, bent and leaning on a sturdy cane. Every person she encountered greeted her, and she cursed them all. "Good morning to you, Old Sophia," a man said, and she replied, "A pox upon your house."

"She is our ticket," announced Othman.

The threesome followed Old Sophia into her cottage, and when she realized she was not alone, she said, "A plague upon all of you. I have nothing for you to steal, you vagabonds."

"Curses upon your head, evil-tongued woman," Layla replied. "Be quiet or I will break your jaw."

"You ill-mannered harlot." She raised her cane to strike, but Layla took it away from her and knocked the old woman unconscious. "Harlot?" asked Layla. "You think me cheap?"

Layla, disguised as Old Sophia, walked to the palace, with Othman and Harhash a discreet distance behind. Passersby greeted her, and she uttered curses in reply. While her friends waited outside, she entered the palace and came across a servant carrying a tray of food in one hand and a candelabrum in the other. The servant greeted Old Sophia, who replied, "May your home crumble upon itself and your thighs remain spread for eternity. Where are you going, my girl?"

"If only I could die and finish with this chore," the servant said. "I have been carrying food to the prisoner for fifteen years. He should expire and save himself the agony. He rots in his cell, and I rot with boredom carrying his food every single day."

"Let me help you. May you be sodomized by an incontinent mule."

"That is so kind of you. Here. Take the candelabrum and follow me."

Inside the cell, Layla saw an unconscious Ma'rouf hanging from chains. The servant began to curse and yell at him to wake up. Layla silenced her with a quick punch. She took her keys and left the cell to fetch Harhash and Othman. In the corridor, one guard said to another, "Do you think this old hag belongs here?"

Layla sighed. "You were supposed to wait for me outside," she said. "Come."

When Ma'rouf heard the voices of Layla, Othman, and Harhash and not that of the servant, he thought they were jinn. "Are you going to break our pact?" Ma'rouf said. "You promised you would leave me to my misery."

"It is I, Layla. We are here to rescue you."

"If you are not a jinni," said Ma'rouf, "stand on my right and speak to me."

And into his right ear Layla whispered, "We are taking you home, my friend."

Othman unshackled Ma'rouf, and Harhash carried him. "Take him to the ship," Othman said. "I have but one more task. I will meet the two of you on board."

King Kinyar's guards drank wine as if it were cool water, and Othman helped them along their journey by adding opium to the vat. Soon the guards were swimming in the intemperate sea of drugged sleep. Othman sneaked into the king's chamber and found Kinyar snoring in his canopy bed. Othman unsheathed his sword and whispered, "For all the suffering and anguish you have caused an honest man." He raised his sword and struck not flesh but another sword, in the hand of a young warrior. Othman thrust at the young man, who parried easily. "I do not partake of wine," he said. "Your unmanly wiles are worthless against me."

Kinyar opened his eyes to see swords clashing above his head, and his mouth dried up and would not release his voice. He pulled the covers up and groaned. The warrior's blows were heavy and insistent, and none of Othman's sword tricks were working. "Kill him, my son," said a suddenly vocal Kinyar. "Avenge the effrontery upon my person."

Taboush, the warrior who was not Kinyar's son, redoubled his attack, and his sword cut Othman's arm. And Kinyar commanded, "Finish him."

The sound of a whip sliced the air, and the sword flew out of Taboush's hand. Layla's second strike forced Taboush to retreat a step, but he drew two daggers from his belt.

"Kill them," yelled Kinyar. "I want both of them dead."

"Run," said Othman. "We cannot defeat him."

"But we can delay him." Layla struck the bedpost, and the canopy came tumbling upon the king's head. She and Othman escaped as Taboush was forced to untangle the screeching king from under the covers, canopies, and falling drapes.

❧

I lay on the couch reading, engrossed in *The Quiet American.* As the afternoon light faded, I switched on the lamp behind me. I felt myself sinking into both the novel and the couch. My father, up from his nap, walked into the den and sat on the opposite couch. He didn't say anything. I expected him to turn on the television, but he just sat there silently, his head bowed, his hands folded.

I couldn't concentrate on the novel. I lay on the couch pretending as the treasure-colored light of afternoon deepened. I kept sneaking looks and catching him averting his eyes. He sat before me, a despondent thinker, involved and disengaged.

In an older time, in a different room, my grandfather used to sit that way. When he was lost and the world befuddled him, when life refused to bow down before his desires and kowtow to his wishes, when my father and Uncle Jihad dismissed him as inconsequential, he sat among us separate and mute, downcast and downhearted, like a punished little boy facing the corner.

I sat up and fiddled with the lamp, a relic once belonging to my grandmother, once adored by my mother. I shifted it back and forth, pretending to be concerned with its inadequacies. I shut my book, stood up, and went out to the veranda. I leaned on the railing, admired the tangerine hues of the sky, watched the sun wilt into the sea, which was dotted with an archipelago of small motorboats and smaller row-boats searching for fish. The sun's sultry reflection on the water triggered all kinds of emotions. I got lost in myself, the Mediterranean as my madeleine.

My father came out on the veranda. He stayed behind me and sat on the deck chair. I didn't look back, but I felt the skin on my neck prickle. My hands were restive, and my sweatpants had no pockets to moor them. I waited a few uncomfortable minutes and slowly walked into the living room, turning on the stalactite lights of the chandelier. I lay on the big couch, my socked feet burrowing under the tessellated cushion. I reopened my book and counted the minutes. Four and a half and my father mutely settled in the living room, across from me.

Over my twelve days in Beirut, my father joined me in every room, moving when I did, following step for step, irate and cheerless, slug-gish and pensive, and not speaking.

❦

Othman, Harhash, and Layla returned with Maʿrouf to the forgiving lands, much to the joy of the great sultan and his people. But back in Thessaly, there were angry calls for revenge. "I will destroy their lands," cried Kinyar. "This is all Baybars's doing. I will not rest until he lies dead beneath my feet. I will call on the French, the English, the Genovese and the Venetians, the Spaniards. We will create a new world order. I will lead the invincible army—no, my son, Taboush, the great champion, will command, and I, his father, will follow. He is a man now."

The calls went out, promises of incredible riches were made, fight-ers swarmed from all across the continent, and an army of fifty thou-sand hungry men was birthed. An army that size could never escape the notice of the invidious Arbusto, and he traveled for days to reach it. He sought King Kinyar, who treated him with the hospitality and respect the evil one was used to receiving from fools. As soon as Arbusto saw Kinyar, he understood that Taboush was not his son, for no loaf of such sturdiness could have risen from the king's yeast. Arbusto said, "I wanted to offer my help, for I have spent years in the land of false believers."

Kinyar invited him to ride to war as his companion and counselor.

Taboush saw great minarets rising in the distance and ordered his army to halt for the day. "What city is this?"

"This is the city of Aleppo," Arbusto said. "Not only are we going to thrash them here, we are going to Damascus and Homs and Hamah, and we are going to Baghdad and Mosul and Jerusalem, then we are going to Cairo to take back the sultanate. Yeeeeaaaah."

"We camp here," announced Taboush. "Send a letter to the ruler of this city and inform him that we declare war upon the sultan. If he opens the city's gates, none will be harmed. If not, we will besiege the city until the sultan arrives."

Baybars received the news within three days and set out with the slave army to Aleppo. The heroes arrived to find the foreign army encircling the great city. Ma'rouf entered the sultan's pavilion and bowed down before his lord. Baybars begged his friend to sit beside him. Ma'rouf said, "My king, the warrior who leads this army is none other than my son, Taboush."

Baybars said, "Glory be. May God gift him with wisdom to help us against His enemies," and he dictated a letter to Taboush: "It has come to our attention that you are not the son of infidels. Your father is Ma'rouf ben Jamr, a hero and the epitome of nobility and courage. Leave your enemies and ours and return to your father's house and ask for his blessing."

Taboush read the letter and passed it to Kinyar and Arbusto, who said in one voice, "The man is a liar and says these things because he fears you. Reject his deceit and call him to battle."

"I will take the field at dawn and throw down my challenge," Taboush said. True to his honest word, Taboush's sword greeted the rising sun upon the field of battle, and his cry sent a shiver through all who listened. One Uzbek warrior rode out to meet him. The fight lasted for two hours, until Taboush finally landed a blow and the Uzbek fell to the ground. On his back, he looked up at the great Taboush, who said, "You fought well. Return to your sultan, and tell him to send out someone stronger."

The Uzbek mounted his stallion and sought Baybars. "That warrior is not the son of the king. A hyena begets not a lion. He is inexperienced in the art of battle because of his youth. If he gains the wisdom and wiles of age, he will be indestructible."

Baybars called on the best fighter of all. "Aydmur, my friend and conqueror. This boy is a great warrior and must be dispatched. Rid me of him so I may launch this war."

Ma'rouf knew that his son would not do well against a veteran hero like Aydmur. With each joust, his son would get stronger and smarter, and he would mature to be Aydmur's equal if not his superior, but he was not yet. Ma'rouf approached Aydmur as he prepared for battle. "I beg you, friend," Ma'rouf said. "Cede your place to me. I fear for my son and wish him not to suffer."

"How can you fight if you do not wish him harm?"

"I will speak to him," said Ma'rouf. "Delay but for a minute, and I will ride to meet Taboush. I chose to disobey the sultan, not you." And father and son met on the battlefield.

❦

"This was a waste of time," I said to my sister as she watched me pack.

"You're so insensitive," she replied.

"He couldn't talk to me. Why did he want me here?"

"He's upset and distraught. It's only been eleven months. What did you expect?"

"A 'good morning.' "

"Well," Lina said, "the next time you're here, he'll be able to say good morning, and the visit after that, he might be able to form a full grammatical sentence."

"I'm not coming back anytime soon."

"Of course you are. Why do you keep lying to yourself? You're coming back in two months, for a longer stay. Fatima will be here. He needs to go through this, and you have to be here to allow him to."

❦

"Does the sultan mock me by sending out an old man?" Taboush asked Ma'rouf.

"Look. Open your eyes, see with your heart. Before you stands your father."

"You are the father of lies. My father is Kinyar. Draw your sword and fight."

Ma'rouf sighed. "Do you believe cowardice could beget courage? Kinyar hides in his pavilion and risks your life. Shed my blood and you shed the blood of your father, and your grandfather, and your great-grandfather before him."

Taboush raged and struck with his sword, but the old warrior was ever quick and parried with his sheathed sword. "Wait," Ma'rouf said, holding out his palm. "If you are to fight, you must learn the skills. I face you because the sultan wished to send the Azeri. You are strong but inexperienced, not yet a match for the slave general. The first blow should never be predictable. How you open a fight is of utmost importance. It must surprise your enemy, frighten and worry him. Begin."

Taboush stared at his father. He struck.

"No," said Ma'rouf. "Still unsurprising. Try again. You rely much on your muscle." And father began to teach son the art of survival. Both armies watched in amazement at the sight before them, lessons being taught and learned. Taboush landed a fierce blow across his father's sword. "Much better," said Ma'rouf, pulling himself off the ground and remounting his horse.

"You are fatigued," said Taboush.

"And you are not yet ready for Aydmur. I will not have my son unprepared."

"Stop," Taboush commanded. "You are my father."

Ma'rouf wept in joy at hearing his son's words.

"Wait for me," Taboush said. He went back to Kinyar's army and stood face to face with his false father. "I am returning to my family," the hero announced. "I will fight alongside my people. Go home, or be prepared to die at my hands. Pack your meager possessions and leave. You are not welcome on our lands."

Taboush returned to his father and accompanied him back to a grateful Baybars.

Ma'rouf told the warrior Taboush about his mother. "She is a Genovese princess. Her father had her kidnapped and brought her back to that cursed city, where he holds her prisoner. She refused to be set free until the day I found you. I will sail today and bring her back."

"You will not sail alone," said the son, and the two heroes sailed to Genoa.

Taboush and Ma'rouf faced the king of Genoa in the royal hall. The king inquired who they were. "I am your son-in-law," said Ma'rouf. "I intend to reclaim my wife."

"You are not part of my family," snapped the king. "Whatever wife you seek does not reside here, for I do not recognize your marriage."

Ma'rouf's face and ears colored with rage. "I have come for my wife, not for your permission or approval."

"You insult us in our court? Not only an unbeliever, but an obnoxious and dimwitted one. Your breath shall leave our port city before you do." The king turned to his guards. "Throw these imbeciles in the dungeon. I never want to hear of them again."

The soldiers took a step toward the heroes but stopped upon hearing Taboush's voice. "Any man who comes within the range of my sword will have to search for his head, after which my sword will divide him in two. Save your life and save our time. Release my mother."

"Are you afraid of one man?" the king berated his soldiers. "Are my guards cowards? This man is nothing but—" He stared at Taboush, his eyes widening. The king saw the brow and cheeks of his father, and his father's father. "This man is nothing but my blood. Be afraid. My grandson. Why was I not informed my daughter had a son? Prepare a banquet. Light the lamps of Genoa. Light the fires of joy."

"Release my mother," commanded Taboush.

The virtuous Maria entered her father's royal hall, her head high and proud. She refused to bow before the king. "Why do you call for me after all these years?"

"My grandson asked for your release," replied the king, gesturing toward the hero.

Maria stared at the visitors. "Time has been unkind to both of us, but still I know you, my husband." And Ma'rouf said, "I bring you the end of your sorrows, my wife."

"How do I know he is my son?" Maria approached Taboush. When she stood before him and saw his eyes, she said, "It is you," and fainted.

Taboush did not allow his mother to fall. He caught her and carried her to a divan.

Baybars offered Ma'rouf, Maria, and Taboush a royal welcome upon their return. The sultan decreed, "Taboush is a king descended from kings. Let all who know him accept this." A tired Baybars lay on his outdoor divan, surrounded by his friends, and watched the youngster disarm every rival he faced. "A magnificent warrior," Baybars said. "You should be proud."

"I am," replied a glowing Ma'rouf. "A son that brings joy to any father's heart."

And Taboush became a hero of the lands.

— *Twenty* —

Sitting on the recliner close to my father's bed, Lina was crying so much she seemed almost happy, relieved to be discharging her sorrows temporarily—in the midst of swimming across the ocean, a few minutes on a raft. "Are you all right?" I asked.

"Not really." She sighed wistfully. Fatigue hunched and curved her. "Why don't you go home and rest for a bit?"

"I think I will, but when I come back, you'll take a break. You'll go home and take a bubble bath. I'll take a drive. I need to see the old neighborhood again."

"Why now? There's nothing there."

I shrugged. "It was Hafez's idea. I want to remember."

"And I want cigarettes," she said.

Once upon a time, I was a boy with potential. I roamed the streets of this neighborhood. Once upon a time, this was a neighborhood with possibility. Now it lay decrepit, dying. A couple of buildings were being erected. A few people walked here and there. Hope, however, was nowhere to be found. Once upon a time, I used to play in these streets, scamper between these buildings. This used to be both my sanctuary and my mystery zone. Under garden shrubs, in concrete nooks, behind ivy-covered metal railings, I hid and observed the world around me. Now everything seemed wide open. The neighborhood had developed new habits. Still, I wanted to find my way home. I wanted to walk through the lobby, take the stairs—not the unreliable elevator—go up past the apartment with the fig tree to the fourth floor, and be there, exist.

But my knees were weak. I stood outside the building leaning against my father's black car, as I had been a few days earlier, staring, lost in a world I knew nothing of. I was a tortoise that had misplaced its shell. The same old man was sitting on the same stool in the same spot. His white hair was still upright, and he still stared through me as if I didn't exist.

I always imagined depression as necrotizing bacteria, and I felt flesh-eating gloom approaching. Think pleasant thoughts.

The tangy, sweet taste of freshly picked mulberries on my tongue. Maqâm Saba.

Fatima holding me. The light on Lake Como. Fatima in a veil.

The noise on Via Natale del Grande. Beirut in April.

Uncle Jihad walking into a room. Uncle Jihad telling me stories. My grandfather drinking maté next to his stove.

Mr. Farouk in the bathtub, the oud on his dry, round stomach, playing his homeland's maqâms because the acoustics were delightful in the bathroom, playing them by the light of candles floating in the tub, playing them to seduce me into playing again.

The Arab voice of Umm Kalthoum.

My father's black hair, thick enough for fingers to hide in. My mother's beehive. The acidic smell of her hairspray. Her ruby ring.

❧

On the seventh day, Shams stopped howling, though he kept weeping. He stood up, stormed out of his room with Ishmael and Isaac keeping pace, and opened every door in the palace. "Layl," he cried, "where are you?" He walked in on the emir's wife admonishing a servant for forgetting to dust under the bed. "Layl, where are you?"

He walked in on the emir lying fully clothed on a bed, berating a naked maid. "How can you not know what Layla does to her husband, Othman?" the emir asked. "Have you not been paying attention to the story? I want you to do to me what Layla does to Othman."

"Layl," Shams cried. "Where are you?"

In the kitchen, he saw the staff preparing meals, but no trace of his twin. In the halls, viziers and ministers ran around chiding their attendants. In the dining room, thirteen servants polished silverware, gossiping and mocking their patrons. Grooms fed horses in the stables, yet there was no trace of his beloved. He ventured out of the palace and into the garden. The line of waiting worshippers remained as long as ever, all weeping and commiserating, thousands of humans, but no Layl. Their idol and his guardian imps broke through the line, back and forth, and none dared reach out to him or utter a word. Shams entered his temple, gawped at the throne. Standing before his altar, he unleashed another howl and was joined by Isaac and Ishmael.

He returned to the palace and retraced his steps, opening every door, checking every room, until he was back at the shrine howling again. For forty days and forty nights, he repeated the faithful process, a ritual of anguish, his feet landing in the same marks each time.

The fall from the worshipped to the mocked is a short one. Those who once prayed to him began to poke fun at him. The idol had become a joke. No longer the prophet or Guruji, he became Majnoun, the crazy one.

The emir's wife woke up feeling light and cheerful. She touched her husband gently, and he jolted up in bed, shouting, "Taboush, hero of the lands." He looked right and left to gauge where he was.

"I feel wonderful this morning," his wife said.

"You are hot," the emir said.

"Really?" She put her hands to her cheeks.

He raised the sheets and looked under. "Your hand is hot. Look."

She tilted her head. "Not now, dear. I am feeling good this morning."

"But look at my member's tumescence. It has never been this big. You are hot."

"Oh," she exclaimed as waves of heat shimmered up from her body.

Majnoun opened the bedroom door. "Layl, where are you?" He walked in, followed by the two red imps, tears trickling down his face. He looked under the bed, behind the curtains, behind the two chairs. He walked out.

"A momentous change has come upon me," said the emir's wife, "and I do not mean menopause."

Needing to be distracted, the emir rose and went off in search of his hakawati. The emir's wife called her maid. "Dress me in my finest." The maid stared hopelessly at the rows and rows of ecru robes. "That one," the emir's wife said, pointing. "And bring out my diamonds."

The line of devotees had not moved for days and days, but when the prophet's mother entered the sun temple, a twitter rose among the believers. The emir's wife sat on the throne, smoothed her robe, patted her hair into place. "Next."

As the tales of Majnoun traveled the land, so did those of his mother. He did not sleep, they said, he did not eat, but kept searching for a love long vanished. Demons of love tortured his restless world. His turquoise eyes had turned ruby.

His mother—his mother, though, was astonishing. She was not the bearer of miracles her son had been, but she gave better advice. She was, after all, more devout. "My child," the emir's wife said to a young woman who was problematically hirsute. "Pluck, pluck, pluck. Never shave. God does not bless those who avoid hard work. You are still young; you do not want stalks of wheat growing there when you are forty." The line grew, and the seekers returned in force.

And on the fortieth day, Majnoun left the palace. In the inhospitable desert where little lived, Majnoun wandered night and day. Every rootless tribe he encountered along the way began by mocking him.

"There walks Majnoun, the insane one. He fell in love with a boy."

"There goes Majnoun, the madman. He fell in love with his brother."

But the desert Bedouins wept upon first sight of Majnoun's unrequited grief.

With each step, Majnoun tore out a clump of his beautiful hair, throwing it behind him. The hair grew back instantly, only to be clutched and torn once more, and again. Following the forlorn one, Isaac and Ishmael walked a trail of sun-colored hair that snaked across the desert. Wind could not move the trail or change its direction, and all the weeping creatures of the desert began to follow the march of grief. Shams roamed until the trail was two hundred and forty-nine leagues, and then he collapsed upon the sand and buried himself underneath.

"Come out, my nephew," said Ishmael.

"Rise, my hero," said Isaac.

❧

The old man leaned forward on his stool and squinted at me. "I know you," he suddenly said. His hand infiltrated his sparse, spiked hair. "I know who you are."

And I awoke from my stupor.

"You don't recognize me," he said, not sounding offended. When he spoke, it seemed only his mouth moved, while the rest of his face remained still. "I remember you as a boy. I remember most of the children of the neighborhood, everyone who used to play on this street. You didn't play much." The neighborhood was eerily quiet. The cars on the main street, three bullet-ridden buildings away, seemed to be running noiselessly, images of cars instead of real. "No one plays on the street anymore." The old man stated the obvious. Anyone not interested in a mud bath would avoid walking on the street, let alone playing on it. "No one cares anymore." He paused briefly. "I didn't really live here then, which is probably why you don't remember me. My sister did. You'd know her. My name is Joseph Hananiah."

I wanted to say, "And I'm Osama al-Kharrat, your relative," but he wouldn't have understood. No one remembered the story of Hananiah anymore. Fewer still would recognize the word "Ananias." Kharrat, Hananiah, liars of the world, unite.

"You don't remember?" he asked. "My sister was Hoda Salloum. The concierge's wife. Elie's mother. Remember?"

Just what I needed. More family.

"My father isn't doing well," I exclaimed, not knowing why. "He's dying."

"I'm sorry," old man Hananiah said.

"I'm sorry, too," I said. "I just had to take a break from the hospital."

"I didn't know him well, but we all respected him. A good man, and decent. He didn't deserve what my nephew did."

"Elie was a good man as well. They were difficult times."

"Elie was a good-for-nothing fake-idealist bastard," the man went on, "bringing disgrace to us all, forcing his parent into an early grave. Even his death did nothing to ease their shame."

"I didn't even know he'd died," I said, and I tried to change the subject. "I wanted to come back here to see, to go up those stairs."

He continued to stare at a point in the distance. "Why?"

"I have never been good with answers," I said. I could tell stories, but explanations always eluded me—an observer, not an expositor, a chronic coward. I paused, felt awkward. I took a deep breath. "Forgive me. I'm just babbling."

"You call that babbling?" He chuckled. "You don't talk much."

I sat down on the sidewalk next to the old man. It was noon now, and the saffron sun stood equidistant from its goals. The world was echoing in my ears, and I had to look up at the old man when he spoke. "There's a nice family from the south living in your apartment. I think the wife and kids are up there, but I wouldn't disturb them if I were you. What's the point?"

"I have to leave anyway. I should go back to the hospital."

From a distance, a muezzin called in his faint megaphone voice, sounding like a boy reciting a lesson. I couldn't lift myself off the sidewalk. A black Toyota Camry parked right in front of us, and Hafez, ever the company man, got out of it. His dark sunglasses made him look like a blind man missing his accordion. "Hello, Joseph. How are you today?"

The old man's face lit up. "Hafez, I have a complaint to make. Your cousin didn't remember me."

"Forgive him, Uncle," Hafez said, sitting on the pavement next to me. "He's been living abroad. He doesn't remember much. That's what we're here for." He put his hands behind him and leaned back. "Did you see your home?"

"No," I said. "I've just been sitting here for a while."

"Come." He stood up and stretched, like an athlete before a run. "Let's go look."

♣

And Isaac commanded the desert's red scorpions to disinter Majnoun. From under the shifty sands he was lifted. Atop thousands of stingers he floated, and upon the trail of sun-hardened hair he was placed.

"Rise, my nephew," spoke Isaac. "Rise and greet the changing landscape."

"Rise, my hero," spoke Ishmael. "Rise and meet the new world order."

Majnoun opened his eyes and moaned. "I long," he said hoarsely, "to see his face once more, to touch his dark and barklike skin, to rake my fingers through his coarse hair. I sigh for what once was and will never be again. I am no longer one who holds the thread to my fate. Longing is full of unmanageable distances. Thus, my life is forfeit."

Majnoun and Isaac and Ishmael wept, as did all the animals gathered round them, the desert swallowing the falling tears, leaving their salt to mix with sand.

The desert snakes lifted their heads into the parched air, and one of them said, "Let it not be forfeit. Consider all pleasures life can offer, those that were and those yet to come."

"Pleasures?" cried Majnoun. "Lewd visions of my pleasures with Layl have collared my wretched soul. My eyes see nothing but his lust, and I wish for nothing but his wantonness."

"Wait," begged a camel. "God rewards the patient."

"Rediscover the enjoyment of eating," cried a vulture. "Think of what it felt like to contemplate a great meal before you, how it felt to be sated."

"Food?" wailed Majnoun. "His skin was what I tasted upon waking, and his flavor was what put me to sleep. I hunger for nothing but him."

"You are power descended from power," announced a lion of the desert. "You are the mightiest creature of above and below. You can rule us all. We will worship and serve you. Does that not entice you?"

"Power?" moaned Majnoun. "I would rather live life on my knees before my beloved than become the master of all realms. For one more kiss of his lips, I would let the Furies torture my soul for eternity. The tiniest kernel of my being has no desire but Layl, for he has melted into my heart. Power means naught if it cannot fulfill my one desire."

"I beg to differ," interrupted the owl.

"About time," said Ishmael.

"Do you remember how Psyche regained the love of Eros after all hope was gone?" said the owl. "How she survived Aphrodite's wrathful vengeance and triumphed?"

"But I am not a helpless little girl," responded Majnoun.

"You are," said the owl. "You are both Psyche and Aphrodite; both the falcon and the partridge. You are Eros as well. You are the demon king."

"That was Layl, not me."

"You are Layl as well," counseled the owl. "Surrender. Pain is proportional to wanting the world to be other than it is."

Majnoun's sun-colored hair rose and burst into flame, his skin darkened and burst into life. "I know you," he said.

"Of course, you do," sneered Isaac. "Of all things, he chooses an owl—in the desert, no less." And Ishmael said, "At least it was not a waterfowl."

"Remove your mask, Uncle," Majnoun said. "I see you."

"And I see you," responded Jacob the yellow owl.

"Rise, my nephew," said Isaac.

"Heed your destiny, my hero," said Ishmael.

"End your sorrow," said Jacob. "Your mother calls."

The emir's wife concentrated on her intention and directed her energy from her stomach up through her right hand to the hairy mole on the supplicant's upper lip. "Heal," she cried. She raised her eyelids discreetly, gently tried to sense with her hand whether the hateful mole was still present, then dramatically swung her arm back, announcing, "Behold!"

The line of seekers gasped and oohed. The supplicant's hand raced to her lips. "It is gone," she yelled, and the line broke into applause. The emir's wife beamed, bowed—she had spent a few hours just that morning practicing her appreciative bows—and sat back on the throne. She waited for the clapping to quiet before calling, "Next."

A full-figured man genuflected before her and kissed her hand. "I am regaining weight, exalted lady," he said. "It is not yet a crisis, but it will be soon. I do not wish to regress to where I was before your remarkable son touched me. I would not be able to bear it. I was hoping your gloriousness could give me a booster."

"But of course." The emir's wife slid forward, moving the ostrich-feather cushion halfway beyond the edge of the throne. "Come closer. I do not bite." She laughed at her joke but then sat bolt upright. A sudden current of heat had shot down her spine, from the top of her head to her behind. "Did you do that?" she asked the man.

"Did I do what?"

She hesitated, looked about her. No one in the temple seemed to have felt what she did. She shut her eyes, recaptured her serene self, and wore her gracious smile once more. "Where were we? Yes, come closer for your booster." She felt it again, stronger, more delicious, more disconcerting. She shivered in momentary glee, considered whether she was having another pleasant metamorphosis. Would that not be delightful? But what if it were not? She had to go on.

"We strive for perfection," she advised the attendees, "to reflect God's. It pleases Him mightily when we achieve our ideal shape. Fat people will always earn lower wages, and they are not pleasant to look at. It is God's plan. To avoid weight gain, you must look to God and worship. He will teach you to love yourself, and love is the cure for obesity."

The line hummed in appreciation. The emir's wife glanced to her left to make sure the scribe was writing down every wise word of her short yet exquisite sermon. An unfamiliar movement in the line caught her eye. She glanced up and noticed a man and his wife raising the robe of the man standing in front of them—thirteenth in line—and fondling his genitals. Before she could open her mouth to demand that they stop, she was struck once more with the surge. This time, she felt her soul shake. This time, she knew it was not going to be pleasant. This time, she was not the only one who felt it. The line was no longer straight; some supplicants looked confused, others terrified, still others lustful. One woman turned toward the temple gate and exposed her plentiful breasts. The floor rumbled, the pillars shimmied, and the emir's wife felt two more surges rush through. Her skin tingled and her vagina buzzed and the temple gate burst into an infinity of tiny shards and toothpicks.

She wanted to exhort her seekers to calm down. She wanted to shout out a warning. Her lips moved of their own accord, and she heard herself whisper, "He comes."

❦

And into the diwan came a messenger bearing a letter from the emir of Bursa to the illustrious Baybars. The emir wrote that the Mongol queen of Kirkuk, a sorceress and half-sister of Hulagu Khan, had threatened to destroy his city if he did not comply with the outrageous duty payments she was demanding. "Let us return that barbarian to the hell from which she came," decreed Baybars. "Taboush will lead an army against her. I pronounce him king of Kirkuk, with all the attendant duties and honors."

The messenger cleared his throat. "Your Majesty, courage and valor may not be a match for this wily queen's witchcraft."

"Then we must certainly send her someone wilier," Baybars said. "Othman, would you be so kind as to ask your charming wife to attend the diwan?"

Taboush led a few battalions of the slave army out of Cairo, accompanied by a most unwarlike-looking group: Othman, Harhash, Layla, and seven of her luscious-dove friends.

"Why are they traveling with us?" asked Othman.

"I do not know much about witchcraft," Layla replied, "so I thought I would ask Maysoura, whose tea-leaf reading is unsurpassed. However, she refuses to be anywhere that Lama is not, and hence I had to ask both. Rania thinks she communicates with the spirits of her deceased paramours, and that might come in handy, although it is hard to imagine what use dead philanderers might be. Umm Jihan says she can conjure jinn, but only on full-moon nights and not during Ramadan. Rouba'ia can do astonishing card tricks, and she has studied necromancy. Soumaya vows that she can change the position of weightless objects with her mind, and Lubna works with potions. I do not know if any of their powers will be helpful, but they are good company, and Lubna brews a marvelously refreshing drink using fermented hops and water."

"Should I start worrying now?" asked Harhash, and Othman replied, "Why wait?"

The witch queen's mighty army laid siege to the fort of Bursa. Upon hearing Taboush's war bugle, the enchantress turned her attention to the slave army. The Mongolian queen babbled, cursed, gestured wildly, and sent forth one of her soldiers to challenge the heroes. The Mongolian's reek preceded him by a hundred meters. Layla held her nose.

"None of them bathe," explained Othman. "They mean to frighten enemies with the stench."

Taboush nudged his horse toward the Mongolian fighter. "I will answer the call. Let us end this quickly."

"Wait," cried Layla. She searched through the saddlebags and brought out a jar. "Allow me." She ran her forefinger inside the jar and dabbed cream beneath Taboush's nose. "A mix of cucumber, lavender, verbena, and rose petals. You will smell nothing but this."

Taboush trotted toward the Mongolian. The barbarian was quick and strong. His arms moved like palm fronds in a swirling sandstorm. But Taboush was a great warrior, a scion of great warriors trained by great warriors, and he parried every stroke the maniac attempted. After an hour of sweat and blows, Taboush saw his opening and with one stroke decapitated his enemy. The Mongolian's head alit five horse lengths away.

"I do not like the looks of this," said Othman.

"That foreigner was not human," said Harhash. "Had I not seen blood spurting, I would have sworn he was a jinni. We must find out how this is accomplished."

Taboush roared victoriously, and another of the witch's men, a

Chechen, trotted out to fight him. The joust followed a similar pattern. An exhausted Taboush returned to his army dragging the two corpses behind him.

"If he goes out tomorrow," said Harhash, "they will wear him down and kill him."

"Both fighters fought the same way," said Layla, "with unusual strength and quickness."

Othman walked over to the corpses. "I will sneak into their camp," he said, sounding nasal because he had his nose covered. "I will be a Chechen."

"His clothes are too bloody," said Layla. "You will have to wear the Mongolian's."

"But I do not look like a Mongolian."

"Who is going to look at your face when your odor is so sickening? You think you will suffer? I am sending my pigeon, who has to endure being hidden on your person."

❧

And Majnoun stepped through the temple he had once possessed. Coral eyes flaring, hair afloat and aflame, he moved across the hall like a lion surveying his realm, like a tiger stalking his prey. His iridescent robe shone and shimmered with the many colors of fire. Three fire-breathing imps walked on his left, three on his right, one before him, and one behind. Neither violet Adam, indigo Elijah, and blue Noah on Majnoun's right, nor green Job, yellow Jacob, and orange Ezra on the left, looked impish. Isaac and Ishmael, sizzling and smoking, carried their agate-and-gold swords. And when Majnoun halted before the emir's wife, every ecru robe in the temple turned an inimitable bright color.

"The prophet returns," the line of seekers said.

"Son," the emir's wife said. "You have returned."

"I am not your son," Majnoun said, "and never was. You never carried me." He snapped his fingers. The emir's wife screamed as Ezra, Jacob, and Job jumped upon her and searched every inch of her body. Job raised his arm triumphantly, clutching Fatima's hand. Majnoun turned around and strode out of the temple with his fighting imps. The emir's wife tried to compose herself. The searching, the touching—she had had a divine orgasm, stigmata.

My feet felt heavy upon the broken and jagged stone of the stairs. Hafez bounded up two at a time, but I could barely manage one. Vigor filled his body—even in repose, as he stood waiting for me on each floor.

"We'll only go to your home," he said. "I don't like the squatters in ours, and they don't like me much, either. The wife in your home is quite nice and will let us in. She's trying to be accommodating, hoping we'll let her stay once the courts start dealing with this neighborhood."

I caught my breath. "Will we?"

"That depends on you. It's your apartment. You decide." He turned, climbed the next flight of stairs, and waited on the third floor. "I'm kicking the bastards in our place out." He lowered his voice as if the walls had ears. "They're insufferable ingrates. I've tried talking to them a few times, but not once have they invited me in. They probably think I'll steal something. They won't allow me to see my own home."

I hesitated on the last step to the fourth floor, but Hafez was already knocking. A young woman opened the door, a colorful scarf hastily wrapped about her face. She held a crying baby in her arms, a toddler clung to her left thigh, and a girl of about four studied us from a few steps away. The woman seemed perplexed but offered Hafez a wan smile. No one moved, and for a moment the family looked as if they were posing for a Diego Rivera mural.

"My husband is away," she said softly, a southern lilt to her accent.

"That's quite all right," Hafez replied. "I apologize for disturbing you. This is my cousin who's visiting from America. I don't mean to inconvenience you, but I was wondering if I could bring him in for a few moments. This is the home he grew up in."

She hesitated, seemed even more perplexed. "I have very little to offer guests," she said. "I haven't been to the market in several days."

"No need to offer us anything. We can't stay long, for we have to return to the hospital quickly to be at his father's bedside. My cousin wishes to recall good memories before he departs."

"Yes, of course," she said, opening the door wider. "Come in."

The foyer was no longer a foyer. It had become a storage room, with cartons piled up. A cheap runner probably covered the absence of marble tiles, which had always made a distinctive clack when my mother's heels stepped on them. The woman led us to a living room that contained nothing but three wooden dining chairs and a rusty metal garden table with a stained-glass top. No curtains covered the windows, which were cheap aluminum-framed sliders. Outside, the balcony no longer had a railing, no whorls of metal roses, nothing to protect one's heart from falling overboard. I hesitated to look at the dining room, where Lina used to practice her piano daily. In what world would the piano exist now?

"Please, sit," the young woman said. "I'll make some coffee."

"No, please," said Hafez. "Allow us a few minutes to look around, and we'll soon leave you be. Don't trouble yourself."

Her face reddened. "Do you intend to look at the back rooms?"

"Not if it'll disturb you. We don't have to go back there. How about the first room here? That's his bedroom. Can we go in there for a moment?" When she nodded, Hafez took my arm and dragged me out of the living room, back through the foyer, and into my bedroom. He closed the door behind him. "Do you remember now?"

We were surrounded by crates piled floor to ceiling. There was nothing else, barely a walkway between them. Spiders had spun intricate webs of desolation in three of the ceiling's corners. I edged to the window. Two bullet holes in each of the top corners radiated jagged scars. Hafez followed me, the crates forcing us closer than I would have liked. I was ill-at-ease and off-kilter, made uneasy by either Hafez's behavior or the past.

When we were boys, Aunt Samia used to force Hafez to spend time in my room so we'd get closer. "He's your brother," she used to admonish him whenever he complained, "your twin."

"I wonder what's in those crates," I said to Hafez. "There sure are a lot of them."

"Toilet paper," he said. "That's what's in all of them. I checked the last time."

He seemed so proud, and it confused me. I didn't know whether he was happy to be back in the old days, or to have known something I did not, or simply to have discovered that a family was storing thousands of rolls of toilet paper in my room. He glowed. "Strange," I said. The skin on my arms itched.

"Isn't it, though?" He held both my hands. "You're upset." He leaned forward and hugged me. I stepped back and banged my head against one of the toilet-paper crates.

"What are you doing?" I whispered.

"I don't know." He didn't seem nervous, let alone guilty. "I'm happy." He smiled and hugged me once more. "Don't worry. It's nothing. Come on, let's get back to the hospital." He led the way out of my room.

✤

"And where is the lair of the monster Hannya?" asked Majnoun.

"I know not," said Adam. "I searched the world, its attic and its basement, but found no trace of her cursed lair."

"And I asked every human, demon, and beast," said Ezra, "but none seemed to know."

"Or was willing to divulge what they knew," said Noah. "A Bedouin tribe gathered at an oasis thirteen leagues away seemed terrified when I asked about Hannya, and their camels shunned me."

"I will crush them," yelled Majnoun. "I will char their flesh, and their bones will speak."

"Wait," said Ishmael. "Gold may get us the information."

"No," said Isaac. "Lust will, with just a touch of the devout. I will announce to the tribe that the fine-looking prophet will offer the informer seven kisses and one lick of the teeth."

A boy and a girl were willing to inform. "A day's camel ride due northwest," said the boy, and the girl said, "You will come across a giant crater. Look for eight palms set in the shape of two diamonds."

"May I have my kisses?" asked the boy.

"May I have my lick?" said the girl.

At the entrance to the lair of Hannya, the imps stood in a circle around Majnoun. Each placed his left hand upon his brother's shoulder and his right hand upon Majnoun's body. "We are with you," they said in unison. "Once and forever."

"There will be seven gates, each guarded by a demon," said Ishmael. "You cannot enter without payment."

"Here are seven gold coins," said Noah. "Give one to each demon."

"And here are two diamonds," said Adam. "Just in case."

"Here are two date cakes," said Elijah. "We need one to get by Cerberus, the three-headed dog, and another to distract him on our way out."

"Be patient," said Job.

"Be wary," said Jacob.

"Be amazing," said Ezra.

And Majnoun, blood and fire shining in his eyes, descended into the crater followed by the imps. Daylight faded with each step, and a flame rose out of Majnoun's hair and lit their way.

The first gate was agate and guarded by a red demon in the shape of a gargoyle with a wolf's head. "Hackneyed," muttered Isaac.

"I seek payment," said the guard, in a voice that sounded like a lapdog's yelp.

Majnoun took a gold coin. He paused for an instant. "No, I will not pay." He raised his hands, and a gush of fire shot out of them, blasting the gate.

"But that is not allowed," whimpered the trembling guard as Majnoun walked by. "You cannot enter without permission. You must surrender something."

Isaac smacked the demon and followed the rest down the path.

"Your style is so different from your mother's," said Elijah. "More Vesuvian, if one were to hazard a description."

The demon of the second gate was not so lucky. He took the form of a giant snake, coiled behind his emerald gate, and hissed poison at the invaders. Majnoun roasted him and pushed through. The bats attacked after the third gate. Elijah swung his arms in the air to unleash his own bats, but Majnoun was much too quick. He exhaled, and the bats fell dead in mid-flight. He shattered the fourth gate with a snap of his fingers. The crows and ravens appeared after the fifth gate. Every one of them exploded when he looked in their direction. Majnoun and his company of imps moved through a cloud of black feathers. When the hordes of walking dead came after the sixth gate, he dispatched them with a flick of his wrist.

After the seventh gate, the fierce Cerberus blocked the path. He was massive, bigger than any demon. "Date cake?" asked Elijah, holding the gift out.

One of the heads snarled, baring its teeth, and the other two barked. Majnoun yawned, and the dog was reduced to ashes. The company followed the path.

"I would like to know who taught you all this," said Isaac. "I certainly did not."

"Nor did I," added Ishmael.

"I surrendered," said Majnoun.

Hannya towered in her underground lair in her most menacing guise. "Swear that you will not attack me," said the monster to Majnoun. "Swear that you and yours will leave me alone for now and forever, that none of you will molest me—not you, not Fatima, not Afreet-Jehanam, and certainly not those silly dolls you travel with." The monster, inhabiting her largest size, was surprised that Majnoun had entered her lair in his awkward human teenage form. Her hair grazed the ceiling, and her arms reached from one end of the cave to the other. Dozens of demons of various shapes and kinds, frozen and imprisoned in translucent egg-shaped crystals, cluttered the lair. Majnoun's mother, Fatima, was in a half-shell, a sword hanging over her unconscious head.

"If you do not swear," the monster said, "she dies. If you swear, she lives. Give me your word that none of you will try to kill me and I will release your mother. All of us can go on as we were before, pretending that nothing happened."

The imps could not keep still. Isaac chomped his teeth. Ishmael cracked his knuckles. Job snarled.

"Release my mother," said Majnoun.

"Leave me," roared the monster. "It is enough that I will not set eyes on any of you again."

🍀

The red pigeon circled in the dark sky until he saw his mistress lounging around a campfire with her seven friends. "What does the message say?" asked Maysoura.

"Every evening, the witch brews a potion that gives her fighters inhuman strength," Layla said. "The men line up at the cauldron in the morning."

"What are we to do?" asked Soumaya.

"Well," said Lama, "we do have a potion expert. What do you think, Lubna?"

"Me?" asked Lubna. "How would I know what to do about a potion like that? If I did, I would be wealthy. The one thing I do know is that if a potion is to succeed, all the ingredients must be mixed exactly right. If Othman can throw something into the brew, it will be ruined."

"He cannot get close enough," Layla said. "Maybe we can—or at least our pigeons can."

"Brilliant," cried Umm Jihan. "I have trained my pigeons to be strong. They can even carry a small olive branch."

"What should we add to the brew?" asked Rania.

"We cannot drop anything large," said Layla, "or it will be noticed. No olive branches."

"I have sage," said Soumaya, "and coriander."

"I have a better idea," said Lubna. "My pigeons will hate me, but I do know how to make one special potion. It comes in handy every now and then."

"Inspired," said Layla. "That is positively inspired."

"My poor pigeons," said Lubna. "I will try to explain to them that the effect will not last long and their bowels will settle in time."

In the morning, the Mongolian queen's men drank the odd-tasting potion out of the cauldron. As soon as the first was within range of Taboush's sword, his severed head lay on the dry earth with an immortalized look of shock. The second soldier to accept Taboush's challenge fared no better and was dispatched in seconds. The sorceress cursed her cauldron. "Have you nothing better?" cried Taboush. "Is there no warrior worthy of being killed by my sword?"

Layla mounted her mare and descended to the jousting field. "Allow me," she said to Taboush. She sat up in her saddle and let out a cry. "You ignorant barbarian. You are nothing but an amateur, a pretender, not a queen. I heap insults and curses upon you. If you have any honor, heed my call. Your minions are not worthy of our warrior and never will be. I proclaim you to be as insignificant as your underlings. Come out and prove me wrong."

The witch queen fumed. "A kingdom that sends its whores to defend its honor has none." She turned to one of her Mongolians. "Come with me. I must prepare. I will teach that scarlet harlot a lesson that will serve her well when she arrives in hell." She entered her yak-skin tent, followed by the Mongolian. "She calls me a pretender? I will show her what a real queen's wrath looks like. I will bring down the force of thunder upon her head. By the way, I do like all that blood around your collar. I shall have all my warriors follow your sartorial example."

When the queen rode out to meet her challenger, Taboush warned Layla, "Be careful. She is a mighty witch. How are you going to fight her?"

"I can tell by the way she holds her head that she is not a sorceress, let alone mighty. She is my beloved."

Othman, dressed in the Mongolian queen's garb, trotted up to them. "The wicked witch no longer breathes. I do not think her men will offer much resistance now."

Taboush blared his war horn, and the army of innocents attacked their enemy. The battle was short-lived, for the barbarians surrendered quickly, having lost the will to fight. The hero of the lands traveled to Kirkuk, where he was to rule, and Othman, Layla, and their friends returned to Cairo.

❦

Fatima's eyes sprang open as she was being carried aloft by Noah, Elijah, Ezra, and Jacob. She saw the mossy cave with shards of marble embedded in the ceiling, the remnants of a shattered gate. "Stop," she demanded, still groggy. "Put me down." She looked around and directed her question to Majnoun, "Where is your brother?"

"My brother is no more."

Fatima disentangled herself from the arms of the imps and stood up. She measured her surroundings and held out her hand, and Job placed her talisman in it. She marched back down the path, followed by the imps and her son, who kept staring at the ground before him.

She stormed into Hannya's lair, and the ground shuddered with each step, the walls quaked with her rage. "Explain yourself before you die," Fatima commanded. "Why did you kill my son? Did you not consider the consequences?"

Hannya let out a long, loud sigh. "We do what we must. Does the extinguished candle care about the darkness?"

"Your time has come," Fatima cried.

"No, it has not. You are bound by your son's word not to harm me. Begone. You and your son may be mightier, but you no longer have dominion over me."

"Foolish, foolish woman. You should have killed me when you had the chance." Fatima raised her arms in the air. "Death will expiate death."

The monster rolled her three eyes. "Useless theatrics. You can cast no spell against me."

"What you have fed upon," Fatima declared, "will now feed upon you," and she unyoked Hannya's imprisoned demons and watched the monster's gigantic face blanch.

"Wait," screeched Hannya. "Wait. Let us bargain. I have something to offer you. I have something you need. I have the—" But the demons, set free from their shackles, descended upon their torturer. Hannya fended off the first three, and the fourth, and the fifth, but she was shortly overwhelmed, was slowly devoured. Her dying scream vanished first, and then her hands and arms, her legs, her head, until naught but space was left of her.

— Twenty-one —

In the early morning, before it was light enough to tell a white thread from a black one, Beirut was pristine and shockingly loud—two apparently interrelated phenomena. The streets were empty except for gigantic green garbage-trucks, and I got stuck behind a particularly noisy one. There were many strange differences between my two homes, Los Angeles and Beirut, but for some reason none seemed more telling than garbage-collecting: in L.A., garbage was picked up once a week; in Beirut, four times a day. Farting and chugging, the truck stopped every few meters and wouldn't let me pass. Finally, when the dark-skinned garbagemen jumped off to the right to empty the next building's Dumpster, I steered left onto the curb and passed the truck. The driver seemed despondent and oblivious.

The hospital's main entrance was still locked. Around the corner, the emergency-room entrance sucked me in with a barely audible hum. The hum of the fifth floor's low fluorescent lights was more than audible. I followed the crayon lines along the floor, past the visitors' lounge, past the unmanned guard's desk, into the cardiac unit, past the rooms with their aquarium-window exhibits of aged, frightened patients.

No one would have recognized my father. What I remembered of him was nothing like what lay before me. I wanted to slap myself, wake up. I stroked his forehead. Fatima was snoring on the gurney. My sister was awake on the recliner, staring at my father's prostrate form.

I went to her, touched her shoulder. "I couldn't sleep," I whispered.

"Neither could I." She reached for my hand, either as a comfort or to comfort me. "Every time I dozed, I dreamed he and I were having a big fight. He was angry and unforgiving." She leaned into my arm. "I'm terrified of sleeping."

"Now that Hannya is no longer in this world," said Majnoun, "I will make her world mine. Her lair will be my home." He began to sweep the floor with a makeshift broom while humming a dirge.

"Your son has not been well," Isaac said to Fatima.

"But he is getting better," said Ishmael. "Night and day."

"He will soon be healthy and thriving, if incomplete," said Jacob.

"It would have grieved me," said Fatima, "had he been anything but devastated. With the aid of time we shall heal him. Yet we must also find his brother."

All eight imps stared at their hooves.

"We have been trying," said Noah. "We have searched everywhere."

"That fornicating demon Hannya cut him up," said Adam, and Fatima wept.

Majnoun swept his broom into a corner and felt a prickle travel up through the handle. He bent and picked up an obsidian box the size of his hand. "Mother," he called across the commodious cave. "I have found him." Fatima and the imps ran toward him. She stared at Layl's heart, lifted it, held it to her own. She let out a piercing wail and was joined by the imps. But grief, the vampire, did not overcome Majnoun. His face shone red, and his hair burst into flames once more. He reached for his lover's heart, took it from his mother. Coddled in the palm of his hand, the heart glowed and pulsed.

"We can rebuild him," said Elijah. "We have the ability."

"Resurrect him," said Adam.

"In our nephew's hand, the heart lives," said Job.

"Layl will rise once more," said Ezra.

"We will need all of him," said Fatima, "as well as a miracle."

With his beloved's heart close to his, Majnoun said, "I know where my adored is."

❦

When Baybars was informed that Othman and Layla were almost at Cairo's gates, he announced, "It is time for our city to honor my friends. Let us celebrate their victory over the Mongolian queen. Taboush has to deal with the affairs of Kirkuk. We will have another celebration when he arrives. Let us surprise Othman and his wife." Cairenes clogged the streets; shouts of joy and ululations erupted throughout the city. Before thousands, Baybars lauded Othman and Layla for their victory over the witch queen and for their longtime service to his kingdom. He covered their bodies in gold and covered their heads with turbans of valor.

"I do not understand," said Taboush as he sat in his diwan in Kirkuk. "Why does the sultan choose to insult me so? He honored the face-cream woman for my victory. Am I not deserving? Have I not served faithfully? How can I show my face in public after being shamed? I led the army. I am the war hero. Why honor his friends at my expense? This cannot be."

And the steward opened the doors of the hall and announced, "There is a priest by the name of Arbusto who begs a moment of your time."

❧

Wan and serene, Aunt Samia appeared in the visitors' lounge, flanked by two of her boys, Anwar and Munir. Salwa, sitting on my right, looked as if she would sacrifice her firstborn to be back in my father's room, or anywhere but the visitors' lounge. Hovik had his arm around her shoulders. She reached out and held my hand. I lifted hers to my lips and kissed it.

"He's coming soon," she whispered. "I can feel it." She mistook my incomprehension for shock and concern. "Don't worry. There's nothing wrong. He's just kicking. He wants out."

"But you're not due for another week, are you?"

She shrugged. "I know when I'm due. I'm not saying he's coming this minute. Soon."

"She would know," Aunt Samia interjected. "I always knew, long before the pain." She paused, looking at no one in particular. "What are you going to call him?"

Hovik started to answer, but my niece was quicker. "We're not sure yet," she said.

"Call him Farid," my aunt said. "That would be such a nice gesture. Your grandfather would be so pleased."

"I don't think I can do that," Salwa said. "I don't see how. I'd never be able to yell at him. How could I punish my child if he was named Farid?"

Aunt Samia looked confused. "Another name, then. Keep it in the family. 'Jihad' wouldn't be good. 'Wajih'? You didn't know him, so that shouldn't be a problem."

Hovik decided that was the moment to begin participating in the family sport: teasing Aunt Samia. "We're thinking of calling him Vartan, after my father," he said.

"Oh," she exclaimed. "An Armenian name. Is saddling your son with such a burden a good idea?"

"It's a great name," replied Hovik. "It means 'the one who brings roses.' "

"In what language?" asked Aunt Samia.

"In the grammatically incorrect one," I heard myself say.

Hovik leaned forward to see if I was channeling a spirit. He chuckled. Salwa smiled. Her turn—she brought my hand up to her lips and kissed it.

"I think it's a good name," Hovik said.

"Isn't the first son supposed to be called Antranig?" I asked.

"I don't know. I wasn't."

"And you weren't called Hagop or Zaven. I thought all of you were called either Hagop or Zaven."

"That's bad," Hovik said, laughing. "That's so unfunny."

Salwa seemed about to break into grateful tears. She brought my hand to her stomach and covered it with her own. "We're going to call him Murad," she told my perplexed aunt. "I've always loved the name. When I was a little girl, Osama used to tell me stories when he came to visit." She paused to settle her voice. "A lot of them were your father's stories."

"And none of my father's stories were true," my aunt said.

"It doesn't matter. One story was about a gorgeous dervish boy called Murat. I swore I would name my son Murat so he would grow up to be handsome and loved."

"We can't use the Turkish form of the name," explained Hovik, "because I have relatives who'd slit my throat for even considering it. We're going with a beautiful Arabic name. Murad."

Aunt Samia clasped her hands around the purse on her lap and said, "And may he grow up to be handsome and loved."

"From your lips to God's ear," said Hovik.

"Help me up," said Salwa. "We should go check on him."

She was so surprisingly heavy that I almost tumbled on top of her as she stood. As soon as we cleared the doors, she began to weep. "You will be Murad's storyteller, won't you?"

❧

First the torso. Up in the sky, upon the carpet, Majnoun said, "I will deal with the lions."

"They are mighty beasts," said Jacob.

"Do not be excessively cruel," suggested Isaac. "They did not kill your brother."

"And in your time of need," said Ishmael, "they were a comfort."

The cave was in a rocky oasis in the middle of the desert. It was guarded by seven lions that roared as soon as the company alit in their midst. The rest of the pride dribbled out of the cave one by one, a solid fifty strong. The king of the beasts announced his arrival by unleashing a forceful roar. "I am here for my son," Fatima said.

"You might as well have stayed at your lair," the king of lions said. "I will not give up our treasure, whose presence has increased our strength a hundredfold." And those were his last words. Majnoun held the heart before him, and the king of beasts exploded into nothingness.

"I will recover my love," said Majnoun, walking toward the cave.

And then the legs. Into darker Africa they traveled, along the Nile and beyond its seven mouths. "Be wary," warned Ishmael. "The monkeys are tricksters, and Hanuman is their god. We cannot allow ourselves to fall for their wiles."

Majnoun pointed toward a dense carpet of sausage trees and baobabs. Upon landing, they were beset by a large band of monkeys, who tried to appear threatening but could only manage irritating. They floated between branches with ease and grace and jumped impossible distances.

"All travelers who pass through my realm must answer my riddle or die." The monkey king's voice, like its master, traveled from branch to branch.

"You said they followed Hanuman," Isaac told his brother, "not the Sphinx."

"I will reduce you and yours to ashes," said Majnoun, "and char your timber into ember."

"Ask now," commanded Fatima.

"Riddle me this," said the monkey king. "What has one voice, is four-footed at dawn, two-footed at noon, and three-footed at dusk?"

"Oh, please," said Job.

"Not that again," said Isaac.

"Who cares?" said Elijah.

"Now give me what belongs not to you or your kind," warned Fatima.

"I will do no such thing," said the monkey king. "Solving the riddle only wins you safe passage. I will not—" The monkey king was no more.

❧

I would be Murad's storyteller, and I hoped he would one day hear me. My grandfather told stories to his children, but only Uncle Jihad heard him, and even he stopped listening by the time he became an adult. My father pointedly refused to listen, neither to his fairy tales nor to his family stories. "I have very little interest in lies and fabrications," he used to say.

A week before he died in that awful spring of 1973, my grandfather told me a story in my room, a tale he hadn't told me before. Maybe it was because he'd thought I had finally reached an age, twelve, when I could understand more, when I could listen better. Maybe he knew he was dying. He was in a good mood, though—ebullient, the corners of his lips pointing toward the ruffles of hair in his ears. His version of the death of Abraham he told me that day.

"And the end approached," he began, "as it always does. Nearer and nearer it came. Abraham, one hundred and seventy-five years old, knew the signs, for his wife had passed away before him. On his deathbed, he whispered to his son, 'I need your health, for mine is fading. I beg you to search for your brother. I promised your mother that I would never try to see him, but I wish for him to see me.' Isaac saddled his horse and rode out to find Ishmael.

"And in a different land, Hagar consulted her heart and knew that her beloved was leaving this world. She woke her son and said, 'Rise, Ishmael, rise, and seek your father, for he will soon be welcomed within God's bosom.' Ishmael sat up and said, 'Come with me, Mother, and we can both say our farewells.' And Hagar declined. 'I have spent lifetimes away from home. My heart has been immured for much too long. Even a hint of what might have been is unbearable.'

"As she bade Ishmael farewell, Hagar wondered, 'Had I done the right thing?'

"And when Isaac came across Ishmael in the desert, he recognized him, for, even though his brother was exiled when he was a baby, Isaac saw his father in his brother's eyes. Ishmael recognized his brother, for he saw his father in Isaac's eyes. And the brothers embraced, for each saw himself in the other, and they rode home to their father.

"But they were not in time, because Abraham had kept his promise to his wife and died before he could see his son. Ishmael and Isaac, kneeling before their father, wept and lamented their destinies. And Isaac said, 'I regret so much,' and Ishmael said, 'I as well,' and Isaac told him, 'Your father wished you to see him,' and Ishmael held his brother's hand. The brothers mourned and grieved together, and comforted each other, for their loss was one.

"Ishmael and Isaac buried their father in the Cave of Machpelah, in the field that Abraham had purchased from the Hittites, what is now the Tomb of the Patriarchs in Hebron."

The arms. The carpets soared above the mountains of Lebanon, past the great cedars, atop which the eagles had their nests. The birds flew in a threatening formation, their king in the lead.

"Return whence you came," cried the eagle king. "Demons are not allowed in our skies. Begone or die."

"Their skies?" asked Job.

"I loathe eagles," said Isaac. "Prissy and pretentious creatures." A popping sound, and Isaac disappeared, and reappeared riding the eagle king's back. He began to pluck feathers one by one. "This little eagle is prissy," Isaac sang, "this little eagle is not going to fly, this little eagle thinks it rules the world, this little eagle shall die." Isaac did not stop until nary a feather was left in its place. The eagle king fell to his death, and Isaac popped back onto his carpet.

And then the head. The hyenas' den was located in a soft desert between the Euphrates and the Tigris. When the company reached the den, not one hyena was to be found, and Majnoun retrieved his brother's head.

"The sultan is a pretender," Arbusto said. "An honorable man metes honors to the deserving, not to his loved ones. The sultanate is being run by whores and thieves and begs to be rescued from its rulers."

Taboush sat upon his throne and pondered the appalling plight of the world. "I do not know what to do. I do not think warring against one's people is either auspicious or admirable."

"A true sultan can distinguish right from wrong," said Arbusto, "an undeserving one cannot. He dishonors you because he fears you. You are a hero descended from heroes, a king descended from kings. He is but a slave whose luck lifted him to the throne, and the throne weeps while it waits for a worthy occupant. Rise, my lord, and claim what is rightfully yours, if for nothing else than to offer the faithful a commendable leader and a righteous example."

"I do not know what to do," said Taboush.

"Call your army. Begin with the city of Aleppo. Once the people see the sultanate's honest hero, they will declare their allegiance to you. If they do not, we will raze their walls as an example to other cities." His eyes lit up, and his pupils moved in every direction. "Not only are we going to thrash them in Aleppo, we are going to Damascus and Homs and Hamah, and we are going to Baghdad and Mosul and Jerusalem, and then we are going to Cairo to take back the sultanate. Yeeeeaaaah."

Taboush did the honorable thing. He wrote a letter to the mayor of Aleppo, warning him of the imminent arrival of the army of Kirkuk. Taboush asked the Syrian city to surrender to his rule, for he did not wish to shed blood. And the mayor of Aleppo sent a message to King Baybars. "Prepare the army," commanded the sultan. "Black days are upon us. Sons will fight their fathers, and brothers will fight brothers. Dispatch a letter to the Fort of Marqab, since the sons of Ishmael are the closest fighters to Aleppo. Inform my brother Ma'rouf of this calamity."

And when Ma'rouf read the letter, he smote his head. "The Day of Judgment nears."

"My heart aches." Taboush stood with his army before the gates of Aleppo.

"The honorable course is rarely easy, and a hero always suffers," said Arbusto.

The defenders of Aleppo cheered as the sons of Ishmael appeared on the horizon, trumpeting the songs of war. The warriors lined up, and their hero rode out toward the invading army and cried, "Return to your homes. I will defend this faithful city unto my death." And Taboush recognized the voice of his father.

"Send a warrior to kill him," said Arbusto.

"None but I will stand before my father," said Taboush, as he jumped on his stallion.

"What are you doing, my son?" Ma'rouf asked.

"I seek to displace a usurper," said Taboush.

"The suit of the dupe does not become you. The honorable sultan is our rightful lord."

"Move aside, Father, for I have no wish to fight you."

"I shall not," replied his father. "No one passes while I still breathe." And neither father nor son moved, but stayed face to face for hours and hours, neither looking away nor surrendering, until the sun finished its daily pilgrimage, for no day is so long that it is not ended by nightfall.

Back in Hannya's lair, Majnoun, Fatima, and the imps put Layl back together. Adam laid the torso down, Elijah fastened one leg and Noah the other, Job and Jacob secured the arms, and Ezra attached the head. Majnoun returned the heart to its place and watched it glow and glimmer before tuning itself to a normal pulse. Fatima closed the wound and cleaned it.

"Something is missing," said Ishmael. "He is not whole."

Elijah said, "He has his penis but no . . ."

"Testicles," said Majnoun.

"Bring me that sycophant," ordered Fatima. "It is time to deal with the mother of betrayal."

Taboush polished his swords.

"You must kill your father," said Arbusto. "You cannot fulfill your destiny otherwise He is as stubborn as you are. You are both cut from the same inflexible cloth."

"I will not."

During the dark night, Arbusto infiltrated the camp of the sons of Ishmael disguised as a Muslim cleric, and in the morning, he approached Ma'rouf as the hero mounted his horse. Arbusto offered him a cup of soup and said, "Drink this, my lord. It will give you strength."

"I have the strength I need," replied Ma'rouf.

"Then drink this because it tastes good."

And Ma'rouf drank the poison before riding to meet his son.

"Move aside, Father," his son said.

"You will have your wish." Ma'rouf swayed upon his horse. "I have been poisoned. Soon I will breathe no more, and you will be able to pass."

Taboush watched his father collapse off his horse and die. Grief and guilt, the inseparable siblings, blighted the son. He rued his stupidity, his pride and impetuousness, and the day he arrived in this world. He wailed, mourned, and suffered.

"Bring me the evil one," Taboush commanded.

When Baybars arrived, he did not find an invading army or a raging battle. He found a contrite hero genuflecting, the corpse of his father on his right and Arbusto in chains on his left. "I have committed sins," Taboush said.

The chief of forts and battlements was buried with full pomp and colors. The funeral lasted three days. After the mourning, Baybars called on the diwan.

"I can no longer be king," Taboush said. "I should not exist among the living. I have failed my father. Justice must be served. I cannot walk among honorable men any longer. I will leave the lands of the faithful and seek exile until my soul is cleansed."

"Stay not away for long," said Baybars. "Your home always beckons."

And Taboush walked away. East was his direction; forgiveness and exculpation, his goal.

❦

The emir's wife no longer dared to set foot in the sun temple proper. She was not afraid of violence or violation—her people were too sweet—but she was terrified of being seduced into the bacchanal. When the prophet made his glorious appearance in the temple, a multi-hued orgy had erupted, and it had not stopped or decreased in inten-

sity since. The liveliness, the combinations, the positions. The emir's
wife had tried to stop it the first day, but as she began to talk to the
seekers, one handsome supplicant, in the throes of receiving oral pleasures, touched her calf, and the bliss was so intense she felt her robe
slowly slip off her shoulders. She had rushed out of the temple, and
had spent every waking second since peeking from behind the sun
altar. Her prurience was in full flowering bloom. The liveliness, the
combinations, the positions.

That morning, she woke and did not bother to wash. She rushed to
her favorite position in the temple, where she had a full view yet was
unseen, to begin her new daily ritual. She watched, entranced, and
slowly her molten insides built up the delicious pressure.

And the colored imps burst in on her secret. Elijah, Ezra, and Job
grabbed her, and she felt herself fading, only to re-emerge in a cave, on
her knees before her nemesis.

She could not tell at first what frightened her most. Was it a furious
Fatima wearing an obvious intent to harm? Was it her almost unrecognizable son, whose red eyes glared with loathing? Or was it the sight of
the murdered one sleeping, obviously no longer dead, still as horrifi-
cally ugly as ever? It had to be Fatima.

"I did not mean it," the emir's wife sobbed. "I did not know."

"You forsook your son," chided Ishmael.

"You killed your son," said Adam.

"And gloried in the killing," said Jacob.

"Your flesh and blood," said Ezra.

"The fruit of your loins," said Elijah.

"For that and more," said Noah, "you must die."

"But it is not yet my time," said the emir's wife.

"I will retrieve my beloved." Majnoun's hand stabbed the emir's
wife. Into her stomach his hand penetrated, and retrieved Layl's testicles. The emir's wife breathed no more.

Fatima knelt before her dead double and touched her wound, healing it. "In death, you are complete."

And Majnoun made his love whole.

♣

Tin Can could not mask his concern. "The dialysis hasn't helped," he
said, "and his liver seems to be failing."

My sister shook her head. She looked as if she wanted to say something but had no idea what. My tongue exploded with the taste of tin and aluminum.

❧

"And what shall we do with the odious one?" asked Baybars.

"Let me kill Arbusto," said one of the Africans, "for all the pain he has caused."

"I will cut off his head," said one of the Uzbeks, "for his betrayals."

"I will hang him," said Aydmur, "for all the deaths he has caused."

"I will burn him," said Othman, "and leave not a trace of him on this earth."

"And what would you do?" asked Baybars.

"I?" said Layla. "I would whip the skin off his body and crucify him in the harsh desert, so that his ignoble soul departs in agony."

"So it shall be," decreed Baybars.

❧

The skin around my sister's eyes was slate-colored, and streaks stained her cheeks. Her world seemed to include not one inch more than my father on the bed, a reverse pietà. Her breathing was a tobacco-raspy susurration.

"Are you all right?" I asked.

She nodded an indifferent assent. Fatima, on the other side of the bed, whispered, "No, she's not." My sister looked at us finally, and infectious desperation and pain flared out of her eyes. "I can rest after," she said, and then, more softly, "It won't be long."

"Go out on the balcony," my niece said. "Smoke. Get out of here." She crooked her head in my direction, then toward the glass door.

"I'll come with you." I took my sister's hand.

❧

Layl opened his eyes.

"My love," cried Majnoun. Layl moaned. He took a deep breath, and his face turned pale. He rolled on his side and began to retch, nothing but spittle leaving his mouth.

"Are you all right?" asked Majnoun, holding Layl.

"Calm yourself," said Fatima. "Take your time."

"I am in pain," Layl said. "I do not belong here."

"Of course you do, my darling," Majnoun said. "You have been away for a while. It will take some getting used to."

"I do not wish to be here."

"Have patience."

"I should not be here," said Layl.

"Of course you should. I have brought you back. Your place is with me."

"No." Layl lifted his head off the floor, and then his torso. He paused on all fours, could not raise himself any more. "I must go." He crawled seven paces in one direction, turned around, and crawled back.

"He is not himself," said Ishmael.

"He will get better," replied Majnoun. "He has to."

Layl crawled in a widening spiral. Majnoun walked behind him step by step, his arms reaching out. Fatima's hands covered her mouth. "I want you," said Majnoun.

Layl crawled and crawled until he was suddenly atop the naked corpse of his mother. "What?" he asked.

"Beloved," Majnoun begged, "you will get used to life."

Layl bent his head and kissed the emir's wife's lips. "Wake," he told her. He kissed her once more. He ran his hand across her forehead, smoothed the hair off her face.

"No," cried Majnoun.

And Layl made love to his mother.

"No," cried Majnoun.

And Layl gave himself to his mother.

"No," cried Majnoun.

The emir's wife opened her eyes, and Layl closed his and died once more.

❧

A solitary pigeon settled on the railing of a balcony a floor below us. Lina lit her cigarette. She looked glum and dignified. She coughed and cleared her throat.

I waited for her to say something. The morning sun bathed our skins in tawny hues.

"I haven't been able to stop thinking of funeral arrangements all morning." She began to cry. "I don't want to go through this now. Not now." She shook her head, wiped her tears with a used tissue. "I'm at a loss. What should we tell people? He's not going to make it through the day. Should we tell Samia? Should we bring her in to see him?"

I grabbed her cigarette pack and lit one. "Let's wait."

"He's not responding to anything. He seems weaker than even an hour ago. He looks like he's in a deeper sleep. We have to talk to him." She sighed. Her hand traveled to my neck and drew me closer. "We have to say goodbye. You should do it. You didn't get to talk to Mom, and you know how that made you feel."

"You do it," I said. I couldn't remember what my father's last words to me were. "I wouldn't know what to say. You're better at this than I am."

"What makes you think I'm better at this?" Lina smiled weakly, childhood shimmering on her mouth for a moment. "You don't have to say the perfect thing. You just . . . just . . . just tell him you're here, that you care for him. It'll be good. Come on. Let's do it now."

⁂

After a day in the ripe sun, even moonlight scorched Arbusto's skin. Yet hope entered his heart when he realized that the guards assigned to him were gone. If only he could disentangle himself from the cross, he would have a chance, but the nails dug too deep, and the ropes were too snug. He prayed for rescue, and his prayers were answered.

A trader appeared in the night, riding a pale horse abreast of seven camels, his beasts of burden, who carried their weighty loads with dignity and grace. "Help me," cried Arbusto. "Rescue me and I will cover you with more gold than you can imagine."

The trader contemplated the suffering man. "I have a wild imagination."

"And I deep gratitude and pockets," replied Arbusto.

"Then this is a most promising night."

The trader dismounted and climbed the cross. He cut off the binding ropes.

"Be careful with the nails," said Arbusto.

"I will be ever careful with you." The trader used both hands to pry out the first nail.

"But . . . ," stammered Arbusto, "but you are not hanging on to anything."

"Have you still not recognized me? I have been looking for you, and you have not been easy to find."

"You are not human," gasped Arbusto.

"Is anyone?"

"O jinni. Do not take me. I can make you the richest demon in the world."

"That I already am. I am so rich I can afford to unburden my camels, laden with the souls of all those whose deaths you have caused."

"You are Afreet-Jehanam."

"I am known by many names. Jehanam is my domain, and it is where I will take you."

"Hell will be my home."

"Most assuredly."

"Death, the scourer, has come for me."

Majnoun held his head and wept. Fatima embraced him and tried to comfort him. The imps surrounded mother and child.

"I cannot bear it," Majnoun said.

"I cannot, either," said Fatima. "Yet we will manage."

"We are with you," said the imps.

"I feel refreshed and rejuvenated," the emir's wife said to herself. "I am so alive."

"Even among you," said Majnoun, "I am so alone."

"Grandfather," my niece said, "can you hear me? We're here." Four of us surrounded his bed. I sat on his right, Salwa and Fatima on his left. Lina stood behind me, her hand on my shoulder. The machines were still going strong. The ventilator inhaled at the same clip. Lina gripped my shoulder.

"Father," I said, "it's me, Osama." I was disappointed, unreasonably so, by the absence of any reaction. I glanced back at my sister, who was crying and smiling at the same time.

"Grandfather," my niece said, "can you squeeze my hand?" She shook her head, then glanced at me. "Grandfather," she said, "do you remember how Osama used to tell me stories when I was a girl? I was talking to your sister a few minutes ago, and I remembered. Do you?

During the war, I used to get so nervous, and he told me stories about your father."

Fatima was trying to cry silently, and failing. Lina kept nudging me. "Yes," I said. "I used to tell her stories. I was there."

"They were wonderful stories," Salwa said. "I always felt that I knew your father, that I was alive when he was. The same for Uncle Jihad. They were odd characters, but I knew them. I'm going to make sure my son gets to know everybody just as well. Do you hear me?"

"The whole family is odd," Lina said, squeezing my shoulder once more.

"I remember a lot," Salwa continued. "I remember that Osama used to say you never listened to your father's stories. Do you know how he came here? It's a wonderful story. Osama should tell you. Let him tell you."

❧

And the lovely face of fate appeared in Baybars's dream. "My son," it said. "You have fought your last battle. The time has come to fulfill your life. New heroes must flourish, new stories must be told. Come home."

At the diwan, Baybars announced, "My friends, I need rest. I wish to travel to Giza."

"Your desire is our command," replied Othman. "I will make the arrangements."

"I wish my friends to travel before me. I wish to sleep in the pavilion my friends painted for me so long ago, in order to remember the best moments of my youth."

And Baybars's friends and companions traveled to Giza and erected the great tent with its quiltlike paintings. They cooked a grand feast and waited for the hero to arrive.

Baybars saddled al-Awwar himself. "It is time, my friend," he whispered into the great warhorse's ear. "We shall have our last adventure together. I am as grateful as ever for your company. With you, I am never alone."

Baybars and al-Awwar headed to Giza. Yet, as soon as the great city of Cairo disappeared behind them, Baybars asked al-Awwar to turn right into the welcoming desert. And the great king, the hero of many a tale, rode toward the immortal sun.

❧

"Do you hear me?" I asked my father. "Do you hear me?" I tried to concentrate on his eyelids and not on the breathing tube taped to his mouth. "I don't know which stories your father told you and which you believed, but I always wondered whether he ever told you the true story of who he is, or the one that seems most true. Did he? He must have, but, then, maybe not." I glanced up at the monitor, hoping it had registered some change, any sign that he might be listening. "Your grandmother's name was Lucine. It's true. I checked it out. Lucine Guiragossian. Your grandfather was Simon Twining. She worked for him. See, you have English, Armenian, and Druze blood. Oh, and Albanian, too. You're a man of the world. We always knew that." I gently held his hand.

"Your grandmother died while your father was still a baby. Another woman raised him, Anahid Kaladjian. Your father loved her most of all, and she sacrificed everything for him. He used to say that she was his first audience, that she was the only one to laugh at his jokes. She sent him away when he was eleven. He used to say that all he remembered was that she told him to go south, hide in the mountains of Lebanon, stay with the Christians. That was before the Turkish massacres of the Armenians. He left before the great Armenian orphan migration to Lebanon. Did you know that?" There was no reaction from my father, but my niece reached across the bed and held my hand briefly.

"Listen. Here's a story you'd like. Your father was born tiny, as tiny as a rat, a jardown. No one gave him any hope of living. His mother, Lucine, concerned that he was so small, took him to the Armenian quarter of Urfa on her day off. She talked to people, interrogated, pleaded, until she was sent to a great fortune-teller called Shoushan. Lucine begged Shoushan for help, but she couldn't afford to pay her. The fortune-teller said that she could do nothing without pay, because if word got out no one would ever pay her again. Lucine swore she'd never tell anyone. Shoushan said, 'You think you can walk out of here without having paid and people won't recognize you got something for free. No, no, anyone can tell when something is free. You must pay me something. Let me think of a form of payment. Wait here while I pray and ask the Virgin what I should collect from you.' "

Lina sat down on the bed behind me.

"After praying, Shoushan asked, 'Do you have someone in your household who knits?' Lucine replied that her mistress did. Shoushan said she wanted Lucine to bring her one of those knitting needles. That would be a fine payment. In her prayers, Shoushan had heard the Virgin say that a devil lived in Lucine's household and knitted every night. Shoushan could do some things with a devil's knitting needle. Would Lucine know if the devil also had a darning needle? That would be a princely gift. Shoushan could perform magic with a devil's darning needle. Lucine promised to get her one of each."

Lina settled her head between my shoulder blades. I felt the rhythm of her breathing, solid and tired.

" 'I'll tell you how to make sure your son becomes a giant of a man,' Shoushan said, 'so listen. For seven days and seven nights, you must bathe your son in warm wine. That will nourish him and make him grow. But here is another secret: heat the wine by placing a red-hot horseshoe in it. He'll grow to have the subtlety of wine and the endurance of iron. You must then cool him off by placing him in the shell of an unripe watermelon. The bitterness will make him wise. Go now, and make sure to bring me back a knitting needle and a darning needle.'

"Lucine left Shoushan's house, and on the way home she found an abandoned horseshoe on the road. 'My luck is about to change,' she thought. That evening, she searched for wine, but the doctor had been on a binge and there was none in the house. She took her baby out to the garden, filched an urn being used to make vinegar. She put the almost-vinegar in a stone mortar used to grind meat. She heated the horseshoe over a fire, and when it turned red, she doused it in the sour wine. And she placed her crying son in the mortar bath. But then she had no watermelon, ripe or unripe, so she cooled her baby in a tub of cold yogurt."

I heard Fatima let out a short laugh. My sister moved her head along my back in response. I tried to ignore the consistent beeping of the monitor.

"Of course, the prescription worked—up to a point, that is. Your father survived, but he didn't grow up to be a giant of a man, now, did he? Like all of us, he wasn't even very big. He didn't inherit the subtlety of wine, but the volatility of vinegar. The yogurt gave him not a bitter wisdom but a sour disposition. And the horseshoe turned out to belong not to a horse but to a mule—Lucine couldn't tell the difference. So he did end up with the endurance of iron, but also with the stubbornness of a mule. That's your father."

Sunlight crept along the floor. The room lit up, but my father's face did not take on any color. I took a deep breath.

"Your father told me that story—one of his best, if you ask me. He also told me how you were born. Do you want me to tell you? He told me all kinds of incredible things about you. He told me how you used to steal meat as it was being fried, how you used to sneak by your mother, grab the lamb from the frying pan, and run." I checked his face for a reaction. "Can you hear me?" I closed my eyes briefly. "I know your stories."

His chest kept rising and falling mechanically, systematically.

"And I can tell you my stories. If you want."

I paused, waited.

"Listen."

NOTES AND ACKNOWLEDGMENTS

By nature, a storyteller is a plagiarist. Everything one comes across—each incident, book, novel, life episode, story, person, news clip—is a coffee bean that will be crushed, ground up, mixed with a touch of cardamom, sometimes a tiny pinch of salt, boiled thrice with sugar, and served as a piping-hot tale. A brief list of sources that provided the most beans: *A Thousand and One Nights* (uncensored), Ovid's *Metamorphoses*, the Old Testament, the Koran, W. A. Clouston's *Flowers from a Persian Garden*, Italo Calvino's *Italian Folktales*, Kalila wa Dimna (uncensored), Ahmad al-Tifashi's *The Delight of Hearts*, Ibn Hazm's *The Ring of the Dove*, Mahmoud Khalil Saab's *Stories and Scenes from Mount Lebanon*, Homer's *Iliad*, Jim Crace's *The Devil's Larder*, *The Letters of Abelard and Heloise*, Ida Alamuddin's *Maktoob*, Shakespeare's plays, numerous Internet folktale sites, and quite a few books of Syrian and Lebanese folktales bought for pennies from street vendors.

This is a work of fiction. It might sound redundant, stating the obvious, but it does bear repeating. Nothing herein should be considered fact or biography. The character of Baybars has little to do with the historical one, the character of the bey doesn't represent any real clan leader or family, and the religion in the piece was invented to fit a better narrative (to the best of my knowledge, Zainab doesn't appear at shrines, nor does anyone worship a Lady Zainab in blue). The tale of Baybars is based on oral stories as well as an actual hakawati's book given to me by Maher Jarrar of the American University of Beirut (a princely gift). Readers who wish to study the history of Baybars might consider *The Lion of Egypt: Sultan Baybars I and the Near East in the Thirteenth Century* by Peter Thorau.

I am indebted to the John Simon Guggenheim Memorial Foundation for a most timely and generous grant. Thanks to my editor extraordinaire, Robin Desser, ever tireless and fervent; to Joy Johannessen, who kept shaking the tree till all the rotten fruit had fallen; to Asa DeMatteo, Barbara Dimmick, Jim Hanks, and William Zimmerman, readers who didn't shy away from pointing out the inadequacies of my writing. I wish to thank Lily Oei, Carlo Togni, and Eric Glassgold for making life easier.

Everything I know about pigeons I learned from Beirut pigeoneers who were gracious enough to tell me their stories. Everything I know about guitars I learned from George Peacock of Peacock Music in San Francisco. Everything I know about maqâms I learned from listening to the inimitable Munir Bashir.

And, finally, this book wouldn't be what it is without the input of almost every Lebanese I know, and even those I don't know so well. Lebanon is a nation of hakawatis, and none had to be asked more than once for a story. Actually, most never needed to be asked.

I heard you're looking for stories. Let me tell you.

You want stories about pigeons? I got pigeon stories.

I'll tell you a story. You can put it in your book, but you can't tell anyone. It's private.

You have to write about my crazy aunt. You just have to. Listen.

Thank you.

PICADOR
...& more

Talk about books with us,
our authors, other readers,
bloggers, booksellers
and others at
www.picador.com

You can also:

- find out what's new at Picador

- read extracts from recently
  published books

- listen to interviews with
  our authors

- get exclusive special offers
  and enter competitions